And then the Penny Dropped

Based on a true story

BP KENNEDY

with Ken Scott

www.andthenthepennydropped.com

www.kenscottbooks.com

Printed in the United States of America

ISBN: 1983774448
ISBN-13: 978-1983774447

DEDICATION

To my three girls and to Mam & Auntie.
Thank you for keeping me strong and believing in me. You are my guiding lights and you always bring me home.
This book is for you.

ACKNOWLEDGEMENTS

The biggest thank you is to my book coach, mentor and ghost-writer extraordinaire Ken Scott, who held my hand throughout and convinced me my story was worth telling to the world. And to my wonderful readers who surprised me with their honest feedback and kind words, Mandy, Suzanne, Trish, Joanne, Kathleen, Louise, Jill, Michelle and Corinne.

And last but not least, thank you to my wonderful editor, Hayley, for her patience and understanding.

1

I'm running, he's running but the distance between us is growing. No matter how hard I try I can't close the gap and the cliff edge is fast approaching. The thorns and brambles rip into my bare feet and I can smell the blood, the salt of the sea, my perspiration. Everything is so real. I want to catch him, I truly do. Despite my pain, my breathlessness, the adrenalin kicks in and I manage to increase my speed and just for a second I seem to be closing in on him. He turns his head slightly and I catch a grin as he powers towards certain death on the jagged rocks below. I'll follow him of course, nothing will stop me, not him, not the cliff edge, not the razor sharp rocks that will cut me to ribbons. We're falling. We are tumbling in slow motion and I reach for him as the sound of the sea thunders all around us. I wait for the pain and the shock but it doesn't come.

The neon light from the bedside clock flashed 4.30 am. I awoke with a start, bathed in sweat. I wondered what the significance was with the time, it was the same time every morning and I knew there was another long day ahead of me.

I gradually reacquainted myself with my surroundings and cursed that nightmare. I'd woken up in this same bed for weeks yet I still can't get used to it, not the memory foam mattress, the units above the bed or the silhouette of the streetlamp casting it's shadow across the curtains. I hated sleeping in a bed with cupboards above my head, it reminded me of a caravan. What was I thinking of designing a room like this? I didn't have to ponder the thought for long as I remembered it was designed for Abigail, a teenager with a shoe collection larger than Imelda Marcos. That was what I was thinking of when I, when we, designed it. Shoes, we were thinking shoes. This bloody room, this bloody mattress. My lower back ached and I curled myself into the foetal position, stretching and arching my back. That felt better, a little better anyway. I wished it were as easy to fix my head. I stayed in the position for some time. Somehow it made me feel safe and cocooned, like a child, a small baby back in the womb. My thoughts drifted back to my own bed. I longed to be back in that bed, my bed, our bed and the luxurious silent night mattress in the room at the other end of the hall with the soft downy pillows.

I visualised him sleeping in that bed along the hall, sleeping like a baby probably, not a care in the world. It never took me long to get back to thinking about him, all day and every day. Where he was? What he was doing? Was he thinking about me?

I'd spent months trying to make sense of it all. I was exhausted thinking about him, about her, about the great mess that my life has become. My head was a mess, like a washing machine stuck in a spin cycle.

I wondered if he woke in the early hours of the morning. Surely he must. How could he sleep soundly? It just wasn't possible because he was responsible for this bloody chaos. I smiled to myself at the irony of the situation because today he was going to tell the girls, our girls that he was leaving. It was Father's Day. Fucking Father's Day. Of all the days to announce he was splitting his family in two, he chose Father's Day. Was he some kind of twisted maniac?

I carried a faint hope that he would change his mind. Surely twenty-three years of marriage meant something to him? He couldn't seriously want to throw it all away like a broken toy?

I wanted to sleep a while longer. Please let me sleep. It was Sunday. It was far too early to get up. I looked at the book staring at me on my bedside table. I had started it when this first blew up. If I picked it up and started reading it might make me tired, with any luck I would drift off into oblivion for another hour or so.

Who was I kidding? I'd barely managed to read past the first few chapters. I was just reading words that meant nothing to me as I was incapable of concentrating on the plot, the characters, anything. It was the same with the TV. I stared at it and barely remembered what it was I'd been watching because I drifted mindlessly and the pain and the ifs and the buts lodged themselves deep within the crevices of my mind. Nothing stayed in my head for more than a second except for the big black cloud that was getting bigger and bigger by the day. Today, Fathers Day, it was going to burst, I knew it is. I could feel it.

An hour later I forced my legs over the side of the bed and let out a deep sigh.

"I've lost the game," I whispered under my breath.

That's what it was, a game. I had lost the game to the other woman, the younger model. I hadn't met her yet but somehow I instinctively knew that I didn't stand a chance. I searched my brain wondering when it had started, the affair, their first kiss, their first sexual encounter. Was she that much better in bed than I was?

At one time, when we were young and I still carried my youthful figure, when my skin was fresh and my jaw line was taut with no sign of sagging, his gaze would follow me around a room full of people and he would see only me. I had the power to hold his attention, I knew exactly when he wanted me. However small the gesture of intimacy I enticed him with, it worked every time. I held a certain sexual power over him and that always felt good.

Now, I was invisible to him. I no longer mattered, no longer existed.

There was no sudden shift in his affection, at first it didn't even flag up in my consciousness. Thinking back in the cold light of day as I sit in the kitchen nursing a lukewarm cup of coffee, I could recall the subtle signs. I began to notice the way he looked at me, the way he spoke to me. I couldn't put my finger on it at first but it was almost as if I irritated him. He started to criticise my every move.

My immediate reaction was to blame his age. What forty plus man didn't turn a bit strange? Tania from the tennis club said her Nick had announced that he wanted to take a sabbatical from work, buy a Harley Davidson and drive route 66 across America. There was no thought of how they would manage financially when he was finding himself around Texas, California and Kansas. In Nick's defence this may have had less to do with his age and more to do with him wanting some space from Tania, that woman could talk the hind legs off a donkey.

At first I kept thinking that Stuart was going through a similar phase but he graduated from a slight look or word of disapproval to a point in time where he didn't even speak to me. He was never a one to waste time on idol conversation but this was far worse. He practically turned mute in my presence.

Gone were the terms of endearment, the shows of affection that had continued throughout our marriage. He had rarely called me by my Christian name, much preferring to call me darling, hun and very occasionally when he didn't want to look too sloppy in public place he'd call me Anna. Now it was just Annette and he made it sound cold and menacing, deliberately drawing out each and every syllable, An ne tte!!! When I questioned him about it, he blamed my vivid imagination.

I closed my eyes and felt the heat of the sun penetrating through the finely veiled kitchen curtains. The birds were in full chorus outside. It was going to be a nice day, for the birds at least. I rested my head on the kitchen table and drifted into a deep sleep.

I woke up suddenly. There was a noise from the garage. My head ached, my neck was stiff and I had a bitter taste in my mouth. I felt like shit, the fatigue had eventually hit hard. What was it? Who was it? It was Stuart. He was lifting his new bike from the bracket on the garage wall. He had taken up cycling. This was his new hobby and it seemed to coincide with his change of attitude. Whatever the reason it was taking up most of his free time. Every Saturday and Sunday he would be away for hours at a time cycling through the Northumberland countryside. Or so he said. How the hell did I know where he went on his fancy carbon framed superbike?

He'd walked past me. Creeping quietly through the kitchen as I'd slept. And yet I wasn't angry. Today I was relieved that he had gone because at least I could avoid the awkward silences or even worse the embarrassing situations when our paths inevitably crossed in the hall or on the stairs or in the doorways, neither of us knowing who should move first. We were both becoming experts at navigating the others whereabouts in the house, both of us wanting to avoid being in the same room together.

It hadn't always been the case. When I first found out about her, I desperately wanted to keep him, to win back his affections but above all I wanted to fight for him because I wanted to protect our beautiful family unit. I followed him around like a lap dog pandering to his every whim. He knew he was in control, the balance of power had shifted, the equilibrium was lost and the pendulum had swung in his direction and had stuck like super glue.

Of course he used this to his full advantage. I had tried to talk to him, tried to resolve the rift. He listened and let me rattle on and on and I would beg him to make things right, make things work. At first

I thought he was listening. He never interjected, never consoled me or offered any resolution. At the end of my performance he would get up and silently walk out of the room. On occasions I'd caught a slight smirk cross his lips and it struck me that just maybe he enjoyed my demise, he enjoyed watching me grovel. My humiliation was complete.

Two weeks ago I finally cracked. I'd endured yet another begging and pleading session, said I'd do anything to give our marriage another chance. He'd sat for some minutes in silence then stood up and announced he was going for a bike ride. I felt as insignificant as a human being could possibly feel. I'd practically sold my soul to the devil and my last ounce of dignity had vanished into thin air.

I followed him into the garage.

He unchained the bike lock and lifted the bike down as I stepped a little closer.

"Can you just move out of my way," he said.

It was not the words, they were benign enough, it was the way he spoke them, sharp, snappy and the look he gave me was one of total disgust. Not only did I now irritate him but I also disgusted him. Something inside me tripped a switch and at that point I lost it. It was the straw that broke the camel's back.

"Who the fuck do you think you're talking to?"

He stood, mouth gaping in stunned silence. In twenty-three years of marriage I had rarely sworn at him. I repeated the words, this time the pitch of my voice even higher. I added in a few more expletives. I wanted a response, a reaction.

"Who the fucking hell do you think you are fucking talking to?"

He composed himself and took a deep breath. He'd been waiting for a moment like this for months.

"Annette we need to talk because this clearly isn't working."

"What's not working Stuart, you tell me what's not working because I'm all fucking ears."

My body was bursting with anger, every emotion I'd suppressed over the months rose to the surface and he sensed it. He played me, moulded me like a piece of play-doh. It was what he'd been waiting for.

"You've changed, you're not the same person I married."

His face was pan straight void of expression. He either felt no emotion or he hid it well.

"I've changed?"

I had to laugh at this point.

"Is that why you feel the need to take off and fuck your young whore?"

He ignored what I said as if it hadn't actually happened. He was building momentum, he wasn't going to miss this opportunity because his wife of twenty-three years had changed and she was wailing like a banshee and swearing like a Tyneside docker.

"I think we should call it a day. I don't think we can go on," he said.

He looked at me blankly. He appeared so emotionally detached as he started to talk sensibly about when he should announce the separation to the family, my girls, our beautiful girls. How could he be so matter of fact about it all? The words weren't sinking in, it was as if I was detached from the conversation and looking down from above. He talked for a good minute or two and I couldn't even be bothered to respond. He'd announced his intention, he got it off his chest, he'd planted the seed and I knew at that exact point in time that nothing could save our marriage. It was so final.

We never spoke of it again as we both resumed our awkward silences. When he sat in the kitchen I was in the lounge and vice versa. Then last Friday he needed to talk again. He came into the kitchen. It was almost like he had arranged a meeting with a work colleague.

"I think we should tell the girls next Sunday."

Next Sunday. There was something special about next Sunday, something registered in my head. Father's Day. I suppressed the desire to hit him with a heavy object. Father's Day. Had it not occurred to him that maybe it wasn't the best day of the year to announce to your daughters that you were walking out on them?

Father's Day.

The day was going to drag. In previous years we would usually go to my Mother's for Sunday lunch. The whole family would be there, my brothers, the nieces, nephews and the in-laws too. It was always a lively event, Mum would excel herself, she could throw a great party and we'd eat, laugh and gossip. The discussions were lively but always good-humoured and the youngsters would hive themselves off to talk relationships, clothes, makeup and music, the usual teenage stuff.

I couldn't face it. Not today.

I wasn't in the mood to field off the questions, they'd pick up something wasn't right, that all wasn't perfect in paradise. Today wasn't the day I wanted to face a grilling. I'd tell the family soon enough but today, right now, it was all about the girls. They were going to be devastated and I had to be there for them. I needed to protect them.

Alexandra looked a bit perplexed when I told her we weren't going to Nanas.

"But we always go to Nanas on Father's Day Mum."

"Not today chick," I said with a sigh.

"Why, and what are we going to eat for lunch Mum?"

Food was the last thing on my mind. I hadn't eaten a decent meal for over a month.

"I'll rustle something up," I said.

"Rustle something up Mum? But it's Father's Day."

I had no answer for her so I just shrugged my shoulders and something in her eyes told me that she realised something wasn't quite right.

Stuart's timing was perfect if I say so myself. He'd been out for a bike ride and as I looked out of the kitchen window he cycled towards us, parked his bike up against the hedge and opened the kitchen door. He stopped for a second, sensed the awkwardness of the situation.

"What is it?" he asked.

Alexandra spoke first.

"What is it Dad? Why aren't we going to Nana's?"

Stuart looked at me for some sort of explanation. I quickly averted my gaze. I think I looked at the floor like a scolded schoolgirl as I took a long slow, deliberate drink from my coffee cup.

"Something's wrong. Are you going to tell me what it is?" she repeated.

Thoughts began to invade my head. What could I say? I had no script, no carefully rehearsed lines prepared for this eventuality. I decided not to say anything, I would let him do the talking, let him tell the girls, after all it was him who wanted to leave not me. I wasn't going anywhere.

Abigail and Victoria had heard their Father's voice and strolled into the kitchen with his Father's Day cards and gifts.

The girls greeted him, planting a kiss on his cheek.

"Happy Father's Day Dad," they said in unison.

He opened the first card smiling lamely. Was the guilt eventually beginning to get to him? He was almost squirming, like a fish out of water. They'd enclosed a voucher for the golf club, if he wanted nothing else he always wanted golf balls. He looked uncomfortable. Was his composure cracking? Maybe he was having doubts.

Abigail and Victoria picked up the vibes.

"What is it Dad?" Abigail asked.

I could feel Stuart's eyes piercing into me. I didn't need to look at him, my peripheral vision caught his look, his stare. He had nowhere to turn. Then I knew what he wanted me to do, he wanted me to break the news, he wanted me to get the ball rolling. I wasn't having it. This was his doing and the coward had to face up to his wrongdoings like a man. I looked up and waited. I stared at him and enjoyed every second that he stood there like a spare part. I waited and waited. His mouth opened and then closed again. The words wouldn't form on his lips. He was trembling, his legs had turned to jelly and he reached out for one of the kitchen chairs. He pulled it towards him and sat down at the table. He shook his head first and then he spoke.

"Girls, there's something your Mum and I need to tell you."

He shuffled in his chair, ringing his hands out, a habit he had when he was nervous. The girls were intrigued; he didn't often have anything to say but today he had their full attention.

"As you know your Mum and I haven't been getting along."

A decent start, although the girls had never questioned me about our relationship. I think they realised deep down that there had been tension in the air for some months. I found myself wondering why they hadn't brought the subject up and yet why would they? A stable home was all they'd ever known. Two loving parents and a big extended family, sisters, cousins, Grandma and of course my mother, Nana.

"We've grown apart," he said.

Abigail was shaking her head. She sensed what was coming. I looked at the other two, their faces were a picture of confusion and dread.

"We've both decided to go our separate ways, I'm moving out."

I forced myself to keep quiet but my blood was boiling. I wanted to rant and rave, tell the girls that there is no 'we,' we had decided nothing. I opened my mouth to speak but the words wouldn't come. This is all down to your father, he's fucking his new lover, I wanted to scream. I had to keep my dignity I reminded myself. He rambled on about how things wouldn't change, he would be there for them like always. Abigail's eyes began to fill up. Of the three girls she was probably closest to him. Abigail was athletic, interested in sport and they had common ground, a shared interest.

He beckoned her to him his arms outstretched.

"Come and give your dad a cuddle."

She didn't move. They were all sitting at the table now. Mute, clearly in shock. The cogs were turning in their heads, they wanted to ask questions but didn't want to hear the answers.

I felt every ounce of their pain.

"But why dad?" Alexandra asked. "What have we done? What has mum done?"

"Nothing," he said. "Nobody has done anything, it's…"

He is wavering, squirming like a worm because he knew that sooner or later the girls would open up and want to know exactly why it was he was walking out on them.

I wanted to plant the words in his head. It's me, I have a new girlfriend and she is more important to me than you lot.

Victoria piped up.

"You're really leaving us?"

He nodded his head sheepishly,

"Don't worry, I'll still be your Dad, things won't change."

Abigail was wiping away her tears with a paper handkerchief and now she looked more angry than sad.

"Of course things will change dad."

She raised her voice.

"Your moving out, how won't things change?"

"I'll go and stay with Grandma, you don't have to go anywhere. It's just down the road."

Alexandra was getting upset, shaking her head.

"This isn't happening to us," she said between the tears. "Please tell me this isn't happening?"

Eventually I spoke.

"That's right Stuart, tell them this isn't happening. Tell them you aren't walking out on them."

He glared at me angrily.

"I'm not walking out on them."

But he was. When a father left the family home and no longer wanted to live under the same roof as his children then what was he doing? Of course he was leaving, of course he was walking out.

Victoria looked confused.

"Then what are you doing?"

"Yes Stuart," I said. "If you're not walking out on them then what are you doing?"

He snapped as he jumped from the table. He looked around the kitchen at the girls then glared at me again. I waited for a response but we got nothing as he rushed from the room. I left the girls alone with their thoughts and their tears as I opened the patio doors and walked up the garden. I breathed in the sweet fragrance of the scented stock, it was the best time of the day, the air was still warm and there was a gentle stillness, quietness and strangely I felt at peace with the world. I sat on the garden chair. I sat for five minutes or so but my maternal instinct kicked in once again. The girls needed me, they needed answers.

Back in the kitchen Stuart hadn't wasted any time. He had packed an overnight bag, was carrying his computer case and his suit carrier was slung over his shoulder. He was ready to go. It was all so final, so quick and I cursed him for being so cold and calculated. He had left the girls with more questions than answers.

I sat at the table. I reached for Victoria's hand and squeeze it tightly.

Stuart picked up the overnight bag.

"Okay, I'm off," hc said.

"Not yet." I said.

He looked at me with a puzzled frown.

"Why not?"

I picked up my cup of coffee. It was stone cold. I swirled the liquid around my mouth.

"Why not?" he repeated.

I stood.

"I'm going out for a walk Stuart. I think you should tell your daughters all about your new girlfriend."

I left the room in deathly silence.

2

Three Months Before.

I noticed something today, something really strange, something that caused my heart to skip a beat. I had just got back from food shopping. I usually went out for odd bits and pieces on a Saturday morning to see us through the weekend. I walked into the kitchen laden with bags. Stuart was sitting in the lounger and he obviously hadn't seen me because I clearly startled him as I dropped a big heavy bag onto the floor. He jumped and his mobile fell out of his hand and onto the tiled floor.

"Shit!" he exclaimed. "What did you do that for?"

I looked at the bag on the floor and back to him.

"We need to eat Stuart, I need to shop," I replied.

He was flustered and more interested in the phone than anything else. It had switched off and he was cursing the fact he thought it might be broken. Luckily when he turned it back on everything was fine. But there was something about his face, his smile, that smug look of satisfaction when he realised his phone was okay that made me wonder what was so precious about it.

As I started to empty the bags, Stuart was surprisingly in a talkative mood and he wanted to chat. I welcomed his conversation. It hadn't been this way of late. I reminisced on how we used to be, how we would talk for hours about something or nothing. Usually he would play golf on a Saturday but not today. He was eager to tell me he was going out for lunch and a drink with an old work colleague, Tom. I'd never heard him mention Tom before but seemingly Tom and he had worked together in his last company. Tom had moved down to London and was up north visiting family. What a great guy Tom was, one of the best, it would be great to catch up with him again. It was as if Tom was like a long lost brother to him. It was a mystery to me.

As it got nearer to the time he was due to leave, he asked me what I planned to do with my day. Was I just going to my mother's? he asked. He knew I would be. I was a creature of habit and that was usually what I would do on a Saturday afternoon.

"I go there every Saturday," I said. "You know that."

"Just wondering," He said with a smile.

Just wondering or just making sure, I thought to myself.

Stuart returned home around six. There was only the three of us in the house, Abigail and Victoria were out on the town so it was just me, Stuart and Alexandra.

Stuart's good mood had carried on from that morning and I was keen to keep the momentum of positivity going so I cracked opened a bottle of red wine. And for once in a long while things seemed okay. There was no negative atmosphere and Stuart and I were actually sitting in the same room. I could feel Alexandra's relief; she wasn't going to be subjected to another evening of torturous silence. We decided to sit and watch a movie together. Alexandra being the typical teenager of course rarely sat without a mobile phone in her hand, no matter what she was doing, she would have one eye on the phone screen the other on the television. As was often the case, her phone ran out of credit.

It was an innocuous request.

"Dad can I borrow your phone for a minute?"

I sat and watched as the scene developed.

"What do you want my phone for?"

She glanced across at him.

"I just want to borrow it for a minute to call my friend Lauren I'll only be a minute."

He looked agitated.

"We're watching a movie, can't you call her tomorrow?"

"But Dad, it's important."

He was grumbling.

"I hate you lot messing with my phone."

I couldn't help myself.

"Just let her use your phone. What's the problem?" I said.

He sighed out loud and shook his head. He had no choice, how could he refuse her? She stood up and walked over to him and he slapped it into the palm of her hand.

"Be quick," he said, "money doesn't grow on trees."

She took the phone and started walking towards the kitchen door as his eyes followed her. I sensed he wasn't happy.

"Where are you going with my phone? I need it. Why are you taking it into the kitchen?"

"I'll not be a minute dad, stop fussing."

But he couldn't stop fussing. He fidgeted and grumbled and sighed, his eyes constantly staring at the kitchen door, almost willing her to walk back through. He had barely waited a minute before it all got too much for him.

"Alexandra where's my phone? Bring it right back now," he shouted.

My thoughts drifted back to earlier in the day when he'd dropped the phone. The look on his face. That phone. What was on that phone that was so important, so secretive?

A strange feeling washed over me, as if everything was falling into place and there was an enormous alarm bell going off in my head. There was something on that phone he didn't want anyone to see and I needed to somehow find out what it was.

After just a few minutes Alexandra returned to the lounge. She handed her father his phone and the relief on his face was clear to see. He placed it back into the breast pocket of his shirt and relaxed again.

I sat the rest of the evening staring at the TV although I wasn't watching the movie. I was piecing it all together in my head. I hadn't realized it before but how bloody stupid of me. How could I have missed it? As the plot of the movie on the small screen developed, I started my own plot in the deep recesses of my brain. How could I get to that phone without him realising?

The only time the phone wasn't on his person was when he was in bed asleep and he would put it on the dresser to charge overnight. That's when I needed to get it, that was the only time… when he was sleeping. Another problem. Stuart was such a light sleeper, any slight movement and he would stir, unlike me, I could sleep through an earthquake. Stuart was rarely in a deep sleep. He had always been the first to hear the girls cries when they were young and he'd give me a nudge, telling me to see to them. He was the first to jump up if there was an unusual sound from outside. My mind pondered over my dilemma. How I could get to that phone and those messages? Shit, I didn't even know how to even work a Blackberry.

I lay awake that night, long after he had fallen asleep and I stared at the little red charge light on his side of the bed. The dresser stood on his side of the room and I was going to have to pass by his side of the bed to get near it. Was it going to be possible without him waking up?

I decided alcohol was the key to my success. Later the next day I became even more cunning as I checked out a Blackberry user's manual on Google. I would spring my plan next Friday evening.

I'd planned everything right down to the last detail and had six days to work it out perfectly as well as six days to build up my much needed courage. Despite being 100% certain that the evidence was on his phone somehow I still felt disloyal to him, checking up on him this way. Every day of the week I thought about aborting my plan and yet the more I thought about it the more positive I was that my suspicions were well founded.

Stuart was always tired on a Friday evening after a long week at work. He wanted nothing more than to eat and curl up on the sofa and watch some rubbish TV. Not this week. I'd told Alexandra that we were going to watch a movie on TV, something someone had recommended, something good, something over two hours long and something that would keep his attention and keep him awake. He wouldn't be falling asleep on the sofa this Friday. I cooked his favourite dinner, roast chicken with all the trimmings and a homemade bowl of gravy and made sure that he had more than his fair share on his plate while I kept my own helping to the minimum. True to form he never noticed. I'd pushed the boat out on the wine front too. The manager in the wine shop recommended it, a good year for a Bordeaux wine, ridiculously expensive. He questioned the price and I told him it was on special offer, less than a tenner. Liar!

He had two big glasses with his dinner and retired to the lounge with a refill. He loved it. I cleared up quickly and Alexandra set the movie away as I walked in.

The movie was good, not a squeak from anyone. Thirty minutes in I got to my feet and retrieved the bottle from the kitchen bench.

"More wine?"

He nodded and gestured a faint smile, I filled his glass to the brim, pouring the few remaining dregs into my glass. Stuart wasn't normally a big drinker, but I figured he'd had most of the bottle

I wanted to keep him in a good mood, off guard. We made small talk about the movie and I saw the sleep in his eyes as he yawned on two or three occasions. The wine had done the trick, he was relaxed, he even appeared to be enjoying himself. Alexandra obviously found this newfound congeniality overbearing and didn't stay until the end of the movie.

"I'm off to bed see you in the morning."

Time was ticking on, it was nearly midnight when the credits rolled across the screen. I kept one eye on Stuart and one on the TV. I knew the other girls wouldn't be home tonight, they were both staying at their friends after a night in town. It was a relief as I didn't want their noise waking him when they came through the front door. It was crucial I kept him awake as long as possible and critical that nobody disturbed him once he fell asleep.

I managed to keep him awake until nearly one o'clock, talking about the girls. He swayed slightly as he walked up the stairs, the alcohol taking effect. He put his phone on the dresser and plugged it in to charge as usual. Other men might forget about charging their phone when a little tipsy and ready for bed. Not Stuart. That phone was everything to him.

I went to the bathroom and by the time I got back into the room, Stuart was in bed with his eyes closed. I looked at him, anticipating my next move. I wanted him to sleep as soundly as possible. I'd need to wait at least an hour. It was going to be hard staying awake myself.

I watched the minute's tick by on the clock, fighting sleep by thinking about nonsensical things and counting the seconds on the clock.

At 2.15 am I decided it was time to act. I looked at the dresser, the phone was feet away from me and I was itching to get my hands on it. I could see the red glowing light from his charger and as the room was pitch black, the light would navigate me towards it. I could hear his heavy breathing, his hypnotic rhythm. The dresser stood by the bathroom door so if he was to wake I would pretend that I needed the toilet. I could always abort my mission and try another night. The last thing I needed was for him to suspect I wanted to get to his phone. If that happened I would never get my hands on it.

I was ready and I gently pulled the bed covers back. My movements were slow and deliberate. I put my feet on the floor one after the other. My fourth step disturbed a floorboard and in the quietness of the death of night the noise seemed deafening. I turned my head towards him and waited, hardly daring to breath. He hadn't flinched, his breathing still heavy and steady. It seemed to take an eternity to walk around the room and with each step I stopped to check he hadn't moved. I was standing over him now, so close I could smell the red wine and toothpaste mix on his breath. I reached for the phone and carefully unplugged the charger cable.

I needed to get into the hall but the difficult bit would be opening the bedroom door. I cursed myself that I hadn't had the foresight to leave it slightly ajar, but no, old habits die hard. There was bound to be some noise when I pulled at the door handle and of course the light would stream in too. I hesitated, I was beginning to have doubts. What would I say if he woke up? He was the lightest sleeper in the world for Christ's sake. I stood while my eyes gradually adjusted to the darkness yet I wasn't sure I would find the door handle. I shuffled towards the door with my hands outstretched and I gently patted my hand on the door panel until I found the handle. I slowly squeezed it down listening all the while to his rhythmic snoring. He hadn't moved. As I opened the door, I could feel the perspiration building on my brow, my breathing growing ever faster. I waited thirty seconds and listened for his voice. What are you doing? Where are you going?

It didn't happen. I was out of the room and I pulled the door gently behind me.

My best bet was to go into Victoria's room as it was far enough from our room and I could turn the Blackberry on. Did it make a noise when it came on? Was the sound turned up? I couldn't be sure. The adrenaline was pumping through my body, my hands were shaking, his blackberry was in my hands and I was so near. I closed the door to Victoria's room and turned on her small bedside light. I recognised the on button and pushed it. The screen came to life. I was tantalisingly close. During the past six days I had expected a bit of trouble fumbling my way around this new gadget but it was exactly the opposite, all too easy. I recognised the envelope icon. Messages. I pressed the button and the last ten of his messages appeared in chronological order, the newest first. I didn't have to look past the first message as her name jumped out at me. Angela Maddison. I instinctively knew this was my missing link. I clicked on her name and opened the message but part of me was still hoping that it would be no more than a business contact, an innocent message about a meeting or an account of a client. I stared down and read the words. Then I read them again. I slowly read each word one by one. It sank in, there was no mistakes this time, no doubts. Each word was like a dagger through my heart.

"Can't stop thinking about you, can't wait to see you and take another hot, hot, shower together. Thanks for making me feel so special, speak tomorrow, love you babe xxxxxxxxxxxxxxxx"

It all made sense. I was enraged. I sank to my knees as I fell forward onto the soft carpet of Victoria's bedroom. I expected the tears to flow but for some reason they didn't. Perhaps it was the anger that kept them at bay. I wasn't going to wait another minute. I needed to confront him. I dragged myself to my feet and reread the message. I practically catapulted myself through Victoria's bedroom door, lurched across the hall and burst through the bedroom door. At the same time I switched on the overhead light. This time he opened his eyes. He was confused. I could see that he was trying to make sense of the situation, trying to focus on me. He gradually lifted himself up into a sitting position and started to rub his eyes. I held the phone in my hand. I wanted him to see that I had the evidence. He looked at me and then to the space on the dresser where his phone had been as he drifted off to sleep. I needed to scream at him, yet I knew I couldn't. Alexandra was asleep across the hall and I couldn't drag her into this. I remained surprisingly calm, my voice was low, almost a whisper.

"You cheating bastard! You dirty cheating bastard!"

He looked again at the empty dresser.

"What fucking drugs are you on you crazy bitch?"

I had him, I had the evidence but wasn't quite ready to spring it on him. I wondered how he would try and wriggle out of it. How devious was he?

"Who the fuck is this Angela Maddison? I've read the text, you're obviously very good friends."

"She … err works with me."

"Yeah, works with you and fucks you at the same time."

He was strangely calm. I could almost hear the cogs turning in his head wondering how much I knew. His stupid wife, might know how to switch on a Blackberry, but that was the extent of her technical ability. She certainly couldn't locate and access messages. She's seen a contact name, that's all, a female contact name and put two and two together to make five. She really is mentally unbalanced. Stupid cow.

"For God's sake she's a work colleague, we work together, we send business related emails and texts. That's how the world works nowadays but you wouldn't know anything about that."

I shook my head in disbelief.

"It's not what you think," he continued. "It's typical of you to jump to conclusions, she's a colleague that's all, you're just being your normal paranoid self."

The tide was turning, or so he thought.

"You've had the audacity to accuse me of being a bad mother, a bad wife." I ranted, but in a controlled way. "So you're just friends?"

"Yes."

I knelt on the bed. I wanted to get up really close to gauge his reaction.

"Then tell me why you shower together."

The penny dropped.

"Tell me why she can't wait for the next hot, hot shower?"

Realisation. He opened his mouth to speak. Silence.

"And all these months you've been making me feel guilty and you've been riding the office bike."

And then I thrust in the final knife.

"We'll see what my solicitor makes of these messages."

It was a red rag to a bull, he was enraged and launched himself off the bed. He went directly for the phone. I quickly turned my back, kept my arm outstretched. He tried to reach from behind me, grabbed my arm and pulled it back towards him. The scuffle continued, I needed to get away from him. We gradually gravitated towards the bathroom while he pulled at my arm, desperate to get to the phone. At six foot two he towered above me and his strength was beginning to overpower me yet the adrenaline kicked in and I felt a surge of strength from somewhere. I fought on, I wouldn't give up. His anger grew with each second that passed. He managed to pull me around to face him as my head cracked against the bathroom tiles. If I expected an exclamation of regret or some sympathy I was sadly mistaken. He was winning. I had practically exhausted all my resources. In a desperate final lunge, he grabbed me by the throat. I could feel his hand tightening. I couldn't breathe. His face was up against mine, his eyes wild and his face red.

"You fucking bitch. Don't you ever threaten me with that again."

I kept my eyes fixed on his trying to be defiant to the last. As he squeezed ever harder I felt myself losing consciousness and let the phone fall to the floor. He released his grip and I fell against the bathroom wall breathing hard. He reached down and picked up the phone.

"You fucking scheming bitch," he shouted. "Do you know what I'm going to do now?"

I shook my head. Suddenly the panic set in.

"I'm going to wipe all of the messages."

He held up the phone to my face as I cowered away from him.

"I'm taking no chances with a devious lunatic like you."

He deleted the messages in front of my eyes leaving no evidence. He then turned his attention back to me. He wasn't quite finished as he raised his hand and slapped my face hard. I was stunned, he had never raised his hand to me before and the shock was harder to take than the actual pain, which hadn't really registered in my brain.

"Keep your fucking hands of my stuff, you ugly bitch."

He smiled as I slid down the wall and burst into tears. He turned around and calmly walked back through to the bedroom.

He turned off the light and I heard him climb back into bed.

3

It was Monday morning, less than twenty-four hours since he had left, the most infamous Father's Day ever. I was grateful it was Monday, grateful for the routine it offered. Alexandra needed to go to school. I needed to get out of bed and get her to school and I definitely needed to tell my mum he had gone. I had no idea what I was going to do with the rest of my life but at least I knew what I had to do that morning.

I had spent the first night back in my bedroom, in my own bed. I planted myself in the middle of the bed spreading my arms and legs across the width of the mattress like a snow angel. I couldn't find a comfortable position and as the night progressed my body naturally gravitated towards my usual side of the bed. The empty spot where he had once been amplified the reality of the situation, he was gone, it was over and even though he'd barely been away for 24 hours, I sensed he would never be back. Stupidly I had thought just by being back in my own room I would be able to sleep. It made not one jot of difference. I still found myself waking at the same time as I had the previous few months, waking from the same nightmare dripping in sweat. Perhaps it would change in a few days. I lived in hope… the eternal optimist.

I forced myself out of bed and sauntered downstairs into the kitchen. I needed a coffee before I could muster up the energy to do anything. Coffee had been my saviour of late; I could not operate without significant levels of caffeine. I filled the kettle and plonked it on the stove. Cilla pricked her ears on hearing the movement and roused herself from her curled up position on the kitchen chair. She jumped down onto all fours and snaked her way across the kitchen floor brushing her fur against my leg. She wanted to be fed. I still had a purpose. The cat needed me.

Usually I would switch the TV on and catch up with the news and celebrity gossip whilst downing my first cup of coffee. Today I wouldn't bother, there was enough drama going on in my own home to fill a book. I didn't need to know about everybody else's bloody mess, I had enough of my own. I needed to keep busy. The girls ironing needed to be done so I pulled the ironing board out of the cupboard and started to mindlessly plough through the pile of clothes that had mounted up over the weekend. I laughed inwardly to myself. At least I wouldn't have Stuart's ironing to do. Jesus, he had more ironing than the girls put together and every item of clothing had to be so pristine and folded to perfection. Hey ho! Every cloud had a silver lining.

No matter how hard I resisted, my thoughts drifted back to the events of the previous day. I knew it was coming but it still didn't make it any less traumatic. I wondered if I could have turned the clock back would I have done anything different. The jury was out. Or was it? I felt for the girls when I dropped their 'fathers girlfriend' bombshell, but they needed to know. I had been reasonably dignified, hadn't called her a whore or a home wrecker and I hadn't cursed or swore.

I wished I could have pinpointed it, the thing that made him stop caring about me. Was it an argument? Did I do something or say something so unforgivable that there was no way back, no room for forgiveness? If I knew what it was, when it happened then I could have put it right. He became distant, that's the best word I could use, distant or detached. I was screaming for him to pay attention to me yet he saw me but didn't hear. I could see him and he could see me but we couldn't communicate, he was getting on with his life and I have no input at all.

We'd known each other for thirty years and had been married for twenty-three of them. I realised we were different people from when we first met. People change, marriages evolve. We weren't the same naïve 19-year-old kids who were arrogant enough to believe that life was going to go our way with no hiccups. But lots of things did go our way. Stuart was ambitious, he had his sights set high and usually he managed to achieve whatever he set his mind to. Promotion was always important to him, the number one 'must have' on his list and he didn't care how many friends he lost or how many people he upset along the way. He was focussed, I'll give him that. Was that when the rot set in, when he put his work before his wife? I lost count of the times I'd had the 'I have to work late' phone call, more often than not when I was all glammed up ready to enjoy a nice night in town or a dinner at our favourite restaurant. The best dress was put back in the wardrobe, the make-up removed and a large glass of wine poured by way of a consolation.

By the time he was thirty, he was CFO of a national manufacturing company based in the North East, by 40 he was the CEO. It had been what he wanted so he went for it. He thrived on his work and equally I thrived on staying at home being the mother to our growing family. He had enough ambition for the both of us and I thought I was happy for him to be cast as the big provider while I revelled in my role as the humble housewife. It was enough for me and I was blissfully happy in my role. I just wanted to bring up my children and love my husband with all my heart. Nothing else.

So life was fine. The pleasant warm winds always seemed to blow in our direction and we were happily sailing along into the sunset or whatever paradise awaited us.

Then it all suddenly changed and we ended up in unchartered territory with no compass and no navigation system to guide us through the fog. The birth of Alexandra was the catalyst of this sudden shift in fortune when I saw something in him I didn't like.

I was expecting our third child and like most expecting mothers I carried a hidden fear in the back of my mind that something could go wrong. I dismissed this repetitive niggling doubt as nonsense. After all we had two healthy children already. Why should our third be any different? The birth was perfectly normal and because I'd been through childbirth twice, I knew what to expect. Yet I sensed something was wrong. There were more doctors in the delivery room and their faces were glum. More doctors were called into the room, they were wearing their sympathetic faces, the face you expected to see on a doctor when he's going to deliver bad news. I knew something bad was coming and they didn't beat about the bush. Our new-born baby girl had Spina bifida. The bone in her tiny back hadn't fused together and the membranes around her spinal cord were exposed causing nerve damage. My beautiful baby girl was disabled.

We hardly had time to turn around before the endless round of hospital appointments began. Soon followed the operations, minor and sometimes major, on her bowel and bladder, the countless sleepless nights and the worry. Alexandra was around six months old when I began to doubt Stuart and questioned his commitment, his compassion. In the beginning he had showed concern, he muttered all the right words, yet after the initial shock he appeared to fall effortlessly back into his old routine. While my life was turned upside down, he went to work, played golf at the weekends and generally got on with life as if nothing had changed.

The burden of responsibility for Alexandra and her welfare fell firmly on my shoulders and yet I knew that would be the case and I accepted it. It was frustrating because the long-term plan for me had always been to return to work. I was an accountant and I loved my job. I now knew that was impossible as the doctor's hadn't pulled any punches. Ten to fifteen years of operations they had said, on-going care possibly for the rest of her life. They also said they couldn't predict the future. There was no way could I return to work, no way I could leave her with someone else.

The hospital appointments, the scans and the admissions took their toll on me. It was always me who took her and it was always me who stayed with her. Sometimes just for a few hours, sometimes six, seven, eight and sometimes all night. I asked Stuart a couple of times to give me a break but his answer was always the same. Why should he take a day off work for me to simply sit at home? He didn't understand how depressing all those hospital visits were and he didn't understand that I was missing out on the quality time with my other two daughters. Alexandra was taking up every ounce of my energy and I needed to direct some of that energy towards Victoria and Abigail and of course Stuart. He wouldn't have it. We argued about it but he never backed down. For a while I stopped speaking to him and I could barely look at him. I was sick with worry, exhausted with the responsibility of looking after a poorly baby and two toddlers and he would just waltz in from work and start talking about whatever crisis he'd had to tackle that day. I'd sit and stare at him blankly while he prattled on and on about work and all the while I was screaming inside, who fucking cares about your work, we have a sick baby, who gives a shit about you and your work.

Of course I didn't say it, I just got on with things, got on with looking after my baby, knuckled down and planned the on-going hospital visits and trips to the doctors.

Gradually her conditions became the routine in our life. I counted my blessings, as it could have been worse. She had her problems but they were manageable, we were lucky I kept telling myself.

Gradually things settled down and Stuart and I patched up our differences. Perhaps I had been unfair to him, after all he had to go to work he had no choice.

I blamed myself for the marital blip, my emotions and hormones were all over the place. I had needed to blame someone and he was close to hand. We seemed to get over it and life fell back into a steady predictable pattern and we were happy and content again. For a while at least.

I still racked my brain trying to establish a timeline of events. When did our relationship shift from a perfect partnership to a dictatorship? I wish I could pinpoint a year when the equilibrium was lost and he took control. I think I started to notice a change when he began to criticize the way I looked, the way I presented myself. You can pick out a stay at home mum out at the school gates, she is usually the one with the unkempt hair, no makeup and more often than not she's wearing a mismatched tracksuit with a food medallion splashed across her sweat top. I was no different; I was one of those women. Five days out of seven I looked like the typical stay at home mum. My focus was on trying to juggle the kids, the school runs and of course the housework. I came last. Come the weekends with Stuart at home (some of the time) and no school runs it was a little easier and I allowed myself a little 'me' time. I'd take a long shower, put on a little make up and pick out my favourite pair of jeans or a nice dress. All this before the girls even stirred.

At first he started to have little digs, nothing big, nothing serious, but he would casually drop in a little joke about my appearance, especially my weight that was surprising. I'd put no more than a few pounds on since we married, my over active lifestyle saw to that. I'd laugh at first, yet after a while, maybe after the hundredth time I'd heard the same old joke, I stopped finding it funny. I would just smile and say nothing. He'd pull me down constantly, tell be I was a bad mother too and if I ever answered Stuart back with a wise crack he would always want the last word which if I didn't back down would always result in a row. I avoided an argument in front of the kids always.

I did myself no favours. I was giving him the right of passage to continue with the put downs, the insults and gradually they turned more sinister in their delivery. They progressively increased momentum and he moved from being critical about my appearance to being critical about the state of the house. Why was the kitchen always a mess? Why did the kids not tidy their bedrooms?

"You let them away with bloody murder," he'd scream at the top of his voice.

It was something else I'd become aware of, that if the children misbehaved or did something wrong it was always my fault. I had to take evasive action to keep the peace. On the odd occasion they broke something in the house or there was some minor mishap, I'd tell them not to mention it to their dad. I couldn't deal with the confrontation, any small event would be turned into a major issue and I could never win an argument so I stopped trying. The Palmer family dictatorship was in its infancy but growing pace by the week.

It became my focus of attention to try and please him as he began to exercise full household power. He made all the rules without any input from the girls or me. I needed to work on my appearance so I obeyed and joined a gym and started playing tennis. I was now conscious about my weight. In addition, I censured whatever came out of the kids' mouths if I felt it was derogatory towards him in any way. I cleaned the house daily, dashing around like a whirlwind trying to tidy things up before he got home.

I started trying to justify my existence and he took pleasure in reminding me that he went to work all day, he made the money and he had sacrificed his life for this family.

And sex. That changed too. As he exercised more power his sexual appetite increased, as did his bizarre demands. Sex became sex. There was no tenderness, no love. At one time he would be desperate to try and satisfy my needs, to whisper words of love, to express his desire. He was no longer interested in making me happy, that had long gone and it had been replaced with a silent selfish urgency and a brutal execution. He made me feel cheap, almost as if I was being raped. It wasn't rape of course, I'd consented to it, I never refused him and always pretended to enjoy it. He notched the sex up to another level. He was keen to experiment, to try new things, different positions, lots of them, things he surely could only have seen from watching extreme pornography. But now he had the confidence to initiate his fantasies because he was the absolute ruler, the king of his castle. He was testing how far I would go to keep him happy, he had the upper hand and I was jumping through hoops to please him. He exploited me and I succumbed to his every whim with gratitude.

It didn't automatically dawn on me that I was been exploited and used as a plaything. In my naivety I thought that if I satisfied him in bed, if I kept him happy it would bring us closer together. We'd be like we used to be so I indulged him. We had more sex, in different places, even on days when he'd barely acknowledged my presence he'd order me upstairs and tear off my clothes without uttering a word. Sex had become our only form of communication, the only connection we had. Of course he loves me, I kidded myself. He couldn't possibly want this much sex if he didn't love me.

Slowly, over time, I confused sex with love. It was an easy mistake to make because the love in our relationship was a distant memory. I was grateful for any attention he showed me, as I was desperate to keep him, but the only attention he ever showed me was in the bedroom where he used me for his own personal gratification. It mattered not, if that's what I had to do to keep our family together then I was happy to do it.

Then one night it hit me like a sledgehammer. I remember it clearly, like it was yesterday. I tried to pull him towards me to kiss him. I wanted to feel connected to him, I wanted him to feel some emotion, any emotion because I couldn't recall the last time we had kissed. As I drew his head towards me he pulled away, all the while continuing to pleasure himself, still going through the mechanics of satisfying his needs. As his head jerked back I saw his face. It was a look of disgust. I'd seen that expression many times before but never in bed, never when we were making love. At that point I realised we weren't making love we were just having sex. He was just fucking me. I could have been a blow up doll for all the difference it would have made to him. I felt the tears well up in my eyes as he continued to thrust into me. His action quickened and his nails dug into the small of my back as he let out a little cry and climaxed.

He lay there for thirty seconds or so breathing hard and then he climbed from me. He walked into the bathroom and I heard him turn on the shower. He came back into the bedroom and threw me a towel.

"Are you going to clean yourself up or are you going to lie there all fucking night?"

At that very moment I felt violated, I felt like a rape victim and as he took a shower to wash my bodily scent from him, I burst into tears. He couldn't hear me above the sound of the shower and by the time he came to bed my tears had subsided.

And still I continued to accommodate him, still I allowed myself to be humiliated, used and degraded.

I now knew that I physically disgusted him. That was bad enough, but it could never be as much as the disgust I felt for myself.

4

I had limped through the first morning after his departure in a total daze. Alexandra swore categorically that she would not go to school but after some ten minutes gentle coaxing I managed to bundle her into the car. The drive was strained, her face was as glum as her mood. At the school gates she climbed out of the car sluggishly and slammed the door behind her without as much as a smile let alone a goodbye. I couldn't blame her. The way I had delivered the news to her and her sisters was shameful, telling them their Dad was having an affair then walking out and just leaving them to it. The guilt was kicking in; maybe Stuart was right when he said I was a poor excuse for a mother.

It had all been pointless anyway, they didn't want to hear the truth and they hadn't taken much convincing that their mother was talking rubbish. He had worked on them when I hadn't been there to argue. It was a bit of a stupid thing to do when I think back. When I returned from my stomp around the town moor, he had gone. He'd wangled his way out of the situation by convincing them that I was being paranoid, over possessive and jealous.

His very words were that I'd put two and two together and made five. I was a drama queen, there was no other woman and then the most sickening thing I'd ever heard came from Alexandra's lips.

"He told me point blank Mum, he said his three daughters were more than enough for him."

It took me all my time to hold onto the contents of my stomach.

The girls were careful not to repeat the exact conversation they'd had with their Dad, they clearly didn't want to add fuel to my fire.

I hadn't needed to witness the conversation, it wasn't difficult to join all the dots together, sketch an outline. He'd told them that I had got up in the middle of the night, sneaked his phone out of the room and read some text messages, one of which was a from a female work colleague. He'd successfully managed to portray me as a psycho deranged bunny boiler, saying I'd misinterpreted it. Although I knew I was as sane as the next person, when your husband and then your daughters begin to question your motives and your mental state of mind it makes you think. One remark above all hurt me. It came from Abigail. She told me that perhaps I read what I wanted to see. She said it was dark, it was in the middle of the night and I'd been half asleep. No, no, I wanted to scream. The screen was illuminated, there was no way I could have misread 'hot, hot shower'. And yet part of me wondered. Was I half asleep? Was I in the middle of a dream like trance?

Maybe I was this person. I had no idea who I was anymore. I certainly didn't feel like a loved and lusted over wife, I certainly didn't feel like a good mother at that point. However, there was one thing I was crystal clear about and that was what my husband was turning into. He was a master of deceit and manipulation; I had believed his lies for so long so why in hell did I think for one minute that it would be any different for our kids? Of course they are going to believe their Dad, after all, I was the one who had walked out after dropping the biggest bombshell ever to have exploded in their short lives. Fuck, fuck! How could I have been so senseless? I gave him the perfect opportunity to work his scheming, manipulative magic for as long as he wanted.

I watched Alexandra walk through the school gates and then drove straight to my mother's house. I needed to break the news before I lost my nerve. I had been harbouring my dark secret for months. I had wanted to keep our marriage together whatever the cost and I didn't want our friends and family treating him differently, judging him, judging me, because I sincerely believed I could pull the situation around. Nor could I have faced their knowing eyes and their sympathetic smiles all the while thinking poor sad cow.

My mother was different. I'd wanted to tell her many times. She was my closest confidant, my greatest ally and yet I'd also kept it from her. She had to know first and as I pulled into her drive I knew I had to break the news that day. She was the matriarch of the family. Widowed at 50, she kept the family afloat, supporting, protecting and never once complaining. Even before Dad died things weren't easy for her. We didn't have a lot. We were kids from a rough council estate. Some of my brothers' friends ended up in borstal and jail and some were junkies. My Mam wanted more for her kids, especially me, her only girl. She worked hard, providing for us and pushing us to achieve.

I hadn't disappointed her. I followed her directive and I was the first in the family to go to University. When I married Stuart, in her eyes, I went up another notch. We were the family success story with a nice house and kids at private school. Stuart was instated as the family's financial guru, he was the go to guy, the font of all knowledge and he revelled in his role. My mother's daughter had married a top, ambitious accountant. At one time Stuart had welcomed my families attention and praise but for some months now I was aware of the fact that they irritated him. These last few months he had avoided them like the plague. As I walked towards my mother's front door the truth dawned on me. In his eyes I was them and they were me and he cared for neither.

My heart was pounding in my chest, my mouth so dry the inside of my lips were sticking to my teeth as I walked into the lounge and saw mam sitting on her favourite armchair. Once I managed to move my lips the words came tumbling out.

"Stuart's left me," I said.

She just nodded. She knew. The wise, old matriarch.

As I spoke I could feel the tension within me dissipate. She said she had suspected for a long time that there was something wrong. She'd noticed the change in Stuart and the change in me. We held each other for some time and we both cried. I felt better after I had cried, more at ease, more unburdened. It felt that every single tear had been a droplet of pressure that had built up over the course of the last year.

My mother was upset for me and for the girls. She asked if there was another woman and I said yes. She was angry with him and all she perceived that he had done to me. She didn't ask any details, didn't pry into anything and I chose my words carefully. If only she knew the half of what had actually happened. How could I tell her what it had been like and how miserable it had all become for the girls and me? I gave her the salient details and no more.

The drive back home was easier than the drive to my mother's and my head was filled with who I should tell next. I thought about playing dumb, after all, surely it would all come out eventually. Perhaps Stuart would start the ball rolling? And there was a new dread that filled my head. How would he tell people? In my mind he'd had an affair. He was having an affair. In my mind he'd left me for that reason, but would that be the way he'd tell it? All sorts of horrifying thoughts filled my head. I tried not to think about it and concentrated on the road ahead. I'd told my mother and that was the first hurdle. That was all that mattered.

When I arrived home Abigail was in the driveway loading things into her car. She hardly acknowledged me. As Alexandra and I were stepping into the house she was stepping out with more and more things. I could see from the amount of baggage she was carrying to her car that she wasn't going for an overnight stay.

"What is it Abigail?" I asked. "Where are you going?"

She let out a long sigh.

"I'm going to stay with Kevin for a few days."

I was taken aback at first, my brain trying to comprehend the situation, process her words. Kevin, the all brawn, no brain bouncer. Kevin the guy who pumped himself up on steroids, women and alcohol. My god she wasn't serious?

"A few days?" I questioned.

She ignored me.

She loaded another bag of clothes into the car and on the next trip from her bedroom she brought a collage of photographs of her friends that were held in a glass clip frame. Then it suddenly hit me.

"Jesus Christ Abigail, you can't be serious?"

"Mum, I've been thinking about it for a while and I definitely think it's the right time. I don't want to be dragged into yours and Dad's problems."

"You're moving in with him for good, you're leaving us too?"

Her eyes lifted to the sky.

"I'm twenty Mum, it feels right."

I felt the tears welling up in my eyes, the panic building up in my chest. Yesterday I lost my husband and today my eldest daughter was walking out too. I stood in stunned silence as my body trembled uncontrollably.

"I need some space," she said. "I don't know what's going on with you and Dad but I won't take sides. Your saying Dad's having an affair, he's denying it. How do you think that makes us feel?"

Again I wanted to hit Abigail with the exact wording of the message, God knows it was ingrained in my mind. But I couldn't, because once that came out there was no turning back. All the while I still wanted to keep a lid on things, imagining, dreaming, fantasising that one day Stuart would turn around and say he'd made a mistake and wanted to give the marriage a final chance.

"I'm telling the truth Abigail," I whimpered.

"You're both pathetic, you especially Mum."

Her mouth twisted in disgust. It was a look I was used to seeing, it was a face her father had pulled many times over the last year.

Then she plunged a knife through my heart.

"When did you become so sad Mum, you're not the Mum I remember, I have no idea where the hell she's gone."

I resorted to begging.

"Please Abigail, you can't go, you hardly know him. For God's sake please don't leave, we'll sort it I promise."

The words couldn't come out of my mouth fast enough, there was so much I wanted to say to her.

In desperation I pleaded with her.

"I'll go see your dad, I'll beg him to come back if that's what you want, that's what I'll do, just please, don't leave."

She stopped at the door her eyes full as she grasped my hands.

" Mum that's not what I want. Do you not realise what it's been like living here these last six months? Don't you think we haven't noticed the tension, the animosity and the hatred between you? I just need some space, I don't want to get involved and I don't want to have to take sides. I want to stay out of it."

I wanted to scream but bit my tongue. I didn't want to inflate the situation.

"I promise you won't be dragged into anything just stay with me and your sisters, we need you. Please."

Abigail continued to fuss around her personal items in the back seat.

"Please Abigail, we can work this out, just stay."

Alexandra intervened, gently taking my arm.

"Mum just leave it, come inside."

Abigail welcomed Alexandra's interruption and seized the opportunity to make her get away and climbed into the driver's seat. I was quick on her heels but by the time I reached the car she had already turned on the engine and was about to drive off. I banged on the window, my voice was screeching, the neighbours would be twitching at their curtains no doubt. I couldn't have cared less, this was my girl, my baby and I didn't want her to go.

"No Abigail, you're not going. Please stay," I wailed.

She ignored my pleas, her eyes focused on the road ahead and she was off. She didn't turn or wave she just drove off and the fumes from her exhaust left a trail as she sped away. Alexandra walked up behind me, placed her arm around my shoulders and guided me slowly back to the house. I sat down at the kitchen table as she held both my hands and broke down. I cried harder than I had ever cried in my life. This was a hundred times worse than Stuart walking out on me.

5

Abigail leaving was the biggest kick in the teeth I had ever experienced. I had been desperate to keep the family together and yet within twenty-four hours it was disintegrating before my eyes and I had no idea how to fix it. She had said she didn't want to take sides but by leaving, that was exactly how it felt. I felt betrayed by my first child and there was no other way to describe it.

The next day the depression set in like a hard January frost. I couldn't even be bothered to put my clothes on. I sat in my pyjamas perched on the breakfast bar stool, crying into my untouched, lukewarm cup of coffee. My thoughts were seesawing from Abigail to Stuart, from Stuart to Abigail and then they moved to her… Angela Maddison. Who the hell was this woman who'd marched into my family's life and flattened it like a steamroller? Ever since the night I'd found the text message, I'd banished her to the back of my mind. I knew her name and I knew she liked HOT, HOT SHOWERS but that was it. I didn't want to think about Angela fucking Maddison. Before he actually left I was so willing to believe him, so eager to give him a second chance and it wasn't so difficult to forget her name. Now her name was at the forefront of my mind and I couldn't simply pretend she didn't exist. I needed to find out exactly who this woman was. If I could, perhaps there was a chance I could rescue the shit situation I found myself in.

There had been no word from Stuart, not that I had expected to hear from him. I knew he wouldn't contact me as he wouldn't be returning any time soon. He was keeping his head down like the coward he was and hadn't arranged any sort of meeting with his daughters. I wasn't even sure where he was although he was supposed to be staying at his mother's house. That was debatable and she had been conspicuous in her silence since that fateful day he had walked out.

I knew his mother had never liked me. She wore a false smile grudgingly, barely tolerating me and I was under no illusion who she came to visit when she came to our house. Stuart and the girls, not her daughter in law. My friends were aghast when I told them how many times a week she would be plonked on my sofa puffing on a cigarette. Recently I'd noticed she had been cooling off, keeping her distance. Had her son confided in her? Had he painted the picture of the man driven into the arms of another women because of an uncaring, frigid bitch of a wife? She had stopped coming around to the house now. The cigs had taken their toll on her lungs, she had emphysema and was on oxygen 18 hours a day. Her world now reached as far as the hose on her oxygen cylinder would stretch, which was about twenty feet. Even then I didn't ignore her, I did her shopping, went to visit, did the odd job around her nicotine stained flat. Latterly she'd started making excuses for me not to go around to see her, yet Stuart who'd happily let me take on the lion share of responsibility for his mother for close on ten years, seemed to be going around to see his mother most evenings. It struck me then that she must have been privy to what had been going on, she knew about the other woman. Had she even been covering for her son when he went about his sordid business? He had to confide in someone and his mother was the perfect choice.

I didn't want to dwell on Stuart's mother. I was more interested in what he was up to and where he was.

When Victoria came in from college she said he had mentioned taking them all out for a meal. Needless to say I was not on the invite list. I was cautious not to ask too many questions, instead I smiled, gritted my teeth.

"Will that be okay Mum? You don't mind do you?"

I reassured her that we were both there for her and we both still loved her. And yet again I wanted to explode, to tell her what had really happened. It was tough but I stopped myself from bringing up the other woman. I had to leave them to make up their own minds, the truth would find its way out and he couldn't hide the fact forever. I was banking on it. It was the last straw that I was clinging to, that my beautiful girls would somehow work it out for themselves and let me back in their lives again.

I knew I needed to do something, I couldn't just sit drowning in self-pity. Abigail and Stuart might have gone but I still had the other two girls at home and I needed to try and keep some sort of normality and routine. I went upstairs, showered and pulled some decent clothes on.

The house was a mess. We had no food left in the fridge as I hadn't shopped all week and at the rate teenage girls ate, the fridge was barren. Each time I opened the fridge door to retrieve the milk the blinding white emptiness dazzled my eyes. I would have to go to the supermarket and restock the cupboards. And then it dawned on me. I had no cash in the house and not a clue what was lying in our current account. A horrendous thought filled my head. What if he had emptied it? Don't be stupid I told myself, that way he would be punishing the girls too. Not even Stuart could stoop that low. A sudden sense of urgency engulfed me. I needed to get to a cash point ASAP. I had to know. I grabbed the car keys from the table in the lounge and ran from the house as fast as my legs would carry me.

All the while in the car on the way to the cashpoint I told myself he couldn't do it. It would be like starving his daughters. I looked at my petrol gauge. It was on empty too. Fuck, fuck, fuck. No, not Stuart, it simply wasn't possible.

I reached the cashpoint and waited patiently in the queue. Within a few minutes I was in front of the machine and I keyed in my personal identification number then punched in my instructions.

Your available balance - £100

The bastard. He'd stripped the account.

My eyes glared at the cash machine, he'd all but cleaned the account out. His message was loud and clear. He didn't want me getting hold of his hard-earned cash. He hadn't even discussed it with me, he had just done it in his true dictatorship style.

Today he'd taken a step too far and I wanted to kill the bastard. Not only had he left me, he wanted me to suffer too. My mind raced around. What was I going to do? Petrol in the car, money for the girls and two days shopping. That was how far £100 would go. I stood pondering my dilemma; I had to make a decision. I knew we had an overdraft facility of £1000. Could I draw on that? As crazy as it sounded, part of me was still scared of what he would say; he absolutely hated us going overdrawn. Nothing annoyed him more than seeing the account in the red, paying unnecessary charges to the bank. Old habits die hard, even though we were no longer together I still feared his reaction. There was a queue forming behind me and I sensed their growing agitation as I stood staring at the screen doing nothing. The maximum it would allow me to take out would be £300; at least it would give me a buffer until I found out what the hell was going on. I tapped in the amount.

Sorry your request cannot be processed - Insufficient funds.

He'd cancelled the overdraft facility.

It had been two days since he had left and he'd wasted no time, that was blatantly obvious. If I had been under any illusion that this whole thing might merely be a blip in our marriage I was left in no doubt he wasn't playing games. He was serious and within 48 hours of his departure he was playing dirty.

As I left the bank I called his mobile number to raise the roof with him. How dare he do this to his own flesh and blood? His mobile rang three times and then he disconnected the call. I was stranded, as helpless as a day old kitten with just one hundred pounds to my name.

When I arrived home, I threw the car keys on the hall table and marched straight into his study. I didn't waste a minute even though I was dreading going in there, I could sense his dominant presence as soon as I opened the door. He had spent so much of his time within its four walls, more so lately. It was his den, his retreat. I could smell his scent as it clung to every fibre of the room. Part of me was a little surprised he hadn't taken more of the stuff with him. I sensed he'd be back pretty soon. I visualized him sitting at his desk, his office chair slightly reclined as he studied his computer screen, chatting on the phone to a client. I'd witnessed the scene a thousand times as I carried a cup of tea into the room, ever the dutiful wife. It was as if he'd only stepped out for a moment, the room was as he'd left it, the desk completely clear apart from his Number One Golfer coffee mug Abigail had bought him, standing on the place mat by the computer monitor. There was half a packet of polo mints looking forlorn in the middle of the desk. Stuart was meticulously tidy and his study served as a showcase for his OCD tendencies. Everything had a place and everything was in its place including his client files that were uniformly stacked on the bookshelf, each one labelled in alphabetical order. Computer paper and envelopes were piled neatly on a shelf as was his CD collection, listed by artist in alphabetical order. The walls were covered in golf memorabilia and family photographs and my eyes wandered from picture to picture. My gaze fell on a photograph of the five of us together. Alexandra could have only been about three at the time. She was sitting on her father's knee with Victoria leaning against his leg looking up at him. Abigail and I were stood behind the three of them and we were all laughing. Something had amused us. We looked so happy, it seemed to be a different world, so distant from the one I inhabited now. Had he really loved me or had it all been a lie even back then?

I stopped myself from looking as I was only depressing myself even more. I'd come in the room for one reason and that was to look for something even though I wasn't sure what it was yet. Cash, Swiss bank accounts? I knew there had to be something as I was pretty sure he hadn't been in here on the night he'd left. Surely there was some evidence of other bank accounts I might be able to get my hands on, it was his room, his financial HQ. I cautiously started to look through the desk draws feeling uneasy. I half expected him to walk into the room and scold me for snooping on him. There was an old diary where he'd pencilled in dates and times of client appointments. I meticulously checked through it page by page, yet nothing jumped out at me. There were no secret codes or abbreviated words with hidden meanings. Everything looked normal. I moved onto his filing cabinet, methodically checking each folder for something that shouldn't ordinarily be there. He had a folder for each of the girls with every school report, merit badge and sport certificate they'd ever received throughout their childhood. In happier times we would take great pleasure in browsing through the files together. Not today. Today it would bring me no joy, only sadness and I quickly put them back in their place and moved on.

There was a file for every household document, insurance certificates, passports, he was meticulous I would give him that. I painstakingly looked at each piece of paper there was. Nothing exciting, nothing usual. This was stuff that I should have looked at in the past twenty years but it was all alien to me. In the beginning I was over the moon that he wanted to be in charge of all the mundane housekeeping accounts, insurance, bills etc. It wasn't an act of altruism on his part, it was an act of control. Anything that involved money or payments, Stuart handled. It was as black and white as that; there were no grey areas. I handled the groceries and petrol in my car and even then he would constantly berate me for the cost of keeping the house and the money I spent on food. He gradually wore me down into submission, my stomach churning when he made me sit down each month in this bloody study to do the household accounts. He would ask for my cheque book stubs and the cashpoint receipts and he would glare at me as he asked me to explain myself when I went ten pounds over budget. It made me feel like a naughty schoolgirl being reprimanded.

"What did you buy at Katherine's florists for £30?"

Let's think about that one Stuart, flowers perhaps?

Of course I didn't say that, I would ramble on trying to justify my spending especially when it came to things like a gift or flowers for a friend's birthday. I sat in his office in the cold light of day and realised how weak and stupid I had been. He would have a heart attack if he could see me now, ransacking his room, disturbing his things.

I had to move on. There was nothing of interest in the filing cabinet and my attention was drawn to the cupboard which stood below the study window. I had always wondered why he had insisted that he wanted his desk facing a wall when he could have looked out across the garden. I looked out of the window and admired the view, the grass was lush green and the summer flowers were out in full bloom, their delicate heads dancing in the gentle breeze. Why wouldn't he want to look onto such a beautiful scene?

I reminded myself I needed to move quickly. Alexandra would be home from school soon and I didn't want to be in his study when she got home. She would start asking questions. It was his turf and we all knew it.

The cupboard was full of books and manuals and then the file labelled Bank Statements caught my eye. He did all his banking online these days; I was surprised he had any hard copies. My initial euphoria was short lived. There was nothing exciting to be found there either; the statements were two years old and related to our current account. It told me nothing. I knew there was another account as the money wasn't hitting our joint account so he had to be putting his salary and fees somewhere else. Stuart had always been canny with money, when he said we had none he meant in our current account. I knew he had money stashed away, these last few years he was very quiet where he was putting it, once it was we and now it was he and he had made it perfectly clear it wasn't my business. It was his money. I started padding around the room, lifting the stationary, looking behind the printer, then my eyes caught site of a strap peeking out from the side of the cupboard. It was barely visible but I recognised it as his spare computer bag. It was wedged between the cupboard and the wall and he only used it when he was travelling. I pulled it with force as it was wedged tightly. As it broke free I immediately felt its light weight. It didn't have much in it, definitely not a computer that would 'reveal all' and I felt a sudden disappointment. I'd already conjured up in my mind that it was the Holy Grail, the laptop I had been looking for. Why else was he was hiding it? I unzipped it anyway. Nothing. I opened the front pocket and there were two white envelopes inside. An involuntary tingling sensation ran the length of my spine. I opened the first of the envelopes. It was a card with a picture of a matchstick man on the front and the words Stuart's are kind, caring, generous and loving.

Someone had taken his or her time to source a personalized card for him. They obviously didn't know him; he didn't meet any of the criteria on that list. I was eager to open it to see who held him in such high esteem. I caught my breath. It was from her… bitch woman.

Dear Stuart

We would like to say a big thank you from all the team at ATOS. We have enjoyed working with you and we appreciate everything you have done for us over the last few months.

We'll all miss you (especially me!)

Good Luck

Love and best wishes Angela xx

It hit me hard. Especially me!

That's where he had met her, at some bloody firm called ATOS. He had done freelance work with so many companies around the country and it was all becoming clear. My mind was racing trying to think if he had mentioned this company before. It didn't ring any bells. I looked over at his client files. I hadn't disturbed them during my search, they were still neatly lined along the shelf in order. He would have a file for the company if he had worked there, that was for sure.

It didn't take long to put my hands on it thanks to Stuart's meticulous filing system. He had his uses even now. I quickly flicked through the pages but then jumped back to the front of the file. It was probably the best place to start. There was a Letter of Engagement and it was signed March 2009. I took a deep breath as I flopped back in the chair. He'd known her all this time, well over two years and the firm was local, she was obviously local. That meant he'd had plenty of opportunities to meet up with her, to forge a relationship and by the tone of the card she would have taken little encouragement.

I quickly switched on the desktop, it was slow to power up. I had forgotten about the other envelope and I hurriedly opened it while I was waiting for the computer to spring into action. In the other envelope was a Barclays pin number for an account ending in 4245. Our account didn't end in 4245. I was no Sherlock Holmes but it didn't take a genius to figure it out. That's where his money was stashed. Just how much was there?

The computer came to life, the bright blue screen reflecting across the desk. It wasn't password protected, it didn't need to be because Stuart knew that never in a million years would I have ventured into his domain, turned on his computer and accessed his files. That had all changed when he walked out on me. I wasted no time in opening a small yellow folder that had three £££ signs at the bottom. It seemed like the right place to start. I found a spread sheet of the account ending in 4245 and as my eyes scanned the entries my attention was drawn to the balance at the bottom of the page. I fell back in my chair as my brain registered the figures. £55078. I was stunned. There were more entries on a separate word document but no amounts this time, just the name of companies such as Marks and Spencer's, BP, Diageo, Smith Kline, St James's Place, British Gas and reference numbers or codes alongside each one. I counted the names of the companies. There were forty-seven of them, some I'd never heard of and were obviously relating to shares that Stuart held or had previously held with them. I couldn't quite take in the balance of the account or the fact he held shares. In twenty-three years of marriage he'd never shown me the balance of any account other than the current account and he had never discussed purchasing any shares. How much was this bastard worth? Had he always planned to leave me? Had this been his secretive contingency plan for donkey's years?

I wasn't finished. I needed to find out about her. I switched to Google search and typed in the name of the company she worked for and the address. It immediately appeared. One click and I was into the company website. If she held a prominent position she would be listed as a director or senior officer. If her role was more menial I would be struggling to find her and yet something told me that Stuart wasn't the type to waste his time with someone like that. Stuart was always ambitious, aimed for the top. Did that include his lovers too?

Their website had a search box. Logical to start there. I tapped in her name, crossing my fingers hoping that something would appear on the screen. I waited a few seconds while it loaded.

Your search yielded one result.

I clicked on the link and within seconds a picture of her face was staring back at me. I was stunned. It was all so easy. It's hard to describe the emotion of that moment in words. If I were to choose one it would be hatred. This was the woman who had schemed and plotted with my husband with the end result being the break-up of my family. I thought about yesterday when my first born abandoned her family home of twenty years. I thought about the dozens of sleepless nights, the tears, the heartache and the confusion of it all and I thought about the times in bed with Stuart and couldn't help wondering how soon afterwards he'd jumped into bed with her. The root cause of two years of torment fixed me in a hypnotic glare. As much as I wanted to put a brick through the screen I couldn't tear myself away from the image.

She had perfectly groomed blonde hair and piercing blue eyes, her smile pearly white. I could only see the upper part of her body but it was enough. She was slim, petite and clearly a lot younger than me. She was pretty, I could not deny it, but she also had hardness about her. Her features were sharp, almost pointed, and rodent like. Here she was, the mystery woman, my nemesis. I wanted her to be ugly and fat but she was none of these things. Who was I kidding? It got worse, below her perfect picture her achievements were listed and the knife twisted, insult was added to injury

Angela Maddison- Assistant Financial Director

Angela joined the company in 2004. She has held a number of senior posts in both the public and private sector. She has previous experience as a board member and is skilled at working at a strategic level. Angela was born and educated in Durham and has two children. She has a BSc Honours in Accountancy from the University of Manchester and is a Fellow Chartered and Certified Accountant (FCCA).

How much salary was she on? At least £50000 a year, perhaps more. And Stuart? It saddened me to think that I didn't have a bloody clue. Then the penny dropped, surely his hourly rate would be on the client Engagement Letter. My eye's immediately dropped onto the ATOS file where the Letter of Engagement glared back at me inviting me to take a closer inspection. My eyes quickly scanned the page searching out anything which would give an indication of Stuarts hourly rate. Nothing. Urgently I thumbed to the second sheet of the document, as soon as I'd turned the page the figure immediately jumped out at me, my eyes which were now standing out like stalks, £800 a day plus VAT and daily expenses. My jaw nearly hit the desk. I searched through each and every client file and they were quoting rates of between £800 and £900 a day! I quickly calculated the maths. Even at £600 a day, twenty days a month that was £12000 and even if he only worked ten months a year he would be earning £120000. I was unable to comprehend the figures and had way underestimated the salary he was earning. What a fantastic life they'd have together with that sort of earning capacity. I made another quick calculation. Even after tax they'd clear £10000 a month between them. Tears of rage fell down my cheeks. He'd left me and his daughters with a fucking pittance. Why had she done this to my family? What gave her the right? At that moment in time I hated her with every fibre of my being. I would have gladly plunged a knife into her heart if she had walked into the room.

I'd seen enough and I needed to get out of that room. Its atmosphere was so repressive I could barely breathe. It was stifling me. A feeling of anxiety began to well up from the pit of my stomach and I was engulfed with a feeling of dread. I sensed his presence all around me, looking and laughing, it must have been killing him to keep quiet about her. He would have been desperate to show off his trophy to rub my face in it. I had obviously been a joke to them. He would have told her I was frigid no doubt, sexless, no longer interested in that side of the marriage. My wife doesn't understand me. Isn't that what they all say?

I was sitting with a £100 to my name while he played the high-powered hot shot with his significantly younger, bitch girlfriend.

I put off thoughts and plans of kidnapping Angela Maddison and torturing her for all eternity. I had to take some action now. I needed to protect the girls and myself. I switched the computer off, not needing to see anymore, not today. Before shutting the door on that bloody room I grabbed the yellow pages.

There was one more job I needed to do before Alexandra came home from school. I turned to the index at the back of the directory and thumbed through the pages until I hit the classified ads.

I went straight to S. I needed a Solicitor and the sooner the better. Surely a solicitor could get me out of this financial mess, or at least point me in the direction of what my monetary rights were.

6

The turmoil of actually getting around to ringing a solicitor had been a nightmare. In my naivety I had thought it was going to be so easy and yet in the back of my mind I still held on to the hope that Stuart would have a dramatic change of heart and come back. I sat at the telephone table pondering my dilemma. Would engaging a solicitor spell the end of any chance we had to save the marriage? In the end it came down to money, feeding and clothing my daughters. I couldn't put it off any longer. I convinced myself it was no big deal yet as I sat with the yellow pages laid bare before me, I realised it wasn't going to be so simple. Suddenly I was overwhelmed by the reality of it all, my heart began to race and a feeling of trepidation engulfed my very soul. I would have to be prepared for the backlash of my actions. Stuart would retaliate with all the force he could muster, I somehow sensed it. He would want the terms and conditions on the demise of our marriage to be negotiated on his terms. If I started making demands he would dig his heels in, there was no doubt about it. The thought raced around my head like a high-speed train. The truth was, I was scared, he frightened me. The thought of his reaction sent a shudder down my spine. Stuart could be ruthless. I hadn't been married to him for twenty three years without realising how he operated. He was merciless in the workplace too. It always surprised me how he could lay off staff without one ounce of guilt, showing no mercy or sympathy. If I questioned his actions his retort would be, "well, you've got to get rid of dead wood, I can't afford to carry them."

I was beginning to realise his bullish tactics weren't exclusively retained for his work place, it was spilling over into his personal life. I was now about to become the dead wood and I knew it. He would dispatch me with the same measure of compassion he afforded his co-workers. None. I sat paralysed, pondering over my dilemma. Should I take the plunge and ring a solicitor or should I sit and wait to hear from Stuart? He might come to his senses, he might eventually do the right thing by the girls and me? I shook my head. Who was I kidding? I realised the stupidity of my thoughts. I was clutching at straws. The light we once had between us had now well and truly turned to darkness.

I had to come to terms with the fact we were finished and get on with my life, the life I still had with my daughters. If I had been in any doubt, his actions over the last few months had spoken volumes to me. I was surplus to requirements. I had been replaced by the younger, rich, bitch girl. I needed to get on the program, snap out of my self-induced coma and check into the real world. We were finished and I had to accept it.

I studied the classified ads with a renewed vigour. I couldn't put off any longer, it had to be done. I traced my fingers across the pages looking for a name that might jump out at me. Nothing struck me. Why should it? I had never had a reason to speak to a solicitor, I had no idea who to go to. Eventually I decided to pick a name using the same selection process I used to pick my horse in the Grand National every year. I had no interest in its form or its past wins I was only interested in how nice the name sounded. The technique worked and my eyes were drawn to Saxtons. I liked the sound off it and it was an easy name to remember with the added bonus that it was a local firm. I grabbed the phone that had been sitting in readiness by the Yellow Pages. My hand trembled as I struggled to hit the correct numbers on the keypad. The phone had barely rang out before my call was answered. I was taken aback but was impressed with the efficiency. But in my eagerness to get on with the job I hadn't rehearsed what I was going to say. The receptionist had her lines off pat and needed no rehearsal.

"Hello Saxtons. This is Karen speaking, how may I help you?"

I began to waffle, a habit I slipped into when I was nervous.

"Its Mrs Palmer, Annette, ah well, my husband, he's left me and I think I need some legal advice. I don't know what to do. I think I just need to speak to someone at the moment."

The voice on the other end was curt, cutting me off the instant she had grasped the gist of my enquiry but once again I admired the fact they seemed to know what they were doing.

"I'll put you through to someone who can help you Mrs Palmer, one moment."

I was put on hold, her bland voice was replaced with music… Clair De Lune. I had a healthy appreciation for the classics having played it on the piano for many years, however this wasn't the mellow sound the piano offers it was obviously being played on a harpsichord. The noise was jarring and equally as irritating as the receptionist's voice. I waited for what seemed like an eternity and my nerve was beginning to go. I could put the phone down and I would try again later. It wouldn't be so difficult. I felt a sudden relief as I slowly removed the receiver from my ear. Then I heard his voice. He had a deep, rich, dulcet tone and the sound drew me back immediately, enticing me to listen.

"Hello Mrs Palmer, my name is John Bennett, I gather you need my help."

A sudden sense of euphoria engulfed me. This faceless angel had uttered the magic words, he acknowledged I needed help. I had forgotten how long I had secretly been harbouring this need for help.

The words exploded out of my mouth. I could contain them no longer and I practically barked them into the receiver.

"Yes Mr Bennett, I desperately need your help."

I went off on another uncensored waffle, he let me drone on until I reached a natural pause "Mrs Palmer I think you and I need a proper chat, maybe you'd like to call by my office tomorrow morning say ten in the morning?"

"Yes, certainly."

"We can talk more then, in the meantime I don't want you to worry."

I had to interject, how would I pay him? I knew little about solicitors fees yet I knew enough to know a £100 wouldn't cut it. He immediately quelled my concerns.

"Let's not worry about money Mrs Palmer, there'll be no charge for this meeting, we'll sort it out tomorrow. By the way Mrs Palmer I'll need the full name of your husband. It's unlikely but I must warn you, if your husband has sought advice from this firm in the past we wouldn't be able to act on your behalf. It would be a conflict of interest. I'll check, it's nothing for you to worry about."

My husband's name tripped of my tongue. I needed to do this. I was I full flow, Mr Bennett had to stop me. I could almost sense him smiling.

"We can talk tomorrow Mrs Palmer, save the details for then."

"Yes, sure, of course, sorry."

As I placed the handset down and I felt a huge sense of relief, eventually someone was going to help me.

My euphoria was short lived. In my haste to find a solicitor I had made myself late for Alexandra and she wasn't happy as once again she was the last child waiting at the school gates. The only cars left in the car park were those belonging to teachers and the cleaners starting their evening shift. The situation was compounded when we got home, in my rush to pick her up I'd left the Yellow Pages open, smack bang in the middle of the dining table. S for solicitor!

As we walked into the kitchen there it was, a big yellow book glaring at us, the words were practically dancing off the page enticing her to look. It took less than a minute for it to attract her attention. Why the hell hadn't Cilla sat on it? She usually coiled herself around everything left lying on the table, purring in contentment. The amount of times I had shouted at that cat to get down from the table. Not today. Shit! Shit! Shit! I busied myself in the kitchen all the while talking to her incessantly in a vain attempt to distract her attention. If I'd went over to the table and shut the book it would have given the game away. She sauntered across to the table. She stared at the page. 'S' for solicitor.

Shit!

"I don't believe you Mum, Dad has only been gone a few days and you're already going to a solicitor, I bet you couldn't wait."

My heart sank, I gave out a loud sigh, here we go again. Doesn't she realise what he was capable of? Does she have a clue about the financial impact this will have on us? I was quickly beginning to realise my life was like quicksand, whichever way I moved I was being dragged down a little further into the abyss. I would have to reason with her, make her see I had no choice

"Listen Alexandra, I've asked your Dad repeatedly what we were going to do about money, he's ignored us. Worse than that, he won't even answer my phone calls.

"What do you mean Mum?"

"I mean he won't answer the phone to me. He earns bloody fortunes and he's left me one hundred pounds in the bank. I've no access to any more money."

I hesitated, I had never wanted to hurt my children and yet she wasn't a little girl any more.

"You want a new pair of jeans or a sweatshirt then you forget it because it isn't going to happen."

"I don't believe it, we've never went without clothes."

It was true. But I couldn't keep her in the dark, she had to know what he was like.

"You've never went without because I begged and pleaded with him."

Alexandra was shaking her head. She was in denial.

"I don't believe you."

"It's true Alexandra, going to a solicitor is my only option. Your dad might listen to him because he sure in hell isn't listening to me anymore."

She gave me a scowl. There were tears in her eyes. "But mum, he'll never come back if he knows you've seen a solicitor."

My heart reached out to her, I knew he wasn't coming back, I'd been fighting for months in a vain attempt to keep the family together, I had been trying to avoid this moment for as long as I could remember. She didn't realise how hard I had tried to keep him, I couldn't do it anymore, we all had to face reality, it was over and I couldn't dress it up to be anything other than what it was. He'd left me for a younger model, he'd left me almost penniless, at times he wouldn't even take my calls. How desperate could it be?

"Sweetheart, me and your dad are not going to be getting back together."

I could see her eyes filling fuller, she didn't look at me, she couldn't look at me, instead she glided past me snatching her school bag she had dumped on the breakfast bar only moments earlier.

I wanted to throw my phone at her, yell for her to call him on my number to see what happened but she beat me to it and sank yet another knife into my heart.

"Don't do tea for me or Victoria, dad's asked us to go out for dinner with him this evening, he's taking us to Gusto's on the quayside."

Gusto's… Gustos! My blood was boiling. Gustos, the restaurant of the rich and famous, Newcastle footballers and WAGS in every corner, where the main course came with a loan application form! I could barely believe it, this man never took them out for dinner unless it was a birthday or a special occasion and even then it was a Toby Carvery or something of equal stature. Now the four of them were dining on the quayside, no expense spared, at fucking Gustos! I couldn't afford to take them for a Happy Meal at McDonalds and there he was splashing the cash.

"And Abigail is coming too."

Ouch.

I hadn't clapped eyes on my eldest daughter since she decamped to Kevin's, in fact she hadn't even called me. I was beginning to feel like an outcast. I was convinced the girls were starting to see me as the instigator of this whole affair, I had no doubt he would be enjoying every minute of it and he'd have another three or four hours of an uninterrupted propaganda push to hit them with, as they chatted over their chateaubriand and lobster thermidor.

When she left I didn't bother with dinner, instead I opted to pour myself a large glass of Pinot Grigio and munched on a packet of salted nuts, which had been left over from Christmas. I flicked the TV channels, nothing seemed worth the effort of my attention so I switched it off and sat in silence stewing.

Was I actually going mad? Maybe it was my entire fault, had I been the catalyst for him leaving? And the girls taking his side, what was that all about? I was an outsider to my own family, that's how it was beginning to feel. It must be me, they were all together enjoying each other's company while I sat alone in my sad old house in the sad old lounge, sad old miserable Mrs Palmer. It was deadly quite. It was like a morgue.

Once my house had been a home, a hive of activity. I would be bustling around the kitchen making the evening meal, chatting to the girls, asking about their day, gently hassling Alexandra to do her homework. There would be laughter, light hearted banter. I relived the memories of those bygone days, the phantom sounds reverberated around the room, I absorbed them deep within me and so wished I could turn the clock back a few years. If I closed my eyes I could almost taste it.

Yet it had all gone. I was standing in a shell of a house and the life had been drained out of it and it was beginning to be drained out of me. I was at the lowest I had ever been. I poured myself another large glass of wine and the tears flowed freely.

When Alexandra arrived home later that evening I had been nodding off drunkenly in the chair. The noise of the front door opening jolted me into life. I had a bitter taste in my mouth as I slowly came around and miraculously my empty wine glass was still in my hand. Cilla had taken the opportunity to wrap herself around my knees pinning me to the chair. Fortunately, I didn't need to move, Alexandra came straight into the lounge, she looked much brighter, happy even, it was a look I hadn't seen on her for a long time. We both gave each other a sheepish smile, I desperately wanted to ask her what he had said, how he looked, was he upset?

Instead I skirted around it.

"Where's Victoria?" I asked.

"She went straight to her boyfriend's Mum. She said she would see you tomorrow."

Another ouch, another knife thrust into me. Deserter number two goes to house of the boyfriend.

"Did you have a good night," I asked.

She nodded.

"Was your Dad okay, did he say anything about me?"

She looked at me, she was processing my enquiry, deciding what beans to spill. "Dad is fine mum, he asked if you were okay, I think he's worried about you." She said sincerely.

I refrained from giving the appropriate reply. He doesn't give a flying fuck about me, I wanted to say as I gathered my thoughts. He just wants you to think he is concerned.

I pulled back from blurting out my true thoughts. Instead I gave her a faint fake smile. "That was kind of him."

My positive response had given her the impetus to spill more.

"Yes, and he was talking about moving into Aunt Peggy's flat."

"What?"

"Aunty Peggy's flat. After the builders are finished." She said.

She came out with it just like that, as if it was the most normal thing in the world. The family had entrusted Stuart with the keys to old Aunt Peggy's flat. He'd looked after it these last few years, he'd rented it out, said the rental income would help with her care home fees. Poor Peggy, the dementia had slowly turned her brain to pulp, she was condemned to a care home for the rest of her life, her frail, sad frame lay curled lifeless in the foetal position twenty four hours every day. The only time she moved was when they woke her for breakfast, lunch or dinner. Good old Stuart, he'd take care of the flat, the expenses, looked after the new tenants and handled the finances. Now the tenants were gone and Stuart had taken a tighter grip. Peggy had no idea and the bastard was taking full advantage that she couldn't even remember what she'd had for breakfast let alone who had paid the last gas bill.

Alexandra was in full flow. "He said he's having it all white inside, he's going for the minimalist look, should look brilliant and we can visit any time we like."

"That's nice."

"I'm probably going to spend the weekends there once it's all finished."

He'd hooked her in too, poor Alexandra. She'd left me only a few hours earlier, convinced her father would be coming back, ostracising me because I had dared to call a solicitor and during the course of the evening he'd described his new, perfect, permanent home and she'd just happened to forget all about our previous conversation.

She could barely contain her enthusiasm. "He's asked Abigail to help him with the soft furnishings."

I couldn't believe my ears, he hadn't been gone a week and now he was playing bloody Laurence Llewelyn-Bowen. Was I actually hearing this or was I still asleep living a nightmare?

I couldn't help myself, I wanted to know more about his plans. "What builders?"

Alexandra looked at me in bemusement. "I thought you must know, he showed me the plans months ago."

"Months ago."

Fucking months ago, I wanted to shout. This bastard was planning his new home as long ago as that!

"I assumed he'd told you, he's changing the bathroom and the kitchen, it's all getting pulled out and renewed."

I had to take a few seconds to absorb what she was saying, he'd shown her these plans months ago!

My voice stepped up a decibel, I was fighting hard to control my anger.

"When did he show you the plans exactly?"

She backed off, sensing my growing anger and boy was it growing by the second. Months ago, she'd said. Months ago I was trying hard to keep him, pandering to his every whim. I was the perfect whore in the bedroom and Nigella Lawson in the kitchen. I meekly obeyed everything he said, never questioned anything he requested of me and all along he had been scheming behind my back. Scheming and plotting with her, even discussing his devious plans with my daughters and yet they had never said a word.

"I don't know exactly mum."

"You have a rough idea Alexandra, I'm not stupid neither are you, I'd like you to tell me when he showed you the plans, because months ago, as you put it, I was fighting the fight of my life trying to keep my family together and he was playing along with it."

She looked to the floor.

"Please Alexandra, tell me."

Her voice was barely a whisper. "Maybe it was Christmas mum. I think it was when we took Grandma to see Aunty Peggy in the home; he was showing Grandma the plans. I thought he must have shown you too. He said he was updating it for new tenants."

"For new tenants?" I questioned.

"Yes."

It was all so obvious. The old tenants had been given notice but there never was going to be any new ones. Stuart had planned it all perfectly; even using poor Aunt Peggy's money for the improvements to a flat he would be moving into. The property was in one of the nicest parts of Jesmond, the most expensive district of Newcastle. It had four bedrooms and a stand-alone double garage. Stuart had said a few years ago it was worth around £200000, all bought and paid for, the mortgage paid off some twenty years ago.

Then an altogether more sinister thought. My property, our property, the house I called home. What was his plans, his ultimate aim for his family abode? A sale and a split of the proceeds? I didn't doubt it for a moment. He'd want his hands on most of that equity and I knew it.

She didn't need to say any more it was all perfectly clear to me. Now I knew exactly why I needed Mr Bennett's help.

7

I had no idea what to wear to visit the solicitor. I needed to look smart and make an effort, I knew that and I had to make my mind up fast as I was due in his office in little over two hours and I was still lying in bed contemplating what I actually had in my wardrobe that would be suitable attire for the occasion. I closed my eyes and tried to picture the inside of the wardrobe. After a couple of minutes I decided it would be as easy to get out of my pit and have a look. I sat up straight and the pain in my head kicked in immediately.

I felt washed out. When I caught a glimpse of myself in the mirror, my worst fears had been confirmed. I looked and felt like shit! I had large, dark, panda like circles framing my eyes, the wine last night had done me no favours and it hadn't helped that I had been up half the night with Alexandra.

She had got me out of bed in the early hours of the morning, her stomach gripped with pain. It wasn't an unusual occurrence, especially lately. She was struggling to manage her bowel condition. Maybe we needed to see her consultant again to see if they had any solution to this problem that showed no sign of going away. We sincerely believed that Alexandra's problem had been solved when surgeons had removed her appendix and used it as a tube that went directly into her bowel. It promised to be the answer to our prayers. The nerve damage to her bowel was irreparable, there was only one way to control the situation and that was to pre-empty it. Although Alexandra hated to do it, she knew it was the only hope she had for a normal life and she had to embrace her daily and nightly routines.

She already catheterised every two hours and then came the nightly procedure of pumping two litres of fluid through the newly created tunnel in her stomach. Her consultant Mr Mackie, had sold the procedure to us as being simple and pain free. It was merely (his words) an alternative way for her to go to the toilet and according to Mr Mackie it wasn't rocket science. I still recall his words as if it were yesterday.

"If you push enough volume of fluid into the bowel, the contents have to come out the other end. It is as simple and as natural as that."

Of course the reality was that it wasn't that simple, it fell miles short of our expectations. Alexandra and I spent many nights sitting in the bathroom together, waiting for nature to take its course. Sometimes it happened quickly, sometimes it took several hours and quite often it didn't happen at all. It was as if her bowel had its own agenda, it was reluctant to part with its contents and when it didn't play ball, poor Alexandra would be in severe discomfort and excruciating pain. I'd lost count of the times she'd roll around in agony, unable to find a resting spot, her skin hot and clammy. At times, the over flow of her stomach projected vomit from her mouth. Mr Mackie hadn't mentioned the possibility of that. There was little I was able to do but console and distract her from the pain piercing through her small body.

Last night had been one of the bad nights when her bowel had refused to play the game. I'd spent the night mopping up vomit and tried to keep her calm as she writhed around in agony on the bathroom floor. I spent nearly five hours with her and eventually, as the dawn was breaking she found relief as her bowel moved. Her ordeal was over, at least for another night. I took her to bed and cuddled her until she fell into a sound sleep. I managed to get one hour's sleep before the alarm clock blasted out its early morning reveille.

Today she wouldn't go to school, we couldn't take the chance, she might have an accident. She would stay at home, this was our secret, we didn't have a choice, the reality was nobody wanted to hear about incontinence. It was a taboo subject never to be mentioned in civil society so we didn't. To the outside world Alexandra was like any other girl of her age, nobody needed to know the grim reality of her condition.

The events of last night couldn't be avoided, or at least Alexandra's situation couldn't be helped, but I had no excuse for the amount of wine I had knocked back. It was one of those nights when the taste of the grape suited my palette and as the alcohol kicked in, the misery of my life drifted into oblivion. I remember someone telling me once, "Alcohol won't help you."

How wrong they were. It did help, it helped me forget. How good was that?

But my pounding head was telling me different now. The deed was done, there was nothing I could do about it. I was paying threefold for my short lived joy from the previous evening. I looked and felt rough but I had to deal with it. The obvious answer was to avoid the mirror and concentrate on the wardrobe. I wanted to look smart, the last thing I wanted to do was to turn up looking like the stereo typical middle aged frumpy housewife who'd let herself go. I browsed through my dwindling wardrobe, everything appeared old and dated. There was only one answer, I would have to resort to my old faithful navy suit, the Tom Ford designer number. It hadn't been cheap. In fact Stuart had nearly passed out when he saw the price. He indulged me for once, I was so happy the day we bought it. It was a spur of the moment purchase, on a weekend trip we had together in London. Stuart was running the London Marathon on the Sunday, the Saturday had been spent sight-seeing and shopping and inevitably we ended up in Harrods, like all good tourists do. That's when I saw the suit hanging on the mannequin, I was transfixed by its beauty, the tailored lines and the stylish simplicity of the design drew me in like a magnet. He immediately noticed the way I was admiring it.

"Go on try it, see if it fits."

"What, are you serious?"

He dared me so I did, and it fitted like a glove. I was sold on it immediately and he could see the look in my eye. Even though it was in the sale, it cost more than I'd ever spent on a piece of clothing in my life, even my wedding dress hadn't cost that much. Part of him wanted to back out but I think he was past the point of no return and he knew it. Those were the good old days and back then there was always the odd occasion where he genuinely wanted to please me, it seemed to give him a sense of pleasure seeing me happy. How the tables had turned, now his only pleasure was seeing me suffer.

Today I was just thankful I still owned this piece of memorabilia from happier days, it was a timeless number, it would be perfect. It had sat neglected in the wardrobe for longer than I cared to remember and as I pulled it down from the rail, shards of sunlight spotlighted the fine particles of dust lifting from the fabric. It didn't deter me from wanting to wear it. It was a windy day, I'd hang it out on the clothes line for thirty minutes, let the freshness of the wind blow through it.

I laughed inwardly. At least I was confident it would fit me. In recent weeks I had totally lost my appetite and skipped most meals. All these years I had been struggling to lose weight and now all of a sudden it was dropping off me at a rate of knots. At least I could take solace in the fact that the divorce diet does actually work. I was living proof of that and it was true.

I hadn't taken long to get ready, once I knew what I was wearing the rest seemed relatively easy. Before I left the house I checked on Alexandra. I could hear the gentle inhale and exhale of her breath. She was sleeping soundly. I would leave her to her dreams while I went to face my worst nightmare.

I parked my car in the only available client parking space, directly in front of the Saxtons' offices. The three storey Victorian terrace loomed above me; its imposing red brick stature cast an impressive shadow across the windscreen. For a moment I wondered if was at the right address but my concerns were immediately quelled when I caught sight of the gleaming brass name plaque. Saxtons' & Co. It was proudly displayed on the sandstone masonry framing the front door. It all looked rather posh, I wondered if I would be out my depth and part of me wanted to throw the car into gear and speed off. I couldn't. I owed it to my girls to get this mess sorted out quick as possible and I needed to safeguard everyone's financial future. I looked up at the buildings as I stepped from the car. I took a deep breath. It was impressive. These grand statures had once been the homes of the affluent middle class, now the streets were a hive of commercial activity housing trendy bars, firms of accountants, solicitors, letting agents and student accommodation. The wealthy families had long since migrated to the outer suburbs in search of peace from the ever growing community of students and thrill seekers seeking a wild night out. For all its commercial activity, the area was still deemed to be desirable, the realty prices reflecting its status and people still flocked in their droves to conduct their business or socialise in the trendy bars and cafes now swamping the area. Without a doubt it was the place to be seen.

I gathered my thoughts, brought myself back to the moment and opened the car door as I jumped out and skipped up the two stone steps to the front door. All the while my stomach was turning summersaults in anticipation of what lay ahead.

The offices were as I imagined them to be, user friendly and welcoming but hardly in keeping with the elegant façade of the buildings outside. The furnishings were plush but modern, any reminder of their Victorian heritage had been ruthlessly stripped away and replaced with smooth lines and up-to-date contemporary furnishing. The immaculately presented, matching receptionist sat behind her paperless walnut desk, her flawless smile fixed in anticipation of my arrival. She certainly complimented her surroundings, her well-honed welcome was emotionless, almost robotic in manner.

"Good morning Mrs Palmer, I'll let Mr Bennett know you're here, I'll take you directly to the conference room and he'll join you in one moment."

She removed herself from the relative security of her desk and glided across the room like a swan cutting through water. I followed her lead as she directed me to my final destination. The conference room was a carbon imprint of the reception area, lavish and sleek. She suggested that I should make myself comfortable and then she quickly left. Once again I was left with only my thoughts, they immediately jumped to the nagging concern I had been carrying since I had spoken to Mr Bennett the previous day. How the hell was I going to afford all this? My heart began to pound so loudly it reverberated throughout my body, I was once again engulfed in panic and fear, every ounce of me wanted to get up and run as fast as my feet could carry me.

8

Bennett sat at his desk amidst a pile of paper work, he barely lifted his head from his intense note taking to answer the internal call from the receptionist, informing him that Mrs Palmer had arrived and was waiting for him in the conference room. He gave a large sigh, he had almost forgotten about the appointment he had made with Mrs Palmer. He tried to piece together their conversation from the previous day. If he recalled rightly she had sounded rather desperate, he had sensed her urgency to talk and unload her concerns and he had listened to her intently until she ran out of steam. He remembered jumping in, seizing the opportunity to put her at ease, win her over. It was his way with clients, especially the women, let them know from the outset they have a sympathetic ear, a friend. Most of them were just desperate to be heard, no doubt their neglectful husbands had been ignoring them for years. John Bennett was more than willing to fill that role. The listener. The ladies loved a man who would listen to them. Over the twenty years he had practiced as a solicitor he had concluded that women loved to talk, they were overflowing with emotion and sentiment. He had long since learned that he wasn't only expected to be their solicitor, his dual role was that of a therapist and he revelled in both. He had to admit to himself, the few men he represented were far less complicated, they had a pragmatic approach and emotional outbursts were far less the norm…thankfully. The men never cried, why was that? Surely it was just as an emotional time for a man as it was for a woman? It was the crying he found the most difficult to deal with. Such a negative trait and in his opinion so utterly pointless, it never achieved anything. It never ceased to amaze him how readily they were willing to pay £350 an hour for his services to sit and blubber or to ramble on about something or nothing while he sat and listened, nodding his head in sympathy every few minutes. They never told you at law school just how easy it was going to be to make money at this game. That's why he preferred to deal with women. More complicated, sure, but complication meant more hours to bill. Not that this prayed on his conscience for more than a second, it was their money to waste. Even taking into account all of their faults, he loved his female clients. Though he was fifty three years old and relatively settled in his third marriage with a wife ten years his junior, he still had a twinkle in his eye for the opposite sex. He enjoyed playing their saviour, there was something sexually fulfilling about it all, no doubt about it. Praying on their desperate vulnerability afforded him the opportunity to showcase his inherent egotistical masculinity. To the outside world he would appear to be a modest man, yet he knew this trait lurked deep within him. Desperate and vulnerable, that's how he liked them. He recalled a few of his past conquests. It was all so easy, the forgotten wife, starved of love, affection and of course sex. The rich, successful and powerful lawyer, defender of the female kind, a compliment here and there, a telephone call after hours suggesting a quick meeting to talk something over. He smiled to himself. It was all so easy, like taking candy from a baby.

Of course they didn't all succumb to his charismatic approach, not all his female clients were weak and helpless, a fair share of them could only be described as being total ball breakers and he could spot them within an instant. In his experience, the ball breakers were confident in their sexual prowess and generally earned sufficient money in their own right that they didn't have to depend upon their husband. These women had a handle on the family finances and were confident enough to appreciate their own worth, both sexually and financially. He hadn't met Mrs Palmer yet, however, something told him she didn't fall into the latter category. She was the sniffling, wailing crying type, he sensed it. He took a few deep breaths as he moved his paperwork away to the edge of the desk. He'd need to clear his mind, prepare himself, because he built his reputation on winning, and winning was all that really mattered. Winning meant higher fees. Within the legal circle he had earned a reputation as being a shrewd, tough negotiator and he was more than proud to be listed in The Legal 500 as being 'exceptional' and 'a highly acclaimed negotiator.'

His reputation hadn't materialised overnight, it had been an art that he had perfected over time. He had worked relentlessly for years building the family law department at the highly respected practice Valentine's. Initially he had started with just a couple of staff but gradually he built the department up and by the time he parted company with the firm after twelve years they employed nearly fifty people and was recognised as the top law firm in the north of England. It was an achievement that had made people sit up and take notice and he'd been able to take a year out to contemplate what he wanted to do with the rest of his life.

Bennett had only been finished a few months when the head hunters came knocking at his door. He could resist anything except temptation. The money they had offered him was ridiculous and he cashed in on his past reputation to secure himself a lucrative contract with the newly established law firm Saxtons'. The practice was owned by married duo Frederick and Elizabeth Henshaw, the couple had both left their hotshot jobs in London to relocate back to their native north east. The Henshaw's specialised in Contract Law, neither had any great experience in family law yet they had set their sights high, they wanted to incorporate family law into their practice, their vision was to provide a service which exceeded anything Valentine's had to offer. Working in London had given them a taste for the big money, they planned to target the high end clients, after all that was where the real money was. To achieve their goal they needed an experienced hand to steer the family law department, it seemed to them that John Bennett was the obvious choice, they were well aware of his reputation as being a bit of a maverick and difficult to handle yet the Henshaw's thought it was a chance worth taking. He alone could be credited with establishing an exceptional family law department in Valentine's, he attracted the money clients, he was the man for the job. He hadn't taken much persuading to join the newly formed team, he jumped at their offer, the fact was he needed the money, the constant financial demands made on him by his wife had taken its toll. She was a beautiful women, he could not argue the point, more than ready and all too willing in the bedroom but it came at a cost. Her outgoings were extortionate, she demanded constant pampering and the amount she spent on clothes was ridiculous. Given his financial circumstances, the Henshaw's offer had come in the nick of time and he snapped it up without hesitation. It could have been a bitter pill to swallow had it not been for the fact he actually loved his work and all it entailed. It was no great hardship to him, he relished being back in the courtroom, arguing his point. Anything else he did in life never quite matched the euphoria he felt when he won a case. No it was a blessing, he had no desire to stagnate, he was ecstatic to be getting back on the horse and riding it to hell and back. He was the best and he knew it. Mrs Palmer could do far worse than have him acting on her behalf. He smiled to himself. True, it would cost her a small fortune but she would get value for her pound. He was as passionate about a case these days as he was twenty years ago.

He rose quickly from his chair, none of his enthusiasm had been extinguished. He was eager to find out the backdrop to Mrs Palmers story, and yes… to see what she looked like. And he wondered how many more conquests he had in him. He enjoyed the thrill of the chase, that first meeting with the vulnerable one. He looked in the mirror, rearranged his hair a little and tweaked an eyebrow so that the hairs fell into place. He cupped a hand and raised it to his mouth as he breathed into it making sure that the stale coffee smell had been eradicated by the peppermint he had popped into his mouth. All of his female clients were under the impression that their particular break up was unique. They weren't of course, he'd heard it all before in some shape or form. Nine times out of ten, husband meets younger model who reignites the sexual touch paper and as sure as eggs are eggs the older model is surplus to requirements. He always held on to the hope that one day he would hear something truly different but to date it hadn't happened. The stories were all too familiar, quite mundane and it was only the settings and the characters that changed.

He picked up his note pad and pen then proceeded to walk down the single flight of stairs into the ground floor conference room.

I had been sitting waiting in the conference room for what seemed like an eternity, my heart still pounding, adrenaline pumping around my body and I could feel the panic rising. Every shred of my being wanted to bolt, to get out of this room and this bloody building. It didn't help that there was a large imposing clock dominating what had once been the fire breast wall. To combat the boredom my eyes had been drawn to watching the second hand glide around its face. It occurred to me that it symbolised my own situation, time was literally passing me by. I had lost twenty-three years of my precise time, I was just about to turn fifty years old and reflected on what had I achieved. My beautiful girls, that's what and yet financially and career wise I had nothing. That's what Mr Bennett would be questioning me about and I had no answers for him. Suddenly my courage deserted me and I decided to get out of the room. I'd make an excuse to the receptionist, a message from school, Alexandra was ill and I had to leave immediately. I was about to stand up and walk when I heard footsteps on the stairs outside. The heavy, wood panelled door to the conference room gradually opened and he was there. The moment he spoke, I knew it was him, it was his voice, its dulcet tone I remembered from yesterday.

"Hello Mrs Palmer, sorry to keep you waiting, I must apologise. I'll get Karen to sort some coffee then you can tell me all about your situation."

He smiled at me sympathetically.

"Sounds like you've had a bit of a time with this fellow of yours."

He had done it again, he made me feel safe. I could physically feel my heart begin to slow as calmness washed over me. He was here to help me and there was something about the way he smiled at me. My once faceless angel now had a face, a very handsome, almost youthful face and I was momentarily taken aback as he had sounded much older on the phone.

I had no clue why I was taking such an interest in his appearance and my face flushed. Maybe he could read my thoughts. He must have realised I was fixating on his face, trying to gauge him, quantifying his worth within moments of our meeting. I inwardly chastised myself as none of his outward physicality mattered to me anyway. It didn't extinguish my enthusiasm to see him, if he could help me sort out this whole mess then he was my man.

For whatever reason I felt at ease in this man's presence. Maybe it was his rich voice transfixing me, I wasn't sure, but I was keen to talk and didn't need much prompting to regurgitate my story relaying the tale with eager enthusiasm. He listened attentively all the while his hand scribbled notes, his eyes firmly fixed on the page. There was the occasional interjection with a question and he was keen to know about the text message. What did it say? I gave him some of the detail although I couldn't bring myself to mention the scuffle in the bathroom, how he had slapped me and the things he had called me. The words were sitting on the tip of my tongue ready to escape yet I couldn't let them go, they were imprisoned within me. It struck me as I sat there unburdening myself, releasing all my angst and anger that those exact words would never be pass my lips, they would never reach another ear. It wasn't as if I held some ill placed loyalty towards Stuart, I wanted Mr Bennett to know what a bastard he was. Stuart was a slippery fish, the net would have to be cast wide to catch him out and he needed to know what he would be dealing with. Yet I couldn't tell all. My motives for being economical with the truth were purely selfish of course and I would never let anyone know the depths to which I had sunk trying to save my doomed marriage. I had my pride and I clung to it like a child clutching its soother and no one would take it from me.

Mr Bennett had been scribbling notes continuously through my interrogation. I was intrigued to know what he was actually writing and I craned my neck to peer across the desk in a vain attempt to catch sight of the contents on the page. He must have felt my eyes burning into him as he immediately raised his head from his activity and looked directly towards me. It was as if he had read my mind and he was quick to interject.

"Excuse my note taking Mrs Palmer, I am listening to every word you're saying, do not fear," he continued on justifying his actions.

"I like to make notes, it's a lifelong habit, instilled into me as a trainee solicitor."

He smiled as he carefully placed his pen on top of his note pad, the movements slow and deliberate, his mind ticking away, processing everything I had told him. There was a millisecond of awkward silence. I scrutinized his actions, and subconsciously my attention fixed on his deep blue eyes.

"Mrs Palmer, to summarise, you believe your husband is having an affair with Angela Maddison and you base your suspicions on a text message you found on his phone." He glanced at his notes as if to prompt himself.

"You say you've noticed a change in his behaviour towards you, he has been cold and secretive, especially with regard to finances, he refuses to discuss his earning and he has a tight control on the amount of money you spend."

I nodded in agreement; the statement was fairly sweeping yet accurate.

He continued.

"He left the family home voluntarily and you believe he is staying at his mother's and he has not contacted you since leaving."

"No," I said, "I've called him a few times to discuss our finances but he won't talk about it."

He took a small intake of breath.

"And you believe the marriage is over."

It was that blunt. He looked over the top of his glasses at me. He had come to the end of the synopsis; it was my cue to respond.

I sensed he was looking for a simple yes or a no as confirmation that his interpretation of the situation had been correct. In typical fashion I couldn't offer the response he was looking for.

"I'm not sure. When can anyone definitively say that something is over?"

I explained that I was in his office primarily to see what my entitlement was regarding money but the text I had found was fairly damming.

He nodded his head, picked up his pen and leaned forward.

"I see," he said, "I can see that you are not absolutely committed to a divorce just yet but you are convinced one hundred per cent that he is having an affair."

"Yes."

"No doubt about it?"

"None."

"He denies the affair?"

"Yes."

He scribbled as he spoke.

"Mrs Palmer, I want you to do something for me."

I waited with bated breath. What did he want me to do?

"Every time you hear yourself saying Stuart said this and Stuart said that, I want you to read this piece of paper. Do you promise?"

He folded the paper and slid it across the desk. I eagerly lifted the paper unfolding it and as I did so, the words met my eyes. They were simple yet powerful.

He's Lying.

Mr Bennett didn't give me the opportunity to say a single word in response.

He came straight in for the kill.

"Mrs Palmer, we men are strange creatures, I can say with almost certainty he will not admit to this affair. He might admit to past dalliances but never this one. For whatever reason, men refuse to admit to the affair which, as in your case, is responsible for the break-up of the marriage."

He took a deep breath as if to get a second wind for his final blow.

"There are many reasons for this. They could be protecting their new relationship, denying the wife the satisfaction of being right, but above all once a husband admits to adultery the odds are stacked in the wife's favour. He know this, he is an accountant and he knows this better than anyone."

The pace of his voice moved up a gear. It was all very well having an insight into the male psyche, however I was still sitting without two pennies to rub together and not a clue how I could afford the services of a solicitor, let alone next week's groceries. I needed to move the direction of this conversation.

"At the moment my main concern is money," I said. "He's left me with nothing and hasn't given the least indication how he's going to provide for me and his daughters."

With a slight movement of his hand, Bennett beckoned for me to continue.

"All the bills are in joint names, he won't jeopardize his credit rating, I can almost guarantee that."

"So you believe the money will be in the account to cover the standing orders and direct debits?"

"Yes."

My voice was beginning to break, emotion was seeping through me as I drove my point to the crux of the matter.

"But that still doesn't feed me and my kids this week and I have no idea how I can afford to pay for your services. As I said on the phone yesterday, I have no money of my own."

"Nothing at all?"

"Nothing, he handled all of our finances."

Did I imagine a flicker of distaste from Bennett when I said that? I felt the tears rolling involuntarily down my cheeks and my bottom lip quivered. I had gone. I had managed to conduct the meeting so far void of any emotion but now it was pouring out of me like a burst pipe as I blubbered like a five-year-old girl.

My outburst seemed to send Mr Bennett into a tizzy as if he was embarrassed for me. He immediately reached for the box of paper tissues conveniently deposited in the middle of the desk, pushing them in my direction with some urgency.

"Now, now, Mrs Palmer, I want you to stop this crying, you have no need to worry," his delivery quickened, "as for my fees, we can sort that out at a later date. Our first concern is to get Mr Palmer to stand up to his financial responsibilities. I believe that we need to send him a letter to ask what his intentions are with regard to your marriage and providing for you and your dependent daughters."

His words brought me some relief. I sincerely believed that he was more concerned about my personal financial quagmire than he was about payment of his fees.

"But how will I manage in the meantime?" I blurted out between the tears.

If I expected my knight in shining armour to come up with a magical solution I was wrong. Mr Bennett shook his head. He had no answer for that, his soothing voice and kind words couldn't solve that conundrum. He was stalling.

"Mrs Palmer, these things take time, even if we made an application to the court today for emergency financial relief it wouldn't happen overnight. At the moment you'll have to seek help from your family for your immediate needs. I will draft a letter to your husband today. We want to give him the opportunity to explain his intentions. The tone of my letter will be forceful enough, he will be left in no doubt we mean business."

I began to feel calmer. It wasn't ideal, yet at least my situation wasn't going to be stagnant any longer, at least things were beginning to happen. As he spoke he gathered his things together. It was a subtle cue that the meeting was drawing to an end. He stood and instinctively I mirrored his action but he beckoned me to sit back down.

"Stay where you are Mrs Palmer. I am going to send my assistant, Louise, to take some details from you, we need your mother in laws address and your ID, the usual housekeeping sort of stuff."

I could see he needed to be somewhere, it was the third time he'd glanced at the clock. He noted down the exact time. And yet he didn't rush. I was grateful for his concern then he offered his final reassurances.

"I don't want you worrying about this Mrs Palmer, you will be provided for financially if he is making the sums of money you have suggested. He will have no excuse not to pay, just give it time."

He reached out to shake my hand, his grip was firm, his hands soft. The exchange lingered a second longer than I felt comfortable with, yet I had no complaints.

As he made his way to the door, he turned as if it were an afterthought.

"By the way Mrs Palmer, I am giving you a bit of homework to do before our next meeting. You need to go back into your husband's study. If he has investments there will be statements. You need copies, any evidence of earnings. Whatever you can find, copy it."

He smiled a sympathetic smile.

"I'll be in touch."

Then he was gone. I heard his footsteps climb the stairs, I was left feeling mentally exhausted yet I realised for the first time in years I was in control of my own destiny. I could do this, I had started to do it. This was the first massive hurdle out of the way and I'd got through it. The sensation was almost euphoric, I felt liberated from the chains Stuart had wrapped me in.

9

When I left Saxtons' plush offices I was full of confidence and hope. The smooth talking Bennett was going to write a letter to Stuart on my behalf. True to his word, the very next day the postman delivered an envelope hallmarked Saxtons. It was a draft copy of the proposed letter. The words weren't intimidating or aggressive; they merely invited Stuart to clarify his position with regard to our marriage and finances. Bennett had asked that Stuart respond within a seven day period. I was grateful that the tone wasn't confrontational; maybe Stuart's response might be conciliatory if we weren't waging war on him.

The tone of the letter, however, made no impact. The deadline came and went without response. I'd been waiting in eager anticipation for his reply yet there was none… he was silent.

Out of desperation I had contacted Saxtons' to see if they knew what was going on. Mr Bennett was out of the office so Karen, the ever so cool, robotic receptionist, swiftly transferred my call to a girl called Louise. I'd briefly met Louise during my first visit and as a fresh faced law graduate she was eager to please. My concerns were dually noted, the call ended with a promise that she would keep me posted. I waited as long as my patience would allow before I made the second call. Karen was once again on the front line fielding the calls and she instantly recognized my voice and knew exactly who I would be chasing.

"Mr Bennett is in court this morning Mrs Palmer, I'll put your through to Louise."

Louise was as helpful as ever however this time my voice sounded desperate and she must have sensed my frustrations and was quick to interject, offering reassurances.

"I did speak to Mr Bennett after your last call. I told him you were concerned that Mr Palmer had ignored the deadline. He has sent Mr Palmer another letter and has asked that he give a response within three days."

We ended the call as we had started with nothing really resolved, only another deadline to wait for.

Several days later the deadline passed again without any communication. My bank balance stood at £14. Stuart's muteness spoke volumes to me. I was receiving his message loud and clear.

Fuck you and your solicitor.

Perhaps Bennett was also getting the message. He had sent me another letter asking to make an immediate appointment with him so we could, discuss the matter further.

When the letter landed on the doormat I called the office immediately.

My appointment with Bennett was at 2pm. It would cut right into my regular weekly meeting with my good friend Rachel but I didn't have time to see both Rachel and the solicitor in the same afternoon and if I was totally honest I didn't have the energy to do both.

I had called Rachel, full of apologies and we chewed the fat about Stuart and the home wrecking bitch. Now my story was out and she was fully initiated into the inner sanctum of my dilemma. It was our main topic of conversation, in fact we couldn't shut up about it. There was no doubt she was on my side, looking out for me. As luck would have it, Rachel lived very close to Stuart's mother's house and she had to pass his mother's home every day in order to reach her own front door. Now she was extra vigilant, my eyes, watching out for Stuart coming and going. I asked her if she'd seen him.

There was a pause on the other end of the phone. Not like Rachel, I thought.

"I think you need to wise up Annette. I don't think he's staying at his mum's house. I haven't seen him or his car. Even when he was living with you, I'd see his car a few times each week. Believe me I've been looking for it and it hasn't been there once."

Of course he wasn't staying at his mother's house, I knew exactly where he was. It hadn't been difficult finding out where Angela Maddison lived. A quick search on 192.com tracked her down to

Sacriston in Durham. It hadn't taken much detective work to realise that of the three possible Angela Maddisons that came up on the search, only one matched the profile on the ATOS website. The words were still etched on my brain 'Angela was born and lives in Durham, she has two children.'

The other two possible Angela Maddisons didn't live in Durham, neither did they have two children. I couldn't help myself. As soon as I found out the information I had taken a drive up to Sacriston to check out the house. It was late evening, already turning dusk as I turned into the street and half way up the road, sure enough; his car was parked outside her house. I sat for a short while staring at the large bay window hoping to see a glimpse of life inside. My emotions were all over the place as I watched on like a peeping tom. I had mulled over the idea of getting out of the car and knocking on her door. They were obviously both there so why shouldn't I give them both a piece of my mind? I dismissed the thought almost immediately. I was a complete coward. Just watching the house had me shaking like a leaf. I couldn't quite believe I had made the drive and there was no way I could get out of my car and make it as far as the front door. Sadly, for whatever warped reasoning going on in my head that even I couldn't understand, it gave me comfort to know where he was. I was still reaching out to maintain a connection, however small and the thought of an official divorce terrified the life out of me. I knew it was pathetic but I couldn't do anything about it.

I still found out the odd snippet from the girls after their weekly outings with him. A pattern had emerged. Their dad would take the three of them out for dinner one night a week and more often than not it was a Wednesday. Typical of Stuart though he had already downgraded the restaurant. There was no more Gusto on offer, no fancy Tapas bar on the Quayside, they had to make do with a cheap Italian on the high street. As was always the case with Stuart, he couldn't keep the pretense up for very long. If he was going to be treating them on a weekly basis it would have to be a little lighter on his pocket. My blood still boiled every time they went on their weekly jaunt but I had to appear, on the surface, as if I was more than happy that they were keeping in contact with their father. I was practically imploding with anger and resentment, yet I couldn't let it out and show the extent of my feelings. It just festered in the pit of my stomach with no outlet other than my mother's ear. I didn't resent the girls their weekly gorge on cheap pizza or the time spent with their father; they might as well take full advantage of the little on offer. My resentment was borne out of the fact that he still hadn't made any attempt to respond to the letters or make any offer by way of maintenance. I was sure in his warped mind he thought he was paying enough out once he'd settled his tab in Pizza Hut.

When Rachel and I eventually ended our call, I went straight back to bed. It was the middle of summer and the warmth of the sun filtered through the house, however it hadn't managed to reach my bones. I'd been sitting on the easy chair by the hall table for the last hour with a phone clenched so tightly in my grip that my hand had started to tingle. The hall was a gloomy place by mid-morning and the sun's rays had already passed it by. Sitting there had made me feel cold while going back to bed appealed as the sun streamed into my bedroom until early afternoon. I could bask in its rays for another half hour or so. It would still leave me ample time to shower and throw on the Tom Ford in readiness for my visit to the solicitors.

I didn't take much encouragement to take to my bed these days. I had no reason to get up, my life had changed beyond recognition. The problem was I had no routine anymore. My two eldest girls had taken on a new independence since their father had left. Abigail and Victoria no longer made any demands on my time and even their regular phone calls to me seemed like a distant memory. They had weaved their way into their boyfriends families, disentangled themselves from their own fractured tribe. I had nothing much to offer them, only love and time and I didn't push them to come and visit. I understood. They were like injured animals hiding away licking their wounds. Do the fathers who do this realise the pain that they cause to their sons and daughters when they simply abandon them? I'd spent countless hours wondering if Stuart ever thought of the sheer agony he'd put his daughters through.

It hadn't helped that Alexandra had broken up from school for the summer. With no lunch boxes to prepare and no school run, my day wasn't anchored with any sense of purpose or direction. In the meantime, Alexandra and I did the best we could to maintain an element of normality. We had even mapped out our own unique routine. For the most part our rituals were silent, neither of us wanted to engage in heavy discussions, conversations were light and superficial, almost meaningless.

Even in our mutual silence we seemed to draw comfort from one another and I'd often think we were like two lone survivors stranded on a desert island clutching to each other for dear life. Our summer days were generally spent together doing the mundane things like preparing a meal and most evenings we'd sit in one another's company, Alexandra stretched out on the sofa messing around on her computer while I'd slump into the swivel chair in front of the TV with a wine glass in one hand and the remote control in the other.

My old friend alcohol had managed to find me again even though we'd parted company years ago. I was high on life and my family and the booze offered me nothing. Now it was back, it was good to meet up again and it propped me up like a crutch, carrying me through the endless nights of boredom and self-pity. I'd even managed to locate Stuart's old wine collection in the far corner of the garage. He'd wanted to build a small wine cellar at one point but it never quite got that far and he lost interest in the project. Nevertheless, he'd build up a collection of about fifty decent vintage wines, some of them quite expensive.

I'd fight my friend alcohol all day but around sixish I'd succumb. What could I say? It was my guilty pleasure, I'm ashamed to admit it and every day I berated myself for drinking that one glass too many. However I also took a perverted satisfaction that one day Stuart would come calling for his vintage collection and the cupboard would be bare.

As the days passed and as my body habituated to its nightly dose, it seemed to take that extra glass for me to find the relief I was craving for. When I drank I knew my same shitty world was still out there, but it wasn't strangling me like it did in the stone cold sober light of day. It was only the alcohol and the box set of Breaking Bad that managed to keep me going into the early hours of the morning. Even when my eyes were so heavy and I was unable to focus any longer I resisted going to bed, the paradox being that once there I'd struggle like hell to get up when morning arrived. I didn't want to start another day. I only moved when my bladder was full to bursting and then I'd scramble out of bed desperate to reach the loo before I peed myself. There had been some close shaves at times and I'd run the last few steps with my hands in between my legs. Today was no different; it was well after midday before my bladder forced me out of bed.

"Shit!" I was now running late.

10

Bennett climbed up to the second floor office with his usual vitality. He took pride in his reputation as a force to be reckoned with in and out of the courtroom, in his game there was no room for such a failing.

Yet today there was a chink in his armour, his thoughts were on this Mr Palmer fellow, there was something about this case that was already beginning to niggle away at him. He hadn't been unduly concerned when Mr Palmer had chosen to ignore his letters, after all it was common occurrence. The perpetrator of the marriage breakdown would often walk away and be unwilling to acknowledge any responsibility for its demise. It happened with such regularity that he had lost count of the number of times he was forced to engage the services of a private detective to hand deliver divorce papers.

Palmer was no different to the rest of the bastards and if the truth be told, his reluctance to play ball would only increase the costs, swelling the firms coffers and adding another few pounds to his end of year bonus. Bennett smiled to himself; whenever there was a negative he could always swing it to his advantage.

But that wasn't the problem. He'd heard Palmer was an awkward bastard to deal with… really awkward, almost to the point of being a bit of a specialist in the field of awkwardness. Would Palmer dare to take him on? Would the unthinkable happen? Would he walk away the victor if battle lines were drawn?

The thought gripped the pit of his stomach.

The snippet of information on Palmer had been channelled through his usual sources. The legal system in Newcastle was a close-knit society. They kept each other informed, operating in much the same way as any old school tie network, scratching each other's backs with regularity. Many of the solicitors, barristers and judges knew each other from Law School, charity events and of course Court and close alliances had been drawn up. The unsuspecting client was under the impression that their legal representative was their best friend and that they viewed the opposition legal representative as the mutual enemy.

Bennett laughed inwardly.

"The stupid bastards," he muttered under his breath.

Little did the poor souls realise that the clients were simply a means to an end, the cash cow, a pawn in the grand legal game of courtroom chess. It was a big, rigged game.

The legal fraternity stood together, almost like a band of brothers and their task was to generate an indispensable service created out of their inflated bluster. The truth was, solicitors were never out of pocket and the client would pay their fees regardless of whether the case was won or lost in the courtroom. Billable hours, that's what really mattered.

The only time Bennett saw his peers as competition was in the courtroom itself. He liked to win but was quick to realise he was only as good as his last case. That's why he had spent so long at the top. The triumph of a judgement held in his favour was his greatest motivation. The courtroom scrap was like the noble art of boxing. They'd trade punches round after round but when it was all finished there would be a glance of respect and they'd shake hands, often whispering that it had been a good fight not to mention a decent purse. Not a clean one like in boxing, but a good one nevertheless.

Like his colleagues he would fight tooth and nail to maintain his reputation, yet outside the confines of their position they would think nothing of enjoying a pint together at the local pub, or one of the clubs in the city centre.

And even more bizarrely, over the years, a get together of some of the more experienced lawyers and solicitors had turned into a Friday afternoon ritual. Bennett and his pals would get together in one of the more expensive bars on the Quayside, a stone's throw from the City Law Courts. More often or not the afternoon hours would extend into late evening depending on their mood. Invariably the cases they were working on would surface, once the conversation pertaining to golf or football had been exhausted. As the evening drew on and the liquor loosened their tongues they would share information to help each other's cause, after all weren't they all brothers in arms? It had been on such an evening that Bennett had first mentioned the Palmer case. He was fishing to find out if Palmer had knocked on any of their doors asking to be represented. If he had approached any of the local firms, Bennett would have found out. However, none of his drinking crew had heard of Palmer. Bennett coloured in the detail in an attempt to prompt any lapses in memory. It wasn't unusual for the memory to slip on occasion especially when alcohol was flowing freely.

Old Bob Swan raised his brow when he heard the name of the street that the Palmer family marital home stood in. Bob had been head of his Company's Family Law Department since the early 90's. He was semi-retired these days and now spent most of his time on the golf course. It beat being stuck in the boardroom, yet it didn't stop him keeping a close eye on his team. The address had rang a bell, and the name 'Palmer' yes, that had meaning too.

He interjected, proud that he was able to make the connection.

"Do you mean Stuart Palmer, plays golf at Ponteland?"

"Sounds like the man, do you know him?"

"Oh yes, I know Palmer," he smirked as he held his glass out indicating it was empty. Bennett took the hint immediately.

"Would that be another double Bob?"

Bennett stood and casually sauntered over to the bar. A couple of minutes later he placed the glass on Bob's table.

"Well, spill the beans old fella, how do you know Palmer?"

Bob gave a mischievous smirk.

"He played golf at my club, but I think he's moved on, apparently he didn't like the winter greens, wasn't a happy chappy."

Bennett sat rather bemused. Where was this going?

Bob took another mouthful, his voice lowered a decibel or two and his tone was more somber.

"He's a crafty piece of work John, in a nutshell Palmer is a bastard, he's a sly one make no mistake and good at it too. If you're fighting him then I'd say you have your hands full."

It was possibly the conversation he'd had with Bob that Friday evening that was now at the forefront of his mind before his meeting with Mrs Palmer. Bennett's thoughts were definitely elsewhere as he made his way to his office. He now shared his room with Louise, his new protégé, her desk directly facing his own. He had no complaints about this new domestic arrangement, after all she was pleasing to his wandering eye and a pleasant distraction from staring at the shelved walls weighed down with row upon row of lever arch files displaying the client names. They were going to be working closely together; it would seem to make sense that she was at hand to see her master at his best. He had even suggested it to the office manager. There were worse things than spying on Louise as she leaned forward to reach for a pen or a stapler. It was inspiration, he told himself and it did no harm. Bennett sat watching her movements for a few minutes, his hand wandered down to his groin region and he squeezed hard. There was nothing on his mind other than the beauty of her female form. If he were but ten years younger she would not have been beyond his reach, yet even he had his limits, he would have to admire her from afar where she was safe from his clutches. But there was one woman who wasn't.

He dropped the Palmer file onto the desk and opened it. Of course Mrs Palmer wasn't out of bounds. She fell within his age range and she wasn't at all bad, quite pretty for her age and she hadn't let herself go like some of the others. He recalled some of the women who had walked into his office, unkempt with no pride in their appearance and they were at a loss as to why their husbands had strayed. Bennett had no doubt why. The mystery for him was why the husbands had stayed around for so long. Stupid bitches. Mrs Palmer on the other hand was well groomed, had a certain style about her and he loved the way she dressed and the way she carried herself. Just what was her husband thinking of? And even in the short period of time he'd known her, there had been a shift in weight, she looked leaner in both body and face, her scales must be touching figures she'd never seen for years. There was something about her that drew him in, just being in the same room as her, taking in her scent, a mix of natural female odour, and expensive perfume that hit the spot perfectly. A bit classy, private school education he'd guess and certainly from money. She may be scrimping for pennies at the moment yet she'd had money to hand at some point. Her whole attire shouted of someone who'd been used to the finer things in life. Her clothes, that beautiful suit she wore, the bag and shoes had not been cheap, he knew that.

Living with his third wife had given him a certain expertise. She would return home laden with designer bags and boxes on a regular basis and he had an eye for well-cut cloths. I've been given no fucking choice, he thought to himself.

He pictured the oh so familiar scene as she stood in the centre of the room, parading on her own personal cat walk, showing off, as she reeled off the designer brands – Gucci, Donna Karen, Dior, Louboutin. Oh how he hated Christian fucking Louboutin and his shoes. He could have purchased a decent condo in Bermuda for what she'd spent on Louboutin shoes over the years.

Mrs Palmer had a vulnerability which was most appealing, especially to Bennett. He hated to use the word but he knew exactly what he was. He was a predator, a sexual predator. Sex was his one and only consideration and he loved using women (usually his clients) as his personal playthings. It was clear Annette Palmer had been under the thumb of her dominant husband for many years, and so brain washed by her philandering husband she was incapable of having one original thought of her own. Every sentence that spurted out of her mouth was peppered with references to her husband. Bennett pitied Mrs Palmer's stupidity. How could a woman of her quality be so naïve, so gullible? As Louise leaned forward again he sighed inwardly. The Mrs Palmers of this world were exactly the type of women he preferred. The vulnerable, the fragile, easily led and eager to please especially when it came to the bedroom. After all they had a point to prove to their legal representative. Once in the bedroom the fragile, vulnerable ones were on a mission and that was to prove that their husbands hadn't left them because of anything lacking sexually.

What would Mrs Palmer be like? He couldn't stop thinking about it and already he had developed a soft spot for the woman. He would give it time, she'd be ripe for the picking soon enough and there was little doubt he would be more than happy to oblige her needs. They all had needs, financial, emotional and especially sexual. He'd need to work on Mrs Palmer starting from today. If his luck was in she might be game, only time would tell. In the interim he would focus his attention on providing her with his legal expertise.

He caught Louise's attention as she sat engrossed, filtering through the mail received that day.

"Louise, can we crack on with the Palmer case? I need to make some notes and push a few more letters out. Do a little research on old cases similar to hers. She's in a little later and I need to show her some activity to keep her happy."

Bennett was fixed in his ways. He didn't write up his own letters, he was dependent on the clerical staff to transcribe his dictated notes. Now it was Louise who was on the receiving end of his secretarial requirements and he wasn't slow to take full advantage of her willingness to please. Louise immediately picked up her pen and note pad. She was aware of her designated role and sat poised in readiness to scribble down his every word.

Bennett was just about to start his dictation when Mrs Henshaw marched into their office. She had a brash manner and was an imposing sight with her flame red hair. She repelled him and he struggled to hide his distain. His voice was light as he greeted her.

"How are you Elizabeth?"

She didn't respond to his question as she jumped straight to the point of her visit to his pokey little office. Her voice was like cut glass. The time spent living in London had all but extinguished her northern accent. On occasion the façade would slip and the odd reference to her Geordie upbringing would find its way into her vocabulary but not today however, her tone was as sharp as ever.

"I was just wondering, are you seeing Mrs Palmer today?"

Bennett lifted his head.

"Yes Elizabeth, I am, after lunch. The husband is proving to be a little awkward. I'm just about to draft him another letter."

Henshaw's face was fixed without expression as both Louise and Bennett set their gaze upon her waiting for a response.

"Has she signed the Letter of Engagement yet, and has she been billed? I haven't seen anything pass through accounts."

Bennett gave a silent sigh. Now he knew the reason for her visit, she was eager to get the money rolling in. Bennett was the top billing divorce solicitor in Newcastle. That's why they had head hunted him in the first place. Bennett was no charity case, that was a given, he had every intention of charging Mrs Palmer premium rates but first he needed to establish what was in the pot to distribute. He had a good idea. The location of the family marital home, the husbands earnings, cash stashed away, it all added up to a substantial sum. They were by no means one of his high-end earners yet there was a pot to be divvied up and it wasn't to be sniffed at. The work he had done so far on the Palmer case was already mounting up to a decent fee. There had been the letters issued to the husband and of course the consultation and the behind scenes that the client knew nothing about and which could be easily exaggerated. The game, the good old game of law. The cost was sure to get heftier once they commenced divorce proceedings. He'd try and get that commitment today then he would start the billing soon enough. Mrs Palmer was already dependent upon his services. He had trapped her in his web of charm and security and she wouldn't be going anywhere else

"I have it in hand Elizabeth, we've already racked up a couple of grand. I would expect us to start billing next month, however we're waiting to hear from the husband, he's rather quiet at the moment."

"Good, I'm glad to hear it John."

"By all accounts, he holds the purse strings and once we know his position then we'll have a clearer idea what our role is going to be. The couple may want to go to mediation, who knows at this stage."

"Not interested John," Elizabeth said. "Billable hours, that's all that matters to me. Get her to sign up and tell her it's gone past the point of no return."

She didn't wait around making small talk. As quickly as she had entered the room she was gone, her flame of red hair in full view as she turned quick on her heels to make her exit.

Bennett looked at Louise, a knowing smirk spreading across his face.

"Shall we get back to where we were Louise?"

Bennett had no desire to make any further reference to Mrs Henshaw, especially to Louise, a new member of the team. She would have sensed his indifference to Elizabeth and it would have been very unprofessional of him to openly criticise his employers. Louise could make her own mind up on the motley Henshaw duo. Bennett was more interested in the job in hand. Time was of the essence and he was looking forward to seeing Annette again. Annette, not Mrs Palmer, he would be calling her Annette from now on. It was time to start the chase. He proceeded to dictate the letter, not wasting another minute. It was short and to the point and it didn't take much thought on his part. Gone was the conciliatory tone. He had a clear message to translate to Palmer:

Dear Mr Palmer

Our Client: Annette Palmer

Despite several letters imposing many deadlines we have still not heard from either you or your lawyer with regards to the matrimonial and financial position.

Please be clear that if we do not hear anything from either you or your lawyer by Monday 25th July then proceedings for a financial order of maintenance will be commenced.

We look forward to hearing from either you or your lawyer as a matter of urgency.

Yours faithfully

Saxton & Co.

Once finished Bennett didn't waste another thought on the matter and he waved his hand as if mimicking a gesture that he was pushing it to one side. His voice was flat as he asked Louise to ensure it was dispatched in the evening post.

"And get me a copy for Mrs Palmer. I'll give it to her at the meeting."

As an afterthought he added, "send it recorded delivery, at least we'll know it has been received and more to the point he'll know too."

His dictation had taken no more than two minutes although he added one hour of billable hours into the client file, another forty five minutes for Louise's preparation of the letter. Daylight robbery didn't even come close to describing it.

11

It had been a couple of weeks since my last visit to Saxtons' plush offices and much had changed. This time I didn't feel the same level of nervous anticipation as I had on that very first visit and my emotions weren't so high. There were no tears lurking behind my eyes ready to burst free as they had done during that visit. Those emotions had all but been extinguished and replaced with anger. I was angry that he hadn't responded to any of the letters, angry that he was obviously shacked up with the girlfriend, angry that he had made no attempt to contact me to sort out the finances.

Anger was my most prominent emotion. I couldn't deny there were times in the evening when my body was drenched in alcohol I would become melancholy, that's when my gentler emotions would rear up making me burst out into tears. Today, thankfully, those emotions were caged away out of sight and there was no alcohol racing around my veins. Not much of it anyway.

The Saxtons' offices had a strange familiarity about them now. I felt like I had got to know the place and the people. Karen was perched behind her desk as usual, as cold as ever. Once she had greeted me, she made her obligatory call to Mr Bennett to let him know I'd arrived. Then like a sloth on speed she disengaged herself from her desk and directed me to the Conference Room.

Karen didn't do small talk and it suited me just fine. For some reason I found her attitude very appealing and I knew exactly how it was with Karen. There were no mixed messages, no nonsense.

Once again I was left in the Conference Room with only my thoughts and that large dominant clock that once again reminded me, as it had on my last visit, of my wasted time and my wasted years in a loveless marriage. I refrained from allowing myself to engage in deep thought, instead I glanced around the room looking for a point of interest, anything to distract me. It wasn't like the waiting room at the doctors where their walls were littered with posters. Saxtons were far too posh to deface their walls with posters. Fortunately I didn't have to debate the lack of anything interesting in there for long as Bennett and his pretty assistant Louise were already making their way into conference room, Louise a step behind her boss in recognition of his seniority.

As he entered the room his hand was already extended in readiness to greet me. In response, I stood up to attention like a soldier on parade.

He spoke. It was always his voice that got me, it transfixed me, quelling my anger.

"Good afternoon Mrs Palmer," he paused for a split second. "May I call you Annette, now that we are a little more familiar with each other?"

I nodded.

"How are you?"

"Fine, I'm okay, trying to stay focussed."

He appeared to look me up and down.

"You look very nice today, radiant in fact."

I was taken aback by his comment. I'd spent a month not eating or sleeping. My routine involved lying in bed or dosing myself up on alcohol. Most of the time I felt like shit and looked pretty much the same. Nevertheless I had made a bit of an effort.

I smiled. I'll take any complement these days no matter how flaky.

"Thank you."

As I voiced my acceptance of his dodgy compliment I found myself lifting my hand to my hair, fiddling with it as if I were preening myself. I caught myself in the act, and feeling foolish I quickly returned my hand to my lap out of sight. So starved of complements, I had desperately latched on to his benign words interpreting them to my own ends.

I brought myself back to the business in hand, noticing my own lever arch file with my name printed across its spine.

Bennett picked up the file and flicked through it. As he did, he held his chin in the cup of his hand as if deep in thought. Louise sat at his side as he studied the file, her role was somewhat surplus to requirements. I turned to Louise to break the awkward silence.

"It's lovely out there today, not a cloud in the sky."

Both of us had half an eye on Bennett as we eagerly waited to hear his synopsis of the situation.

Eventually he raised his head ready to speak and we both listened intently.

"Mrs Palmer, err Annette, how are you managing at the moment, financially I mean?"

I was ecstatic he had asked, overjoyed that this was the first thing on his mind because to me, that was the crux of the matter. It wasn't the other bitch woman or Stuart walking out on his family or divorce proceedings. No, when push came to shove I was barely surviving, sorting the finances out had to be the number one priority. I was barely scraping through with the help of my family and a small piece of ingenuity on my part.

"Not too well," I said. "I've even had to resort to a little bit of dishonesty in order to get a hold of some money."

Bennett raised an eyebrow.

"Tell me."

I couldn't wait to tell him. Sherlock Holmes would have been proud of my detective work and subsequent execution of the plan. I explained to Mr Bennett how difficult it had been getting Stuart to stump up cash. He'd blocked most of my calls when I had tried to contact him to ask what I would do for money. I never got a response. When he did answer the phone he listened to me for no more than a minute or two as I presented my case of hardship and then, as if he didn't have a care in the world, the same four words.

"Talk to your solicitor."

A hundred pounds here and there was all that he had come up with. He was making me sweat, keeping me hanging on. I was in a state of desperation. It was at that point I realised that desperate times called for desperate measures. I wasted no time setting myself up with on-line banking, something I had never done in the past. After a few computer glitches and my constant pleas to Alexandra requesting her assistance, I had managed to navigate my way round the on-line banking system much to my surprise. It was a joint account after all. The bank called me and asked me my date of birth and a few random questions that only I would know the answer to. Then bingo! I was on line with full access to our joint account. I was quite chuffed with myself and even more so when I'd had a quick peruse around the joint account and realized that all the direct debits were in either joint names or his name alone.

Mr Bennett leaned back in his seat and smiled. I think he knew where this was going.

"The payments are due out of the account on the 1st of every month," I said, "and based on my calculation they amount to £726. I know Stuart well enough to know he wouldn't forgo the direct debit payments. He's never missed a payment or a bill in his life, he is so conscientious when it comes to things like that. Like a kid with a new toy, I constantly accessed the account waiting for him to deposit the money to cover all of the payments."

Bennett nodded.

"Go on."

"Sure enough, the Gods were on my side for once. At around two in the afternoon on the last working day of the month, £726 was deposited into the account in readiness for the payments on the first of the following month. I'd kept watch on the account the whole day. My perseverance had paid off for once and I practically ran down to the bank to retrieve it. My face was beaming like a Cheshire cat as I withdrew every last penny he'd deposited."

Mr Bennett was laughing, Louise too. They were on my side.

It had been the only lift I had experienced in the last month, the euphoria of the moment was like a drug. The same day I received a phone call from Stuart, the first in a long time. I expected him to raise the roof but he didn't. I told him his daughters had to eat but he ignored me and calmly stated that he would be putting a new system in place the following month. It was easy enough to transfer the direct debits to his sole name account, I knew that, but nevertheless I had a little money in my pocket and it felt good getting one over on him.

But now I was back too square one and once again I was sitting in front of Bennett desperate for his help.

I explained my monthly requirements.

"And of course there's your bill too. When will I be getting the first bill and how much will it be?"

Bennett pulled out a page from the file and studied it. I half expected him to push a bill across the desk but he didn't."

"Don't you worry about that Annette."

"But I am worried Mr Bennett, I don't even know your hourly rate."

Rachel and I had discussed his hourly rate. She said it could be as much as £150. I nearly fell off my seat, surely Mr Bennett wouldn't charge that much?

Bennett ignored my appeal. Instead, as was his manor, he listened to me intently whilst I relayed my financial dilemma. This time he didn't have his pen in hand scribbling notes, that job was left to his able assistant Louise. He sat with his hands crossed in his lap whilst she frantically made notes.

Eventually, after he'd heard enough, he interjected in his usual style.

"All very good, and I don't blame you for doing that, but it hardly helps with next month's finances."

His voice was slow and deliberate.

"Annette, I believe that your husband is proving to be rather stubborn. I think our softly, softly approach thus far has yielded nothing."

He checked his notes on file.

"We have given him one deadline after another and he's ignored them all. Are you sure, you've given us the correct address for his mother's home?"

I reassured him there was no doubt I had given him the correct information.

"And he's definitely living with his mother? I mean there's a girl involved here, could there be a possibility he is living with her?"

Bennett knew. He had been in the game too long and if a husband had left his wife for a younger model then there was a massive possibility that he would want to share a bed with the girl who had enticed him into her bed in the first place."

"Yes," I said, "I think that could be a distinct possibility."

He nodded at Louise and almost telepathically she picked up her pen as it hovered over her legal pad.

"And would you have an address for the other woman Annette?"

"Yes Mr Bennett, I have."

I reached into my handbag for a notepad and pen. The address of the bitch woman was etched into every corner of my brain. I wrote it down, even the postcode and slid it across the desk.

He pondered a moment then grinned at me as he removed his

glasses.

"I think we have no choice but to be a little more aggressive Annette. Your husband needs to know we mean business. I intend, with your permission of course, to send him a letter today saying that if we do not hear from him or his lawyer by next Monday then we will have no option but to commence proceedings for a financial order of maintenance."

He looked back at me and smiled.

"It won't do any harm to let Mr Palmer know that we are well aware of his alternative domestic arrangements."

He showed me the letter and I read it carefully. He turned to Louise.

"Send the letter to both addresses."

I sensed a slight agitation in his voice. Mr Bennett wasn't used to been ignored and it didn't sit well with him. I was depending upon his wealth of knowledge and experience to sort things out.

"We will get this sorted Mrs Palmer, just you wait and see, you will have your day with him."

He showed me a copy of the letter and then reached into his file for something else. He handed it over to me, explaining exactly what a letter of engagement was and I signed it.

"It all seems rather final," I said meekly, "rather official."

Bennett leaned forward.

"It's not Annette, but sooner or later you need to face the facts."

I shook my head, I wasn't sure what he was getting at.

"The dreaded D word Annette. Divorce. In my experience it's an inevitability."

It was three days later when it came in. Louise had opened the post as usual and she thought it important enough to stand and take it personally to her boss. She walked the short distance to his desk and laid it down.

"I think you should see this Mr Bennett."

The letter was headed Richfield Grealish, a firm based in Durham. It had been sent on behalf of their client Mr Stuart Palmer. He raised his eyes above his reading glasses that were balanced on the end of his nose. Bennett scanned the content, years of practice looking at legal documents had trained his eye to go directly to what really mattered. Immediately he homed in on two sentences. It was a long letter full of bluster, none it relevant apart from two simple sentences:

We write to confirm that we are instructed by our client in relation to Divorce Proceedings

And further down:

We are instructed by our client that he considers it would be possible for him to petition for Divorce based upon your client's 'unreasonable behaviour.'

A big smile pulled across his face.

He didn't need to read any more and he looked back at Louise who was sitting awaiting instructions. She didn't have to wait long. Bennett had digested the information. The firm was based in Durham and the solicitor was a Simon Steedman. He'd heard of neither. He wasn't surprised at the content, it was what he had eventually expected.

His direction to Louise was straightforward.

"Send a copy of the letter to Mrs Palmer today and ask her to make another appointment with me to discuss the matter further. I should imagine after this she'll want to get things moving."

"Yes, Mr Bennett."

The case file was on his desk. He reached for it and opened it at the accounts page. He entered the figure '3' into the accumulated billable hours section of the page.

"At last a result," he muttered to himself. "Worth at least another three hours of my time."

12

Simon Steedman of Richfield Grealish had eventually taken up the mantle and started banging Stuart's drum for him, fighting his cause, squaring up to Bennett.

When Saxtons had sent me Steedman's first letter and I had read the contents I was raging like a woman possessed. The postman had deposited the letter directly in my hand while I was standing in my front garden passing the time of day with Mr Hannon my next-door neighbour. I remember the day clearly. It will be embedded in my memory for as long as I live. The sun was shining and the air was warm and scented with the sweet smell of cut grass. Maybe it was the fine weather that had lifted my mood, because that particular day I had set about doing some jobs around the house, jobs I had put off for far too long. I'd even managed to get myself out of bed as the birds were still singing their first dawn chorus. It had been the first time I had been up that early in a long while. I had taken the opportunity to sit outside on the patio drinking my first coffee of the day. It was just after 7am and I was enjoying the gentle warmth of the early morning sun and the stillness that accompanied that time of day. The early rise had also given me renewed vigour, I felt good, it had even prompted me to spend some time in the garden, weeding and cutting the grass. In fact I had spent the whole morning doing jobs outside in the fresh air and for once in a long while I had felt like my old self again.

I remembered a notice on someone's desk once upon a time, though I couldn't think where. It read, 'It's been a great day, watch some bastard spoil it.'

I swear that quote could have been written for me.

I was pulling stubborn weeds from between the block paving on the front drive when he ambushed me. Ted Hannon was a retired schoolteacher and had been our adjoining neighbour since we first moved onto the street. He had always struck me as being a man who had possibly been a weasel in a previous life. He was tall and skinny with a narrow face, sharp features and a beak like nose. There had been a Mrs Hannon at some point before my time on the street, but the neighbourhood rumour mill churned out that she had left him for another man, not that Ted had every shared such information. He was the local busy body and far too interested in other people's affairs to let slip any gossip about himself.

He never went out of the house. Who needed a burglar alarm or a Rottweiler with a fearsome bite when you had someone like Ted living next door?

Admittedly there was one drawback. Ted was like a cat waiting to pounce on an unsuspecting mouse. He would jump out from nowhere and you would be stuck for an age, listening to him spout off about something or other. The amount of times I had stood praying for someone to rescue me.

That day I had been crouched in a kneeling position pulling weeds when I had the urge to stand up to relieve the throbbing ache in the base of my spine. That's when he had walked up behind me and nabbed me. My heart sank just a little when I realised who it was. Here we go again, he'll keep me talking at least an hour about some crap or other.

"What about the bloody council's new bin policy," he said.

And so it began. We discussed the City Council's bin collection policy, totally inadequate in Ted's humble opinion, then the conversation moved on to the decline of the global Honeybee population, how our ecosystem would collapse if these pollinators were obliterated. I had been depressed enough over these last few weeks and the last thing I needed was Ted Hannon's doomsday predictions. I was just about to make my excuses when the subject of Stuart came up. The thought had crossed my mind that Ted might have noticed Stuart was no longer living with us. He would probably think he was working away again. I had decided to run with whatever story Ted had formulated in his own imagination. As predicted he had noticed a change and couldn't resist mentioning it.

He cocked his head to one side like a bird weighing up his prey.

"I haven't seen much of Stuart lately at all. Is he busy?"

I had always prided myself as being an honest person, lies didn't easily roll off my tongue, however I was not averse to avoiding giving a straight answer

Fucking his new women Ted, living his new life in his new home, that's why you haven't seen him, I wanted to shout out.

Instead I played the diplomat, giving Ted an answer that would give him no room for gossip.

"You know Stuart, very busy at the moment, here, there and everywhere."

I kept my eyes directed at the mass of weeds that I had piled up ready for the recycle bin. I avoided looking directly into his beady eyes, I didn't want to be locked into that particular conversation. It was always the eye contact that drove me to giving in to total honesty.

It didn't deter Mr Hannon, he had something on his mind and he wanted to say it.

"I thought he must be busy," he said. "I shouted across the fence when he was going into the house last Sunday but he totally blanked me, not like Stuart at all I thought, he's usually happy to have a little chat, you know, pass the time of day."

I wanted to stop him in his tracks and rewind the conversation. Did he just say he saw Stuart going into the house? Last Sunday, he'd said. Of course that's what he had said, Stuart knew the house would be empty on a Sunday afternoon. As sure as night followed day our family would always make the weekly pilgrimage to my mother's house for Sunday lunch. The sneaky bastard knew that. Steam was practically billowing out of my ears. How I kept calm I'll never know. My face glazed over with a fake smile.

I couldn't help myself and stood up.

"Was that last Sunday Ted, about three O'clock?"

I had made a calculated guess that he would have waited until mid-afternoon to creep in like a cat burglar, knowing for certain that at that time we would all be happily ensconced at my mother's house.

"Yes that's right Annette, spot on, he was in a real rush, he was barely in ten minutes then off he dashed, loaded up with paper work."

Mr Hannon laughed.

"The poor sole was working on a Sunday, you'll drive the fellow into an early grave."

I smiled weakly.

"You know him Ted, a real workaholic."

I was livid but had barely got the words out of my mouth when the postman popped a letter in to my soil covered hands. I looked at the postmark 'Saxtons.'

It was my cue to get the hell out of there.

"I must go Ted, I've been expecting this letter, it's quite important and I have a bit to do."

I dashed into the house and quickly ripped the letter from the envelope. My eyes quickly scanned the page. I read the first few lines, legal jargon, small talk. I read further and it was at that point I read the words that turned my world upside down. My husband claimed that he had grounds to divorce me for my unreasonable behaviour. I am embarrassed to admit, I turned into a women possessed. I picked up an empty coffee cup and hurled it across the kitchen. It smashed against the far wall and broke into a hundred pieces. The rage engulfed me. I was shouting out loud, totally flabbergasted at what I had just read.

"A total fucking joke. He has the affair, he leaves me and I'm being the fucking unreasonable one."

I picked up a plate and that flew in the same direction as the coffee cup.

"The bastard, the utter bastard."

I had never known rage like it. I thought back to all the mental turmoil he had dragged me through, the pain and suffering, not knowing where the next ten pound note was coming from in order that I could feed my children, the fact that I'd only went to a solicitor to talk finance.

"The fucking miserable bastard."

And why the hell had he been sneaking around the house behind everyone's back? My head was practically exploding trying to process both bits of information. I collapsed onto the kitchen chair and felt the tears welling up inside me, but this time they were tears of rage, not sorrow.

"What was the bastard looking for?"

I rose slowly from the seat and found myself moving around the house taking a general stock of its contents. Everything seemed as it should be. In the bedroom his clothes were still hanging in his wardrobe, his cufflink box and his assortment of manly junk housed in his bedside drawer were still there, untouched. It was obvious that his secret missions to the house were directed towards recovering paperwork, Ted had mentioned he'd been loaded up with paperwork.

There was only one room left to visit. I marched in to his study, the room I had been avoiding for weeks. I could feel his presence; his scent still lingered in the air, yet now it didn't bother me as it had when I had last opened the door into his inner sanctum. His imprint was gradually being erased and I decided at that very moment I would reclaim the room and use it as my own. I needed to move forward. It would no longer be the private lair of Stuart Palmer. I sat in the office chair in front of the computer trying to control my anger. I was still raging, I was heavy handed, opening draws then banging them shut once I saw the contents were still intact. Who was I kidding anyway, with so much paperwork filed away in one draw or another how could I tell what he had removed? I was still swearing out loud but the decibels were decreasing. My anger had reached its peak and was on a steady decline. I forced myself to take deep breaths, and as I did so, my eyes scanned the room. What was it he was looking for? My eyes settled on the shelf and at the neat row of client files he'd had lined up there. They had been depleted and the gaps had caused the remaining files to fall over. The once regimented display now looked dishevelled, their line had been broken. Now I knew exactly what he had been looking for. Every file had a letter of engagement with dates and of course his daily rate. I quickly scanned through three or four files. Every single letter of engagement had been removed. I breathed a sigh of relief. Thank God I had had the presence of mind to photocopy one of them the first time I'd gone in there after he'd left.

I made a decision that I wanted the locks changed that day. If he had started divorce proceedings he wasn't getting in my house. I rang a few locksmiths in the Yellow Pages and although they weren't outrageously expensive, I realised I couldn't afford to pay them. I could hardly send the bill to my husband and he was still making sure money was in short supply. It made me realise what a desperate financial situation I was in. Fortunately, I didn't need one. As luck would have it my brother Darren called later that day and I blurted out my sorry predicament. He was more than willing to help me as I told him about my unwelcome guest. He went straight out to purchase the new locks and came across that very day to fit them. I was so relieved to see his happy smiling face as I opened the front door. It lifted me just a little and I was grateful that he'd taken time out of his day to help me out. As he went about his work removing the old Yale locks and replacing them with new ones, I hovered around him, offering refreshments and keeping him company. When he had finished he held the new keys in the air shaking them together, indicating the job was done.

"There you go sis, he can't just walk in when it suits him now."

I felt no remorse or guilt. Stuart had made it abundantly clear he had moved on. I couldn't walk into his new home so why should he think it was okay to visit mine whenever he felt like it? I sent the girls a text saying I had changed the locks and new set of keys would be at home for them. I knew there would be some sort of reaction when Stuart found out what I had done and as it turned out, I didn't have to wait long for it to happen.

It all kicked off the following Sunday. I half expected that Stuart would make another visit to the house. How I would have loved to have seen his face when he realised he couldn't get in. I was enjoying my usual roast beef Sunday lunch at my mother's when I heard the phone ring. My brother Roger did the honours and answered the call.

"It's for you Annette, it's Victoria."

I knew what was coming and I wasn't keen to go to the phone but reluctantly I left my half-finished plate to answer the call.

"Mum!"

It was Victoria and she was upset, I heard the gentle sobbing with her very first word.

"Mum, he knows He's been to the house again and can't get in."

I'm ashamed to admit it but a smug smile of satisfaction pulled across my face. However it quickly disappeared.

"He's blaming me Mum. He said I must have known." The floodgates opened and the tears flowed. "I'm sick of this Mum, totally sick of it all."

I wanted her to be with me right at that moment. I wanted to protect her, comfort her. Suddenly I had lost my appetite. She was right, she hadn't wanted any of this, none of my daughters were to blame for any of it.

She was crying hard now.

"He's sent me a text saying I must have known about you changing the locks and he said not to go near him again. He said he's finished with me."

If Stuart had been standing in the room at that moment I would have happily choked him. He had to blame someone so he had picked on the weakest link in the chain, the most sensitive child of our three children. Once again I could feel the anger well up inside me.

I had always protected them, always tried to intervene in whatever Stuart had thrown at them over the years. During arguments I instinctively stood between him and the girls whenever he set about them with his verbal abuse. I'd try and mediate to keep the peace and at times he could be quite vicious and hurtful, two or three heavy sentences being enough to reduce them to tears. When the girls had turned from children to teenagers they had dared to voice their own opinions. I took it as a normal phase of development, but not Stuart. It appeared no one had an opinion on anything, especially not his daughters. Stuart had attempted to raise his hand to them but I would never let it happen. I always stood in front of them fearful he may strike them but he never did. On a few occasions I took a few blows myself as he vented his frustrations on me. To my knowledge, he never got to any of them, physically at least. Mentally it was another matter. It surely must have taken its toll over the years. Ever since they could talk they'd had to walk on eggshells and dance to his tune in an attempt to keep him happy. We all did it with such regularity it became the norm. Now they were alone and vulnerable and I felt so helpless. I could no longer shield them from his verbal attacks and of course there was nothing I could do against the power of a cutting text message.

Still I tried to keep the peace.

"Calm down Victoria, you know what he's like. He says these things and he doesn't mean it. He's annoyed at me and taking it out on you. He'll realise soon enough it has nothing to do with you."

"He won't Mum," she sobbed, "he means it. He doesn't want to see me again."

Stuart was running true to form again. He always had to blame someone, generally the weakest. It was the same at work. He had to create turbulence in calm waters and then apportion blame. He'd walked away from our relationship with his girls still onside. Why couldn't he be happy with that?

And yet I knew it wouldn't be long before the cracks would start to show. I was convinced that his run in with Victoria was just the start.

I managed to calm her down, telling her that it would all be forgotten about in the morning. I said it was our family home and he was quite naturally upset. As our conversation came to an end I found myself defending him and making every excuse under the sun. What the hell was wrong with me?

Nevertheless, as I had predicted, Stuart's temper subsided enough to at least invite Victoria to the weekly pizza fest. All appeared well on the surface as the girls met up at home and left together in a taxi. It was business as usual as I settled down in front of the TV, wine glass in hand with Cilla curled up on my knee. I was convinced the cat was trying to stop me from drinking and found ways to deliberately pin me to the chair so I couldn't get to the fridge where the chilled wine would sit calling my name with frequent regularity.

That evening, just after ten, all three girls waltzed in together. I knew something was wrong as normally, after their meal, Abigail and Victoria would go racing straight off to their boyfriends. They rarely called back to the house as a unit. I could gauge by their sullen faces that something was up and yet I was glad to see them all together because it had become something of a rarity these days.

I tried to raise a smile and lifted my empty glass.

"So who's going to get me a refill?"

Abigail did the honours and brought the bottle to refill my glass. I'd had two glasses already and my mood was relaxed, yet I could feel their tension. It was almost tangible, the prickliness of their demeanour as they had walked into the room. I tried to make light of it, trying to defuse whatever tension was building. At that point I was feeling far too giddy to care. The alcohol had well and truly kicked in.

"What's up chicks?" I asked. "Has daddy downgraded the restaurant again?" I raised an eyebrow. "Tell me it wasn't McDonalds?"

The joke wasn't well received as none of them raised a smile. I sensed it and changed tack. Suddenly I was concerned. Maybe there was something upsetting them other than a bad pizza.

"What's happened, he's not having a go at you about changing the locks is he?"

As usual Abigail took the lead. She shook her head.

"No, not that mum."

"Well what is it then?"

"He's going on a golfing holiday with his friend Andy and a group of lads."

I could feel the anger rising again. Even the alcohol couldn't work its magic and keep me calm. I was sitting on the bones of my arse and he was planning a holiday. I was trying to suppress the anger in my voice but it didn't work. It was rising from the pit of my stomach and eventually came out.

"I do not believe that man. He refuses to give me any money and he's off on his bloody holidays. He is unbelievable."

I sat shaking my head in total disbelief.

But there was something else. There was more. I could read their faces and the girls were angry, upset. I had shielded them from most of the finance issues and they didn't know the half of it. Dad going on a golfing break would not have distressed them that much.

"What is it?"

Abigail flopped into a chair.

"He lied to us Mum. It was as plain as day, we all noticed."

Alexandra was next to take a seat.

"He's lying mum, he's not going on a golf holiday. I bet he's going with her and he sat there all evening and lied to all three of us, his own daughters. Lie after bloody lie and he wasn't even very good at it."

From the tale they had told me it was apparent that his story didn't add up. At first he had said he was going to the South of France, then it was the north. I imagined them cross-examining him once the first few fibs had fallen from his lips. He mustn't have expected an interrogation. If he had, he may well have spent a little more time on his story.

According to the girls, at one point he had said that the 'golfing group' were going by coach then it was by car.

"I asked him how many was going," Victoria said, "and he said he didn't know exactly. A little later he categorically said there were twelve of them."

"His story was full of holes," Alexandra piped up. "It all sounded odd, however the final nail in his coffin was the fact he had no idea which golf courses he would be playing."

"That just wasn't dad," Abigail said. "He would have researched every bloody course, every hole, including the yardage and the quality of the greens."

The girls knew that a golf fanatic like their father would know exactly which courses he would be playing and that bit didn't wash with any of them. I sat dumbfounded as they reeled off lie after lie. They described how he had looked… uncomfortable. A trip like that would have excited Stuart and he'd be like a schoolboy waiting for Santa Claus on Christmas Eve. But no, Stuart had been uncomfortable, shifty, squirming and lying his way through dinner.

I expected to feel joy, after all they had finally seen through him and his seedy affair but I looked into my beautiful girls broken faces and felt only anger and despair. He had tormented and hurt me for months and now he was doing the same to his own flesh and blood. A seed had been planted in their heads and it was beginning to grow. I had always suspected if he had enough rope he would hang himself and from the comfort of my swivel chair, glass in hand, I sat and watched the rope tighten.

13

The shenanigans of Steedman's letter and the changing of the locks caused a flurry of activity between the warring solicitors. Stuart and I had almost stopped speaking completely and even the text messages had dried up. The one time husband and wife no longer communicated, our legal team did it for us. It was a crazy situation and I knew it. All I could think of was the mounting costs and the charges for every phone call, every message, every letter and every meeting. Everything involved a minimum four-way conversation where messages were passed from me to my solicitor who forwarded it onto his solicitor and then to him. Stuart would digest the communication and then contact his solicitor again, then the magic bloody roundabout would turn again. And of course it had become a line of Chinese whispers and like most chains it was sometimes open to misinterpretation.

The arguments escalated after that initial Steedman letter and then things turned nasty. I received another letter of only two lines. Bennett wanted to see me urgently. I placed it on top of the ever-growing pile and picked up the phone. Within forty eight hours I was sitting in his office again.

He was not happy.

"With your permission Annette, I'd like to write straight back to him."

He handed me the drafted letter.

Mrs Palmer has made it quite clear to us that she does not

consider that the marriage breakdown is any of her fault and should your client choose to issue proceedings based on unreasonable behaviour they will be defended vigorously.

Mr Bennett, or John as he preferred me to call him now, was on the warpath, gunning for Stuart. He leaned over the desk and smiled. It made me feel a little uncomfortable. I could smell a little mint on his breath and if I wasn't mistaken, a whiff of expensive smelling aftershave.

"My original thoughts were that we should petition for divorce on grounds of unreasonable behaviour Annette, but that letter from Steedman has thrown a spanner in the works. I believe we should go for the jugular. I think we should consider petitioning for divorce on grounds of adultery with an unnamed women."

I voiced my concerns.

"But why would Stuart publically admit adultery when he refuses to admit it privately?"

He edged ever closer.

"In my experience, the last thing a cheating husband wants is for the name of their mistress to be made public. That is without doubt the worst-case scenario. Whilst they won't be happy that they've been ousted, the threat of naming the other woman usually makes them see sense and they'll rarely want to admit to the affair which was the catalyst for their marriage break up in the first place. I'm convinced Stuart will not want Angela Maddison named and don't forget he will also be under pressure from her. The last thing she wants is to be named in court proceedings."

I'd love to name and shame the bitch, I thought to myself, but I could see his point. If he admitted to adultery with an unnamed woman it will all be so much cleaner. It all made perfect sense.

He shuffled a few papers on his desk.

"We know all about Miss Angela Maddison and if he concedes that we will keep her name out of the picture."

John suggested that we utilised the services of a private detective and as we had the other woman's name and address to save time it might be the best route to take.

"We'd get proof that he was living there at least a few days a week and then we would name her, detail the exact dates of Stuart's little stopovers with photographs of his car throughout the small hours of the night. A picture of him leaving her premises at daybreak would put the ball firmly in our court."

I shook my head. I could only think of one thing.

"But Mr Bennett."

"John."

"Sorry, John. A private detective, won't that cost a fortune? I hate to remind you, but I have no regular income. I don't know where my next penny is coming from and I haven't a clue what my bill stands at."

John steepled his hands together as he leaned back in his seat. He seemed to take a moment considering his response.

"You keep worrying about the money Annette."

"Can you blame me?" I replied.

He leaned in again, this time closer than ever.

"Don't worry about the financial side Annette, I'm on your side, I'll take care of the accounts.

Bennett couldn't have been happier. Money was all Annette Palmer had on her mind, or rather the lack of it. He hated to admit it but sometimes he even felt quite sorry for them, the broken ones, the ladies that had been wronged and cast to one side. It was hot in the office today and Annette had removed her jacket. She wore a thin white blouse, its tightness accentuating the shape of her breasts. Bennett liked what he saw; he'd need to be careful not to stare too much.

The bill was mounting and the time was probably right to at least give her an idea of how much it stood at. That always put the fear of God into them. It was a hammer blow, like a right hook from a heavyweight boxer and what made matters worse was that they knew for certain they had only just dipped their toe into the water. It wasn't over by a long shot. There was an awful long way to go and starting over with a newer less experienced and yes, less expensive solicitor would be madness because they'd have to start all over again and starting all over again meant paying two sets of bills.

"The private detective is quite reasonable Annette. We use a retired ex-policeman, who doesn't really charge an awful lot."

"How much?"

Bennett smiled again.

"Expenses, he really only takes his expenses."

It was true. Bill Harris was good and had retired on a full pension but like most coppers liked a good drink. Bill was paid a pittance from the firm, around seven quid an hour, cash in hand, but a few days work each week kept him in beer money. Bill was happy, the firm was happy, Bill's missus was more than happy that he was out from under her feet and that their bank account always remained in the black.

"It works out at about forty pounds an hour Annette."

He studied her carefully. She was expecting more than that. Forty pounds in the grand scheme of things didn't sound so bad. She could relate to a figure of forty pounds.

She sniffed a few times, then blew into a paper tissue.

"What does it entail?"

Bennett liked this bit. It made him sound as if he knew what he was talking about.

"It's all very straightforward Annette. Bill will fit a tracker device to your husband's car, a small device no bigger than your thumbnail. He'll place it into a wheel arch. As the name suggests, it tracks the car and Bill will follow it on a lap top computer. As soon as it starts heading for Sacriston, he will spring into action."

Bennett explained that the ex-policeman had a powerful zoom lens camera that would also take quality photographs in the dark.

"We will track his movements and log them all. Every time he parks his car outside her address is another nail in his coffin. Photographs of him coming and going are priceless. We'll give him and his solicitor all the evidence they want, accurate details of his visits there and his sordid stopovers."

"My friend think he stays there quite often," she responded.

Bennett raised an eyebrow.

"And what makes her think that?"

"She lives in the same street as Stuart's mother, at the address he claims to be living at." Annette paused momentarily. "She says he's never there."

A smile pulled across Bennett's face.

"Excellent news, just excellent."

Bennett smiled because Annette was smiling too. At last there was something going on, a little light at the end of the tunnel, a brief glimmer of joy in her miserable life. He could only imagine the despair and frustration she had gone through over the last few months, perhaps even years. When was the last time she had been held close? When was the last time a man had kissed her, whispered in her ear and dragged her into the bedroom telling her that she drove him wild? They liked that, the vulnerable ones. They loved to hear that they were still attractive, desirable, a turn on, but most of all they loved to be told that they still had what it took to make a man lose complete control.

"It's nice to see you smile for a change," he said.

Annette shrugged her shoulders and her face flushed a little.

"I haven't had a lot to smile about lately."

Bennett paused.

"Annette," he said, as he reached for his diary pawing through a few pages, "I need to talk to you a little more but can't see any space in my diary over the next few days. I was wondering."

He looked up, made eye contact.

"Yes?"

"I was wondering if you would possibly meet me for a little dinner one evening?"

Annette hesitated, unsure of what to say.

"Nothing too fancy, just a couple of hours somewhere where we can talk without distraction."

"If you are sure that's appropriate."

Bennett stood.

"Of course, a working dinner that's all. Unfortunately needs must, there's not enough hours in the day. I'll fix something up and call you soon."

Annette reached for her handbag and jacket and rose from her seat. She took the hint, it was time to go. Bennett had spent enough time with her for one day.

As she said goodbye and turned to leave, Bennett's eyes followed her as she walked out of the room. He took in the elegant shape of her back and then his eyes continued downwards until they settled on her beautifully proportioned backside and something stirred deep inside him. He let out a small breath and sighed. He just had to see what lay beneath that classy outfit. He was desperate to get Annette Palmer into a hotel bedroom, or better still her own bedroom. That was something that would really hit the spot.

What was abundantly clear to me was that John had been there and done this all before. He knew exactly what should be done, right down to the private detective. It all sounded a bit Hollywood to me, but then all he would be doing was logging Stuart's visits to the other women and then confronting him with the evidence. There would be no shootouts and no high speed car chases. An admission to adultery with an unnamed woman. Grounds for divorce.

Part of me wanted to name Angela Maddison, wasn't she the reason for this shambolic mess in the first place? But I was clever enough to do whatever John advised me to do. Why would I question his judgement? He had a wealth of knowledge on the subject. He had given me his personal mobile number and insisted that if anything was worrying me I should ring him immediately.

I admired his commitment yet still worried about the cost. I knew it was mounting and I still hadn't seen a bill. John insisted that there were ways to sort the fees out but never explained how.

He copied me in on a letter he had sent to Stuart, asking him to return any documentation relating to investments directly pertaining to me. Something jogged my memory and I remembered something about an ISA Stuart had persuaded me to take out and it had to be in my name for tax purposes. I never kept the receipt book of course, Stuart had squirrelled that away with all the other investments. He had a file and it was loaded with share certificates, bank details, endowment statements etc. That was long gone. It would have been the first thing he lifted on his secret house visits. I called John at the office and when I told him about the investment he appeared to be over the moon.

"Oh Annette, I am glad you remembered that. Anything in your name you are entitled to have and I will make it my business to ensure he hands it over pronto. It could amount to quite a few thousand."

My heart skipped a beat. John was right. I recalled an initial investment of three thousand pounds but then Stuart had added to it for several years. The thought of six or seven thousand pounds would easily cover John's bill and still leave me with enough money to treat the girls to a small holiday, a weekend break or something like that. It would be a Godsend. He wasted no time contacting Steedman to demand the return of the ISA payment book and I was grateful for his prompt action.

However, the on-going battle about maintenance was still raging. Stuart had been asked to provide evidence of his earnings, yet despite the repeated requests made by John, his side were not forthcoming. He had however made an offer of maintenance. It was Louise who called to break the news.

"It's rather a paltry offer I'm afraid," she said, the anxiety clear in her voice.

"But at least he's made an offer," I said optimistically.

"Yes."

How much?"

"£600 per month."

I was speechless as I almost dropped the handset. £600 a month to keep the house, feed and clothe Alexandra and myself and although the other two girls were spending most evenings away from home, Stuart did not know that.

"Mr Bennett is fuming with the offer Mrs Palmer," she said, as I returned the handset to my ear. "We are well aware that Mr Palmer charges out £800 per day for his services and works at least twenty five days each month."

John was quick to write back to the other side requesting that Stuart needed to 'inject a little realism into the equation.'

He didn't stop there. He wanted Stuart to know that he wouldn't be calling all the shots with regard to finances and he ended his curt letter 'we note your client's attempt to dictate all matters to our client in relation to finances and indeed in relation to the marriage. You need to impress upon him that this is not going to happen.'

They were strong words and they got an immediate response. They asked what steps I was taking to gain employment and also wanted to know what appropriate benefits and Tax Credits I had applied for. What the hell were they? They were saying that because of the ages of our daughters I was no longer Stuart's responsibility. It was harsh and it hurt. He made me feel like an unwanted pet deposited at the Cat and Dog Shelter, the owner shirking away from the on-going responsibility for their upkeep. I'd sacrificed my career in order that he could pursue his, I was the mother, the child bearer, the cleaner, the cook and the housekeeper. But now I'd served my useful purpose it was time to let me go. I was the old incontinent sheepdog that was no longer needed, the one that curled up in the corner of the kennel, the mangy dog that no one noticed anymore.

It was one of the few letters from Stuart's solicitor that caused me to break down into tears.

And the lock changes hadn't gone unnoticed.

'My client has a right to enter the house to retrieve his personal belongings.'

He had prepared a list of his personal belongings that he wanted made available to him. There was nothing unusual, clothes, spare car keys, items in his bedside draw, files out of the study, golf clubs, bicycle etc. The solicitor reiterated that his list was not exhaustive; he needed to have a proper look around the house and was demanding to be allowed to 'come into his own home to retrieve them.'

John was not happy with that and responded accordingly.

'Should your client make any attempt to enter the family home the police will be called.'

When I read this, even I thought it had been a step too far. How could I call the police? How had it come to this?

Yet once again John reassured me with a phone call. He said that he knew what he was doing and it was all part of the fight that only one party could win.

"It's a war," he said, "and to gain victory in the war, we need to win as many battles as we can."

As a way of calming the situation I had suggested that maybe I should put the items he had requested together, and one of the girls could take them around to their dad. John was not keen. He was happy for the clothes to be returned to their owner, however he was adamant that the files and any other paperwork were to stay in the family home.

"I think it may be wise if I come round to your house and take a look at the files myself. It's clear there's still a lot of paperwork that is very important to him, paperwork that perhaps he doesn't want anyone to see."

At first I wasn't keen for him to come around and invade my personal space, however, if nothing else, John was persistent and frankly I had no more excuses to put him off. He said that his trained eye might just discover the one thing that would hang my husband out to dry.

He had invited himself around 'one afternoon' but he wasn't specific about which afternoon.

"I'll text you beforehand," he'd said, "to ensure you're in."

I increasingly felt on edge waiting for his call though couldn't quite figure out why. I found myself constantly checking my phone and sure enough, after a couple of days the message 'pinged' through.

Hi Annette wd it be ok to call in next hour?

I panicked. Hi John, no hurry, don't put yourself out.

Returned. It's ok, I'm in the area. CU in 30 mins

I had been knocking around the house all day in tracksuit and trainers and visually I was falling well short of the facade I had been presenting at the Saxtons' offices. I didn't want Bennett to see the real me in my natural habitat. Fortunately the house was already tidy as I had spent the morning cleaning it so I could spend my time on me. But I'd barely had time to change my clothes and touch up my make-up before he was at the front door ringing the bell.

He stood at the door in all of his finery, smiling. He looked a little different, though I couldn't pinpoint exactly what it was that was different about him.

"Well, aren't you going to ask me in?" he said with a shrug of his shoulders.

"Yes, of course John, come in."

"Thank you."

He appeared quite focussed on the job in hand.

"The study Annette please, I assume it's upstairs, and that's where his paperwork is with the evidence of earnings, bank statements, investments?"

"Yes, follow me, that's where all the files are."

As we entered the room I could see John's eyes darting around. He was absorbing his surroundings, feeding off the imprint left by its predecessor. It struck me that John had been the first man to step into the study since Stuart's departure, the first man I'd taken upstairs. I pointed my hand towards the bookshelf that housed Stuart's work files.

"That's his work stuff John. As you can see he has taken some of the files, the shelf is looking a bit depleted."

I sat at the desk and removed one of the files from the shelf and proceeded to thumb through it. I had my back towards him yet I sensed his head peering over my shoulders. His body was so close he was practically touching me and I could feel the warmth of his breath. Mint again. The strong scent of his musky cologne drifted through the air and my heart began to pound. It had been a long time since I had been this close to any man and ashamedly I felt a slight tingle rise within me, a more than pleasant sensation. For a moment I was transported back to when I was first married. Stuart and I would lie in bed on lazy Sunday mornings, me dozing off, taking advantage of the fact I didn't have to jump up to go to work. Stuart wouldn't let me sleep as he always wanted my attention, snuggling up against me as he wrapped his arms around me. I would feel his breath against my ear as he gently kissed my neck, his erection pressing against me as his hands slipped into my panties, focusing all his energy on trying to arouse me. It wouldn't take much back then. I was always his. I closed my eyes and held the moment, for a fleeting second at least I could pretend I was back to that time.

I came back to reality with a bump as I realised the body practically grinding up against me was my solicitor John Bennett. He stood with my hand resting on the file as he placed his own hand on top of mine.

"He left with a load of paperwork as you know, I'm not sure what else is here," I said.

He spoke as if nothing was amiss.

"He didn't take everything that's for sure."

He held up a sheet of A4.

"Look, a Letter of Engagement for one of his clients."

It was the one I had photocopied. I sat there almost paralysed and the discomfort of the whole situation had become unbearable. I pulled my hand away and jumped up swinging my body around with such force it jolted John to take a step back. He leaned in smiling and kissed me gently on the lips but so slightly I thought I might have imagined it.

I was breathing heavily and I needed to break whatever was going on and get out of the room.

"I'm going to leave you to it John, you'll work much better without me under your feet."

He smiled again. The man was totally unflappable.

"Don't worry Annette, you would never get under my feet."

It was my imagination I convinced myself. I was creating something out of nothing, he hadn't just kissed me. I'd picking up the wrong vibes. Was it possible that I was attracted to him in some odd way that was making me imagine things?

I concluded that I had obviously been starved of male affection for so long that I was letting my imagination run away with itself, after all I was a woman with needs, and although sex was off my agenda at the moment, it hadn't escaped my mind completely. It was always there lingering in the background.

After about ten minutes he came out of the study, his hands loaded with lever arch files. I couldn't quite believe how much Stuart had left behind.

"If you don't mind Annette, I am taking a few of these files away with me. I would like our Forensic Accountant to take a quick look at them. I feel it may be worthwhile."

Forensic accountant. How much was this all going to cost?

John once again pre-empted the thoughts running through my mind.

"Don't worry about cost Annette, my forensic accountant and I do each other favours all the time. That's how I like to work."

He stood outside my bedroom door. It was open and he subconsciously looked in. He may not have realised but he did, and another pleasant sensation rippled through me.

He looked back over at me.

"It's not always about money you know."

This was crazy. This was my imagination again. I cursed myself as John seemed to loiter at the top of the stairs.

He looked at his watch.

"I really should be going?"

"Yes."

"Unless?"

"Yes."

He stepped forward. He stepped forward to kiss me. I wasn't imagining it this time and it was about to happen again. John kissed me full on the lips and I allowed it to happen as his tongue probed gently between my lips and my whole body trembled. I realised how nice a tender kiss was. Stuart and I hadn't kissed like that in years. But John Bennett had overstepped the professional mark and I knew it, yet as I pushed him away I realised I had enjoyed every second.

"John."

"Yes."

"You really should be going, Alexandra will be home any second."

John straightened his tie and looked at his watch.

"I think you're right Annette, I didn't realise it was that late."

John almost skipped down the stairs and walked down the hallway. When he reached the front door he turned to face me.

"About dinner."

"Yes."

"How does Thursday suit you?"

"Great."

He took his mobile phone from his pocket, punched in a few digits.

"I'll make a note and get Louise to book somewhere decent."

He looked up.

"Nothing but the best for my favourite client."

Before I could reply he had left the house, got into his car and was gone.

14

It was the eve of my Maintenance Pending Suit hearing and the anxiety was building up within me like a pressure cooker about to blow its lid. Total dread had engulfed me as soon as I had opened my eyes that morning and I realised what day it was. I had the overwhelming urge to bury my head under the duvet and not come out until it was all over.

My fear was born out of the fact that I had to attend court the following day and air my dirty washing in front of a bunch of strangers. I cursed Stuart for putting me through this ordeal. If only he had agreed a realistic maintenance figure to tide me over until we could resolve the finances properly. The MPS, as John referred to it, could have been avoided altogether. Yet if I was honest it was no surprise, I knew it was coming and I had realised weeks beforehand that nothing was going to be resolved outside of a courtroom. It would take a judges intervention to settle the discord as neither of our solicitors appeared anywhere near reaching a resolution. The war was still raging. There would be no amnesty any time soon. Battles were being fought on two fronts and neither party could agree who was at fault for the break-up and it didn't bode well for reaching an amicable financial settlement. The signs were already there, Stuart was keeping his cards close to his chest refusing to disclose anything relating to his income. To gain an inch of common ground on either issue involved dozens of solicitors letters, time spent on emails, faxes and phone calls and of course they were reaping the rewards from our discord. During my frequent visits to the Saxtons' offices, I could see the lever arch file proudly displaying my name across its spine, literally bursting at its seams.

My only thoughts, as we discussed our next course of action, was the mounting costs of which I didn't have a clue. I could see no way out other than to continue on the path I had chosen to take and hope that maybe a settlement could be reached before the costs got completely out of hand. As much as I hoped and prayed, I could see no end to the madness. In between the worry there were now small interjections of pleasure and satisfaction because I was beginning to see the light at the end of the tunnel.

After the study incident and the second kiss John had firmly planted on my lips that I couldn't discount as my imagination, I had been left feeling totally gobsmacked. I recalled standing in the hallway with the front door wide open, watching him make his getaway in his fancy sports car. I couldn't quite believe what had just happened, yet there was no denying I had welcomed it and hadn't recoiled from his advances. I had even felt a tingling sensation ripple down my spine as his lips had touched mine. They were soft and the kiss was gentle and tender. Something had definitely stirred within me and these were feelings I had not encountered in a long time, years in fact. Yet surely it couldn't be. Was it possible that I harboured feelings towards John Bennett? I had no doubt he would be married. He had never mentioned a wife and he wore no wedding band on his finger, yet he had talked about his son and I could only conclude that where there was a son there was usually a wife in tow. I felt ashamed of myself, what if he was married? A feeling of nausea swept over me. Alexandra had even noticed there was something wrong when she had returned from the cinema shortly after John had made his exit.

"What's wrong Mum, you'd think you'd seen a ghost?"

My face flushed over with embarrassment as I dismissed her observation as being unfounded.

"Nothing's wrong with me chick, I'm fine. John Bennett called by to pick some files up, it just stressed me a little having him in my home."

She moved the conversation on swiftly. Alexandra had made her feelings very clear from the onset, she had no interest in being drawn into the marital dispute, despite the lies her father had told her. From the moment I mentioned John Bennett's name she had already disengaged, picking her bag up from the kitchen counter and making her way upstairs to her bedroom. I was left nursing a mug of freshly made coffee whilst I played the whole John Bennett scenario around in my head like a revolving door.

The thought wouldn't budge. How could I face him again? How hypocritical was I? Condemning Stuart as an adulterer and there I was kissing my bloody solicitor five minutes after I had engaged his services. The whole situation did not sit well with me. I was many things but I didn't have myself down as a hypocrite.

I made a decision that same afternoon that I would disengage from any attempt John made in future to flirt with me or worse, put me in a compromising positions as he had done that day. If there was a Mrs Bennett I would not be her nemesis as Angela Maddison was mine and more importantly I would not let my girls down. They had one sexually active, wayward parent and they didn't need to deal with a second.

It was fair to say that even though I had drawn a line in the sand that I had promised myself I would not cross. Pandora's box had been well and truly opened. I cried off sick from the dinner date he had arranged for the following Thursday and to my immense relief he seemed to take it in his stride. He didn't press me to commit to another day when I had rang him on his mobile to say I couldn't make it.

"Oh dear Annette, we will have to rearrange it when you're feeling better," he'd said.

Cancelling the meal had left me with mixed emotions as although I was relieved, a small part of me was disappointed, a romantic and yes, sexual seed had been planted and it was growing by the day. As the weeks progressed I began to realise that even though I could control my actions, I had no control over my thoughts and my mind had its own agenda. I wrestled with what had happened in the study and after much self-analysis I concluded it was possible that John Bennett was the embodiment of everything I had lost and yearned to have again, a husband, a protector and security. He ticked all the boxes and I am ashamed to admit I even built up my own fantasies around him. As much as I hated to admit it, a small part of me melted every time I heard his voice or was in his company. He made me feel safe and like a moth to a flame I was drawn to him. He had turned the light on in my bleak sexless world and it had opened up the possibility that perhaps another man was sexually attracted to me. Over the years, Stuart had stripped away the layers of my womanhood as I had become invisible to him. He didn't desire me, I was a plaything and he had used me like a doll. John had inadvertently allowed me to rediscover my femininity and he had certainly revitalised my confidence.

I was turning into the stereotypical wronged woman, desperate to prove I was still a desirable commodity. I had started to take more time on my appearance, even making a deliberate attempt to cut out the boozy nights. I was achieving my nightly dopamine fix with exercise rather than my usual bottle of wine. I was hitting the shady end of my forties, yet with the divorce diet, exercise and the reduced alcohol intake, I was starting to look better than I had in a long time. It hadn't gone unnoticed by John as he acknowledged my glowing complexion and ashamedly I soaked his complements up like a sponge.

There was now a familiarity between us which hadn't been there before and although I didn't encourage it, deliberately ignoring any compliments he sent my way, it was still there in the background, ticking away, waiting to strike like the oversized clock in the Saxtons' conference room. My gut instinct was telling me that John was playing with me like a cat with a mouse.

I focused my attention on my own growing mess where unfortunately John was a central player. I took solace in the fact that he was certainly not playing games with Stuart's solicitor. I watched as he outflanked his opponent time and time again and was glad that I had him on my side.

It might have been a different story if Steedman had not continued to insist that his client had grounds for divorce based on my 'unreasonable behaviour'.

Steedman Letter

"Your client does not consider the breakdown of the marriage is any of her fault; however your client has changed the locks to the property and requested that our client move out. As you can appreciate, this is clearly not the actions of someone who wishes to remain in a relationship and certainly would be sufficient to satisfy the test for unreasonable behaviour in relation to a Petition for Divorce."

On receiving the fax John rang me at home. He wanted to fire back a response immediately, however he needed to update me on the situation and was seeking my permission to suggest to Steedman that it was possible for us to name Angela Maddison as the Co-Respondent.

Bill Harris, the private detective, had staked out Angela Maddison's house and had the proof that Stuart had spent the night with her. According to John, Harris had produced a report that clearly stated and proved with photographic evidence that Stuart's car had been parked up outside Angela Maddison's house overnight. Bill had seen the pair enter the house together late in the evening and he had watched as the lights had gone on in the kitchen. Eventually they had been switched off and he saw the bedroom lights going on. After a while the house was in darkness. Stuart never came out of the house. His car was photographed every hour, a time display on each photograph. Bill had sat outside the house all night only leaving at 5.30am the following morning. John relayed the details of the report with childlike eagerness.

"We have caught him red handed. All we need to prove to the court is that your husband had the opportunity to commit adultery. In the old days we would literally have to catch them in the act," he laughed raucously. "Thankfully it's not needed these days. We have proved he was there all night and he had ample opportunity to commit the act."

John said now we had the evidence, it would be an ideal opportunity to send a letter Steedman's way suggesting that unless his client cooperated we would name the other woman. I wasn't about to argue, the alternative would be Steedman pursuing the Divorce Petition on grounds of my unreasonable behaviour and I was prepared to fight that allegation tooth and nail if necessary. I had no hesitation saying yes and so it was, John set about drafting his response.

Bennett 1st August 2011

It appears clear that our client could petition for Divorce based on your client's adultery. It would also appear that she can name Angela Maddison as the Co-Respondent.

It occurs to us that the simplest way to proceed with the divorce would be based on your client's adultery with an unnamed woman. We invite your client to agree to the Petition to proceed on that basis.

If your client is not prepared to agree this then we will proceed with a Petition that will be on the basis of adultery with a named woman.

Steedman did not respond to the bait. It had gone quiet and I had a good idea why. Stuart had already gone off on his so called golfing holiday with his friends. With him on holiday and in another country, Steedman was left tapping his fingers on his office desk waiting for his return.

I had the exact dates that he would be away. Stuart had forewarned the girls about his golf holiday and Pizza Hut would have to wait a couple of weeks. He didn't flinch from his story, sticking to it like a clam to a rock, yet it didn't wash with either his girls or John.

As soon as Stuart had left the country John asked his assistant Louise to check the story out. Like a young Miss Marple she rang the ATOS offices acting as one of Angela Maddison's clients. The unsuspecting receptionist dropped her boss straight in the brown stuff when she confirmed Mrs Maddison was on annual leave and wasn't due back until 15th August. It was no surprise that it coincided exactly with Stuart's golfing holiday.

John wasted no time informing Steedman that he knew the score. He was turning the vice a little tighter in the hope it would yield a result.

Bennett

Further to our latest fax to you, we are now aware that your client has gone on holiday with Angela Maddison.

We have invited you to agree to a Petition based on your client's adultery with an unnamed woman.

We have not had a response from you.

If we do not have agreement to the position within five working days then we will proceed based on your client's adultery with Angela Maddison.

Please be clear that we shall make sure that all necessary evidence can be produced regarding your client's adultery, that will include interrogatories being served upon him, should he deny the adultery.

Steedman responded to Bennett on the deadline date and he obviously hadn't been able to speak to his client. They were clearly the writers' own words as he suggested that John should inject some realism into the situation. He confirmed that his client was on holiday and on that basis he suggested it was 'unrealistic for your client to expect a response within five working days.'

John fired straight back with a sarcastic response carrying on the realism theme that both parties had now latched onto as their new buzzword.

Bennett

Thank you for your fax.

We had hoped that you would have heard of the invention of the telephone and text message to contact your client.

Perhaps you would take some advice with regard to these devices as we believe they may ensure that you can speak to your client almost instantaneously.

We are prepared to extend the deadline three working days. We assure you that is realism!

On reading John's letter, I remember laughing out loud and was keen to share the joke. I had immediately phoned my mother and recited the entire letter to her. We both laughed like two naughty children playing a prank although we didn't appreciate the madness we were being drawn into.

At the time I didn't dream to question John. Wasn't this how wars were fought and won? His approach had produced results, it got the response John was looking for. Sure enough it arrived.

Steedman.

Our client entirely refutes the allegation of adultery with Angela Maddison. The allegations are entirely incorrect and grossly exaggerated. However our client does accept the marriage has irretrievably broken down and on that basis our client sees no practical point in defending these proceedings and will therefore consent to a Petition based on adultery with a unnamed person.

Our client is prepared to put forward the dates for the alleged adultery as between March 2007 and December 2008 in Manchester.

When John showed me the letter giving the dates of the adultery in Manchester, it was the final blow to the already shattered illusion I had held of Stuart. I knew the dates and location were entirely feasible. He had been involved in a management buyout for a company in Manchester and for the best part of three years he'd worked there Monday to Friday barely spending more than two nights at home in any given week. Once again my world had spun off its axis. I was devastated that he had owned up to another affair to protect his new bitch of a woman and stop her name from being dragged into court.

John had called me into the Saxtons' offices to disclose his find and as we sat in our now familiar chairs he casually slid Steedman's letter across the desk, his hand lingering next to mine a little longer than necessary. I was starting to pick up on all of his micro signals since our kiss. Once they might have gone over my head yet now I couldn't help but notice how his eyes would look me up and down as I entered the room, lingering a little longer than acceptable upon my breast area causing me to instinctively raise my hands across my chest. Usually it would bother me or make me feel uncomfortable, yet that day my thoughts had moved to the letter he had slipped in front of my eyes and it had touched a raw nerve. I was struck with a sharp, almost tangible pain. It was much the same as the pain I had felt when I found out about Angela Maddison first time round. I couldn't be one hundred per cent sure if Stuart was telling the truth, or if he was making the affair up to spare Angela Maddison the indignity of being named as the other woman. That was equally as hurtful. He wanted to spare his new woman any embarrassment yet he couldn't have cared less about the pain he was inflicting upon his wife, the mother of his three children. The bastard was dishing it out to me by the bucket load. And yet to my simple mind, why would anyone lie about such a thing? Hell would have frozen over before I would have admitted to an act I hadn't committed. Whatever the reasoning for his admission it had destroyed what little stock I'd had left in our marriage. It was just over two months since he had walked out and I had been holding onto the misguided belief that our marriage hadn't all been bad. We'd had our good years, building a home, producing our three beautiful daughters together. Yet now I realised our marriage had been built on quick sand. It had no substance and it never had. Once the tide had turned it had been washed away. The man I thought I had married had never existed in the first place. He was just a figment of my imagination. How many more women had there been? For all I knew he could have been a serial adulterer. My mind boggled as I started to build a chronology in my mind of the times he had worked away which would have given him the ideal opportunity to play the field, while I sat at home taking care of his three children. Of course John wasn't the least bit phased by the admission, but it hadn't occurred to him that it would knock me for six.

He claimed he had seen it all before.

"You discover one affair then they all come out of the woodwork."

I was full of hell again and as usual John employed his calming, reassuring voice, throwing water on the flames and dampening down the rage growing inside me.

"Take the positives from this letter, he has conceded and you'll get your divorce on your terms. Isn't that all that matters?"

He was right.

And so it was agreed between the two parties that the divorce petition would be submitted to the court on the grounds of Stuart's adultery with an unnamed woman.

But incredibly, at the eleventh hour, John had a change of heart.

It was towards the end of the summer when Louise Visser made her way to the Newcastle County Court to hand deliver my Divorce Petition, the grounds for the divorce being Stuart Palmers adultery with the named Co respondent, Angela Maddison. For good measure John had thrown in the adultery committed with an unknown woman in Manchester between 2007 and 2008.

I had agreed to the Petition. John had persuaded me it was the way to go and to be quite honest I didn't take much persuasion. If I was honest with myself, I saw no logical explanation for naming her as he'd already confessed to adultery. It was a tit for tat retaliation, no more and of course it was my heart felt desire to name and shame my husband and his bitch Angela Fucking Maddison.

John didn't have such sentiment for moving the goal posts and going back on his agreement with Steedman. Stuart and his solicitor had been less than forthcoming about his financial situation. After repeated letters there was still no clarity, nothing forthcoming. He was doing all he could to understate his earnings and withhold information. With his hands tied, John Bennett hit the only place he knew it would hurt. He named the woman Stuart was so desperately trying to protect. Steedman reluctantly accepted service of papers for both his client and surprisingly enough, the co-respondent, Angela Maddison. Stuart's acceptance of the divorce papers was sufficient acknowledgement that they were no longer refuting the allegations of adultery with Angela Maddison. John had proved him to be a liar and an adulterer and for that he was my knight in shining armour. The reason for doing so, he claimed, was that the judge would start to question Stuart's honesty and integrity when he attempted to understate his earnings, which we knew he would do. Only time would tell.

One thing I did know for sure was that Stuart would be as mad as hell and determined to seek revenge.

Now that the start of proceedings was but hours away, the prospect of facing Stuart and his motley crew across a courtroom table was testing my nerves. On that day I reverted back to the old me, not wanting to get out of bed and it was only when I heard the phone ring and then Alexandra shouted up the stairs saying that Mr Bennett was on the phone that I raced out of bed. I made my way to my newly claimed study and plonked myself on the study chair reaching to pick up the receiver as I did so. I was grateful that he couldn't see me on the other end of the line as I was a complete mess, sitting in a pair of pyjamas that had seen better days and my bed hair sticking out all over the place. Even my voice was croaky and dry and in need of a glass of water.

"Hi John."

There was a delay and for a second I thought he had put the phone down. Then as my ears strained I heard mumbled sounds in the background. He was obviously talking to someone. I waited, resisting the temptation to hang up. My patience was rewarded as his soft voice exploded in my ear and calmness was restored within me. Yet again he was my faceless angel, as he had been since the very first day we spoke.

"Good morning Annette, have I got you out of bed by any chance?"

I lied.

"God no John, I just didn't hear the phone."

"Sorry to interrupt your morning. I'm catching up on a bit paper work at home, getting ready for tomorrow and I am just going over you statement of income. Could you remind me the benefits you receive? I have a rough idea but need the exact amounts. Could you email me them sometime today?"

I was relieved that it was all he had wanted. Now that he was on the phone I took the opportunity to voice my concerns about the following day. He reassured me there would be nothing to worry about, we would be in the judge's chambers not a court room. No one else would be in the room other than the judge and the two opposing parties.

"Don't worry Annette, I will be there for you, all you need to do is turn up you do not have to say a word. In fact I'll collect you myself, save you the worry of getting there."

I was about to interject and tell him not to bother, but before I could get the words out of my mouth he had closed the conversation.

"Pick you up 10.30, be ready."

Then the line went dead. He had hung up.

There was nothing to worry about, John would be there to hold my hand. I stood up and walked out of the study and back into my bedroom. I felt wide awake now, with thoughts of my handsome solicitor filling my head. I walked into the en suite and opened the shower door. I smiled as I threw my pyjamas onto the floor and climbed in. The hot water felt fantastic as it cascaded over my body and I drifted away into a fantasy world.

15

Bennett had just ended his call when his wife Alma interrupted him yet again. She was silhouetted in the doorway of his study, hands on hips, waiting for an answer to a question that he hadn't even picked up on. She had already interrupted him at the beginning of his call and it had irked him that as usual she was totally oblivious to the fact he was working.

"Well?" she asked.

She was back again, with another axe to grind he suspected. He sat ensconced behind his battered, old, mahogany desk, flanked either side by bookcases filled with volumes of his well pawed law books. Cautiously he raised his eyes to greet his wife. She was sporting her lycra gym wear which was no surprise to him. Exercise was as important to her as breathing and each day she put her body through a rigorous routine and Sunday was no exception. She had a towel over her shoulder and on closer inspection the Lycra was stained with sweat around the arms, her chest, her crotch and the top of her thighs. Alma had finished her exercise regime and was ready to embark on the next part of her well-planned Sunday.

"You are coming John, aren't you?"

Bennett raised an eyebrow.

"Me coming darling? That would be nice."

A smile almost crept across her lips, almost but not quite.

"Sarcasm doesn't become you John," she said. "Leave the jokes to the comedians."

Then it dawned on him. They were going out for drinks then lunch with friends and it had completely escaped him.

They weren't his friends of course, these were friendships Alma had forged at the up market David Lloyd Club, at the spinning classes, the indoor pool and the Spa, the state of the art gym and of course in the 'Relax and Socialise' lounge afterwards. God how he hated that place.

He anticipated how the day would pan out. He would be stuck making polite conversation with a bunch of men he barely knew, talking football no doubt or even worse and as was often the case once they realised he was a solicitor, they would be seeking his advice on some legal point which was invariably outside his area of expertise. He was filled with dread at the prospect, yet he dismissed the thought as she started to undress. This was no seductive striptease, just practical. His once cautious eyes danced in admiration at her perfectly formed figure and her full, voluptuous, enhanced breasts that had cost a small fortune. She dropped her sports bra to the floor, standing in front of him as naked as the day she was born. He was transfixed by his wife once more and his annoyance was downgraded to a slight irritation that she had interrupted his work and more importantly his chat with Annette. How he wished it was the shape of his favourite client standing in front of him right at this moment. Bennett conceded and the task of getting Annette into bed could wait a little longer. He'd already dipped his toe in the water to gauge the temperature and the response to his kiss left him in no doubt she was definitely warming to him. He had felt her body tremor during their short embrace and it was no shock to him. The vulnerable ones were always the easiest to please and her desperation for attention was almost palpable. It was certainly pleasurable and something he wanted to repeat. He felt himself getting aroused as he slipped a hand into his trouser pocket.

He hadn't been the least bit deterred when Annette had cancelled their dinner date and her coy exterior after the event hadn't fooled him for one second. He would play along for a while, he wouldn't rush her even though she was now occupying his mind, invading his thoughts on a daily basis. As Alma bent over and picked up her bra from the floor he groaned out loud. He wasn't about to abort his mission, especially now he'd marked his territory. Now each time she sat in the Saxtons' office, barely an arms width away from him, he could feel the energy growing. Like an alchemist he had created the chemistry between them. To his mind his motives weren't totally selfish because the attention he was giving the poor deserted woman could only serve to brighten up her otherwise dull little life. The truth was he couldn't get her out of his head. He wanted her so badly and he wanted her now.

As his wife stood before him he put aside his transgression for a little while at least, her voice booming in his direction had made sure of that.

"John, why the hell are you still sitting here? You know we're going out for lunch."

Her curt words echoed her facial expression and he could not help notice the look of annoyance spread across her face. Her voice had a deep husky pitch and a sharpness that contrasted with his own mellow tones.

Bennett smiled and reached for the statement.

"You're up to the limit on your fucking credit card again."

Her demeanour changed slightly. She hesitated, temporarily lost for words.

"Yes darling, I meant to say, I errr… had a rather large unexpected bill I'd forgotten about."

Bennett shook his head.

"Naughty girl."

His erection was in full bloom as it poked uncomfortably against the material of his trousers. He reached down and unzipped his flies, fumbling inside to free himself.

"John, no," she said. "We haven't got time for that."

He had her exactly where he wanted her. He looked at his watch.

"You're probably right dear and I won't have time to clear this little bill until at least Thursday or Friday."

She was nothing more than a prostitute.

"John… please. I'm meeting some of the girls tomorrow for shopping and there's a table booked on the Quayside."

She had no choice, she knew the game.

"We've got no time."

Bennett waited patiently, wafting the statement like a fan. Alma let out a sigh as she dropped to her knees.

"You'd better be quick."

"That's in your hands dear," he laughed, "so to speak."

He surprised himself at how witty he could be sometimes. His wife lowered her head and took his erection in her mouth. She sucked slowly at first before building up her expert rhythm, working her hand at the base of his shaft. She was clearly in a hurry with no time for any sort of foreplay but he didn't care as he gazed down at the top of her head. Almost the same colour and same hairstyle as Annette Palmer. How convenient. Bennett spread his legs, closed his eyes and as he tilted back in his seat he reached for a handful of her hair and moaned out loud.

"Quicker," he whispered quietly.

Alma obeyed his instruction and as he cried out loudly he exploded into her mouth.

Alma stood, picked up her clothes and got ready to leave the room.

"Hurry up," she said, "you got what you wanted so hurry, please."

He directed his attention back to the paperwork sprawled across his desk.

"Jump in the shower Alma, I've a little bit to do."

He picked up his ballpoint pen as if he intended to write.

"I'm working darling, you might like to try it sometime."

He counted the seconds in his head before she started again. One, two, three. Then she was away, the demure figure had turned into a she-devil yet again.

"Fuck you John, you don't appreciate anything I do for you. I've been a good wife and mother who brought up our son while you were working every hour god sent."

John gave a weary sigh as he removed his reading glasses to rub the bridge of his nose with his thumb and index finger in an attempt to defuse the annoyance building up within him. He'd heard it so many times and it was wearing thin and yet the first thing he would do tomorrow morning was to clear that bill. What a fucked up relationship. What a fucked up sex life. Thinking about another woman every time they got intimate. Would he have done anything different if he could turn back the clock?

As soon as he had set eyes on her, he knew almost immediately she had to be his. She hadn't taken much coaxing. She was a woman driven by money and ambition and living with a husband who had neither. Bennett appeared to be the better option, a means to an end.

He was at the high end of his game, offering her the world and she snatched the opportunity and ran with it. Alma's husband was the first to get the chop, quickly followed by the then Mrs Bennett. Bennett showed no mercy for his mild mannered first wife, the mother of his two girls. She had been dispatched with the same callous determination he employed on his clients behalf. His ruthlessness had minimized the collateral damage; with his purse strings relatively intact he walked away with his prize. Now as the years passed he found himself questioning his foolhardy decision again and again. Alma was unquestionably a beautiful woman and at times when he watched her from across a room he could barely believe his luck but then at other times, he doubted his own sanity. A blowjob for the price of a credit card bill summed her up, that was Alma, she was a whore and there was no other word to describe her. But she was a force to be reckoned with, her feet would stamp until she got her own way and for peace's sake he invariably gave in. The truth was he had no time for her antics and with two court hearings lined up for the following day he needed to prepare. He would have to be the diplomat once again, holding his tongue and letting her loose with his credit card. That always did the trick. Fucking slut.

Bennett was once again alone in the relative sanctuary of his study. He looked over the paper work strewn across his desk, his thoughts drawn back to Annette and her case as his eyes caught sight of her sworn affidavit. He looked through her case file in an attempt to refresh himself with the details. He noted with annoyance how many times had he requested details of Palmers earnings from Steedman. Nothing had been forthcoming except one tax return from three years ago. That would be of no help when they tried to pin him down to produce a figure for his current years earning. Not knowing his exact income flagged up a concern in Bennett's calculating mind. It would be an uphill struggle to convince a judge to award a temporary maintenance order favourable to Annette as they were bound to underestimate Palmers earning. He hated the fucking self-employed, the bastards who could squirrel funds away in contingency accounts and delay invoicing. There was all manner of ways to reduce their bottom line and Palmer was an accountant so it went without saying he knew the game inside out. Without a doubt he was Bennett's worst nightmare. Luck would have to be on their side and they would need an amenable judge, a Bennett boy, someone who he enjoyed a pint or a whisky with now and again. The old school network, he needed them now more than ever. He strummed the fingers of his right hand across the desk as he contemplated the argument he would present to the court the following day. This was a fight he wasn't prepared to lose, Palmer was niggling away at him, getting under his skin.

And yet he could picture the scene in his mind as he painted the canvas with clarity. He would be Annette's hero, the man who had given her everything she had dreamed of.

"Thank you John," she'd say. "How can I ever repay you?"

"I'll think of something, don't you worry about that."

The dreaded day had arrived. Within hours I was going be in court confronting my biggest fear, Stuart Palmer. How times had changed. Once upon a time I'd have counted the minutes until we were together, especially in the early years. Now I dreaded the thought of being in the same room as him. How had it come to this? The last time we'd shared breathing space was the day he had left the family home three months previously. It seemed like a lifetime away. A great deal had happened since that day and I knew we were fractured beyond repair, yet despite everything that had passed between us there was a still a small part of me that wanted to see him one more time. Whatever was going on with my fucked up emotions I was still totally unprepared for the day ahead. The girls had tried in vain to put my mind at rest the previous evening as they watched me going into a blind panic thinking about the prospect of the next day. I had noticed that all of my children had a growing allegiance to me as relations with their dad cooled and soured and that comforted me in a strange sort of way. Lying about his holiday had started that ball rolling and now it was all team Annette. Now he had nailed his true colours to the mast. Yet despite the reassuring support I still didn't feel calm.

I had been struck with fear as soon as I opened my eyes that morning and a feeling of nausea had swept over me. I was unable to even contemplate drinking my usual cup of morning coffee, which in normal circumstances would have done the trick and brought me back to life. I sipped some water and avoided breakfast altogether as the mere sight of food made me want to retch. As the time drew closer to the event my heart started to pound so hard I could practically see it leaping out of my chest to a staccato beat. My head was already throbbing from lack of sleep and way too much alcohol consumed the previous evening. In truth I was back to looking like shit and felling equally as bad.

In my dazed state I had lost all track of time and before I knew it, I had given myself less than an hour to get ready before John was due to pick me up. It was a mad dash. I was racing around the house in a blind panic trying to get sorted. The inevitable stumbling block was what should I wear for the occasion? John in his wisdom had suggested that I should be understated. In his opinion it was always an advantage to play the vulnerability card in front of the judge. I knew exactly what he meant, he wanted me to rock up looking like a stereotypical broken housewife, a bit jaded around the edges with grey roots on display for all to see, a shopping bag in hand and probably wearing an anorak. As much as I valued John's advice, on that matter I had no intention of taking it. He obviously had no understanding of how the female mind worked, not one clue I surmised. When he suggested it, I practically fell of my chair laughing. Which woman in her right mind, who had been jilted by her husband for a younger model, would turn up presenting herself like some down and out hobo? Not this woman that was for sure. I wanted Stuart Palmer to see that I was still standing. Whatever pain and humiliation he had inflicted on me over the years, he had not broken me down into submission, not yet at least.

And so it was, when John turned up, spot on 10.30am, I waltzed down the path to his car donning my Tom Ford outfit once more. It was inevitable I would wear it. What other formal outfit did I have in my wardrobe that could out style it? At one point I wished I had worn trousers. Getting into John's sporty little convertible had been a tricky task and the effort of manoeuvering myself into the low bucket seats without allowing my skirt to ride up had been a challenge. I had no doubt that during the kerfuffle John would have been ogling my legs or whatever other bit of flesh that was on show during the process. I felt his eyes burning into me as I settled down and drew the seat belt across my chest. It was only when seated that I gave out a sigh of relief and looked across at him. He smiled back at me, placing a hand on my thigh and patted gently. No words were needed as calmness was restored within me once again. At that point I sincerely believed I could get through the ordeal. John was by my side after all.

Newcastle Crown Court was an impressive sight and a dominating feature on the recently regenerated quayside. I had no doubt I would have passed the building on numerous occasions over the years, however I had never paid it much heed. It had never occurred to me that one day I would be one of its occupants. That day, as I walked up the steep steps to the main entrance, I had the opportunity to appreciate the size and magnitude of the building, with its orange Corsehill Sandstone set off by vast panels of tinted windows. It was imposing. On any other day I might have marvelled at its grandeur and appreciated its prime position facing out towards the River Tyne, but unfortunately its qualities were wasted on me. The only thing I wanted to see of that building was the back of it.

As we climbed the last step and reached the entrance I could see that Louise was waiting in the foyer, a large smile planted across her face even though she was loaded down with paperwork and files. John wasted no time on greetings. Theirs was a new working relationship yet it was obvious their rapport was quickly growing. The courts were their daily stomping ground and they had their routine off pat. They ushered me up to the second floor that was home to the family courts. I followed them like an obedient dog walking to heel. Having not been in the building before I scanned my surroundings, observing the rhythm of its workings. We walked through a vast reception area onto a narrow corridor housing private consulting rooms and Louise led us into the first available room and immediately dumped the files on to the desk.

As soon as we got into the room, John was on the move again.

"I'd best go and have a word with the other side," he said and then he was gone.

Louise seemed keen to keep me in the loop and filled me in. John would be off to find Steedman and also let the Court Usher know we had arrived. They would call for us over the court tannoy when the judge was ready to see us in in his Chambers.

I was trying to remain calm, yet I could feel the anxiety slowly creeping in again. Louise did her best to distract me, talking about anything and everything and I appreciated her effort yet it wasn't working. Eventually John came back into the room, carrying a document in his hand.

"Your husband is in the next room with his solicitor. I've had a word and as we suspected they aren't being very helpful."

John let out a sigh of frustration.

"He's just provided us with his income and his list of outgoings."

He passed the paper across to Louise for her to study while he sat down and took his battered old Casio calculator from his briefcase. His head shook in disbelief as he surveyed the numbers.

"He has his earnings at £63000, which is a complete nonsense. As you know, he's on at least double that."

John remained very calm yet I was bubbling away inside. It didn't help that he proceeded to read out the list of Stuart's outgoings, which any idiot could see were totally exaggerated.

"Rent payable on flat £1000 per calendar month."

I let out a squeal of derision.

"That's his aunt's flat and she's in a home. He's her power of attorney so there's no way will he be paying that sort of rent. He's her nephew, he'll be living there for buttons."

John looked up.

"Exactly," he said, before continuing. "Maintenance charges on flat £110, Petrol £800, Car Insurance £50, Food £200."

My jaw nearly hit the ground, £800 for petrol?

"Entertainment £300, House insurance £50, Clothing £100, Light and heating £100 Council Tax £80, Water £50."

As he read out each amount I observed his immaculately manicured fingers tapping the numbers into his calculator and as he reached the end, he slowly read out the total.

"£2840."

I wanted to laugh although I refrained and let them continue with their work. Stuart thought that £600 a month was enough for his family to live on yet he needed practically £3000 to get him through the month.

John looked up.

"This is by no means exhaustive. Steedman's already put it out there that we need to add the Child Support Agency payment you've just been awarded for Alexandra."

He shuffled through his paper work in search of the email I'd sent him the previous day. He needn't have as I knew the amount off by heart. I had been over the moon when the letter from the CSA had arrived through my letter box stating I had been awarded £197 a week towards Alexandra's upkeep. I hadn't yet received a payment but I wasn't worried too much because Stuart would have no choice but to pay up. I was told the CSA didn't fuck around. They had the power to access bank accounts and confiscate assets. I knew without doubt, Stuart would be eager to pay it on or before the day it was due. John quickly tapped the additional amount into his Casio. "Hmm and no doubt he will be adding outgoings such as holidays, Christmas, birthday gifts."

He looked at his watch, time was ticking on. Conscious that we had precious little of it left, he started to do the maths out loud as if to quicken the process.

"If he's saying he has an annual income of £63000 that would still give him a net take home pay of around £4200."

He looked in the direction of Louise for her agreement. I sensed a slight impatience in his voice, which was unusual. I had never seen him other than calm and laid back. "Louise, go through Annette's list of income she sent me yesterday."

Without a seconds hesitation, Louise lifted the now crumpled sheet of paper and ran through the numbers while John scribbled away on his notepad.

I moved my seat a little closer and studied the figures.

Family Allowance £20.30

Income Support £42.95

CSA £197.00

Child Tax Credit £112.98

He pondered the numbers he had jotted down, he was a study of concentration. Then his focus once again shifted back to me.

"You know he's playing funny buggers don't you? He's understating his salary and racking up his outgoings."

He threw his pen down on his pad. He had made a decision on something and wanted to share it with me.

"Two can play at that game, I'm knocking the Child Tax Credit off, if he can understate his income we can do the same for yours."

Something didn't feel right. Wasn't that lying to the court? But I offered no argument. Wasn't he right, wasn't John always right, why would I doubt him? He gently rubbed my hand as he slowly raised himself from the chair.

"I'd better go and give them a list of your income and outgoings, they'll only have a couple of minutes to look at it which is what we want. It gives them less opportunity to question it when we get into court."

I gazed into his eyes in admiration. He stood and left. He'd barely been gone a moment when he entered the room again. This time he had a twinkle in his eye, something had cheered him up.

"We're in front of Judge MacNab and the good news is that he's a reasonable man, no nonsense yet fair."

There was now a rush to get everything packed away. Our names had already been called out across the tannoy and we were expected in Judges Chambers pronto.

Both John and Louise started to pack up their belongings. In the short time we had been in the room they'd managed to make it their home and the desk was covered in their paperwork while bags and briefcases littered the floor. I noticed solicitors didn't travel light with every vital piece of paper being carried about their person just in case it was needed.

We left the relative safety of the small characterless room and we entered the hustle and bustle of the busy corridor. My legs were like lead as I watched the people milling around, some loitering, others drawing up their personal battle plans with solicitors and friends. Then I saw him. He was walking with his solicitor, no more than ten yards ahead of me. Even though he had his back towards me I recognised his tall outline towering above most of those around him. My heart began to pump as the adrenaline raced around my body. I stopped in my tracks as every bit of my soul wanted to turn around and race off in the opposite direction. Both John and Louise had noticed my hesitation, and they both turned. Louise smiled and John spoke.

"You're fine, I'm here for you, all you have to do is sit in the room and I will do all the talking."

Once again his words had released me from my torment. I felt safe and secure and justice would prevail. I can do this I whispered to myself as I made my way through into Judge MacNab's Chambers.

16

On the day, I wondered if I would make the long walk through to the Judge's Chambers. When I had stopped dead in my tracks on the first sighting of Stuart, I knew I might not have taken another step if John and Louise had not been by my side coaxing me along like two nervous parents taking their child to school for the very first time. Stuart turned his head and for second he fixed his gaze on me. I wanted him to tell me it had all been a big mistake instead he looked away and scurried on ahead. Stuart and his solicitor came to an abrupt stop as they reached the ushers checkpoint. It seemed to me no one passed that point without first been vetted and checked off their list. The five of us stood awkwardly together while the aged old court attendant slowly shuffled through his court timetable looking for our names. We waited in silence, neither party acknowledging the other. As I stood staring at the back of Stuart's dark outline I immediately sensed that I was in the presence of a total stranger. He was alien to me and the sad fact was that I now knew I hadn't known him at all despite our years together. I thought he was a man and yet he hadn't even had the balls to hold up his hands and do the right thing. He'd been forced to own up to two indiscretions, he was the modern day Don Juan but was it just the tip of the iceberg, had there been more? How many lies had he told throughout our marriage?

And I just knew he was about to lie all over again.

As the thoughts swirled around my head I knew if I didn't distract myself we'd be calling Court Security, so desperate was my desire to smack him in the face. I needed to turn my attention away from Stuart and fixed it on Steedman. It was the first time I had clapped eyes on the man, but because of the number of letters he had penned and I had read, I felt as if I knew him well enough. I had a good take on just what sort of character he really was. I hadn't needed to see him to know that I didn't trust him and his appearance only served to endorse my already preconceived ideas. It was true to say I wasn't impressed at all with the cut of his jib and he looked unkempt in his ill-fitting suit, the hem of his trousers cut way too short, displaying the most unattractive mustard coloured socks. Was he serious? He had the figure of a man who had lived well on his immoral earnings, overweight with an ample paunch hanging over his tight trousers. He and Stuart looked an unlikely combination, as Stuart stood tall and skinny. In another life they could have passed for Laurel and Hardy.

The tannoy made an announcement. It was our turn and the somber convoy was once again on its slow death march to Judge MacNab's Chambers.

The old court attendant who'd led the procession ushered us into the room like a bunch of naughty school kids being summoned to the headmaster's office. Judge MacNab barely raised his head from his paperwork to acknowledge the assemblage proceeding to take our seats at opposing sides of the table.

Like a Mexican standoff, the tension was mounting. I sensed John and Steedman were already squaring up to each other, preparing for the battle ahead, yet they were equally respectful of their referee, Judge MacNab. He was a portly little man with a ruddy complexion, sitting at the slightly elevated desk presiding over the room. He, metaphorically speaking, held the gavel, which would rule both our fates that day.

No time was wasted. With a maximum of one hour to present our case, there would be no icebreakers or courteous exchanges between the parties. After doffing his cap to the Judge, John immediately opened up the argument. All eyes were fixed on him in anticipation. Steedman sat, his hand poised in readiness to start his note taking and I was beginning to realise that solicitors were obsessed with taking notes. However, there was no able assistant by his side scribing for him, unlike John who had Louise at his heel.

It was the first time I had seen John Bennett at work in a court. Our meetings had always been in less intrusive settings where his manner was demure, understated even, but now in his natural habitat, I suspected I was witnessing a master at work as his assertiveness filled the room. Steedman seemed to be no match for John who was now banging on his war drum, the beat increasing in momentum as he forced his point, reaching a crescendo as he listed Stuart's shortcomings.

"Here we have a man, who leaves a marriage of twenty three years for another woman. His wife and the mother of their three children have no means of income other than the benefits Mr Palmer insists she should claim."

He lingered on the word 'insists,' wanting to plant the seed in Judge MacNab's mind that Stuart was a man happy to shirk his financial responsibilities, which was true of course. John had barely begun speaking, yet I noticed the fury was already building up in Stuart. He wasn't happy at all. I had caught a glimpse of him out of the corner of my eye, his head shaking in defiance and his hand cupped next to Steedman's ear whispering some line of defence he was no doubt expecting Steedman to offer up to the judge when it was his time to respond. I had to bite my teeth into my lower lip to stop myself from smirking. Yet my initial smirk turned to fear as I began to reminisce at how it used to be and my stomach began to churn as it had done when we had lived together. He scared me. He was about to blow, I just knew it. I'd seen it so many times at home. When there was an argument he would outshout me, driving me into submission. How would he let today be any different?

Stuart kept glaring at us yet his menacing manor didn't seem to deter John as he marched on with his appraisal of the situation.

"He refuses to make a reasonable offer of maintenance to Mrs Palmer, in fact other than paying the utility bills, which are in his name, he has not provided for either his wife or his children since the day he left."

John barely stopped for breath as he drew to the crux of the matter, his voice forceful and directed towards the Judges ear.

"Mr Palmer has refused to provide any evidence of his current years income, although we have requested it on numerous occasions.

Mrs Palmer believes her husband's earnings to be in excess of £100000 a year. The only evidence he has provided of his income is a tax return of three years ago which show earnings of £107000"

Judge MacNab raised his hand slightly indicating to John to pause while he searched through the bundle of papers. John, realising that he was actually looking for the old tax return, quickly directed him to its whereabouts.

"The document is in the Appendices, item 2, page 43, Sir."

The judge slowly thumbed through the array of paper while John sat on the edge of his seat, obviously willing him to find his place quickly so as not to interrupt his flow.

Judge MacNab wasn't going to be hurried. Instead he took the opportunity to seek clarity on the issue from the other side.

"Mr Steedman, why is your client refusing to disclose his earnings? How can we establish what is a fair maintenance payment for both parties if you client refuses to share this vital piece of information?"

He had just got the last word out when Stuart, unable to hold his tongue any longer, jumped in, his agitation displayed in the sharpness of his retort.

"I haven't got, I -"

His sentence was cut off abruptly as the judge stopped him mid-sentence, his voice slightly raised.

"Mr Palmer, my question was directed at your solicitor Mr Steedman. Can you please refrain from interrupting? If I have a question for you, I will direct it to you. Is that clear?"

Stuart drew back in his chair, sinking into submission. Outranked, he was wise enough to realise he wasn't going to win that argument, which surprised me. Didn't he win every argument? I could now see through him for the coward that he was.

Steedman jumped to the defence of his client, his voice low and submissive in an attempt to calm troubled waters.

"I believe what Mr Palmer was going to say Sir, is that he is currently a partner of a company, the final partnership accounts for last year are not yet available. Their year-end is 30th June, however, he has provided Mrs Palmer with an estimate of his earnings for the current year."

John wasn't going to let the opportunity pass him by. He'd found the chink in their armour and he wanted to unravel it. He jumped in.

"Your client will obviously have his earnings for last year, can he enlighten us as to what that figure might be, because he hasn't provided it despite several requests?"

Brilliant, I thought. The way John had delivered that sounded so simple, so obvious.

Steedman's gaze darted to his client as Stuart once again shook his head and whispered in his solicitors ear. His body language gave the game away; he didn't want to part with that figure either. Steedman listened intently then spoke to the judge.

"My client doesn't have that information available as the Partnership accounts for both years have not been finalized. He cannot provide information he hasn't got."

John saw red, or at least acted that way. His head shook in total disbelief and a look of exasperation set on his face. At that moment I was so grateful to have him on my side, he was giving everything he had to fight my corner. John didn't shout or scream, his response was measured and his tone was as transfixing as ever.

"Your client is an accountant. I believe that he is very good at his job, in fact so good, he's a bit of a trouble shooter, going into companies who are in such dire straits they need someone of Mr Palmer's caliber to sort them out."

John paused for effect. He glanced at Stuart then turned to the judge.

"That's why I find it so hard to believe that he has no idea as to what his earnings were for the last two years. Mr Palmer is meticulous in his personal accounting and knows to the penny his income and expenditure, it's his nature. It's an even bigger mystery to me that Mr Palmer is projecting his current year's earnings to be £63.000, practically a fifty per cent drop from the last legitimate tax return."

For the first time since we had entered the room I focused my gaze on Stuart, as did John. Stuart's face displayed an expression I'd seen many times before, the last time being when he slammed me against the bathroom wall slapping my face. Once more I was transported back in time and my heart began to pound.

Stuart was livid but he had been backed into a corner and he had nowhere to turn.

John goaded him. There was no other word to describe it.

"Times are very difficult for you aren't they Mr Palmer. First your salary drops to the floor which coincides with your marriage break down and to add insult to injury you are forced to rent your Aunt's flat at a rate of £1000 per month, not forgetting the service charges of £112."

He didn't let up and kept prodding away.

"That must have been a blow to you Mr Palmer, your aunt charging you premium rental when the last tenant only paid £750 per month. Of course your aunt is incapacitated isn't she? She isn't capable of making such decisions."

John looked at Stuart as he leaned forward.

"You make those sort of decisions for her don't you?"

Stuart looked at the floor.

"Because I'm led to believe that you are your Aunt's acting Power of Attorney. Is that not the case Mr Palmer? Was it you who took the decision to increase your own rent by nearly thirty per cent?"

As Stuart sat, arms crossed in front of him, his face red with rage, John gave him a dismissive glance before turning his attention back to Judge MacNab who had sat passively listening to the exchanges between the fractured parties. John took a sharp intake of breath before he delivered what was to be his final statement.

"Mrs Palmer has been a housewife and mother for over twenty years. Unfortunately, taking into consideration her age and the fact that she has no current work experience, she would find it difficult to obtain work immediately. There are three children, two of whom are still dependents and living at home. The youngest child, Alexandra, unfortunately has a disability and Mrs Palmer has been her main carer since she was born. These two factors alone make it very difficult for Mrs Palmer to find work at this present point in time. The family have enjoyed a fairly affluent lifestyle. The marital family home is in a pleasant area of Gosforth and the children have attended private schools. The family have always enjoyed holidays abroad and a skiing trip each winter to Canada or Austria. Mrs Palmer has stated that her immediate monthly requirements are £2615. This is not an unreasonable amount given the lifestyle the couple have enjoyed throughout their marriage and taking into account Mr Palmer's earnings which we have to base on the evidence he has provided, not his hearsay. Mr Palmer has offered £600 per month by way of maintenance which is wholly inadequate."

The Judge listened intently, all the while his eyes fixed on the bundle laid before him. His expression remained pan, giving no indication where his sympathy lay.

Bennett turned to the judge and paused while he removed his glasses.

"Mr Palmer has offered to provide a monthly amount to his wife and family which is less than his daily rate of pay. Quite frankly Sir, I find that insulting."

John looked across at me and gave a gentle smile as he relaxed back in his chair waiting for Steedman to present his defence. I gave a weak smile back at him, it was all I could muster as my insides turned to jelly. I knew Steedman was going to be gunning for me. He wouldn't spare me, especially after John had relentlessly provoked his client.

Steedman started off in much the same vein as John, however he focused on his clients attributes rather than his shortcomings. Mr Palmer was the great provider who had been the breadwinner for the whole family, his wife had offered no financial support even though apparently she was more than capable of finding employment. Steedman focused intensely on my qualifications. Stuart had spent years knocking me down and undermining my intelligence. Yet now all of a sudden here they were painting me as this intelligent intellectual who would give Einstein a decent run for his money.

John once again sat bolt upright in his chair, not waiting for Steedman to finish his sentence before he interjected cutting Steedman down to size.

"With all due respect, this hearing is concerned with Mrs Palmers immediate financial needs. Her qualifications at this point in time are irrelevant as my client has not been in the workplace for a number of years. She would need to retrain and she also has to consider the needs of her youngest daughter, Alexandra. Not only is she dependent but need I remind you that Mrs Palmer is also her carer."

Ouch, that hit home. My bastard of a husband wanted me working full time while our disabled daughter was left home alone.

With his point well made, John sat back in his chair again, resuming his cool, unruffled exterior. The focus was once again on Steedman as he continued, frustration written all over his face. He picked up on John's point in an attempt to turn it in his clients favour.

"If we consider Mrs Palmer's immediate needs, they have been adequately met by my client. Since leaving the marital home Mr

Palmer has deposited £3500 into the joint account. He has hardly left your client destitute. Mrs Palmer has her own income amounting to £63.25 per week and she has also been recently awarded £197.00 per week from the CSA, which is more than adequate to meet Alexandra's needs."

I watched as Steedman spoke. Obviously I was already predisposed to disliking him, yet there was something else about him that niggled away at me, as he was a slimy little character. He wasn't finished with his character assassination either, he reviewed the schedule of my immediate outgoings and picked through them one by one, challenging each item listed.

John put across a persuasive argument for every expense Steedman questioned, all be it until it came to the petrol where neither the Judge or Steedman were buying that a woman who didn't need to travel to work would need to spend £270 per month on fuel. John didn't push the point. He wanted to brush over it and not alert Judge MacNab to the possibility that other items on the list were questionable too.

Once Steedman had finished dissecting my monthly expenditure he turned his attention back to the girls. Victoria, he suggested, was hardly a dependent. She was at Newcastle College doing a Health and Social Care qualification and she also had a part time job giving her an income of £400 per month. He pointed out Alexandra had a Saturday job and she was also in receipt of Disability Living Allowance. According to Steedman they were both bringing an income into the house.

John retaliated almost immediately.

"So I would be correct in saying, your client doesn't feel it is his duty to contribute to the household bills, he wants to shirk that responsibility and he expects his children to use their pocket money to help to meet these needs. He walks away and doesn't want to pay, that seems to size Mr Palmer up doesn't it?"

John was looking directly at my smouldering husband challenging him. Stuart sat stony-faced glaring back in defiance. He didn't bite, yet I knew every part of him wanted to bound across the table and tackle John head on. The situation was getting very tense and Steedman was about to engage in the debate once more but wasn't given a chance. Judge MacNab had had enough. He raised his hand. Both Steedman and John looked in his direction and stopped dead in their tracks.

"I think I have heard quite enough from both parties."

The room went silent as he studied the court bundle and the notes he had been diligently jotting down throughout the hearing.

We waited for what seemed like an eternity.

Eventually he looked up and turned his attention to Stuart's solicitor.

"Mr Steedman, it concerns me that your client is unwilling to provide evidence of his earnings. I cannot accept that a professional accountant is unable to do so."

I suppressed a smile.

"I also have concerns with regard to your clients outgoings, specifically rental payments and petrol. However you have shown evidence of a rental agreement and on that basis I am inclined to accept that this is a genuine payment. With regard to petrol usage of £800, it does seem excessive in my opinion, but I am aware that your client does travel with his work and his usage will be high."

He then turned his attention to John who was once again poised on the edge of his seat.

"I would also question Mrs Palmers outgoings relating to petrol. I believe it is an excessive amount and I consider it to be unrealistic. Having said that, Mrs Palmer's budget in general appears to be reasonable."

As he slowly and methodically recited the reasons behind his judgement amount my heart raced. Why could he not just get to the point and tell us the bloody figure? I looked to John for reassurance however his head was down taking notes, as was Steedman. Both solicitors were scribbling away as if their lives depended on it.

He continued.

"Mr Palmer has not provided sufficient evidence relating to his current earnings and on that basis I am inclined to make an assumption that Mr Palmer's income is in line with his 2009 tax return which was stated to be £107000."

My heart slowed slightly as I heard his words. Mr Steedman and Stuart had not fooled the judge. I quickly glanced at Stuart, his eyes were fixed on Steedman, his mouth contorted in such a way I knew it was taking him all his effort to hold his council. Steedman was either unaware or uninterested in his clients glare as he like John, was hanging on every word Judge MacNab had to say.

Again a concern flagged up in my mind. We had omitted the Child Tax Credit from my income. Wasn't that equally as misleading? I dismissed the thought almost immediately. Why would I doubt John, he hadn't let me down so far? I sensed the pendulum swinging towards me and I wasn't going to let that little niggle bother me.

I returned my attention back to Judge MacNab who still hadn't delivered his financial judgement, yet I was sure it was going to be within his next breath and so it was.

"I am going to order that Mr Palmer should pay maintenance of £1000 per calendar month payable on the 1st day of every month. This payment shall commence immediately and shall continue until further order."

I could barely contain myself, the endless days of worry, the sleepless nights, now at last I had a result. With my tax credits, the family allowance and the payment from the CSA my income would be pushing two thousand pounds a month. But better than that was the fact it was all legal. Stuart had no choice, he had to pay it.

Judge MacNab continued.

"In addition I am awarding costs of £1320 to Mrs Palmer, this amount is payable in the next seven days."

Halleluiah!

Finally it was over. Within seconds we were all rising to our feet and doffing our imaginary caps once more. We filtered out of the room. No words were spoken and all eyes were fixed to the floor in an effort to avoid contact. We walked down the eerily quiet corridor, past the usher's checkpoint and into the public area. The formal atmosphere of the courtroom was replaced with the hustle and bustle of the everyday functions of the court, people sitting, standing, moving, solicitors and barristers consulting with their clients. It was over. I had survived. I had almost broken out into a smile when he reached me and confronted me face on. I stopped in my tracks as my estranged husband stood merely inches from me and I could smell the venom on his breath. It was the anger on his face and the darkness in his eyes that struck me as he squared up to me. Those very same eyes had once been filled with love but now I only saw hatred and disgust.

He spat his words out with such bitterness I felt their force cut into me.

They were as painful as any physical blow he could have dealt me and sharper than any blade he could have plunged into me.

"You fucking greedy bitch, you fucking leech."

How I wanted the ground to swallow me up.

"You pathetic, money grabbing cow."

Time stood still and I was aware we had an audience watching us, waiting for the battle to erupt. Fortunately, before he could speak another word, Steedman pulled him away. At the same time John grabbed my arm and pulled me into a client conference room that stood conveniently empty just feet away from us. The euphoria I had felt leaving the Judge's Chambers had been replaced with an overwhelming sense of shame and sadness. How the hell had we reached this point and how could he hate me so much? I was in court to protect our home, to make sure our daughters, his daughters could eat, be clothed and could have the things they wanted and enjoyed, the things they had had all of their lives. My hands trembled as I struggled to fight back the tears that were so close to flowing. His words were sinking in. I so wished I had been able to answer him but I could barely bring myself to speak. The three of us sat in silence trying to take in what had actually happened.

Louise placed her arm gently around my shoulders in an effort to comfort me, I knew she didn't know what to say.

John broke the ice first.

"Louise, would you mind getting Annette a cup of coffee from the canteen, I think she might need one."

Immediately she rose to her feet, as eager as ever to accommodate John's every command and probably relieved to escape.

John wasted no time pulling a chair up beside me. I had barely noticed his move as my head replayed the event that had just taken place. He lifted my hand gently and squeezed it. The gesture was simple enough and I immediately I felt safe as he brought me back to the moment. I could feel the warmth from his body and smell the light fragrance of his musky aftershave, my senses were aroused once more. Why was I allowing myself to feel this way, hadn't I promised myself a line would be drawn? Then he spoke. It was always his reassuring voice that made my heart skip a beat.

"My dear Annette, I think once Louise gets back and we have a little chat about the events of today I am going to run you home. I have a hearing at 2.30pm so I have plenty of time."

I blushed.

"No, its fine, I'm happy to get a taxi home, you've done enough for me today already."

I felt flustered. I didn't want a repeat of his previous visit. I sensed he knew what I was thinking and he seized upon it.

"We never managed to go out for dinner did we? I think you need cheering up. I'll check my diary and ring you to arrange it and this time I won't take no for an answer."

I was feeling totally exhausted after the events of the day and I didn't have the energy to protest. I don't know what came over me, the words just tumbled out of my mouth. What was I thinking?

"What will Mrs Bennett have to say about that?"

As I said them I wished I could have retrieved each and every word. Why didn't my mouth have a two second delay, like the send button on my emails? It was too late, they were out there floating around that bloody dingy room.

He didn't even blink, it hadn't caught him off guard or offended him. He smiled and looked longingly into my eyes as he spoke.

"That ship sailed a long time ago Annette. I find myself just like you, all alone at sea."

17

As I turned onto the street I felt a huge sense of relief. I was on the last fifty yards of a three mile run and my front door was now within sight. I'd made it and I was damned proud of myself, even though the run was interjected with frequent pit stops as I gasped for breath. I quickened my pace in a last ditch attempt to reach the finishing line, the effort practically killing me but I did feel proud and elated. I was no Paula Radcliffe that was for sure and as I reached the gates of the driveway I was overcome with exhaustion. I slumped back against the pillar of the gatepost, my head bent forward in an attempt to recover. Tightness engulfed my chest as my lungs desperately struggled to expand and fill with air. Like two lead weights, my legs anchored themselves to the pavement unwilling to move another inch as the blood rapidly pumped around my body leaving a red blush on my skin. And yet some chemicals coursing through my body made me feel good. The sweat was pouring out of me and the staccato beat of my heart reminded me of my day in court. On that occasion its rapid pace had been borne out of fear, yet today it was symbolic of my efforts. Today I felt invigorated.

As much as I tried to focus on my running achievement, memories of that day in court flooded back to the forefront of my mind. That day had been a milestone, there was no other word to describe it. It occurred to me as I wiped away the beads of sweat from my forehead that it was a day that had changed me forever. I had got through it and I was still standing.

When I left the courtroom and wedged myself into John's little sports number for the short drive home, my hands were still visibly shaking. We didn't speak much in the car apart from John gently grilling me about Stuart's anger issues as he'd witnessed how he had reacted. What he was really eluding to, that Stuart had been violent towards me in the past? I didn't offer up any information in that direction as the courtroom fiasco had been bad enough and I had wanted the ground to swallow me up when Stuart had confronted me. I wasn't about to share the slap in the face incident or the mental abuse he'd subjected me to in recent years. My humiliation would well and truly have been complete if I had told him everything that Stuart had put me through.

Wouldn't it just beg the question of why had I stayed married so long? Sadly I had no answer to that, other than a misplaced loyalty towards a man I had loved and who I thought had loved me back.

John had realised I was reluctant to talk and hadn't pushed the matter. He just let me be with my thoughts as I sat gazing aimlessly out of the passenger window.

Strangely enough it hadn't been an awkward silence as I was content to sit quietly in his company as my angst and anger gradually faded away. At last my trembling subsided and my rapid breathing returned to normal. By the time the car pulled to a halt outside my front door calmness had once again been restored. He put his handbrake on but left the engine running. There was a soothing, gentle vibration and a low, growling noise from the engine. I had been relieved that there was no expectation of an invite into the house and I was keen to make my exit and get back to the comfort of my family and he obviously sensed that. Before I opened the door I once again proclaimed my undying gratitude for his help.

"You're more than welcome Annette," he said in a matter of fact way but as I looked at him his eyes twinkled and a beaming smile spread across his face. I offered a weak smile in return, it was all I could muster, my energy levels were at rock bottom. I reached for the handle on the passenger door and as I did so he stretched across and placed his hand on mine.

"Let me help you with that Annette."

My heart began to race yet again, as I coyly turned my head back to meet his gaze.

I knew our relationship had entered a new phase. It was on the cusp of changing into something quite different from the formal harness which had restrained us in the Saxtons' offices. His admission that he was no longer with his wife had opened up new possibilities and we both knew it. That ship sailed a long time ago Annette. I find myself just like you, all alone at sea.

He has been my saviour in the courtroom that day. He had been my knight in shining armour, standing up and defeating the foe that had wronged me. His dominant presence drew me to him like a magnet. When he said he would ring me to arrange another dinner date I gave the only response that came to my head.

I smiled.

"I'll be waiting for your call John."

I ended up almost skipping into the house that day, with a spring in my step and lightness in my heart. I was greeted in the hallway by Abigail, Victoria and Alexandra's frozen, anxious faces. They'd heard the engine of John's car and were waiting for me. I knew they had been stressing about the hearing. Their upbeat manner the previous evening had been false, obviously a ploy to spare me further distress and now the worry was clearly etched on their faces. My heart sank just a little as the guilt crept through me. The pain their father and I had put them through was unforgiveable. It dawned on me at that moment that they were going to carry the scars of our separation for the rest of their lives. I was desperate to make amends and instinctively I held my arms out, beckoning them to come to me. They ran towards me as they had done when they were small children, expectation, relief and tension exuding from their bodies. That day they were my babies once more.

The four of us stood huddled together, our heads nuzzled into one another. One of the girls was sobbing though I didn't know who. I felt safe again; I was with my girls and at the end of the day that was all that mattered. I told them about the award and we cracked open a bottle of Prosecco to celebrate. Within a few short minutes the sobs and frowns of concern had changed to smiles and laughter filled the room.

The news travelled fast around family and friends. My mobile was buzzing with text messages, while the house phone rang off its hook; everyone wanted to know what had happened at court. What did Stuart say? How did he react? Was she with him?

There was a whole host of questions fired in my direction and I recounted the events of that day so many times that by the time the story reached the Sunday dinner table, as I sat once again with my wonderful family, I had become totally desensitised to Stuart's vicious verbal attack. While recounting the story yet again upset my mum and brothers, it no longer stuck in my heart as it had done on the day in court.

The family listened intently yet again, their eyes gawping and mouths set ajar as I recited my story once more, adding the odd embellishment along the way to heighten the drama. Darren, my youngest brother, shook his head in disbelief unable to retain his anger any longer.

"The bastard." he said. "Give me one good reason why I shouldn't kill him?"

I wasn't the least bit surprised by his response as he'd always been first up to fight my battles, yet my oldest brother Roger, the less sensitive of my three siblings, saw the court scenario as an opportunity lost.

He broke the somber mood as he chipped in with his misguided (I thought) words of wisdom.

"You should have taken a punch from him sis. He wouldn't have had a leg to stand on, it would have been game set and match."

I laughed at the thought of me egging him on to take a punch and slapped Roger gently on the arm by way of a reprimand.

"Yeah, and it might have been game over for your sister as well, have you seen the size of the man?"

Once again we all laughed and for a change there was joy in the house that afternoon as we made a determined effort to celebrate my small victory.

Laughter had begun to gradually seep its way back into my life where it had been almost alien to me. There was no sudden transformation, only small incremental changes in my general demeanour. I was still riddled with guilt having had to put the girls through the whole charade, even though I felt I had no choice.

I couldn't deny it, I was mightily relieved and if I was honest, even a little smug that I had got to the bastard and had hit him where it hurt, deep in his pocket.

The spring in my step had returned once more and for the first time in months I wasn't filled with trepidation going on my weekly food shop. I almost floated around Sainsbury's no longer having to justify every penny spent or subject myself to the humiliation of having to put items back on the supermarket shelf when I discovered there wasn't enough cash in my purse to get me through the checkout. I was once again enjoying life's small luxuries and I even treated myself to a visit to my favourite hairdressers and a coffee with friends afterwards. I was merely reinstating elements of a lifestyle I'd taken for granted before Stuart had cut himself loose from his family and his commitments.

I noticed the change in the girls too. They were more relaxed and the caution and tension they had displayed on that day had melted away as they saw their once downtrodden mother reclaiming some of the joys of life without the worry of money. Inevitably, John had once again drifted into my thoughts. It had been a few days since I had spoken to him and as if by magic I had no sooner started to think about him when he rang me. I nearly didn't answer his call when number not recognised flashed across the screen of my phone. I had been very tempted to ignore its menacing bleat, thinking it was probably one of those bloody call centres touting for business.

I answered with my sharp, no nonsense tone.

"Hello can I help you?"

"How is my favourite client today?"

I recognised his voice immediately, the rich deep tones as distinctive and captivating as ever. The words just popped out of my mouth automatically while my initial harsh tone changed to a schoolgirl giggle.

"All the better for hearing your voice John."

Oh my god, had I just said that?

"I'm glad to hear that Annette," he said with a chuckle. "No more bother from your husband I hope?"

I lost the girlish giggle immediately. The mention of Stuart's name had that effect on me now.

"No nothing John, I haven't heard a thing," I replied seriously.

"There's a couple of things I need to talk to you about Annette," he said. "I was hoping that we could discuss them over dinner tomorrow evening."

As he said it I could literally visualize my girls faces, wondering how they'd react. I was struck with fear. How would I tell them?

I didn't care, I would work something out. I wanted to see him, wanted dinner with my handsome and caring solicitor.

"That sounds lovely John although it will have to be early because I really can't be too late for Alexandra."

"That's not a problem. What time would suit you best?"

I dithered for what seemed like an age then finally it was agreed that we should meet at 6pm. John suggested a little pub, The Fox, just outside Ponteland. He offered me a lift which I declined for no other reason than I wanted to control the time of my arrival and my departure. John gushed about the cuisine and the homely atmosphere of the place but I could only think of one thing. What would I say to the girls? I knew it couldn't be avoided and I wouldn't lie to them. Their dad had blatantly lied to them throughout the duration of this debacle and I wasn't about to follow suit.

Fortunately the big date fell on the same evening as the girls usually dined with their Dad, although I had my doubts whether it would come off now. His initial enthusiasm to 'always be there for his children' was dwindling and the daily texts had faded out almost as quickly as they had started and now the one meal a week was sporadic. His work commitments had to atone for that misdemeanour.

As it turned out, my announcement that I was having an early bird dinner with my solicitor was met with a degree of indifference. I had sold it to them as he had to me, he wanted to discuss a few things.

Apart from the odd comment from Victoria saying "ugh what freaks," and a couple of wise cracks they didn't see it any other way than what it appeared. The fact that he was my solicitor and they had no idea that he had made a pass at me in their Dad's study, threw them off the scent and refrained them from concluding it was anything other than a business meal. Stuart had called earlier that afternoon and confirmed their Pizza fest was on. I was grateful for that at least and I left them as they fought over who was going in the shower first.

I found The Fox with the ease John had told me I would. It was as I imagined it would be, a Jacobean façade with a low, oak beamed ceiling and heavily patterned carpets that carried the tread indicant of the establishment's popularity. John was already seated at a candle lit table squirreled away in the corner. Although it was bright sunshine outside, the light was sparing in the aging establishment. I noticed he already had the menu in hand and was using the reflective glow from the flickering light as way of support in his attempt to read it. I hadn't been nervous at all up to that point, it was only when I approached the table that my anxiety kicked in and I began to think this had not been a good idea. What had I been thinking? I scolded myself for my stupidity. But it was too late to back out. He looked up from his menu and caught my attention. I was hooked on his line and he was drawing me in, I could feel it and there was nothing I could do about it. Immediately he rose from his chair as if he was greeting a long lost friend and a gentle peck was planted on each cheek. I could smell his aroma as he commented on mine.

"You smell lovely."

We went through the awkward introductory formalities, the weather and the mundane events of our respective days.

John said his had been a bugger of a day with one awkward client after another. He laughed then gave a mock gesture of being exasperated. He made me laugh with his light hearted banter and it served its purpose of breaking the ice.

The waiter loitered within earshot of our conversation but gave us a courteous length of time to settle ourselves into our surroundings. Then before we knew it he was practically on top of our table desperate to take our drinks order. John suggested that maybe we should place our food order at the same time, that way we would be free to talk undisturbed. He'd obviously had time on his hands waiting for my arrival, because without a moment's hesitation he ordered the house special, beef and ale pie and that put me right on the spot. I wanted to order quickly as I admitted to myself that I couldn't wait to be alone with this man. I pondered the menu for what seemed like an age then in total desperation I resorted to my familiar favourite.

"I'll go for Caesar Salad."

Relief, decision made, we dispatched the waiter with his menus and John took centre stage once more. His was cheeky with an easy charm and I suspected he was controlling the conversation like a master puppeteer guiding me in the direction he wanted to take me but I didn't mind. I felt at ease in his company as he asked about my background then I asked a little about his past life. He said that law ran through his veins, it was in his genetic make-up. His father had been a barrister and his father before him.

I could see the passion on his face as he spoke and I sat captivated listening to his numerous anecdotes each as amusing and entertaining as the last.

We both stepped around the subject of our ex partners and I avoided asking about his for fear he might broach my mess of a marriage. I hadn't wanted to taint what was turning out to be a pleasant evening.

It surprised me when he got down to business, I thought it would never happen. I was waiting to be seduced, there was no other way to describe it but I sensed our mutual business would inevitably rear its ugly head.

His voice was tentative and I was guessing he was reluctant to put a dampener on the evening.

"There are a couple of things we need to discuss."

It sounded serious, I was all ears.

"Steedman has been in touch and reading between the lines they are getting fairly worried we might use Alexandra's condition to our advantage."

Now my ears had totally pricked up, he had my full attention.

John sighed, his finger tracing along the tablecloth as if he was sketching the event out.

"Basically if we don't reach a settlement and it goes to court, a judge may be more favourable to you in the settlement with regard to maintenance and distribution of assets."

He pressed the point home as if he were back in the courtroom.

"They are worried that if a judge decides that you're Alexandra's main carer, then he'll figure that will impact on your ability to go out to work and earn a living."

"I am her main carer," I said. "I do need to be there for her so of course that may affect my work situation."

I looked at him blankly, was I missing the point? Why would this be bad for my case?

He got to the nitty gritty, obviously spotting the confusion on my face.

"Your husband is threatening to get independent medical reports on Alexandra's condition. He wants to try and disprove your claims. He claims she is independent enough and doesn't need a carer."

That was it. I wanted to kill Stuart fucking Palmer. I tried to keep calm.

"He doesn't need a bloody medical report John, his daughter has

Spina bifida, irreparable nerve damage to her spine. It's a chronic lifelong condition and he is well aware how much she needs me. He's seen me when I've sat up with her during the early hours of the morning, he's seen us both collapse into bed through sheer exhaustion after a night of torment. He's witnessed the pain she goes through."

John nodded his head in agreement

" I know that, and so does he, but the court will look at the evidence presented to them. They will need to see something and it's best we get our own report from her own Consultants. They are the people who have the better understanding of her condition."

I shook my head in disbelief, once more flabbergasted at the depths Stuart was willing to plunge to deny me a reasonable settlement.

Yet John wasn't finished. There was more.

"To complicate matters further, Mr Palmer has said he has an eye condition which will affect his ability to work in the long term."

John raised his eyebrows as if he was searching the recesses of his brain in an effort to try and remember the name of the condition.

I prompted him.

"Glaucoma," I explained, "it's a eye condition where the optic nerve is damaged by the pressure of fluid inside the eye. He's had the condition almost as long as I have known him."

"What's the extent of the condition?" John asked.

"An odd flare up," I stated. "Some blurred vision in the morning as he got out of bed. The doctors prescribed eye drops to keep the condition at bay."

"That's it?" John said. "It worked?"

I nodded.

"That's it, it hasn't impacted on his life in any way, for Christ sake he plays golf to a handicap of two, he runs marathons, has been a county squash play and holds down a full time job down spending at least ten hours a day looking at a computer screen. He's hardly walking around with a dog and a white stick."

I couldn't quite take in what I had just heard. Was this the man who vowed to love me forever? First Alexandra's condition and now this? How low could a man go?

John sensed my utter disbelief. The mood of the evening had changed after these two revelations. He lifted my hand that had been resting on the table next to the now cold cup of coffee and his touch soothed me.

His voice was quiet.

"The bottom line is Steedman is threatening to produce medical reports on Mr Palmers condition, I'm surmising what they are going to say is that your husbands medical condition could mean he may lose his sight."

I sighed once more. John didn't have to paint a picture, I knew where this was heading.

He made light of the situation in an attempt to lift my spirits.

"Look on the bright side Annette, you have me on your side and I'm not going to let him get away with it."

His kind, reassuring words made me feel better. Within a short time he had managed to bring me out of the doldrums. I had witnessed first-hand John Bennett at work in the court room and I did not doubt for one second he would fight tooth and nail on my behalf. Both claims were ridiculous. Surely a court would see that?

He moved the subject on although it was still in the same vein.

"You need to come in the office next week, we need to make a stab at completing Form E."

I nodded in agreement. Completing the form didn't faze me. It was where each party had to list their bank accounts, assets, investments, shares and liabilities such as credit cards etc. I had nothing to hide, unlike Stuart, who I knew had been stashing cash away for donkey's years.

It was time to leave and John insisted on picking up the tab when our impatient waiter delivered it on a small silver tray with mints. I argued that we should go Dutch, but he wouldn't hear of it, he was insistent and eventually I gave up the fight.

We meandered back to our cars, with autumn almost upon us there was a slight chill in the evening air and I shivered slightly as the cool breeze touched my skin. John instinctively placed his arm around my shoulders, shielding me from the cold. I didn't flinch, in truth I didn't want to. I felt safe with him by my side and as we reached our respective cars, he leaned towards me and gently kissed me on the mouth. It wasn't urgent as it had been in the study, his lips barely touching mine. He kissed me slowly yet it still had the same effect. He had aroused all of my senses again leaving me wanting more.

He broke the kiss, looking tenderly into my eyes.

"You know I want to see you again, I hope you feel the same way."

I didn't speak. To be honest I felt a little stupid, a middle-aged woman standing in a car park kissing her boyfriend like a teenager.

He leaned in and kissed me again, his tongue probing gently between my lips and his hips eased forward as he drew his arms around my waist and pulled me into him. What was I thinking I kept asking myself, as I wanted to pull away? But I returned his kiss eagerly and I slid my arms around his waist. I couldn't help it. I was drawn to him like a dog to a bone.

After some minutes we separated.

"I want you so much Annette," he said. "I want to take you away for a weekend, far away from here and explore every inch of you."

I knew I was going to see him again, I wanted to see him again.

"Tell me you feel the same way," he said.

I was totally lost for words but nodded helplessly.

He smiled.

"Soon, we'll do that soon, somewhere like London, perhaps even Paris."

My mind had cruised into overdrive and I could almost picture a small hotel in the Sorbonne, in the heart of the Latin Quarter, just me and my handsome protector. But in an instance practicality kicked in. It was impossible. How could I leave Alexandra for a whole weekend and what would I tell the girls? I could lie of course, like their father had lied to them for God knows how many years. But that wasn't me. I couldn't bring myself to lie to my girls, I never had and I never would.

He was talking about Paris as if he had already settled on the venue for our weekend break. He loved the Champs Elysees and the restaurants and bars around Montmartre. My head was in the clouds as I dared to daydream.

"By the way, I think we should keep this between ourselves, I'd rather the Henshaws don't get wind of our dinner date or they'll want to bill you for my time."

It never dawned on me that there would be a fee structure put in place for our evening together and yet we had talked business.

"The bill," I said, "I still haven't seen hide nor hair of one."

John pulled me in close yet again. He kissed me once again on the lips.

"Don't worry, it won't be as bad as you think. I've not charged for anywhere near the hours I've worked on your case."

He gave a sigh of dismay.

"But my hands are tied unfortunately, the Henshaws are my masters. If they found out about this date tonight I would be finished."

He looked deflated as he said the words and my heart went out to him.

"Don't worry," I said, "it will be our secret."

The journey back to Gosforth was all a bit of a blur. The rain started after about twenty minutes, the drops of water and the windscreen wipers blended into a kind of giant hypnotic screen and I did well just concentrating on the road ahead of me. As I pulled into the drive and stepped out of the car a wicked grin pulled across my face. My God, I thought, if I walk in looking like this then surely the girls would know exactly what had happened. It was written all over my naughty face.

Nothing could have prepared me for what happened as I opened the door and walked into the hallway.

18

Barely a week had passed since my evening with John and I found myself back sitting in the conference room of the Saxtons' offices with the oversized clock ticking away behind me. My heart was skipping to its own joyful beat anticipating his arrival. I hadn't seen him since that evening yet the dialogue between us had been on going and sometimes quite naughty. It was John who had initiated a text conversation the very next day, reaffirming his eagerness to arrange another evening. His texts had been a consistent flow over the week, their content increasing in intensity and the language between us developing a flirtatious theme as our familiarity with one another grew.

I was grateful for his texts and he had been the only light in what had turned out to be a bleak week.

As I sat recollecting those events, my attention was drawn back to the present as the conference room door opened and John walked in with Louise at his side. I said good morning to Louise and John greeted me with the same formality as in previous meetings.

As usual it was Louise who made light conversation whilst John set about sorting through the bundle of paperwork that he had dumped on the desk when he entered the room. As he sat flicking through my file, clearly in pursuit of some specific document, he took the opportunity to cut through our conversation apologising for the interruption.

"Did you receive the blank copy of the Form E we sent you Annette?"

He didn't wait for an answer, seeing that I had placed it on the desk in front of me.

"Hopefully if you've managed to complete most of it we'll not have much to do today. It will save you time and money," he said with a wry smile.

He reached into his briefcase.

"Talking of which, I have something for you."

He slid the envelope across the desk. I knew exactly what it was.

"Open it," he said. "It won't be as bad as you think."

I reached for the envelope and opened it with the same fear and trepidation I had had when I was a teenager receiving my A level results, half of me wanting to know, the other too terrified to look. Like my A levels, the result wasn't good. The numbers jumped from the page, each digit offending my eyes in equal measure and then my eyes fell on the bottom line, £6239 with the option of a 5% discount if I settled within 28 days. My mind went into a blind panic wondering where the money would come from and John noticed the fear in my eyes.

"The bill is covered, don't worry about it."

What was he talking about?

He reached into his briefcase again and pushed another piece of paper across to me.

"That's the amount from the ISA and the costs awarded by Judge MacNab."

I looked at the total. £6430.

I looked up at John he smiled.

I was safe. Relief, nothing else mattered and there was even a couple of hundred quid left over. I didn't question the amount as I browsed the attached breakdown of the hours both John and Louise had spent on my case but how could I argue anyway? I had no idea how much time the pair had spent working on my behalf, I had to trust their word. I was just grateful I had them on my side and there had been enough pennies in my purse to meet the bill, this one at least.

John had another surprise for me as he retrieved the document he had been looking for, pulling it from the file and placing it on the desk.

I read the words Decree Absolute and my heart sank. This scrappy piece of paper represented the end of my marriage. It hardly seemed a worthy trade for the investment I had made over the years. My eyes dropped as I inhaled deeply in an attempt to catch my breath. John's tender voice reached out to me again drawing me back. He was my anchor keeping me steady. I clung to his every word and each day my dependency on him grew stronger.

"Why are you looking so sad Annette? You're a free girl now your divorce is complete. You can enjoy a new life. Isn't that what you want?"

"Yes," I said, "But…"

I couldn't find the words to describe my emotion, my feelings of failure to simply hold a marriage and a family together.

He smiled. I gave a weak smile in return.

Unlike John I didn't see it as freedom. It was a stigma in fact, the divorced woman, a leper among those insecure soles who had a husband or a partner. They would see me as a threat. I was already seeing it with a few friends and acquaintances who now inadvertently marked their territory in their less than subtle ways. No longer was Mrs Palmer automatically included on the guest list of a social event. No one wanted the unwanted guest, the gooseberry, or worse still the singleton praying on their partners.

As I sat pondering over my new status my eyes remained fixed on the Decree Absolute. I could hear John's voice in the background diligently going through the Form E section by section, yet the sound trailed away as my thoughts returned to Stuart and what had happened when I returned home from the dinner date with my solicitor. He had been cutting the strings that bound our family together, one by one, but now his relationship with his children had sunk to a new level.

It was the night they were supposed to go for dinner with their dad, the same night I had headed up to Ponteland to the pub called The Fox.

The three girls had been waiting for me when I returned, lined up on the sofa like the Three Stooges. Seeing them there together with faces trailing the floor I instantly thought I was about to face the Spanish Inquisition about my night out. It wasn't the case. To my shame I breathed a sigh of relief when it became evident that it was their dad they were gunning for that evening and not me. He had failed to turn up for dinner. They'd ordered a drink or two and then called him to ask where he was. He'd made an excuse about work commitments and said he wasn't going to make it. Abigail just knew he was lying and her fury built as they finished their drinks and headed outside. In a fit of rage she had driven up to Angela Maddison's house with her sisters in tow. It appeared that Abigail knew exactly where to find Angela Maddison, in fact she'd been quiet the detective taking it upon herself to follow her Dad home after one of their weekly Pizza fests. Unbeknown to Stuart he had led his daughter right to the bitch's front door. His car was there again the night they drove up to Sacriston, which prompted Abigail to get out and she stormed towards the house. Victoria and Alexandra were too scared to get out, they remained huddled together in the car. She rang the bell and it was Angela who answered the door. She obviously recognised Abigail immediately, she needed no introduction, and the cold hearted bitch hadn't been the least bit intimidated on seeing Abigail's disgruntled face on her doorstep.

I started to cringe as Abigail retold the tale. I was desperate to hear the outcome yet part of me wanted to plug my ears up and drown it out altogether. I knew the story was going to get worse and so it did. Abigail, unable to contain herself, had started shouting and screaming when her Dad appeared at bitch's shoulder.

"You're both bloody liars and you're a complete cow. Do you get off on breaking up families?"

The woman was the complete ice maiden and hadn't been the least bit daunted by Abigail's emotional outburst. If Abigail had expected her father to calm the situation she was sadly mistaken.

The bitch's retort was sharp and unflinching.

"If you do not remove yourself from my property I am going to call the police."

Stuart made no attempt to comfort his own daughter who was clearly distressed. Abigail continued her onslaught.

"You didn't have time for your daughters, yet you had plenty of time to come up here to see this home wrecker."

Eventually he took control of the situation but directed his anger at Abigail.

"Have you vented, have you vented?" he repeated over and over again. He offered no excuses for failing to turn up at the restaurant.

Abigail said there had been no let-up in his bellowing attack and no opportunity for her to respond.

"How dare you come up here," he said. "You have no business to be here."

He shouted at Abigail until she broke down in tears and, humiliation complete, she retreated back to the sanctity of her car and drove home.

As she sat on the sofa recounting the tale, eyes full of tears and mascara running, I had wanted to kill both him and his bitch Maddison. He was letting them go little by little, day by day, sacrificing his children for her. And his money of course, it was always about the money.

John's voice gradually filtered back to me as I released myself from reliving that particular nightmare.

"Annette, I think all you need to do now is get copies of your bank and credit card statements from the last twelve months, plus don't forget you also need a pension statement from the last company you worked at, Proctor and Gamble wasn't it?"

I nodded in agreement only half interested. John started to scribble once more. The room was silent as John and Louise engrossed in their form filling and taking notes.

John spoke.

"Louise, we need to ensure that the form is typed up today and back with Annette tomorrow at the latest, if we are exchanging with the other side on Monday it needs to be done pronto."

He turned his attention to me.

"Would you be able to pick the form up from reception tomorrow Annette and take it to the solicitors across the street?"

I nodded.

"You need to sign a sworn affidavit, it only takes minutes and there's a small charge but unfortunately its only you who can do it." His voice was light and chirpy. "I can't do it for you I'm afraid."

As he spoke, Louise was already packing away her notepad and papers, keen to get on with the job in hand. John didn't move an inch. I assumed that our meeting wasn't quite over as he had not cast his eyes to the clock on the wall, that in the past had always been his final calculation on billing hours and my cue that things were drawing to a close. He continued to skim through my file and I wondered what else he was going to pull out of the hat like some macabre magician. Eventually his hand landed on the page he had been searching for and traced his finger across its contents, reacquainting himself with the subject matter before he divulged its contents. I sat eagerly waiting in anticipation. Once read he was keen to share.

"It seems that since the court hearing we've managed to ruffle your ex-husbands feathers."

John had adapted quickly to my new status as the ex-wife.

"Steedman is demanding to see any evidence we plan to produce relating to Alexandra's condition."

He glanced at me sheepishly as he remembered the conversation we had at dinner.

"You need to speak to Alexandra's doctors and start the ball rolling."

He didn't linger on the issue. We had thrashed the subject to death the previous week, he knew my thoughts as I did his. He swiftly moved on, his voice slow and deliberate. "He's also threatening a court injunction against you if you make any attempt to sell or dispose of any household belongings, specifically the Norman Cornish painting, the two Alexander Millar paintings and the baby grand piano."

I was flabbergasted, speechless yet again. Selling the artwork we'd chosen together had never entered my head, but obviously Stuart was ready to rip the family décor to pieces for the sake of a few more quid in the bank. And I played the piano daily in case my ex-husband had forgotten. It wasn't an instrument of pleasure to him, it was more money in the bank.

Un-fucking-believable was the thought running through my mind at that moment, my head shaking in sheer disbelief. John seemed oblivious, turning his attention back to Louise.

"That reminds me Louise, the artwork and the piano need to be added to the form," He glanced back in my direction, "have you any idea of their value Annette?"

Both pairs of eyes were now firmly focused on me as I hesitated, trying to think. "Well I can only tell you what we paid for them, I have no idea what the resale value would be."

I relayed what I could remember relating to the costs and both John and Louise made note of the purchase figures on their notepads.

John looked down at the notes he had scribbled, then lost in his own thoughts once more he proceeded to bounce the pencil off the pad of paper to a rhythm less tune. I stared at him while he performed his little gig, yet he was completely unaware of my uncomfortable demeanour. I realised there had been no flirtatious gestures on his part that morning, his business like mode carrying on throughout the meeting. He remained lost in his work, his focus fixed.

"I think we need to be conservative when estimating both the value of the house and the artwork," he said. "If, as you've indicated Annette you want to stay in the family home it might serve our purpose to put a lower value on the house. If we undervalue the house significantly they'll insist on an independent valuation. I think if you agree we should value the house at 600k."

I nodded my agreement. Being honest I was totally confused, I had no idea why we would choose to over value or undervalue anything, wasn't it best to avoid the game playing?

Both John and Louise continued to discuss the merits of undervaluing as opposed to overvaluing assets and vice versa and I listened on as the debate ran its course. I had nothing to offer as I had no clue as to its significance. The figures were eventually agreed, Louise amended her notes to reflect the changes needed, then she repacked her belongings said her goodbyes and made her exit.

We were alone once more yet he continued to write. My heart began to sink slightly as he had been more attentive the previous week. My feelings stirred once more as my mind regressed back to our candle lit dinner then the kiss in the car park. He continued to scribble and I felt like some love struck teenager biding my time for his attention.

He obviously sensed my growing agitations and with one final flurry, he practically stabbed the paper with his final full stop.

He raised his head and smiled.

"Alone at last with my newly divorced client."

His choice of words irritated me slightly. The first divorced woman joke and it had come from his very lips. I realised John was an expert at reading body language and I imagined all his years as a solicitor dealing with people, had only served to hone his skill and he changed his tact realising he had struck a raw nerve, pulling up his chair to meet mine as he did so.

He was now so close I could feel the warmth from his body and could smell the now familiar musk from his cologne. Without being able to do anything about it my heart raced at a galloping pace, my stomach fluttered and all my senses came to life. No words were spoken. Without invitation he reached his hand towards my face, skillfully manoeuvering it to the back of my neck and as he did so he gently pulled my head towards him until our lips were almost touching. There was a faint smell of mint as his breath met mine. As our mouths finally reached their inevitable destination there was an explosion within me and the feelings increased as he kissed me harder and more passionately. His hand gripped my neck firmly as he drew me even closer to him. Like school kids behind the bike shed we pawed at each other and he raised his free hand sliding it between the fabric of my jacket and blouse before cupping my breast. His skilled fingers found a gap between my bra and my skin as he eased through the tight material and located my now erect nipple and squeezed hard. What the hell was happening? It wasn't long before his hand was on the move again and he glided it gently down towards my skirt, first resting it on my knee before making the bold move of placing it between my lower thighs. My body was now on fire, every sexual desire I had been suppressing all these months had been ignited once more and my body was almost limp with desire. Eventually I snapped out of it and pulled away gasping for breath. I jumped to my feet.

"No John, no. This is wrong."

We were in the Saxtons' offices for God's sake and I was behaving like some cheap whore.

He wasn't in the least bit deterred by my sudden rebuke.

"You know I can't stop thinking about you and I know you feel the same. I want to prove to you how much I care."

He pulled me physically into his lap and nuzzled his head against mine, his mouth softly whispering in my ear.

"Do you know how difficult it was to sit across that desk from you today, pretending it was business as usual when all the while I wanted to grab you and kiss every part of your body."

As he spoke he gripped my hips firmly, pulling my buttocks hard into his groin.

I pulled away once more and stood, struggling to catch my breath unable to find a pitch.

"Just not here John, not here please. I'm not a quick grope in the car park or a fumble in the office"

He held my gaze as I spoke and he replaced his smile with an expression I had only seen in the court room when he was fighting my cause.

"Then spend some time with me, a weekend, a night or just an evening as we did last week."

His voice softened.

"Just let me get to know you more Annette, that's all I ask."

Before I had a chance to reply there was a gentle tap on the door.

"Come in," John said completely unflustered.

It was Karen and in her usual brisk expressionless manner she walked into the room.

"Your next client is here Mr Bennett, she's in reception."

I took the hint and reached for my handbag that had been perched on the end of the desk and swiftly made my exit.

Bennett stood at the conference room window staring out into the rapidly darkening, grey Newcastle sky. The rain was falling hard, bashing against the pane of glass with such force it obscured his vision slightly. He rubbed the inside of the window with his hand in an attempt to clear the build-up of condensation.

He was deep in thought, deep in thought about only one person. He had to concede Annette Palmer was never far from his mind. He cast his mind back to earlier in the day. The soft touch of her breast and the warmth of her thighs, he'd been so close. He groaned as the blood surged around his body pooling in his crotch.

He let out a heavy sigh. He had to have her. She wasn't without passion and it was clear from her response to his advances that she was as keen as him to take it further. Her coy exterior didn't fool him. Beneath it all he guessed there was a little minx trying to get out. After their little tete a tete the previous week, he thought it would be so easy to get her into bed, yet after her parting shot today he realised he might have to put more work in. Perhaps poor vulnerable Annette wasn't so vulnerable after all, maybe she did have a backbone.

It wouldn't deter him, he loved the challenge of the chase and the prize would be that much more rewarding.

As he stood lost in his thoughts looking out of the window, the conference room door opened. His nostrils were filled with the familiar smell of a sickly sweet odour of perfume, too cheap in his opinion. It was the fragrance favoured by Elizabeth Henshaw.

He acknowledged his boss in a matter of fact manner.

"Yes Elizabeth can I help you?"

She stood just inside the office door, her hand set on her waist looking ready for combat.

"Was that the Palmer woman leaving earlier on? Did she say anything about the invoice?"

Bennett continued to stare out of the window, his eyes raising to the ceiling as she broached her favourite subject, money.

His normal expressive voice was now flat void of emotion.

"No she hasn't complained about the bill, she's happy to pay it as I knew she would be."

Elizabeth twisted her face, a smug smirk set upon her lips. Both Bennett and Elizabeth Henshaw had a mutual hatred for one another, their allegiance to one another was purely business. The negative atmosphere was so repressive it filled the room, stifling communication but it didn't hold Elizabeth back, so desperate was she to get her point across.

"I hope you're not getting any ideas about that Palmer woman, I've noticed the way you look at her." Her voice was slow and menacing. "Remember John, I know of your reputation both in and out of the court room."

For the first time since she had entered the room, John turned his head to face her, a false smile planted across his face disguising the fact that his teeth were clenched tightly together in an effort to suppress his rage.

"Elizabeth, you have such a high opinion of me, I would hate to disappoint you."

A silence fell over the room, the only sound was the rain hammering against the window pane. Elizabeth held his gaze with a steely defiance, the anger building up within her. It was clear she was determined that the last words should fall from her lips not his. The smooth sophistication she displayed in front of her clients was now replaced with a crudeness saved for the unfortunate few. John was one of the elite group.

"Keep your fucking dick in your pants John and just do the job your paid to do. We're not offering any free rides just so you can get into her knickers. It's all about hours billed, just remember that."

"As if I could ever forget Elizabeth."

Her point made she stormed out of the room slamming the door behind her.

Bennett, unperturbed by her outburst, turned back to face the window once more. His thoughts returned to Annette and the encounter they had just had that morning. He could just about smell the remnants of her perfume as it lingered on the fabric of his jacket and remembered how soft her lips were as he had kissed her.

But there was one thing that Elizabeth was right about. There were no free rides. Everything had a cost. Annette's bill had been on the low side, of that there was no doubt and of course he'd based it on exactly what had come in from the ISA and court costs so she had the ability to pay. He laughed inwardly to himself. The next one would be different, all together much higher and there were items and hours he'd held back deliberately.

Bennett picked up the phone receiver and punched in his home number. After a few rings his wife answered.

"Hi."

"Hello dear, just me. Just to let you know I'll be home about seven."

It was a curt, quick conversation, no pleasantries.

"Did you get your trip booked," he asked.

"Yes, we're staying in the Park Lane Hilton, got a real bargain, three nights for the price of two."

Bennett cringed. Always a fucking bargain. The woman didn't know the meaning of the word.

"We leave on Friday afternoon from Newcastle Central, arrive Kings Cross just before six, first class upgrade for next to nothing."

First class fucking upgrade.

"I'll be back in Newcastle by midday on Monday."

"That will be lovely dear, I'm sure the girls will love it."

Bennett said his goodbyes and replaced the receiver. For once he wasn't unduly annoyed at the extravagance displayed by his wife.

He picked up the phone once again and dialled Annette's number.

"Hi Annette, just a quick one."

"Sure John, what is it?"

"No big deal, no business this time, just you and I and a little dinner once again."

There was a slight hesitation before she answered.

"I suppose so. When?"

"Saturday 19th."

"Just a minute."

Bennett heard the phone being placed on a table, the rustle of pages in a book or a diary.

"That would be nice John, I'll look forward to it. Where are we going?"

Bennett had her in a corner, there was no going back.

"It's a surprise Annette, a beautiful place with a real homely atmosphere, nice and intimate."

"Sounds great."

"It is, I promise you'll love it."

19

It had just turned 7.30am and Bennett was already stationed at his office desk, a steaming cup of freshly made black coffee by his side and pen poised in hand reviewing the days agenda.

The office had stillness about it at that time in the morning. He liked it, the calm before the storm so to speak. He was always the first person to enter the building, Karen, next in, was manning her receptionist desk at 8.15am on the dot then the Henshaws around about nine.

Bennett had been in the game for longer than he cared to remember and as a result he had a dogmatic approach to work. His schedule was precious to him and while court appointments took centre stage, attending to his clients was his bread and butter and as such it always took priority.

When the Henshaws had originally approached him, Bennett had neglected to take into account that the company was still in its infancy and as such staff resources were limited to such an extent that he was required to do some of the more routine, monotonous donkey work. The situation was beginning to niggle away at him. All work and no play makes Jack a dull boy. Bennett didn't want to be dull Jack, he wanted to play and this weekend was certainly earmarked for some playtime with his favourite client. Favourite for now.

Bennett wasn't a one to let things fester and as a result he'd requested a meeting with both Elizabeth and Neil Henshaw at 3.30pm that day. Part of his planning was preparing the figures that he would throw at them, figures they couldn't possibly dispute. Bennett was confident he had the measure of the pair. Elizabeth was the mouthpiece of the motley duo yet it was Neil who gave her the ammunition and more importantly he had the final say in all matters relating to staffing and ultimately the finances and that was the very subject Bennett wanted to discuss.

When he agreed to join them on a £1000 per week retainer and twenty five percent of all the fees he generated, it was on the understanding he would have an experienced team working under him and enough of them to cope with the business. He had already invoiced £269000 in fees with a further £280000 of projected hours to be billed in the next six months. It was beyond the Henshaws' wildest dreams that he would generate that sort of income within his first calendar year.

He punched a few buttons on his keypad and opened up his Excel work planner, a document he kept for his eyes only. He had no trust in the Henshaws. The best way to ensure he got every penny due to him was to keep his own record and at the end of each quarter when he received his fees, he would check the sum against his own calculation. He scrolled down the sheet to his projected earnings for the year. £189000 give or take a few quid. It simply wasn't enough he thought to himself. Didn't they realise how much tax he paid on that?

He closed off the Excel spread sheet and opened up another file. With his glasses perched precariously on the end of his nose he gazed at the list. There were 120 active client accounts split into three categories.

The first group were billed hard and fast but in reality the workload was very little. Prenuptial or postnuptial agreements as they were called. Clients who wanted the finances predefined should the relationship turn sour. It was Hollywood celebrities like Brad Pitt and Angelina Jolie who had brought it to the public's attention and these arrangements made up about one third of their entire client base. Bennett laughed to himself. These contracts weren't exactly watertight and when the shit had hit the fan and one of the party inevitably disputed a clause or a sub clause or even a full paragraph. He was only too happy to rack up the billable hours talking and arguing about it.

The second group of clients were Bennett's particular pet hate. These were the couples that wanted an amicable divorce. How his heart would sink when he heard those two words. These people would waltz into the Saxtons' office with a list of their joint assets in hand, terms and conditions already agreed between themselves. All they needed from Bennett was a draft agreement and a stamp of approval from the judge. A simple task yet little reward for Bennett in either satisfaction or money. Invariably it was the prenuptial's and amicable agreements that he offloaded onto his less than able assistants whilst he focused his attention on the big money cases.

These were the individuals who excited him and made his job worthwhile. His eyes scanned the client list and rested on the name of Annette Palmer. She was his prize client, at least for the time being. He took a deep breath. The perfect storm. Money was power, sex was power and Annette had both. Her husband and his solicitor were playing hard ball and Annette was fighting for what she truly believed to be hers and she wasn't giving an inch. It was perfect. Who was he to try and discourage her? After all it meant more billable hours.

She had been on his mind for weeks and as his loins stirred once more and tonight he would know if she lived up to his expectations. His wife had been safely dispatched to London that morning and he had invested a considerable amount of time supplying Annette with a steady flow of text messages and phone calls reiterating his commitment to her. He had nurtured this manufactured relationship and like a prized fruit, tonight he was sure Annette would be ripe for picking. Inevitably he knew his interest would wane once he had accomplished his mission, it always did. He didn't mean it to end that way, it was just something in his nature, the hunt, the chase, then more hunting and more chasing. It went back to Neanderthal Man. Bennett would continue to hunt his beautiful clients, a lion does not become King of the jungle by hunting mice.

His curser hovered over Annette's name and as the black writing turned blue he clicked. It opened up another page. He smiled. He was now in receipt of Mr Palmers Form E and it was apparent that when all was said and done there was just over a million in the pot to divide up. Not one of his high-end earners but still a healthy sum to play with. Even with the assets as they stood, it was clear the husband was still hiding cash and underestimating his earnings considerably. From what Bennett could make out from the illegible bank statements Steedman had sent him, Palmer had managed to take a

£55000 balance in the savings account down to zero in the matter of weeks post break up. Bennett the solicitor kicked in and he was irked. Stuart Palmer had got under his skin. Then Bennett the man kicked in. Screwing Palmer's wife would be that much sweeter.

His right hand moved down between his legs and he squeezed hard as he whispered under his breath.

"Oh Palmer, your wife is going to be so good to me tonight."

He pictured his bedroom, the king sized bed and those silk sheets that only came out on special occasions. He still had work to do, of course he did, but was more than confident in pulling it off. He checked his diary again, seven hours until the meeting with the Henshaws. Nothing like a corporate victory to get the juices flowing. Yes, today was going to be one of those days, he could feel it.

It was the Palmer's First Direction Hearing next week and he already had a hundred questions to put to Steedman and Palmer as well as Annette. But tonight wasn't about that, tonight he would need to avoid the conversation. He needed to keep Annette's mood upbeat and didn't want her sinking down into the doldrums that invariably happened once the ex-husbands name was mentioned. Time was of the essence and the fine champagne would flow but he knew she wouldn't stay the night. A taxi back home in the early hours, that was the best he could possibly hope for.

He checked his watch. No court today and only one client meeting just before lunch. He called Louise and asked her to prepare the client files he needed to work on. No more than four hours work he thought. It would give him plenty time for yet more preparation before the Henshaws' meeting. They wouldn't know what had hit them.

There was one more thing he had to do. God forbid, surely she hadn't managed to miss the train.

Bennett picked up his phone and dialled out.

"Hello darling," he said, "did you get the train alright?"

There was a sound of laughter in the background and he breathed a sigh of relief as he heard the faint sound of the train's engine rumbling on in the background. Bennett had the answer to his final question. Nothing could go wrong now.

Her voice was giggly.

"Yes, the train was on time. We're all settled in our seats, the champagne has already been cracked open."

Bennett looked at his watch. It was barely nine o'clock in the morning. He was desperate to get off the phone now he knew she was hurtling her way towards London Kings Cross with the champagne on ice. And with her David Lloyd friends in tow, it wouldn't be a British Rail Cava or sparkling wine. There'd been four bottles of Dom Perignon on the credit card bill during her last visit to London, not to mention a bottle of Cristal in some fancy Mayfair nightclub. How he hated her and her bitchy friends.

She started to tell him where the train was, as if he'd be remotely interested. He cut in raising his voice slightly in an effort to block out the background noise on the train. "Very good, I'll ring you tomorrow at some point, enjoy your trip." On my fucking money.

More laughter, he didn't even hear what she said.

"I have to go darling, I have a phone call coming in."

He placed the receiver into the cradle and the phone went dead.

"Mission accomplished," He mumbled to himself with a smile.

He leant back in his seat and sighed deeply. There was no other word to describe it. He was feeling smug.

The meeting with the Henshaws was less than an hour away. He contemplated whether to ring Annette beforehand but decided to concentrate on his big speech. It needed fine-tuning and it would have more of an impact if he memorised all of the critical figures.

He knocked on Freddie's office door at 3.35pm. It was the biggest office in the building with sweeping views over Jesmond Dene and beyond to Armstrong Park. Freddie felt justified in taking the prime office spot as he was the senior partner. He sat poised behind his desk as he beckoned Bennett to take a seat opposite him. Elizabeth preferred to remain standing alongside him, her arms crossed and her back against the wall. As theirs was purely a business relationship there was no pretense of congeniality. Bennett got straight to the point whilst both the Henshaws looked at him stony faced. He scanned both of their reactions as he explained his dilemma in his usual calm reassuring tone.

"The bottom line is that by the end of the year I will have generated over half a million pounds of income for this practice," he paused for effect, "whilst at the same time managing and dare I say training your team of novices."

Bennett could see they were shocked at what he had just said but neither of them said a word. Elizabeth stood with her arms still crossed, her foot tapping on the floor in an attempt to channel her agitation.

Bennett continued. It was time to get to the crux of the matter that he did without hesitation or embarrassment.

"I have been reflecting on my situation and I believe I am justified in asking for thirty five percent of the income generated."

He let that sink in and waited for a reaction that wasn't long in coming.

Elizabeth folded first.

"You must be fucking joking John. Is this why you called this meeting, to fly us to Fantasy Island."

It was no fantasy. Bennett looked at Freddie as the colour had drained from his face.

Elizabeth couldn't stop herself.

"We might as well terminate your contract now if that's the level of respect you have for us, coming in here asking for a £50000 a year pay rise. For fuck's sake John, even the MPs don't vote themselves that much."

Bennett did his best to ignore her.

"I also need another qualified solicitor, someone with a little more experience who can share the load. Quite frankly it's only a matter of time before the office implodes under the workload from my clients."

Bennett leaned back in his chair waiting for the inevitable response. Freddie sat quietly as expected, hands clasped in front of him and it was Elizabeth who jumped in feet first again.

"You take more out of this practice than Freddie and I do and we're both senior partners. You're bleeding us dry for Christ sake."

"I'll say it again," Bennett said, "my current clients will bring in a minimum of £500000, £549000 actually, and that doesn't include any new clients I bring in by the end of the year."

Freddie had picked up a pen and scribbled a few notes on his desk pad. The knife had been planted and it was time to twist it.

"When I joined the company there was no contract signed. We all know I could walk out this office now and set up across the street. I could take my clients with me and you would have no claim on them whatsoever, after all they are my clients."

Freddie was beginning to panic. Bennett thought that any second

Elizabeth would explode yet they both knew the situation they found themselves in. He had no notice period or any restraint of trade agreement. They had been so eager to get him on board that the protocol and sensible housekeeping had gone out of the window. For two go getting corporate lawyers who had cut their teeth working for major law firms in London they were oh so fucking naïve.

Freddie, the wise one of the pair, was beginning to realise the situation they were in. His silence spoke volumes. Elizabeth was less astute as she continued to bang out the accusations and insults but they were meaningless.

"Do we have a deal Mr Henshaw?" he asked.

Elizabeth turned to her husband fearing the worst.

"Don't let him blackmail us like this."

"Elizabeth please," Bennett said in the same dulcet tones, not a fraction of a decibel higher. "I'm simply negotiating a contract which should have been put in place some months ago. What's more, I've proved to you both just how much I'm worth. Not in your wildest dreams did you expect me to bring in half a million a year."

Freddie knew he had been backed into a corner. Bennett could see it in his eyes.

"Okay John," he said, "we'll meet you half way. Thirty percent."

For the first time in the meeting Bennett allowed himself a smile. He shook his head. "The percentage is not negotiable Freddie, it's thirty five percent. I thought I'd made that clear."

Elizabeth's tone went up a decibel or two such was her anger.

"And how do we know that you're not up to your old tricks. I'm not convinced you've invoiced that Palmer woman for the time you've spent on her case recently. She certainly seems to have captured your attention and I've heard all about your past track record."

At that point Bennett sensed the victory, it was all that Elizabeth could throw at him.

He didn't bite, he merely stated the facts.

"I think if you check Elizabeth, her bill is clocking up nicely, she's already paid over £6000 and there's another £4000 to invoice at the end of the month."

He let out a little chuckle.

"In fact, if her husband continues to play hardball they'll be paying most of my modest pay rise themselves."

Freddie had booted up his computer and punched in a few keys.
"Can they afford to pay that much?" he asked.
Bennett nodded. "The E20 details over £1000000 in assets."
He had them over a barrel and Freddie Henshaw and his wife knew it.
By 5pm they had drafted out a provisional agreement and all parties had signed it. As Elizabeth put her signature to the document she was trembling visibly and nearly in tears. At one point he nearly felt sorry for her. Nearly… but not quite.
He had gone in and pitched the ball high and it had landed exactly where he expected it to. They had even agreed to place advertisements for a new solicitor by the end of the month.
As Bennett climbed into his car in his allocated parking space on the Saxtons' forecourt, Elizabeth stood and watched him from her office window, her face etched with anger.
"Bastard," she mouthed under her breath.
The dye had been cast yet she wasn't prepared to be outmanoeuvered by John Bennett. He was now in her sights. She picked up the phone and dialled an internal number, the recipient picked up.
"Hi Louise, would you mind dropping the Palmer file into my office before you leave please. Many thanks."

He had a busy night ahead of him and he was keen to get on with it. As he climbed into his car, he gently slung his briefcase onto the passenger seat while he reached into his jacket pocket to retrieve his mobile. He tapped the number in, his fingers automatically landing on the appropriate digits, so ingrained was the process in his memory. The number rang once.
She picked up instantly.
"Hello," she said, her voice low, almost timid.
"Just a quick call Annette," he didn't wait for a response, "I'll send a taxi for you at 8pm and no rushing home, I have a night of celebration planned for us."
"A taxi?"
She was confused.
"Where are we going? What are we celebrating?"
Bennett smiled to himself, his confidence high. It had been a fabulous day and tonight would be the icing on the cake.

"We're celebrating me and you and I can't wait to see you."
"But where are we going and why are you sending a taxi?"
It was time to tell her.
"I'd pick you up myself but I'll be busy in the kitchen."
It was a second or two before it sank in. Annette could hardly say no at this late hour. "At your place?"
"Yes and if I say so myself I'm pretty handy in the kitchen."
"But I thought ......"
"Don't be late. 8pm."
Bennett pressed end.

Busy in the kitchen wasn't exactly the honest truth. Marks and Spencer's food court just off the Haymarket in Newcastle gave Bennett everything he needed for the evening, all he needed to do was heat up the main course and make sure the cartons and packaging were out of site in order to claim all of the credit. He'd settled on a goat's cheese salad to start with and a chicken herb crusted lattice with a creamy garlic & parsley sauce. He didn't want anything too heavy for obvious reasons. Marks and Spencer, however, couldn't cater for his taste in champagne. He needed to go to a specialist wine merchant for the bottles of Taittinger 2002. He figured that with a £50000 a year pay rise, negotiated that very day he could well justify the ridiculous cost.
Annette arrived on cue, just after 8.25pm. As he opened the door she genuinely took his breath away. He was almost speechless. But not quite.
"My God Annette, you look absolutely beautiful."
And she did. He kissed her gently on the lips and took her coat as he ushered her into the hallway and then through to the kitchen. In the middle of the room was an elegant marble island. He'd set two places with elegant place mats, crystal champagne flutes and four jasmine scented candles.
"I hope you don't mind," he said, "but if I'm messing around in the kitchen it's far easier to eat here."
"Of course," she said, "it's lovely and something smells gorgeous."
Bennett spent the next few minutes telling her about the food he'd cooked, saying on more than once occasion that he hadn't gone to that much trouble. He uncorked the chilled champagne and poured

two glasses. Annette looked at the bottle as she said she had never heard of it. Bennett watched closely as she put the glass to her mouth and took a sip. It was clearly the first time she'd tasted quality champagne as her face seemed to explode in ecstasy.

"Now that's good," she said, "that is so good."

Bennett raised his glass.

"Cheers. Here's to a great evening and there's plenty more where that came from."

His plan had been laid out meticulously. During the starter he had complemented her on almost anything and everything, flirted outrageously and managed to lay his hand on hers several times. She hadn't pulled away from him that was a good sign. As he served the main course he leaned over and kissed her neck and as she responded by tilting her head back he slid his hand around to the front of her chest and squeezed gently on her breast. There was no resistance. He was home and dry.

The main course was perfectly heated through and it was Annette's turn to dish out the compliments as Bennett sank back in his seat and took in the adulation. It had been a great day and the food and champagne were perfect.

"How are you feeling?" he asked. "I've a nice selection of cheeses or would you prefer something sweet?"

Annette eased back in her seat.

"Not at the minute John, that was beautiful and I've had more than enough for the moment."

Bennett nodded.

"A great idea. Let's relax for an hour or so, we can always come back to it."

He was already on his feet easing Annette from her seat.

"I'll put some music on, we can go into the lounge."

There was a token resistance but no more than that as Bennett led her through by the hand. The lounge was almost in darkness save for a small strategically placed lamp in the far corner.

"What sort of music do you like Annette?"

"Anything John, your house, your choice."

He walked over to a small speaker docking station and placed his iPhone onto it. He pressed a few buttons and the unmistakable sound of Van Morrison echoed around the room. He turned the music down a little and turned to face her.

"I love Van Morrison, do you?"

She nodded meekly. She was putty in his hands and she knew exactly what was coming next. As he walked forward she simply closed her eyes in a gesture of submission. She'd drank far too much of that wonderful champagne and as he approached her, he slid his hands around her waist and pulled her towards him. He kissed her hard as his hands moved down to her buttocks, his erection growing by the second. He pulled her into him as she gasped out loud. She could feel him that was for sure. He slowly moved his hand around to the bottom of her skirt and crept his fingers up to her panty line. He slipped them inside the fine material and located her wetness. She moaned gently as he pushed his fingers up inside her and she responded by grinding against him. She kissed him harder and he thrust his tongue deep into her mouth. He had her now, there was no turning back. Even the spot where he'd kissed her had been preplanned. As he pushed her gently away from him she took an involuntary step backwards and as the back of her legs came into contact with the sofa her knees buckled and she fell backwards. Bennett didn't move. Annette made no attempt to regain her composure as she lay back on the sofa, her legs slightly parted revealing the black lace of a small pair of knickers.

Bennett pulled slowly at his belt buckle.

"You've no idea how long I've waited for this moment Annette."

"This doesn't feel right John," she said. "I've been married to the same man for twenty three years, I don't know if…"

He said nothing as he removed his belt and let his trousers fall to the floor. He stepped forward and kneeled on the sofa as he took a handful of her skirt and pulled hard. She lifted her hips to help him and the skirt fell to the floor. In the same movement she hooked her thumbs either side of her panties, removed them and reached for him. Everything had gone according to plan. She was his now and while the lovemaking would be gentle at first, the night was still young. They would have sex three times, in many different positions. It was all part of the plan.

20

Maybe it was the way my naked body had been lying precariously across the bed which pricked me into a level of consciousness. I woke up flat on my stomach, one arm stretched above my head, contorted in such an awkward position that my hand had turned numb. Instinctively I moved, releasing the uncomfortable pressure throbbing down my arm.

The sheer effort had the effect of lifting me from my comatose state and I gradually became aware of the dryness of my mouth and the bitter taste of stale alcohol swamping my palate. I gradually raised my heavy head from the mattress, the movement sending a drilling sensation through my brain. I grimaced in pain as my heart galloped away at an unregulated speed. It was a familiar sign that I had drank far too much alcohol. For a moment I was totally disorientated, nothing in this bedroom was familiar to me, not the sheets or the pillows, even the near darkness was somehow alien to me, a different type of darkness if that makes sense. I was not in my bedroom, it even smelled differently. I looked across the bed and to my horror sensed someone else lying there with me. Then it came back to me. I realised that it was my friendly solicitor lying in a position not dissimilar to my own, eyes firmly closed in a sound sleep and a gentle snoring emanating from his half open mouth.

Reality struck me like a sledge hammer. Immediately my thoughts raced. Christ, Alexandra, shit, what time was it?

Now, almost fully conscious, I pushed myself up into a sitting position, my eyes searched around the room looking for a watch, clock, mobile phone, anything that would give me a time reference. There was nothing, only the evidence of our evening lay around us like a crime scene. There was a champagne bucket on the dresser, empty glasses on the bedside table and clothes littered across the bedroom floor. It was evident that there had been some urgency to get undressed as our clothes were all over the place. I shook my head in an attempt to erase the ever darkening thoughts. I had no time to think about it, I needed to focus my attention on getting home. I looked at the bedroom windows and breathed a sigh of relief as I realised it was still dark outside so obviously still the early hours of the morning. In my mind I still had time to recover the desperate situation. Without further thought I reached across the bed and gently shook his arm.

"John, please, wake up. I have to get home."

He opened his eyes and it took him no time to come to his senses. A smile radiated across his face and without hesitation he attempted to draw me towards him. For a split second I was about to succumb and melt back into his body, yet my maternal instincts kicked in. I pushed back with forceful determination. "No John, I need to get home now!"

As I sat in the back of the taxi, handbag clasped between my folded arms like some sort of comfort blanket, I became conscious of the taxi drivers eyes peering at me through his rear view mirror. I felt the warmth of my blushing face as I made a lame attempt to rearrange my disheveled clothes which were only half put together. I dreaded to think what I looked like with my hair all over the place and my make-up plastered all over my face. Definitely not in the place where it had been originally applied.

"Have you been partying pet? Good night was it?" he said with a hint of sarcasm lingering in his voice.

I now knew it was 4.30 in the morning. I felt like a criminal unable to hide my guilt and I was sure he had the measure of what it was I had been doing for most of the night.

"Yes, it was a good night," I replied shamefully.

He had seen it all a million times before, an occupational hazard no doubt. He proceeded to drone on about how busy he had been, the town had been heaving with people and he'd not stopped. His voice trailed off into the background as my mind involuntarily flashed back to my activities of the previous evening and the early hours of the morning. It had been a drunken sex fest, there were no other words to describe it. The events were blurred yet the sequence was clear. Drink, food, more drink, my head spinning as it hit the sofa for the first time and our gentle love making as he explored me and I him. Then it went blank but there was definitely more champagne. We were in his bedroom and the alcohol must have taken its toll at that point because the subsequent events were less clear, yet still flashing images filled my brain. He was behind me, my breasts cupped in his hands, my head buried in the pillow as he thrust hard into me. I recalled that the gentleness had been replaced with an animalistic urgency, he was using me as he wanted and I was enjoying every second of it. Blank again, I had no grasp of the timeframe yet the images kept coming. He was down on me, his head between my legs, his tongue inside that most intimate of places as I begged him not to stop and with expertise he probed and teased and brought me to an earth shattering orgasm. It was a given that the act would be reciprocated, a sort of telepathic understanding as he pulled me from the bed and I dropped to my knees as he took a step forward and pushed his fully erect penis deep into my mouth. I was eager to please and we fell into a natural rhythm as I sucked hard and our pace quickened. I remembered a loud cry of ecstasy as he gripped my hair in his hands and exploded into my mouth.

"Stop!"

The driver slammed his breaks on and my body jerked forward from the seat such was the velocity of his action.

I was in the moment once more.

"Sorry," I said timidly, realizing that I'd shouted far too loudly.

"Could you pull over to the side? I'll just get out at the end of the street."

I had obviously shocked him shouting out like that yet he was happy to oblige and take his payment.

There was method in my madness, Alexandra's bedroom was at the front of the house. The last thing I wanted was for her to hear the rumbling engine of a mini cab as it drew up outside the front door at this ridiculous hour. If she did wake up she would definitely check what time it was and I was desperate to save myself the embarrassment. As I stumbled down the street, still half drunk, I couldn't help but think of my mother and what she would think if she could see me in this state. She would be so disappointed, it was without doubt the walk of shame and every ounce of me felt lower than the pavement I was walking on. I'd let them down, all of them, my daughters and my mother, yet John Bennett had me under his spell and I was like a moth drawn to his tantalizing flame.

I sneaked into the house but like most drunks trying to be quiet I made more noise than usual, first stumbling into the hall as I swung in through the front door clinging onto the key which was still firmly lodged in the keyhole. I immediately removed my shoes and crept up the stairs as the familiar creaks in the floorboards amplified in the stillness of the early hours. Alexandra's door remained closed. Momentarily I stopped outside her room listening carefully for any indication that she might be awake. Satisfied she hadn't stirred I made my way to my own room. I had a terrible vision that any second her door would burst open and she would be out on the landing giving me merry hell.

I stumbled into my room ripping my clothes off as soon as the door shut behind me. I was desperate to climb into bed, close my eyes and sleep away my shame and my hangover. I wanted to block out the evening's events yet my mind wouldn't switch off, the images were still relentlessly flashing in front of my eyes. It didn't help that he wasn't only in my thoughts. I could smell the mixture of his musky cologne and his bodily odour lingering on my flesh. It was no good, I got up and headed towards the bathroom, switched the shower on and fell into the cubicle. The hot water washed over my body as I slumped my back against the tiles for what seemed like an age, cleansing myself, soaping and rinsing every last trace of him from me. Eventually I finished, toweled myself off and fell into bed.

It was 11am when I eventually opened my eyes. My head was still banging and I was engulfed with a feeling of dread. Inevitably my mind began to race once more and the images became more vivid. As my amnesia lifted and I was able to fit each little piece of the jigsaw together I sank further into despair. How could I have gone that far? Stuart had been the only partner I'd ever had. Now I had severed that last tie with my past and from the flashbacks I was having I had really gone to town, no holds barred and I had enjoyed every minute. There had been no half measures on my part as all my inhibitions had flown out of the window, blown apart by John Bennett's charm.

As I lay half-awake nursing my hangover I couldn't help thinking back to my old life. Where had it all started going wrong and why? When I had first made love to Stuart it was a very different scenario. We were barely out of our teens yet our lovemaking was pure and gently paced. He was my world and I was his and neither of us could see a future without the other in it. Incredibly I felt an overwhelming sense of disloyalty towards that young naïve couple who were once so in love. Both Stuart and I had let them down badly.

As I regressed back to those happy, long gone days, I realized how different it had felt from the events of the previous evening. That first sexual encounter with John had been wholly based on lust not love. There was no expectations for a future together only the hard earned knowledge that the moment would be fleeting. The school of hard knocks had taught me nothing lasted. As much as I recognized what had been the catalyst for my encounter with John, I had no clue what had come over me. I didn't recognize myself and neither did I feel proud of my actions. Yet I could not deny it had happened and as much as I tried to hide the truth, the fact was I had welcomed John's advances, enjoyed the intimacy and the explicit sexual encounter.

It was inevitable I would have to face the consequences of my actions sooner or later and from the look on Alexandra's face as she walked in my bedroom at that moment it would be sooner.

She pounced immediately.

"What time did you get home last night?"

I had not lied to any of my children about going around to John's house the previous evening, as much as I hadn't wanted to tell them I felt an obligation to do so. I so prided myself on honesty and wouldn't follow their dads example and spin them a yarn. If there was someone in my life, if I went on any sort of date they needed to know from the outset. Unlike the dinner date with John at the pub, where they had been very accepting of the situation, the news that I was going around to his house for the evening was a different matter altogether. It hadn't gone down well at all, particularly with Alexandra. There had been questions, their suspicions were aroused and boundaries were being crossed and they were bright enough to know it. As much as I wanted to keep on track with honesty and openness, I wasn't yet prepared to venture into the minefield of Mum's sex life. With that at the forefront of my mind Alexandra started once more with her probing questions and I told my first lie.

As the words crossed my lips I realized my morality had sunk to a new level. Once again sadness enveloped me.

"I wasn't too late getting home darling, I can't remember the exact time," I said sheepishly my eyes fixed on the duvet cover in an effort to avoid eye contact. She didn't give up as she sat on the end of my bed. More questions were fired in my direction, none of which I had an honest answer for.

"Why were you at your solicitors house anyway?"

"A little bit dinner and some business," I answered honestly.

"Was anyone else invited?"

"Well … no."

"What did you do all night?"

By the end of my interrogation I had told more tales than Hans Christian Andersen and flatly refused to answer some of the more personal questions. She eventually left my bedroom not one hundred percent happy yet appearing to accept most of my responses to her questions. I breathed a huge sigh of relief but once again was wracked with guilt. I was shameful of the little white lies I had told to my youngest daughter but also at the way I had acted with John. I had behaved like a Hollywood porn star. The moral high ground I had took when looking down on their father had been lost completely. Now I was treading the same path as him and I didn't like the feeling. My girls deserved more than that.

The reality was that it was way too soon for me to be getting involved with another person and it was definitely far too early for my children to accept the change in circumstances. They were already struggling with how their father had abandoned them and it was unfair to complicate their lives any further. I sincerely wanted to step back from John Bennett for the sake of my family. We all needed time to heal and this was my resolve as I lay in my own bed that morning overcome with remorse. Yet as quickly as the thoughts entered my head I was already doubting myself. I wondered how long my willpower would last if John enticed me in to his lair once more. Not long I suspected, he was like an opiate drug to me, he had left me wanting more and it would take all my strength to resist him and the sex he was so good at.

My day went from bad to worse. Apart from nursing a banging headache my body was tender and sore and I felt like I'd had ten rounds in a boxing ring such was my discomfort. I could feel muscles

I never knew I had.

Alexandra didn't let up either, and it wasn't long before she marched into my room once more, ranting about me leaving the front door key in the outside lock.

"Honestly Mum, anyone could have walked in during the night, you must have been in a right state," she said, the loud vibes piercing my head like a sharp blade.

The last straw, so to speak, set the tone for the rest of the day. I was definitely in the dog house and by the time text messages had been exchanged between her and her sisters it wasn't long before the other two were on the war path too.

As I had suspected my charming solicitor kept a low profile. Since our night together I'd received only one courteous text message from John thanking me for a pleasant evening, nothing else, not even the slightest reference to the events that had occurred. Surely he couldn't have been that drunk? What did he mean pleasant evening? You have a pleasant evening when you sit relaxing in front of the television or enjoy a drink in a busy bar with an old friend, that would be pleasant. I could feel my anger rising. He had been privy to my most intimate desires, I had given myself to him wholeheartedly and the best he could do was sum the night up as being a pleasant fucking evening. I tried as best as I could to suppress my feelings, wasn't that the way it needed to be? I remembered the promise I had made to myself on the Saturday morning, to put my family first.

By the Thursday of the following week, I still hadn't heard a word from him but I convinced myself he was doing me a favour. I was better off by myself and I didn't need John Bennett. From now on our relationship was going to be on a purely professional basis. Once I had made my decision I was relieved, things had settled down with the girls and the dog house was a distant memory. Harmony had been restored at home and in my mind and I was focused once again on my divorce settlement. We had another court hearing coming up and as much as I had put it off, I needed to go through the bank and credit card statements Stuart had sent via Saxtons. Louise had sent a letter out and said I needed to flag any suspicious amounts. With a large pot of strong coffee by my side I painstakingly went through each of the bank and credit card statements line by line. The print on the bank statements was so faded I strained my eyes to read the figures. Had they done that deliberately? Surely their photocopier couldn't be that bad.

Louise had noted that "Mr Bennett was concerned about the bank account."

No wonder, within three months Stuart had managed to take a £55000 balance to just a few hundred pounds. Some of the transfers out were easily explained but I saw enough to know that some payments were at best extravagant and others transacted in just a way to strip the account for the sake of it. Since Stuart had left he'd not only had a holiday in France but he'd also had a week in Dubai and a weekend at Gleneagles. I googled the webpage, its plush five star hotel and luxury spa, "situated within three of the best golf courses in Europe," was a far cry from the cheap and cheerful accommodation we had to endure when me and his kids had an overnight stop somewhere.

I made notes as I went through each and every item on the bank statement. My blood began to boil, surely a court would see what he was up to. I needed to show John the breakdown of the accounts yet I was loathed to ring him. Maybe I would send him an email with an attached spreadsheet showing the analysis of my research. I diligently created an excel document breaking down each and every one of Stuart's outgoings. Once completed and feeling proud of my achievements I was keen to share my efforts with both John and Louise. I wasted no time attaching it to an email destined for John's attention and took great pains with the wording, ensuring that its content was professional with no indication of any growing familiarity between us.

I was just about to send it when my mobile phone rang and Saxtons' number flashed across the screen. I scrambled to pick it up off the kitchen table like a love sick teenager.

"Hello," I said calmly in an attempt to conceal my eagerness to answer. It was his voice and despite myself I melted when I heard his reassuring tones.

"How's my favourite client?"

My response was cool, yet polite. I wasn't giving anything away.

"I'm fine thank you."

I offered no more and there was no intention on my part to be gushing as it appeared to go over his head. He continued on oblivious with not even a mention of his pleasant evening.

"We need to speak about the hearing next Monday Annette."

I immediately jumped in telling him that I'd put a spreadsheet together and was just about to send it across.

"Yes that's very good, send it across and I'll take a look at it, thank you that will be most helpful," he said, his voice sounding less enthused than I was expecting.

The stuffing knocked out of me my response was flat.

"You're welcome."

There appeared to be an awkwardness between us now, or was it my imagination? I felt the need to clear the air and was about to jump in and at least acknowledge our night together when he got there first.

"I've been thinking about you all week Annette."

My heart skipped a beat, the chemicals in my head began to dance.

"Can we catch up in private, I am in the area tomorrow?"

I was totally tongue tied. No! I wanted to scream but the words just wouldn't form on my lips.

"I'll pop over for a coffee and we can go over the spreadsheet."

Then he was gone. He had tested my resolve. I could have easily said no but I didn't. All I could think of was that night, the passion, the intimacy and the raw sexual desire that took over my entire being. He had me exactly where he wanted me and I could do nothing about it.

Bennett replaced the receiver as a smug look pulled across his face. He knew that Alexandra stayed late at school that day. Annette Palmer would be his yet again and the blood was rushing in the direction of his groin at the very thought of what he might do with her. And yet already his interest was waning just a little. If it hadn't been for the splendid performance she'd put it on Saturday evening she would already be yesterday's news. No, he wanted her again, there was no doubt about it. But she had to go the journey like all the others, the real excitement was in the chase and then seeing just how far they'd go in the sexual stakes. Mrs Palmer had gone further than most and he sensed there was more on offer.

The phone on his desk let out a high pitched shrill.

He picked it up and answered it. "Bennett."

"Hi Mr Bennett, it's Louise, I have Joanna King on line two."

"Thanks," he said, "put her through."

Bennett listened as the call connected. He waited until he heard the click of Louise's handset.

"Hi John, how are you?" a soft female voice enquired.

Bennett smiled.

"Fine Joanna, and how is my favourite client?"

21

Newcastle Crown Court didn't appear quite as imposing as it had done on my first visit two months previously. As the Taxi drew up outside the dominant structure and I stepped out on to the pavement at my journeys end as my eyes were still drawn to its sheer magnificence sitting as bold as brass, parallel with the River Tyne. This was my second visit to the building yet I was still swamped with the same degree of fear and dread as I had been on the first occasion. It was an important day, Settlement of Issues Day, or in layman's terms the day we would lay bare our finances to the Judge and he would decide what was relevant and what should be thrown out. It was a place that ruined lives, a place that gave justice but also put people in prison, tipped many over the edge and perhaps even pushed some to the brink of suicide. It was almost as if this building was somehow alive, a building with a soul. I was still nervous, apprehensive and the feelings compounded as this time I would walk in unaccompanied.

I looked at my watch. I was due to meet Louise and John at the Family Law Courts on the second floor at 10.30am and already I was running a little late. I grew more frustrated as a queue to the entrance of the court had formed and I couldn't get past. I stood patiently straining my neck to see the cause of the delay. It was evident that a bottleneck had occurred at the security gate and the culprit for the holdup was a gentleman in a tracksuit, trainers and decked in a selection of chunky jewelry. He had set the alarm off as he attempted to walk through the scanner. The court guard wasn't in any particular hurry, he appeared unfazed as he calmly set about the business of trying to locate the offending item with his wand like metal detector held against the fabric of the man's clothing whilst the perpetrator of the holdup stood like a stone statue fixed to the spot. My impatience grew as my desperation to get to the relative safety of John and Louise increased. I looked at my watch again. It was already 10.40am and my anxiety went up a notch. My eyes darted around aimlessly looking at the hotchpotch of people going about their business. Eventually my focus settled on a familiar shape as my heart missed a beat. It was Stuart standing amidst a crowd of people with his seedy solicitor Steedman. He couldn't see me in the queue at the other side of the barrier but even so, I subconsciously dropped my shoulders as my knees bent and I hid myself behind the bulk of the man standing in front of me. Stuart was engrossed in conversation with Steedman. Inevitably my breathing quickened as my mind regressed back to our previous encounter when Steedman had to drag him away from me. I tried to resist the temptation to look in his direction but it was no good, I just couldn't help myself. My eyes settled on him. I couldn't remember the last time I had actually looked at him properly. He'd walked out on me five months previously and even before his departure the eye contact between us had been almost none existent. We just hadn't looked at each other anymore and there was no closeness, no intimacy, and we would deliberately looked anywhere rather than each other. Now I had an uninterrupted view of him, as if I were the operator behind a TV camera. I could see him but he couldn't see me. He appeared different, something about him had changed but what was it? The hair on his temples looked a little greyer and he was now sporting designer stubble, something he wouldn't have entertained when we were together. His body was definitely leaner, no doubt he was hitting the gym with renewed vigor in an effort to claw back some of his youth. The changes hadn't stopped at his appearance, family and friendships had been mercilessly sacrificed, his golf partner of thirty years no longer had any contact with him and neither did any of our joint friendships survive the cull. He had wiped almost everyone from his life. Even Stuart's old running friend and our close neighbour Barry had been sacrificed for his new lifestyle with the other woman. What did they expect? He had been callous enough to turn his back on his wife and his children, why would a friendship be any different? He couldn't give a flying fuck about any of them as long as the younger woman was on his arm, couldn't they see that?

As I studied Stuart from my safe vantage point it was clear his physicality might have transformed yet the man behind the image was all too evident to me. I could see there was fighting talk going on. Stuart's arms were flaying in all directions as he barked instructions at his slippery solicitor.

When I eventually got through the security barrier, Stuart and Steedman were nowhere to be seen. I had taken my eye off them for a second as I checked my bag through security they were gone. I breathed an involuntary sigh of relief.

I made my way up the staircase to the second floor, my breath becoming laboured as I neared the top. As soon as my foot had stepped off the last stair I caught sight of John and Louise waiting for me in the main waiting area. As I walked through the double doors they spotted me.

"I'm so sorry," I said, "there was a hold up at security."

Louise gave a courteous smile whilst John made the less than subtle gesture of looking at his watch followed by a weak smile which I interpreted as a reprimand for being late.

"Shall we go through ladies?" He said, his hand pointing towards the glass door leading to the Judge's Chambers.

The narrow corridor was crowded with people as Louise, who obviously had doubts about finding a vacant client conference room, quickened her pace in an effort to get whatever was available. However, at the very end of the corridor next to the ushers checkpoint, she found a room and signaled a thumbs up gesture to John and I who were trailing in her wake. She waited for us to catch up, her back propped against the heavy fire door.

Once settled, John didn't hang around. He picked up his note pad, scribbled something down and without as much as a glance or an apology he left the room to find the other side, as he preferred to call them.

I watched him leave and in a way I was relieved. Seeing him only reminded me of the things we had been up too and I was desperately trying to put our sexual encounters to the back of my mind. It wasn't working. As much as I tried, I couldn't help but think about the night I had spent at his house then his later visit to my home on the pretense of looking at the spreadsheet I had created of Stuart's outgoings. On both occasions my initial intentions had been good yet ultimately thwarted by John's persistence. After the events at John's house I had been quick to blame the alcohol. But when he had then visited my home I had been as sober as a judge. I had consciously set my mind om keeping him at arm's length and my mission had been successful while we sat around my kitchen table drinking coffee, discussing the hearing. It was only when our meeting migrated to Stuart's study to look at the spreadsheet did the whole atmosphere change from business to raw sexual lust.

John had been interested in viewing the detailed spread sheet for all of five seconds, that's when his attention waned. He was standing behind me as I navigated the computer curser around my work as he watched on. At first I could feel his breath against the back of my neck as he bent down nuzzling his head against mine. I did nothing to encourage him and even less to stop him. He progressed, as he started to caress my hair, kissing my shoulders. He had an arrogant confidence about him that I struggled to resist even though every bit of me wanted to. With no alcohol in my system I was a little coy at first yet it didn't take long for my senses to be aroused as he explored me once more. His hands moved inside my blouse, skillfully maneuvering the strap of my bra as he located my now hard nipple. The mouse and the keyboard were frantically pushed to one side as he turned me round and started to kiss me hard. His hands moved to my hips as he lifted me onto the desk, positioning me exactly how he wanted me as if he was working a mannequin on a shop display. My panties were unceremoniously ripped off. He threw them to the floor as he unbuckled his belt and dropped his trousers. He stepped forward, saddling my thighs around his hips and he thrust into me as I let out a little squeal. With no alcohol in my system to dull my senses the sheer pleasure notched up to a new level. We were both so absorbed in our own self-gratification our inhibitions were cast aside once more and the boundaries of our sexual exploits were pushed even further.

I sat in the characterless room with only Louise by my side, legal papers strewn across the desk but I could only think of that afternoon, staring over his shoulder as his nails dug into my bare backside and he brought me expertly to a quick, earth shattering orgasm before coming himself.

"How are your girls Annette? Are they all okay?" Louise asked.

I smiled, Louise was both bright and astute. She had chosen a safe topic, one that I would talk about endlessly without much interjection needed on her part.

Without further encouragement I told her what the girls were up to before inevitably the subject moved to the breakdown in relations with their father. She sat back in her chair and listened as I droned on about the girls not seeing or speaking to their Dad for weeks. I told her about Abigail driving up to his girlfriend's house and confronting them both.

Louise looked genuinely shocked.

I told her that even their own grandmother, Stuart's mum, had turned her back on them. Abigail had gone to see her grandma looking for support. She had made the mistake that her grandmother might have had some sympathy for me. Abigail had spilled the beans, telling her grandmother the cat was out of the bag and Stuart's new girlfriend had been the reason for the break up, the reason he had walked out on the family home and the reason he had deserted her own grandchildren. Stuart's mother had always been Abigail's biggest advocate. The standing family joke was that Abigail could do no wrong in her grandmothers eyes, 'the sun shone out of her backside.'

But now it had all changed. Angela Maddison had even ripped apart the strongest bond in the family. Grandma was ready and willing to ignore everything her son had done, to forgive him in the blink of an eye even if it meant turning her back on her granddaughters. Abigail didn't get the sympathy and understanding she was expecting, but instead a scolding from Grandma for invading her father's privacy.

"His private life is his own business," she had said.

An argument had inevitably broken out, Stuart's mother defending her son and his new girlfriend and even criticizing me, the ex-wife. Abigail didn't relay what was said word for word but she didn't need to. According to granny I was a terrible mother who had been feeding off her son for years, unwilling to go to work while he worked himself into the ground. The argument had ended when Abigail flatly refused to listen to any more disparaging comments about her mother. She had stormed out of her grandmother's house because she'd refused to apologise for some rather cutting remarks about me. Abigail wouldn't divulge what her grandmother had said. She came around to see me straight away. She was in floods of tears, sobbing that she would never set foot in her grandmother's house again.

Despite myself, I put my wicked thoughts to one side and encouraged Abigail to speak to her Grandmother again. I argued that she was an old woman who through ill health was ebbing towards the end of her days.

A few days later, after she had calmed down, Abigail had taken my advice onboard and rang her Grandma to make her peace. It fell on deaf ears. Her fucking Grandmother had slammed the phone down on her. Abigail called straight back, innocently believing that they had been cut off. She did it again, then again until the penny finally dropped. There were more tears as she realized yet another piece of her family life had been ripped away from her because of her father's actions. She sat in my kitchen and I held her while she sobbed her heart out and if her father had walked through the kitchen door I would have gladly killed him. I could take the pain and the misery, I was strong and tough enough but what I couldn't bear was the pain my daughters were taking on an almost daily basis.

Louise listened intently, her soft almond eyes fixed on me as I talked on. I had no idea why I was relaying the story to her, she probably had no interest in it and it didn't have any bearing on my case, yet I suppose it stopped me thinking about the fucked up mess I found myself in. As I was about to continue John burst into the room, his manner more brisk and upbeat from when he had left it. Speaking to the other side had obviously given him a new lease of life. He pulled his chair up at the table and fixed his attention on Louise.

"Pass me the Statement of Issues Louise, we need to go through it quickly."

He looked at his watch. I sat next to him and I could see it was a Rolex. I'd recently had a small insight into John's lifestyle and I sensed money wasn't in short supply. His life was a far cry from my own. Money or lack of it was a constant worry for me these days. Even though I was now receiving maintenance from Stuart, I was struggling to keep up with the legal bills. Irrespective of our extra-curricular activities I was still racking up a bill at a rate of knots and there didn't appear to be any friends or family discounts on offer despite the fact that we were bed mates. The vicious circle I found myself in had no end. Without Saxtons representing me Stuart would walk all over me. Even with John's wealth of experience in family law he was finding it a struggle to get to the bottom of Stuart's finances and if I didn't have legal representation I would have no chance. Yet the cost of getting to the truth was one I could ill afford and I was spending a small fortune in my quest. I had barely settled my first legal bill when another one had dropped through my letter box. I put off opening the envelope because I knew exactly what it was and unlike the first bill there were no ISA funds or awarded legal costs to settle this one.

Eventually, when curiosity got the better of me and I could wait no longer, I tore open the envelope. My intuition had been right. The figure was staggering. I was so shocked my knees started to buckle beneath me and I staggered back into the hallway chair that was situated conveniently behind me.

In bold print the numbers stood out like a beacon. £5670. I didn't need a calculator to work out that in the short time Saxtons had been acting on my behalf, I had incurred costs just short of £12000. What was worse was that I knew we had barely scratched the surface.

As I sat in the dingy meeting room waiting for John's return I was hoping that he would come back with positive news. More than ever I knew I needed a settlement. It was my only hope before the legal costs totally spiraled out of control. I hadn't a clue where the money for this bill was coming from, let alone the next bill or the one after that.

When John walked back into the conference room he appeared all buoyant and upbeat and I sincerely hoped and prayed that perhaps Stuart had come to his senses and was willing to compromise.

My optimism was short lived.

"It's not good news Annette. They are unwilling to agree any of the issues we've raised."

My heart sank, I couldn't take much more of this. The pen and paper were now out as he started to scribble his illegible notes once more and after no more than a minute he spoke.

"You do realize that this is only a first direction hearing Annette, Steedman will be asking you about your finances and the judge will decide what can and cannot be asked at the second hearing. Nothing will be resolved today."

All I could think of was the increased costs and another bill. The costs associated with the last court hearing had been ridiculous considering we had been in and out in less than an hour.

He continued.

"We're trying to iron out any discrepancies in the financial disclosure and unfortunately Annette there's quite a few with regards to your husband's finances and your shared assets. It should be black and white but this bastard is giving nothing away and his solicitor is just as bad."

As he proceeded to list the issues, my mind had already switched off. I was now more concerned with the questions Steedman might ask me. Although I had nothing to hide it still didn't stop me from worrying. Throughout our marriage, during any disagreement, Stuart had had a canny knack of turning the tables. He always had to have the last word. My stomach began to churn and I could feel the colour draining from my face at the prospect of a close interrogation.

John talked on as he collected his papers together.

"Annette, one more thing, you mentioned that Mr Palmer's mother was in her eighties and in poor health."

I nodded in agreement, my face twisting as my thoughts turned once more to the bitter old woman and what she had done to Abigail. But where was this going?

"Yes," I said reluctantly.

John's right eyebrow raised slightly.

"And he is likely to be the only beneficiary in her Will, if anything should happen to her?"

I explained that Stuart was the only surviving son, his brother Frank had died ten years previously from Motor Neuron Disease. It was true that Stuart was very likely to inherit a substantial sum of money when the old bitch eventually took her final breath. She not only owned property, she also had land that gave her an income of £25000 a year.

"What figures would we be talking about?" he asked.

It didn't take me long to answer John's initial question because Stuart had been counting up how much he would inherit from his mother for donkeys years. When he had had a couple of glasses of wine on a Friday evening, he'd slip into another altogether relaxed dimension and tell me how wealthy he would be one day. (Pre Angela Maddison of course.) He practically knew the value of her estate to the penny.

"With the land and property, investments bank accounts and

shares her estate is worth well over a million pounds."

"Really?" he said, "as much as that?"

"Yes."

"I think we need to ask him about his inheritance."

I shook my head in disagreement.

"I think that's a step too far John, I really couldn't ask that. Surely I'm not entitled to any of it?"

He looked at me as if I was talking another language, it was evident that for John there was no level he wasn't prepared to stoop.

"Well you might not be prepared to ask the question, I am however your solicitor and my duty of care is with you. If he is likely to inherit that sort of money it will impact significantly on your settlement, particularly from a maintenance point of view."

He bent forward, as if he was divulging a secret for our ears only. Louise twisted uncomfortably in her seat. He sat so close I could smell the scent of his breath, his voice low and deliberate.

"If his housing and income needs have been met, which they would be if he had his mother's house to live in, then there would be a stronger argument for you to keep the house and for him to continue to pay you maintenance for a longer period of time."

I liked the sound of it but I didn't like the sound of it. Was John playing for time? Was he waiting for the old bitch to die?

It sounded viable, yet the clock on the bill was ticking every day. I wanted this over with yet John sounded like he was playing for time.

He smiled as he rose from his chair, straightening his tie as he did so. Right on cue, the tannoy announcement boomed out from the inconspicuous speakers situated in the corner of the room. The high pitched, almost undistinguishable crackling noise pierced my ear drums.

"Could Palmer make their way to the Judge's Chambers please."

Louise jumped to her feet, racing around picking up the bits and pieces as John walked slowly towards the door. He turned to look at me, he was clearly getting psyched up for the event ahead, straightening his back, his expression was one of sheer determination.

"No Annette, you might not be able to say what needs to be said, however I am more than happy to raise the issue."

I wanted to speak, wanted to tell him that it was a step to far and I wanted no part of it but I said nothing.

"Leave it to me," he said.

Once again we were making our deathly march to the Judge's Chambers. The fear was rising in me. I walked in. Stuart sat with Steedman, both stony faced, deliberately avoiding eye contact. I studied both Steedman and my ex-husband. I looked at the focused determined look on the solicitor who I was engaging in regular sex.

I started to tremble. It appeared everyone was ready for a fight. I looked at Stuart again. The man could start a fight in an empty room.

22

It was a different room and a different Judge, yet the set up followed the same format. We entered the chambers where District Judge Maitland was already settled at his slightly elevated desk ready to referee the forthcoming events. Unlike Judge MacNab who was round faced and portly, Judge Maitland looked a considerably younger man. His manner certainly appeared more interactive than his predecessor. He lifted his head from his paper work to eye each of us up and down as we quietly filtered in to take our seats.

"Are we all present and correct and ready to get on with this?" he said with a with a slight smirk on his face.

My initial thoughts were that he had a little too much of a cocky confidence about him and it was clearly all in a day's work for our Judge Maitland. I wondered how many divorce cases he'd presided over in his time. He had clearly reached the point of indifference where one case seemed like any other, the faces having merged into one as he became desensitized to the unique circumstances of each of our plights. This wasn't another day in the office for me, it was an excruciating ordeal I had to sit through whilst my life was played out in a public arena.

We took our seats and there was barely three feet of space between me and my ex-husband as we sat parallel to one another across the table. It was awful and I could feel the electrically charged tension between us. I knew he was seething with anger because I had dared to challenge him. Beneath the calm, outward exterior his resentment and anger were festering at a rapid pace. He may not have realized it, but his hostile, threatening manner had the effect of transporting me back to the insecure person he had left all those months ago. I tried hard to fight it but I could feel my confidence ebbing away as I sat facing him waiting for the proceedings to start.

It was Steedman who jumped in first, eager to take up the mantle, listing the chronological events in a bland, monotone voice. I sat with eyes glued to the floor trying to mentally disengage myself from the proceedings as once again dates of our doomed marriage were recited like a role call in a military parade. Judge Maitland sat forward in his chair with his copy of the chronology in hand, skimming the pages as Steedman twittered on. I wasn't sure he had anything constructive to offer yet the Judge was keen to wade in, making us all aware he was orchestrating the show, leaning even further forward in his chair to the point where his upper body practically stretched across his desk.

"So I assume mediation has failed and both parties have failed to reach an amicable settlement."

He answered the rhetorical question himself.

"Obviously. He said, gazing across at me then settling his eyes firmly on Stuart.

It was clear he was shrewd enough to know who was in the driving seat with regard to finances and it wasn't me. Stuart ignored the inference as he stared back unwavering in his stance. Arrogant bastard, I thought to myself.

The Judge asked several almost mundane, insignificant questions and both solicitors jumped through their respective hoops. It was only a matter of time before the subject of the finances reared its ugly head.

Steedman wasn't performing particularly well and at times he looked rather uncomfortable. He was scratching around hoping that somewhere there would be evidence of illicit earnings or a hidden stash that I had squirreled away. I knew he would find no financial skeletons in my closet so to speak.

They were wasting their time, there was nothing.

Still, despite this knowledge, Steedman's piercing eyes reached across the desk to me and made me nervous. His attack on me may have had a weak foundation, however he compensated with steely eyed intimidation. John had been provoked by Steedman's tactics just enough to start speaking. He sprang into action like a greyhound out of its trap, sitting bolt upright in his seat. Steedman started to throw questions in my direction but John did my talking for me. Even the irrelevant benign queries, he questioned the validity of the necessity for me to answer them. Steedman ploughed on without any real success as Stuart's agitation mounted. He was already showing the signs of his pent up frustration, his lips pouting together tightly in an effort to keep control.

I had seen it all before. Stuart clearly had anger issues, he couldn't help himself and I suspected that his solicitor now had his own insight into his clients bad temper.

I had to give Steedman credit, he soldiered on.

"Mrs Palmer has a direct payment made payable to B & Q of £76.52 going out of her current account, number 95219566. Could she explain what this payment relates to?"

My God he was clutching at straws!

I had already explained to John that I had signed up a credit agreement on behalf of my mother for a bathroom suite. It was black and white. The statement clearly showed that she deposited the exact same amount into my account a day before the direct debit payment came out.

In his calm, unflappable voice he turned directly to the judge. He shook his head and flicked a brief smile in Steedman's direction.

"Mrs Palmer set up a credit agreement on behalf of her mother."

He flicked through the pile of bank statements until his hand stopped on my account statements.

"If you notice Sir, Mrs Palmer's mother credits her daughters account on the 28th of every month with that exact amount."

He passed a copy of the statement across the table to the Judge.

John gave him a second to absorb the information, his timing was fine-tuned, like that of a veteran comedian.

"I don't think it is necessary for Mrs Palmer to provide any further details, a nine year old mathematics student could work that one out."

Steedman appeared to see a window of opportunity and stepped in.

"Mr Palmer would like to know what the item relates to and to see a copy of the credit agreement."

It sounded pathetic, it was pathetic and it took the judge just seconds to dismiss it and see it for what it was.

He spoke in a mocking manner.

"I'm satisfied from the entries on the bank statement that it is a payment relating to Mrs. Palmers mother and quite frankly Mr Bennett is correct, a nine year old could have worked it out. I hardly think Mrs. Palmer is decking herself out in expensive jewelry or other luxury items. If the direct debit had been from Harrods or Fenwicks, I may well have taken a further look."

He leaned over and stared at Steedman.

"But from a DIY store Mr Steedman, are you serious?"

They were scraping the bottom of the barrel. My husband had stolen a King's Ransom from his wife of twenty three years and his three beautiful daughters and they were seemingly concerned about a small payment to a DIY outlet. They had shot themselves in the foot, there was no other way to describe it and the Judge had seen right through them.

Steedman sat down shaking his head. It was a clear admission of defeat as he penciled through the question on his pad.

Inevitably their questions moved from wanting copies of Pension statements, explanations of various cheque payments, account deposits and more personal probing enquiries but I got the impression that the Judge had not been impressed by the B & Q debacle. As we continued the reoccurring theme of my job searching and qualifications hit the agenda. They wanted evidence of my qualifications and my searches for work if any. John appeared exasperated with the repeated requests, yet I sensed it was a kind of mock frustration he was displaying. He was a first class actor as well as a comedian. As always his response was measured and calm.

"I am surprised that after twenty three years of marriage Mr Palmer does not know what his wife's qualifications are."

He looked directly at Stuart.

"I suppose however, that a man so self-absorbed in his own life and agenda may have absent mindedly missed the achievements of someone they had lived with seven days a week for twenty three years."

Ouch! I had to refrain from outwardly smiling as I watched Stuart cupping his hand against Steedman's ear once more, no doubt venting his outrage onto his sidekick.

John turned to the Judge.

"My client will be more than happy to list her qualifications"

At that point I wanted to melt into John arms. With each metaphorical swipe he made in Stuart's direction my emotions were stirred a little more.

My joy didn't last long however, as my heart sank to the pit of my stomach when Alexandra's condition was brought into the equation.

John quite naturally defended my decision not to go to work. He spoke eloquently and with compassion to match the sentiment.

"Alexandra, unfortunately, has a disability. Mrs Palmer is her only carer now that her husband has walked out on his family home and her daughter is dependent on her mother for both psychological and physical support."

It was at that point that my ex-husband stooped to a level lower than a snake's belly. He couldn't help himself and mumbled just loud enough that we could all hear.

"She's never been disabled, that is a total exaggeration."

My insides were raging with the most explosive anger I had ever felt. Without thinking I began to push my seat back and rose to my feet. How dare he devalue all the pain our daughter had been through with his glib, hurtful comments. How could he ignore the pain and suffering she had been through, the nights of mental and physical torment? John had picked up on his remark and my resulting anger and immediately he grabbed my hand from under the desk pulling me down, forcing me back into my chair. For a moment he gripped my hand tightly, his reassuring face looking directly at me.

"Don't rise to it," he whispered. "We've got them on the back foot, the judge has seen right through them."

I took a deep breath. John was right. The judge was well aware that Alexandra had been diagnosed with Spina bifida, it wasn't as if we were making up a bad back. They were digging themselves into a hole and covering themselves in shit.

I regained my composure, I was determined not to sink to Stuart's level. We both knew our daughters condition yet it wasn't the first time he had tried to pass it off as less than what it was.

As the proceedings dragged on I had an overwhelming urge to leave the room to breath some fresh air. I was suffocating in that oppressive environment, yet I knew there was no end in sight. We hadn't touched on the questions John had for Steedman and the list was long. Steedman was back on his feet again and was still throwing more wood onto the fire, stoking up the flames. His whining voice whimpering on about another grievance.

"Mr Palmer has repeatedly asked for his personal belonging to be returned to him. He has no access to the family marital home and although we have provided Mr Bennett with a detailed list of the items, Mrs Palmer has refused Mr Palmer access to the house and has even changed the locks."

All eyes were on me at this point and I sat nervously waiting for my solicitor to deliver. The Judge looked a little perplexed. Was this a genuine objection at last?

"Why are you refusing to reunite Mr Palmer with his personal belongings Mrs Palmer?"

He stared at me waiting for a reply.

My handsome solicitor came to my rescue.

"On the contrary Sir, Mr Palmer is in receipt of all his personal belongings, his clothes, watch, jewelry etc. Even his study has been cleared of all his personal effects and of course he has removed everything relating to his business."

The Judge looked directly at Stuart.

"Is this true Mr Palmer, are you in possession of everything Mr Bennett has just mentioned?"

Stuart squirmed. Was he about to lie his arse off and deny it?

"Err.. yes sir," he muttered, "but there are other things still in the house, like books and DVDs a cross trainer for example."

The Judge paused and waited for Stuart to continue. Stuart said nothing.

"And, Mr Palmer… anything else?"

Stuart looked at Steedman for support. Before he could say anything John jumped in.

"Mrs Palmer believes that items such as the DVD collection, the books that they have built up over the years belong to the whole family and not just one person. Even the cross trainer that Mr Palmer mentioned is used by his daughters and Mrs Palmer on a regular basis."

Brilliant, I thought, sheer bloody brilliance. How could Stuart or Steedman argue with that?

The judge was satisfied but as way of a compromise it was agreed that Stuart would prepare a list of items that he believed were his personal belongings and arrangements would be made through our respective solicitors to organize repatriation to their owner.

Now the pressure was off me and it was Stuart's affairs under the spotlight. I felt my body relax back into the chair as I watched John at work.

However, it didn't start off well at all. The Judge immediately denied John the right to ask the first two of his questions. The first question asked how many nights a week Stuart spent in the house of Angela Maddison and the number of nights she stayed at his house. Steedman argued the question was irrelevant to the proceedings, there was no debate on the subject and the Judge agreed with him. The next question was the same. John had put forward a question about Stuart's August holiday. We already knew he'd spent it in France and he went with the bitch girl, however John wanted it to come from the horse's mouth and not second hand. Request denied. Another irrelevant question in the Judge's opinion. I was beginning to think every question would be rejected, yet the tide was turning in our favour once more.

"Will the respondent please confirm that it is his intention to cohabit with Angela Maddison in the future?" John asked.

I sensed immediately Stuart didn't want to answer that question, his head shaking in defiance whilst Steedman fought his hardest to justify its exclusion.

No, it had to remain in the questionnaire said the Judge, much to my satisfaction. He would lie of course but at least he would have to answer the question. John was on a roll now. For every question he posed and as much as Steedman argued against it, the Judge thought them reasonable requests. At the end of the twenty itemed questionnaire only the first two had been rejected. Steedman had a growing list of information that his client had now been ordered to provide including the exact breakdown of his £50000 spending spree. John had requested partnership accounts, pension statements, current year tax returns and current year's earnings. As the list went on I could see Stuart sinking further into his chair. Steedman, once again, kept a close eye on his client wondering if he would explode with anger. I breathed a sigh of relief as John announced he had no further questions on the list.

It was at that point that John brought up Stuart's mother and her Last Will and Testament. Stuart's mother was very ill but it still seemed wrong. As the words fell from his mouth I cringed and realized that he had no shame. Addressing the judge once more he waded in.

"I am led to believe that Mr Palmer's elderly mother is seriously ill and he is the only surviving son."

A shame, an embarrassment washed over me as I felt my face burning. I wanted to plead that I had no hand in this line of questioning. Stuart was once again sitting up in his chair, brought back to life by the direction of the statement. John continued in his cool manner and his probing, antagonistic style was all too evident.

"The mother has a significant estate and Mr Palmer is the only likely beneficiary. His only other brother died ten years ago. He will inherit a substantial sum of money but specifically land and property."

John had just got his last words out when Stuart, unable to contain himself any longer leapt out of his seat,

He was in John's face, literally spitting out the words like some rabid dog.

"How dare you bring up my mother and my dead brother, that is totally disgusting. You're sick completely sick you twisted bastard."

At one point I thought he was about to climb over the table and launch a physical attack. John was completely calm and unperturbed at the outburst as he continued to fix his eyes on Stuart and if I wasn't mistaken, there was a hint of a smile rising from his lips.

Steedman was panic stricken as he stood behind Stuart gently coaxing him to sit back down.

My insides quivered as I looked from John to Stuart and back again. As I stared at the pair I realized the man I had shared my bed with and the one I was currently having sex with weren't poles apart. They were cut from the same cloth, both strong willed and ruthless and used to getting their own way. It was only their delivery that was different, smooth talking John against hot headed Stuart. The thought bothered me, a seed had been planted in my head. I was still drawn to John, my enthusiasm hadn't waned and there was something about his demeanor that attracted me, that turned me on, but I was as mad as hell he'd brought Stuart's mother into proceedings.

Judge Maitland stamped his authority on events, his voice slightly raised and clearly unimpressed.

"Mr Palmer will you please sit down otherwise I will have no other alternative but to have you removed from my chamber."

Stuart sank into his seat slowly as I knew he would. Beneath all the show he was a coward, only able to hit out at defenseless women.

Stuart's eyes remained fixed on John as if challenging him to dare say another word, but his intimidation was lost on him and within a heartbeat he dismissed Stuart immediately and continued on with not the slightest change in his voice.

"As I was saying before I was so rudely interrupted," he shot Stuart a disapproving glance. "Mr Palmer is likely to inherit a substantial sum of money which will undoubtedly impact on his financial circumstances. Above all he will inherit a large property in a much sought after area. In the event of his mother's demise the property will provide a roof over his head."

I didn't know at that point in time how prophetic John's words would be or what it was he was trying to establish. I would later find out that if Stuart were to be left a property before a settlement was reached, it could have a huge impact on both our circumstances. I wanted to stay in my home, Stuart wanted it sold to purchase a house for himself. His argument would collapse if he had a readymade home to move into, especially one that he owned outright. His mother's mortgage had been paid off twenty years since.

John didn't get the chance to say exactly that as the Judge held his hand up stopping John mid flow.

"I do not think Mr Palmers potential inheritance is relevant, Mrs Palmer would have no entitlement to it anyway."

John shook his head.

"On the contrary Sir, Mrs Palmer certainly -"

The Judge cut him short.

"Enough, I've made my decision. This line of questioning will have no place in our discussions. The question will be erased completely, end of."

John objected in the strongest possible manner arguing his point which seemed to make sense. The Judge reminded him that the old lady was very much alive and as far as he was concerned the subject could not be raised until the event of her death. He did however concede that it was a relevant point, but again he emphasized the matter was not to be brought into his courtroom while the lady was still living.

Soon after the Judge called time on our meeting.

As we trudged out of Judges Chambers, I sensed that neither side was waving a triumphant flag as a sign of victory. Stuart and Steedman bolted ahead of us eager to get away. I was relieved. At least we wouldn't have a repeat of the last fiasco yet my stomach was still churning as feelings of guilt and anger were building up inside me.

Why did he have to bring up such a subject? I felt sick at how callous and calculating we had looked. Up until that point we had fared well and I felt the Judge was certainly on my side and he had seen right through Steedman's pathetic straw clutching.

John was oblivious to my concerns, the events in the court room hadn't dampened his spirit, and he was clearly pumping with adrenaline after the tensions of the court room.

His voice was bright and enticing as ever.

"All is not lost as far as his mother is concerned, the Judge is wrong."

I turned around to face him.

"The Judge was with me up until that point John. Why did you have to bring it up?"

"I'm looking after your interests. If she dies it will make a huge difference to you."

"But you heard the Judge, John, she's still alive."

He placed both his hands on my shoulders and his voice dropped to a whisper.

"In the unfortunate circumstances she should die before your financial settlement is reached, your husbands inheritance would have to be taken into consideration, irrespective of what has been said today in court. The land provides £25000 a year income alone."

"But it's not Stuart's money yet," I cried out in exasperation.

"But it could be."

"Then bring it up if she dies, but not now John, it makes us look callous and uncaring."

I wasn't prepared to listen to him, it just felt plain wrong. He tried to offer more of an explanation but I cut him short. His face was now wearing that familiar smile and his tantalizing eyes stared right into mine once more. For a moment I was lost in them again, my gaze only interrupted by Louise who was now standing right by my side. John immediately cut the silence.

"Louise would you mind taking the files back to the office, I'll just drop Annette off at home."

"It's okay John," I said, "I am happy to get a taxi home."

John looked surprised.

"Are you sure?"
I nodded.
Louise looked at her notepad.
"You have the next three hours blocked out Mr Bennett."
John looked as if he had been taken by surprise.
"Yes," he said. "I need to make a home visit."
"I'll make a note Mr Bennett, who with?"
"Mrs King."

As I climbed into the taxi I was still boiling with rage. I never considered for one moment that John could have been correct, but to my own disgust I found myself calculating my mother in laws estate. How wrong was that?

Stuart had mentioned his mother's will on more than one occasion, saying the girls would be well taken care of, whatever that meant and the rest would come to him. I had no idea what her investments were as he kept that card close to his chest, but her house was surely close to £200000 and if her land was producing £25000 a year income then how much must that be worth? I hated myself. I was working it all out and of course John was right. If anything happened to Stuart's mother the money was his and therefore had to be taken into account.

Despite shouting no, no, no, I'm ashamed to admit, I did the rough calculation in my head. Stuart was her only surviving child, his only brother had died ten years ago. Her estate would be valued close to £1.5 million. John was right, the financial law was on my side. If Stuart inherited his mother's money it would impact significantly on my settlement.

23

It was the middle of December and the month had kicked in with a roar as storms raged throughout the country. In the north we were used to the harsh north wind, yet conditions were so bad even the most hardened Geordies had battened down the hatches as hurricane force winds swept across the country leaving devastation in its wake.

I was already dreading Christmas so this was all I needed. Houses had been flooded and there were power cuts right across the north. But we'd fared better than most, relatively unscathed by events, apart from a couple of loose tiles falling from the roof. One had smashed into the bonnet of my car but there had been no lasting damage to our property.

I should have been feeling relieved, even a little smug, as I watched the dramatic television footage of the raging rivers and poor pensioners being rescued by boat. Normally I couldn't wait to start the Christmas celebrations, it had always been my favourite time of the year and my enthusiasm and excitement always rubbed off onto the girls and dare I say it, even Stuart. Despite his somber disposition throughout the year, as Christmas approached, I could see his mood visibly lighten as his childlike enthusiasm to embrace the festive celebrations grew by the day. Like many families, our own annual merriments were steeped in tradition and rituals. Some were inherent from both mine and Stuart's childhoods yet others were unique to our family unit and these were the most treasured traditions, the one's we'd made our very own. Buying the 'real' Christmas tree had been one such 'Palmer' tradition, a special family ritual and it marked the start of the Christmas festivities. We even dressed up for the occasion, donning our winter woolies, coats, scarfs and gloves, even wellington boots come rain or shine. We would bundle into the car for our annual pilgrimage to Chopwell Woods to select our 'must have' pretreated Norwegian Spruce. Laughter and excitement would fill the car as the Christmas songs blasted out from the CD player and we sang along in unison to Jingle Bell Rock, or some other similar Christmas anthem.

As soon as we had parked up, the girls would dive out of the car losing themselves in the forest of felled trees stacked up for sale, scrutinising every single one. They took the task of finding the right tree as seriously as their mother. As we snaked our way around the rows of felled pines propped up against a makeshift fence, Stuart would start to grumble about the cost of forking out for a tree. We ignored him of course, our focus fixed on finding the biggest, bushiest tree of the lot.

Stuart was always designated the job of holding each tree upright so we girls could view the full effect from a vantage distance and eventually there would be a unanimous decision on which tree we wanted and his next designated role was to pay for it.

Reluctantly, his moth balled wallet would be pulled from his back pocket and the forester would bear a dismissive smile as Stuart cracked the same old annual joke about how he could have bought himself a whole forest for what he'd paid for that one tree. Invariably, his light hearted moaning continued as he laboriously dragged the netted spruce to the car and loaded it onto the roof rack.

"I think next year we should just get an artificial one," he'd say, "we're only going to put it out for the bin man in a few weeks time."

It was an annual standing joke as the girls delivered their well-rehearsed response in unison.

"Bah humbug Dad!"

And he'd moan and protest all the way home and I'd drown him out by gradually turning the music up a little louder as we belted out yet more seasonal tunes. Once home the tree would be ceremoniously placed in its resting spot then there was a flurry of activity to adorn it in all its finery. I'd always let the girls hang the baubles on the tree from being tots, it was part of the fun.

By early evening the house would be festooned with an array of Christmas decorations and a light fragrance of pine would waft through the air from the tree which at this point was bedecked in sparkling fairy lights, their reflective glow showcasing the meticulously placed baubles.

It was only when the Christmas spirit had been ignited, so to speak and the drink had softened Stuart's uncompromising shell exterior, did he reluctantly admit the trip and the cost had been worth the effort. The house looked beautiful he would say in sheepish admission. And so another tradition was borne. Stuart would retain his festive spirit throughout the Christmas period. He somehow miraculously changed his whole demeanor. Even when his mother arrived with her small suitcase in hand on Christmas Eve, entrenching herself in our home for several days, he would smile, even though I knew he hated every minute of her stay. When family and friends arrived with their children full of heightened spirts, he would continue to smile as unruly kids raced around the house spilling their drinks on the carpets all the while quelling his OCD tendencies to scream at the chaos unfolding around him.

But the previous Christmas that all changed. The fun and the festivities and the laughter had all but died. We went through the usual motions of course, pretending things were fine, but there was no magic, the spark had gone. There was a tension in the air and my heart remained firmly in my mouth as my family gathered at our home. There was plenty food and drink, one or two tipsy relatives and the inevitable spillage occurred but his usual amnesty was nowhere to be found, his festive spirit a distant memory and he snapped and barked at everything and anyone, even his own daughters. As my family bid us goodbye after a day of supposed Christmas celebrations I knew they were glad to be going. Although I wouldn't acknowledge it to anyone, I somehow sensed that we would not celebrate another Christmas together as a family.

I stood at the window watching the raging storms outside and reflected on the previous year and realized that my prophecy had come to fruition. This year Christmas was going to be a very different affair.

Stuart was gone and I knew his mother wouldn't come anywhere near the house, but the biggest wrench of all was Abigail. She had moved in with her boyfriend and announced one night that she had no plans to return home for Christmas dinner, in fact she'd already made tentative suggestions that her and Kevin would be having

Christmas dinner with his family. It was all matter of fact, so casual. The task would have been far easier if I had been rolling in money. At one point I wanted to take the two girls away on holiday and get as far away from Newcastle as possible, but the Christmas hotel prices and flights were ridiculous. I was nevertheless quite proud of myself because through good housekeeping and money management I had managed to put aside some money to spend on Christmas presents and the general festivities. The legal bills were crippling me though and I knew the latest one was overdue. Elizabeth Henshaw had made it abundantly clear that Saxtons' services could be suspended if I couldn't afford to settle my account.

Her call came out of the blue as I was planning to go into Newcastle to start my Christmas shopping. When my mobile rang and Saxton's appeared across the screen. I instantly thought it was John and like an excited puppy I grappled with my phone desperate to press accept and hear his voice once more. I was sorely disappointed when instead of John's dulcet tones I was met with a strange voice which was alien to my ear.

"Hello Mrs Palmer, it's Elizabeth Henshaw from Saxtons."

My heart sank to the floor. I kind of guessed the reason why she would be calling me and immediately sensed her coldness.

"Hello," I said hesitantly, unsure what else I should say.

"We haven't met yet," she said, "but John has kept me up to date with your case and I gather from what he has told me you've had a bit of a rough time."

She didn't stop for breath, her voice dragging on.

"Fortunately you have John on your side and he doesn't suffer fools gladly, he has quite a reputation in the court room. Are you happy with the service you're receiving Mrs Palmer?"

"Yes, yes, definitely, more than happy."

"Oh good," she interjected. "Yes, he's really very good at what he does."

Clearly she wanted to drive the conversation forward as she got to the point of her call. Her voice lowered and the tone sounded compassionate but I sensed it was fake.

"I've been reviewing client accounts Mrs Palmer and you have a rather large bill still outstanding which we really need settled before we can proceed any further."

"Proceed any further?" I mouthed silently to myself.

Does she mean they are going to down tools until the bill is settled? I panicked, my heart pounded once more. If I didn't have John working on my case, Stuart and his lynch mob would eat me for breakfast.

I jumped in.

"Yes I am aware of the outstanding bill Mrs Henshaw and you must be aware that I am waiting to receive a settlement on a joint endowment policy my ex-husband and I have together. It's being cashed in."

She hesitated. She clearly didn't know anything about it.

"And when will that be Mrs Palmer?"

"Your guess is as good as mine. You know what these companies are like when it comes to parting with money."

She was quick with a reply.

"I'm afraid guessing isn't my game Mrs Palmer. If you don't know when the funds are due and you have no means to settle the bill then it could leave us both in an awkward situation."

I couldn't believe her attitude towards someone who had already paid her company almost £7000 and it was obvious she didn't know anything about the policy.

I enlightened her anyway. Stuart and I had taken out an endowment on our first house for £50000. When it became clear in the mid-1990s that these policies had effectively been mis-sold and the expected return was unlikely to cover the capital repayment on the mortgage, Stuart, not wanting to be caught on the back foot, switched to a capital repayment mortgage but still continued to pay the endowment. If I had anything to be grateful to Stuart for, it was the fact that he had kept the original policy running and in my hour of need John had discovered the joint policy and I was entitled to half. Even Steedman couldn't wriggle out of that one. I continued to explain that John and Steedman had already agreed that the policy could be surrendered ahead of the final settlement.

"And how much is that likely to be Mrs Palmer?"

I took a deep breath.

"We are still waiting to hear from the Insurance Company as to what the final surrender figure will be, the estimate is just short of £40000."

"And will that be paid before Christmas?"

I knew John was pushing Steedman to move things along, I had seen the correspondence to that effect, although Steedman seemed just as keen as John to release the funds because he would want his bill settled too, no doubt. But with Christmas only days away it was likely to be mid-January before either of us would see a penny.

"Unlikely," I said.

"Well Mrs Palmer, from what you have told me I think that it is important Mr Bennett forges ahead to ensure you receive a settlement quickly."

I almost breathed a sigh of relief, the smell of the money had won her over. Where was the problem? It was more than enough to cover the bill, surely that would placate her?

"So as soon as I receive the funds I will settle my account," I said in a submissive voice. Convinced she had been sufficiently appeased I wanted to get off the phone but she hadn't quite finished.

"Mrs Palmer, in order to pacify our accountant I will still require a part payment before the Christmas holidays."

Before I could say another word she spoke again.

"The outstanding amount is just short of £7000. If you could possibly see your way to paying £2000 we will still be able to act for you into the New Year."

I was mortified and stood rooted to the spot. I didn't have £2000. I'd managed to put aside £1000 but that was for Christmas for the girls. I'd scrimped and saved that money by cutting back, not buying a single item of clothing since Stuart left. The odd take away meal and a night out was a distant memory. The only time I'd been over the door was when John had taken me for dinner. My girls, I thought, what about my precious girls?

I couldn't bring their Dad or their Gran back for Christmas but I didn't want my children to suffer. I wanted to ensure that they had as normal a Christmas as possible. We might not have the same numbers around the dining table but surely we could have nice food on the table and the same number of presents under the Christmas tree as other years? Now this woman wanted the lot.

I would have to do something. My mind was in turmoil, wondering where and how I would magic all this money from.

But I was too proud to make Elizabeth Henshaw party to my dilemma, she would get her money come hell or high water.

"That's not a problem," I said biting my tongue, "I will have the money to you in the next couple of days."

Behind the calm voice I was seething. As soon as I had pressed end and the call had finished, I searched through my contact list for John's mobile number. Why the hell hadn't he given me an idea that she wanted the bill settled? He constantly reminded me not to worry about the legal fees, everything would be fine.

His phone rang out but he didn't answer. It went to voicemail and as usual when faced with the challenge of leaving a message I rambled on nonsensically. But he would get the gist of my message. Within the hour he called me back all apologetic, saying it had been a huge mix up, his voice as persuasive as ever.

"I am so very sorry Annette, it is nothing personal, she goes through the outstanding accounts on a monthly basis but I didn't get the opportunity to explain the endowment policy."

He continued to apologize profusely yet I wanted him to know that I hadn't been the least bit impressed with her tactics. I explained the £2000 part payment and said that I had no option but to pay it.

"She threatened to withdraw your services if a payment isn't made before Christmas."

"That won't happen," he said, "don't worry Annette, I will speak to Mrs Henshaw but in the meantime you have my word that my services will not be withdrawn, I promise you that."

"I know it won't," I said, "because I have promised a payment."

Although his voice was reassuring, for the first time I detected a slight agitation. It struck me he was annoyed she had gone behind his back, it had irked him.

His voice softened to almost a whisper.

"How can I make it up to you Annette? I've been thinking about you, in fact, I can't get you out of my mind."

He was winning me over again as I thought about our previous encounters. The sex was electric and neither of us had found any difficulty expressing our sexual desires. If he had been in the room at that very moment I know where it would have led. However, he wasn't in the room and my priority at that moment in time was sorting out £2000 for Mrs bloody Henshaw.

"I need to go John," my voice direct and to the point. "She wants me to find £2000 this side of Christmas and quite frankly I haven't a clue where to get it from."

As much as I wanted to succumb to his charm, I forced myself away from dangerous territory because there was only one thing on my mind and that was money, or rather the lack of it. I was angry with myself. I should have stuck it out with Mrs Henshaw and told her the money was on its way. What could she have done about it?

And I was in the house alone. One word of encouragement and I knew he would be round in a heartbeat. There was a pause. I was so tempted to ask him to come round, it was like an itch plaguing me, demanding my attention and even though I felt compelled to ignore it, I couldn't get rid of it.

He spoke again.

"Can we arrange another night out?"

His soft voice was drawing me in. I closed my eyes willing myself not to break, the temptation was so enticing.

"We'll sort something out John, I need to go."

I ended the call before my willpower caved in completely.

Asking my mother for a loan of money wasn't that difficult. I knew she wouldn't mind and what made it easier was that I knew I could pay her back in January when the endowment money came through. I still didn't enjoy the prospect of going to her and I hated putting my dear old mam in this position. The woman was eighty years old and the last thing I wanted to do was let her know that her daughter was on the bones of her backside the wrong side of Christmas. And yet I had no choice, my options were limited. I wasn't working so a bank loan was out of the question. My mother was my only salvation.

I waited for the right moment when the two of us were by ourselves which in my mother's house was a task in itself. It was always full of family members and her friends and neighbours popping in for a cuppa. Eventually I caught a moment when the last visitor of the day had left, shortly after six o'clock, two days before Christmas Eve.

"I need to borrow some money to pay my solicitor…"

I'd barely finished my sentence before she stopped me. She didn't need to hear another word. "Pass my bag, I'm writing out a cheque for them, if you drop it off tomorrow they'll have their money."

"I'll give you it back in January, I promise."

Her head was shaking in disagreement and she reached out for my hand as I knelt down beside her chair, holding her fragile fingers. Her skin was thin, like crepe paper, age was taking its toll and I wasn't helping. How many extra worry lines and wrinkles had I given her I wondered.

"I don't want a penny of it back," she said with determination.

I protested.

"I wouldn't have asked Mam if I had no intention of paying it back. I have the money, it's just a cash flow problem that's all."

My mother was old but her will was strong and as sharp as ever.

"Listen to me, I don't need the money, I just want you and those bairns to see your day with him. If it takes my last breath and my last penny I want to make sure you're all alright."

I was on the point of tears as she continued.

"I hate that man and what he's done to you."

Her voice was animated and full of venom. I had never known my Mam say that she hated anyone, she had always seen the good in everyone. How sad it was to hear her say that. Stuart had introduced this beautiful old woman to the meaning of the word hate.

Saxtons and Elizabeth Henshaw got their money. I delivered it by hand the very next day. With the problem of the legal fees at least resolved until the new year, I felt a little lighter within myself, however it still didn't solve the problem about what I would do for Christmas presents. I'd bought a few bits and pieces of food and drink but not one present for the girls, except that is for the novelty Christmas pyjamas the day before we went to Chopwell Woods. As usual, when faced with a financial conundrum, I resorted to the wine bottle. It was two days to Christmas Eve and I had just over £43 in my purse. On the verge of tears and pondering my sorry predicament the answer came to me like a lightning bolt. How stupid of me. Why hadn't I thought of this earlier? Half staggering at this point, two thirds of the way through a bottle, I made my way to my bedroom. I sat down in front of the dressing table and lifted my neglected jewelry case out from the bottom drawer of my dresser. I rarely looked at my old jewelry these days, let alone wore it. Stuart had worked in Oman for three years before we were married. Gold Souks were two a penny in Oman and the gold was a fraction of the price of the UK and much better quality. Each piece of jewelry he had bought me was eighteen karat gold and skillfully hand crafted. Keen to impress me, every trip home, Stuart would come bearing gifts and over the three years I had built up an impressive collection. I had almost forgotten about the pieces because they never saw the light of day once we got married and had kids. My collection was sitting collecting dust along with my wedding band which I had cast in there the day Stuart had left me.

As luck would have it gold prices were at an all-time high. As stocks and share prices dived, the bombed out investor looked for a tangible alternative to invest their cash. Gold was the obvious answer. I picked up each item and reminisced. The gold pear drop earrings Stuart had given me on his first trip home along with a gold bangle. Each piece had a history to it, one I was now trying to desperately forget and thankfully Stuart appeared to have forgotten about them too.

One by one I placed them all into a silk pouch. The last piece to go in the bag was my wedding band. I held back for a moment wondering if I could bring myself to drop it in. I had always loved the simplistic elegance of it. There had been a delicately etched pattern running around the main ring but over the years it had worn away, now it was barely visible. It seemed ironic that it somehow symbolized our love, that too had worn away over time. It had no place in my new life and I quickly I placed it in the pouch and tied the knot.

I'd never been into a pawn shop before, although I'd passed them many times, the display window showcasing row upon row of second hand jewelry. The shop was packed with people, some selling, others buying. If I was honest it all seemed a little seedy. The young girl at the counter barely out of her teens handed me a small silver dish and I dropped my trinkets into it.

"Len, we got a lady here wants to pawn her jewelry," she shouted at the top of her voice.

My face flushed with embarrassment, it sounded so wrong to hear that. Len, a rather large man with greying greasy hair and a grubby appearance hauled himself up from his chair and waddled like a fat goose towards the counter. Fixed in his eye socket was his jewelers eye loupe. It didn't move an inch, his squint fixing it into position like glue. He lifted each piece raising it to his eye to peer at them closely. He wasn't looking at the craftsmanship or its beauty, he was looking for the hallmark, what karat the gold was.

He slung it into another plastic dish and nodded his head in my direction.

"Good," he said, "it's real."

I looked on with sadness as the sentiment behind each of my little gems was evoked. When he mauled his dirty podgy fingers over my wedding band my heart sank. That ring once meant so much to me. Who would have thought that when Stuart had placed the sparkling band on my finger all those years ago that it would end up in a pawnshop. For a second or two I desperately wanted to retrieve it, yet I did nothing as he picked the dish up and put it on the scales.

When I walked out of the Pawnshop I was clutching £1800 in my hand, an empty silk pouch and the feeling that I had just prostituted my life to the fat man. I tried to cast my doubts and regrets to the recesses of my mind, convincing myself it was all in a good cause and I forced myself to move on to more positive thoughts. I would be in Newcastle City Centre by 9 a.m. tomorrow morning and I was going to shop until I dropped. The traditional Christmas Eve joint of ham would be placed in the oven, set on the timer and as long as I could get back around six that evening, I'd have time to prepare the potatoes and salad and pickles. I'd buy a few quality cheeses from Marks and Spencer's and the Christmas chocolate log. A bottle of Moet and Chandon and a bottle of Baileys. I was going to push the boat out. It would be just like old times except Stuart wouldn't be there moaning about how much everything had cost.

My beautiful girls would be celebrating Christmas as they had always done, I was going to make this a Christmas to remember.

24

Adrenaline and caffeine got me through the Christmas period. As I walked out of the Pawnbrokers with the money in my hand, I went onto autopilot, racing through the list of jobs I had to do before the big day.

As planned, I hit the town by 9am Christmas Eve morning and it turned out to be an exhausting experience. It was far removed from the joy I had been expecting. Stepping out of the front door that morning I could feel the cold freezing air as it hit my face, yet to my relief the storms had died down and mercifully the torrential rain had stopped. My job had been made just that little more bearable not having had to face the biting strong winds or diving for cover in shop doorways to escape the rain.

Nevertheless, Newcastle City Centre was bedlam, a hive of activity, full of shoppers, but surprisingly somber faced shoppers with little or no Christmas cheer left in them. It puzzled me at first. I expected joy and laughter, but smiles were at a premium. It came to me after a while and I realised why. We were the desperate ones, the last minute dot com zombies, the bad planners, the ones who had secured last minute funds just like me and were ready to grab our last minute purchases and escape town to start our last minute festivities back home.

I told myself I was more prepared than them, at least I had planned. I tackled my way through the crowds as I diligently worked down my list. Occasionally I stopped at Costa or Starbucks to replenish my caffeine levels or when my arms that were so laden down with heavy bags and boxes cried 'no more.'

Every few hours I hobbled back the car to relieve myself of the burden before taking a deep breath and starting the whole process all over again. I discovered that Christmas Eve shopping was a drab experience, the shops were almost stripped of stock and although the staff were kitted out in Christmas hats and pieces of tinsel draped around their necks, they too were sick of it and couldn't wait to go home.

The Christmas songs were still blasting out over the tannoy and whatever seasonal stock was left on display by late afternoon started to be reduced in price. I couldn't deny there was significant bargains to be had for those who had the balls to wait until the very last minute, yet there was precious little Christmas spirit on offer and I couldn't help but wish that I was at home with my presents all wrapped up, and placed under the tree. I recalled previous years when all of my shopping had been done the week before and all I had to worry about was the traditional Christmas Eve dinner. I looked at my watch, it was just after four o'clock. I'd normally be in the kitchen by now, the smell of the roast ham wafting tantalizingly through the house and all I would be worrying about was what time I'd have my first glass of Moet & Chandon. I couldn't help thinking that this tiresome day was all Stuart's fault.

By six o'clock I had almost reached the end of my tether but thankfully I'd also reached the end of my shopping list. Strangely enough the atmosphere in the town had lifted somewhat. Gone were the urgent shoppers with their dismal faces, being replaced by what appeared to be a contingent of half drunken male stragglers and office workers heading to the shops for last minute gifts for their wives and girlfriends en route to the nearest pub to continue their celebrations.

With little energy left in me I decided to call it a day. I made my way slowly back to my gift laden car and once slumped behind the steering wheel, breathed a sigh of relief and allowed myself a big smile of satisfaction. I had achieved my own personal miracle. My body ached and the soles of my feet were burning in pain but still I felt a sense of euphoria. There were going to be gifts under the Palmer Christmas tree and that's all that mattered. I had done it. I didn't know how but I had done it.

The rest of the evening seemed relatively easy in comparison to the Christmas Eve shop. The alcohol helped I suppose. Abigail and

Kevin arrived after seven and we sat around the dinner table eating and chatting until well after nine. The Christmas Eve dinner was perfect, I'd excelled myself in every department. The only slight worry was about how much I had spent, there were barely £50 left from the money the pawnbroker had given me.

But I didn't care. As I reached for the bottle of Moet and replenished my glass I said a silent toast… to myself.

The girls were brilliant. They somehow sensed what I had achieved on my own and appreciated the effort I had made. They could see how exhausted I was, I barely had the energy to lift my glass and they scurried around clearing dishes and tidying everything away. I made a halfhearted attempt to help but they wouldn't hear of it.

Afterwards we all sat down to watch 'It's a Wonderful life," another family tradition in the Palmer household.

By midnight the house was silent. Abigail and Kevin had gone home with a promise to return the following day for Christmas Day tea while Victoria and Alexandra had long since made their way to bed and for the first time all evening I felt totally alone. It was in stark contrast to the madness of earlier on. I reflected on the day. It had been a success but I couldn't help feeling a little melancholy.

I realized that Stuart's absence from the dinner table had been the great, big elephant in the room, none of us wanting to mention him for fear of dampening our spirits, yet he was present in all but person.

Beneath the façade we had all been wondering where Stuart was and what he was doing. As I sat drinking my solitary glass of Baileys, midnight carols from St Paul's Cathedral played on the TV in the background and the thoughts of Stuart's whereabouts occupied my mind.

I had no doubt he would be ensconced at Angela Maddison's house celebrating Christmas with her and even more cutting, her children.

I pictured the scene. It would be the family Maddison's traditions this Christmas, Stuart would be happy enough with that. After all, why would he come between a mother and her children? He'd be making a special effort as it was his first Christmas with his new family and he'd want to create a good impression. That was Stuart… false. And now, Maddison's children were likely in bed and Stuart would be curled up on the sofa with the bitch.

I gazed over the top of my glass, the flames from the fire danced in time to the carols on TV and I looked at our Christmas cards on the fireplace. This was a special place, the place reserved for family cards. There should have been at least three more cards there this year, three cards from a father to his daughters but the space was bare. Stuart hadn't sent a single card and not one present had been delivered. I wondered what sort of man could do that, turn his back on his own flesh and blood yet be willing to embrace another man's children. And he would embrace them and there would be presents, decent presents and kind, friendly words and gestures of love and respect not to mention the display of affection for their mother. Look at me he'd be saying, look how caring I am, look how much I love your mother, don't you know I am going to treat her like a princess until Hell freezes over.

It was all about first impressions with Stuart. I knew the man inside out.

It was to become a reoccurring theme in my thoughts throughout the Christmas period as again he was with me when I got up early on Christmas morning to light the fire and switch on the Christmas lights. I liked to make the house warm and cozy and wouldn't open the curtains for some hours as the daylight spoiled the effect of the Christmas tree and the lights. He was there when the girls appeared to open their presents and he sat at the dinner table too, despite his vacant chair. And of course there were two more empty spaces, the chair his mother would normally occupy and of course Abigail. How I managed to make it through dinner without breaking down I'll never know.

As the evening was drawing to a close and in our usual style, I sat at the piano and made my best attempt to play my entire repertoire of Christmas carols as the family tried to sing along in unison, covering up the endless flaws in my notes. My mother and Aunt Helen were sitting in their usual seats, smiling sincerely, appreciating the soft tones of the piano as opposed to the din of the TV. Abigail and Victoria were sprawled over the sofa and floor with their respective boyfriends, arms hooked around each other whilst Alexandra, not wanting to miss out on the warm love, nuzzled up with her Nana.

Once again my thoughts returned to Stuart. Not as much as a phone call or text message to his three beautiful daughters. How could he live with himself? At one point I even felt a little sad for him, giving up his family for what, another woman, money?

'Stock is better than money,' my grandad's voice echoed in my head. They were words I remembered him using when I was young girl and I had never known what he meant by it, but that evening as I sat physically exhausted and with barely a penny to my name, I eventually came to understand the meaning of those words. It was at that point that I realized how fortunate I was.

The New Year arrived with a flurry of snow and the promise of new beginnings. I had made the best of Christmas and New Year, yet if the truth be known I was glad to take the tree down and re-establish a degree of normality.

With the decks cleared, my thoughts inevitably returned to my pending divorce settlement. I hadn't heard from John Bennett for nearly two weeks. He had been conspicuous by his absence during the festive season and I hadn't even received a text wishing me a Merry Christmas.

I had felt a little hurt by his lack of acknowledgement yet despite my misgivings I could feel that familiar itch rising once again. I took the letter he had sent from the kitchen drawer and reluctantly admitted to myself that I was looking for any excuse to contact him. The letter he'd sent listing Stuart's belongings had arrived a couple of days before Christmas and I had shoved it away in the drawer determined not to let it spoil the celebrations. With normality resumed it was time to take a look at it again. I laid it tentatively on the kitchen table and cast my eye over exactly what it was that Stuart wanted. John was right, there was nothing exciting on it, an odd item of clothing he was insisting I still had, some golf memorabilia of which he was more than welcome to and the same was true for his collection of Star Wars DVD's and the set of seven Dune books. He wanted his cufflink box, his gold watch, ring and wrist chain. The jewelry, he wrote, was to be located in the top draw of his bedside table. He wanted his dad's record collection and a spare set of golf clubs that were in the loft. Finally, the most laughable of all the requests, he wanted his Father's Day Tigger toy.

I couldn't quite understand the irony of that final demand. He didn't want to be the girls Dad any more but he sure as hell wanted a keepsake of the position he had once appeared to hold in such high regard.

I decided to get on with the task in hand. I was now driven by anger and my lethargy had been outdriven by a sheer determination to get the last traces of this fucking man out of my home. I set about the task of retrieving each item on the list and placing it in a large brown box . The golf clubs and record collection were a bit more of a challenge and I needed to draft in Alexandra's services to help me lift the heavy load down from the loft. She whined and moaned as I had interrupted her viewing of Desperate Housewives yet after gently cajoling her, she stood fixed at the bottom of the loft ladders whilst I lowered the heavy loads down to her. Eventually, all his personal belongings were sitting in the garage waiting to go, all that was, except Tigger. For some reason I couldn't bring myself to place it in the box. I remembered vividly when the kids had bought it for him. Abigail couldn't have been more than ten years old at the time and I'd taken the three of them on a shopping trip so they could buy him a gift for Father's Day. Like most kids, they didn't consider anything practical, they wanted to buy something they'd want to have for themselves. Sound children's logic. That year it was a small Tigger toy holding a plaque saying, Best Daddy. The bright orange toy had caught their eye in Clintons Cards and all three were immediately sold on it. They had been so excited when they passed their gift across to their Dad, along with a card that had been signed by each of them individually, then row upon row of kisses planted along the bottom for good measure. It was the thought of that memory which had stopped me from letting go of that shabby little toy. I couldn't quite bring myself to put him in the box. Stuart didn't deserve his Father's Day Tigger, especially when the bastard had chosen that very day to walk out on his precious girls. I took Tigger into the kitchen and decapitated him with my boning knife. I cut off his hands and one foot then sliced him open from throat to belly button and after I made sure he was well and truly dead, I took a photograph of the sorry looking little chap with my mobile phone. I sent him the picture, explaining that the mice had somehow got to Tigger before I did.

Once again it was Abigail who volunteered to take her Dads belongings to him.

"I'll text him Mum and arrange to take the stuff around."

I hadn't asked her, I didn't want to put her on the spot yet common sense told me it was the most sensible approach to take. I couldn't take them, we were way beyond civility and if the solicitors got involved the letters would be flying and costs would be incurred on both sides. "Are you sure you're happy to do that?"

"Yes," she responded immediately, "of course, he's not going to bite me."

I breathed a sigh of relief. Thank God for Abigail, what would I do without her?

I had no clue what had been said in the text messages between Abigail and her father but there had been sufficient information relayed between them to establish she would deliver his belongings to his Aunt Peggy's flat on the Wednesday night, a week after Christmas. Abigail came around that evening to collect his things from the garage. It dismayed me that I could somehow sense she was keen to take them, excited that she would be meeting up with her Dad again and who knows, would there also be a small present for her?

As we loaded everything into the back of her car, I wasn't sure why she appeared so eager because I was as nervous as hell for her, my stomach churning and the anxiety building. As we finished loading her car and I slammed the boot down I questioned her once more. "Now, you're fine about dropping this off aren't you?"

"Yes, yes Mum, why wouldn't I be?"

"I don't know," I said, "but once you've dropped everything off ring me, okay?"

She raised her eyes to the sky.

"Alright Mum, I will do, but don't worry."

I couldn't shake my fear, I wouldn't be there to protect her and I had witnessed his anger first hand having been the recipient of a slap across the face. I didn't want a similar fate for my daughter.

After she had gone I was unable to settle. I paced the floor checking my phone continuously to make sure I hadn't missed a call or a message. I looked at my watch. Damn! Why was she taking so long? It was only ten minutes away.

After what seemed like an age, I heard her come through the front door and immediately knew she had something to tell me. Her face said it all as she stormed into the kitchen pulling out a chair as she almost fell into it.

She rubbed both eyes, pulled her hands away and then looked up at me.

"He is one nasty, ignorant bastard that man."

My jaw almost fell to the floor in shock.

"Sorry for swearing Mum but he is."

Her eyes were full of tears and I waited patiently until she continued.

She started to recite the tale, the cracks in her voice almost breaking as she desperately tried to hold the tears back.

"I rang the bell but before he answered I thought I'd go back to the car and start unloading his stuff. By the time he opened the door I had already unloaded the golf bag."

She paused while she pressed a finger into the corner of her eye. Her decibels increased, her voice was now full of rage.

"I heard the door open and looked up as he walked towards the car. I looked at him and smiled."

She could no longer hold back her tears as her pent up emotion exploded.

"He just walked straight past me Mum, not a word, no eye contact, no smile, nothing and started to unload the boxes from the car."

Abigail explained that she lifted up the box of records and followed him to the door.

"And what did he do?" I said desperate to hear what happened.

"Nothing," she screamed. "The bastard stood at the door and literally snatched the box from my hands and slammed the front door in my face."

She had difficulty speaking as she sobbed like a child.

"No thank you, no Merry Christmas, Happy New Year, nothing. Not a bloody word."

I couldn't quite believe what I was hearing, he had slammed the door in her face? His own daughter. I retraced her story like a detective cross examining a witness.

"So he opened the door and didn't say hello?"

'No."

"And you didn't say a word to each when you were unloading the car?"

"No."

"Maybe he said bye before he shut the door and you didn't hear?"

"For Christ sake Mum, NO, NO and NO. He said nothing to me, not a bloody word."

She buried her head in her hands and the tears fell onto the table.

She looked up and wiped away the tears.

"I'm done with that man Mum. It's finished, it's over."

I pulled up a chair and nudged in beside her.

"I'll make you a cup of tea," I said.

"Thanks Mum, that would be nice."

Stuart's festive spirit shown towards his daughters didn't end there. The day after Abigail's encounter with her Dad, Victoria had her own run in with him. Like most teenage girls, her mobile phone was practically glued to her hand but today the phone was seemingly playing up, she couldn't make or receive calls and the internet service was down. Her first reaction was to contact her service provider. The contract was in her Dad's name but once she gave them the agreement number and a password the voice on the other end of the call was happy to chat.

"Mr Palmer has paid the contract up, he has effectively terminated it."

Victoria was gob smacked.

"There must be some sort of mistake."

The member of staff suggested that she contact the bill payer. Victoria rang her father as soon as the call ended.

Stuart wasn't very talkative.

"There's no mistake," he said. "That's your Mum's responsibility now, I'm paying her to cover that sort of expense."

I could see Victoria almost shaking with rage.

She held the hand set at arm's length.

"He's hung up on me Mum."

"He's what?" I asked.

"He's cut my phone off Mum and hung up on me, didn't even say goodbye."

What on earth was the man playing at? These were his own daughters.

"I hate him," Victoria said as she burst into tears. "He's a total creep."

I calmed her down reassuring her that it wasn't a problem.

We'd jump in the car there and then and sort her out a new contract.

We were just days into the New Year and Stuart had already set out his stall. He had unnerved me and I wondered how much more shit he was prepared to throw at the fan.

Like always, when I needed reassurance, I turned to John. I'd been looking for an excuse all week to ring him and hear his voice. He was my shield against Stuart and his bully boy solicitor Steedman and I needed to speak to him. The following day when I was pacing the house on my own once more I picked up the phone. Victoria and Alexandra were hitting the Christmas sales one last time, spending what little they had left. I rang the Saxtons' office, Karen's cold unwelcoming voice greeted me.

"Happy new year Karen," I replied. "I hope you had a good Christmas. Can I speak to Mr Bennett please?"

"No sorry, he's on holiday until Monday."

"No problem." I replied before ending the call.

It took a little nerve for me to ring John's mobile number directly. My justification for ringing was Stuart's awkward behavior towards his daughters and the pretense that I needed to know if we'd received anything from Steedman with regard to the Endowment policy. I felt vindicated in interrupting his Christmas break as John was always preaching that his client service was available twenty four seven, no question too silly, no problem too small.

He picked up immediately, the phone hardly had a chance to ring out.

"Hello Annette, how lovely to hear your voice."

I took a deep breath, his voice was low and sultry and I immediately forgot about the pretense of my call, I had even cast aside my dignity. It was all lost to his alluring voice.

"John," I said in almost a whisper, "I've been thinking about you, can you come round, I need to see you."

John Bennett had been sitting in his study when his mobile rang and Annette Palmer's name flashed across the screen. His immediate reaction was to ignore her call, the fascination for Annette Palmer had long since passed, the thrill of the chase and the capture long since forgotten. Yet despite his initial misgivings he pressed accept as he recalled how his prey had surrendered meekly, without so much as a struggle and complied with every sexual request he threw at her.

She rushed straight in, not giving him a chance to speak. A grin swept across his face as he heard the desperation in her voice. She wanted him to go around, needed to see him. His groin immediately began to stir as he heard her words and remembered his previous visit to her house. He could almost feel the intensity of their encounter on the desk in the study. His thoughts were lost in the moment, but only for a second, as he quickly weighed up the practicalities of going round there. Even though she rambled on about something or nothing, her call could only mean one thing, she wanted to repeat the experience. He gathered himself together, how could he not oblige the woman, his was a bespoke service he was offering and it was the least he could do after Elizabeth Henshaw had harassed the woman over her outstanding bill. For a moment the annoyance he felt towards Elizabeth took over his planning for an afternoon of hardcore sex with his ready, willing and able client. When he had picked up Annette's voicemail telling him Henshaw had demanded payment of the outstanding bill he had been fuming. Already his relationship with the Henshaw's was on rocky ground since he had bent them over the barrel when he had demanded a bigger cut of the profits. Now that Elizabeth was starting to interfere directly with his clients he would have to rethink his position. The woman was becoming a thorn in his side.

As Bennett sat at his study desk listening to Annette's almost desperate voice, with an element of amusement, he found himself considering her request. And why not? It was obvious she wanted sex and he was more than willing to provide it. There was definitely a sexual chemistry between them and a reciprocal gratification where few words were needed.

"Are you sure today is good Annette? I mean, the girls won't want to be seeing me, they're still on holiday aren't they?"

"Yes John," Annette replied, "but they're both off to Newcastle for the sales."

John couldn't prevent his hand, which had been resting on his knee cap, trace a line in an upward direction as it came to rest in between his legs.

"They're out for the day?"

"Yes John."

He squeezed his rapidly growing penis and a warm expectant feeling flowed through his body.

He lowered his voice to barely a whisper.

"Well now Annette, you know what that means don't you?"

There was a brief silence on the other end of the phone but John knew that his next, well-rehearsed line would strike a chord.

He lowered his voice to a whisper.

"It means I simply won't be able to keep my hands off you, that's what it means."

Annette was breathing deeply, he could just about hear her. She would be considering her next course of action, the briefest and sexiest of lace underwear would be lying on the bed ready to change into and without a doubt the mere sound of his voice and his suggestive words would be beginning to work their magic and she would be moist and expectant.

"I'll be round there within the hour," he said. "I hope you are going to be a good girl."

"I will Mr Bennett, I will."

He ended the call, straightened the papers scattered across his desk and searched for his car keys which he eventually found in his jacket pocket. He didn't want to waste another second, now that he had been aroused he was desperate to get to Annette's house and make good on his promise.

There was only one minor problem to solve. His wife.

He threw on his top coat and walked out of his study, down the stairs and into the kitchen.

Alma stood at the marble island staring vacantly into Jamie Oliver's latest recipe book. She looked up.

"Are you going somewhere darling? You haven't forgot we're taking my mother out for dinner this evening?"

"Fucking clients," he said in a display of fake anger. "Sometimes they just take the piss." She reached out grabbing the lapels of his coat to draw him close to her, there was always a motive for her to instigate affection and it usually involved him spending money. At least screwing Annette Palmer wouldn't cost him any money and although he was reluctant to admit it, she was far more responsive.

He pushed her away gently.

"Sorry darling, I haven't got time, I need to call by the office to pick some paper work up and then get to a client's house double quick. I haven't forgot about dinner this evening."

She located his flaccid penis and felt him through the thin material of his trousers. The temptation to take her in the study and save himself the bother of leaving the house to attend to Annette Palmers needs was a tantalizing thought and a one he almost succumbed too. He weighed up the options. Alma's hand slid down towards his groin.

"Are you sure you don't want to cancel that meeting?"

"I wish I could dear, but you know what that Henshaw bitch is like."

He planted a light kiss on his wife's cheek.

"This shouldn't take long darling, I'll be back before you know it."

25

I was lying in my bed crippled with lethargy, not wanting to make that initial exertion of pushing back the duvet cover and putting my feet on the bedroom floor. Why would I want to do that? It would only act as an acknowledgement that the day had officially started. It was here, today had dawned and quite simply I didn't want this particular day to begin.

I glanced at the bedside clock hoping that a visual image of the time might give me the impetus to start moving. I knew it was late, too late. I only had to look out of my bedroom window at the sight of low winter sun bouncing it rays off the windowpane to know it was way past nine.

My cautionary peek at the clock confirmed the reality, it was 9.35 am. Shit! I thought as I turned my head back to my pillow closing my eyes tightly in an effort to block reality out for a few more precious seconds.

I took stock wondering if I could possibly make up the mother of all excuses that would allow me to swerve the day completely. There wasn't an excuse big enough except if the bloody house caught fire. Victoria had dropped Alexandra off at school to spare me the bother, she knew exactly how hard this day was going to be for me.

I lay there thinking about the night before. I was beginning to realize that when faced with a major challenge I would either take to my bed or the bottle. The previous evening I had broken my impressive run of sobriety, the wine had been flowing once more and a few Baileys too. I remember almost falling up the stairs but that was the last thing I could recall, most of the latter part of the evening had been a complete blur.

Now I was suffering the consequences, the signs were all there, banging headache, dry mouth and a vague sense of nausea lingering in the back of my throat.

The truth was that alcohol hadn't solved the problem. Yes it allowed me a few hours of temporary release, yet the problem still lingered there.

I kicked off the duvet, placed my feet over the bed and stood up. Oh my god! What was happening to my head? In less than three hours I was expected to look good and face Stuart and his lynch mob in a court room for yet another round of bare knuckle fighting.

How I was beginning to hate the sight of Newcastle Crown Court. I was no longer impressed by its striking character or the fact it overlooked my beloved River Tyne. I now loathed the site of the bloody building and all the pomp that went along with it. I hated the criminals who congregated in and around the building and the suited and booted men and women who prosecuted or defended them. I hated the Judges and their ushers, their secretaries and security. The place was the pits, I hated it with a passion. Why had my ex-husband forced me into this situation? It was a thought that recurred over and over again.

According to John, today was going to be the biggy and everything rested on today's hearing. All the previous bitter exchanges between John and Steedman and the disclosure of our financial information, or as in Stuart's case, his endeavours to hide financial information, had all been geared towards this one momentous occasion. There would be no more opportunity to ask the opposing party for information about their finances, this was it. What we knew about Stuart's income and savings was all we were ever going to know and it was precious little. Steedman had come back with answers to some of the questions we'd posed in the previous hearing, yet the information Stuart and Steedman had cobbled together had only served to pose more questions. They'd supplied us with copies of his accounts and his tax returns yet it was all historical and we were no further forward as to what his actual current year's earnings were.

I vividly remember puzzling over them for a good hour as I sat at my kitchen table staring blankly at the copies of Stuart's previous two tax returns John had forwarded on to me. Stuart had sat and told me that he estimated a fifty to sixty per cent rise in income at the very least, that was the very reason he had been persuaded to join the partnership in the first place.

By the middle of the second year of Stuart joining the partnership he was run off his feet, dealing with several clients at once and although he wasn't forthcoming with information about his earnings I knew the rewards were significant. Stuart was earning a fortune and he was as happy as a pig in shit and I'd latterly found out that he had been billing the partnership between £800 and £1000 per day.

I knew how many days he worked, I could do the math's.

The conundrum was why hadn't the figures on his tax return reflected the increase in his income? After much contemplation and several cups of coffee it eventually dawned on me and I scolded myself for taking so long to unravel the mystery. Back in the day I would have figured it out in no time, nowadays I had to mentally work through my rational. His tax returns were estimated, based on the previous year's earnings. Stuart had played the system but had done nothing wrong and there was nothing I could do about it. Reluctantly I picked up a pencil and began to make the financial calculations. After no more than fifteen minutes the figures were displayed on the page of a Marks and Spencer's notebook.

Stuart had worked 240 days last year and I calculated he had billed the Partnership for over £212000. I looked at his last tax return which showed a total gross income of just short of £107 000 and I swear my heart dropped into my stomach. That was the figure we were going to court with, that was the figure my solicitor would be trying to get a slice of for me and the girls and I was left feeling angry. Despite all the questions, letters, phone calls and confrontations we were no further forward. I could accurately calculate his earnings but as John had told me time and time again, it was what was on his tax returns that mattered. As I sat fixed on the two figures mulling it all over in my mind, I had to wonder what had been the point of it all? Stuart had effectively told us nothing, he had fiddled the system. No wonder I'd resorted to the wine bottle and the Baileys on the eve of the hearing. I was expected to try and reach a settlement based on figures that had been legally falsified. What chance did I have of gaining a fair settlement if the odds were so stacked against me?

I had already been warned that if we failed to settle then matters were going to be taken out of our hands and a Judge who knew nothing about either me or Stuart would be making the decision on our behalf. Furthermore, the figures he would be assessing the settlement on, were the official, legitimate figures from the Tax Office, not my scribbles on the page of a notebook.

John had been brutal and frank in delivering the importance of this Financial Dispute Resolution hearing.

"Annette," he said," "if Stuart doesn't make an acceptable offer at the FDR, and I have serious doubts he will no matter how hard we negotiate, it will be a case of you resigning yourself to either accepting the offer on the table or going to a final hearing."

My heart had slumped on hearing the words final hearing. More money, I thought. More legal costs and solicitors fees.

The New Year had actually brought with it a change in financial fortunes, or so I thought. The endowment payment had materialized and after paying Henshaw the balance of the outstanding bill, I was left with just short of £15000 to bank. For once I had been able to breathe a sigh of relief, it was the first time since Stuart had left that I had a financial safety net. However, I somehow sensed it wasn't going to last long. I paid back my mother despite her protestations and even treated myself and the girls to a new wardrobe which was long overdue. The next kick in the teeth came a week later when Henshaw slapped me with another jaw dropping, eye watering invoice for £6300. I had been so incensed on receiving it I hadn't been able to stop myself from tackling John about the ever increasing legal costs. Now that I'd literally had John's dick firmly wedged in my mouth, on more than one occasion, the formality in our client solicitor relationship had lapsed and our conversations were a little more candid.

"How much is this all going to cost John?" I said, "The bills are getting out of hand, I can't keep going."

He stood over me, dressing himself after another vigorous sex session, beads of sweat still standing out on his forehead and his breathing laboured from the sheer exertion of our love making.

"Believe me Annette, I am trying to do all I can to minimize your bill."

He shrugged his shoulders as he buttoned up his shirt.

"You've experienced Elizabeth's wrath, she's not an easy woman to deal with and unfortunately she's the organ grinder and I'm just her monkey."

He went on to tell me that he had checked the account personally. There was no discrepancies, every hour and every cost had been accounted for. He left me with a positive in that the bill was now up to date. He stepped forward, kissed me and said goodbye. Both our needs had been satisfied once more and at least I didn't have to pay for the afternoon quickie. For some reason I sensed a growing animosity between John and Elizabeth and I had no doubt she was keeping a close eye on my account. There would be little in the way of wriggle room for John to trim my costs, even if he'd wanted to. After all, surely he was on some sort of percentage of the fees his clients paid.

It was time to make tracks. I closed the notebook and pushed it into a drawer yet the figure of Stuart's £212000 income somehow wouldn't filter out of my head. I knew it would stay with me for most of the day.

We had to settle today, surely it was in everyone's interest to do so? If we didn't settle today and it went to a final hearing I couldn't even begin to imagine what the costs would be. What little I had from the Endowment would quickly run out and deep down I knew the likelihood of a settlement was looking bleak. I only had to look at the past record of negotiations between John and Steedman to realise that the odds were stacked against that. It was unlikely that Stuart had suddenly developed a conscience and would want to do the right thing for me and his children.

Still, secretly, I willed him to try and make amends and not burn all of his bridges with his children altogether. The girls were already losing patience with him, but if I could walk into the house and tell them that their father had agreed to a reasonable settlement and that we would be financially comfortable, who knows what might happen.

Victoria would take more persuading however, cutting her phone off had been the last straw for her and had even gone as far as changing her surname to my maiden name.

I'll never forget as she walked into the house and dropped that bombshell. No discussion, nothing. In Victoria's usual stubborn, rebel style, she'd made up her mind and gone ahead and done it without mentioning one word. She was almost smug as she strutted into the kitchen. I knew something was wrong.

"Hi mum," she grinned. "Just call me Victoria Jane Garwood

from now on."

"What?"

"I've decided I no longer want the name Palmer as my surname," she proclaimed as she slapped the legal looking paperwork down on the kitchen counter.

I had been peeling potatoes in preparation for the evening meal. I dropped the knife into the sink.

"What are you talking about now Victoria?"

"There, look," she said, pointing to the paper, "I've changed my name by deed poll. Downloaded the paperwork, paid my £30 and bingo, I'm now Victoria Jane Garwood."

I reached for a towel, dried my hands quickly and grabbed the paper from the bench. My eyes quickly scanned it. It all looked official and there was her new name printed in the centre of the page.

"What in hells name did you do that for?" I yelled in exasperation.

Her voice carrying its usual tone of measured determination, she answered.

"Because I don't think Stuart Palmer deserves the privilege of any of his daughters carrying his name."

I stood motionless, unable to speak as she continued.

"He's a disgrace to fatherhood and I no longer want to be called Palmer."

"But… he … I"

"I'm not a child anymore Mum and there's nothing you can say or do that will make me change my mind. "

She reached for her papers that were clenched in my trembling hand.

Victoria Jane Garwood strutted off with a clarity of mind I wished I could replicate and not such a small piece of me admired what she had done. My annoyance gradually subsided over the course of the evening as I began to realize she was dealing with her dads rejection in her own particular Victoria style. I was proud that I had raised such a strong and feisty girl, I had no concerns that she would breeze through this thing called life, with or without her estranged father.

Alexandra on the other hand had her own unique way of coping. She was more the ostrich burying her head in the sand hoping it would all go away. Whenever her Dad's name was mentioned, Alexandra maintained a dignified silence, offering no opinion either way. The only time her voice could be heard was when I had tentatively broached the subject of the house and the possibility that we might have to sell it. She was adamant she didn't want to move, her eye's filled with tears. It was the only home she'd ever known.

"If he makes us sell the house Mum, I'll never forgive him."

I was carrying that one thought in my mind too. If we didn't reach a settlement that included the house, she may not forgive me either. I panicked at the very thought because I knew that Stuart had no intention of allowing us to stay in the house, in fact I had almost resigned myself to the fact that however the settlement went, we would have to sell up. Even if an agreement was reached today, I knew I would be coming home with the news that would break Alexandra's heart.

I'd arranged to meet John and Louise at the Saxtons office. John had made it clear on more than one occasion that it was imperative we were at the court an hour before the hearing. Clearly he was getting wise to my timekeeping and I knew the underlying reason for him wanting me to meet them at their office was to ensure that I was walking into the court at the same time as him and Louise and not lagging behind by half an hour.

It had been a race against time to get there, but after a quick shower and gulping down a cup of strong black coffee I had managed to pull things together and miraculously I was sitting in Saxtons' reception in full view of the emotionless Karen, dead on 11.15.

Karen greeted me with her usual dead pan face and wasted no time ringing through to John to let him know I was waiting for him in reception.

"Mr Bennett has asked me to show you to the client room and offer you some refreshments."

I laughed inwardly. I could have made my own way to the bloody Saxtons' client room blindfolded I had been there so many times. However, we followed the steadfast Saxton protocol and she led the way. I sat in my usual chair beneath the giant ticking clock.

"What would you like to drink Mrs Palmer, tea, coffee?"

"Nothing thanks Karen," I said, "we are due in court soon. I should imagine Mr Bennett will be here soon."

Karen glanced at her watch.

"Yes, he shouldn't be too long. He had an unexpected visit from his wife, that's the reason he is running a little late."

Had I heard her correctly, did she say wife?

Without thinking the words dribbled out of my mouth, immediately I had wanted to retract them.

"Ex-wife I think you mean."

Pan faced, Karen gave me her first insipid smile.

"No Mrs Palmer, it's definitely his current wife though he does have two ex-wives somewhere. Perhaps you picked him up wrong."

I sat stunned. I hadn't picked him up wrong, I remembered his words with clarity.

I'd asked him about his wife and he'd answered quite clearly. That ship sailed a long time ago Annette. I find myself just like you, all alone at sea.

A nauseas feeling started to build up in the pit of my stomach. What the hell had I been doing?

Karen's voice was still bland and without feeling yet her deliverance had hit its intended target and had managed to knock me for six.

"He'll be here shortly Mrs Palmer, don't worry," she said, as she walked through the door.

Somehow I had the feeling Karen knew exactly what she was doing. It might have been my imagination yet my intuition told me deep down in her cold heart, her mission had been accomplished. Now I was left to fish through the debris of the knowledge that all these months he had led me to believe that his relationship with his wife was over. The bastard!

Alone in the room, panic swept over me as my stomach tightened. I was starting to drown in my own guilt. Me, the self-righteous Annette Palmer was doing to another woman exactly what Angela Maddison had done to me. How could I forgive myself and what about my kids? If they ever found out, how could they ever respect me again? I had already been less than honest with them about my relationship with John. They knew we'd been out for dinner and he'd been around to the house, but they had no idea that their meek mother had turned into some sex starved maniac desperately luring her solicitor around to their home at every available opportunity.

I held my head in my hands and fought back the tears. How pathetic can one woman be? I wondered how many lies John had told his wife and had she, like me, been gullible enough to be taken in by them. With my head almost exploding my gut instinct was to cut and run out of the office and get as far away from John Bennett as I possibly could, but before I had another moment to think, the door swung open and he and Louise stood in the door way.

"Sorry you've had to wait Annette," he said, "we need to dash. I'll run over things when we get to court."

I sat for a moment unable to move.

"What's wrong Annette? You look like you've just seen a ghost."

I eased myself slowly to my feet. It took a great deal of effort but it took even more not to slam my fist into his face.

"Is everything okay?"

Is everything okay? I wanted to say. Do you know what I've fucking been through? Do you know how much I've suffered because of what my husband did to me behind my back?

And my solicitor, my rock, my knight in shining armour, Mr Integrity has been doing exactly the same fucking thing.

I'd poured my heart out to him, told him the pain and suffering I'd gone through because of my husband. He'd made me feel worthless, unattractive, thrown me away like a used handkerchief, a worthless machine, long past its sell by date. I'd told him all of this and more.

My anger was building.

"Annette say something."

I smiled.

"It's nothing John, it's just that I'm not exactly looking forward to this."

I'd bide my time. It wasn't the right place and it certainly wasn't the right day to confront him with the bombshell that had been dropped firmly in my lap. Today was about me and the girls, it was a fight, the biggest scrap I had ever been involved in and I had to focus for the sake of my family to see that we got what we were entitled too.

He placed a hand on my arm. I tensed up in disgust.

"I understand," he said.

He handed a large box file to Louise and she took it from him.

"C'mon, let's get going, we don't want to keep the judge waiting. That wouldn't do at all."

And like the proverbial lap dog I followed him without further question.

The trip to the court had been an arduous one. My face was like thunder and even Louise had little success in getting any conversation out of me. I wondered if John was oblivious to my disposition because as always he rambled on regardless, his eyes seeking mine through the rear view mirror as I sat slumped in the back seat, arms crossed in front of me in an attempt to quell my fury. For Christ's sake we'd fucked in his wife's bed, how bad was that? I thought back to that fateful night of passion and realised what a devious bastard he'd been. There was no signs of a wife in that house, no photographs, no clothes, nothing. He was good, I'd give him that because I'd suspected nothing.

His voice managed to pick its way through my thoughts and draw me back to the moment. "Can you hear me in the back Annette, you're very quiet?"

I nodded.

He continued.

"I was saying we need to be at the court an hour before we go before the Judge, he will expect both parties to have put forward our best offers to each other before we go into his chambers. To be honest it's an exercise in negotiation, think of me as your own Herb Cohen."

He laughed while I glared at him.

"Sorry?" I said, my voice totally flat.

Louise piped in clearly understanding the underlying joke.

"Ignore him Annette, John flatters himself that his negotiating skills compare to the world renowned negotiator Herb Cohen."

I stared blankly at Louise. It was lost on me. Who the fuck was Herb Cohen? Shouldn't he be comparing himself to Hugh Hefner, the world renowned womanizer?

My own guilt trip kicked in as we approached the courts. Should I have been asking more questions? When was the split? What had happened? Who wronged who? In reality I'd asked nothing because I didn't want to know.

We pulled into the car park near the court building, parked up and got out of the car. John continued to talk as we walked towards the court house.

"Are you sure you're okay Annette? I've never seen you this nervous."

"I'm okay," I said, "just let's get this over with."

He stopped dead in his tracks and turned to face me as he stretched two hands out and placed them on my shoulders. To say it was an uncomfortable moment would have been the understatement of the year. He looked me in the eye the way he did when he normally kissed me and for a second that's exactly what I thought he was about to do. I could see Louise in my line of vision. She was displaying a mixture of confusion and embarrassment.

"Annette," he said. "I'm here for you, I'm here to look after you and don't you ever forget that."

Louise about turned and started to walk towards the entrance, she could stand it no longer.

"You're truly here for me?" I questioned.

"I am," he said.

I placed both hands on top of his and removed them from my shoulders. I placed them by his side and pointed towards the court building.

"Let's go then Mr Solicitor, it's what every woman could ever wish for."

"What's that?" he asked with a frown.

"A man like you by her side."

He grinned a big Cheshire cat, schoolboy grin.

The sarcasm was lost on him completely and at that exact moment in time I questioned just how intelligent my wonderful solicitor was.

26

We walked through security and as usual the foyer was buzzing with people waiting around. The scene had become all too familiar to me and I was now practically oblivious to it, especially today when both my mind and body wanted to be anywhere other than that building.

Louise did the usual task of finding a client conference room and almost immediately John made himself scarce as he went on the hunt for the other side. Louise tried her best to strike up a conversation.

"Are you nervous Annette? You seem quiet," she said cautiously, not wanting to be too invasive with her questioning.

"Oh I'm fine," I said offering her a smile as reassurance.

"You never know," she said, "at the end of today it might be all over."

I fixed yet another weak smile on my face.

"Let's hope so."

The words were barely out of my mouth when I looked up and John was walking back into the room. I was grateful that he had ended the stilted conversation. His smile had disappeared. He was in work mode because I now recognized the look of determination fixed across his face. It was the same expression I'd seen on all of our other court visits, as if he had flicked a switch and morphed into another person.

He took out a handkerchief and mopped at his brow.

"Mr Palmer has brought a barrister along. They call him Bentley."

I think I detected a glint in his eye, clearly he was enjoying the prospect of a fight with a different opponent. For the first time since we had left the Saxtons' office, I was engaged, my mind focused once again on the hearing, instead of my fucked up love life.

"Stuart has a barrister? Should I be worried?" I asked. "Should I have had one too?"

John was clearly hurt by the remark, his face couldn't disguise the fact that my comment had wounded him for a fraction of a second but it didn't take long for him to bounce back. I was slowly realizing that John had a confidence and an underlying arrogance about him."

The look on his face said it all.

He smiled a smug smile of conceit.

"You don't need a barrister Annette, you have me."

Every part of me wanted to slap his face there and then and challenge him about his wife. I took a deep breath and counted to three. I stopped myself… just. I had to focus. First of all I needed to get rid of the other waste of space clogging up my life, Stuart Palmer. Perhaps it would be my lucky day and I might get rid of both of the bastards, kill two birds with one stone. It was with that thought in mind that I was prompted to give the response he was expecting to hear. I would leave his ego intact to fight my case.

"Yes I do have you John," I gushed, "what a lucky girl I am."

He smiled, completely taken in as he stood there motionless basking in false adulation. I had given the correct response and he turned his attention back to the case. He looked at his notes.

"We could wait for the other side to make their opening offer or we could set out our stall, go in high of course and see what they come back with."

I wasn't sure if he was seeking a response from me. Surely this should have all been decided back at the office?

His eye's lifted to meet my gaze before answering his own rhetorical question.

"I think we'll wait for Mr Bentley to come to us. Let's see where they want to start before we jump in with both feet."

He handed a piece of A4 paper to Louise and turned to face me again.

"In an ideal world Annette, what are your expectations on what you want to walk away with?"

That was an easy one. The house of course. I wanted to go home and tell my daughter that we didn't have to move out of the family home.

"The house," I said. "I want to keep our house, plus I'll need maintenance for a period of time until I can get myself sorted with a job, perhaps when Alexandra is a little older."

They knew what I wanted, it had all been written down in the Statement of Affairs which was now sitting in front of the Judge. Alexandra's face swamped my thoughts every time the subject of the house came up. How could I tell her it would have to be sold? How could we take away the foundations she had built her life on?

Both Louise and John looked at me as if I was asking for the moon. I knew it was a ball buster, a one which Stuart was unlikely to agree to.

John, clearly thinking a pie chart would be the best way of giving me a reality check and bring me back into the real world, drew a circle with a line vertically down to the middle and then another line horizontally.

"You see Annette, if you take your assets in their entirety, well over three quarters are in the house and the pensions. What's left are the investments, cash in bank accounts, the art work and other valuables."

I knew exactly what he was getting at.

He pointed to the pie chart.

"This small section represents your liquid investments, the larger section the equity in the house and the pension funds. It's unlikely a Judge is going to allow you to keep the family marital home because Mr Palmer will argue he needs sufficient liquid funds to buy his own home. As you are aware, a pension fund can't be liquidated and the only way to give Mr Palmer anywhere near what they are asking for is to sell the house and utilise the equity."

His voice was sympathetic yet the underlying tone suggested I would be fighting a losing battle. The gentle tap on the door stopped our conversation dead in its tracks. John immediately picked up his note pad.

"That will be Bentley, he must be opening up the negotiations."

He kicked back his chair as he rose to his feet quickly and made his way out of the room desperate to see what was on offer. For some reason my heart began to pound, the room was silent and calm, yet inside my head there was a war breaking out. Within ten minutes he was back in the room and shaking his head in a show of disbelief.

"Well," he stalled as if lost for words, "as I anticipated he has started low, very low. He believes it should be an equal split for everything. He wants a clean break, capitalizing any potential maintenance payments by giving you an extra five per cent of the house sale and all other assets."

John's head was still shaking as he slumped back in his chair.

"I've told Bentley to put our opening offer to his client, I've said you want to keep the house and five years maintenance at £2000 per month. He can keep all other investments and assets and his pension funds remains intact. I'll give it a few minutes then I will go back and tell him you've rejected Mr Palmers offer."

His eyes glanced towards me as if awaiting my agreement.

"Yes, that's what I want in an ideal situation, the house and a reasonable maintenance payment. Let's start there."

I was aware that my voice was flat, matching my demeanor when usually just being with John could ignite a spark in me and rekindle a passion that I thought I had long since lost. Today not even his hypnotic voice could stir me. It was as if I had been doused with a bloody big water cannon and the flames of passion had been well and truly extinguished leaving only smoldering embers.

We continued to wait in the small, airless room, John and Louise going over every conceivable permutation of figures that could possibly be brought to the negotiating table as a viable solution for a settlement. I only half listened, it was early days but already I knew Stuart wasn't going to give an inch, he'd come prepared for a fight, in fact he'd come more than prepared, he'd added a barrister as his corner man. They were expecting me to seriously consider his derisory terms. I could accept them and get on with my life or I could fight. Stuart was gambling on thinking I didn't have the stomach for a fight. Going to a final hearing would cost me dearly, not only financially but emotionally and I had to ask myself was I ready for the fight? Already it was slowly sapping the life out of me and todays revelation about Mrs Bennett had hit me like a right hook. Should I cut my losses, walk away and just get on with things?

Another gentle tap at the door. I looked up and John was on his feet once more and then he was gone again. When he walked back into the room he didn't hold back, he was direct and to the point.

"Palmer has rejected our offer. He will not entertain you keeping the house, let alone pay maintenance. It's a stalemate."

The Mexican standoff continued, neither party willing to shift from their stance. The room reflected the tension, it was still and silent. My mind was racing once more and my heart pumping as I contemplated the prospect of agreeing a settlement. I wanted to settle but could I bring myself to accept an offer knowing that he was being less than honest about his income and savings and more to the point could I face going home to my girls saying we had to sell the house?

The silence and my personal torment was eventually broken by the crackling tannoy in the corner of the room.

Palmer, can you make your way to Judge's Chambers please.

Louise, as usual, scurried about collecting papers whilst John took his time, first straightening his jacket then his tie. I could see he was psyching himself up for the battle.

He took a deep breath and smiled.

"Let's get on with it ladies."

We walked in to the chamber and the three men team were already seated, Stuart propped in the middle, Bentley, his new bully boy sitting to the right of him and Steedman to the left. Not surprisingly, neither Steedman or Stuart looked in our direction as we entered the room, their eyes were fixed to the floor. But not Bentley. His eyes locked on me as soon as I entered the room, clearly he wanted to see what all the fuss was about, why the gloves were off and the fight so dirty. I met Bentley's gaze head on, my stubborn pride wouldn't allow me to recoil away from his glare and equally I wanted the measure of him. He had a sharp, uncompromising look, sunken cheek bones, sallow skin and black hawk eyes which bore into me. He was trying to put me under pressure, intimidate me, he wanted me to look away, round one to him and a huge psychological advantage.

I couldn't help myself.

"What are you looking at?" I asked.

He was lost for words, his jaw fell open. Has she just said that he thought to himself?

"Sorry…I … nothing."

Round one to me. But even so alarm bells were now ringing in my head. There was something about him that unsettled me.

We took our seats. My fixation on the opposition had not only unnerved me, it had distracted me. There was a fleeting silence before

Judge Blake introduced himself. The Judge made it clear he didn't need a rundown of events, stating he had familiarized himself with his copy of the court bundle cover to cover. John, who had been sitting poised on the edge of his chair was about to make an attempt at outlining events. He'd barely managed to get two words out of his mouth before Judge Blake cut in, his voice bright and eager with no hint of the cynicism I'd often heard in his predecessors

"I've read the chronology and the case summary Mr Bennett, I think we can move on."

His eyes glanced at the bundle of papers as his fingers flicked through each page like it was one of those flick books we played with as children. But in this file there was no matchstick character on each piece of paper creating the movement of the image with the speed of the flick, it was just the documented life of Mr and Mrs Palmer passing through his fingers.

As I watched his movements, I could hear his voice, upbeat and bright, directing proceedings.

"Can we move directly to the settlement please? Have both parties managed to reach an agreement?"

His eyes scanned the table like a hawk, the open ended question had been thrown into the air and it was Bentley who caught it first. John slumped back in his chair as his opponent held court. It was the first time the sound of Bentley's voice had touched my ears apart from his initial stumble. This time he hadn't been caught by surprise and although his voice had a slow drawling pace with no defined pitch, it oozed confidence and professionalism and it unnerved me.

"My client is looking for a clean break Sir, however Mr Palmer is not unsympathetic to Mrs Palmers plight, he is aware that she will need a period of time to retrain before she seeks paid employment. On that basis my client accepts Mrs Palmer will require maintenance for a reasonable period of time."

How magnanimous I thought to myself as his slow drawl headed towards the punch line.

"Mr Palmer wishes to capitalize the maintenance, moving the split of all the joint assets to 55% in favour of the applicant and the remaining 45% to my client."

Bentley slowly recited the valuation of all the assets listed on the schedule.

"Joint assets including pension funds amount to £968.053.16."

Bentley, a man clearly economical with his words, didn't drag his presentation out, he'd pitched his offer and his work was done for the moment. His dark pitted eyes made a courteous glance towards the judge before resting on John. Now it was our opportunity to show our hand.

Since coming into the room I had been trying to avoid eye contact with John. I was still fuming and having to look at him only heightened my anger. Yet now he was on the stage and in full glare of his audience, I was drawn to watch his performance. Unlike Bentley, who didn't exude showmanship, John had an element of theatrics in his performance and definitely wasn't economical with his words. But, he didn't wade in to push our terms, he wanted to set the scene, get the Judge onside and conjure up some sympathy and drama. He started with all the shortcomings of Stuart's disclosure. It was all in the case summary of course that the Judge had at hand, yet it didn't stop John reiterating it.

"It has been difficult for my client to propose a settlement figure as she believes the assets Mr Palmer has declared are not an accurate reflection of their joint assets. Mr Palmer has already disposed of considerable sums of money after the separation, including £50000 from a savings account. Mr Palmer has failed to provide my client with his actual earnings for the current year even though we have repeatedly asked for the information, nor has he detailed any share holdings."

His eyes moved from Stuart to the judge as he continued to berate the opposition.

"At best Mr Palmer has been economical with the truth, at worst he has lied."

As much as I was still seething with him, at that moment I found myself admiring his gung-ho enthusiasm as he listed Stuart's shortcomings. He didn't hold back. He continued his onslaught, citing how Stuart had turned his back on his children, moving in with his girlfriend whilst insisting that he was living in his aunts property and paying a premium rate to do so. I watched my ex-husband's reaction as John prodded away, his relaxed posture becoming more rigid as the assault continued.

Judge Blake had been patiently waiting in the wings, anticipating a suitable break. Once he found it he stepped in, his enthused voice now carrying a hint of frustration beneath its upbeat exterior.

"Mr Bennett, could you get to the point. What is Mrs Palmer looking for by way of settlement?"

I knew John wasn't the least bit optimistic that I had any chance of keeping the family home, yet it didn't stop him from presenting his argument with a conviction that could only lead his audience to believe he meant every word of it.

Under my direction he presented my terms and admittedly, even to my own ears, they sounded unreasonable. Why did they sound unreasonable? Who had pushed me to that conclusion? Why shouldn't we be allowed to stay in our family home. Was that too much to ask?

"My client shall remain in the family matrimonial home and continue to receive maintenance on an ongoing basis. In exchange, Mr Palmer will keep the entirety of his pension fund, cash in his company drawings account which currently stands at £40000, all other investments and the valuable art work."

I thought about the pie chart. Approximately 70/30.

Bentley was pitching at 55/45. We were miles apart. Bentley had sat mute since he had presented his clients settlement proposal but could keep his council no longer. The knot in my stomach tightened as he spoke.

"It is totally unreasonable for Mrs Palmer to expect to keep the marital family home. Mr Palmer is currently living in rented accommodation and is dependent on his share of the sale of the house to purchase his own property. He works on a self-employed basis and his income cannot be guaranteed."

Then he pulled out his trump card, the one I'd been waiting for him to play since Steedman first mentioned it months previously.

"As for maintenance payments, Mr Palmer has made a very generous five percent concession to Mrs Palmer, one of the reasons being he has a degenerative eye condition which may well stop him from working in the future."

I glanced at John waiting for his response, none was forthcoming. For Christ sake John retaliate. The judge beat him to it.

"Mr Bentley, your clients idea of a 55/45 split in the applicants favour and no maintenance whatsoever is not in my opinion an appropriate offer and not acceptable to the court."

Had he just said that? A warm pleasant feeling welled up inside of me. Was the Judge siding with me?

For a moment I hung on his statement. Could I dare to dream that we might just be staying in our house, the only home my girls had ever known?

It was short lived however as he turned and stared at me.

"At the same time it is wholly wrong for Mrs Palmer to have the former matrimonial home in its entirety. There has to be a significant transfer of capital to Mr Palmer and I can see no other way to do that than to put the house up for sale."

My whole body slumped forward. I felt like bursting into tears.

His hands rested on the bundle of papers as he picked a couple of sheets up and studied them. Everyone sat in silence blankly staring at walls and floors.

The Judge continued.

"I would like both parties to take another half an hour to try and reach an agreement. I do not expect either party to come back into this room without having reconsidered their offers. It is imperative that both sides move from their current stance. As a guidance to where you should be heading, I would expect Mr Palmer to be paying periodical payments to Mrs Palmer but whether this is capitalized is for the respondent to decide. I would also expect these payments to be not less than three years yet no more than five and furthermore, I think a starting point for the split of all assets should be 60/40 in Mrs Palmer's favour."

He started to gather his papers together.

"We'll adjourn for thirty minutes. I expect in that time that you both make a concerted effort to reach a settlement," he said in a scolding voice.

We shuffled out of the chamber in silence, neither party wanting to be in ear shot of the other before a word was spoken. Stuart and his team rushed ahead of us and scurried out of the room, the chitter of their voices carrying through the otherwise empty silence of the outer chamber. Only when we were back in our airless box of a room did John let his voice be heard.

"Well what did you think of that? The question is how much weight do you put on the Judges opinion? He cannot enforce this judgement, he can only give us an indication of what judgement he would make if it went to a final hearing."

I listened as he summarized what had taken place in the court. Usually in times like this John was the one reassuring voice that could calm me yet today he irritated me, his presence in that small, characterless room was getting on my nerve endings.

"I think I'll have to concede the house," I said, my voice almost on the brink of cracking. "The judge is adamant I wouldn't get it so let's try and reach a settlement that mirrors his suggestion."

John picked up his notepad and his calculator which he seemed to rely on to do the simplest of calculations. He started to tap away.

"Ok, if we say that you want £2000 per month for five years, that give us…"

Usually out of politeness I would let him continue tapping his calculator but not today.

"You don't need to work it out John, it's £120000."

"Quite," he said, "so it is Annette."

"Well, if we say to capitalize maintenance at £120000 and accept that they might knock us down to four years, would you take the 60/40 split plus an additional £96000?

He looked up from his scribbles to gauge my reaction. I nodded in agreement.

"Then I think we should go for a 65/35 split on all other assets. They'll want to knock us down a little so let's concede five percent.

Once again I nodded in agreement, yet the truth was I wasn't sure. The house and the thought of selling it was still lingering in my mind. What would I say to Alexandra, that I'd caved in, I'd conceded defeat?

It was too late. John rose eagerly from his chair and quickly exited the room to find the other side once more. Louise filled the gap with light conversation. I could do nothing but bury my head in my hands. My stomach was doing summersaults in anticipation that maybe this was it. I'd conceded to everything the Judge had asked, surely it was a matter of a formality that the other side would do likewise. Moments later John burst back into the room, his head already shaking. Clearly it wasn't good news.

"I started at sixty five percent and then dropped to sixty but they won't go with it, nor are they willing to even talk about maintenance."

I was confused.

"But we've all heard the Judge's opinion. 60/40 he said plus maintenance of between three and five years. If I've agreed that then surely they should be doing the same?"

John sighed.

"In an ideal world Annette, yes."

I couldn't believe it. I was tearing my hair out. What sort of legal system was this, what the fuck was the point in a Judge being here at all?

It was a game, a big stupid corrupt game, a game dragged out for the sole purpose of creating wealth for lawyers, barristers, judges and their hangers on.

"Go back John, I'll go 60/40 only if I get the maintenance. I am not going to forfeit both the house and the maintenance."

John looked at his watch, the half hour was almost up and he wasted no time dashing out of the room in one last attempt to reach an agreement. Five minutes later he was back shaking his head once more.

"The bastards won't budge an inch, I can't understand them."

We marched back into Judge Blake's chambers. He was already sitting at the helm and got straight to the point.

"Have both parties reached an agreement?" he asked, surveying the room once more, looking for a response from either party.

It was John who delivered the news.

"Unfortunately Sir, we have not reached an agreement. Mr Palmer's barrister is unwilling to even talk about any maintenance."

The judge looked exasperated and then his face took on an altogether different look, that of sheer anger.

He turned to Bentley.

"Mr Palmer is going to be paying maintenance Mr Bentley, I can assure you of that and I would expect it to be in the region of £1500 a month."

Bentley turned to Stuart and they spoke in whispers for no more than a few seconds. Stuart was shaking his head. I knew Stuart well enough to know he wouldn't budge on his decision.

Bentley spoke.

"I'm sorry sir, but my client sees no valid reason why his wife can't work to support herself."

The judge continued to direct his criticism at the other side as the three men sat looking anywhere but directly at the Judge. He looked down at his notes.

"Then do we have an agreement on the asset split?"

John couldn't get to his feet quick enough.

"My client is happy to go with your recommendation Sir, a 60/40 split but only if she receives maintenance payments either monthly or capitalized."

I had to admit that it was a big play from John. He sat down smugly, knowing what would pan out next.

The judge looked at Bentley.

"And your client is happy with that Mr Bentley?"

For the first time Bentley looked lacking in confidence, almost lost for words. The drama was building. Had Stuart at least conceded to that?

"No Sir. My client will not concede to a 60/40 split. He feels it is unreasonable."

The judge looked furious. He glanced at his watch, his voice now raised. "I am going to adjourn for another thirty minute break and I want both parties to try and use that time to reach a settlement"

John, unable to resist made a valid point.

"Mr Palmer is categorically unwilling to move on maintenance payments Sir, is there any point?"

The Judge saw red.

"Point Mr Bennett, point! There is every point in trying to avoid a costly final hearing. Have either of you thought about how much this could cost you if it did go to a final hearing?"

He looked directly at Stuart, his voice increasing further as he struggled to conceal his ever growing frustration.

"Has it crossed your mind Mr Palmer that the amount you are fighting over could easily be swallowed up in costs if your case goes to a final hearing?"

His voice was now full of rage, his angry glare swinging from Bentley to Bennett in a non-discriminative manor.

"Mr Bentley, has your client been given an estimate of the cost if the case should go to a final hearing? Can you share it with us?"

Bentley looked vacantly at Steedman who until that point had had so little input in the whole event he was practically snoozing in his chair. Clearly pulling a figure out of midair Steedman offered his best guess estimate.

"I believe that it could cost in excess £10000 Sir."

Without adding to the statement the judge rested his line of vision directly onto John.

"And you Mr Bennett, how much do you think it will cost your client to go to a final hearing?"

I was confused. Why was he having a go at us? I had agreed to what the judge had suggested.

"About the same Sir," John answered.

I could have leaned across the table and quite happily strangled Stuart Palmer. On top of everything he had done to me he was going to take another twenty grand out of the equation through his sheer, pig headed, stubbornness. Hadn't he heard the Judge? 60/40 he had said, maintenance payments he had said and yet my arsehole of a husband knew better. What sort of advice was he paying for? Surely his Barrister should have urged him to settle on the Judge's recommendations?

We marched out of the room a final time back into our airless pit.

John was the first to break the silence.

"What are your thoughts Annette? Do you feel like conceding any more ground?"

"What?"

"This is our final chance, "he said.

In truth I had none other than an overwhelming urge to get out of that bloody building as quick as I could. I was physically and mentally tired from the events of the whole day, from Karen dropping the bombshell that John was married to the toing and froing in the Judge's Chambers. I was exhausted, I could barely think straight, yet in my heart of hearts I knew one thing. I had conceded enough and furthermore an independent Judge had drawn the line in the sand and I would not go beyond it. For Christ's sake I had conceded the family home, what more did the bastard want? No, the Judge had said maintenance payments and I would not walk away from the court without an agreement.

"No John, I'm not prepared to move another inch, if we go to a final hearing so be it, but that's it."

I was adamant. I had reached my base line and either grit, pride, stubbornness or a little bit of everything wouldn't allow me to concede another penny.

John sighed as he arranged his papers.

"Oh well, who knows, perhaps Bentley and Steedman have talked some sense into him this time."

John didn't know Stuart like I did. I knew he wouldn't budge an inch and he didn't. The time in that little, dingy office had been wasted as we sat strumming our fingers and John bounced his pen off his note pad as he usually did when he was bored. Eventually we made our way back into Judge Blake's court for the final time. He listened in silence, shaking his head as both John and Bentley attentively argued why their stance had not changed. He looked at us in total disbelief, yet he too admitted defeat. In his opinion Mr Palmer was £100000 out on maintenance and about £50000 on the asset split based on the facts presented before him. On the face of it I should have been happy as he concluded my ex-husband's shortfall but I wasn't. The facts that had been presented before him were rigged. I knew the real income, I knew about the hidden money and the shares and the fact that he was living with his girlfriend and had no intention of buying his own home. These were the facts which that never come to light. I also knew just how ill his mother was. Surely it was just a matter of time before Stuart became a very wealthy man and me and the girls wouldn't see a penny of it.

We walked down the court steps, having been in the building most of the day. The dusky light seemed in sharp contrast to the bright winter sun we had left behind on entering the building several hours prior.

"Well Annette, you shall have your day in court after all." John said, his voice bright and cheerful.

I looked at him, wanting to slap the smugness from his face. No wonder he was happy, we'd just agreed another ten grand minimum for his crooked firm. Not today, not now, I wouldn't slap him because all of my energy had been drained from me. I would save it for another time, a different time when I could hit the cheating bastard so hard I would knock him into the middle of next week.

27

When I arrived back home from court it was almost dark. As the taxi pulled up outside my front door, I knew the girls were already home as both cars were in the driveway and the house was lit up like a beacon. Strangely though, today it was a sight I welcomed and I couldn't wait to pay the driver and fall into the cushioned security of the place I called home. As I expected, the three of them were in the kitchen eagerly waiting for me. Their eyes locked on me in anticipation as I entered the room. I was feeling tired and bedraggled after the day's events and took a deep breath as I reached the kitchen table, pulled out a chair and flopped down into it. I knew they wanted a blow by blow account of what had happened yet the truth was I didn't have the stomach to dredge over it all and yet I knew I would have to fill them in with at least some of the major points. But not right at this minute, I just wanted to change my clothes and pour myself a strong drink. As a pacifier I offered them the briefest of synopsis in an attempt to abate their hunger for information.

I looked up from the table as they hung on patiently. I shrugged my shoulders.

"Not much to tell, we didn't settle, the Judge said your Dad was over £100000 out on his offer."

I shrugged my shoulders again and leaned back in the seat and let out a long sigh.

Victoria was the first to pitch in.

"You look tired Mum. Are you alright?"

"Yes I'm fine," I said, lying, as I took the opportunity to take my jacket off.

I stood up and dismounted from my stiletto heels which were now killing my feet.

"I just need to get changed and have five minutes. It's been a long day."

Alexandra stood behind me and started to rub my shoulders. Her soft hands were welcoming as I felt the tension leaving my body.

I couldn't tell them the whole story of course, the other reason I was so wound up, why I felt so low. They could never know that the man their mother had been screwing at every conceivable opportunity was married and now a big part of the reason why I was looking so dejected. But that aside, it didn't detract from the fact that their own father was the biggest arse hole on the planet, a man who had not only dragged me to court and put me through this ordeal, but was refusing to make his family a realistic offer on the day. It wasn't my settlement, it was theirs too, his daughters, his own flesh and blood.

The depth of my distress would have to remain locked within me. They would only ever know the edited version. I had to get away upstairs and change, think through what I was about to tell them when Abigail stopped me as I started to walk towards the door.

"So what happened Mum? You can't just drop a bombshell like that and walk away, we have a right to know."

She was right of course. They did have a right to know, they were no longer little children who I could fob off. I sat back down at the kitchen table.

I looked at Abigail and smiled.

"First things first," I said. "You'll have to indulge me with a large Baileys. I need one like never before."

Abigail moved quickly. She lifted a glass from the bench top, pushed a few ice cubes in and poured a generous measure of Baileys over the top.

She handed me the glass and I took it straight to my mouth and consumed a large measure. The exquisite cool liquid hit the spot almost immediately. I looked up, smiled and took another mouthful.

The girls sat down at the table almost in unison. It was time to relay the theatrics of the day, there was no escape route.

I went through the figures not leaving anything out. I explained how we had all been ostracized by the judge, how I'd backed down and agreed to what he had suggested but how their father hadn't budged an inch and flatly refused to pay maintenance even though the judge had told him he'd have no option.

Eventually I got to the story's conclusion. I looked at Alexandra and fought hard to keep control of my bottom lip which was vibrating like it had a life of its own.

"The bottom line is that your Dad is unwilling to let us stay in the house. The house makes up the bulk of the assets and has to be sold so that he can purchase a house of his own."

I glanced at Alexandra trying to gauge her response. She'd been unusually quiet the last few days and gave no hint of her thoughts in her facial expression. Her elbows remained on the table, whilst her head rested in her hands as she passively listened on.

The other girls weren't so calm.

"The bastard," Abigail said. "He'll have a home when his mother kicks the bucket and God knows that won't be long."

"Two homes," Alexandra piped up. "don't forget Aunty Peggy. Her flat is as good as his anyway and that's where he claims to be moving into once the improvements are completed."

Alexandra lifted her head from her hands and spoke softly.

"He'll have three homes."

We all looked at her in silence.

"His Mum's, his Auntie's and where he's living now," she paused for a second. "The bitch's house."

The silence was deafening as the enormity of the unfairness of the situation sank in. Alexandra was right. He'd have three houses to choose from and yet he was more than willing to kick us out of the only family home we had ever known. I looked around my beautiful kitchen, the kitchen that we had sat in as a family for twenty three years. I looked at the view from the window, the strategically placed solar lights had kicked in. And then I looked back to my beautiful girls, angry, devoid of hope. Hope for their mother.

Once the first tear fell it was like an avalanche I couldn't cap. The girls were all up off their chairs buzzing around, consoling me as best they could.

Victoria was the first to burst in with her logical advice.

"Mum you have to do what's best for you and Alexandra at the end of the day, me and Abigail are barely at home these days."

Between the tears I managed to blurt out a sentence.

"It looks like we'll be going to a final hearing, God only knows how I'm going to afford it."

My voice cracked along with my spirit, broken by the day's events. I reached for the Baileys bottle again as I started to go into melt down.

Abigail spoke this time.

"If you want to fight on, you've got my support but don't feel you have to do it for us, we don't need his bloody money."

Her response was fueled with her usual pent up emotions. Of all three girls, the hurt her Dad and Grandmother had inflicted on her appeared to have cut the deepest.

"Let the bastard keep his money."

The venom in her voice was almost tangible yet within an instant she reverted back to the gentle tone I was used to hearing.

"Sorry for swearing Mum, but that man gets me so angry."

We were all aware that Alexandra, at this point had lifted herself from her chair.

"I'm tired mum," she said, "I'm going to bed to watch some television."

We sat in silence as she slowly left the room, clutching a glass of juice in her hand. My youngest daughter was broken too, she had no heart for a fight and it was clear she had no intention of having any more input in the conversation. Despite her lack of words she couldn't have made it any clearer, she had accepted the inevitable and was truly devastated.

I spoke with Abigail and Victoria for about an hour but eventually they left me alone with my thoughts.

I spent the remainder of the night sat on the sofa alone, the unwatched TV blaring in the background, a glass gripped tightly in my hand. I'd already polished off a bottle of Sauvignon Blanc, drank what was left of the Baileys and had now started on the remains of a bottle of gin I'd found collecting dust in the bottom of the kitchen cupboard.

Admittedly gin tasted better with tonic but as I had none in the house, diet coke had sufficed and to my drunken palate it turned out to be an agreeable alternative.

My emotions were raw and the alcohol wasn't helping the situation. Thoughts of both John and Stuart were spinning around my head at the same pace as the room. They were both number one prize bastards I thought to myself and I couldn't escape Alexandra's analogy of the three houses my ex-husband would have at his disposal while we would have none.

It was all so bloody unfair.

To escape the three house torment I drowned myself in yet more alcohol and eventually everything became a blur, even the television screen.

It was in the midst of those lost hours I made the cardinal sin of thinking the most appropriate way of expressing myself was by texting the two men who had been the catalyst of my drunken stupor. Rooting out my phone that had become wedged down the sofa I thumbed through the contact list. My eyes could barely focus as I tapped out the letters of my messages on the key pad.

It all seemed so perfectly logical and clear in that moment in time, they needed to know exactly what I thought of them. The first of my messages was sent to John and this was quickly followed by a second message to my ex-bastard husband, Stuart Palmer. It was a complex task, I could barely see the letters but once I was happy that the messages had tripped through cyber space I congratulated myself and settled back on the sofa in the company of my good friend, the gin bottle. I was totally pissed by then and eventually I passed out on the sofa.

It was the cold and my stiff neck which first made me stir. The heating system was programmed to switch off at 11pm and come back on at 6am daily. At 3am on a February morning the house was at its coldest and I woke up with my body twisted across the sofa, shivering, my hands and feet like blocks of ice.

Slowly I raised myself up. My heart was racing, my head still groggy yet sufficiently clear enough for me to realize that I needed to pick myself up and make my way to bed to find some warmth. Gradually I started to come to my senses as I stood upright and little by little the events of the day came together in my head once more. Instantly my eyes were drawn to the mobile phone which was now lying on the floor beside an empty glass that had been knocked over onto its side and the dregs pooled on to the carpet.

More memories of the evenings events started to materialise, the flashbacks becoming stronger and stronger as my eyes focused more intently on the mobile. Oh shit! Shit! Shit! Oh fucking shit, tell me it was just a dream. I reluctantly bent down and grabbed the phone. But it wasn't a dream and I knew it.

Please, please, please, don't let it say what I think it's going to say.

I pressed on my text messages and to my horror of horrors it did exactly that.

11.05pm - John Bennett:

I need to see you ASAP. I know about your wife. You bastard.

11.09pm – Stuart Palmer:

You bastard, I can't believe that you'd throw your own children out of their home . YOU FUCKING WANKER!

11.15pm Reply- John Bennett:

Annette you seem upset, I think you have the wrong end of the stick. Now is not the time to talk. I will call around tomorrow lunchtime to sort this out. x

As I climbed into my freezing cold bed early that morning, my body was still shaking from a combination of the biting cold and the shock of what I had actually done. I couldn't believe that I'd text both of them in that state. Why the hell had I done it? Especially the message to Stuart letting him know he'd got to me. I'd exposed my heart felt desire to stay in the family home and I knew he would never let it happen. He simply didn't care, there wasn't an ounce of feeling in his entire soul.

It was fair to say that sleep didn't find me for the rest of that night. I tossed and turned puffing my pillows, thrashing my restless legs around the bed unable to find a resting spot. By 7am that morning I'd given up the ghost as my daily alarm switched the news channel on the radio, my eyes were already wide open as I listened to the daily traffic report. The information filtered through my head but none of it registered. My head was filled with the two men in my life and the texts I had sent to them. And yet again I lay lifeless, like a zombie, feeling totally exhausted and dreading the day ahead.

John Bennett turned up at my front door at lunch time. He had text me early that morning enquiring if the coast would be clear that were our code words for would my children be at home.

I hadn't put him off. Alexandra was going to be at school all day which meant I had the house to myself and to that end I was grateful.

I wanted to sort it out and didn't want another day to pass with it hanging over my head.

Once he confirmed he was coming around I couldn't wait for him to arrive. I'd been holding on to this pent up anger for over twenty four hours, planning exactly what it was I was going to say and as the time drew near I was practically exploding with the need to vent my spleen. I had stationed myself at the bedroom window, looking out over the front garden, awaiting his arrival and spot on 1pm his car glided up to the front door.

As he got out of the car I leaned back into the shadow of the curtains in an attempt to hide myself from view, the last thing I wanted was for him to look up and see me standing there waiting for him like some love struck groupie. I watched his every move from the safety of my bedroom. He looked at his phone before placing it in his jacket pocket then as his heavy stride made its way up the drive to the front door, he attempted to undo the top button of his shirt. He was nervous and the starched white collar was so stiff he struggled to release the fiddly button with his fingers.

I was still smoldering away yet there was a small guilty part of me skipping in delight on seeing him. I scolded myself. What the fuck was wrong with me? As he walked slowly towards the door I bounded down the stairs. He had barely pressed the doorbell when I opened the door, greeting him with an expression of anger firmly planted across my face. John was now so familiar with my home he no longer stood on ceremony and instead he marched past me uninvited. But today his face was not wearing its usual charismatic smile, today he was donning the look I'd seen so many times in court and it unnerved and yet excited me.

"What's this all about Annette?"

His voice was calm yet displayed a slight hint of irritation behind the façade.

I didn't waste a second, unable to hold my tongue a minute longer.

"I'll tell you what it's about John, your wife and the fact that you have one. That's what this is about."

"Yes I have a wife," he replied as a deliberate puzzled look spread across his face.

"So what? he said.

I couldn't quite believe he'd just said that.

"Is there some thing you're missing here John? Do you want me to spell it out for you? You have a wife for Christ sake, one you are still living with and don't try to deny it because Karen told me and why should she lie?"

I could see he wanted to jump in and plead his defense but I wouldn't allow it. Barely stopping for breath I continued on with my relentless onslaught.

"When I asked you about your marriage you categorically stated that the ship had sailed long ago. Well, it seems to me that it hasn't and in fact it's well and truly anchored in dock. How could you lie to me especially knowing what I've been through with my husband John? How could you do that do to me after everything I've told you?"

My voice was almost screeching.

"And how could you do that to your wife?"

I could see by his expression he was taken aback. He'd only ever heard me talk to him as an emotionless client or like a love struck teenager. His brain was struggling to comprehend the fact that mild mannered Annette Palmer harboured a troubled soul, an unattractive dimension to her personality. It was far removed from the nymphomaniac persona he was normally privy to. Usually he would barely get through the front door before we were ripping each other's clothes off, desperate to make full use of the snatched time we had together.

Why hadn't I put two and two together? Of course it was snatched time, it was always exactly that, snatched stolen moments, that's all it ever was. Twenty minutes here, an hour there. Apart from one visit to a pub together and a night at his house, our affair was conducted entirely at my house when my kids were conveniently out of the way. Our time together was filled with sex and precious little else. There were never any noises of intelligent or meaningful discussions, only groans of satisfaction and laboured breathing.

I berated him for another five minutes and only when my voice had ran out of steam and there was little breath left in my lungs, did I fall silent.

He used my muteness as an inroad to state his defense. His arm reached out to draw me to him, instinctively I slapped it away.

"Don't even go there," I shouted.

His voice pleaded with me.

"Annette, please, just let me explain."

I wondered how he would talk himself out of it. What game would he play? And yet I had no doubt, if anyone could talk himself out of a situation it was John.

He hung his head slightly and lowered the tone of his voice.

"Yes I live in the same house as her, but we're not husband and wife in the truest sense."

A look of sadness now replaced the look of agitation and his eyes seemed to glass over. He was good, I would give him that, he was putting on one hell of a performance. Part of me wanted to step forward and console him and yet the other part of me sensed the acting I had seen so often in the court room. Nevertheless his voice, unfortunately for me, was still as enchanting as ever and almost too hard to resist.

"We live together for the sake of our son," he continued, "but we have our own separate lives, we don't have a sexual relationship, it's just," he paused, "well… convenient."

That old chestnut, I thought, my wife doesn't understand me has to be his next line.

"You are seriously expecting me to believe that John, for Christ sake credit me with some intelligence."

"It's true," he said, his voice pleading with me. "The only reason I have been discreet is for the sake of our son and Elizabeth Henshaw, let us not forget you're my bloody client. I can't possibly go public with our relationship until after your divorce settlement."

His head was down, the violins were well and truly playing in the background as he rolled out his selfless reasons for having an affair.

"It's only my son who keeps us together, if it wasn't for him I would be long gone. I need you Annette, it's been so good since I met you and I almost feel born again."

I was trying hard not to listen to the shit spewing from his mouth. He droned on about how hard his life was, how cold and hostile his wife was towards him and even how they ate dinner separately and at different times.

Clearly thinking he'd done enough to convince me he was telling the truth he stepped towards me as I took a step back towards the wall. He was so close, I could feel his breath against my face, smelling the familiar combination of mint and expensive cologne. My heart began to race as he tried to press his body against mine.

But my primitive instincts to oblige my sexual desires were outranked by my principles and disgust for myself and him. As my conscience came into play his touch gradually made my skin crawl and a feeling of disgust swamped me. I'd been having a sleazy, sexual affair with a married man. My instincts took over once more and I pushed him away from me and slapped him hard across the face. I offered no words, I didn't need to. I could see the look of surprise spread across his face. He thought his job was done, he thought he was home and dry, another quick fuck with Annette Palmer.

"Don't you ever touch me again," I screamed. "Don't put your fucking hands anyway near me."

Shocked at my own outburst, I lowered my voice to a whisper, its tone mocking.

"Go back to your wife John, she'll be waiting for you. You're a good fuck… she's a lucky lady."

He looked like a rabbit caught in the headlights.

He made one last attempt to win me over.

"Stop being ridiculous Annette, I'm telling you the truth."

I burst into a manic laugh, the sound so alien to me even I wondered where it had come from.

"Ridiculous John? It's you who's being ridiculous thinking I'd believe that cock and bull story for one moment."

"But Annette," he pleaded, "listen to me please, you've got this all wrong, we can make this work, we can be good together."

I took a deep breath.

"Fuck off out of my house John, there's a good boy."

His head sagged and the colour seemed to drain from his face. That was it, he had nothing else to offer. We'd never moved from the hallway and it only took me two steps to reach the front door.

He turned his head.

"But don't let your mood fester too long. Remember your case is going to a final hearing. We need all the time we can to prepare for it."

He looked around the hallway. His smooth rich tones had returned.

"You want to keep this house and I don't blame you and there's only one man who can help you do that and I don't mean that cunt of an ex-husband of yours."

Those last few words took on a hint of menace. The C word, he had never used that before. His face changed as he stepped towards me. Suddenly I wasn't so comfortable and my confident manner had deserted me. In a flash his two hands slammed into my shoulders and he pushed me hard against the wall.

"You're not fooling me for a minute you pathetic little bitch. You want me as much as I want you."

"John, please, no, get off me."

He pushed an arm across my throat and I felt the breath drain from my body. Within a split second his hand was in between my legs and he grabbed a fist full of my knickers as I struggled hard.

"I could take you any time, just remember that," he said, as he pushed harder into my throat. He pulled down hard and the thin material of my panties split in two. He held them up to my face.

"Well, well," he grinned, "Mrs Palmers knickers are off yet again."

He threw them onto the floor and stepped back as I slumped against the wall breathing hard.

He laughed.

"I'll be around tomorrow at the same time. Make sure the coast is clear."

He walked through the door and my body began to shake uncontrollably. What the hell had just happened and why had I poked the biggest stick in the world into the hornet's nest?

28

Bennett eased his car onto the driveway of his house. It was a welcome sound to his ear, the tyres crunching against the red gravel on the ground as he pulled to a halt in front of the garage door. The security sensor light perched high up on the eaves of the building burst into life, its intense beam shinning directly into the plush, leather interior of the car.

He sat for a moment, his head cushioned against the backrest of the seat and closed his eyes before taking a deep breath and exhaling slowly. He welcomed the few moments of silence, no car radio, no mobile phone, no screeching hysterical woman's voice ringing in his ears. It allowed him a little thinking time. His dramatic encounter with Annette Palmer was fresh in his mind. What a sour ending to the day. As his thoughts returned to their rendezvous in the hallway of the house she was so desperate to keep, the blood in his groin began to stir and he so wished that he had forced himself on her. Damned woman, were any of them worth the fucking effort?

He'd expected a little resistance from her, that was to be expected and he knew there would have to be some display of anger on her part in an effort to save face and retain her position as the victim. And even taking that into account, he had been more than confident that once he had turned on the charm and poured his heart out about the plight of his failed marriage she would have fallen into his arms once more, clothing cast to one side in an all too eager effort to quench her sexual thirst. Unfortunately events had not turned out as he had expected and he was at a total loss as to why his words had fallen on deaf ears. Instead of offering a shoulder to cry on she'd put up one hell of a fight. He now realized Annette Palmer was not the meek and mild vulnerable soul he'd first perceived her to be when she walked into his office all those months ago. Apart from the fact that she had turned out to be as skilled in the bedroom as any backstreet whore, he had also discovered to his cost that she had a feisty bite if provoked, but this trait wasn't so appealing and she needed to be put in her place. She was certainly full of surprises one of which was the fact she had managed to retain his interest this long, and yet he knew if it had not been for her sterling performances in the bedroom, their affair would have been over long ago.

His mind couldn't help but wander to their previous encounters, they'd found a rhythm in their sexual relations which had needed neither direction or provocation from either party and more importantly it had not yet reached the stage of being boring or tedium.

He cast a casual gaze towards the house. Reluctantly he found himself thinking of Alma and the mundaneness of their sex life. He couldn't argue that she was prepared to satisfy his conjugal rights under duress, but he knew it was rarely a voluntary act on her part and usually there was more than a hint of it being a staged performance. Her thespian skills were such that she knew when to grunt and groan in the right place in an attempt to fake orgasm and the bigger the climax normally mirrored her financial request, a holiday or repayment of a particularly high credit card.

He smiled to himself as he smugly realized the irony of the situation. Just the opposite was true in the case of Annette. He laughed out loud. She was the one turning tricks and paying him a handsome fee for the pleasure. The stupid cow. After the day's outburst he no longer had any qualms about doubling the billable hours. He would make her pay. From now on, whatever time he or his team spent on the Palmer file, the figure would be at least doubled. He had to admit, it had been a godsend having Steedman and Palmer in opposition as a double act. Those two knew how to drag the job out. His work had been that much easier knowing that every tempting piece of bait he'd dangled in front of the cantankerous twosome they'd snapped it up like two hungry piranhas. The extortionate costs for both parties were mounting up by the day.

He turned off the engine, opened the car door and climbed out. He stood and looked up at the house. Another thought permeated his mind, the little problem of Annette jumping ship. A smug smile crossed his face. There was no way he was going to give that gift horse up and she'd quickly come to her senses once she realized how difficult it would be to find another solicitor. It wouldn't take much, an odd phone call here and there to his old boy fraternity. Newcastle wasn't such a big city and any solicitors with worthy credentials were almost certain to be a part of his old boy network. It would take an hour or two of his time, no more and she'd be top of the blacklist.

No, he wasn't quite done with his rebellious client and in a strange way the day's events had only served to fuel his desire. He recalled her slapping his face and pushing him away. He instinctively raised his hand to his face brushing the light stubble on his cheek where her hand had fell. He shook his head as if trying to disengage from the memory. Slut, she'd pay for that. He leaned into the car and picked up his briefcase from the passenger seat as he slammed the car door behind him. He stepped across the drive and walked towards the front door. The house appeared to be in darkness as he walked into the hallway. He placed his briefcase on the telephone table and noticed a reflective glow radiating from the lounge. He walked towards the welcoming light and as he entered through the doorway his wife looked up from the sofa.

"Hello dear."

"Alma," he responded. "How are you?"

She nodded politely.

"Fine."

Alma turned back towards the TV. A bottle of Bollinger chilling in a cooler sat on an occasional table in front of her and she held a champagne flute in a pincer like grip. Without taking her eyes from the TV screen, she spoke.

"There's a Beef Bourguignon in the microwave, I've had mine," she said, her voice slightly softened by the alcohol.

Bennett raised his eyes to the ceiling. Fucking typical, working every hour God sends and she can't even put some food on the table. Bitch.

He lifted a glass from the drinks cabinet and poured himself a generous measure, lowered himself on the sofa.

She looked at him. "A rough day?"

"You could say that darling," he said, as he emptied half the glass into his mouth, the alcohol kicking in almost immediately.

Bennett met his wife's eyes. She is beautiful, he thought, why is she never enough?

As he left the memories of the day behind him his attention once again turned back to his wife.

"It's been a bastard of a day darling."

He reached out for her and pulled her towards him, he felt the tension in her body as she held back. Undeterred, he continued to pull her closer.

"I just need a cuddle it's been an awful day."

"Please John," she said, "I'm really not in the mood I'm watching this."

After the earlier rejection he wasn't prepared to suffer the same again. He wasn't going to take no for an answer. He reached for her glass and placed it on the coffee table. He could feel his erection growing. He wasted no time grasping the back of her head pulling it towards him and kissed her hard on the lips. Again she pulled back.

"John, for fucks sake no."

He ignored her pleas as he guided her down onto the sofa sliding his hand up her thighs. Her skin was soft to the touch, the scent of her perfume filled his nostrils. Quickly he unfastened his trousers and pushed them to the floor.

"Please John, no."

His desire was now mixed with a little rage, his desperation to release himself almost overwhelming. The fact that his wife didn't want him didn't matter in the slightest. He loved the feeling of power, knowing that she had no real choice in the matter. He wanted sex right now and at some time in the very near future she would want a bill paid. It had been the unwritten marriage vow for well over a decade.

"Mouth or pussy?"

He turned and smiled.

"I have needs, your choice darling."

She was too slow to react. A blow job was her normal preferred choice. He came quicker that way and it was altogether less hassle for her.

"Neither John, can't you see I'm watching the television."

He'd given her the chance and she hadn't taken it and within seconds he had pushed her face down onto the arm of the sofa.

"Please John, no, stop right now."

He had gone past the point of no return as his hand lifted her skirt and reached for a fistful of her panties. He pulled them down while his free hand reached underneath and lifted her backside high into the air. He wasn't about to stand on ceremony and as he roughly parted her legs he guided his penis into her moist vagina and began to pummel against her with increasing pressure.

"John your hurting me for Christ sake."

Her cry went unheard as he relentlessly took his pleasure, gradually increasing momentum. His eyes glazed over as he thought about Annette and their urgent lovemaking, how he wished he was pounding against that bitch. He closed his eyes as he imagined her beneath him, with no thought of Alma. His performance was quick and brutal as he hammered away selfishly until he had released every ounce of his pent up rage. His body quivered in pure delight and with one final thrust he came and felt the anger and rage dissipate as he slumped down, the full weight of his body lying on top of his less than satisfied wife.

There was a moment's pause before the full force of Alma's rage pushed him away.

"Get off me John, I can barely breath, you selfish bastard."

Bennett fell back onto the sofa and took a few moments before his breathing returned to normal and he stood up. He pulled up his trousers and buttoned up his shirt.

"Dinner in the microwave darling is it?" He bent down and kissed her on the forehead. "I really don't know what I would do without you dear."

"You bastard."

He removed his tie, placed it on the table and headed towards the kitchen.

His mind was now clear, the pent up tensions had been released and the weight lifted from his shoulders. As he busied himself in the kitchen with cutlery, plates and the microwave, he poured himself a large glass of brandy. As he waited, his thoughts returned to Annette, feeling more benevolent than he had earlier in the day as he re thought his strategy. It wouldn't do any harm to give her a few days to cool down and she would soon realise there was no one else to turn to. He smiled to himself. The bitch would be begging him to help her, he'd oblige of course but she'd be paying dearly for it in every sense of the word.

I had remained slumped on the floor in the hall, paralyzed to the spot for what seemed like an age. Had I really been sat there for hours? The light had faded and it had almost turned dusk. I kept bursting into tears and then tried my best to compose myself, my mind seesawing between the disgust and anger I harboured for John Bennett to a feeling of complete terror and what my solicitor was actually capable of. He had been like Jekyll and Hyde, it was a side of him that I could never have imagined.

It had seemed so long ago. I couldn't forget how he'd pushed my neck so hard against the wall and his ghost of a grip still lingered long after he'd slammed the front door behind him. I vividly remember my fear and terror as he towered above my limp body and his eyes had turned cold and dark as he lost himself in his rage.

John never lost his external composure, his actions were always gauged and measured and as I was discovering, every one of his actions had a sinister connotation. In those few short moments when the pressure of his arm stopped the air reaching my lungs, I was terrified he was never going to stop but eventually he did and I folded to the floor like a rag doll. The incident had lasted all of a few seconds but it seemed like forever and would live with me for a long time. I tried to fight it but it was the overwhelming sense of fear I felt in those few short, horrific moments I couldn't shake. When he'd gone, I lay there like a broken toy and I wondered if I could ever find the strength to rise to my feet again. And I told my inner self that I should be used to it because how many times had Stuart kicked me down over the years?

"Get to your feet," I urged myself. "Don't let the bastards grind you down."

But by Christ they both had. My ex-husband had stamped on me so hard and so many times, the soles of his feet surely had the imprint of my face on them and now John Bennett had managed to do the same.

It was the knock at the front door that brought me to my senses. For a moment I thought he had come back and I cowered on the floor like a whipped dog frightened of his masters boot. At first I ignored the repetitive knock hoping whoever was calling would give up and go away. I sat in silence almost too frightened to breath, yet the person on the other side of the door was persistent.

I heard a female voice project itself through the letter box.

"Hello, Mrs Palmer, its Alexandra's teacher," she shouted.

My maternal instincts immediately kicked in and I was up on my feet in an instant.

Alexandra? what was she talking about, she was at school? Something was wrong, something was very wrong. I wiped my face with the sleeve of my jumper, a mixture of snot, snivel and mascara imbedded itself into the woven fabric and I instinctively hid my arm around my back. I straightened my skirt and flung the door open.

To my relief Alexandra was standing alongside the jolly looking woman. Despite the smile on the teachers face I knew something was wrong. I looked at Alexandra, her contorted ashen face cried out silently in pain.

"Alexandra, what is it?"

I held out my arms and as she gripped her stomach, she barely managed the step over the threshold before she fell into my arms.

The teacher offered an explanation, her voice compassionate in its delivery.

"Alexandra hasn't been well this afternoon, she seems to be in a lot of pain. We did try and ring your mobile Mrs Palmer, but we couldn't get a reply." She paused to take a breath. "So the Headmistress thought it best we should bring her straight home."

No, I didn't answer my phone because I've been sitting on the bloody floor feeling sorry for myself.

I offered my apologizes and gratitude as we both helped Alexandra shuffle into the lounge where she collapsed on the sofa. At that point alarm bells were ringing in my head, God knows I'd seen her in pain since the day she was born, yet something was telling me this was different and I didn't know what the hell it was.

It had happened again, the fickle finger of fate had poked me in the eye and showed me that what appeared to be a catastrophe was merely an inconvenient turn of events in comparison to the real drama happening right now.

As Alexandra started to moan I picked up my phone and called Dr Carrion and described her symptoms. This was a regular occurrence, something that Dr Carrion encouraged me to do. By now Alexandra had curled up tightly into the foetal position. I described the way she was lying on the sofa to the Doctor.

"Take her up to A&E," she said.

Within thirty minutes we were in the A&E department of the Newcastle RVI. As soon as we walked through the sliding doors a nurse took one look at Alexandra and called for some oxygen promising that she would be seen very quickly. Even with the oxygen mask fitted she was struggling to get her breath.

It all seemed to happen to happen so fast, one minute we were entering the A & E unit the next they were racing her along to the Observation Unit where there was a bed ready and waiting for her. She was more or less unconscious as they lifted her onto the bed and a team of nurses sprang into action with machines and tubes and an IV drip.

I stood there helpless while they connected everything up and as the monitors settled down, the readings they were almost screaming at me. They were telling me her blood pressure and her oxygen levels were at a dangerously low level.

They worked on Alexandra for about twenty minutes and one by one the nurses drifted away. The communication was poor, in fact the communication was none existent. Every time I asked a question I was informed that the doctor was the only one who could give me answers but he or she was nowhere to be seen.

I tried to remain calm and retain a modicum of understanding. This was a busy place, Alexandra certainly wasn't the only person on the ward. And yet every time a nurse or an auxiliary passed within ten metres of the bed I would unashamedly harass her to get some information or a commitment that someone was on their way to see my daughter.

I pleaded and begged at every opportunity. At first they were sympathetic with my plight but eventually after my constant badgering their patience ran out.

My voice was now noticeably louder, I was getting desperate.

"We've been here nearly two hours, how long does it take a doctor to get here for God's sake?"

I sat for most of the afternoon, perched on a hard plastic visitors chair holding onto Alexandra's hand as she drifted in and out of consciousness. They had dozed her up with painkillers and God knows what else and I had to admit she looked quite comfortable. All the while my eyes were fixed to the entrance of the ward, willing a doctor to make an appearance. Eventually my patience paid off when two doctors arrived on the ward. They walked over to the nurses station discussing various patients notes. I wasn't imagining it, on more than one occasion both doctors looked over towards Alexandra. Within five minutes they were at her bedside. As they started to examine her I could see by the look on their faces that they were concerned. My heart began to race as the moisture from my mouth evaporated leaving my lips so dry I could barely speak.

The older of the two doctors removed his glasses and spoke.

"Can I have a word in private," he gestured for me to head towards the nurses station. "In the room over there."

I looked at Alexandra, she was barely conscious.

"I'll not be a moment chick, I promise."

The doctor had already started to walk away and I followed him. By the time I reached the small room he had turned to face me and I could see by his expression he wasn't going to be telling me any good news.

"Come in Mrs Palmer, take a seat," he said.

His voice was slow and deliberate as he searched for the right words.

"Your daughter is very ill, Mrs Palmer."

"What do you mean very ill? How ill is very ill? "Its not serious is it?"

It was an easy answer to give, he simply needed to reassure me. I looked at him. Talk to me I wanted to shout, tell me what I want to hear.

But he didn't.

Instead he shook his head as he spoke.

"I'm afraid until we know what the problem is we just don't know."

"What do you mean you don't know, you're a hospital and she's been here five hours, surely you know what's wrong with her?"

He shook his head again.

"She needs a scan. We're going to send her down immediately. Time is of the essence."

As the words came out of his mouth I thought I was going to fall to the floor again, yet this time I wasn't going to hit the ground because some man had kicked me down, this time my legs were buckling beneath me because my heart was breaking in two. Time is of the essence he had said. I knew exactly what that meant, it meant if they didn't do something quickly my beautiful daughter might die.

The flood gates opened again and if I expected the doctor to offer me any sort of reassurance, I was left wanting. He told me to compose myself and be strong for my daughter. I walked to her bed with both doctors and two other nurses.

She was conscious and I could see her frightened eyes pleading with me to give her some answers. She was looking for the same reassurance that I had been looking for only moments earlier. She pulled the oxygen mask away from her mouth so she could speak, her voice staggered as she gasped for breath.

"What did they say Mum? Am I going to be alright?"

I took a deep breath and gave her the biggest smile I could muster.

"Are you kidding me Alexandra, of course you're going to be alright, stop being silly. Everything is going to be just fine."

29

The hospital porter arrived minutes after the doctor had delivered his devastating blow and then followed up with a hasty getaway. Normally I would have jumped for joy seeing a porter appear so quickly. God knows, in all the years Alexandra had been in and out of hospital we'd had our fair share of waiting around for one of these overworked foot soldiers to transport her either to or from a ward.

Today it unnerved me. This was an emergency, a real emergency and I knew as soon as the chirpy figure bounced on to the ward that the doctors had wasted no time requesting an emergency scan. This was serious and I could feel the fear building within me as my mind worked overtime extrapolating every negative word the doctor had shared with me and recreating my very own doomsday scenario.

"Your Chauffeur's arrived," the porter said in an upbeat voice quickly casting his eye over the name plate displayed above Alexandra's bed.

"Miss Alexandra Palmer is that right?"

She was barely conscious but the strange voice mustered albeit, a very weak smile beneath her oxygen mask. The porter lifted the safety gates on either side of the bed while the ward nurse who had followed him to the cubicle, hurriedly connected the oxygen supply to a portable cylinder. Then the porter was off and whistled away as he expertly weaved the bed off the ward and down through the maze of corridors to the X-ray department.

I walked along side, trying to keep pace with his long stride and to maintain eye contact with Alexandra. She wasn't stupid, she had registered my fear, my pain, my anxiety and all the while what little breath my daughter had left in her lungs she squandered asking for reassurance from the one person she had put her whole trust in.

"Mum I will be okay wont I?"

I had no good news to offer only false reassurances. I told her what she wanted to hear, my face wearing its own deceitful mask of calmness and positivity.

"Of course you are, it's going to be fine, you're having a routine scan that's all."

I could hear the false sentiment in my dismissive voice. In an attempt to avoid any more awkward questions I quickly deflected the conversation onto the chirpy porter, interrupting his birdlike tune.

"Have you had a busy day?"

I confess I haven't a clue what his reply was but I continued with the zombie like conversation until we came to an abrupt halt as he anchored the brakes at the reception of the x-ray department. Two nurses were waiting there ready to pick up the baton and direct the trolley the final few yards to its destination.

"Would you mind waiting in reception Mrs Palmer?"

"Can't I stay with her. It's only a scan."

The nurse ignored me.

"We shouldn't be long Mrs Palmer, thirty minutes at the most."

I wanted to protest, I wanted to tell the nurses that my daughter needed me. I looked at Alexandra. She had slipped into unconsciousness again. I quickly weighed up the options and decided to leave it. What mattered most was the scan and I wasn't about to start a five minute argument which would do nothing but cause an unnecessary delay.

The stillness of the waiting room was broken as the double doors of the scanning room flew open and to my relief I caught sight of Alexandra's head bobbing up from the bed. She was dazed but semi-conscious, her eyes darting around the corridor looking for me.

One of the nurses spoke to me.

"A porter is on his way to take her back to the ward and the consultant will be with you very soon."

Very soon, she'd said. The alarm bells in my head had now reached a deafening pitch.

I hurried along by the side of the trolley as the porter headed towards the ward. He looked up and pointed.

"I've been told to push her into the cubicle, she will be on her own."

A cubical? What was the significance of that I wondered?

As the bed disappeared into the room I looked up and caught sight of a consultant meandering along the corridor. He didn't seem to be in such a hurry. A good sign? He stuck out like a sore thumb, most unlike the trainee and ward doctors who wore their stethoscopes around their necks like a chain of honour. He wore no such encumbrance, instead his bright red braces and dickie bow tie were the only indicators of his senior rank. He was on his mobile phone and I couldn't avoid picking up on his conversation.

"So she's on her way back to the ward now, I'll go straight along to see her."

Alexandra… it had to be.

"Hmm, not good, she's seventeen you said?"

My legs turned to jelly and I propped myself against the wall and my heart began to thump.

I walked into the cubicle and as the porter positioned the bed into the bay, the consultant walked in and flicked a halfhearted smile in my direction.

There was only one reason a consultant would be on the case so quickly, it was clearly bad news. Edging his way further into the cubicle he pulled the curtains around the bed and turned towards me. I could barely breathe. Apart from the claustrophobia of being in such a small space, the fear of what he was about to say was almost paralyzing. I fought to maintain a calm exterior as I knew Alexandra's frightened eyes were now watching my every move. She was gauging my reaction and if I weakened I knew she would fall.

I turned my attention towards the consultant and feigned a smile. A man in his late fifties, I suspected he'd been practicing for years, dishing out pessimistic prognosis's like the grim reaper that had clearly honed his skills and toughened his skin to the point where human emotion couldn't quiet penetrate and detract him from his work.

After introducing himself as Mr Blair, the Senior Gastroenterologist, he waded straight in. This man wasn't going to pull any punches. His deep voice softened as if this would somehow lessen the blow. It didn't.

"I'm afraid Alexandra has Peritonitis."

"Sorry?"

I had no idea what Peritonitis was.

He continued on in simple layman's terms.

" I believe your daughters appendix has ruptured. As you know since her operation Alexandra's appendix has effectively been used as a tube to administer fluid into her bowel."

I nodded in agreement.

"We believe that the wall of the appendix has broken down and the contents of her bowel is leaking into her stomach slowly poisoning her."

Slowly poisoning her? Had he just said that?

"There is no way of knowing what the damage is until we operate and the sooner we do that the better."

I could feel the panic building up in my body.

"Is she going to be alright, can you sort this Peritonitis thing out?"

He sighed, reluctant to give a definitive answer.

I wanted to scream at him. Tell me she's going to be alright for fucks sake!

I looked at Alexandra. My calm exterior had slipped and my face now painted a less than pleasant picture.

He turned and looked at Alexandra.

"We're going to do all we can for you Alexandra. We need to open you up and clear as much of the leakage as we possibly can."

I needed air and I couldn't bear to listen to him a moment longer. I ushered him out from behind the curtain which I had managed to successfully open.

"Can I have a word in private?" I said.

He obliged, following me into the corridor.

"She's seriously ill isn't she Doctor?"

He ignored the directness of the question.

"Alexandra is very sick Mrs Palmer. You need to focus and keep calm for the sake of your daughter. She'll be going down for surgery in the next hour, she needs to be prepared." He looked at his watch. "I need to get going."

Blair walk away from me and I went straight back into the room.

My daughter needed to hear this.

"You're in safe hands darling, I've had a good chat with Mr Blair and he reckons this Peritonitis malarkey is just like appendicitis. How many people do you know who have had their appendix removed?"

I rambled on and on, our neighbour down the street and a boy in

Abigail's class had had their appendix out. By the time I'd finished, Peritonitis was as common as a nose bleed. Eventually I stopped.

"Talking about Abigail, I'm going to ring your sisters and tell them to come to the hospital, they'll keep your mind occupied until you go down to theatre."

She nodded in agreement.

"I'd like that," she gasped.

I took a deep breath. I could avoid the subject no longer. It was a decision she needed to make, not me.

"Will I phone your Dad Alex?"

Her eyes opened wide as she glared at me and I could tell from her reaction she was horrified as she shook her head from side to side. It was the most energy she'd expended for several hours.

"I don't want him here. Where's he been all these months? Promise me you won't let him come anywhere near me Mum, promise me."

I hadn't expected such a strong objection but secretly I was pleased. Stuart was the last person I wanted here and the thought of calling him sickened me.

"Don't call him Mum, please."

"Okay, okay, don't worry, I won't call him, I promise."

It was a surreal, defining moment and a sad one too. My daughter was about to undergo a serious operation, a dangerous operation and no one, least of all her, knew what the final outcome would be. I sincerely believed that she would want her father to be there, after all that had happened he was still her father. How had he let it get to this level? Hate was a strong word but my daughter's reaction at the thought of her father being by her bedside at the most critical period of her life left me in no doubt what her feelings were towards him. There was no time left for any more words as our cramped quarters suddenly burst into life as an anesthetist fired questions in our direction whilst a nurse prodded away at Alexandra's veins trying to insert a cannula.

It had all happened so quickly. One minute she was going for a scan and now she was being wheeled away into an uncertain future. Abigail and Victoria had just made it to the hospital before she was taken away. They allowed the girls a few minutes together but made it clear that time was of the essence. They hugged and kissed her all the while offering her the same reassurances I'd been overdosing her with. We followed the trolley and continued to chant our support all the way to the operating theatre until we reached the point where we could go no further. It was the end of the road. The rest of her journey would be a lonely one.

"I love you darling," I said. "We'll see you very soon."

I had no clue what they were going to find or the extent of the fight that lay ahead. I only knew my heart was breaking in two and if I could have taken her place I would have done so in a heartbeat. In those final moments together I witnessed her true strength.

She turned to her sisters.

"Look after Mum. I don't want her to worry, make sure she's okay." Every ounce of me wanted to pull her back and not let go. If I kept her in my sights everything would be alright. But no, it wouldn't be alright because I could see that she was slowly drowning, fighting for every breath. My youngest daughter was slipping away and the only chance she had was for me to release my grip on her hand and allow Mr Blair do his work.

The waiting was the most unbearable part. Every minute seemed like an hour and my mind was going crazy wondering what they were doing. To make matters worse I had jumped onto Google and searched Peritonitis while going to the toilet. What I read on an official NHS website was like someone slowly sinking a blunt knife into me.

Peritonitis needs to be diagnosed and treated quickly to prevent fatal complications developing.

This was my worst possible nightmare.

I read on. Peritonitis can be fatal if the infection spreads through the bloodstream to the major organs. Peritonitis caused by a bowel perforation is the worst and it is estimated that 1 in 10 people will die from the condition.

No wonder Mr Blair was so evasive. I read it over again. 1 in 10 people will die from the condition.

I sat in the toilet for some time and spilled a bucket load of tears. It was Abigail who came to find me, she said I'd been away for too long. From behind the cubicle door I assured her I was alright and said I was just having a few minutes peace. I joined the two girls soon after I had washed my hands and face and put a little lipstick on.

Out of nowhere my brother Roger made an appearance and he found us huddled together like lost souls in the general waiting area.

We were all overjoyed to see him as his presence and chit chat was a pleasant distraction. The joy was short lived however as the time dragged on and eventually all four of us fell silent receding in our own torment. We had nothing left to say to each other, we were lost for any more positive words.

Four hours had passed and still there was no word from theatre. My thoughts ventured into the dark place, rational thought had long since escaped me. At one stage I even thought about what sort of funeral she might like and I couldn't get the statistic of one to ten out of my head. The waiting was becoming sheer agony and my only outlet was to harass the nursing staff at every available opportunity asking if they'd had any word and was she out of theatre. Each time a quick phone call to that department would be politely answered.

"Sorry Mrs Palmer, not yet."

What the hell were they doing? Four hours under the surgeon's knife. This was not good, the odds of the one in ten statistic was increasing with each minute she spent in theatre.

The cycle rolled on for a while or at least until the A & E department started to fill up with its usual quota of Friday night drunks and druggies who's own self-inflicted stupidity had brought them to the hospital doors.

I watched a handcuffed patient arguing with a burly policeman. He sat waiting for an injury to his head to be attended to. He didn't let up as he harangued the nursing staff at every opportunity.

"How fucking unfair." I whispered to myself.

The policeman was struggling to keep him quiet and how I wished the policeman would subdue him across the back of the head with his truncheon. The injustice of it all were my only thoughts and I could restrain myself no longer.

I walked over to where the twenty stone, six foot plus oaf sat and slapped him hard across the face.

"Shut the fuck up," I shouted at him. "There are people in here at deaths door so stop fucking complaining."

His mouth fell open with shock. The policeman stood rooted to the spot and for just a few seconds the whole of the waiting area lapsed into a stunned silence.

"Show some respect you drunken bastard."

His eyes filled with tears and his bottom lip started to quiver.

"Do you hear me?"

Slowly but surely he nodded his head.

"Good. That's good, there's a good lad."

I took a deep breath and nodded at the policeman. I needed to do that I thought to myself and turned to walk away. Abigail, Victoria and Roger couldn't believe what they had just seen.

"Mum," Abigail said, "he could have killed you."

I patted her knee as I sat down beside her.

"But he didn't darling so everything is alright."

Roger was shaking his head and a grin pulled across his face.

"I've seen everything now, bloody everything."

At last a nurse walked over and delivered the news we were all waiting for.

"Mrs Palmer, if you make your way up to theatre she's in recovery. They are going to let you see her before they take her up to ICU."

On hearing those words I could breathe once more. Everything was going to be alright. Little did I know the news that Mr Blair would deliver a several days later.

Thankfully when we all arrived at ICU she wasn't on a breathing machine as predicted, yet it was still a scary sight seeing her wired up to every piece of monitoring kit imaginable. However, now that the operation was over, we quite simply had to be patient and wait for her to improve. Mr Blair arrived after a few minutes and said he'd cleared as much of the toxic fluid as he could, the antibiotics would have to take over the next part of the fight and kill off any remaining infection.

I sat with Alexandra for five days and nights. Her temperature never dropped, it was sky high and her breathing just as laboured. Each day drifted into the next yet I rarely left her bedside, only venturing home once when her sisters insisted that I should go home for a shower and a change of clothes. I was never away for more than two hours. Alexandra never noticed I'd gone. She was rarely able to stay awake for more than half an hour at a time, drifting in and out of consciousness and on more than one occasion she woke up delirious, looking startled and anxious and convinced that I'd been shouting her name.

I held her hand the whole time, I held her hand until my fingers were numb and I only moved my chair a little to change hands. My eyes were permanently fixed on the monitors, watching for any sign of improvement, praying that they would somehow change and give us some positive news.

As the days rolled on my initial euphoria of getting her through the operation gradually dissipated as I began to realise that despite the twenty four hour nursing care she was receiving she wasn't improving. Blair came onto the ward twice a day and his face showed increasing concern. She wasn't getting better, if anything she was going downhill.

On day five he called me into a private room.

"I'm sending her for another scan."

His deep voice echoed his frustration as he relayed his instruction to the staff who buzzed around him.

"When will her scan be?" I asked.

"Now," he said, "if we don't get to the bottom of why she isn't recovering we are going to lose her."

I don't know if Mr Blair should have told me that or what the rules were relating to dropping such a bombshell on a mother. At that point in time I actually respected the fact that he was speaking from the heart and any rules went out the window. His words slowly sank in. We're going to lose her.

I had no energy left to respond. Lack of sleep and total exhaustion had rendered me almost as helpless as my sick child. I knew I was at rock bottom, was I losing the will to continue? I thought of my husband and my creep of a solicitor and losing my self-respect and my beautiful home and the pending court cases and I could handle all of that. They meant nothing. I could give everything up, Stuart could have the whole fucking lot, but what I couldn't handle was losing my beautiful daughter. It couldn't happen, I wouldn't let it.

And a part of me experienced a flicker of joy because now I was grateful that Blair had also seen what I knew had been happening, that she was losing her own fight day by day.

Blair was on his feet and at the door while I sat there motionless.

"Mrs Palmer," he said, "do you want to accompany her down to x-ray?"

"Yes Mr Blair," I said. "For sure, I'll go with her."

I said goodbye to her the same place as I had the last time. Not that she knew I was there. By this stage she was totally out of it. As the double doors opened automatically on a sensor and they wheeled the trolley through I wondered if that was the last time I would see my daughter alive.

The scan happened almost as quickly as it had the first time and Blair was once again swinging through the ICU unit doors almost at the same time as Alexandra was returned back to her bay.

I looked at his face and tried to read him. He didn't look so happy and I suspected there was more bad news heading my way. He saw me and called me over.

"Things aren't going well at the moment."

The words wouldn't sink in.

"The infection is beating us. It's a battle and we're losing it."

My heart was skipping to its own beat, I was running on autopilot.

He let out a sigh.

"I'll get to the point, we found another pool of fluid that we weren't aware of."

I remembered the NHS website and about how fatal peritonitis could be if it poisoned the major organs. And yet a glimmer of hope I thought, now we know why she wasn't improving.

"But unfortunately we can't operate."

"What?" I said. "You have to operate. That fluid has been in her body for at least five days."

"We can't," he said.

"What do you mean can't? You've got to do something."

"She isn't strong enough Mrs Palmer, another major operation would kill her."

"But the poison…"

He cut me off.

"She wouldn't manage another operation, her right lung has collapsed."

I wanted to scream. Every part of me was desperate to run off that ward and away from the nightmare. I glanced across at Alexandra who thankfully was blissfully unware of our conversation.

I covered my eyes with my hands.

"No, no, please tell me something, just give me some hope."

He reached for my hands and pulled them gently from my face.

"Come around here and take a look at the scan."

He beckoned me around the desk where with the wonder of technology Alexandra's scan results were already displayed on the computer screen. Patiently he explained, pointing his finger to the outline of computer image of her pelvic area.

"That's where the fluid is sitting, just behind her pelvis and that's why we are so lucky."

I looked at him. Luck? What the hell was he talking about bloody luck? Where did luck come into this equation? Still, I wasn't going to argue with him and for the first time I even noticed a smile break across Mr Blair's face.

"If we open her up again I'm not sure she would cope with the operation, however where this pool of fluid is situated I'm more than confident we can drain it off if we go up through her rectum."

He smiled again.

"This is what has been making her so ill Mrs Palmer. We can drain it off and she doesn't have to be put through an operation."

I could see the delight in his face as he delivered his counter attack plan.

"If we remove this last reservoir of fluid I'm very confident that we'll see an improvement."

"And she'll recover?" I asked expectantly.

"Yes, at the moment the infection is winning but if we get rid of this last pool of poison we can turn this thing on its head."

As I listened intently I basked in his positivity. How I needed to hear something good. I doubt he would ever realise how he had made me feel that bleak afternoon. For the first time since the nightmare began I could see a chink of light in the form of hope and for that I was eternally grateful.

The procedure was successfully carried out that same day and she was back on the ICU unit to be monitored for another twenty four hours. I wasn't sure if it was my imagination playing tricks on me but within just a few hours I could see the first signs of improvement and inside I rejoiced, sincerely believing the worst was over. I knew I looked rough, I had barely left her bedside for six days and my body ached from sitting balled up on a chair hour upon hour, yet that afternoon nothing could dampen my spirits, well almost nothing.

My mobile phone rang and I looked at the incoming number. My heart sank to the floor. John Bennett had not entered my mind since our run in almost a week before. His name flashing across the screen on my phone brought some of the memory of that day back to the forefront of my mind. I was almost tempted to ignore his call, yet I remembered his last words to me, his threatening manner and I also recalled how pathetic I had been. Things were different now. I had been to hell and back and this man would never intimidate me again.

I lifted myself gently from the chair by Alexandra's bed.

I pressed accept, unable to resist its taunting any longer and instantly his rich enticing voice tried to cast its spell once more.

"Annette it's John."

I remained silent.

"Annette?"

"Yes what can I do for you John?

"Annette I've been thinking about you. I can't stop thinking about you. I just want to make things right between us. Is the coast clear?"

His voice was now almost seductive.

"Annette, you know what you do to me, I need to see you again. Are the girls in?"

"No." I said.

"Good," he replied, "I'll be around within the hour."

He pressed end and the line went dead. The silly, silly bastard, I thought. It didn't bother me that I'd sent him on a wild goose chase, in fact it felt quite good. He'd be in his car stroking his growing erection convinced that a wild sex session lay ahead. Nothing mattered to me anymore, the only thing that did was my children.

It took an hour before he called back.

"Where are you Annette? I'm at the house and there's no reply."

I stroked Alexandra's head. She was breathing normally and her blood pressure was coming down too.

"You said the coast was clear, you said the girls weren't in."

"They're not?"

"But…"

"And neither am I."

"But Annette, I don't understand, I've had a wasted journey."

"John, can I stop you there please. I'm in hospital with Alexandra, she is dangerously ill and quite frankly I'm not interested in what you have to say or how long you've driven expecting a fuck at the end of your journey. All that matters now is Alexandra, not you, not me, not my ex-husband or my home or the court case or the fucked up twisted lawyers and bent barristers."

"But Annette please."

"You need to go through what I've gone through in the last week to know what really matters."

"Yes, Annette I know, I understand."

"No you don't John, you know fuck all."

He got the message. His solicitors hat had now been firmly positioned on his head as he spoke.

"Does Stuart know what's happened?"

I began to give him an outline of the story and he listened looking for an angle that would be to our advantage, I could almost see him starting to take notes.

"Her Dad doesn't know and Alexandra doesn't want her Dad anywhere near the hospital." I said.

"Annette we must tell him about his daughter, if we don't it's not going to look good when you go to a final hearing. Believe me he has a right to know."

I could feel the anger building up inside me. Why did I even tell him? And yet he was right. I knew Stuart had to be told.

"You're right John, I know. Call his solicitor and tell him about Alexandra but make him aware that Stuart is not to come anywhere near this hospital. I don't care how it looks. This is his daughter's decision and nothing at all to do with courts or solicitors. She is seventeen and she has a right to make her own decisions."

"Do not worry Annette, your ex-husband will not be coming anywhere near the hospital. I'll speak to Steedman and make sure he gets the message. In the meantime, you need to give me updates every day."

I'd had enough of John, his voice was draining the energy from me and I wanted to concentrate on Alexandra, make sure I was there for her.

"I need to go John."

"Yes, you need to focus on Alexandra, I'll deal with Palmer and Steedman. I'm going to make things right and when you get home we can get back to normal and concentrate on the final hearing. I promise I'll work it all out and we can start all over again."

As I listened my skin started to crawl. I knew exactly what John was getting at and he wanted to pick up where we had left off a couple of weeks previous.

"I understand," he said.

"Do you John?" I asked.

"Yes Annette I do."

"Great," I said. "And make sure my husband gets the right message."

"Of course."

"Tell him we almost lost Alexandra. Make sure he knows how close we were and make him aware that when Alexandra knew she was about to undergo an operation that might have ended her life, the last person she wanted to see was her father."

"Yes Annette."

"Just make sure he knows that, will you?"

I pressed end. I didn't give my solicitor the chance to answer me.

30

Mornings on Ward 37 were unquestionably the busiest time of the day. Life kicked into action at 7.30am when the day staff trickled onto the ward to start a grueling twelve hour shift and they were quickly followed by the cleaners, armed with mops and buckets who clattered along in their wake.

Alexandra's cubicle sat directly opposite the nurses station and hearing the early morning chorus of exchanges between the flagging night shift staff and the early bird team was inevitable. The thinly veiled curtain that screened her bed offered little by way of defence against the onslaught of noise. Not that I had any complaints and it had little impact on Alexandra, she barely flickered an eyelid until at least ten in the morning. I had started to welcome the daily ritual, it marked the end of another long night on my makeshift bed of three chairs saddled together in a row. I had now been sleeping next to Alexandra's bed for twenty seven nights. I took a few calls from Bennett updating me on developments but not one call from my ex-husband. I checked with the nurses daily as they wrote a list of the people who had enquired about Alexandra. Not one call from Stuart fucking Palmer.

At first, it was impossible to catch even the briefest of naps yet as exhaustion took its toll, my aching body became accustomed to the contours of the moulded plastic of the seats and somehow despite myself, sleep managed to find me. It had all been worth it. Each day I counted my blessings that I was just able to lie next to my daughter, just to be within breathing distance of her, to smell her, to touch her, to stroke her hair. I was there watching her beautiful face when she eventually opened her eyes. It was a priceless moment that words could never describe. I couldn't deny there had been times in the beginning when I had doubted she would make it but she had proved us all wrong and battled hard to stay in this world. Mr Blair's prediction had been spot on, removing the last reservoir of poisonous fluid from her failing body had turned everything on its head. Gradually she won the fight and after eight days on ICU she was able to go onto a regular ward.

The relief I first felt when she left ICU was indescribable, yet once the initial euphoria passed there were still occasions when both my optimism and hopes were intermittently dashed as she faced one set back after another. After twenty eight days in hospital the evidence of her fight was etched across every inch of her frail, weak, pin pricked, emaciated body. Aside from wound infections and her disrupted bladder, her bowel management was now in total disarray. The ongoing worry throughout her illness had always been her breathing. At first Mr Blair had thought her collapsed lung was the reason for the pain she was experiencing with each tentative breathe she took, but it was only when her condition didn't improve and his concern grew that he subjected her to another battery of tests which identified fluid on her lung as being the culprit. As always he was eager to share his prognosis.

"There is no magic pill," he said, in his now familiar matter of fact tone, "her recovery will take months because the lung is like a sponge and it needs time to dry out naturally."

He went on to tell me there was no treatment he could prescribe. It was a natural but long recovery process and we just had to be patient. Unlike our first meeting when I'd marched him out of the cubicle, infuriated with his tactless manor, my respect for Mr Blair had grown during the weeks that fate had thrown us together. Every word he uttered I clung to like a life raft in a storm. I trusted his opinion, he'd saved my daughter's life and I was indebted to him. Today we would be saying our goodbyes to Mr Blair and his team as at last we were going home and I couldn't help feeling a little sad. He'd delivered the news the previous day as he spoke with an uncharacteristic smile and a glint in his usual somber eyes.

"We'll check your bloods and if they come back clear Alexandra, you can go home tomorrow and continue your recovery there."

Alexandra was over the moon to be going home whereas my reaction was a little mixed. Of course I was overjoyed that she was well enough to leave, however beyond that I was struck with fear and trepidation. In an odd sort of way hospital had offered us a sanctuary away from the real world, we were living in our own micro environment where our biggest domestic concern was what time the lunch trolley would make an appearance on the ward. I was more than confident that she was in safe hands and was constantly under observation and the enforced incarceration had given me temporary respite from my divorce and the mess I found myself in with John Bennett. Admittedly my predicament with both my ex-husband and now my ex-lover hadn't disappeared entirely. It was still stewing away in the background. I couldn't quite escape it altogether especially when I was in constant contact with John giving him regular updates on Alexandra's condition. John had insisted that I touch base with him every couple of days so he could at least keep the other side updated with her progress. Reluctantly I would call him but made sure that the conversations were as short as possible, my voice always curt and to the point. John seemed oblivious to my stance and he put my obnoxious attitude down to tiredness and fatigue. I was always insistent that Stuart should stay away from the hospital.

I sensed his frustration.

"Annette, your ex-husband has asked to visit the hospital. He wants to see his daughter."

He emphasized his daughter, which only served to raise my heckles.

"For God sake woman they'll use it against you at the final hearing."

It fell on deaf ears, John's silk smooth voice could no longer sway me or break me into submission as it once had.

"It's my mistake to make John, not yours, Alexandra doesn't want to see her dad and that's final."

"But Annette."

"I'm giving you regular updates and that's all he's going to get. I have her phone with me and he hasn't even sent her a text, never even called the ward, it's all bluster, bullshit, he hasn't seen her for seven months so why would he want to see her now?"

"But in court," John said, "it won't look good."

"I couldn't give a shit, I'm abiding by my daughter's wishes. That's all that matters to me and if he comes anywhere near this place I'll be waiting for him and he won't get anywhere near her."

Whenever he sensed my anger, he would interject his berating with messages of concern for me, invariably this would lead him to suggest that he couldn't wait for us to get back to normal and pick up where we left off. I no longer had the time or the tolerance to listen to the shit that was coming out of his mouth and by the time the conversation had digressed in that direction I would use my usual defence tactic and cut him off dead before he had the chance to utter another word.

"Got to go John, goodbye."

"But Annette."

End call.

I no longer valued John's opinion as I once had. He had lost me when he'd held me against the wall with his hands around my neck in a vice like grip. It begged the question why I was still allowing him to act as my solicitor when other sane minded people would have ran for the hills. Yet despite my misgivings and his shortcomings I knew John Bennett had the measure of my ex-husband and his sneaky little solicitor Steedman and that I needed him to fight my corner. With barely two months to go before the final hearing, to start over again would be financial suicide. I knew it was only a matter of time before he would come knocking on my door again thinking he still had the leverage and hold on me for his own selfish sexual gratification. I wouldn't let it happen again, I would do whatever it took to stop him. Any passion I had for him had been well and truly extinguished. It had been a hard lesson but I now knew John Bennett's interest in me extended to a lunch time fuck in-between clients.

Nor did I need his advice relating to Stuart and Steedman. I knew they would use whatever ammunition they could find to fire at me yet I no longer cared, my only concern was Alexandra. John failed to acknowledge this when he was constantly berating me about my ex-husbands right to see his daughter. Furthermore, Stuart hadn't caused a great ruckus when I had laid down the law that he was not welcome at the hospital. There were no guards around Alexandra's bed and I tried to put myself in his situation. There was no way anyone would have prevented me from walking into the ward and demanding to see her. As I lay next to her bed night after night with only my thoughts to keep me company, I often wondered how Stuart had stayed away so long. He had made no obvious effort to contact her. Her bed was surrounded by get well cards, none of which were from her father and while we were inundated with messages and calls on a daily basis, there wasn't so much as a text message from him. His action had made me question his sincerity and I couldn't quiet shake off the feeling that his motivations to see his daughter were selfish ones. I'd voiced my concerns to John during our weekly telephone spats but he pulled my argument to bits.

"It doesn't matter what you believe his motivation is for wanting to see his daughter, the court will only take into account that he's made a written request to see her and you've flatly refused."

I repeated that it was my daughters wishes and that as her mother I had to respect that. As I packed our things and prepared to leave hospital, I couldn't help feeling that my decision to deny him access was going to come back and bite me on the bottom but quite frankly, after all we had been through, I couldn't and wouldn't care.

It was late afternoon when we eventually received Alexandra's discharge letter and enough prescription painkillers to knock out a small horse. As we said our heartfelt goodbyes to both staff and patients, Tony, one of the regular ward porters arrived right on time and helped her into a wheelchair. As he pushed her out into the bright sunshine and headed for the taxi rank I could see the look of delight on Alexandra's face as she inhaled fresh air for the first time in weeks. The stale recycled vapors of the hospital ward could be forgotten about for a while at least. Her smile remained intact as we made our silent journey home, her attention fixed on watching the passing scenery from the car window and soaking up her new found freedom.

The house was cold when we eventually made our way through the front door. It was early April but there was still a winter bite lingering in the air. As soon as I'd dropped our numerous bags onto the hall floor and sat Alexandra down in a comfy chair in front of the television, I made it my first job to race to the boiler and turn the heating on to full blast. The house had been empty all the time we'd been away, Abigail and Victoria had only made fleeting visits to feed the cat before scurrying back to their boyfriend's places. Within minutes it felt like home again as the warmth began to permeate through each room. Even Cilla the cat had made an appearance brushing herself back and forward against my legs, purring with contentment now that we were home at last. It didn't take long for me to dispel the fears I had earlier in the day about leaving the safety of the hospital ward. Now I had been in the house half an hour I was glad to get back to reality and was already looking forward to a good night's sleep in my own bed.

As I was beginning to learn, happiness in my life came in very short increments and within an hour of arriving home my newly found enthusiasm was being put to the test. I heard Alexandra's weak grasping voice call me through from the kitchen to attend to her. She was sitting in the chair in the bay window, her back propped up against cushions to help her breathing with a catheter bag standing on a fixed frame by her side.

"What is it?" I asked.

My attention was focused on the deep clouded urine dripping slowly into the bag. Alexandra had built up quite a reservoir of the murky fluid and it needed to be emptied. I was immediately struck by the reality of the situation. She still looked like a hospital patient and even though she was in her own home I was fully aware that the care she needed was constant. I was her own personal nurse and it was my job to make sure that everything was just right including administering a concoction of drugs and pain killers every couple of hours. The only thing that had actually changed was that we were now prisoners of our home and not the hospital ward.

She spoke again snapping me out of my thoughts.

"Mum, are you listening to me?"

In an attempt to set my feelings of doom to one side I graced my benevolent daughter with the biggest smile I could muster.

"What does madam want? Your wish is my command."

She cast me a sympathetic smile as way of payment for my sad effort to amuse her, yet I could see from the way she was looking at the TV control there was something amiss.

"Mum, we've got no broadband or internet connection, it's all off, plus the phone's dead."

Disappointment was etched all over her face. No TV or internet connection for Alexandra was a big deal but my concern lay with the land line. The hospital, GP and District Nurse all had our landline number as our focal point of contact. How would they get in touch? Eager to dispel her worry and put my own mind at rest, I jumped straight onto my mobile, determined to get to the bottom of the problem even though ringing my service provider at 6pm was the last thing I wanted to do on our first night home. After what seemed like a lifetime listening to a barrage of irritating mindless tunes I was eventually rewarded with the sound of a human voice.

"Hello can I help you?"

After answering the obligatory security questions and explaining the situation, I listened on whilst the call handler tapped away on his computer trying to resolve the issue. I waited patiently occupying my time checking Alexandra's medicine chart. Another painkiller due in ten minutes time.

His voice popped up again interrupting my concentration.

"There's no problem with the service Mrs Palmer, you terminated the contract at the beginning of the month by email. That's why you have no service."

I was confused.

"No, I think you have it wrong, I haven't terminated anything."

"I've just checked the records twice and the contract was cancelled at the beginning of the month. I have it here in black and white, there's no mistake."

"You're not listening to me, I haven't cancelled anything."

"Stuart Palmer," he said. "The email came from Stuart Palmer."

I breathed a sigh of relief.

"There's the mistake," I said, "my husband doesn't live with us so he had no right to cancel anything."

The man started to apologise.

"The contract was set up in his name so I'm afraid he does."

"But the last bill was paid," I said, "I don't want the contract cancelled."

"It doesn't matter Mrs Palmer, the contract was in your husband's name."

"But this is ludicrous," I said, "I need a phone, can't you reinstate it?"

"I'm sorry Mrs Palmer I can't, however I can set up a new contract in your name and we can get a line engineer out within the next five days."

"Five bloody days!"

The man went on to explain that it was easier to simply transfer the contract to my name, moreover, my bastard of an ex-husband was told exactly that but he chose to cancel the contract completely.

"There must be some way of reinstating it?" I said.

"No, I'm sorry."

The man had no morals. His daughter had been at deaths door and still he was happy to cut off her only life line to the outside world. I thanked the messenger of doom politely for all of his help and pressed end.

That phone call set the tone for the rest of the evening. We sat flicking through the terrestrial channels trying to find something Alexandra could watch, while I failed miserably trying to put on a brave face and maintain an upbeat mood. As usual, when things went wrong, I was drawn to the Gin bottle. It was such an urge to reach for the bottle and knock back a healthy measure, yet it wasn't willpower that made me resist the temptation, it was the knowledge that I was alone in a house caring for a sick person. She had no one… only me.

The next day ran into a blur. I spent the first morning ringing Alexandra's care team and anyone else I could think of to change my contact number, then in-between caring for Alexandra who needed as much help as a new born baby, we had a steady stream of visitors wanting to welcome her home. In between the endless flow of tea, coffee and biscuits I called more people, explaining the situation and passing on the new number. I rang them all, doctors, dentists, pharmacists, Ward 37 and of course my good friends and family. Abigail and Victoria turned up early and tried to help as best they could but I carried a mixture of rage and helplessness for the rest of the day. When the last visitor left I had a tight sinking feeling in the pit of my stomach and the only thing keeping me going was the thought that I couldn't let Alexandra down.

Those first days back at home were bleak and I thought things couldn't get any worse. I kept trying to convince myself that it was only a phone number but it wasn't, it was so much more than that. At the end of the first week, just when I thought I was getting over the phone line debacle, a bill came in from my utility provider. I opened the envelope and it notified me that I owed them £2500. I couldn't help but smile. Someone had clearly screwed up. There had been a monthly £250 direct debit payment for as long as I could remember. It was high and if anything I thought they might have miscalculated and even owed me money. I had no enthusiasm for the phone call yet I knew it was one I had to make. This was a huge mistake and they needed to know about it. I calmly relayed my grievance to the operator and the phone went silent as the faceless voice on the other end tapped away on her computer bringing my account details up. When she did eventually speak her bland voice cut me to the quick.

"No Mrs Palmer, it isn't a mistake, your husband left the property on the 19 June 2011, the account was in his name and at the time he requested that his name was removed which is his entitlement. We didn't do that," she paused, I was half expecting an apology. "It was an oversight on our behalf so we have had no choice but to reimburse him with the direct debit payments that have been made since that date."

"But I made those payments not him."

I could hear her tapping at the key board.

"They came from a joint account."

Now I couldn't refrain my anger, it was the last straw. I argued that it was my money that had been paying the bills.

"I'm sorry Mrs Palmer but that joint account should have been stopped and you should have set another account up in your sole name."

The devious, tight bastard had exploited the oversight, challenged the company and accused them of a legal cock up. They had no alternative but to return all payments in full.

When I eventually came off the phone I was visibly shaking. I could barely believe the levels to which Stuart would stoop. He'd left his youngest daughter without her life line now he was happy to take away both her light and heat.

I telephoned him immediately. He picked up.

"Just what the hell do you think you're playing at, you bastard?"

"What are you talking about you crazy bitch?"

"Alexandra's mobile, the utility bills, that's what."

"Speak to your solicitor," he said and hung up.

John Bennett was at the forefront of my mind and he was the only person I wanted to speak to at that precise moment in time. I called the office number and Karen recognized my voice immediately when I connected to the Saxtons' reception. Without even asking, she knew who I wanted to speak to.

"I'll put you through to Mr Bennett, wait one moment."

His voice was almost gushing when he picked up the phone. There had been a time whenever I heard his voice my heart would melt. Now every word that rolled off his insincere tongue made me want to reach for a bucket to vomit.

"Annette, how lovely to hear from you and how is Alexandra?"

I ignored his question and for the first time in a long while I spoke to him like any client would do to their solicitor. I needed to offload everything Stuart had done and above all I needed my solicitors help. He listened as I relayed my tale. I sat outside on the garden wall, well away from Alexandra's keen ear. The sun was already beginning to set and the cold, northern wind was biting into my skin, yet for the most part I was oblivious to my discomfort and far more focused on my conversation. Once he'd heard enough he offered his reassurances.

"Annette, first and foremost I will write a letter to Steedman. It will take some time but do not fear, you will be reimbursed with the utility money."

I took a deep breath. I could feel the pressure drifting away as I heard the reassurances I had been seeking. He paused and in usual John style his next sentence was tentative and gauged.

"I was going to ring you today Annette, Steedman has come up with an offer." He paused for dramatic effect. "A very good offer Annette."

My ears pricked up. I was physically and mentally exhausted. Was this the offer I had been waiting for? Would this offer be the answer to all of our problems. Could we finally put it all behind us and move on?

I looked up towards the pink, glowing sunset and out of nowhere I thought of what my parents would frequently recite when sighting a similar skyline. Red sky at night sailors delight.

"Annette, did you hear what I said? Mr Palmer has made an offer. Alexandra's illness has them running scared. He wants to settle out of court."

I'd heard him alright I just didn't know if I wanted to hear what the offer was. I knew I was fragile. Could I make a wise, informed and well thought out decision?

I forced a response. "Tell me what the offer is John, put me out of my misery."

"He's offering sixty five percent of everything. No maintenance of course, he wants a clean break."

He was waiting for my response. I wanted to say yes, how easy it would be to say yes and put an end to the perpetual misery. After all I had been through with Alexandra wasn't health and family the most important factor. Wasn't money a mere irrelevance?

"He's upped his offer by ten percent Annette."

I was calculating the maths and it sounded good. I could put an end to the endless shit I'd suffered for so long, the word closure sprang to mind.

My thoughts returned to Stuart. He'd want closure too. I wondered if he was sitting under the same sunset as I was, looking for answers. I could only imagine the task his solicitor had, persuading him to up the offer to 65%. I pictured the scene. Stuart, arrogant as ever, convinced he knew best but Steedman reminding him what the Judge had said when he came up with the 55% offer.

"I never expected a ten percent increase at this stage," John interjected.

"It sounds good."

"It is good Annette, we should be proud of ourselves."

It did sound good and yet I couldn't shake the thought that as a father he had given up on his girls. They were irrelevant in his perfect new world, he'd made that clear in the last few weeks.

"You can settle everything, buy yourself a small place and still be in a position to put away a couple of hundred thousand to cover the maintenance," he said.

I quickly worked the figures out in my head, about £630000. He had originally offered just five percent extra to cover the maintenance. Now it had increased to fifteen. John was right, it was a huge difference.

John continued to ramble on, taking the credit for the deal.

"I knew they would crack," he said, "I told you so."

I still couldn't keep the house. Sell the home and move on I thought. It's over.

"Annette what are your thoughts? I hate to push you on this but as soon as its agreed I can start to draw up the paperwork."

John told me it was a verbal offer. We had to act fast because there was nothing to stop them changing their minds.

"Well Annette, what do I tell them?"

I took a deep breath as an involuntary smile pulled across my face.

"Tell them to go fuck themselves, there's no deal."

31

It had been a week since I had rejected Stuart's offer and it played over and over in my mind that maybe I had been a little hasty in my response. If I had accepted the offer it would all be over, the pain and anguish gone and more importantly I could say goodbye and good riddance to the two men who had made my recent life a misery, namely John and Stuart.

It wasn't too late to go back and reconsider the offer but that would only expose my weakness and my stubborn pride wouldn't allow me do that.

I couldn't help the reoccurring doubts, they usually came late at night when the house was still and Alexandra was fast asleep. However, I'd convince myself to think about everything my daughter had gone through and my financial dilemma resolved itself. There was nothing more important than Alexandra and I told myself I'd done the right thing. It was all so very simple, Alexandra didn't want to move house and if I had said yes to Stuart's offer, there would have been a for sale sign planted outside the front door quicker than the blink of an eye. Alexandra needed her home at least for the foreseeable future and if I could delay the inevitable then so be it. I knew the inevitable would happen, I knew I couldn't hang on to the house indefinitely but if I could fight long and hard, when that time eventually came she would be strong enough to handle the turmoil, the upheaval and the emotional drain on her mind and body.

Day by day I could see slight signs of improvement in her health although she still slept more hours than she stayed awake and her breathing concerned me. I would watch her walk as ten steps or more rendered her weak as water, like a Puffing Billy, her lungs struggling to catch each breath and yet I saw glimpses of the old Alexandra emerging from the dark. The catheter bag was no longer required, the painkillers had been gradually reduced in quantity and frequency and her appetite improved almost daily. The old Alexandra humour made a welcome appearance and as normal I was generally the focus for the butt of any joke. But it was all music to my ears and I never tired of hearing her well-practiced repertoire. Her throaty laugh was as welcome as a newborn baby's first cry.

On the fifth weekend since she'd come out of hospital we reached another mile stone. For the first time we ventured out. Not far, only to my Mother's house for the weekly Sunday roast, but we couldn't wait, desperate to escape the confines of the same four walls and the repetitive monotony each day brought us.

The family had all promised to be there to welcome her home and I knew how much she was looking forward to mixing with her cousins and catching up with the teenage gossip.

I sat with the oldies, chewing the fat as we relived the dramatic events of the last couple of months. Inevitably the conversation turned towards my pending divorce settlement and how Stuart had fallen well short of the father they'd all expected him to be. I basked in their sentiment knowing it wasn't just me who thought he was the most selfish bastard on the planet. Stuart Palmer's fan club was dwindling by the day.

By the time we'd made our way home that evening, Alexandra was so exhausted she lay flat out, stretched across the back seats of the car. I drove along in silence, my mind retracing the day's events. I wasn't surprised she was so tired, she'd been fighting sleep all afternoon, resisting the urge to shut her eyes for fear she'd miss out on something. The day had turned out just as I had imagined, absolutely perfect. My Mam's house was always bursting with activity, yet even by her standards today had been extra special. It had been a perfect balance of family love and sheer chaos at times. All of my brothers had turned up with their families, all making the effort to be there. It was what we called a 'full house.'

By the time Alexandra and I arrived my three brothers had adopted their normal slouched positions in the living room whilst the sister in laws and nieces helped in the kitchen preparing dinner. I popped my head around the lounge door to say my hellos. While Darren and Peter sat next to each other talking about something or nothing Roger's attention was completely drawn to his new granddaughter, Penelope, who he held in his arms, his eyes transfixed on her crown of red hair and cherub like features. The newest member of the family had just arrived into the world a few days before Alexandra had taken poorly and there'd been no chance for us to introduce ourselves. As soon as we walked into the room we instinctively made a bee line towards the small swaddled bundle desperate to see what she looked like.

Roger looked up as we stood over him.

"Isn't she gorgeous?" he said, barely able to contain his bursting pride.

"She is," I responded holding out my fingers to touch her perfectly formed little hand which seemed so small in comparison to mine.

"And where did the red hair come from?" I said in mock surprise.

He shrugged his shoulders as baffled as I was as to how the rouge red gene had found its way into our family DNA.

"I don't know, but I feel like the luckiest man alive having her." He nodded in the direction of Alexandra. "We're both lucky to be sitting with these two today," he said.

Alexandra sat down beside him, desperate to relieve him of his nursing duties but he held onto the baby as if his life depended on it.

"If I won the lottery tomorrow I'd get her the best medical treatment money could buy, I hated seeing her in hospital," he said as he eventually handed the baby over into Alexandra's waiting arms.

I laughed out loud, how many times had he said he was going to win the lottery I thought.

"And when's this going to happen Roger, sometime never?"

"You just wait and see," he said with total conviction. "I'm convinced I'll win it someday."

I sat with my oldest brother for some time unable to tear myself away from his soothing tones, his eternal optimism and the promises that whenever his ship eventually sailed into port he would be the most generous man on the planet. I had no doubt that he would do exactly as he said and I couldn't help thinking that he was the exact polar opposite to Stuart. While Roger would have parted with his last penny to help his family and friends, Stuart, in acts of meanness and spite had kicked his youngest daughter in the teeth time and time again over recent months.

As I drove home that evening recalling the conversations I'd had that day, not least the ones I'd had has with Roger, I began to smile.

Little did I realize at that moment in time that by the next morning our lives would never be the same again.

It was Monday morning and with nothing to get up for I lay in bed until past nine o'clock. The morning was bright and even through the closed curtains, the sun's rays managed to penetrate the fabric of the drapes casting a warm amber glow throughout the room. It occurred to me as I anticipated the day ahead that maybe I should venture out into the garden to cut the grass whilst the weather was in my favour. Alexandra was sound asleep. I knew after the previous day's activities it would be hitting noon before she'd raise her head from the pillow and the long sleep would do her the world of good.

As was my ritual each morning, I picked up my mobile phone from the bedside table, switched it from vibrate to ring tone and checked to see if I had any messages. As I lifted the phone to my eyes and slowly focused in, I noticed the small red notification bubble registering nine missed calls. My heart skipped a beat, someone was keen to speak to me. My first thoughts were that it could only be Victoria or Abigail, no doubt they'd forgotten something and want me to drop it off at work. It wouldn't be the first time I'd swung by their offices with packed lunches, phone chargers and gym kits. My curiosity pushed me to check the missed calls. They were all from Roger and he started making them at 5.30 in the morning. My heart began to flutter as instinctively my thoughts turned to my mother. I hope she's okay. I jumped out of bed, now wide awake, the adrenaline pumping around my body as I fumbled with the phone trying to press return call.

The phone rang out only once.

"Hello, Roger?" I pounced, "What's wrong?"

A female voice, Roger's wife.

"Hello Annette, its Marion. I'm using Rogers phone," she said.

I found myself gasping for breath.

"Is there something wrong Marion? Where's Roger?"

Her response was instant, I could almost feel the desperation in her voice.

"Roger collapsed during the night, he's had an aneurysm on the brain, we went to the Queen Elizabeth and- "

I cut in struggling to keep pace with her bullet point dialogue. We'd been together less than twenty four hours previously, he had been totally fine. I struggled to comprehend what she was talking about.

"He's what?.... Is he okay?" I asked in desperation.

"Annette, I'm in an ambulance, they are blue lighting him to the RVI."

Her voice was now cracking as she struggled to find the words.

"They've put him into an induced coma, the doctors say they're not sure he'll make the journey otherwise."

Make the journey? My head began to spin into its own cycle of turbulence, her voice brought me back.

"Just get to the RVI as soon as you can Annette."

Then just as she was about to cut off she said.

"Your Mam doesn't know yet."

The line went dead and she was gone.

I don't remember feeling panicked after the call, it all felt so surreal as if it wasn't actually happening. An aneurysm? A stroke? I tried to tell myself it was nothing to worry about. Strokes could be slight, surely that's all that had happened to Roger. He'd be fine, a couple of days in hospital and then he'd be home laughing and joking as normal. I pictured the scene, when I get to the hospital he will be sitting up in bed saying panic over, what's all the fuss about?

I left Alexandra lying in bed asleep with a note by her bed saying that I'd be back before twelve as I just needed to pop out for a while. I gave her no more information other than that. Why worry her unnecessarily? I wanted to find out what was happening before I shared the news with the three girls and especially my mother. In my mind he was going to be fine, perhaps that's why I stayed so composed, it couldn't be happening, not now, not after everything else we had been through. I dived in the shower, not even waiting until the water ran hot and showered in double quick time. I threw on my clothes, didn't bother with any make up and raced to the hospital desperately wanting to believe that poor Marion had simply been over dramatic.

My hopes that it had been a slight stroke, that Marion had been pessimistic were instantly dashed when I caught sight of Roger's entire family huddled together in the A&E waiting room. The two girls, Hannah and Faye, were sitting either side of their mother propping her up, while young Robbie who had spotted me coming down the corridor, jumped up out of his chair and bounded up to greet me like an excited pup, as if somehow my presence would make everything better. I remember thinking my six foot two, strapping nephew looked as helpless as a vulnerable child and my heart reached out to him immediately. The four of them embraced me into their small, tight clan, desperate to offload what little they knew. They told me that Roger was in a critical condition. My blood turned to ice. I knew what critical meant in hospital terminology, it meant the worst, it meant the most concerning condition a living person could be in. We all sat in silence, watching like hawks for someone to give us an update on what was going on. We waited for what seemed like an age, my mind reliving the events of the previous weeks when I had waited in the same room for Alexandra to come back from surgery. Roger had sat with me that night, consoling me, offering his support. It seemed such a cruel twist of fate that here we were again only this time it was Roger fighting for his life.

I can barely remember how we got through the endless waiting. We were there for what seemed like hours. I kept an eye on my watch conscious of the time, my loyalty torn between wanting to stay at the hospital and knowing I needed to get back to Alexandra before twelve. We filled the endless vacuum of minutes trying to downgrade the seriousness of the situation. Maybe it wasn't so bad, a simple operation would stop the bleeding and everything would be fine.

"Isn't modern science a wonderful thing," Faye said. "These doctors just about fix anything these days."

We all nodded and agreed, offering reassurance to Marion who looked devoid of hope. I wanted to give her a shake, tell her to be more positive but she just kept looking around the waiting area like a Zombie.

We had almost convinced ourselves of a positive outcome when there was a burst of activity around us. Two doctors in masks passed us and then a nurse arrived and guided us towards a private waiting room. The doctors were waiting for us, their masks removed and their gloomy faces gave the game away before a word had left their lips. They were about to deliver a bombshell, I just knew it.

The Aneurysm was right next the brain stem, one of them said. None of us needed a degree in medicine to know that was bad. Even with my limited medical knowledge I knew the brain stem controlled our most basic of functions, it was the building blocks for life and controlled our breathing and heart rate. The doctors told us that because the damage was so close to the brain stem there was no hope of opening up the head to halt the flow of blood.

"But there's a chance?" I asked desperately, "surely there's another way?"

The older of the two Doctor's nodded.

"The only chance of repairing the damaged artery was to go up through the major vain in his groin and follow a path leading to his brain."

"There you are," I said as I forced a smile. "He's going to be fine."

But the doctor wasn't smiling. He looked like Marion did, devoid of hope.

"Hang on," I said. "I'm not feeling too much optimism in here, what are you saying exactly?"

I remember the scene vividly, two gently spoken surgeons sitting in their blue scrubs opposite us, tentatively searching for the right words to tell us in their very professional opinion that my brother's life was hanging by a thread.

They were going to try and repair the damage, give him the best chance of survival they said.

I asked outright.

"So what are his chances of survival?"

The taller of the two surgeons looked me in the eye.

"Very slim."

"We'll do our best," the other surgeon said, barely audible.

I wondered what the other four were thinking as they sat by my side listening to the pessimistic prognosis and I knew, as I gripped Faye and Hannah's hands willing them to be strong and positive, that my dear brother was going to die. Something deep inside told me there was no way back, yet I sat calmly consoling them, offering reassuring words. It was false hope, I was kidding myself, because I knew in my heart of hearts it would take a miracle to turn things around and miracles were something that didn't happen in the

Annette Palmer world.

Two weeks later Roger was still with us. I sat by his bed watching the artificial ventilator push his chest up and down keeping him alive. He had cheated death, that were the very words of the surgeon a few days after surgery and we dared to believe that he was going to make it. The operation had been a partial success, they'd managed to stop the bleeding temporarily but its position had made it impossible for the doctors to cauterize it. The operation had bought them time until they could think of a more permanent solution and we were all relieved that at least he was still with us. Two days after the operation they'd reduced his sedation, gradually bringing him out of the induced coma and back into the world. Marion said he had been a little confused yet he had still managed to hold a conversation. Just as I was about to visit him on the ward he fell unconscious once more, the temporary dam had ruptured and they were forced to put him back into an induced coma while they looked for another solution.

My days had turned into the stuff of nightmares once again. Since Roger's aneurysm, Alexandra and I had practically upped sticks and moved in with my Mam to give her the support she needed. She took it badly. My Mam's house was the nerve centre of everything, where all the family members congregated to get an update on Roger. Marion and his kids would automatically make their way to her house in-between hospital visits and we would make them food and encourage them to eat. I spent my life looking after Alexandra while spending as many hours as I could by Roger's bedside. Somehow it seemed better when we were together, trying to think of positive outcomes whilst my Mam just sat silent most of the time, her eyes looking blankly at the wall or the TV in the corner that played to itself. She would always look to me for reassurance and I'd be happy to give it.

"He'll be alright, nothing will happen to him," she'd say, her eyes pleading with me to give her the answers she wanted to hear.

"They've got him sedated, the doctors know what they are doing," I would say, with no genuine conviction in my voice.

No one was prepared to tell her how bad the situation was. She was eighty one years old, how much more pain could she take? She'd already endured my divorce and Alexandra's illness yet this was undoubtedly the worst she'd had to deal with. Roger was her oldest child and I could only imagine what she was going through. Fortunately she didn't want to go into the hospital herself, seeing him on all those machines would be too much for her she said. I was grateful for that at least. It meant we could hide the truth a little longer. I didn't want her hope extinguished and as long as he was alive at least she still had that.

In those desperate days, all thoughts of my divorce drifted away as my mind fixed on my brother. It all seemed irrelevant, as it had done when Alexandra was so ill. There were times where I simply didn't care and if Steedman had walked in with an agreement where Stuart took the lot I would have happily signed it. John had left me numerous voice mails asking me to ring him and eventually, out of desperation and to shut him up, I eventually did. When he heard my voice on the other end of the line he went ballistic, scolding me like a naughty school girl. I held the phone two feet from my ear and took it all, I didn't care, nothing seemed to matter anymore.

"Where the hell have you been Annette? I've been trying to contact you for days. We have a court date and we really need to agree the Barrister."

He carried on without waiting for a response.

"I'm thinking Mr Gilbert, he's a good man."

He gushed on about him being a good fellow and I knew it was going to cost me another small fortune. I had to stop him mid-sentence. How could I talk about something so trivial when my brother's life was hanging by the slimmest of threads?

"John I can't talk at the moment, my brothers very ill and my divorce settlement is the last thing I want to think about."

There was no anger or frustration in my voice, just flatness as I explained my latest and gravest current crisis. He listened attentively as usual before agreeing to hold off any decision about the barrister for a couple of weeks.

"Whatever you think John, I really couldn't give a shit."

The following day a bouquet of flowers arrived with a handwritten card attached.

'Thinking of you. Lots of love John xxx'

The delivery man smiled and as I thanked him I watched as he walked down the drive and out towards the gate. I binned both the card and the flowers as soon as he had disappeared from view. Two days after the flowers another Saxtons' gift arrived through the letterbox, a bill for £5500. John's concern hadn't stretched as far as holding off on the monthly bill or the amount of billable hours. He was almost certainly on some sort of percentage and he was a lawyer. No matter what crisis his clients battled through it wasn't his concern. I cast a dismissive eye over the figure before slinging the letter into the waste bin. I hadn't a clue where I was going to find that sort of money but it was the least of my worries. An hour after the letter had been thrown away I was called back to the hospital. Roger's condition had deteriorated and they wanted me to get to the hospital as quickly as possible.

During the drive through the city, although I feared the worst, I still clung to what little hope I had left. It was precautionary I told myself. Roger would bounce back, he always did.

I walked into the hospital and along the corridors that were now as familiar as a second home. I joined Marion and the kids in a private room, a minute or two later Peter and Darren arrived.

The doctors were waiting for us and wasted no time in telling us they were going to switch his life support machine off. They'd done the tests and said there was no pattern in his brain activity. The surgeon told us that the neurons were firing off in every direction which meant in medical terms Roger was brain dead. The surgeons words confirmed what I had known for two weeks. My brother was going to die, but even so his words hit me like a thunderbolt.

The other surgeon explained the details nobody wanted to hear.

"The machine is going to be turned off soon but the doctors have reassured us that the end will be quick, he won't linger and the end will be painless."

The surgeons and the nurses left us to our pain and grief but within a short period of time some sort of sensibility and normality kicked in. Marion and the kids decided that they wanted to donate his organs to the hospital. They said the transplant teams should be gifted with his heart, lungs and kidneys. Within a very short period of time a transplant coordinator arrived. Her name was Helen and she went through the process in a kind and sympathetic manor. She had a jolly face and I recall thinking that someone with that kind of job shouldn't have a jolly face, she should be gloomy and miserable and morose. I sat listening to her, staring at her, all the while wondering what sort of person could do this job day in day out. She told us so matter of factly that after he died they would allow us a few minutes with him before they took his body in to the operating theatre. A transplant team would be standing by to harvest his organs. It seems so cold and clinical, as if they were talking about slaughtering a beast in an abattoir but still we were consoled by the fact that some good would come of it.

We walked down to his bed. I held his warm hand, listening to the suction of the breathing machine pumping up and down keeping his organs alive. I sat staring at his blank, lifeless face and couldn't help thinking how ironic it was that none of his precious organs would sustain his life yet they offered hope to other poor souls. In a strange way I valued those final moments we had together. I told Roger how much I loved him and how I couldn't have wished for a better brother and I reminded him of our last conversation, the one we'd had that Sunday afternoon and how he was going to win the lottery.

"I hope you win the lottery today Roger and go to a better place than this sad world with so much heartache and pain."

I wonder to this day if he heard my last words.

Peter and Darren said their last goodbyes and we held each other as a united family, our hands linked together in grief and then the real tears started to flow by the gallon. There can be no worse feeling in the world than to know for sure that in the very near future, less than a few hours in fact, that your brother is about to die. You are part of the macabre plot and there is nothing you can do about it. Even worse, you have been a part of that decision to end it all. But I drew strength from my brothers and Roger's family as we shared the pain and torment together.

A team of nurses and doctors appeared and silently performed the tasks they needed to do. They disconnected some tubes, flicked a few switches and we all knew this was the end.

The room was in darkness except for the dimmed fluorescent strip lighting running down the centre of the ceiling and a night light above Roger's bed. The room was filled with the sound of his staggered breathing. Marion, Hannah and Faye sat at the right side of his bed, Robbie to the left. Peter suddenly jumped to his feet and announced he couldn't stand it any longer. Between the tears he sobbed that he couldn't watch his brother die and left the room. I understood exactly where he was coming from. Part of me wanted to run out after him.

But I stayed. Darren and I hung around at the foot of the bed to savour those last precious moments.

I'd expected a calm, silent, dignified passing but wasn't to be like that. His breathing laboured on and almost in unison Marion and the children began to chant his name as if they were willing him to fight on and prove the doctors wrong. Robbie bent over his Dad's bed, his hand clinging to his chest as if his heart was going to burst out, his husky sobbing echoing around the stillness of the room. I didn't cry, speak or move, my body was fixed to the spot taking in the ghoulish sight as if I was watching a nightmare unfold. I was watching a nightmare unfold.

His breathing became more and more staggered as their chanting grew louder and louder, then suddenly Roger's eyes flared open and for a fraction of a second I really believed something had changed within him. He was fighting for every breath, willing himself to live on. Was this the miracle we were waiting for? My hope only lasted a few seconds as his black, coal like eyes stared back at me and I realised they had no life in them. They closed as quickly as they had opened and then my gorgeous, kind, generous, protector of a brother took his last breath of life. I watched Robbie stagger back into the chair as if he were about to collapse. The big bear of a young man knew that his father was dead and he began to sob like a baby. I watched my brother's face as a wave of death appeared to wash right over him turning his body into an alabaster cast and then he was at peace with the world.

A strange sort of shiver, something I had never experienced before, rose from my feet and coursed through my whole body and at that precise moment I knew that Roger had left us.

32

After Roger died I found myself thinking about him every minute of every day. But now, three weeks on, my thoughts were more intermittent and I could go a whole four or five hours without his image entering my head and I soon realised that I was able to function quite normally following this cycle of behavior. It was only when in situations like visiting my family, that he was constantly in my thoughts again. There were other things that would trigger a flood of tears, more often than not happening in the full glare of the public eye. Whenever I heard a song Roger loved, seeing his mobile number glaring at me in my list of contacts or passing a lottery kiosk, knowing he wouldn't have been able to resist buying a ticket I was reaching for the paper tissues as it hit me like a bolt of lightning that he was gone and I would never see him again. During these moments I would be wracked with guilt and sadness, annoyed with myself that I was getting on with my life when he couldn't. Whenever a smile crept across my face or I laughed at a joke or something funny on TV, I'd reprimand myself for daring to even think about having some fun or a fleeting moment of joy. By way of penance I'd force myself to relive his final moments as the machines were switched off and the horror of that night would unfold in my head in startling technicolour detail. At once he was back in the forefront of my mind and I sincerely believed that is where he should be… permanently. How selfish of me to forget him, even for an hour.

My cycle of grief would start all over again and I welcomed it because at least the guilt had gone, at least for a few hours until his voice, inevitably, whispered in my ear again, or he laughed, or smiled and his wonderful form once again filled my head and although I was sad and angry I was also content and happy that he was somehow with me again.

I began to realise that each member of the family was battling through their own cycle of grief too, but somehow life still managed to wheedle its way in, giving each of us reason to go on. We shared our experiences occasionally, but for the most part it was a private war that nobody appeared to be winning.

I wondered how my mother would cope, doubting that she would ever find a purpose to go on, but my concerns were short lived as it soon became apparent that she was focusing her energy on me to ensure I got a fair divorce settlement. Roger's death had served to sharpen and intensify her disgust for my ex-husband and her resentment was born out of the fact that her son had been cruelly snatched away from his family yet Stuart, who was in the fortunate position to have his family, had willingly given up on each of his three daughters. Stuart knew about my brother's death but if anyone thought that such a tragedy would bring him to his senses and make him realise how precious his daughters were then they were sadly mistaken.

I knew my Mam struggled to speak about Roger, she said there was a hole in her heart that could never be filled and instead she had buried the loss of her eldest child under a blanket of hatred for Stuart Palmer. I knew that it was my legal battle that gave her a reason to get up in the morning and keep on going.

A few weeks after Roger's death I went with Marion back to the neurosurgical ward where he had lay in a coma for the best part of two weeks. The night his machine had been switched off, we'd all rushed out of the hospital with not a word or a simple thank you to the staff for their hard work and dedication. She felt it was time to go back, to pick up his belongings and to say our belated thank yous. As we slowly trudged towards the ward a sudden chill ran down my spine as it had done on the night he had died. Instantly, I began to regret my decision to accompany Marion back to the RVI, a place that held too many bad memories for me and I wasn't sure I was ready to deal with them. I could see Marion in a similar state, if not worse, the colour had drained from her already pale face, her strong voice that had propped up most of the conversation in the car journey to the hospital had gradually faded away as we drew closer to our destination. Once on the ward she crumbled. She had been fighting the tears back since we had entered the building but going back on to the ward had been a step too far. Forced to take the lead, I thanked the staff who'd cared for him, presenting them with the generous donations we'd received in lieu of flowers at his funeral. The ward sister, Rebecca, handed over his scant belongings. I noticed his glasses, a shaving bag, wedding band and his Rotary watch. They were sealed in a clear plastic bag, his name printed in bold black marker pen across the front. ROGER GARWOOD. In a weird way I was glad to see his name in print, hear his name spoken out loud and a warm glow seemed to flow through me. It made me feel that somehow he was still with us and not just a few pounds of ashes sitting in a urn awaiting collection from the crematorium.

I handed the bag to Marion, who quickly drew them to her chest as if she was reclaiming part of her husband and at that precise moment I felt an overwhelming urge to get out of there. Our mission had been accomplished. We said goodbye and walked down the corridor, out of the hospital and into the car park.

As I looked up I saw what I thought was some sort of ghostly apparition, someone who had his back to me fumbling for change in the hospital car park, yet the contours of his body and the way he stood left me in no doubt that my eyes had focused and settled on the form of my ex-husband. There was no mistake. It was the dark satanic outline of Stuart fucking Palmer heading back towards his car. Since Alexandra had taken ill and then Roger had died, all thoughts of Stuart and our divorce had been firmly placed in the deepest recesses of my mind, purposely cast to one side, but now that he was in plain sight all my anger and frustration bubbled to the surface like an ocean of volcanic molten lava. The residue energy of its force propelled me forward in his direction. Slowly at first but then faster as I broke out into a sprint across the car park. I was getting closer but I had no idea what I was going to say to Stuart fucking Palmer when I caught up with him. Within fifteen or twenty seconds I had almost caught up to him as he made his way towards the entrance of the hospital. I had left Marion stranded by the car totally unware what had caught my attention making me bolt like a greyhound out of a trap. All I knew in that frantic moment of time was that I needed to get to him, I needed to vent my anger and tell him how he had failed as a husband and a father and of the damage he had inflicted upon us. On any other day I may well have ignored the opportunity, allowing him to go about his business undisturbed, yet not this day, not after what I'd been through. I couldn't let the opportunity go. I needed to give him a huge piece of mind. He needed to know what a total bastard he had become, how he had ruined his family's lives. He had reached the revolving door to the main entrance and I knew he was within ear shot. I struggled to catch my breath, a combination of nerves, adrenalin and exertion had emptied my lungs of its reservoir of air and I had to dig deep within my abdomen to exhale sufficient breath to carry my words to him.

"Stuart!"

He didn't turn.

"Stuart!" I screeched in a desperate gut curdling voice.

I sounded like a cat run over by a car, the poor creature expelling its final cry. He still didn't turn yet I knew he had heard because the other visitors who walked in close proximity to him turned their heads towards me, unsure why and where the ungodly noise was coming from. The attention from the onlookers didn't deter me one bit. I was in a zone that excluded all bystanders, it was just me and him and all dignity escaped me.

"Keep running Stuart, your good at that aren't you?" I shouted.

He was desperate to get through the door and into the sanctity of the hospital building, yet by a strange twist of fate the revolving door froze trapping him in the entrance.

"I'll keep following until you hear what I have to say," I screamed with no less intensity than my first cry although my throat burned with the sheer effort.

He pushed at the door gently and then harder, clearly reluctant to turn around and face his antagonist.

I had reached the entrance too, I was almost within touching distance of him, so close I could smell his cologne. The other hospital visitors took a step away, not wanting to get involved in what they thought was a domestic dispute.

"You need to listen to me your heartless, pathetic excuse of a man."

He had no choice but to turn and face me, his nostrils flared like a raging bull ready to charge. He was mad, as mad as hell, it was a sight I had witnessed too many times in the past yet not one fibre of my being was afraid of him. In my mind I had been taken to the depths of hell and confronting my cowardly ex-husband was light work in comparison.

"You've managed to find the hospital, I thought you must have forgotten the address."

He was lost for words. I looked around at the shocked onlookers and continued with my onslaught.

"Your daughter nearly died you selfish twat, and not once did you even attempt to come and see her, not once did you try to call her, no messages, nothing."

He started his defence with a roar.

"You stopped me from visiting her so don't fucking start that you bitch."

"When have you ever listened to me Stuart, not once, so don't give me that shit."

I was in full flow, wild horses wouldn't stop me from saying what I had to say and he knew there was no escape from my verbal attack.

"It was Alexandra's decision not mine and she had every right because you hadn't bothered to speak to her for seven months."

His head shook in a mocking gesture.

"Yeah, yeah, always my fault."

The volume of his voice had turned down a decibel now, it was merely mocking and dismissive, serving to intensify my anger and frustration.

"You disgust me," I spat at him, "of course it's your fault, you deserted her not once but twice."

He looked back towards the revolving doors and gave them a hard shove. Still they wouldn't budge an inch.

I stepped forward.

"You turned your back on her."

A woman in the entrance of the other doorway tutted.

"Annette leave it."

It was Marion, understandably in no mood for confrontation.

"You poisoned them against me," he protested.

I went for the jugular.

"You chose a cheap whore over your three daughters. What do you fucking expect?" I bawled.

"Bastard," the woman onlooker cursed.

He took a step closer, our noses were inches apart.

"Fuck off out of my face," he snarled demonically.

I wasn't going to let him have the last word. We'd built up quiet an audience around us. A thick set man had joined us in the doorway looking like he was ready for a fight.

"Fuck off out of my face," he repeated as he pushed past me.

Since Alexandra's illness and Roger's death there was a massive part of me that no longer cared. I dug deep and found enough wind in my lungs to bellow my parting shot as he scurried back in the direction of the car park.

"That's right Stuart, piss of back to your back street tart, forget about your daughters you selfish bastard."

I watched his dark silhouette getting smaller and smaller as the distance between us increased, he didn't look back once, his old life was well and truly behind him.

Marion and I walked back to the car in relative silence, my embarrassment apparent as I rushed away from the startled onlookers who'd had ringside seats to my shambolic outburst. When I reached the car I couldn't wait to get in a close the doors. It was as if we were shutting out the drama behind us.

Days after our run in I was still mulling over the event, reliving it in my head, constantly wondering if I could have handled it better or if I could have come up with more scathing insults. Ashamed as I was to admit it, I was pleased that he'd heard the truth, the words I'd been wanting to throw at him for so long.

I hadn't given much thought as to why Stuart had been visiting the hospital in the first place. It had been late afternoon when our paths had crossed and he was in his work suit. I had assumed he must have finished work early to attend the Eye Infirmary for one of his regular checkups. A day or two afterwards I began wondering about his mother. She wasn't a well woman and could that have been the reason he was visiting the hospital?

Even though it had been Stuart's mother who had severed all links with me and her granddaughters, I still felt a pang of guilt that perhaps we hadn't made more of an effort to patch things up even though that was counterbalanced by my annoyance at the fact that the once overzealous grandmother had cut all her grandchildren off dead since she and Abigail had argued the previous September.

The thought prayed on my mind for the rest of that morning until eventually I could struggle with the thought no longer. It was easy enough to find out, just ring the hospital and find out if she was a patient.

It took a simple phone call to the RVI main reception,. They put me through to Admissions and within minutes the helpful voice on the other end of the phone gave me the answer I had been looking for.

"Yes, Mrs Palmer was admitted to Ward 52 last week."

That's all I needed to know and I hung up almost immediately.

Now I had the information, I knew I couldn't keep it from the girls, especially Abigail. I knew she was big enough and strong enough to swallow her pride and go and see her Grandmother in hospital. It had hit Abigail particularly hard when she had rang her Grandma to voice her concerns about her Dad and she'd put the phone down on her mid-sentence. That act had brought home to her that her Grandmother's loyalty lay with her son. It still played on Abigail's mind that they hadn't spoken for so long and they'd parted on such bad terms.

I made the phone call to Abigail and Victoria that same afternoon to tell them their grandmother was in hospital. Victoria's response was the most measured, she wasn't sure what to do.

"I'll have a think about it Mum, I might go into the hospital to see her, I'm just scared I bump into Dad."

I sensed the genuine nervousness in her voice, I hadn't wanted to push her either way.

"Have a think about it and do what's best for you," I said, attempting to keep my voice as neutral as possible for fear its very tone might influence her decision.

When I broke the news to Abigail minutes after putting the phone down to Victoria, her response was less gauged and far more cavalier as I knew it would be.

"That's it, I'm going in to see her today," her voice full of emotion, "I don't care if my Dad's at the hospital when I get there."

I could sense the frustration and anger in her voice.

"Why the hell couldn't the bastard have told us she was in hospital? I just hate that man," she screamed down the phone.

Oh God, what have I just done? I wondered as I ended the call.

Alexandra and I were both sitting at the kitchen table eating dinner when Abigail came hot footing it through the front door, slamming it with such force it shook the whole house. She marched into the kitchen and I knew by the look on her face something was seriously wrong. Her eyes were puffed and bloodshot. I drew my own conclusion thinking she'd been to the hospital and had had a confrontation with her dad. Surely that was the reason she was so angry and upset.

"What's wrong Abigail? What has he said to you?" I asked as I jumped from my chair to go and comfort her.

She just came out with it. There was no preparation and no forewarning to make the blow easier for Alexandra's fragile ears.

"Grandma's dead," she sobbed, her hands smearing the remains of her make up as she wiped the tears from her eyes.

It was the last thing I had expected to hear. My heart skipped a beat as I automatically cast my eyes across to Alexandra to see how she would cope with the dramatic turn of events. Her eyes had filled with tears I could see that, but beyond the initial reaction she said nothing. I could see that her main concern was for Abigail who had now placed her head against my shoulder and was breaking her heart.

"What happened?" I said, my voice tinged with sadness as I tried to make sense of it all.

There had been no love lost between us, yet it was still a life that had been lost and she was my daughters' Grandmother, a Grandmother who would go to her grave knowing she hadn't made peace with the girls who had been the world to her since they had been born. For a moment I wondered how her last moments had been and I felt pity towards her. I suspected that she had died almost alone, unlike my brother who had been surrounded by love when he took his last breath. It would have been her and her cold hearted son. Nobody else.

Between the sobs Abigail relayed the story. She'd gone into the hospital that evening making her way to the nurses station to find out where her Grandma was.

"I knew something was wrong straight away," she said between sobs. "They said someone should have told us that Mrs Palmer had died." She looked up into my eyes. "She's been dead two bloody days Mum, two bloody days, why the hell couldn't he have text me and let me know? I hate him so much," she screamed.

I couldn't argue, there was no excuse I could offer up for her Dad's incredible behaviour. And then a thought crept into my head, a thought so wicked that I cursed myself for even thinking it. Surely it was nothing to do with her money?

Unexpectedly I felt the tears starting to flow down my face. I was sad the woman was gone yet the tears weren't for her. Each drop I shed was for my gorgeous daughters and their pain and suffering. Since that day Stuart had walked out on them their world had shifted beyond recognition. How much more could they take I wondered? The thought sneaked into my head yet again. What possible reason could their own father have for not telling them that their Grandmother had died?

33

Sleep eluded me for much of that night. I was still awake into the early hours of the morning listening to the occasional unnerving creek and groan of the house as it settled into its dormant state. In between the occasional nightly disturbances the silence was almost deafening , outranked only by the noise in my head as my thoughts were inevitably hijacked by the incredible drama of Stuart and his late mother. Why the hell hadn't he told his children their Grandmother had died? My fertile mind could almost see her chalk white, lifeless body. A shiver ran down my spine as the image burnt itself into my brain forcing me to suddenly open my eyes in an attempt to erase the sight from my mind. The selfish bastard I thought, he'd made no attempt to contact any of his girls, if he really cared and wanted to make amends wouldn't this have been the ideal opportunity to bring them all together, once more united in their grief? What sort of man was he? It was a question I'd asked myself so many times over the months since he'd left us. He was a monster not a man. He was a cold hearted creep.

Inevitably as I lay questioning his motives, it led me to wonder about his mother. Again, surely when she had realized the emphysema was winning the battle, strangling her lungs, suppressing her every breath, she would have wanted to make peace with her three grandchildren. Hadn't they been her world all of these years? As I thought back I recalled how she had been the first in the queue at the foot of my bed in the delivery suite after each of my children had taken their first breath. From the moment they were born she was determined to be a constant in their lives, forcing herself to the forefront at every event and every occasion throughout their childhood. More often than not she'd had the privilege of being the first to witness important milestones in their childhood. She'd heard Abigail babble her first audible word, Dadda, watched Victoria take her first tentative steps unaided before stumbling head over heels into her delighted Grandmother's arms. She relished being a grandmother and was vocal and opinionated in every aspect of their lives, from the food they ate, to the clothes they wore and to the schools they attended. Reluctantly, I had allowed her to wheedle her way in to our family in the full knowledge that any kindness she displayed towards me was disingenuous and merely a means to an end to get to my children. She tolerated me at the very best. No more than that.

Abigail was always the favoured granddaughter, the first born, the most treasured and she made no secret of the fact that she adored her and told her so on every occasion she could. This was irksome to me and strangely enough, to Stuart too. He would become very defensive when her favouritism was glaringly obvious and on more than one occasion I'd see him pull his Mother to one side, snapping his disapproval when he witnessed Victoria or Alexandra being starved of her attention, the bulk of which was always focused on her eldest grandchild.

Yet despite her obvious preference for Abigail, they had all given her pleasure in one way or another, filling a huge void in her otherwise empty life, giving her a renewed purpose, especially in the latter years. So I couldn't understand for the life of me why had she turned her back on them, especially her golden child, Abigail. My blood boiled as I played out my anger, punching my pillows into submission in an attempt to find a more comfortable position for my heavy head. It was glaringly obvious, my beautiful girls had been like sacrificial lambs led to the slaughter. Both Stuart and his mother had deliberately opted to break all ties with them as they didn't want to place them in a situation where there was a chance that they could carry gossip or dare I say evidence of his affair back to me. Once again it boiled down to money. If there was no proof of an adulterous affair, the Judge would be more sympathetic to Stuart. The timing was obvious, the rot had set in after the girls picked up on his lies about his holiday with Angela Maddison. It was at that point that he must have realized everything he did or said would be under close scrutiny by his watchful children. It was a situation he couldn't control and something had to give. He'd taken the decision to sacrifice his relationship with his children and his mother had backed him one hundred percent, so much so that she had decided to follow suit and disown them. How could she so callously cut them out of her life? What plan had they hatched ? Was it really about money? What sort of father valued money more than his own flesh and blood? My eyes flickered open yet again as I stared at the ceiling. It was clear as crystal, everything in that family was geared towards money and the preservation of their wealth.

Question after question raced through my head like a high speed train. Stuart was her only surviving child, his brother Frank had died ten years previously. The subject of money, or rather Gran's money, had been discussed countless times. We all knew she had a bob or two to leave, it was common knowledge and she'd been dangling that carrot in front of Stuart ever since his brother had died.

The two brothers had been at each other's throats for years and years and even after Frank's premature death, the feud lingered on as Stuart's animosity and resentment redirected towards his widow, Tina. The resentment between the siblings started at an early age. Frank had been Olive's favoured child, the first born. Stuart had lived in his older brother's shadow his entire life, constantly striving to gain his Mother's love and approval yet always falling a little short of his older brothers achievements. Stuart said his mother would burst with pride talking about Frank's feats, yet any accolades bestowed on Stuart were met with a luke warm reception. Having an insight into Stuart's childhood I had often suspected that one of the reasons he was so keen to have children of his own was to win favour with his mother. He knew she had always hankered after grandchildren, something Frank had failed to provide her with. They'd had the conversation countless times, Stuart and his mother, normally in my kitchen after lunch or an evening meal. I could still see Olive's face as she deliberately raised the sensitive issue.

"You'll be well off when I'm gone."

Stuart would grin.

"Don't be silly Mam, you'll be around for another fifty years."

It was a stupid statement because we all knew Olive had no more than a few years at best.

"Half to you Stuart," she'd say, "and the rest to these little darlings."

There would be a pregnant pause… a long deliberate pause and then she'd chip in that she owed it to Frank to leave something to his widow.

"£50000 to Tina, that's only fair."

And immediately Stuart would bite. I think Olive did it deliberately, her way of a little fun because when it came to her daughter in laws, she treated us both like something she had just scraped from her shoe.

"That's far too much Mam, Frank left Tina well taken care of and you know it."

There was also the slightly worrying concern that Tina had taken up with a new man only months after her husband's death. Then there had been gossip that she'd met this fella while her terminally ill husband lay in his sick bed. That hadn't gone down well with Olive Palmer.

And Olive would sit staring into space as if she was reviewing the situation. After much bickering and calculating the estate they both came to the decision that £20000 was a generous amount to leave to Tina. Stuart didn't care for her at all, twenty thousand was a fraction of Olive's estate but even that didn't sit well with him.

I could only wonder what was going through his head now his mother was gone. I expected that Olive had written her Will several years back but now that he was estranged from his children would he be hostile to any money left to them? Another thought jumped into my head. Surely his mother wouldn't have changed her Will? Even Stuart couldn't stoop so low as to persuade his mother to leave her entire estate to him? No, that just wasn't possible. I was sure of it.

Olive had a bit to leave by way of land and property. I recalled the evening Stuart had worked it all out. He'd sat at the kitchen table with a pen, a notepad and a copy of the Estate Agent's section of the local newspaper. Being the capable accountant that he was, it hadn't taken him long to calculate that his mother's estate was in excess of 1.6 Million. He sat beaming as he boasted she was completely mortgage and loan free, in fact she didn't even possess a bloody credit card!

Invariably, as we sat around the kitchen table more often than was healthy, she'd say how well off the girls and Stuart would be when something eventually happened to her. It was always just the girls and Stuart. I was conveniently left out of any inheritance planning, I was never mentioned, never considered. The crux of the matter was that even as long as ten years ago, it was as if they were trying to make sure that whatever happened, none of her money would ever find its way into my pocket. I couldn't help wonder, had Stuart always been planning to leave me? Had this been part of his long term plans and was growing old gracefully as a couple never been a factor.

I'd been lying half the night torturing myself and just as dawn was on the cusp of breaking, the penny dropped and everything fell into place. This was the only reason Stuart had tried to hide his mother's death. Stuart had coerced his mother to cut his daughters out of the will. He was more than capable. I sat bolt upright in bed. He would be the sole beneficiary of 1.6 million pounds. He'd cut his daughter's loose from his life so why should they get a penny?

And then another more pleasant thought. The court would have to take this into account when they divided our joint assets. I could feel a tinge of excitement stir within me, then within seconds my conscience instinctively rebelled. The woman was barely cold and already I was thinking of how it would benefit me and mine. Yet no matter how hard I resisted I couldn't fight my inward glee that maybe just maybe there was still a glimmer of hope that Alexandra would get her dearest wish and we'd be allowed to keep the family home. It made perfect sense to my now razor sharp mind. If Stuart had his mother's house to live in the court would be more amenable to me staying in the family home. There was also the small matter of about another 1.6 million quid to soften the blow. Surely the judge and the courts could see that? As I lay there plotting and scheming in the last dregs of quiet night hours, I had to question my own integrity. It dawned on me that somewhere along the line I had changed. My once soft gooey centre had crystalized into hardened rock. At some point, probably a couple of months after Stuart left me, the old Annette Palmer had disappeared. She got up and walked. This new version of myself was prepared to go to any lengths to protect my family and I was willing to dance with the devil to achieve that end. Hadn't I done just that, hooking up with John Bennett, a married man? I was exhausted, I couldn't stay awake a minute longer but as I drifted into a hypnagogic state, on the brink of sleep but not quite there, I remember making one last mental note, ring John first thing in the morning.

Karen was her normal pleasant self.

"Good morning, Saxtons."

"Hello Karen."

"Hello Mrs Palmer, John's in court this morning can I get him to ring you when he's available?"

"Please, it's fairly urgent Karen, so if you could get him to ring me back as soon as possible."

The mobile phone sat dormant all morning. Fortunately I had something else to keep my mind active. I was on a mission to find out where and when Grandmother's funeral was being held. It was clear Stuart was not going to be forthcoming with the information as in his mind none of us were remotely aware that she was dead. He'd get one big shock if the girls waltzed up on the day I thought, as my mind began to imagine the scenario for a moment before returning to the realization that it might be a little too much to expect them to cope with going to a funeral where they clearly wouldn't be made welcome. At least if I found out where it was being held they would have the choice of whether to go or not. I'd already tentatively broached the subject of their Grandma's funeral with all three of them. Victoria and Alexandra voiced a unanimous no, unless their Dad contacted them directly and asked them to attend. They were genuinely upset and saddened on hearing about her death, tears pricking up in their eyes as they both bit their lips in an attempt to hold back the flow of tears. They were wracked with guilt not to mention a large slice of frustration that they hadn't seen or spoken to her before she died.

"It doesn't sit well with me Mum," Alexandra's weak voice piped up. "I didn't contact her after the argument about Angela Maddison and Dad's holiday."

Her eyes looked at me sheepishly, guilt written all over her face.

"It's not your fault Alexandra, your Grandma had ample opportunity to contact you and she didn't, so don't beat yourself up about it."

My voice was deliberately firm and unflinching in an attempt to eradicate the nonsense she was thinking. And yet Victoria felt much the same and I knew from speaking to Abigail the previous day that she was still distraught that she hadn't made up with her Grandma.

She had been in tears.

"If only I'd gone around to see her after she put the phone down on me."

My own frustration was now becoming apparent as I tried in vain to convince all three of my children that it wasn't their fault, the argument had been a convenient guise for their Grandmother to cut all ties with her grandchildren at least until after my divorce settlement had been finalized and I had no further claim to her son's money.

I busied myself trying to find out when the funeral was because sure as hell, I was going to be there. There simply had to be a representative from our family, it was down to respect, it was as simple as that. However, there was another reason I wanted to be there, I wanted to know who was taking my children's rightful places in the mourning cars and I'd be dammed if I was going to miss that show.

John eventually rang me back late into the afternoon.

"I'm glad you contacted me, I need to speak to you Annette, we've got the court date, two weeks tomorrow."

I wasn't expecting to have a court date so soon. My heart fluttered, somehow I didn't feel the least bit prepared for its eventuality. He must have sensed my anxiousness.

"Don't worry Annette, Stuart may well make another offer before that date but in the meantime we need to firm up a Barrister to represent you."

He rambled on without a break in his breath.

"I'm thinking Mr Gilbert, the firms used him before, he's very good."

Now he'd mentioned the court date I'd lost my train of thought and the reason why I had wanted to speak to him in the first place. I followed the direction of the conversation.

"We need a meeting next week, there are a few things we must discuss. Can you free yourself from Alexandra for a little while. She'll still be recovering at home is she?"

He was on the case again, probing to see if there was an opportunity to call around. Well, that simply wasn't going to happen.

"She's absolutely fine, making great progress," I said, ignoring his main question.

There was a brief pause, a moments silence.

"Did you want to speak to me about something?" he prompted and immediately Olive Palmer's image sprung to mind.

"Yes I do want to talk to you. It's about Stuart's mother, she died a few days ago."

My voice was calm, matter of fact and shamefully without an ounce of emotion. He didn't need me to shade in the detail, we'd already had the court room fiasco when John's provocative suggestion that Stuart was likely to inherit from his mother had caused Stuart to have a courtroom outburst referring to me as being sick. For the first time in the conversation I could hear a hint of enthusiasm in my solicitors voice. Although I couldn't see him I just knew that a huge smile had pulled across his face.

"Such bad timing for Mr Palmer."

It wasn't good timing for Olive Palmer I thought, but I didn't offer up my thoughts knowing it was inappropriate given the circumstance.

He dropped in the mercenary comment without any coaxing from me.

"We need a copy of the Will, it could be brilliant news. I'd better get on to Steedman first thing"

"No," I jumped in.

"Annette we need it, if what you say is right he stands to inherit a significant sum of money."

"I know," I said, trying to explain myself before he went off on another tangent

"I want you to wait until after the funeral on Friday. My girls may well decide to go and I don't want to add fuel to the fire."

I explained about their father's actions.

"Stuart kept her death a secret for some reason, he didn't get in touch to tell the girls that their Grandmother had died."

"You're joking?"

"Nor has he told them about the funeral. We found that information from the funeral director."

I heard John let out a deep sigh.

"That man is a different level of bastard," he said.

"I couldn't agree more."

I was just about to say my goodbyes as the line of conversation drew to a natural end when John brought up a subject I was hoping to avoid. His voice dropped down a decibel or two as was often the case when the subject of money cropped up in conversation.

"I'm loathed to mention it Annette, but you still have quite a large bill outstanding. I know family circumstances have prevented you from dealing with the matter promptly."

My face flushed slightly as my eyes began to fill with tears, my brother and Alexandra's trauma was dragged to the forefront of my mind once more. I wondered when I'd last thought of my brother, had it been that morning or the day before? The guilt trip struck me once more as I struggled to remember. I bit my tongue and swallowed hard.

"Don't worry about my outstanding bill John, I'll have the account settled by Monday."

The words just popped out of my mouth before I could put the leash on and stop them. The truth was I had no idea if I had sufficient funds left in my deposit account to cover the fee which I knew to be £5500. Yet again another crisis jumped up and slapped me in the face.

"Thank you Annette, it's not me you understand, I'm getting pressure from Elizabeth, she likes to keep on top of the accounts."

Yes right I thought, nothing to do with you John, of course not.

"It's okay John, the account will be settled by Monday at the latest."

"Don't worry Annette there's always ways around these things. I try to give as much of my time as I can without adding it to my time sheet. Perhaps I could come around to the house when Alexandra's otherwise engaged. I can do a little work with you there where no one can clock up the hours."

I took a sharp intake of breath. I couldn't quite believe he had made it that obvious. Prostitute yourself he was saying. My anger was building, my hatred for this weasel of a man was growing by the second and if I had been standing in front of him I surely would have gone for his throat.

"As I said John, I'll settle the account by Monday."

I hung up on him before he had the opportunity to say another word.

34

I sat I my car in the Crematorium grounds. It was only 10.30am, the funeral service wasn't until 11am but it had been my intention all along to get there early. Despite my best intentions and my sheer determination to turn up at the funeral and face whatever flak came my way, in the end I couldn't be 'in your face,' I'd bottled it, I was quite happy to blend into the background but at least I'd be there, that was what mattered. I stood under a large willow tree within thirty yards of the small stone chapel and discreetly camouflaged by the surrounding foliage. At around 10.45am the first few mourners started to arrive. I knew I wouldn't be watching my own children in the congregation as all three girls had decided to boycott the event. For Victoria and Alexandra it had been an easy decision to make, their Dad hadn't been in touch to tell them their Grandmother had died let alone make them privy to the funeral arrangements. They could only draw one conclusion, if they did make an appearance they were going to be greeted with hostility and for the sake of their own dignity and out of respect for their Grandmother both had decided to stay away. For Abigail, the decision had been a more arduous one to make. She'd toyed with the idea of attending and her mind was almost set to go. That was until she made an spontaneous visit to see Auntie Peggy, her Grandmothers sister, who lay almost forgotten in a care home. I don't know why she had decided on visiting Auntie Peggy, but I suspected she was grasping at straws, somehow convinced that it would bring her closer to her dead Grandma.

After her Grandmother's death she had got it into her head she needed to visit Aunt Peggy, her aunt was a reminder of the grandmother she'd just lost. Whatever her reasoning, the day before the funeral she'd trundled along in her car to the Care Home determined to see her. I knew nothing about the planned visit, I only heard the whole story after the event, when she stormed into the house full of rage and anger.

"The bastard, I totally hate that man."

Her outburst took me by surprise, her voice full of venom as she burst into the kitchen.

The words were now all too familiar and I knew she could only be referring to her Dad.

"What's he done now?" I said hesitantly, lifting my head from the pile of ironing.

My heart went out to her as I glanced up at her red rimmed eyes, she'd obviously been crying.

"He's banned us from going to visit Aunt Peggy in the home," she said, throwing her car keys on the bench before plonking herself down on the kitchen chair with such force I thought she'd break its legs.

"Have you been to see your Aunty Peggy?" I questioned.

"I tried," she nodded, "but they wouldn't let me in. Dad has stopped me."

She explained that she had been filling in the visitors book when the manager had approached her. She was full of apologies but said visitations were limited.

She mimicked the manager's voice.

"Mr Palmer has Power of Attorney for your aunt and therefore the authority to say who visits her and the instruction is quite clear that only your father and Peggy's brother should be allowed in."

She shook her head in disbelief.

"Her brother hasn't seen her for fucking years."

She looked up sheepishly instantly acknowledging her slip.

"Sorry mum I didn't mean to swear."

The washing pile was totally abandoned at this point as we thrashed out the reason why his vindictiveness appeared to hold no bounds. In truth, I was no longer surprised by his actions, yet still the fact that he could sink to such depths never ceased to amaze me.

"She did tell me Auntie Peggy was on the Liverpool Care

Pathway," she added as an afterthought. "You know what that is Mum?"

"Yes I do."

Liverpool Care Pathway was for patients in their last days of life. They were sedated and all fluids withdrawn to hasten their death. I knew exactly what she was referring to and it made the situation that much worse. Peggy had only perhaps days left to live and Abigail had been denied the right to say her final goodbyes.

As we talked, sitting around the kitchen table, my naïve eldest daughter came to the realization that her Dad, through his thoughtless selfish actions, had made his position crystal clear. Not only had he cast his three daughters adrift, he didn't want them at the funeral of their Grandmother or anywhere near any other member of his family. She didn't say as much but behind her bold exterior she was fearful of his reaction if she turned up unannounced at the funeral. Stuart had always held the power of fear over his children. She was adamant she didn't care what he thought but it was all a façade. I knew she and her sisters were still frightened of him and there was no way they'd willingly want to be on the receiving end of his temper. She'd once been on the end of an incident that could have escalated out of control, over a mobile telephone bill a couple of years back. I'll never forget it as long as I live. It had all seemed so innocuous, the bill was about £15 higher than the monthly account limit their father had imposed on them. He was holding the bill in the air as she walked in through the kitchen door. Abigail shrugged her shoulders, apologised and Stuart's voice notched up another level. He'd had a bad day, I could tell, but what did he want her to do?

That was exactly what she said.

"What do you want me to do dad? I'm sorry."

"Well that's not bloody good enough."

She lit the touch paper.

"I'll do a cartwheel if it makes you feel better."

It escalated quickly from that point.

Stuart was in her face screaming and wailing what a ridiculous excuse for a daughter she was. Not one to walk away Abigail gave as good as she got, said her friends bills were way higher than hers and their parents didn't make half the fuss. She twisted the knife by saying he was on far more money than any of her friends fathers, and as the screaming got ever louder she called him a mean bastard.

Stuart exploded and picked up a wine glass and threw it against the wall. That was Abigail's cue to run and she made for the door. I heard her footsteps on the stairs en-route to her bedroom. To my horror Stuart took off after her. I gave him a few minutes convinced he would calm down but then I heard more screaming and a dull thud and then complete silence. I hesitated, waiting for something, some noise, a voice, a shout, anything. When I reached her bedroom door I couldn't believe what I was witnessing. Stuart was on top of her on the bed, his hands around her throat squeezing hard and Abigail was turning blue. I stood frozen in shock for some seconds until I realised that if I didn't do something he would quite possibly kill her. I looked around. Abigail's heavy shoulder bag sat on her computer desk and I reached for it and lifted it above my head. I remember thinking it was a little heavy as I swung it like an athlete's hammer in a full 360 degree circle and connected with Stuarts cheekbone. There was a sickening crack as Stuart flew over the bed and landed in a heap on the floor. Abigail was gasping for breath but the colour was slowly returning to her cheeks. I looked down at the sheets between her legs and noticed that she'd wet herself.

I took her through to the bathroom and cleaned her up while Stuart was lying on the floor, holding his hand to his jaw, squealing like a baby in pain. Abigail and I went to bed. Stuart left and didn't return until the following morning. The incident was never mentioned again.

Secretly I breathed a sigh of relief knowing that she wasn't going to the funeral. I knew that it was likely to turn nasty and it was no place to settle family scores.

As I waited for the other mourners to arrive I felt nervous as the adrenaline pumped around my body and every ounce of my being wanted to run. But I stuck it out and at seven minutes to eleven I witnessed the small procession of cars coming up the main drag of the crematorium. The hearse led the convoy followed by just one official black mourning car then a few random vehicles close behind. Olive Palmer wasn't well liked, there would be no more than a dozen people to pay their last respects. Nevertheless, at least they had had the opportunity to attend which was more than me and my daughters had been given. I shook my head in disbelief. How sad I thought, he could have afforded his own children the same rights.

As soon as the deathly procession had glided to a dignified halt outside the chapel, the black clad pallbearers prepared themselves to lift Olive's wicker casket from its glass encasement allowing the chief mourners time to disembark from their vehicles. Stuart was the first to step out of the car, his long lean figure framed in his immaculately tailored suit and was I mistaken, but was he actually smiling? Then my heart skipped a beat as the bitch stepped out behind him, her flowing blonde hair and slight figure were unmistakable, it was Angela Maddison alright, standing as proud as a peacock, confident in her place by his side. He reached to take her hand. Their hands were intertwined, his large shovel like mitt appearing disproportionate against her small skeleton like fingers. Their sign of affection had barely touched a nerve, admittedly there was a fleeting reminder that it was my hand he had once reached out to hold, yet that was it. Beyond that I felt nothing other than hate for him and his whore. It was only when Maddison's children stepped out from the mourning car to position themselves behind their mother and my ex-husband did I feel the first tangible pain piercing through my chest like a burning hot poker.

"The fucking bastard," I muttered to myself through gritted teeth, "the dirty, loathsome bastard."

My mouth fell open in disbelief and I slapped my hand hard against my hip bone in an attempt to release the frustration building up inside me. How could he allow that bitch and her offspring to stand where his own flesh and blood should have been? I looked again. He turned his head to speak to the gangly teenage boy, then his gaze fixed on the girl, daughter of whore and I wondered what he was saying to her as he smiled a sickening smile. One thing was for sure, she wouldn't have been subjected to his shouting and screaming as my children had throughout their lives. More infuriating was his body language, he looked relaxed and inviting as he beckoned the pair of them forward. They moved together, all four of them huddled behind the coffin like a normal family in mourning for the dearly departed. The beautiful close knit, plastic family barely knew the woman lying in the casket. It was almost farcical. My gaze followed the line of the congregation as they formed an orderly queue behind the main party. Some of the faces were familiar, neighbours, old family friends, her cleaner Mildred was there I noticed. And then I focused in on Tina Palmer, snaking her way up the line as she positioned herself behind Stuart. As she reached him, she tapped his shoulder to draw his attention. He turned to greet her, smiling again, their manner friendly and the chat flowed between them as if they were long lost friends and not arch enemies as I knew them to be for more years than I cared to remember. The pleasant scene puzzled me as I closely scrutinized their body language. When had they formed such a close alliance? Had they reconciled their differences when Olive became so ill? I had no answers, I could only draw one conclusion from the sight unfolding before me. Poor Tina Palmer hadn't inherited anything of significance in Stuart's mother's will. I knew my ex-husband well enough to know he wouldn't have been so affable to his sister in law if she'd had any significant claim on his mother's estate.

As I digested the situation my mercenary inclinations coaxed their way to the forefront of my mind once more. If Stuart had inherited his Mother's entire estate, surely I would be allowed to stay in the family home. How could a court deny me that? If Stuart's housing needs had been met by way of his Mother's large house and he had £1000000 on top they couldn't possibly deny me that right. I couldn't stop the thoughts racing through my head nor could I dampen my excitement at the prospect that there may be a good chance we would be allowed to stay in our home. As the party filtered their way into the chapel, I knew I couldn't follow. I had paid my respects. Job done. I walked towards the car, climbed in and started the engine. As I drove down the long drive and out of the cemetery gates my thoughts turned to John. I imagined he would have already set his pen in motion, requesting a copy of the will from Steedman. I knew he was almost as keen as me to find out what Olive Palmer had left in her Will and who the beneficiaries were. Yet at that point I no longer needed to question its contents, I knew it was Stuart who had inherited the bulk of it. Tina may well have received a little something in Olives will, but clearly Stuart was more than satisfied with the amount otherwise he wouldn't have given her the time of day at the funeral. I recalled vividly the conversations that took place between Stuart and his mother relating to her Will. He probed his mother regularly about money and what would go where when she died. He claimed his curiosity was never borne out of any self-interest, his benevolent cry was always yielded towards the concerns he had for his children and their wellbeing.

"I don't want a penny of my mother's money," he would say in his self-righteous voice. "as long as she leaves it to the girls I'll be more than happy."

As Olive's health deteriorated and her reliance on her family and friends increased, I began to realize that she pacified her sons scrutiny of her affairs by enticing him with appetizing snippets of information. I knew he'd voiced his concerns to his mother about Tina Palmer receiving £20000 and she justified her decision by saying she was Frank's widow and it was the least she could do for her. The conversation had always stuck in my mind as it occurred to me at the time that they were willing to discuss death and money so openly. It would never have been a conversation I would have ever had with my own mother, the prospect of talking about her demise filled me with dread and whenever she had tentatively broached the subject of her dying and what should happen to her house and belongings, I'd cut her off immediately. I couldn't bear the thought of losing her, yet Stuart's family were another matter, money was never far from their minds.

By the time I completed my journey home and pulled the car onto the driveway of our house I was convinced beyond a shadow of a doubt that Stuart had inherited everything, lock stock and barrel. Why else would he look so happy at his Mother's funeral? I'd seen how he'd welcomed Tina with open arms, if he hadn't known what was coming to him, I was sure there would have been far more hostility towards her.

As I sat on my driveway looking up at my beloved house I dared to breath a sigh of expectant relief. Perhaps when Stuart got the letter from John enquiring about the will he might even see sense and make a realistic offer, one which included the house and ongoing maintenance. He knew it was Alexandra's dearest wish to stay in the family home, now at least he could afford her that privilege, surely it was the least he could do.

Whatever happened, I knew at the very least I would be in a stronger position to negotiate a settlement. If my theory was correct and I was sure it was, he'd have to dish up and agree to give me a larger split of our joint assets now he had his mother's estate all to himself. I knew I just had to sit tight and let John Bennett do his work.

"Shit!" I exclaimed. "The bloody account."

Of course they wouldn't do much more work for me unless I

settled my account. That's what I needed to do I thought, as I reminded myself that I'd promised to pay the bill in full by Monday and I was almost certain that I didn't have enough cash to settle it.

As soon as I stepped foot through the front door I went straight to my lap top and checked my deposit account. My worst fears were confirmed. I'd been putting off for days, burying my head in the sand as usual, pretending the problem would go away. The money situation had been bad but not as dire as I had expected. I was £2000 short of what I needed. I considered my options yet again and at that point I realized I had only two alternatives available to me, either take my few remaining gold trinkets to the pawnbrokers or alternatively, ask my mother for another loan to tide me over. I knew how angry my mother would be if I pawned any more of my jewellery, so cap in hand, swallowing my pride yet again, I climbed into the car and headed towards her house.

I found mam in her favourite spot sitting by the window, eyes fixed to the TV watching her daily dose of Countdown. As usual I took a moment to appreciate the image before me, the light streamed through the window and bounced off her silver white hair and her eyes immediately lit up as I walked into the room. The warmth of her welcome touched my very core and instantly all apprehension melted away. The words hadn't been so difficult to get out after all and I could almost hear the glee in her voice that she was able to help me.

"Pass my cheque book across Annette," she gestured towards the sideboard where a collection of papers and envelopes stood propped up against the unit, their position fixed by a heavy crystal vase wedging them into line.

"Is that all you need?" she said, lifting her eyes to meet mine before committing to filling the details out on the cheque book.

"Yes, yes that's all I need," I insisted gingerly.

"You'll get every penny back as soon as I get sorted mum."

"I don't want it back."

Her voice was so strong and determined, it evoked memories of my childhood when she would give us merry hell if we stepped out of line.

"I just want you to see your day with that Palmer, I don't care what it costs, we'll sort the money out don't you worry."

She meant every word, her warmongering talk filled me with pride.

"You want maintenance off him Annette and I wouldn't accept any offer unless it included it."

"Yes Mum."

First thing on Monday morning I waltzed into the Saxtons' office to settle my account. Karen sat in her usual fixed position behind the reception, her face pan straight with no hint of emotion evident. She looked so pretty I thought, as I walked across the room towards her desk, her attractive image enhanced by the vase of flame red lilies perched on the desk by her side. As I approached, my nostrils caught a whiff of their strong aroma and for some strange reason the fragrance lifted a slight smile to my face. Today was going to be a good day, I just knew it. Clearing the bill was a weight from my shoulders and surely John would be in possession of a copy of the will. I slapped the envelope containing the cheque onto Karen's desk.

"Could you pass this on to Elizabeth please?"

"Thank you, I'll give it to her as soon as she gets in."

The relief of having settled my bill was short lived. I knew as soon as I'd placed the cheque on the Saxtons' desk I was already in debt to them again, the clock was ticking, every minute spent on my case would be listed on a time sheet and the bills were only going to crank up as John and Louise prepared for the final hearing. On top of this would be the Barristers fees and I'd yet to find out what he would be charging. My mind raced at the thought and I could feel the onset of panic sweeping over me but refused to let it affect me on this of all days. I convinced myself that nothing was going to spoil it.

I was almost in a trance like state as I headed into their offices. Louise greeted me with a smile and I reciprocated before turning my eye towards John. His face didn't light up, it bore a sullen expression. I could see they had been to court as both their desks were weighted down with papers and files. It was a sight I had been familiar with on a number of occasions when I had met them at court. Louise was about to take a chair when John disrupted her plan sending her on an errand to locate my file.

I watched her leave the room, the door closing quietly behind her.

"How have you been Annette? You look gorgeous ," he added, his voice rich and sultry.

He was playing with me and despite myself I could feel a tingle run down my spine as I recalled the intensity of our love making.

And yet equally, I loathed the man nearly as much as my ex-husband. Before I could answer, Louise walked back into the office, a large bulging file under her arm. Immediately I noticed John's attitude change, he straightened up in his chair, instantly resuming his business like composure. I could see how easy it was for him, he was able to turn the charm offensive off and on like a switch.

"Back to business," he said, a weak smile planted across his face.

I knew he had something important to tell me, I could feel it and I knew at that moment he had seen Olive Palmer's Last Will and Testament.

And yet there was no devious sparkle in his eyes, no fire, no look on his face that said 'we've got the bastard by the balls.'

"What's the problem John?"

My eyes glanced from John to Louise searching for the answer.

"Well," he said, as he flicked through the file Louise had just presented him with.

"Mr Steedman has come back very quickly regarding the letter I sent him requesting a copy of Mrs Palmer's Will."

He paused for a second or two before reiterating the important point in his previous sentence.

"Very quickly indeed, I got the copy first thing this morning."

"And?" I said impatiently. "What does it say?"

John removed the document from the lever arch file before placing it on the desk in front of me. I glanced at the paper before making eye contact with him once more, my impatience was such I didn't want to have to wait to read it I just wanted him to summarize it in one sentence.

"C'mon John, I don't need to read it word for word just tell me what it says."

He took a deep breath.

"Steedman sent us a copy of the Will as requested."

He paused again. I was infuriated.

"Come on John, what do you want, a fucking drum roll?"

Poor Louise nearly fell off her seat. Something was wrong, something was very wrong and I could see it in his eyes.

"Tell me what the Will said," I exclaimed in desperation. "How much is the bastard getting from his mother?"

He sighed, his voice loud and deliberate as he wanted me to fully take in the devastating news he was about to deliver.

"It would seem that Mr Palmer didn't inherit one penny from his mother. Her entire estate was left to her daughter in law, Tina Palmer."

35

The name went over in my head as I tried to make sense of the information. Tina Ann Palmer, surely not? That can't be right I thought as I lunged for the document on the desk, my hands now shaking uncontrollably, making reading the text almost impossible.

"That's impossible." I screeched as my eyes scanned the page.

I took a deep breath, told my hands to stay still. It was Olive Palmer's Last Will and Testament alright, I'd read that much, yet I couldn't focus my concentration sufficiently to read it word for word.

"The whole thing is a sham, totally absurd," I said, almost screaming. "As much as his mother had a warped mind, there is no way she would have left everything to her daughter-in-law. She hated her."

Louise and John sat in silence while I ranted on.

"And absolutely nothing at all to her only surviving son? It simply defies logic."

I wanted them to say something. I wanted to hear John say it was a big scam and that he could see right through it but they both just stared blankly across the table.

"And," I added, as I had a sudden flashback to the funeral the previous Friday, "Stuart was at the funeral and very pally with Tina Palmer. I know for a fact that wouldn't have been the case if his mother had disinherited him and left the whole bloody lot to her."

I was on the verge of tears, such was the enormity of the distressing news, as I felt my bottom lip begin to tremble.

"He wouldn't have been greeting her with open arms, more likely he'd be hitting her over the head with a baseball bat."

It was all so obvious now. They had never been close, Stuart slagged her off continuously.

John's eyebrow raised very slightly.

"You think they have pulled something underhand?"

"Without a doubt." I replied.

I was getting more and more flustered as I tried to explain that I'd stood by a tree watching the whole thing, like some perverted peeping tom. A slight warmth spread across my face as I blushed with embarrassment. I knew how ridiculous it all sounded, as I mentioned the funeral. This supposedly normal family were not so normal after all. A voyeur at a funeral and a father so warped that he hadn't even told his daughters of their Grandmother's death.

And now, on top of everything I'd been through, the glimmer of hope I'd held onto for just a few days that there was a possibility that I might just be able to stay in my home had been dashed on the rocks. I gave a heavy sigh, as I held my head in my hands. How could I adequately encapsulate the fucked up dynamics of the Palmer family well enough to make John and Louise understand? No one could understand, let alone a Judge in a court room. The funeral scene kept repeating over and over in my head. Her hand on his back and the smile as he recognised who it was. They would never truly know how significant that was. It was all the evidence I needed to know there was a rabbit off, that something didn't smell right, yet it meant nothing to anyone who didn't know anything of their past relationship. They had stitched me up well and truly. They had swindled me out of the right to remain in my home and I was one hundred percent convinced.

"There's more," John said. "If you read the Will, both Stuart and Tina Palmer are executors."

I glanced down at the document. Was I being given some hope?

"Your ex-husband and sister in law are executors of the will Annette, which means they both have a responsibility to distribute the Estate, but what's strange are the witnesses."

I looked down at the two witnesses signatures just below their printed names.

John continued.

"The signatures are those of your husband and Angela Maddison which means your ex-husband knew exactly what was in that will. Look at the signatures," he paused giving me time to take the information in before adding.

"It was signed by Olive Palmer and witnessed in the presence of Stuart Palmer and Angela Maddison."

My eyes traced the outline off all three signatures.

I shook my head in total disbelief.

"Impossible," I cried again, "Stuart would never have agreed to witness a will that left him nothing and everything to his sister in law, nor would he have agreed to be the executor."

My words reached fever pitch as I held my head in my hands once more.

"It's all very peculiar," Louise added, "irregular to say the least."

John was shaking his head.

"I would think that any son being asked to witness a Will like that would be furious."

I nodded in agreement.

"And yet he wasn't. They were all best buddies at the funeral and he'd supposedly known for five months he'd been left fuck all."

Louise twisted uncomfortably in her seat, not impressed with my choice of words.

John pushed the document closer.

"Look at his mother's signature again Annette. Are you sure it's definitely hers? It could have been forged."

I looked at the signature. I knew instantly it had been her hand that had penned the signature.

"Yes it's definitely hers, I've witnessed it numerous times before."

"Are you one hundred percent sure it is her writing?"

"Yes it is."

"How was your mother in laws mental health? Was there any likelihood she was suffering from Dementia?"

"No definitely not," I said, "she was as sharp as a tack that one. There was nothing wrong with her mind."

John sighed again.

"Are you sure she hasn't been pressurized into changing her Will to disinherit the children?"

"No," I said dismissively, as much as I wanted to believe they had forged her signature or coerced her into something against her will I knew that it wasn't the case. Whatever plan had been hatched she was a willing party to it.

I looked at the will again. More incredible revelations. She'd left small bequests to her neighbours and a few family friends, even something to a cat and dog charity but absolutely nothing to her only son.

I wanted to rip the thing apart.

"All these bequests yet nothing to her son or her grandchildren, does that not just stink to you?" I threw the paper across the desk. "Take a look John, it makes no sense, it's a scam, it has to be illegal."

He picked it up and looked at it again.

"I appreciate where you're coming from Annette, but even though its highly unusual to disinherit your only son, its not against the law."

"It has to be," I cried in desperation.

"And get him to witness the signature and to execute the estate." Louise said quietly.

A disapproving frown crept across John's face as he glanced at Louise.

"As I said Louise, highly unusual but not against the law."

He placed it down on the desk.

"If it's a legally binding document the court will accept it, they'll only question it if they think there was some skullduggery going on."

"Exactly," I said, "there's no doubt about it, it's a fiddle. There's no mention of her assets. Look at what it says."

I pointed to the line and read it out.

"I give the residue of my estate both real and personal to Tina Ann Palmer."

I was fuming, John could see it in my eyes.

"This was my one last chance to stay in my home. If Stuart inherited that much money they would have to take it into account."

John started to talk money. I knew the figures off by heart, Stuart had talked about it so much, often referring to his mother's assets as the family crown jewels.

John's eyes were now well and truly sparkling. I had wet his appetite. In the past he had been slightly dismissive of my mother in law's wealth but now it was real and tangible it was a very different story, now the wicked witch was dead I could see his brain ticking over. How much of my ex-husbands potential new found wealth could hit his pockets? More money for Annette's higher fees for him. His attention immediately turned to Louise, his voice sharp as if he didn't have a minute to lose and I'll admit, I was pleased that something had eventually rattled his cage.

"I want you to get onto Steedman and ask him for the notes relating to Mrs Palmer, there will be records of letters and conversations she had concerning her Last Will and Testament."

Louise looked bemused, then, as if he could almost read her mind.

"Mr Parkland drafted the Will and he's a partner at Richfield Grealish, seems that they are the family solicitor, so the notes should be easy to get a hold of."

He was in full flow. It was amazing how the mere mention of £1.6 million changed his whole persona.

"Oh and Louise, we need to get onto Land Registry, see who the registered owners are for both the land at Redburn and the property in Jesmond."

His mind was working like a high speed computer as his eyes swung back to me.

As he worked he continued to talk.

"I have an appointment for us to meet Mr Gilbert at his Chambers, 5pm Thursday. Can you make it?"

He momentary took his eyes away from his files giving me a sideway glance. I nodded yes in agreement. Then his voice changed, he had a glint in his eyes again and I knew the direction his thoughts were going.

"Can I pick you up? I'm more than happy to drive by your house?"

I bet you are I thought, that wasn't going to happen.

"No I'll meet you there," I said sharply "I'll find my own way. No need to worry about that."

Thompson Chambers stood barely one hundred yards from the court house. The building was far more discreet and the entrance to the premises was almost hidden from view and only accessible via a wrought iron gate leading onto a narrow side alley. When I eventually found my way into the building I was greeted by John who was sitting in reception, his knees piled high with paper and files.

"Oh I'm glad you've arrived," he said. "Gilbert is ready to see us."

"Sorry I'm late," I said as he jumped to his feet and headed out of reception towards Gilbert's office.

It was clear he was familiar with the layout of the building as he found his way to the barristers office with no directions needed. Clearly it was a path he had tread many times before . One heavy knock on the door and a loud pompous voice shouted out from the other side.

"Come in."

As we entered Gilbert was on his feet and heading towards us his hand outstretched ready to exchange greetings. From the depth of his voice I had expected to see a much larger gentleman yet instead I was greeted by this small squat man with a ruddy complexation and tight curly hair that only served to emphasize the roundness of his face.

"Take a seat please," his hands gesturing towards the deep green velvet sofas which had been strategically placed to complement an ornate marble fireplace.

"Can I get you tea, coffee?"

We both declined, eager to push on with the meeting. I knew John was clocking the time, no doubt ensuring he added every second as billable hours. My anxiety reared its head once more as I wondered what this was all going to cost, I could only hazard a guess. I only had to look at the cut of Gilbert's suit and the location of his offices to know his services would not come cheaply. My heart began to skip to its own beat once more as my thoughts were inevitably drawn to my ongoing dilemma where the hell was I going to find the money to pay for all this?

My worries were temporary suspended as I heard Gilbert's voice demanding my attention.

"Lovely to meet you Mrs Palmer, I've had the opportunity to read your file."

He smiled at John before opening up the file on a page he'd earmarked with a post it note .

"Let's start with Mr Palmer and the other woman, Angela Maddison."

John took a deep breath and then relayed the whole sorry tale whilst I sat back listening, nodding in agreement when it was my cue to do so. The conversation followed the catalogue of events from Stuart leaving, to him emptying the bank accounts, understating his earnings, the list went on and on inevitably ending at his Mother's death and the subject of her Will. A good hour had passed and Gilbert was still probing, asking question after question. The file lay before him on his desk, each relevant section conveniently sectioned off with his favoured yellow post it notes. As the conversation progressed, his small stubby fingers pawed back and forward through the pages. It was clear he'd read my case cover to cover, he needed no prompting to remember names and dates. As the meeting progressed I was gradually won over to the fact that at least he had a good understanding of my predicament and the measure of my ex-husband, perhaps he was the man to represent me at a final hearing.

I soon realised that it was Gilbert leading the meeting which seemed very odd as I was used to Bennett running the show. He wasted no time laying bare his opinions as to how the case should be handled

"I think we need to call Angela Maddison as a witness."

Good start I thought.

John raised his head from his notes. He had a puzzled look on his face and I could sense he wasn't convinced.

"Are you sure we should summon her?" John questioned.

"Oh yes, no doubt about it. We need to discredit Palmer, He said he didn't start a relationship with Maddison until after he left the family home yet within four weeks he is holidaying in France with her and her children and that's just a joke."

John nodded reluctantly as Gilbert took centre stage.

"We need to show Palmer to be the liar and cheat he is. He planned his departure all along and emptied the bank accounts in the process."

Now I was totally on Gilbert's side but I wondered if I was up for confronting Angela Maddison in the court room. Damned right I was. She was the bitch who'd driven a monster sized wedge straight down the middle of my family.

John didn't argue against calling Angela Maddison, instead his hand was already jotting the instruction down on paper, yet his body language was signaling quite the opposite, he wasn't in agreement, occasionally shaking in disbelief.

Gilbert continued.

"Let's not forget, Maddison witnessed Mrs. Palmer sign her Will. We need to find out what she knows about it, Palmer must have discussed with her how he felt about Tina Palmer inheriting everything, which leads me onto The Will."

His nimble fingers flicked through the file and he pulled out a copy of the document.

He turned and looked at me.

"This is a joke is it not? Highly suspicious to say the least. You don't leave Jack Shit to your only son and then ask him to witness the will and be the executor too."

Beautiful I thought and so eloquently put. Surely the Judge at the final hearing would see through the scam exactly as Gilbert had?

John updated him.

"We've requested a copy of Mrs Palmer's file from the solicitor. It's unlikely there will be a copy of her old Will, more likely its already being destroyed. It all looks very suspicious and we are thinking there may be some sort of secret trust set up." Gilbert agreed immediately.

"It is a substantial sum of money we are talking about £1.6 million you mentioned Mr Bennett."

"Yes, that's a ball park figure," John said.

Gilbert raised his hands in the air as if he'd just had a brainwave.

"We need to call Tina Palmer as a witness. We want to know exactly what she has inherited, the will tells us nothing. What if there is a secret trust? We need to get to the bottom of it."

My eyes focused on John who I could see was getting slightly flustered at the prospect. He pulled his tie away from his neck loosening the top button of his shirt as he did so. There was something concerning him yet he was keeping tight lipped as he continued to scribble his notes.

Still Gilbert wasn't finished. Once again his fingers were pawing through the file and he continued to speak as his eyes glanced up and down the pages.

"I also have grave concerns about Mr Palmer's earnings. We know for a fact that he is understating his income," he said as his hand landed on the income tax returns.

John shook his head for the umpteenth time.

"We haven't got long until the hearing, four weeks."

John was clearly apprehensive at the prospect of calling witnesses yet Gilbert's fighting talk enthused me, he was winning me over. I wanted to see Angela Maddison and Tina Palmer hauled over the coals. I wanted the Judge to see what I knew to be true, they were all in it together and if they were forced to give evidence I was sure the lot of them would be outed. While John and Gilbert continued to talk through some of the more technical details that were way above my head, I mulled over my finances once more. Whatever the cost I knew I needed to pull together the cash because I wanted Gilbert to represent me. But more than that I was desperate to see both of those sad bitches take the stand. The home wrecker and the bitch who was trying to swindle me out of the right to stay in my home.

Gilbert seemed confident he could break them down and that was good enough for me.

Still I had to pose the question.

"What are your fees Mr Gilbert?"

The pair stopped mid conversation as they turned their attention to me. John glared at me whereas Gilbert didn't flinch as he fired back his response.

"£6000 Mrs Palmer, that's my fee and its fixed. If the case rolls over into a second day, that's still my fee."

"Oh good," I responded positively before taking a deep gulp.

That was a lot of money yet I wasn't prepared to share my concerns with either Mr Gilbert or John Bennett, my pride wouldn't let me even though I barely had a pot to pee at that moment in time.

"That's fine," I said as if it was small change for me.

"I look forward to taking on the case Mrs Palmer," he smiled before adding, "over the coming weeks I want you to chase up medical reports for Alexandra. We must put across to the court how reliant Alexandra is on you both financially and emotionally."

His words were almost stern as he delivered them.

"It's vital you get me this information, a lot hinges on it."

It was agreed Gilbert would represent me and we said our goodbyes. It seemed like we'd been there for hours and both John and I were both keen to make our get away. John lagged behind me as he packed his briefcase with papers. I had taken the opportunity to add a little pace to my step and marched ahead of him through the reception then out into the small alley. I had no intention of waiting for him, I just wanted to get to my car and go home yet he caught up to me before I reached the wrought iron gate leading back onto the quayside.

"Wait Annette," he said as he caught my arm to stop me in my tracks.

I turned to face him.

"We need to talk Annette, do you want to go for a quick coffee?"

"Sorry John, I need to get back to Alexandra, she's not been well today," I lied, desperate to get away.

He persisted.

"Annette I don't know why you're so reluctant, I just want to see you again, get back to where we once were."

My hackles were now up, my voice remained low yet now it had a sharp edge to it.

"Get back to what John? You coming around to my house and having a quick fuck behind your wife's back? Oh and let's not forget about the odd throttling, you enjoy that too or was that just a bit of foreplay to get me excited?"

He shook his head, his voice pleading.

"Let's not go there Annette, I'm sorry about that, I let my frustration get the better of me." He inched closer. "You know what you do to me."

His hand reached out towards my face, immediately I slapped it down.

"Do not even think about touching me."

He changed his tack coming at me from a different angle, yet his voice no less tantalizing trying to draw me in.

"We can help each other you and I, I'm happy to work out of office, that way Elizabeth will have no clue, you could really reduce your legal bill."

I smirked.

"And what will that cost me John. How many blow jobs do you want in exchange?"

A look of disgust spread across his face.

"What are you getting at you bitch?"

I could almost feel the anxiety rising within me as he stepped closer. I could smell his sweet breath, his after shave. Hold your nerve I thought to myself.

"John," I smiled confidently, "you're my solicitor let's leave it at that, there's a good boy."

I could see his hand lifting, it was if it were in slow motion, my body tensed anticipating his hand strike me but it wasn't going to happen, I wouldn't let it.

I grabbed his hand as he launched it towards me, amazed at the surge of strength that appeared to take over me.

"Don't even fucking think about it you little fucking creep. You work for me and I'm calling the shots so don't even begin to threaten me."

I slammed his knuckles into the brick wall behind him and he winced in pain.

"Let's just get that clear and bear in mind I will be scrutinising every inch of your next bill, so if it's just a single penny out I'll be knocking at Elizabeth's door raising some fairly sensitive issues about their high flying cunt of a solicitor."

His legs seemed to buckle at the knees as he fell against the wall, totally lost for words. He staggered against the wall, panting heavily as his briefcase fell onto the ground. I stood over him for a few seconds wondering where my strength and courage had come from. It was as if I had floated above the scene, looking down on the drama unfolding in a Hollywood action movie.

I bent down and picked up his briefcase.

"Here you are Mr Bennett, you've a lot of work to do, you need to take care of this."

I threw it into his lap.

"Now, if you'll excuse me this little lady needs to get home. There's somebody there who needs me."

36

Bennett dropped his pen onto the desk and flexed his hand in an attempt to relieve the cramp in his fingers. As the pain registered he instinctively looked down at his right hand, at the grazed, scabbed, knuckles pulling as the tort skin cracked a little more with each flex. His face flushed with embarrassment as his memory recalled the events outside the Thompson Chambers.

"Stupid fucking bitch," he muttered quietly under his breath.

He could barely acknowledge to himself let alone anyone else that an insignificant, whimpering woman got the better of him on the night. And he couldn't deny it no matter how he viewed it. She'd put him on the bottom, on the floor and she sneered at him and ashamed him as he was to admit, a shiver of fear and apprehension had crawled up his spine. She had made him look like a fool. A definite smile played at the corner of his lips. He wasn't prepared to leave it at that. He had a prearranged meeting with Elizabeth to discuss the Palmer case and he had it all planned out. He may not have been able to turn the tables in the alley way but the bitch would live to regret what she had done. He would hit her in the hardest place possible, in the most sensitive area of her entire being... her pocket.

Peering over the top of his reading glasses he punched in the four digits of the internal number on the key pad, the line beeped no more than once before his innate charm sprang into action.

"Good morning Elizabeth, how are you today?"

Not waiting for a response, he continued.

"I was wondering if you had a few moments to spare so we can have that meeting you requested?"

His fingers strummed on the desk as he waited for her reply, it wasn't long in coming, she quickly obliged clearly intrigued to find out what was going on.

"That's lovely Elizabeth, I'll be along in a few minutes."

A smug smile crossed his face once more as his mind worked overtime on the cunning plan that would bring Annette Palmer down a peg or two. All he needed do was plant a seed in Elizabeth's gullible mind and then she would do his bidding for him.

He was going to make the little bitch sweat, he had nothing to lose, because it was too late in the day for her to jump ship and change solicitors. He held all the aces and with less than two weeks to the court hearing it would be sheer madness to start all over again. His mind started to wander again, he couldn't stop himself. She'd served her purpose on the sexual front and he'd ridden her like she were a young filly. He could hardly contain himself on the occasions he'd visited her at home and she was as keen as him at first, always up for their experimental frolics.

And then everything changed.

His wife. Annette's anger and distaste when she'd realised the shocking truth. And who could blame her? After all she'd been the victim too. But he would blame her. She should have been grateful, she should have enjoyed it for what it was, she should have been thankful that he'd been so considerate, so keen, so willing and ready to risk so much.

He jumped to his feet as he grabbed his pen and legal pad in one hand while his other hand adjusted the crotch of his trousers. He opened the office door and headed off along the corridor towards Henshaw's office.

Elizabeth's greeting was guarded as she raised her head from the mountain of paperwork on her desk.

"Hello John," her voice sounding less than enthusiastic.

Bennett gestured towards the chair, she acknowledged the hint.

"Yes, do take a seat."

Bennett took his time as he pulled out the chair slowly and sat down.

Elizabeth looked at the notes in her diary.

"Yes, the Palmer case isn't it? What seems to be the problem?"

He sighed.

"Well Elizabeth, no real problems as such, it's just that I thought

I'd better bring you up to date. I would appreciate your advice on a rather sensitive matter."

She raised an eyebrow as she placed her pen on the open page of the diary as she sat back in her chair, mirroring Bennett's posture.

"What advice can I offer?" she asked with a hint of surprise in her tone.

"You may already be aware but Louise and I are spending a considerable amount of time on Mrs Palmer's case"

"Is there a problem with that? Is it affecting your other work?" she said.

He gave a weak smile.

"No, it's not infringing on my other work, not at all."

He had it all rehearsed, his face remained pan straight as he delivered the line that he knew would grab her attention.

"However there could be a problem with the fees. They are mounting up and my fear is that Mrs Palmer won't have the resources to meet the upcoming bill."

Money was always the Henshaw's be all and end all, their God. He watched as she referred to Annette Palmer's timesheet.

"She settled the outstanding account last month, a little late admittedly, but never the less it was paid in full."

"Yes," he said, "but I do know she struggled to pull that money together."

Elizabeth flicked her hair back from her face. Still she wasn't unduly alerted.

"She's up to date John, so there's no problem. Don't forget she won't be the first client to not pay after the divorce settlement has been reached."

She picked up the pen and made a note on the timesheet.

"We can wait until after the hearing for any outstanding monies at which point she'll have a settlement. What's the value of their joint assets, it's around a million isn't it?"

Bennett was about to spin the biggest lie of all, he had deliberately not filed Mrs Palmer's Last Will and Testament, there was no way she would get to know any of the details until it was far too late.

"Yes," Bennett confirmed without hesitation, "but her husband's mother has died and Palmer is an only son and her estate has come into the mix and Mrs Palmer is now adamant she should get to keep the marital family home should Palmer inherit."

Bennett paused as he looked down at his hands and was faced yet again with the sight of the bruised scraped skin across his knuckles. It was time to go for the killer line.

"And if that happened there is nothing that would go to Mrs Palmer by way of liquid assets, everything is in property and pension funds."

Elizabeth shifted uncomfortably in her seat.

"What figures are we talking about John, will it have a significant impact on the case?"

Bennett teased her.

"Oh yes, it could have a significant impact on the outcome.

Elizabeth sat forward in her chair, the mere hint of money and her mouth was almost salivating.

"Well spit it out man, what sum we talking about?"

"Mrs Palmer believes that the estate is in the region of £1.6 million but as you know she is not legally entitled to any of that."

Elizabeth slipped her pen into her mouth and started to chew nervously.

"So the Judge could quite easily come down on the side of Mrs Palmer and grant her the right to stay in her home but it will not leave her anything by way of cash, nothing left to pay our fees."

Henshaw grinned. There was a solution.

"She can remortgage the house."

Bennett shook his head.

"She can't, no legitimate income, no bank will touch her with a barge pole."

The realisation of the situation was beginning to sink in.

"How much are you forecasting the final bill to be?"

This time Bennett leaned forward in his chair. He paused for dramatic effect, lowered his voice to almost a whisper.

"As much as £25000 including the Gilbert fee."

Henshaw didn't know whether to laugh or cry.

"Good," she said without too much conviction.

"But it should be a whole lot higher," he said.

It was Elizabeth's turn to lean forward, their faces were barely inches apart.

"Explain."

He'd planned the moment well as a look of guilt swept over his face. Bennett's dramatics now came into play, a life time in the court room had fine-tuned his art and overflowing with sincerity he began to try and justify his actions. He slumped back in his chair.

"It's all been very time consuming and unfortunately I've made a bit of a mistake."

"What do you mean?"

Her voice was sharp.

"Louise and I have spent a great deal of our own time working on the case."

Elizabeth's face was now turning the same shade as her flame red hair, her previous civil voice replaced with a harsh cut edge.

"What the hell do you mean John, you and Louise have spent your own time on the case?"

He shrugged his shoulders apologetically.

"We, err... I've been spending a lot of time at her house working through her case."

"Her house?"

"Yes," he said. "As you know her daughter has been very ill and it has been more convenient to meet there. I've also asked Louise to pull hard on this case and the long and the short of it is that there's an awful lot of hours that haven't been logged on the office time sheet."

Standing up from her chair, both her hands anchored to the desk as she leaned towards Bennett to bellow her point in his direction.

"There is no 'your' time John. You know how I disapprove of out of hours visits and it's for this very reason that hours get missed." She lifted her hand and gestured. "Do you think these offices pay for themselves and how do you think we afford your extortionate salary?"

Bennett was quick with his defence.

"But I haven't forgotten them Elizabeth, I have them logged."

"Yes, but the woman has been our client for practically a year and she's paid her bill on time month in month out and now you're telling me there's the little matter of twelve months missed hours?"

As she sat back down she turned her attention to the computer screen pulling up the client account ledgers. As she waited for the program to load John relaxed in his chair trying to retain his smugness knowing his mission was almost complete.

"How many hours have you and Louise spent on the case and not charged out?"

Her hands clicked furiously on the keypad.

"Oh," he pondered, "that's a difficult one, thirty hours, maybe more."

"For fucks sake John, that's ridiculous, that's another £9000."

Her head shook in disbelief. Bennett could barely stop himself smiling.

Her attention was now drawn back to the computer, with the program powered up she nimbly tapped in the Palmer name. Her eyes glared at the screen.

"You're right, there's over £8000 in billable hours on Mrs Palmers account at the moment and now we are going to have to weave in these additional hours."

"We can't do that to the poor woman Elizabeth. I really wish I hadn't mentioned it."

His performance was almost reaching its finale.

"Well you have," she snapped, "and now it's my problem." She rubbed her temples with her forefinger and thumb then looked up. " And I agree we need to inform Mrs Palmer that her bill is getting rather large and it would be advisable that she pays at least half of the outstanding amount before the final hearing."

"Yes Elizabeth."

"I do agree if liquid funds are low and there is the chance she is to remain in the family marital home, she needs to understand that she's going to have to find her solicitors fees from somewhere."

"Yes Elizabeth. Should I request payment or would that be better coming from you?" Bennett said tentatively.

Elizabeth sighed deeply.

"I'll send the letter to Mrs Palmer asking her to make an interim payment, leave it to me."

Bennett nodded in agreement.

"I think that's best Elizabeth, I'll leave it in your capable hands."

Bennett made his way back to his office and collapsed into his chair. He closed his eyes and took a deep breath then slowly exhaled.

He spoke out loud. There was nobody in the office, no need to whisper or mutter under his breath.

"Nine fucking grand that's cost you Annette Palmer, nine fucking grand." He laughed out loud. "I did warn you."

He leaned forward and picked up his mobile, keyed in her number. Annette picked up the phone on the third ring.

"Hi Annette, how are you?"
"Fine John."
"I just wanted to give you the heads up."
"About what?"
"Just a little bad news I'm afraid. Elizabeth has made a terrible mistake with your bill."

37

I couldn't stop thinking about the night outside the Barrister's office. I felt ashamed of myself, when had I turned into such a hard faced bitch? Admittedly John had provoked me, yet I could have handled it in a more dignified manner and not behaved like some common fishwife in a pub house brawl with the language to match. And when had I ever used the 'C' word? For years I'd cringed whenever I'd heard anybody use it and on an odd occasion even rebuked the perpetrator. It was without a doubt the worst word in the English language but now it had found its way into my common vocabulary and my thought pattern on a regular basis.

Since that night I had been dreading having to speak with Bennett on the phone again or worse still a face-to-face meeting but his phone call out of the blue took me completely by surprise. I had expected him to be cold, yet surprisingly his manner was casual, relaxed, even warm, as if nothing had happened between us.

He was giving me the heads up that Elizabeth had made a mistake with my bill.

"What do you mean mistake, John?"

"There are a few hours you haven't been charged for. I just wanted you to know because I appreciate funds are tight"

"How many hours John, how much are we talking about?"

My voice was almost frantic as I fired questions at him, yet still I tried to keep my cool, I didn't want to break down or worse still start shouting my mouth off using the 'C' word again.

"I really can't say Annette, I just know she said that a couple of timesheets had been misplaced. Unfortunately I have nothing to do with the finances, that's strictly Elizabeth's department I'm afraid."

It could have been my imagination or did I detect a hint of joy and satisfaction in his voice? I persisted in my attempt to get some information out of him

"She didn't give you any indication of the sum we are talking about?"

I was barely able to disguise my anxiety at this point, but still my pride wouldn't allow me to show my vulnerability especially to John Bennett.

"I'm sorry Annette, she just mentioned it in passing and I was dashing off to court so I didn't have time to talk. It's probably nothing. I wouldn't worry. I'm sorry I mentioned it, I didn't want to upset you."

Well if there was nothing to worry about why had the bastard phoned me?

I bit my tongue.

"I appreciate you telling me John, thank you."

The rest of the day I was so crippled with worry I could barely function. I ran over and over in my mind how many hours they could possibly bill me for. Was it just a few as John had said or was it a lot more? Should I ring Elizabeth and ask?

By the end of the day I'd convinced myself it couldn't be that much because she hadn't contacted me direct which was a good sign. I'd already paid nearly £30000 in fees, it was impossible I could owe that much more. This was John's way of a little bit payback. Yes, that was it, this was his way of a little revenge and John Bennett was trying to spook me. Well it just wasn't going to work.

The phone rang early the following morning and as I walked towards it my heart was in my mouth as I convinced myself that it would be Elizabeth.

I was so relieved when the caller announced he was a Mr Flanagan, an auctioneer from Flanagan and Aitchison.

"Hello is this Mrs Palmer I'm speaking too?"

"Yes speaking," I replied, my attention only half drawn to the call as my eyes remained firmly fixed on the Sudoku I'd challenged myself too complete before I reached the dregs of my first coffee of the morning. I knew who the auctioneers were, in happier times when I had cash to splash I had occasionally visited the antique auctions on the lookout for an unusual piece of furniture or some artwork. I'd often wandered around the showroom filling in an hour or so before I picked the kids up from school.

"Yes, how can I help you?" I said cautiously, wondering why in the hell the man was ringing me.

"I've had a phone call from Mr Palmer and he's asked me to pick up some pieces of art work from the family home. He'd like us to auction them in our next sale"

I'd never spoken to Mr Flanagan before, yet after that sentence I'd already made up my mind I didn't care for him.

"Excuse me?"

My voice displaying indignation while I tried to remain dignified and calm.

"Mr Palmer has explained the unfortunate circumstances which has led to the need for the artwork having to be sold. He mentioned the Norman Cornish and two Alexander Millers, is that right?"

"I think that's my business Mr Flanagan," I said as my anger sat beneath the surface of my calm exterior.

"With respect Mrs Palmer, but that's not entirely true, Mr Palmer has equal ownership of the artwork and he wants them sold. He has tasked me with the job of doing just that."

I imagined the conversation Stuart would have had with Flanagan, no doubt he would have been raging as he portrayed me as the villain of the piece, changing the front door locks to stop him getting into his own house. Mr Flanagan would be left with the impression that I was the awkward one and now my defensiveness would only serve to prove the point.

I couldn't stop myself.

"Well Mr Flanagan, I haven't tasked you with the job of selling the paintings and as you've pointed out already, its equal ownership."

"Mrs Palmer, I remain entirely neutral, I am not acting on behalf of Mr Palmer, I have no bias either way but Mr Palmer did say that the money would be useful to both parties given the extent of the costs of your divorce."

I couldn't disagree with that as I thought about Bennett's phone call and the extra hours.

Flanagan rambled on.

"If I pick up the artworks they will be in held in my safekeeping but I do need them quickly, they need to be in the show room if they are to make the next sale at the end of the month."

"I'll need to talk to my solicitor Mr Flanagan."

"I understand. Mr Palmer also mentioned the baby grand piano."

Now he'd touched a nerve, the piano had always been my hobby.

"What?" I said.

"The grand piano Mrs Palmer, that falls under joint ownership too and Mr Palmer said it could be worth as much as £10000."

I lost it.

"I don't suppose my husband has mentioned his Ping golf clubs or his titanium framed fucking bike. Those two will fetch about ten grand too."

Inside I was screaming, outwardly I tried to keep my composure. There was silence on the other end of the phone.

"Well?" I asked.

"Err... no."

"No, I thought as much. I'll task you with the job of telling him the piano is not his to sell, it's going nowhere and when he throws his golf clubs and his bike into the mix I'll be happy to let the paintings go."

Flanagan composed himself and found his voice.

"I'll ring you in a couple of days Mrs Palmer."

"Tell my ex-husband to go and fuck himself Mr Flanagan."

Before he could answer me I slammed the phone down.

Could he do that? I thought to myself. Could he force me to sell the paintings and my piano? This divorce was getting messier and more personal by the day. I was furious and the only place I could turn to for advice was my solicitor. He'd been civil enough the previous day so I tried to compose myself and picked up the phone. I tapped in Saxtons' number, which was now imprinted on my brain.

Karen answered and I explained about my conversation with the auctioneer.

"Wait one moment Mrs Palmer, I'll transfer you to Mr Bennett."

My heart pounded as I was reminded about the 'terrible mistake' relating to my legal bill and just as I prepared for another awkward talk with John, without warning, I heard Louise's voice instead. I couldn't help but breathe a sigh of relief.

"Morning Annette, John isn't available at the moment, can I help?"

"I hope so Louise."

I gave her an edited version of the morning's events.

"I'll have a word with John and get back to you. In the meantime, I think you need to consider whether you want to keep the artwork and the piano and if so, it will have to be included as part of your settlement."

Her light voice then took on a more serious tone.

"The other side will be expecting to get market value for each one of the paintings and the piano so it could amount to rather a lot of money but he can't force a sale at this point."

I'd found two receipts that confirmed we'd paid £10000 for the Cornish and £6000 for each of the Miller paintings. Could I really afford to keep them I wondered? Louise's answer had appeased me sufficiently for me to realise my hand couldn't be forced by my ex-husband or Mr Flanagan. I could wait until the final hearing and make my mind up then. I was just about to say my goodbyes when Louise had an afterthought.

"By the way, you don't have Tina Palmer's address, do you?"

"Unfortunately not Louise, I know she lives in Gosforth but that's it. Why do you need to know?" I asked

"We need it to serve her the witness summons. As I told you she needs to be given sufficient notice by law, seven days, otherwise she doesn't have to appear and her home address is the easiest place to find her."

"But she has to appear," I said. "We have to find out what happened with that will, it's vital she gives evidence Louise," I said, my voice full of concern.

"Don't worry about it Annette, we'll find her in time, but I'll need to get onto it immediately."

Sensing the anxiety in my voice she tried to lift my spirits.

"We served the summons on Angela Maddison and she was livid. She went to court to try and overturn it. I wish I could have taken a picture for you Annette, it was a sight."

"You were there in court?" I asked.

"Yes, and the Judge wasn't having any of it. Maddison said she had important meetings on the day of the hearing but the judge told her to rearrange them."

As she spoke I could feel my spirits lift just a little, if I could make Angela Maddison feel a fraction of the pain she'd put my family through, to my mind it would be all worthwhile. I needed them both to appear in court, to experience some of the worry and pain that I'd been subjected to for more than a year now.

"Annette, one more thing," she said, "we got Alexandra's doctors report you sent us, which is brilliant, it's just what we need to present in court."

"That's good," I replied.

I'd had to approach Dr Carrion and explain about my pending divorce and how I needed a doctor's report to explain Alexandra's medical condition for the court. She was more than obliging, yet it was still embarrassing that I felt I was somehow trying to profit from my daughter's condition, it made me feel uncomfortable and I was glad when the surgery said the report was ready to be picked up and my ordeal was over.

"We just need one amendment made to the report. With your permission I'd be happy to ring Dr Carrion and speak with her myself." Louise added.

Immediately the alarm bells started in my head.

"Is it normal to ask for the report to be amended Louise? What is actually missing from it?"

"We need the doctor to say it would be beneficial for Alexandra to remain in the family home. It will strengthen your argument to keep the house."

I couldn't disagree, I was desperate to stay in our house and whatever the cost I was prepared to pay it and I wasn't going to argue.

"That's fine Louise you have my permission to speak to Dr Carrion."

A Saxtons' letter arrived through the door the very next day. My eyes scanned the covering letter with horror as each word slowly filtered through my brain and the realisation of what I was actually reading sunk in. The letter wasn't from Louise or John it was from Elizabeth Henshaw. It started friendly enough but I knew what it was about:

Dear Annette

Herewith the latest interim account which very much reflects the amount of work done on your behalf. This bill also includes the total hours submitted on behalf of Louise. This has not been included in previous accounts.

We would be grateful if you could make an interim payment before the Final Hearing. Perhaps we could have a word about how best the fees can be met.

I would hope that there will not be too much involved in further fees, in that the Final Hearing is of course coming up very shortly.

You will see from the time entries that the fees we are charging are rather less than the actual time recorded and costs involved and I can confirm that both John and Louise have not recorded all of the time in an effort to assist you.

Yours Sincerely
Elizabeth Henshaw

I could barely bring myself to look at the invoice that was stapled to the covering letter and behind that was the Time Ledger Report she was referring to. Was this the terrible mistake John had referred to, they'd missed Louise's hours? The heavy embossed paper and the fact there was more than one time sheet made for quite a weighted bundle that only served to add to my distress. My hands were shaking with fear as I gingerly turned the page. It couldn't be right, it must be wrong I thought. Yet it wasn't. It was in bold print and hit me like a sledgehammer.

Balance Due for Payment - £16,453.85.

Surely she wasn't expecting me to pull together that amount within days of the hearing?

"What's wrong Mum?" Alexandra said as I walked back into the kitchen clutching the papers in my hand, my face drained of colour and a feeling of nausea engulfing me that only added to my general demeanour

"Are you sure you're okay, you look as if you've just seen a ghost." Her witty voice was wasted on me in that moment.

"I'm fine, I just need to make a phone call immediately."

Elizabeth Henshaw in her overly gushing manner was very understanding of my plight. I pleaded my case. Wasn't it short notice expecting me to find that sort of money?

"I totally understand Mrs Palmer, however when cases go to Final

Hearings the costs do tend to rack up. I didn't want you to be presented with a huge bill at the end of the hearing and not be prepared."

The plastic sincerity was oozing from the phone. I didn't believe a word. I tried to keep my composure but my voice was beginning to crack.

"Mrs Henshaw -"

"Please call me Elizabeth," she interrupted.

"Elizabeth, if your agreeable I would prefer to settle the account after the hearing. I have some artwork going to auction at the end of the month, (I'd just decided in that moment) that will free up some funds."

My nerve was barely holding and I knew she sensed desperation in my voice. The line went quiet for a moment.

"The thing is Mrs Palmer, we have invested a great deal of time and resources on your case, time that could have been employed on clients who are in a position to settle their account."

Ouch that hurt, the cutting bitch I thought as I bit my tongue.

"We'll need at least fifty per cent of the account settled immediately."

I decided to put her on the spot. There was no way could I find £8000 in such a short time.

"And if I can't pay before the final hearing?" I questioned. "What will happen then?"

I heard her take a deep breath.

"I'm sure it will not get to that point Mrs Palmer, however if your unable to settle at least half of your account we would have to consider withdrawing our services until payment is made."

She had me and she knew it, with only days to the hearing she was threatening to pull the plug again. I simmered with rage as she continued.

"Mrs Palmer, please do not worry, there are loan schemes available, the interest rates are reasonable, if you need to make an application we can help you with that."

Her voice was even more gushing, but she couldn't disguise the underlying threat. I found myself between a rock and a hard place and the bitch knew it.

"I haven't got any income Mrs Henshaw, how do I get a loan?"

She took another sharp intake of breath.

"I'm sorry Annette, it's really not our problem. We've done the work and the account needs settled, it really is as simple as that."

As simple as that. Her words hung in the air.

"I'll have £8000 to you by the beginning of next week Elizabeth."

"I'm sure you will, that's fine Annette, believe me we just want to help you and I didn't want to present you with a huge bill after the hearing."

She bleated on until I could bear it no longer.

"As I said, your money will be with you next week so if you'll excuse me I'm very busy at the moment."

Since Elizabeth's call, apart from an occasional formal email, all communication with John ceased. It was Louise who took my calls and Louise who rang me on a regular basis. On one occasion I demanded to speak to him but was brushed off with a lame excuse that he was with another client. I told Karen that I would be in the house for the rest of the day but she said he was running behind schedule and had given strict instructions not to be disturbed. I was desperately trying to find out if they had managed to serve a summons on Tina Palmer but feared they'd all but stopped working on my case, waiting for me to cough up the money. If we couldn't serve the summons, she would not have to appear. I was paralysed with fear, what the hell was I going to do? Dark thoughts invaded my mind; maybe they'd all be better off without me. What would it take to swallow a few tablets then the misery would be over? And yet as soon as the thought entered my head I knew I had to fight it, I would not allow it to take hold. I rebuked myself for even entertaining such thoughts. Pull yourself together; stop feeling sorry for yourself and think, just think.

I paced the house, trying to think. I needed £8000; surely there was something I could sell. I looked at the artwork adorning the walls, at the piano. Even if I rang Mr Flanagan that very moment the paintings wouldn't go to auction until the end of the month. The jewellery had gone already and I wasn't prepared to go back to my mother, I would not do that, she was too old for me to keep burdening her with my financial woes. I looked out of the hall window and my eyes were drawn to the one possession I had left to sell. My car.

As I looked at its gleaming paintwork glistening in the late afternoon sun, I knew there was way more than £8000 worth of British engineering sitting on the driveway and an involuntary smile pulled across my face. Not wasting a minute, I jumped onto my computer and logged into Auto trader. I was right, a two-year-old Mini Countryman with one careful lady owner was worth in excess of £13000 and I knew exactly what had to be done.

First thing the following morning I was at the sales showroom. Matty, the slimy car room salesman with the exaggerated sideburns and slicked back hair, took some convincing that buying my car was a good deal. After all they were in the game of taking money off punters and not giving it to them but I was desperate and he sensed there was a bargain to be had. It took me more than an hour to strike the deal. I accepted an eight-year-old Ford Fiesta with dodgy paintwork and rust erosion under the front wheel arch and £8500 in cash. It was at that moment I knew my life was back on track and it was game on. I persuaded him to do the transfer there and then and as soon as I got home I wired the money to the Saxtons' account.

I called their offices immediately and relayed the news to them and as they transferred me to Louise my heart was in my mouth as I waited patiently to hear her voice.

More bad news. With little more than 48 hours to go to the hearing, Louise told me they had not been able to issue Tina Palmer with the summons but she tried to reassure me that at least they still had the rest of the day.

I was elated that I had managed to cover the Saxtons' account but more than a little angry that they hadn't done what they promised to do and that was to issue the summons. Surely it couldn't have been that difficult? Louise promised to call me as soon as she had some news. My stomach churned all afternoon as I paced the hallway staring at the phone, willing it to ring. All three girls were with me offering their support, trying to keep my mind occupied, but of course nothing worked, my mind was anywhere but in the present but they did their best to distract me. Now more than ever I was willing the phone to ring, come on Louise just ring me, have we got Tina Palmer or not? It was a big deal, the biggest deal of my life. If we got Tina Palmer into the witness box there was just a possibility that she would crack and disclose the fraudulent nature of Olive Palmer's will that would ultimately end in a victory and give me the right and the financial means to stay in my house... our home.

The phone eventually rang at 5.15pm and I ran towards it almost knocking the table over in my urgency to pick up the receiver.

"Hello Louise," I said, desperate to be put out of my misery

"Yes Annette it's me," her voice was loud, trying to drown out the noise of the car engine in the background.

She's driving home I thought, on hands free. I wasn't interested in pleasantries; I asked the one question I needed an answer to.

"Did you get her?"

"We got her with two minutes to spare."

I sighed, falling back into the chair. It felt like I'd won the lottery, the Euro Millions three times rolled over.

I could sense that Louise had a huge smile plastered right across her face as she relayed the story.

"She refused to take the summons off the server, she was getting out of her car and when he tried to hand it to her she put her hands behind her back, point blank refused to take it. But that doesn't matter, legally all he has to do is place it in front of her, the court will be satisfied with that."

I still wasn't convinced.

"What if she still refuses to turn up?"

"Well Annette, the Judge would order her to be picked up and she would go to prison for contempt of court."

"Prison?"

"Yes, it could be for twenty four hours or even for a few days, it depends on the Judge."

"And she'll know that?" I asked.

"I would be fairly sure that she'll be Googling that eventuality right at this very moment."

I allowed myself the luxury of a smile.

"Good, that's good Louise, thank you, thank you."

I was elated and couldn't wait to get off the phone and tell the girls but Louise interrupted me. She told me something else had cropped up and she wanted me to come into the offices first thing tomorrow.

"It's Aunt Peggy's will. There's been a very interesting development."

38

I was sad, yet in a way relieved, that Peggy had finally been put out of her misery, her quality of life had been zero. The girls hadn't been surprised or shocked by the news either, they knew it was on the cards after Abigail had made her unwelcomed visit to the Care Home and had been refused entry. Although they were expecting it they were no less angry that their Dad hadn't told them she'd passed away. It was all rather Déjà vu and they were greeted with the information in the Births and Deaths section of the Evening Chronicle two days after she had gone.

Once again they'd faced the same dilemma they'd had with their Grandmother, should they go to the funeral or not? After much debate around the kitchen table and a couple of spats between Abigail and Victoria as tensions and emotions collided, it was finally decided they would take the same stance as they had with their Grandmother and stay away. I lingered on the memory of the heated discussion for a second before Louise interjected.

"We received a copy from Mr Steedman only yesterday."

She paused and I could sense a hint of excitement in her bright voice as she eagerly shared its contents.

"It's very interesting because thirty per cent of her estate goes to Mr Palmer and the rest is to be divided between your three girls."

I stiffened up.

"What?"

She smiled.

"Yes. Seventy per cent of the estate to the girls."

I was almost lost for words.

"Well I never, at last a financial break for the family."

"The estate is valued at around £360000, her flat in Jesmond just short of £180000 that will need to be sold of course but once it is, that will be over £80000 each for your daughters."

"Fucking hell."

I immediately apologised for my language.

"That's okay Annette, I forgive you," she grinned as she continued.

"Mr Palmer is the executor of the estate and Steedman has stated -"

I interrupted her. "Whoa, what did you say?"

"I know, not the ideal situation but at least he has to do everything by the book this time. We can demand to see the estate accounts and every transaction he makes in relation to winding up her estate. He can't pull anything funny this time."

As soon as she said the last sentence I couldn't help myself.

"You don't know Stuart," I said.

She seemed to hesitate for a moment. There was something else.

"What is it?" I asked.

"There's something else I think you should know about."

"What?"

"A note from Peggy's solicitor, the solicitor who drafted the will."

Louise read the note verbatim. It appeared that there had been an application to change the will two months ago. The application was lodged by the executor who was Stuart. The solicitor had visited Peggy's care home along with Stuart but had categorically stated that the old lady was not of sound mind or deed and therefore the instruction could not be carried out.

I swore for the second time that day.

"The bastard."

"No need to apologise Annette," she said, "I agree one hundred per cent. He tried to change the will of an old woman who clearly didn't know what she was doing."

I flopped forward and leaned on the desk for support. Surely this was all the proof the Judge needed to see the type of man that Stuart was. He'd managed to change one will and attempted to change another. This was surely the sort evidence that should be shared with the court. Louise was reading my mind, she was one step ahead of me.

"I'll talk to John and see what sort of case this new evidence gives us. If nothing else it should be raised in court."

My mind was doing summersaults. Another hundred grand to my thieving bastard of an ex-husband. In the grand scheme of things it was nothing to the amount he would be receiving from his Mother's estate once his little scheme came to fruition.

Louise interrupted my thoughts.

"It's good news all round, a substantial amount for the girls and even more money to take into account for Mr Palmer."

I was looking at the details of the will when my eye read something that turned my stomach.

I pointed to what looked like some sort of clause.

"It says something about the girls being twenty five before they inherit the money."

Louise was already shaking her head.

"Don't worry Annette, that isn't legal, it was just a suggestion to the executor. As soon as the house is sold he will have access to the funds and have the authority to pay out."

"But he doesn't have to?"

"No, but what possible reason could he have to deprive his own daughters of their money?"

Despite everything that had happened, Louise clearly didn't know my arsehole of an ex-husband. She went on to tell me that it was only in extreme circumstances that executors withheld payments, if the recipient was in prison or a drug addict for example. She spoke with conviction; she sincerely believed that Stuart would be paying out quickly with a big smile and a fatherly pat on the back.

I knew differently. They would have to wait until they were twenty-five years of age. There was no doubt in my mind.

I tried to put Aunty Peggy and her Will to the back of my mind, although it was niggling away there was little I could do, all three girls were adults, if it got to the point of challenging their father, which I was sure it would, they needed to make their own minds up, I couldn't be a warmonger and incite discord. Fortunately Louise didn't linger long on the subject, there was a number of points listed on her faithful notepad I noticed as I peered across the desk curious as to what else she wanted to talk about. I couldn't help but think of John, my absent solicitor, as Louise sat absorbed in her paperwork clearly enthused by the fact John had bestowed her with the responsibility of taking charge of my case. Everything seemed much the same as it usually did. We sat in the Saxtons' client conference room, me in my usual chair under the oversized wall clock, its loud second hand even more deafening in the absence of John's mesmerizing drawl. My mind was only half focused on Louise as she extrapolated the salient details of my case in an attempt to dot the I's and cross the T's. I couldn't help wonder where the hell John was, we were appearing in court the very next day and he was nowhere in sight. My anger was brewing once more, Saxtons had once been a safe haven for me, a place of sanctuary, now it seemed its inhabitants posed as much a threat to me as Stuart and his bull dog Steedman. Still I took some comfort in the fact Louise appeared to be genuinely committed to fighting my corner, her pen posed steadfast in her delicate manicured hand as she flicked through the groaning bundle of notes on the desk in front of her. For what seemed the umpteenth time we dissected my finances, my eyes rolling to the ceiling when the subject reared its head once more. It seemed ironic that I'd been married to Stuart all those years and I had no clue what we paid in utility bills or any other bill for that matter, he insisted on dealing with everything. Now I was reeling off my monthly outgoings to the penny without a moment's hesitation and no need for a prompt to remind me. How my life had changed in the short space of a year.

Louise's voice chipped in.

"The hearing is in the old Moot Hall just by Newcastle Keep, unfortunately it's a busy day for hearings, there aren't enough court rooms so the overflow has to be heard in the old court house."

But I was no longer listening, I was desperate to get away.

"Louise, are we about done here, I really need to get going?"

She appeared startled by my sudden outburst. Usually I would sit diligently listening, only acknowledging the end of the meeting when John instigated it. Realising my voice had a sharpness to its tone, I back peddled

"Sorry Louise," I said, "I'm getting stressed to bits about this hearing tomorrow, my life's hanging in the balance and John Bennett's nowhere to be found. Where the fuck is he anyway?" I shocked myself, I could have cut my tongue out with a blunt knife.

"Sorry Louise, I didn't mean I wasn't happy with seeing you," I rambled.

"It's perfectly alright Annette," her soothing calm voice offering welcomed reassurance

"John is working in the background on your case, he's dealing with both Steedman and Gilbert so don't worry on that front. He's still working tirelessly on your behalf."

Poor Louise I thought, how naïve was she that she still held some misconstrued belief that the practice of law was for the greater good of others. How wrong she was. Now I saw solicitors for what they really were, vultures swooping in on a dead carcass ready to pick off the bones.

She gave me an awkward smile as she stacked the scattered papers into one neat bundle ready to pick up.

"I'll walk out with you Annette. I have to run down to the courthouse and submit Dr Carrions amended letter."

"Oh you got it?" welcoming the digression into lighter topics

"Yes. She sent it through last night so I need to get it submitted. It has to be included in the Judges court bundle ready for tomorrow."

"And she rang me this morning."

"Dr Carrion?"

"Yes," she said, "apparently your ex-husband contacted her digging for information about Alexandra's health."

I shook my head in disbelief.

"She's been ill for months and he hasn't looked by or even messaged her and he waits until the day before the hearing to contact her doctor."

Louise nodded.

"Incredible isn't it? He can only be interested in something that helps his case."

A shiver ran up my spine wondering if the Doctor had given him anything he would use against me in court.

"Did Dr Carrion part with any information?" I asked.

"No, definitely not," she said, "Alexandra's over the age of sixteen so the Doctor can't divulge any information to anyone, not even her father."

I breathed a sigh of relief. Louise fished in her bag, eventually retrieving a set of car keys and pressing a button on the fob. The beep echoed around the car park as the hazards on a neat metallic grey Audi flashed twice.

"Where are you parked Annette?"

"Just over there Louise," as I pointed towards the battered Ford Fiesta which now looked even more shabby in comparison to her pristine sporty number. She looked puzzled, she was used to seeing me waltzing up in a gleaming Mini.

"Is your car getting a service?" she said.

I laughed just once.

"No Louise, that's my car, a twelve year old Fiesta, that's what it's come to."

A puzzled frown swept over her face.

"But why? I loved your Mini, it was so you."

"I've hocked just about everything I own to pay your firm's accounts."

She shook her innocent pretty head.

"But-"

"Anything of any value has been pawned to keep the Saxtons' crew in the manner to which they have been accustomed."

She shook her head slowly as I continued.

"All my jewellery and my wedding ring and not to mention the money borrowed from my dear old mother."

"I had no idea," she answered meekly.

"I've paid your firm nearly £30000 to date and I can guarantee before this is all over you can double that figure." I was in full flow. "They've nailed me to the cross Louise and what's worse is that they won't even wait for their money until after the settlement, Mrs Henshaw has even threatened to pull the plug and hang me out to dry."

"The bitch," Louise whispered softly.

I ranted on about the paintings and the piano and told her exactly how much I received for my car. I detailed Bennett's hourly rate and hers and at one point I thought she was about to faint. She told me her hourly rate of pay, a fraction of what Saxtons charged me and at the end of my three-minute tirade she leaned forward and gave me a hug, tears in her eyes. No doubt she felt a little guilty climbing into her year old Audi as she keyed the ignition and lowered the electric window but at least little, naive, Louise was slightly more clued up as to the wicked world of lawyers, the men and women whose salaries depend on conflict, a conflict that they stoke and fuel themselves and as long as that conflict continues the longer the revenues last.

As she pushed the car into gear she told me not to be late tomorrow morning.

"9.30 pronto Annette, the hearings at ten and we need to meet with Mr Gilbert beforehand."

My stomach churned at the thought. I planted a weak smile across my face.

"Yes, I'll be there, 9.30 on the dot"

That evening I wanted to drown myself in a bath of Gin, yet despite my overwhelming urge to escape the horrors of my own imagination I opted to abstain. Above anything else I wanted to look the best I possibly could, because I was going to be coming face to face with my nemesis, Angela Maddison, for the first time. I had no plan to look anything less than polished for my performance in court. The time I'd had spare between leaving the Saxtons' offices and getting home to make Alexandra's evening meal I'd invested in the local beauty and nail bar and had been pruned, plucked, manicured and pedicured to within an inch of my life. When I got home my preparation was no less rigorous, rummaging through the contents of my wardrobe with a fine tooth comb, trying on every conceivable combination of outfit before deciding to play safe and wear my understated little black dress. I was taking no heed to the advice I'd been given by Louise a few days earlier, who said I should turn up to court adorned in rags like some sort of bedraggled bag lady.

"You want to get the Judge on side your Annette, show him your vulnerability."

It was the same advice Bennett had given me months previously.

"It needs to be glaringly obvious that you're a middle aged housewife who'd struggle to find work in the real world."

"Well that's not going to happen Louise," I said, "I'd prefer to boil my head in hot oil than turn up at court like an aging housewife who'd let herself go."

We eventually agreed to disagree.

If I say so myself I looked radiant as I left the house the following morning.

Abigail had been adamant she was dropping me off at court because I flatly refused to take the battered old fiesta. There was no way I'd let Stuart or the bitch see me in that. I tried to put her off insisting I could take a taxi yet she was having none of it.

"I'm staying with you mum until you go into court. I don't care if Dad sees me, I want him to know you have my support."

As much as I tried to put her off I was delighted that she would be with me. I paced back and forwards in the hall awaiting her arrival. Eventually as I saw her car pull onto the driveway, my trembling hand instinctively reaching to the latch on the front door in desperation to open it and get moving on the day's events. As my gaze fixed on her bright, familiar, smiling face peering over her steering wheel. A huge surge of strength seemed to rise within me.

Moot Hall was no less impressive than the new court buildings. As we stepped out of the car and walked across the gravelled courtyard my eyes couldn't help but be drawn to the opulent Georgian building with its sandstone steps leading up to a columned portico on the front of the building.

I turned to Abigail.

"Okay, thanks, you can go now."

She smiled and reached for my hand.

"I'm going nowhere," she said.

Abigail held onto my hand as I walked tentatively up the sandstone steps to be greeted by Louise who stood statue like at the oak panelled door awaiting my arrival.

"Come through Annette."

She beckoned me to follow her.

"Mr Gilbert is waiting for us in the main reception, unfortunately there aren't any client waiting rooms."

Gilbert stood beneath the main central stairwell, his back propped against the wall, his stockman's long waxed oilskin coat sitting over his shoulders like a cape, shielding his business attire beneath.

"Good morning Mrs Palmer."

His loud voice projected around the hall drawing attention to our whereabouts that only served to increase my anxiety as I wondered where my Stuart and his solicitor were hiding.

"Good morning Mr Gilbert, this is my daughter Abigail." I said as I gestured towards my eldest girl.

"Nice to meet you Abigail," he was quick to add. "Shall we find ourselves a little cubby hole, Mrs Palmer and park ourselves for a few moments?"

He walked towards a wooden bench seat placed precariously by the main entrance and in full glare of anyone entering or leaving the building. Not very private I thought

"What do you think of Moot Hall? You're very fortunate to have your hearing in this building, it's only used as a necessity."

I wasn't feeling overall lucky or privileged and his flamboyant voice still fixed on telling me the history of the Hall.

"Yes it's a very old building, 1852 I believe, steeped in history. The back of the building is fashioned in the style of the Parthenon in Athens."

I smiled yet inwardly my irritation was growing, as was the feeling of nausea intensifying to the point where my mouth was beginning to salivate.

"Excuse me, where is the ladies?" I said quickly.

Louise obliged.

"Straight ahead then turn right."

Not wanting to attract any unnecessary attention, at first I didn't rush. My feet only gathered pace as I moved further away from my party but I could feel the acidic taste of vomit hitting the back of my throat. Slamming open the bathroom door I threw myself over the toilet basin, retching as I did so. The contents of my stomach consisted of yellow bile that was now trickling down the side of the white porcelain pan. The acid burnt into the back of my throat and I swallowed hard in an attempt to relieve the symptoms.

"Mum are you in there? Are you okay?"

I heard the concern in Abigail's voice as I pulled the toilet chain.

"Yes I'm good," I said as I walked out of the cubicle my eyes still smarting.

"I saw Dad" she said urgently "He's out there with his Barrister and some other dodgy looking slime ball."

I stood by the toilet sink and splashed water into my mouth and onto my face.

"That's your Dad's solicitor, Steedman," I said, trying to make myself heard above the noise of the dryer.

"Go home Abigail, this no place for you. You've delivered me here safe and sound and I appreciate that."

"But Mum, you need me."

"I'm with Louise and Mr Gilbert. Everything is fine chick, I'll ring you as soon as I'm done here, I Promise."

Despite my protests, Abigail insisted that she would deliver me safely into the hands of Louise and Gilbert. She somehow realised that we would inevitably come face to face with her Father and didn't want me to be on my own.

She was right.

As we made our way to Louise and Gilbert I caught sight of Stuart and Steedman out of the corner of my eye and I could almost feel their eyes burning into me. If I expected any sort of reaction from Stuart as his eldest daughter passed him I was wrong. There was none and as I looked up his head tilted forward and his eyes found the floor.

"That's right, hang your fucking head in shame."

I looked to my right, shocked at what Abigail had just said.

She'd taken a step nearer to him as he looked up, his face ashen.

She continued.

"You fucking snake in the grass, you obnoxious twat of a man, how dare you put our Mum through this ordeal."

Steedman was on his feet as he bridged the gap, no doubt expecting a full fistfight to break out.

But Stuart did nothing and in a blink of an eye it was all over as Abigail tugged at my arm and pulled me towards my corner.

She looked at me and smiled.

"I feel better for that," she said, "been wanting to say it for months."

"Mrs Palmer your back," Gilbert said, "I'm just going to have a few words with the other side, I need to know in what order witnesses are going to be giving evidence."

Louise told me the name of the judge, a man called Stokes."

"Is this good thing or a bad thing?" I asked.

Gilbert responded, whispering in hushed tones.

"Well he's decent enough," he paused as he chose his words carefully. "But not my first choice, a bit of a male chauvinist to be honest."

I shook my head in disbelief. Fantastic

"You've got a good case Annette, let us not underestimate the strength of that," he muttered before leaving.

Once Louise and I were alone, it gave me the perfect opportunity to ask the obvious.

"Where the hell is John?"

"He said he's on hand if we need him Annette, he'll come straight down, but he can't do anything in the court room today, that's Gilbert's job and it would work out rather costly for you to have him sitting here doing nothing."

I couldn't argue with her logic yet I was infuriated that he'd not had the decency to even pick up a phone over the last few weeks. He'd been as elusive as the bloody Scarlet Pimpernel.

Gilbert returned within a few minutes.

"Right we have agreed a schedule. The Maddison woman is up first."

My heart skipped a beat or two, the acidic taste returning to my mouth. Gilbert looked at his watch. He was on his feet as he lifted his bulky wax coat and placed it across his arm.

He looked at his watch.

"We better make our way into the court, it's on ten already."

His short, stout body minced its way across the huge elegant hall as Louise and I trailed behind in his wake. He was brought to a sudden standstill at the entrance to the courtroom as the court attendant checked the listing. We drew to a halt behind him, then suddenly panic set in. I could feel my legs begin to buckle as the anxiety mounted in my chest, cutting the air from my lungs. I'm going to pass out I thought as I struggled to catch my breath. Louise held onto my arm.

"Are you okay Annette," her calming voice acting as an anchor bringing me back.

I managed to catch a deep breath then slowly exhaled.

"Louise, I don't know if I can do this," I said, but as I turned my head I saw Angela Maddison striding through the main entrance, but with not such a confident swagger to her step.

"Annette are you Okay?"

The genuine concern in Louise's voice was apparent, yet it wasn't her voice that made me dig deep to find my fighting spirit once more, it was the sight of the arrogant blonde bitch heading in our direction. She looked like her photograph, but ten years older. She clearly hadn't slept, black rings under her eyes and her face was masked with make up in a vain attempt to hide every wrinkle, every line of worry. Her hair was dull and lifeless and I drew strength from her pathetic appearance. I could feel the anxiety being replaced with raw anger, ripping through the core of my sole like I was being possessed by demons.

“Yes Louise I'm fine,” I said, my eyes now firmly fixed on the cheap suit she wore as well as the patent leather, ridiculously high heels .I wondered what the hell had possessed my husband to leave me for this woman.

“I'm good,” I said, “couldn't be better in fact.”

Louise looked at the bitch and then at me and our thoughts collided. She smiled.

She took my hand.

"C'mon Annette, let's do this.”

39

When we stepped into the elegant oak panelled courtroom with its raised witness box and the Judge's bench sitting under an oak canopy, I was immediately transported back in time to a bygone era. It looked like something out of a movie and not the venue I'd expect my divorce hearing to be heard in. Was it really necessary to play out the demise of my marriage in such a large public arena? Mercifully the exceptionally large, public viewing gallery that looked directly down onto the court was completely empty of unwelcome onlookers. I breathed a sigh of relief. As we walked in and shuffled our way along the worn, oak bench seats, Gilbert continued to spout forth about the grandeur of the room and on any other day I may well have been impressed by his apparent wealth of knowledge on the building's history.

"It's absolutely splendid isn't it Mrs Palmer? There is something so special about this place."

His face was absolutely bursting with pride and I wondered if he had forgotten for a moment why we were actually there.

"And look," his small chubby hands pointed to the dock, my eyes cast it a glance and I immediately imagined the numerous criminals who'd stood in that very spot awaiting their fate and here I was, not a criminal, yet still my life was hanging in the balance.

"If you ever have the opportunity to have a proper look around this place, you'd see there is a trapdoor in the dock which leads directly down to the cells."

Gilbert's face was glowing with uncontainable excitement.

"The studded door and shackles in the cell are original, they date back to the 1870's."

"Mr Gilbert."

"Yes Annette?"

"I'm not interested in the fucking slightest," I said. "It's all very graceful but I'd don't need to know what was going on in the 19th Century, my interest is only focussed on what is going to happen today. In case you've forgotten a stranger is about to decide the pathway to my future."

Before he could answer me our attention was drawn to Stuart and his crew who were slowly making their way into the courtroom with no sense of urgency. Stuart's mouth was going as usual (no surprise there) and reading his body language, he was not too happy. No doubt Abigail's outburst earlier on hadn't helped his mood, he was going ninety to the dozen barking instructions to Bentley who as usual acted like his diligent little lap dog.

Same barrister I noticed, Bentley, how could I ever forget that man with his hawk like eyes and menacing glare. A shiver ran down my spine as I remembered he'd had much the same effect on me the last time I was unfortunate enough to encounter him. This time it would be worse, his questions would be fired directly at me and I wouldn't be shielded by my solicitor. I could feel my anxiety rising to the surface once more as a feeling of nausea pricked up at the back of my throat, my saliva glands were working overtime as I gulped down hard. Forcing my attention away from Bentley, my eyes fell onto Stuart once more, he was playing the dress down game that was for sure. His usual immaculate suit had gone and he was sporting the dishevelled look, casual pants that were so aged the fabric had a worn sheen. The top button of his shirt was undone, he wasn't even wearing a tie. No tie! My God, Stuart would never be without a tie in an office environment, he'd even wear a tie if he visited a stationary shop. The finishing touch, the old battered ski jacket with a haversack anchored over his shoulder. When the hell had he ever been caught dead in a formal environment without a suit on? I wanted to laugh out loud, the last time I'd caught sight of him wearing that particular jacket was on a family skiing holiday in Canada, ten years ago. Stuart didn't do casual, I had a feeling it was all part of the sneaky bastard's grand plan to get the judge on his side.

I whispered under my breath, "you sad cunt," as my eyes pulled away from him in total disgust. That word again.

"Court rise."

I jumped to attention, my knees jarred against the back of the oak seat. Judge Porter wasted no time taking his seat on his would be throne, shielded beneath the oak canopy. I studied the Judge, Gilbert had been right, mollycoddled was also my first impression. He was a slight balding man, his horn-rimmed glasses perched on the bridge of his nose couldn't disguise his small slit like eyes.

"Be seated," he said, his voice flat with no edge or backbone to it, his vocal cords probably bashed into submission by a dominant mother then a wife to follow.

I suspected the courtroom was the one place he could wreak revenge against his female oppressors.

Gilbert gave his opening statement, the usual catalogue of events going totally over my head. In the grand scheme of things it was no great loss, I'd heard the Palmer's divorce chronology umpteen times now, it was boring, mundane.

Porter interjected as Gilbert reached the end of his summary, his hand wafting in the air beckoning him to sit down, his low voice, boosted by his mic.

"I think we need to move swiftly on to the first witness if we hold out any hope of hearing all the evidence today. You have two witnesses Mr Gilbert?"

His narrow, slit eyes stared in our direction. I could almost detect a hint of disapproval across his face. Gilbert jumped to his feet like a jack-in-the-box.

"Yes sir, it has been agreed between Mr Bentley and myself that it might be advisable for Mrs Maddison to give her evidence first."

"And the second witness," he glanced at the witness summons sheet, "Mrs Tina Ann Palmer?"

"Unfortunately Tina Palmer hasn't arrived at the court and we aren't entirely sure when she will get here." Gilbert answered.

The judge shook his head, he didn't appear too impressed. He tilted forward in his chair slightly, bringing his mouth closer to his mic once more.

"Can Mrs Maddison be brought in?" he said, turning to the usher slumped on a chair by the entrance to the courtroom. He stood, opened the door and disappeared. My stomach churned at this point, yet still my eyes were fixed on the large, oak panelled doors the usher had walked through. I knew that within just a few seconds, the bitch would be making her grand entrance. I was going to savour every second of her ordeal and I only hoped Gilbert was going to do me justice and have her squirming in her chair.

As she walked in to the courtroom there was total silence, the only sound to be heard were her stiletto heels clicking against the stone floor. I listened to the rhythm, even the sound of her shoes against the hard surface seemed angry and reluctant and I could almost feel the tension radiating from her body. Apart from the brief glimpse of her in the courtroom foyer it was the first time I had been given any time to study the women in great detail. My family had callously been torn to shreds by her and I couldn't help wondering to myself that the 'thing' sitting in the witness box had been responsible for this whole bloody mess. I wanted to scream out at my ex-husband.

Is that what you gave everything up for, that insignificant piece of shit? You sacrificed your children for that hard faced cow?"

She was no Cameron Diaz or Kate Moss that was for sure, she looked nothing, plain, too much makeup, skinny rather than slim and not well toned at all.

Gilbert was on his feet, his papers in hand, standing at the bench directly in front of me. I could easily see his scribbled notes over his shoulder, they were practically illegible yet I had managed to make out that they were a list of questions he planned to ask the opposition. I knew he wasn't going to press Maddison too much, he'd already warned me that he couldn't harangue the witnesses, the Judge wouldn't look favourably on that sort of approach.

But I reminded Gilbert who was paying the bills. This was our only chance, I wanted them both hauled over the coals, wasn't that the point of calling Maddison and Tina Palmer, to put them on the spot? The one thing on my mind was a £1.6 million fraud that they had both been involved in. There was also Stuart's understated earnings and the missing investments. We needed to leave the Judge under no illusions.

Once she'd been sworn in offering to tell the truth and nothing but the truth, Gilbert stood and prepared to question her. He started off gently at first with benign and formal questions.

I'd immediately sensed from the very first word she spoke and her general demeanour, Maddison resented being forced onto the witness stand. She was hating every second of it and she didn't want to be there. I gave a sideward glance to Louise, who'd already started scribbling notes.

Once the formalities were over, the questions became more interesting, Gilbert wanting to know when her own marriage had broken down. She shuffled uncomfortably in the chair.

Gilbert was suggesting her and Stuart had met two years prior to her marriage ending.

"Had you started to form an association prior to your divorce?"

The insinuation was an obvious one.

"We were friends," she said, offering the minimum response.

She'd been coached on what to say, it was obvious. Tell them as little as you need to.

Eventually Gilbert got to the crux of the matter.

"Was there a sexual relationship prior to your divorce?"

My heart began to gallop, why did it still sting I wondered?

"No," she snapped, clearly resentful of the intimation.

She explained that they were close work colleagues, no more than that.

Gilbert moved it on as he mentioned the text I'd found prior to the separation.

"We were contacting each other by phone and text, the texts became flirtatious. Mrs Palmer found out, she wasn't happy."

She shrugged her shoulders, my blood was boiling as my eyes cut into her.

"So when did you begin a relationship?" Gilbert said, as he fidgeted with the corner of the paper now laid on the bench before him.

"The summer of last year, after he separated from Mrs Palmer," she responded.

Bloody liar I wanted to scream. It was all so clear; the missing pieces of the jigsaw were fitting together. She'd separated from her husband in the previous New Year, which not surprisingly coincided with the worst Christmas and New Year I'd experienced throughout our entire marriage. I remember Stuart being particularly strange that Christmas, the festivities had been ruined, they had died a death before it had even begun, now I knew why. Him and his bitch were already planning their escape. All the months I'd begged him to try and sort our marriage out yet my pleas had fallen on deaf ears, all the while he'd been waiting to make sure Maddison was committed to leaving her husband before he jumped ship. Crafty bastard, he had played me like a fiddle all along. I cringed as I remembered the memory before I buried it back into the murky recesses of my mind, where it belonged.

"Mrs Maddison," I heard Gilbert's voice filtering its way back into my head.

"So you started a relationship with Mr Palmer in the July, yet in August you went on holiday to France together. A bit quick wasn't it?"

Maddison was beginning to squirm, she looked at her counsel, she needed to be rescued.

"No, I was with my children, we were staying in a cottage owned by a friend."

"But Mr Palmer was there too, wasn't he?"

"Yes, what's wrong with that? It isn't against the law."

Gilbert smiled, looked at the judge and then to Stuart.

"No law against it, that's correct."

Maddison's mouth turned up at one side, a half smile formed before it quickly disappeared.

"I'm just puzzled," Gilbert said, "why Mr Palmer told his family that he had been on a golfing holiday with his male friends. He clearly had something to hide or something that he was ashamed of."

"Objection!"

All hell seemed to break loose as the Barristers argued the relevance and whole point of the accusation. In my mind my Barrister was trying to show the court that my husband had walked out of the family home and furthermore he had planned to do so at least a year in advance. Of course it was relevant.

Not in the eyes of the Judge.

When he had eventually chastised and silenced the two barristers he began to speak.

"Quite frankly Mr Gilbert, I'm not really interested in which party was to blame for the breakup of the marriage. It's irrelevant, the law isn't interested, it will have no impact on the financial settlement."

But it was relevant, I had discussed the relevance with Gilbert. There was an inheritance fraud, not to mention the possibility that Stuart would ultimately have three properties he could quite easily call home, whereas if the judgement fell short of what I needed, I would have none. That was the relevance.

"Come on," I whispered under my breath, "do your job Mr

Gilbert, do what I am paying you to do."

Gilbert was back on his feet attempting to rescue the situation.

"Have you any intention of cohabiting in the near future Mrs Maddison."

His laid back line of questioning was gathering a little pace, although still lacking any real bite.

"None what so ever," she said, "it's early days."

The judge intervened.

"Mr Gilbert, please get to the point."

He looked up and smiled.

"I will your Honour."

He looked back to Maddison.

"Are you friendly with Tina Palmer?"

"Not especially, I've met her a couple of times but that's it."

"And what about Mr Palmer's late mother, Mrs Olive Palmer? Did you meet her at all?"

"A couple of times, no more."

Gilbert paused.

"But you were a witness to Mr Palmer's mother's will weren't you?

"Yes. There's no law against that is there?"

Gilbert shook his head as he deliberately adjusted his glasses.

"No law, but don't you think that was a little strange?"

Maddison shrugged her shoulders, looking over towards Stuart and Bentley. Her whole demeanour said get me out of here.

Gilbert continued.

"Something so monumental as the Last Will and Testament of a lady with an estate of over a million pounds and they ask a stranger to witness it."

This was more like it, he was getting to the point.

Gilbert established that the bitch had gone around to Stuart's mothers for a cup of tea and by chance had been asked to witness the will along with Stuart. She was adamant that there had been no discussion before or after the will had been signed even though she'd seen Tina Palmer was the only beneficiary.

"And you both knew the will disinherited Mr Palmer?"

Her response was snappy.

"Yes, he knew he would not get anything from that will."

"And yet he appeared more than happy that as an only child he had not been left one single penny of his mother's estate?"

Yet again Maddison shrugged her shoulders.

"You don't think that it was strange that he knew the content and he was still happy to act as the executor?"

"No."

"Distribute the estate in its entirety to a non-blood relation?"

"His choice."

I noticed a line of perspiration building on the bitch woman's lip as she began to visibly shake. She was lying, just a little more questioning and she would break.

Gilbert returned to his notes, pawing through a couple of pages. He looked unsure of where to go next.

My frustration was rising.

"Louise," I whispered, she raised her head.

"Why isn't he asking her to explain herself?"

My voice hushed yet my annoyance was evident. Louise shrugged her shoulders, her mind was way too focused on keeping up with her note taking to be bothered with answering any of my queries.

Gilbert looked towards the judge.

"No further questions."

I sighed in total disbelief, was that it I thought, Gilbert had her by the jugular, all he had to do was squeeze.

"Thank you Mrs Maddison," the Judge said, "that will be all."

Bentley didn't even bother lifting his backside from the seat.

"No questions."

Porter, realising the interrogation was at an end looked at his watch and then leaned towards the microphone.

"If there are no more questions from either side," he paused a moment, no response was forthcoming as both Gilbert and Bentley buried their head in their files. I stared at Gilbert, willing him to push Maddison a little further, surely there were more questions to ask, buttons to push in an attempt to get to the truth of the fraud. Wasn't that why we had called her?

The court fell silent momentary as Maddison manoeuvered herself out of the oak encased witness box. My eyes fell to the floor as she marched out of the room, I didn't look up but I could hear the spring in her step as she clipped her heels against the stone flooring, the rhythm of her pace brighter than when she had entered the room and why wouldn't it be? Some ordeal that was I thought, she was off the hook. Gilbert hadn't made the worm squirm and I was as mad as hell.

Porter spoke.

"We will take a fifteen minute recess, we'll resume at 11.30."

"Court rise," the usher bellowed, as we all stood and Porter made a hasty retreat to his chamber.

We'd managed to find a little private area in the corner of the hall by the female toilets. Gilbert was about to bang on again about the architecture of Moot Hall, his eyes focused on the ceiling.

I brought him back to reality.

"What the hell was going on in there? She ran rings around us, understating her relationship, pleading ignorant to knowing what was going on with the will," I said in sharp, hushed tones fearful that the opposition would be lurking somewhere in the background.

He was flustered I could see, I realised Gilbert was all wind and bluster, there was no substance to the man. He wasn't used to being questioned or criticized, he was used to lesser mortals like myself hanging off his every word.

"I told you Mrs Palmer, we couldn't put too much pressure on the witness especially when we'd called her to give evidence."

My back was slumped against the wall relieving the weight from my feet, although I'd been sitting most of the morning in court my legs had turned to jelly.

"You had her where we wanted her and you let her go, she was lying Mr Gilbert, about the length of her relationship and the will, it was all so obvious but you didn't follow it through." I slapped my hand against the wall hard. "No wonder she skipped away so fucking happy."

I was about to continue my onslaught when Louise burst in, interrupting my flow, she'd been checking with the court ushers to see if Tina Palmer had arrived. Her voice was urgent, it was 11.29am and we had to be back in the courtroom at 11.30am. Slightly out of breath she threw her words between myself and Gilbert, breaking up our dispute.

"Tina Palmer hasn't turned up, you're on next Annette and we've got to get in there pronto. The Judge is ready to take his seat."

Oh fucking hell I thought as my hand grabbed Louise for support as my legs began to buckle. I took a deep breath drawing strength as I exhaled. You can do this, I chanted inwardly to myself over and over again.

I prayed that Bentley would be as easy and courteous on me as my barrister had been on the bitch woman. Then I'd have nothing to worry about. I looked at Gilbert as he stood and recalled the price he'd set for his services. What a ridiculous amount of money? I'd have done a better job representing myself.

40

After all the puffed up confidence I'd mustered while standing in the Moot Hall foyer waiting to come back into the courtroom to give evidence, I found when push came to shove and I was forced to make my way to the witness box I'd lost my nerve and felt like a frightened, cowering dog waiting for a beating. It didn't help that once seated in the raised parapet I realised the vantage point offered me full view of the entire courtroom that sadly brought into clear focus the overbearing frowns of the opposition.

I was breathing hard but trying not to show it, as Stuart and his hench mob stared in my direction, all three sets of eyes piercing into me like sharp pins, depleting my confidence by the minute.

I was still seething at Gilbert's inept performance and drew strength from the anger coursing through my body. I resisted the urge to run from the room although my feet, which were tap, tap, tapping on the oak flooring in a staccato beat, were urging me to do just that.

I tried hard to focus as the court usher stepped up in front of me and handed an ancient leather bound copy of the Bible.

"Can you place your right hand on the Bible please?"

It all added to the farcical game playing out in front of us, an atheist swearing on the Holy Bible. I obliged, shaking slightly as he placed in my free palm a copy of the Witness Oath. The artificial lighting in the windowless room bounced down from the rafters hitting the sheen of the plastic card and momentarily my eyes were dazzled by its bright reflection. It all seemed so bloody surreal, me sitting there pledging an oath with my hand planted on an old Bible. I struggled to read the small print, my distorted vision causing me to squint, yet still I ploughed through the short and meaningless passage with relative ease.

It hadn't escaped my mind that I'd already listened to Angela Maddison's pledge to tell the whole truth and nothing but the truth and as it turned out every word she'd spouted out of that vicious cutting mouth of hers was pitted with lies from start to finish. It was a fucking joke, a game, a fucked up, perverse, rigged theatre with ham fisted actors and storytellers and I was slap bang in the middle and couldn't escape. The words of the Eagles classic drifted in from nowhere. 'You can check out anytime you want but you can never leave'. It was a farce, from the jumped up overpaid pompous pricks in cloaks, to the Bible and the pledges and the promises and the obvious lies that everyone told. We are just prisoners here, of our own device.

Thankfully and to my relief it was Gilbert who was first up, his small stout figure barely stood head and shoulders above the bench he was anchored behind. Just knowing it was Gilbert and not Bentley opening the gambit of questions gave me a false sense of security, the panic I'd initially been feeling gradually subsided and it was replaced with a sense of calm as he guided the court to the relevant section in the bundle of papers pertaining to his first query.

"Mrs Palmer, please look at the statement in section C on page one, this sets out your financial position with regard to all your monthly income and expenditure. Is it correct?"

"Yes," I answered without need for thought on the matter, I knew the figures off by heart.

"And it is fair to say that you produced a sworn affidavit stating that the income and expenditure listed on your Form E is correct and accurate."

Gilbert laboured on his words as he swooped his head around the court like some Shakespearean thespian trying to heighten the drama.

"Yes."

He moved on. Bentley was furiously scribbling his notes whilst Gilbert baited me with a very gentle stick, his questions ranging from the type of house I lived in to Stuart's affair with Maddison and Alexandra's medical condition. Eventually as his audience began to shuffle in their seats, their attention waning as the stuffiness of the room and late morning fatigue began to take its toll, I sensed a general stir in interest as he brought up the subject of the mothers will.

"In relation to the husband's late mother, I believe she decided to disinherit her son and your children."

"I believe she did."

"Could you explain the relationship she'd had with your children."

"It was a close relationship," I said.

Gilbert raised his eyebrows slightly, prompting me to expand. The words flowed from my mouth, I took no coaxing, I spoke of the only life my children had ever known with their Grandmother.

"From the moment I had the children their Grandmother had a great deal of interaction with them, she visited the house three times a week, picked them up from school, came on holiday with us, stayed over at Christmas, that sort of thing. All three girls were her world."

My dialogue drifted on for some minutes as it dawned on me I was within a hairs breath of beginning to waffle, it was a sign my nerves were threatening to get the better of me. I stopped, allowing silence to invade the space for a microsecond before Gilbert filled the gap.

"Did you ever discuss her estate with your husband?"

I hadn't expected the question to be so direct.

I pondered my reply once more racking my brains as I recalled the conversations he'd had with his mother about how she wanted everything divided up when she was gone, I vividly recalled the conversations about what Tina should get and how she couldn't forget her Little Darlings as she often referred to her grandchildren. Stuart knew what was coming to him, he'd often have a joke referring to her property and land at Redburn as the Family Crown Jewels. It all raced back to me as I lingered on the question.

"Mrs Palmer," he pushed me, "can you answer my questions?"

"Yes he talked about inheriting from his mother and I'd often overheard him and his mother talking about how she planned for Stuart and her grandchildren to inherit her estate."

"Was Stuart close to his mother?" he interjected.

"Yes he was close to his mother, especially after his brother died. She visited our house regularly and latterly when she was too sick to leave her home, Stuart would visit her every night."

"Every night?" Gilbert questioned.

"Yes," I said without hesitation, "every night."

Gilbert nodded as he took his time to take a long lingering look at Stuart.

"So it would be fair to say that when you found out that Mr Palmer's mother had disinherited her only child you were a little surprised?"

"I was lost for words, it simply didn't make sense."

I wanted Gilbert to continue, I wanted him to mention the fact that Stuart was the executor, I wanted him to get to the nitty gritty, I wanted him to paint the picture of fraud, of an old woman changing her Will just a few months before her death to something so ridiculous that it belonged in a fairy story.

"Thank you Mrs Palmer," he said as he bobbed his head to the Judge before taking a seat, "no further questions."

"What the fuck?" I muttered under my breath.

My mouth turned dry as my foot began to tap, tap, tap, against the wood panelled floor once more. Bentley rose from his seat. I could see him composing himself, straightening his back up, flicking through his notes as his cold, hawk like eyes fixed upon me.

I will not be intimidated by this man I thought as I lifted my head to meet his gaze, my eyes locking onto his like a magnet.

He spoke and I remembered the pitch of his voice from our last encounter, his slow menacing drawl, how could I forget it?

He dived straight in.

"Your children haven't seen their Grandmother for several months have they Mrs Palmer?"

I wanted to counteract, deny it, but it was true.

"The fact is that you have driven a wedge between you children and their Grandmother, isn't that correct?"

"No, not at all."

"Which led to Mrs Palmer changing her Will, which she was entitled to do given the change of circumstances in her son's life."

I looked at him directly.

"She was entitled to disinherit her grandchildren but there was no reason whatsoever to cut her son out, that was just ridiculous."

"What are you saying Mrs Palmer? What are you accusing Mr Palmer of?"

"A fraud," I said, "resulting in an illegal transfer of £1.6 million."

"Objection."

I shouldn't have said it, I knew that and the judge reprimanded me for doing so. He asked that it be struck from the court records and yet I was glad to have at least planted the seed.

But Bentley stepped up the grilling and baited the hook. He called me bitter and twisted and reeled me in like a prize salmon. It was a red rag to a bull and I lost it.

I ranted about the fraud and Angela Maddison and the golf holiday and the night up at Sacriston and I pulled out just enough rope to hang myself. I obliged him, unknowingly playing right into his hands. Bitterness latched onto every word as I let rip and he let me rant on for two or three minutes. I was aware of Louise trying to catch my eye as she slowly moulded into the shape of her seat with embarrassment.

Why the hell was I telling him all this? I could feel the heat rising, sweeping through my body like a bush fire, instinctively I raised my hand wafting it across my face like a fan. I was becoming flustered but still I kept going.

"You feel very strongly about Angela Maddison don't you Mrs Palmer?" Bentley said.

I was beyond rational thought.

"Yes, you could say I have strong feelings, I fucking hate the bitch for destroying my family."

The judge was almost on his feet.

"I will not tolerate language like that in my court."

Bentley was glaring at me, taunting me, daring me to dig an even bigger hole for myself.

"In fact, you told your children you didn't like her and you also told them that their Dad had been having an affair."

"I told my daughters the truth. My husband had been having an affair for some time and chose to leave on Father's Day."

I looked over to Stuart.

"Classy."

Bentley continued.

"Is it true that you embroiled the children in adult issues."

My anger was starting to rise, I could almost feel the hairs on the back of my neck stand up, still I attempted to keep calm.

"I embroiled my children in nothing, it was their Dad who lied to them about his relationship with Angela Maddison then he continued to lie about his golf holiday. He was the one who stopped contacting his children."

They weren't the words Bentley wanted to hear, he was a calm man, his body language gave nothing away, no visible ticks to be seen, yet as I sat defiant I could see in my peripheral vision his hand was stroking the corner of his note pad like a comfort blanket. Was I touching a spot, was there an inkling of agitation stirring within him I wondered?

"You involved your children in everything, you showed them documents from your solicitors, you actively encouraged them to turn against their father."

His voice was still calm yet increasing in momentum as he delivered his final cutting remark.

"It's what you wanted wasn't it? You felt like the injured party and you were determined Mr Palmer was going to suffer as well."

His dark, hawk like eyes drilled into me willing me to retaliate. My hands lay on my lap hidden from view, I screwed them into fists, my manicured nails cutting into the flesh of my palms. Instantly I felt a sense of relief, at least if I could feel some physical pain I would be spared the mental torture this man was trying to put me through.

"They aren't children Mr Bentley, they are grown women who have minds of their own and a right to know what's happening. I've got nothing to hide from them, I've done nothing wrong other than marry a man who is incapable of monogamy. If they ask me a question I will answer it as honestly as I can and that is exactly what I have done with regard to my marriage breakdown."

I told Bentley about the pizza fests and how they stopped once my daughters saw through the tissues of lies and I tried to steer the conversation back to the will and the fraud that had quite clearly taken place. Bentley was having none of it as time and time again he prodded and poked and tried to stir the hornet's nest with cutting, personal comments that I reacted to time and time again.

My words were defiant and defensive. I wondered how long I had been on my feet, it seemed like an eternity and I remember wondering why Gilbert hadn't put in a performance like this. Bentley looked on as he chipped away, slowly destroying my character in front of Porter and the open court.

I thought my ordeal was coming to an end, Bentley was slowing up.

He shuffled a few papers.

"Let's move on to finances," He looked at me directly. "You're a trained accountant aren't you Mrs Palmer? Good with money would you say?"

I hesitated, was it a trick question I wondered.

"I suppose so."

"Being good with money you would be fairly sure you were able to calculate your income quite easily?"

"Yes." I was at a total loss at his line of questioning.

"But at the Maintenance Pending Suite hearing last year, the statement you made about your income was completely untrue."

My face flushed, I knew exactly where he was going and it wasn't up any blind alley, it had direction and he was delivering it right to my door.

"You lied Mrs Palmer, you made a statement that you were not in receipt of Child Tax Credits, however the truth was you were receiving it at the time of the hearing."

My eyes scanned around the courtroom like a missile detector, seeking out Louise, she knew the truth, surely she'd jump up and tell the court what had actually happened. Her head raised from her note taking as if she knew I was looking for her, for a moment our eyes fixed on to one another. My eyes were pleading with her tell me what to say Louise, what should I say. She gave a weak smile shrugging her shoulders, was that it, was that all the help I was going to get? It was Bennett who had lied to the court and she'd witnessed it yet that didn't matter, the buck stopped with me, I was on my own, my handsome solicitor was nowhere in sight.

"Well Mrs Palmer, maybe I can show you the bank statement, it gives the dates you received Child Tax Credit and it proceeds the MPS hearing."

My eyes jumped back to my antagonist as he wafted a copy of the bank statement mid-air. I bit hard into my lower lip. The court was silent, all eyes were on me, I had to say something.

"At the time of the hearing any money I was in receipt of I listed and gave that list to my legal team."

Bentley glared at me.

"You lied Mrs Palmer."

He turned to the Judge.

"A deliberate blatant lie your honour."

Humiliation swept over me. I looked at Bentley then Stuart who was sitting directly behind Bentley, smug smiles planted right across their faces.

Without a hint of emotion in my voice, my eyes fixed once more on Bentley I delivered my response.

"I don't lie Mr Bentley, I told my solicitor everything, he will confirm that the Child Tax Credits were fully documented."

I'd stepped into the trap and as soon as the words fell from my mouth I wanted to grab them back.

"Excellent Mrs Palmer, then we shall do just that." He looked slowly around the courtroom mimicking surprise. "And where is you solicitor?"

I looked at Louise at then at Gilbert. Louise started to scribble, Gilbert just looked away.

"Where is Mr Bennett, Mrs Palmer?"

I shook my head and looked towards the floor.

"That's right Mrs Palmer, he's not here and therefore conveniently for you he can't confirm or deny your little oversight."

Bentley turned to the Judge, who seized the moment.

"I think this would be in ideal opportunity to take a lunch break."

There was silence as we walked from the court, Stuart and his crew were directly behind us neither side wanting to give anything away to the opposition. Anger was still raging inside me, I was absolutely furious, it couldn't have gone any worse. Not only had I been painted a bitter and twisted woman who had purposely turned her children against their father, I was a liar as well. But more than that I had received no support from my legal team, the legal team who had fucked up good and proper.

Without John to hand it was Louise who was on the receiving end of my wrath.

"What the hell happened there? Why didn't Bennett document that he hadn't disclosed the Child Tax Credit? I warned him that it would be picked up but he chose to ignore me."

I turned my attention to Gilbert.

"And you, aren't you supposed to throw in an occasional objection when your client is under pressure?"

My legal team gave me no answers.

"And where is Bennett? Surely he should have been here, surely he could have stood and admitted his oversight? At least I wouldn't have been painted out to be a liar."

I buried my head in my hands, I was on the verge of tears.

"Fucking useless, he's fucking useless."

Louise was guarded, hesitant to give a response, I realised there and then no matter how friendly she'd been, above all else she was John's girl, loyal to the last. I pushed her for an answer once more.

"What was I supposed to say in there Louise," my hand pointing in the direction of the courtroom we'd just vacated. "I looked like a bloody liar." I said.

I could see the concern on her face, she was about to speak when suddenly Gilbert interjected, his voice had an authoritative edge to it.

"Louise don't say a word, Mrs Palmer is still under oath. Mr Bentley hasn't finished cross examining her," he glared at Louise who was looking unusually flustered.

"What did you say Mr Gilbert?" I questioned.

He shook his head,

"Unfortunately we can't talk about your evidence because you're still under oath, we can't be seen to coach you with your answers. You are on your own Mrs Palmer."

My head shook in disbelief and wasn't that the truth I thought the moment he had said it.

"I'm on my own alright, over £50000 on legal advice and you tell me I'm on my own."

"I'm sorry," he said, "but it's the law."

"It's the law?" I questioned. "It's a fucking circus, a charade, an absurd pretense played out by men who like to dress up. It's a nonsense, the whole truth and nothing but the truth, what the fuck's all that about?"

Louise tried to cut in but I stopped her dead.

"The only person in there who was telling the whole truth and nothing but the truth was me." I jabbed a finger towards my barrister. "What am I paying you for Mr Gilbert? You tell me, because from where I'm sitting I think I could have done a hell of a better job."

Gilbert ignored me and looked nervously at his watch.

"And they convinced the Judge I was a liar. Me, the only person in there telling the bloody truth."

Gilbert stood.

"Anyone like a sandwich?"

When I stepped back up into the witness box after our thirty-minute lunch break I felt anything but refreshed. I'd managed to grab a black coffee from a Subway sandwich shop that was conveniently situated on the corner of the street yards from the old court house. I'd sat drinking it, perched on a window seat, like a zombie, flashbacks of the debacle that had played out earlier in the day spinning around my head. I was just hoping that I could hold out this next show.

Bentley stood up once more, eager to begin the second part of his interrogation. He started off gently enough asking about my qualifications and my efforts to find work. I waffled for a while explaining how it had been impossible to look for employment since Alexandra's illness. His questioning smoothly moved onto my daughter's medical condition.

"Alexandra has been poorly hasn't she Mrs Palmer?"

"Yes," I responded, "very ill, we nearly lost her."

"Alexandra's on the mend now isn't she?" he said, his tone slightly upbeat which I instantly flagged up as unusual.

"She's improving day by day. There's still a long way to go." I was quick to add.

I knew where he was leading me, he wanted to hear that Alexandra was an independent girl who didn't need her mother as her carer.

"She'll be resuming her studies in September."

I shook my head in disagreement.

"No, Alexandra will take a good year to recover, her consultant has said as much."

Bentley gave a weak smile, I knew immediately he was jostling with me, setting out his stall ready for an attack.

He glanced across to Stuart.

"Mr Palmer didn't known what was going on with Alexandra when she was ill. You wouldn't allow him to go and visit her in hospital, is that true?"

My blood was boiling at the man's condescending manner. I rushed back at him.

"No, that isn't true. That was Alexandra's decision not mine, when I realised how serious her condition was I asked her if she wanted to see her father, don't forget he hadn't seen her for seven months."

My voice was on the verge of cracking as the nightmare flooded back into my head. I looked across at Stuart, he avoided my gaze staring blankly ahead, not one ounce of emotion evident.

"What did Alexandra say exactly Mrs Palmer?"

"Alexandra said she couldn't cope with seeing her Dad at that point."

I was aware that I had raised my voice again. My emotions were beginning to get the better of me.

"Are you sure you didn't plant the seed Mrs Palmer? Are you sure you didn't take that decision for her?"

"No."

"You are telling the truth Mrs Palmer aren't you? We've already heard today that you can be economical with that sort of thing."

I was floundering again. I looked at Gilbert expecting an objection at least.

Nothing.

Bentley was going for the kill.

Bentley lifted an email from the indexed bundle.

"I have a letter written at the time of Alexandra's release which you passed to your solicitor and he in turn passed to us. It states quite clearly, 'Under no circumstances should Mr Palmer contact Alexandra, Abigail or Victoria.' His voice took a more sinister tone.

"It would seem that you not only wanted to keep Mr Palmer away from his sick daughter in hospital you also wanted him to stay well away from all of his children and indeed the family home."

"Yes, it's what they wanted."

"Not what you wanted Mrs Palmer?"

"No."

Bentley fell silent for a moment as he looked around the courtroom. I knew what he was doing, he was letting it all sink in. He was skillful, I'd give him that. My head was in a different place and my eyes began to fill with pools of tears as thoughts of my brother invaded my head once more.

Bentley spoke.

"Why did you stop your husband coming to visit Alexandra when she was recuperating at home?"

By now I was sobbing gently.

"Alexandra had been so ill, in hospital for over a month, we'd only just got home when my brother had a brain haemorrhage and..." The words were strangling my voice chords as I tried to get them out, “he died, my brother died.”

A court official rushed forward with a box of hankies, then suddenly, out of nowhere Stuart, who’d sat and said nothing while I’d spoke about his daughter's illness jumped up from his seat, tears in his eyes.

“You didn’t tell me about Roger,” he shouted across the courtroom.

He took me by surprise. Of course he knew about Roger, this was staged, pre-planned. I could feel all the anger and hate rise up in me and I couldn’t stop myself, everything burst out of my mouth like a volcanic eruption.

“You’re a lying bastard. I sent a letter to your solicitor explaining everything. I told him Alexandra couldn’t cope with any further stress neither could the other girls. That’s why they didn’t want you there.”

“I didn’t know about Roger, I swear I didn’t know,” he shouted across the room.

Porter jumped in immediately.

“Please Mr Palmer sit down.” His attention focussed on me “Mrs Palmer, be quiet please and do not attempt to speak directly to Mr Palmer again.”

I nodded meekly. Stuart sat back down and buried his face in a paper handkerchief, still sobbing. I looked around, I couldn’t quite believe what I’d just witnessed. Wasn’t I just the baddest bitch on the planet? I turned to Louise and Gilbert. They looked away. I was aware that Bentley had started to speak again. He’d stuck the knife in me and now he was starting to twist it.

“Not only did she stop her husband seeing their gravely ill daughter, she stopped him from seeing her when she was quite clearly on the road to recovery. Furthermore she stopped Mr Palmer from seeing his other two daughters as well and although she denies that, we have already seen today that fact and fiction are much the same thing to her.”

I opened my mouth to defend myself. The words wouldn’t form on my lips.

Thankfully Porter stepped in to save me from further punishment.

“If you have no more questions Mr Bentley, I think Mrs Palmer can stand down.”

Bentley was unmoved.

“Just one more question for Mrs Palmer, Sir.”

"Well hurry along Mr Bentley," Porter snapped back.

My heart was still racing and my anger still at its peak as Bentley turned on me once more.

"Mrs Palmer you asked for Alexandra's Doctor to provide you with a medical report so you could present it to the court. Is that right?"

"Yes I did."

"Could you then explain why, after she diligently produced the report giving her opinion on Alexandra's health and future medical needs?"

He paused. My eyes flared up like a rabbit caught in headlights.

"Why Mrs Palmer did you then ask Dr Carrion to alter the report to include a statement saying that it would be in Alexandra's best interests to stay in the family home?"

I shook my head.

"No.. No .. No.. That was not the case Mr Bentley."

"Yes it was Mrs Palmer, you asked her to amend the report did you not, attempting to influence the Judge's decision?"

"No."

"Because you want to stay in the family home."

"No, yes…"

Bentley reached into his file.

"Your honour, I have here two reports from Dr Carrion, both dated the same day, both identical apart from the final paragraph."

The Judge held out his hand.

"Let me take a look."

I watched the court usher take the paperwork to the Judge and he started to study the two letters. I knew what was coming, I knew my legal team had fucked up in grand style yet again.

After no more than two minutes the Judge handed the sheets of paper back to the court usher and turned to face me.

"Would you care to explain this Mrs Palmer?"

41

The Judge called another recess and we made our way to a quiet area of the court building. My attention turned to Louise, with John nowhere to be found she was in the direct firing line for my wrath, it hadn't escaped my attention that I was being accused of being a liar and yet I'd paid thousands of pounds in fees to Saxtons and they'd hung me out to dry on one of the most important days of my life.

"Where is John? Why isn't he here Louise? He's fucked up from start to finish and he's nowhere to be seen."

She had nowhere to turn. While I was angry with her my real venom was directed to the man who was conspicuous by his absence.

"He should be here, he could have explained the tax credits, admitted he'd made a mistake but instead the Judge thinks I'm a compulsive liar."

Gilbert was trying to placate me, telling me it wasn't as bad as I imagined.

"And how do they know about the amended Dr's report?"

Louise let out a deep sigh.

"That's my fault, I'm sorry. We were late adding Dr Carrion's amended letter to the court pack, as a consequence they got sight of the original letter as well as the amended letter. I'm sorry Annette," she said.

"For Christ sake," I snapped, shaking my head in total disbelief, "it looks terrible in there, Osama Bin Laden would get a better reception. Have you any idea how it looks?"

I buried my head in my hands as I took stock of the day's proceedings and realised it couldn't have gone any worse.

Gilbert turned to whisper in my ear.

"Well done Mrs Palmer, you did brilliantly all things considered, your ordeal is over now."

He was right, my ordeal was over but that didn't stop me from wanting to hit him. He had been useless, silent, non-descript and he had left me like a lamb to the slaughter. What had he done to justify his ridiculously large fee?

A court official walked over and whispered something in Gilbert's ear. He smiled.

"Tina Palmer has arrived," he said, "if you'd been listening instead of talking you would have heard Judge Porter ask who was taking the witness stand next. This is what we have been waiting for." He glanced at his watch. "If we don't get moving we'll not get through everything today. It will go to a second day."

As I walked across the courtroom to reclaim my seat directly behind Gilbert, my eyes were instinctively drawn to Stuart, handkerchief still dabbing at his eyes. I was still totally perplexed by his sudden outburst, when had he given one jot about my family? His performance had been worthy of an Olivier Award.

I breathed a sigh of relief as I spotted Tina Palmer in the courtroom. Could I dare to hope that something was about to go my way? Were we were going to get to the bottom of the Will and where Palmer's money had gone?

Gilbert was on his feet.

"Our next witness, Tina Ann Palmer, I propose we hear her evidence next if that's agreeable sir."

Porter nodded.

"Mr Bentley are you agreeable?" he queried.

"Yes Sir."

Tina Ann Palmer tottered into the witness box like butter wouldn't melt, another one playing the game were my initial thoughts. She was wearing her work attire, Karen Millen suit, court shoes with a matching neutral, oversized Mulberry bag slung over the crease of her arm, her whole persona reeking designer. Apart from the brief glimpse I'd sneaked of her at the mother's funeral, I hadn't clapped eyes on the woman since Frank's funeral ten years previously. There'd been no great change in her appearance, a little older looking for sure, jowls had appeared where once there were none, yet all in all she was much the same. The bleach blonde hair was still bleached and the most prominent feature on her face, the large hooked nose, was still hooked which surprised me a little as I was sure she'd have afforded herself a plastic surgeon after the pay-out she'd received from Frank's premature death. By all accounts, Frank had left her mortgage and debt free with a couple of hundred grand in the bank for good measure, not bad for a woman who was in her mid-thirties when she was widowed and young enough to start a new life.

As she perched herself in the witness stand, her bag cradled on her lap for fear the £800 piece of precious cowhide might pick up dust if it were to hit the floor, she placed her hand on the Bible and went through the formalities.

"Can you confirm your name and address?"

Already something was beginning to niggle away at me as Gilbert began to bat the questions to her and she volleyed the answers right back at him in a mouse like voice.

"You married Mr Palmer's brother in 1990?"

"Yes."

"He sadly died in 1999?"

"Yes."

"You both worked at the same firm of accountants?"

"Yes."

"It's true to say that the two brothers were not close?"

"Not particularly," she replied, not caring to fill in any of the detail of their ten year rift. Why didn't he ask about the rift I pondered as I clasped my hands together tightly in an attempt to channel my growing frustration. Olive Palmer hated Tina, question her on their relationship, never mind the brothers. My list of questions to throw at Tina Palmer was building by the minute. Unfortunately Gilbert wasn't on the same wavelength.

"And what was your relationship like with Mrs Palmer?"

"Very good, we were quite close."

Liar!

"And her relationship with Stuart Palmer?"

"Like a normal mother and son relationship."

"So you didn't think it was strange that she cut her only son out of the Will in favour of you?"

She shrugged her shoulders.

"Her decision."

Gilbert appeared to hesitate but it was all part of the act.

"You do know that Stuart lived with his mother when he parted from his wife?"

"Yes," she said, not a flicker of change in her voice.

He picked away, said that the fact they were living together hardly painted a picture of any problems between them.

He continued.

"We know Olive Palmer made a new Will several months ago. In that Will you became her sole beneficiary. Did you know about that?"

"I found out about it last week."

"Really Mrs Palmer? I find it that hard to believe, especially as you were joint executor."

I held my hand in a fist like grip in front of my face, willing my mouth to remain shut.

"Stuart told me at the funeral," her voice weak as her eyes filled with her own brand of crocodile tears.

"And that surprised you?"

"Yes, I suppose so."

"Quite," said Gilbert, "a lady who was almost a stranger leaves you £1.6 million and you suppose so."

"Objection."

Bentley wasn't happy he had used the word stranger and said that Tina Palmer was entitled to dignity and respect but Gilbert claimed she had seen Olive Palmer no more than half a dozen times in the last ten years and the description was accurate. The Judge over ruled, instructing him to continue. Was he at last earning his corn?

"Was it true that Mrs Palmer wanted nothing to do with you after you took up with another man so soon after her son's death?"

"Objection."

This time the Judge sided with Bentley. Gilbert was warned.

He carried on, his enthusiasm to get to the crux of the matter apparent. The crux of the matter was fraud.

"And Mrs Palmer, did she discuss with you that she was disinheriting her son and her grandchildren in favour of you?"

"No."

"Again, don't you think that's rather uncalled for?"

"Her decision."

"They were the only grandchildren of Mrs Palmer?"

"Yes"

"You don't have children?"

"No."

"So all of her grandchildren are Stuart's children?"

"Yes," she sighed either out of resentment or boredom I wasn't sure which.

"Mrs Palmer was very close to all of her grandchildren?" Gilbert asked.

"Well she was close to them when they were small children."

My ears pricked up, hardly believing what I was hearing. For the first time since the beginning of her gentle interrogation she'd found her voice, desperate to add meat to the bones of her argument. She went on.

"As they got older she had less and less to do with them. For the last few years she hasn't been close to any of her grandchildren at all."

Her sweet, innocent voice pitched her deceitful sentiment directly at Porter.

Instantly I saw red, my entire body was raging with anger and frustration, not giving myself a moment to think I sprang into action jumping up from my seat with such force the turbulent air caused the papers on Gilbert's bench to catch on the breeze and fall to the floor. As he bent to pick them up I was already on my feet screeching.

"You liar, where do you think Olive spent her time? At my bloody house that's where."

"Mrs Palmer sit down." Porter said, trying his best to project his weak insignificant voice.

I continued, ignoring him completely.

"Not close…she spent every weekend at my house, every Christmas, Easter, we went on holiday with her from when they were babies up to when they were young adults."

"Mrs Palmer sit down."

"They stopped going to see her when she took their fathers side so don't give me that shit."

"Mrs Palmer sit down!"

Porter was now practically eating his microphone in an effort to get his voice heard. I may have well gone on and continued to ignore his command if it were not for Louise pulling at my arm urging me to sit down.

"Please Annette sit down, you must sit down."

I slumped back in my chair as Porter regained control of his courtroom.

"If I have one more outburst from you Mrs Palmer I will stop proceedings and the case will have to be rescheduled for another day."

He didn't stop, for the first time there was more than a hint of authority present in his voice.

"Let me remind you if I am forced to do that you will be paying Mr Palmer's court costs for today's proceedings."

His eyes fixed on me, my shame and humiliation complete as I shrunk back in my chair.

Gilbert, still flustered and clearly not at all happy took the stage once more as Stuart and his crew looked on, desperately trying to conceal their smugness.

He asked Tina to continue. Her eyes were cast to the floor once more, lips contorted.

"Olive said she was disappointed with the way she'd been treated by her grandchildren."

For the first time since she started her performance her eyes met mine. She was trying to taunt me I had no doubt, her voice was sickly sweet, that was her instruction from the other side.

"She said she didn't want Annette to benefit from her estate. I thought it was a kneejerk reaction to their divorce. I didn't think she would do it. We never spoke of it again."

Her voice trailed off as Gilbert latched on to her mistake.

"So you had discussed the Will with Olive Palmer, Mrs Palmer, you said a few minutes ago you hadn't."

She hesitated for a second.

"Just generically in conversation, we never discussed specifics, she never mentioned that she wanted me to be a beneficiary."

Gilbert smiled.

"Don't you mean the sole beneficiary?"

"I suppose so."

"So when did you see the Will?"

"Last week when I went to see my solicitor about changing my own Will."

Gilbert shook his head, I could only see the back of it as I sat directly behind him yet I knew there was a hint of drama about to be delivered.

"And your solicitor is?"

"Mr Boulton."

"Who happened to be Olive Palmer's solicitor?"

"Yes."

"You all use the same solicitors?" he questioned.

"Yes that's right"

"And Olive didn't ask you to hold on to her estate and hand it over to Stuart at a later date?"

"Objection."

"You may answer the question."

"Of course not," she said, "that would be ..."

Gilbert found the word she didn't want to say. "A fraud Mrs Palmer, a fraud."

"Yes."

We had her, she was floundering, she was looking worried and even Bentley hadn't objected to the F word because everyone present in the court building, including the Judge knew the farcical nature of Olive Palmer cutting her own son and grandchildren out of the her Will and leaving it to someone who severed links with the family ten years ago. I sat back, for once looking forward to what lay ahead and wondered what Gilbert's next question would be.

"No furthers questions," he projected across the room before sinking into his seat.

42

I was numb with rage when Stuart Palmer took the stand with the self-assurance of a man who'd been dealt a good hand in a poker game. The stakes were high yet he knew the odds were rigged in his favour. All he had to do was keep his nerve and his cards close to his chest and how could he fail to scoop the prize?

Not that Judge Porter would recognise his cock sure arrogant nature, my devious ex-husband had disguised it well, the dishevelled look, the downcast eyes and that alien, low submissive voice were all props in his well-rehearsed act. I wasn't without fault, I'd helped his cause with my dramatic outbursts and I looked every inch the liar, the cold-hearted ice maiden determined to seek revenge because my husband had the audacity to get up and leave me for another woman. But I knew where the real blame lay and that was with my legal team who had not only made two monumental errors in open court, but had also failed to guide me and failed to defend me against a highly skilled and vicious barrister. Now I knew with outright certainty naming the other woman had done me no favours, the courts were only interested in dividing the assets up between the fractured parties, they had no interest in attributing blame. At the eleventh hour when I was sitting at the final hearing, it had dawned on me Judge Porter and the rest of his fraternity couldn't give a flying fuck whether my ex-husband had been screwing half of Newcastle throughout our twenty-three-year marriage, they couldn't care less. Why hadn't Bennett warned me it wouldn't be in my best interest going for the jugular and name Angela Maddison. As I watched Stuart take the age old Bible in his right hand and swear to tell the truth the whole truth and nothing but the truth, it occurred to me that it was more likely that pigs might fly.

Bentley took his time painting the scene. He cast Stuart as the loving, dotting father, the big provider who'd selflessly given up the best part of his life working hard to provide for his ungrateful family.

"Mr Palmer, relations between you and your children have been strained in the last few months, can you tell me why the communication has broken down?"

"I blame their mother for turning my daughters against me."

There's a surprise.

"When I first left the family home I would take the girls out of dinner every week, we had a good relationship but gradually things deteriorated. I eventually realised Annette had started to feed the girls lies about me, showing them letters from her solicitor. They began to blame me for the marriage breakup."

"And were you to blame Mr Palmer? Did you start a relationship with Angela Maddison prior to separating from your wife?"

Already Stuart's head was shaking, a look of shock in his eyes as if his brain couldn't quiet comprehend such an outlandish thought.

"Never, I just wouldn't do that, I didn't start a relationship with Angela Maddison until my marriage was completely over and I'd left the family home. We were work colleagues and friends, however as usual, Annette was irrational and concocted the whole affair in her mind. I was faithful throughout our marriage."

I began to fidget in my chair, trying to resist the urge to jump up from my seat and plant the bastard. He was making me sound like some deranged bunny boiler. Louise, sensing my agitation reached out and gently tapped my arm.

"Don't rise to it Annette, one more strike and Porter will have you out of the court," she warned in hushed tones.

I took a deep breath; reluctantly I leaned into the hard back of the bench seat deliberately casting my eyes to the floor no longer giving myself the opportunity to look at Palmer's smug self-righteous face.

"And what about Alexandra and her recent illness?"

He was shaking his head once more.

"I tried to contact my daughter, I was desperately worried but once again," he threw me another glance, "Annette wouldn't allow me to visit the hospital. I was out of my mind with worry."

He didn't convince me, there was no hint of emotion in his voice and it dawned on me there and then that he had no real idea how ill Alexandra had been. He didn't have an inkling because it wasn't him who'd had to witness the Consultant saying he'd do what he could for my daughter, it wasn't him who'd camped by his daughter's bedside for a whole month whilst she lay there struggling to breath, her head delirious with the concoction of drugs she was force fed just to keep her relatively pain free. He was supposed to be eaten up with worry, yet the best he could do was send one letter via his solicitor. I tried to contain myself, the pressure building up to the point of bursting.

"Do you plan to contact your children in the future?"

"It's my dearest wish," he said, his voice almost pleading as he got to the purpose of the orchestrated question.

"I want to buy a four bedroomed house so the girls can stay over and we can start to build our relationship again."

How rehearsed I thought as Stuart's response led Bentley nicely into his next question.

"Are you dependent on the sale of the family home to be in the position to buy a house for yourself and your children to live in?"

"Yes. I would be dependent on the money from the sale of the family home to buy a property. I'm not able to get a mortgage which is partly due to my medical condition but also there is the factor that I haven't any work on at the moment."

"Yes, your medical condition," Bentley said, with more than a hint of enthusiasm, he was wise enough to know this was his clients ace card when it came to maintenance payments and he was going to capitalize on it.

"I believe your referring to your eye condition is that right Mr Palmer?"

"Yes. I have Glaucoma."

The words rolled off his tongue. I'd heard it all before, he'd been dinning out on the bloody condition for as long as I could remember.

"My eyesight is deteriorating rapidly, I don't know how long I'll be able to go on working."

My frustration was growing once more as I surveyed the room. Although he didn't have my sympathy I could almost feel the vibe of compassion from the court swaying in his favour.

Bentley wasn't slow to build on the advantage he had gained, without hesitation he whipped out a report and rattled off the key points of an eye specialist, Mr Aziz's prognosis.

Oh it was bad, white stick and guide dog bad. He handed a copy of the report to the Judge.

"If I can sir, I would like to draw your attention to the second paragraph of Mr Aziz's letter."

He recited every word of the damming diagnosis as he savoured every word.

"Over the last year Mr Palmers vision has deteriorated. Unfortunately this deterioration that we see is significantly affecting him in everyday life and will probably continue to do so until such times as he may even lose his sight altogether."

Bentley paused, allowing Porter a moment to read the letter in its entirety. The court was silent for a couple of minutes before Bentley reclaimed the void.

"I think the report speaks volumes sir."

He glanced in Porter's direction, who still appeared to be engrossed in the Aziz's letter. It was not a good sign.

My hand reached out for Gilbert's shoulder once more, his head snapped around and his eye brows raised, agitation at my disruption written all over his face. I leant towards his ear, my hushed tones still carrying sufficient noise to attract Bentley's attention who shot me a cold glare.

"You can't let him get away with this, he's practically portraying himself as blind and he's far from that, he plays golf off 3 for Christ sake"

I knew my last rumpus was still on Gilbert's mind as his sharp blunt whisper cut me down

"Please let me get on with my job Mrs Palmer. I will have my opportunity to cross examine Mr Palmer in due course, do not worry."

He turned away leaving me with the view of the back of his head once more and worse still, the sound of Bentley and Stuart's voices going through their pre rehearsed dialogue.

Having exhausted the eye condition, Bentley built on his advantage, turning to the next subject he knew could sway the judgement in his clients favour, work.

Stuart was speaking again.

"I haven't got any work on at the moment. With the economy

taking a downturn a lot of companies are going into liquidation."

Judge Porter interjected.

"You aren't working at present Mr Palmer?"

"No Sir, I'm unemployed."

How fucking convenient for him. It was perfectly usual for Stuart to have an odd few weeks off in between jobs, it was par for the course for a self-employed accountant but he was milking the situation for all it was worth.

You fucking liar, I wanted to scream out and I may have well have done if it had not been for Porter calling time on Bentley.

"I think we'll take a ten minute refreshment break before Mr Gilbert starts his cross examination," he glanced at his watch. "Court rise."

Then he was gone.

Once again I was venting my anger towards Louise and Gilbert for the shambles unfolding in the court room. What a perfect session Bentley had just conducted. It was measured, precise, emotional and effective. We only had ten minutes huddled together outside the cubbyhole by the ladies loo and I wanted to get everything off my chest.

"What the hell is going on? It's a bloody mess from start to finish. If it had been a boxing match they would have stopped it by now."

"Can I get you a coffee Annette," Louise whispered softly, clearly thinking it was caffeine withdrawal which was responsible for my irritability.

"No, I don't want a fucking coffee," I snapped although as soon as I'd said the words I wished I could have retracted them. I would have killed for a strong back coffee, preferably laced with a decent cognac.

Gilbert offered his reassurances in an attempt to dampen my rage, his fat chubby hands waving around in the air as if he was juggling a set of balls.

"Mrs Palmer, when I begin my cross examination I will go over all the issues Bentley has raised. However I warn you we have to be careful, I don't want to dwell on Mr Palmer's eye condition or the fact he is now saying he has no work at the moment."

I was flabbergasted.

"You don't want to dwell Mr Gilbert?" I took a deep breath. "I want you to dwell, I want you to dwell on his eye condition and his unemployment because he's lying. I want you to pick holes in his story and make him out to be the liar that he is and I want you to tell the world about his phony income and his fucking hidden millions."

"You need to calm down Mrs Palmer."

"Calm down! For fuck's sake is it not obvious? Stuart has had this bloody eye condition for as long as I can remember. It hasn't deteriorated in the last fifteen years and he's unemployed because he's between contracts that all."

The irritation and frustration in my voice was all too apparent as I rubbed the temples of my brow in an attempt to release the growing pressure.

"Mr Gilbert is right Annette," Louise chipped in, her calming voice a welcome sound for my battered ears. She went on as I reluctantly listened to her logic.

"If we dwell on Mr Palmer's eye condition it gives him more air time on the subject which we don't want. Don't forget, whether he's exaggerating or not he's provided the Judge with evidence that there's a realistic chance his eye sight may well get worse."

Gilbert nodded his head.

"Exactly, I'm going to have to focus on Mr Palmer's historic earnings but will make the Judge well aware that Mr Palmer's unemployment is a temporary setback. Specialist accountants like him, with his experience and qualifications, won't be unemployed for more than a few weeks."

I wanted to give up. I couldn't have possible felt lower, never in a million years did I expect the biggest day of my life to go as bad as it had and I wanted to turn back the clock and start all over again. As we stood in that stinky cubbyhole with the faint stench of urine rising from the toilets I felt totally defeated.

I turned to Gilbert.

"It's over, I'm not going back in there."

"Annette, don't be stupid you -"

"I'm not going in. You and Louise sort it out between you."

Louise was on her feet. She had a calm voice but was on the verge of losing her temper with me. I wasn't listening. Fuck her, fuck Gilbert, fuck them all, fuck the wigs and the Judge, fuck the game and fuck the system.

"Wild horses won't drag me in there. Do you hear?" I said.

"Mum."

My ears pricked up as her voice echoed across the foyer. I turned my head, she was back, without a second thought I raced across the vast hallway and sank into the warmth of her body and sobbed. I could smell the fresh soapy fragrance lifting from her skin as I inhaled deeply, savouring every moment of our embrace.

"It's a nightmare in there Abigail, a complete mess and I'm not going back."

She drew away from me, her strong hands gripping my shoulders as if she were about to shake me.

"Mum calm down," she said, her voice almost scolding. "You're going back in there and you're going to face the music. You can do this. Show that bastard how tough you are Mum. Forget the money and the settlement, get in there and tell him it doesn't matter, what matters is that you have your girls. No Judge in the world can take your girls away."

I looked at her tear filled eyes as she stood.

"We are so proud of you Mum, just get in there and keep your head held high. It's not the money, it's about dignity and pride and you are the most dignified and proud person we've ever met so get in there and don't let us down."

I was aware of Louise standing beside us, gently stroking my arm. She also had tears in her eyes.

"I love you Abigail," I said, my words shamelessly reverberating around the room.

"I love you too Mum," she bounced back, her words drifting away as Louise led me towards the doors of the courtroom. Within a few short seconds they slammed shut behind us. I looked at the Judge and Stuart and his pathetic little team. I smiled. Do your worst, I thought to myself, you can't take my girls away.

Gilbert started his cross examination at the obvious point, the catalyst of the entire mess, Stuart's affair with Angela Maddison.

"So Mr Palmer, you state you didn't start a relationship with Mrs Maddison until after you left the family home."

"That's right," Stuart snapped back, his defences already on heightened alert.

"Yet Mr Palmer you admitted adultery in the divorce petition as did Mrs Maddison."

Stuart hesitated before answering.

"Errr…Yes."

"But you are now saying you didn't commit adultery."

I almost smiled as I saw my ex-husband put on the spot, his posture already beginning to change as his back stiffened and his doe like eyes were replaced with a menacing stare, it was a look I was familiar with when his hackles were up and his patience was being tested.

Stuart looked over to his team before answering.

"I started a relationship with Mrs Maddison in July, after I left the family home."

"So there was no adultery during the marriage?"

"No."

"But you admitted to the adultery in the divorce petition?"

"Yes."

Gilbert looked at the judge.

"There you have it Sir, Mr Palmer has clearly confessed to telling lies."

"Objection."

The Judge removed his glasses and spoke.

"I fail to see what you are trying to establish Mr Gilbert. It matters not who is to blame. The law does not apportion blame when deciding any financial settlement. What is your point?"

Gilbert explained that he was trying to prove that Mr Palmer could also be economical with the truth. He cited that he had more than a strong suspicion that he had lied about the adultery, his medical condition and the fact that he was unemployed.

"I intend to prove to the court just what sort of man Mr Palmer is and how he is trying to steal what rightfully belongs to my client."

"Objection."

The judge allowed him to continue.

"Mr Palmer, did you commit adultery with an unnamed person in Grimsby?"

Stuart grimaced.

"No."

"I beg to differ," Gilbert said. "It clearly states in your divorce petition you admitted to adultery with an unnamed person in Grimsby between March and June 2009."

He looked directly at Stuart.

"Are you saying you lied again Mr Palmer?"

Stuart's head went down as his theatrics started in earnest.

"I did it to protect my children," he said, the handkerchief was out once more as he dabbed his eyes although there were no tears evident. He continued with his sob story.

"I didn't want the girls to go through any more anguish. I thought if I admitted adultery the whole thing would be over and done with. Annette was determined that I should admit to having an affair," he threw me a dismissive glance, "so I was prepared to do it to spare my children any more heartache."

"So you freely admit you lied?"

Stuart remained silent, Gilbert continued.

"You categorically stated you did not have sexual relations with Angela Maddison or an unnamed person in Grimsby before your marriage break up and yet said exactly the opposite on a legal binding document?"

"Yes, yes," said the Judge, "you've made your point Mr Gilbert, now can we move on?"

It was a victory of sorts, Gilbert had outed Stuart as a liar, not once but twice.

"Let's move onto some more lies," he said.

"Objection."

The Judge was beginning to look weary. Gilbert explained once again that he believed Mr Palmer was a serial liar and intended to prove it. Although Bentley voiced strong opinions the Judge allowed Gilbert to press on.

"You're keen to blame your wife for the breakdown in the relationship with your children. Yet it was your own fault, didn't you lie to your children about your holiday with Mrs Maddison, didn't you tell your children you were going on a gentlemen's golf holiday?"

"I didn't want to upset my children, they'd been through so much."

Gilbert continued to probe.

"So you lied to them. Wasn't that the reason for the rift, because they found out about your romantic week away with your girlfriend? Once the cat was out of the bag and the girls knew you were having a relationship with Mrs Maddison and going on holiday with her and her children behind their back, that's when relations soured wasn't it?" Gilbert took a deep breath filling his lungs with air to finish his onslaught.

"It wasn't Mrs Palmer who was responsible for the fall out with your children, it was you Mr Palmer, you lied to your children just as you had lied to your wife about your affair with Angela Maddison, just like you lied to her about your income and the bank accounts and your investments."

"Objection."

"You are a compulsive liar Mr Palmer aren't you?"

Stuart wasn't slow to retaliate, although he desperately tried to contain his fury.

"Annette turned the girls against me and Abigail came unannounced to the house shouting and screaming using foul and abusive language."

"I think you turned the girls against you yourself Mr Palmer, affairs in Grimsby, affairs in Newcastle, romantic holidays away a matter of weeks after you walked out on your family. It all adds up."

"No." Stuart screamed, as he leaned out over the dock.

I saw a hint of a smile cross Gilbert's lips and then it was gone as he changed tact once more.

"When you left the family home there was £55000 deposited in a bank account in joint names. Is that right?"

"If you say so," Stuart replied being as obstructive as only I knew he could be.

"Well it's not if I say so is it?" Gilbert snapped. "You're the accountant, did you have £55000 deposited in an account?"

"Yes."

"Thank you Mr Palmer. But within a couple of weeks of leaving your wife you managed to spend the whole lot leaving nothing but a few pounds in the account. Is that correct?"

"Yes."

"What did you buy Mr Palmer? My client tells me you're usually a very careful man."

Stuart shrugged his shoulders.

"I had bills to pay, I'd borrowed some money from my mother which I paid back, I can't remember every last penny."

Gilbert looked towards the ceiling in mock disgust.

"We don't need to know about the pennies Mr Palmer, just the £55000, what did you spend it on?"

"I renovated my Aunt's flat, that took up most of it."

"Ah I see," he said, "and does your wife have a financial interest in that property?"

"No."

"And did you happen to call her and ask if she was agreeable to the spending?"

"No."

"That money belonged to you both, it was in a joint account and you spent it on a property she had no financial interest in. As well as being a liar you are also a thief."

Gilbert was right, he was a thief but the other side and as it turned out the Judge, didn't quite see it that way. He earned a stiff rebuke from his Lordship who warned that if Gilbert continued in the same way, he would have no alternative but to suspend proceedings.

"Shall we move on Mr Palmer?" Gilbert said with renewed energy.

True to his word Gilbert was cautious when tackling my ex-husband about his earnings and his eyesight. Stuart remained insistent that he was to all intents and purposes unemployed, as no work had materialised over the last few months. I doubted that very much. The man was an outright liar it seemed he had no shame as he kept the pretense up when Gilbert suggested that maybe he was exaggerating his eye condition especially considering he played golf with a handicap of three. Stuart remained unmoved in his stance and simply referred back to Mr Aziz's letter.

I could feel my frustration grow as Stuart circled around Gilbert and it didn't help that I knew the afternoon was drawing to a close. The day had been long and my head was searing with pain. I was in desperate need of a strong coffee or a stiff drink. Still, I wasn't ready for the day to be over, there seemed to be so much ground to cover and Mr Gilbert hadn't made any great inroads in his attempt to discredit his witness who sat leaning back in his chair, his demeanour now relaxed, thinking the worst was over. When Gilbert eventually got around to broaching the subject of his mother's Will, Stuart's relaxed posture was replaced with a visible display of tension.

"Mr Palmer, your mother died in May this year and you were her only surviving child?"

"Yes"

"Were you not shocked when you mother disinherited you and your children in favour of Tina Palmer?"

"No."

"Were you not angry that your own mother bequeathed money to friends, charities and her daughter in law but not one penny went to you or your children?"

"No, it was my mother's money, it was her decision."

Gilbert smiled.

"Her decision, yes. We've heard that quite a lot today, is that the words your counsel told you and Tina Palmer to use?"

Stuart didn't even bother to answer.

"So you visit your mother casually one evening and she asks you to witness her Will and you agree in the full knowledge that your mother was leaving everything to Tina Palmer."

"Yes."

"Did you not challenge your mother?"

"No I did not."

Gilbert looked over to the judge and then to me and Louise.

"You seriously expect us to believe that?"

Stuart shrugged his shoulders.

"It's the truth," he said.

Gilbert picked out something from the file and walked over towards Stuart.

"And your daughters, you claim your mother didn't get on well with your daughters?"

"As I have said, she was close to them when they were young but in the last few years they didn't bother with her and she was hurt by their attitude."

"Really Mr Palmer, that's hard to believe because I have bank statements from just a few months back and your late mother deposited £3000 in each of their accounts. Doesn't sound like the act of somcone who wasn't close to their grandchildren."

Stuart remained poker faced as the lies continued to pour out of his mouth.

"So you are not the least bit upset that you have been disinherited from your mother's Will?"

"No," he said, his voice slightly raised as he struggled to keep his composure.

"And not upset that she has left nothing to her only grandchildren?"

"No, not in the least."

The bastard, I tensed in my seat every bit of me urging Gilbert on, desperate for him to keep the pressure up, surely he would crumble and admit it was one big con to ring fence Olive's estate from the divorce settlement. Wasn't it as clear as water to Porter, wasn't it so blatantly obvious what had happened?

"Was there an agreement made between you, your mother and Tina Palmer that Tina would hand your mother's estate across to you at some later date?"

"No."

"Have you set up a secret trust?"

"Definitely not," he answered.

"If your medical condition is as precarious as you would have us believe, would your mother not have wanted to leave you well provided for? She had property and rental income from land, surely a mother would want to ensure her only son was financially secure."

"I'm sorry, I cannot speak for my mother," he said, "she's no longer here. It was her decision."

Gilbert pounced.

"Well Mr Palmer, I have some good news for you."

Stuart glared, unsure what was coming next, he wasn't used to going off script, his lines had been well rehearsed for every eventuality, well maybe not every eventuality.

Gilbert seemed enthused and keen to share his findings.

"You're entitled to make a claim on your mothers estate, on the basis that your mother should have made provision for you."

A frown crept across Stuart's face as he continued, my ears were standing to attention.

"You are entitled to claim under the Inheritance Act of 1975. Do you intend making a claim?"

Without a second thought the response was hurled across the courtroom back at Gilbert.

"I have no intention of contesting my mother's Will."

I leaned back in my seat letting out a huge sigh that could no doubt be heard throughout the court. I no longer cared. If the wigs and solicitors couldn't see this for what it was they were bloody idiots and didn't deserve to practice law if this was their level of stupidity.

"Of course you won't claim Mr Palmer, because if you did you would likely win and if £1.6 million suddenly found its way into your bank account it would have a dramatic effect on this settlement wouldn't it?"

"I have no idea what you're talking about," Stuart said.

"I'm talking about the grand plan you've put in place with Tina Palmer, a fraud."

"Objection."

Gilbert had gone too far according to the Judge. He asked if he had any proof that a fraud had been committed and of course he didn't. The Judge stood him down and then Bentley gave his closing statement. I had just about switched off, I wanted to get up and find myself a bottle of wine to drown myself in.

Porter eventually piped up, his weak voice still struggling to carry around the room.

"Could I have an indication of legal costs both parties have incurred thus far?"

His gaze met Gilbert who immediately jumped to his feet shuffling through his paperwork to find a tally of costs. I had a fair idea yet it wasn't until the words come out of his mouth did it hit me like a sledgehammer.

"Mrs Palmer's costs at the end of proceedings will be approximately £60000 sir," he said, so matter of fact.

For the first time I saw real emotion on Stuart's face as he bent his head forward to look across in my direction, his jaw had practically dropped to the floor. Why was he so surprised? Wouldn't his costs be equally as steep?

Porter didn't turn a hair as he turned towards Bentley and asked him the same question. Bentley needed no time to give a response, the costs tripped off his tongue.

"My clients costs to date are just short of £14000 Sir."

Had he just said that? It couldn't be right, the discrepancy between Bennett and Steedman's fees were far too great, weren't the charges for phone calls, letters, faxes and court hearings like for like? How could there be such a difference in costs? I was totally floored.

I'd had a fucking pisser of a day and this had just about topped it off. As I walked out of the courtroom, feeling sick and bedraggled with a gapping big hole in my stocking to match the bloody gaping hole in my argument, I had one thought on my mind, John Bennett. I grappled with my handbag and retrieved my phone.

I rang Saxtons' office and for some strange reason I was put straight through to Elizabeth.

I took a deep breath.

"I need to speak to Bennett right this moment."

"I'm afraid that won't be possible Mrs Palmer," she said.

"And why not?" I questioned as my rage built up.

"Because just over an hour ago he handed me his resignation letter."

43

Elizabeth Henshaw stood with her back pressed hard against the door post that led into her office, arms wrapped in front of her looking every inch the back street scrapper waiting for her next fight. She'd heard the front door to the offices open and being as it was gone 6pm, she suspected it wasn't a client making the racket downstairs, it was the one person she'd been waiting to see for the last few hours. Louise trundled up the steep staircase pulling a box trolley behind her full of the Palmer case files. As she glanced up the stairwell her tired eyes caught sight of Elizabeth who was clearly waiting for an argument, her face full of hell. Louise sighed, she had so wanted to head straight home but had no alternative but to return the files to the place they belonged. Now she had thrown herself directly into the eye of the storm.

"My office straight away," Elizabeth barked.

Louise took a deep breath and hesitantly made her way into the unwelcoming lair of Elizabeth Henshaw's office.

"Shut the door behind you," Elizabeth said sharply.

Louise quickly obliged and at the same time slipped her hand into the side pocket of her handbag to retrieve an envelope she'd been carrying around her person for best part of a week. Pre-empting Elizabeth's next words Louise took a deep breath and threw herself in before she had the opportunity to change her mind.

"Elizabeth I'd like to give you this," she said, placing the slightly crumpled envelope on her employer's desk. "I am handing in my notice and if its agreeable I'd like it to be with immediate effect."

Elizabeth's eyes swung between Louise and the envelope and for a moment she was caught off guard and unusually for her, tongue-tied. But it didn't last long, suddenly she found the voice she'd lost and Louise who had now taken a seat was the single recipient of her wrath.

"So you and John were in cahoots all along, I don't fucking believe it," she shouted, her voice and posture fuelled with aggression as she continued her rant.

"No warning, how the hell are we supposed to operate?"

Louise so wanted to say 'not our problem,' but she bit her lip, Elizabeth looked as if she could throw a punch across the desk at any second.

"Where are the pair of you going?"

"I don't feel I want to disclose that information at the moment Elizabeth," she said, her voice remaining calm yet noticeably fatigued, the troublesome day in court relentlessly scribbling notes was beginning to take its toll.

"That is absolutely ridiculous Louise. I want to know where you're going. I am still your employer after all, you have an obligation to tell me."

Louise's stance remained resolute, she shook her head, her composed manner only serving to fuel Elizabeth's fire.

"I thought you were a loyal, honest girl, obviously I was wrong."

Louise shrugged her shoulders, she had no answer for her employer, only the unflinching belief that John's advice to keep quiet was her best course of action.

"Do you want to be John's side kick for the rest of your career? You do know he's only interested in feathering his own nest, he couldn't care less about you. He's bled us dry, it's impossible to negotiate with someone like him," she said, slapping her hand on the corner of her desk.

"I'm sorry you feel I've been disingenuous, it wasn't my intention," Louise said.

"Well you have been disingenuous, we've invested time and money training you. There had even been mention of giving you a pay rise. John was very keen on the idea until we made it clear it would come out of his share of profits."

Elizabeth leaned across the desk, her raised voice turning down an octave.

"He wasn't so keen when he knew it would be coming out of his pocket."

Louise checked her watch, she just wanted out of there. She had delivered the files and her resignation letter and she wasn't going to sit in Elizabeth's office any longer.

"If it's alright with you Elizabeth, I'd like to get home, it's been a long day."

"You'd like to get fucking home Louise, well I wish I could do the same but unfortunately I've been fending off John's clients most of the afternoon. And then there was the Palmer woman. What the fuck happened today? She was as a mad as hell?"

Louise stared for a moment wondering what to say. She opted for diplomacy.

"Her husband's team put up a strong defence, most of which we couldn't argue with, he had the evidence to back it up."

"And you two decide to walk before we have even heard the judgement. Have you no shame?"

Louise chose to ignore the cutting comment.

"Gilbert presented a persuasive argument," she said, "Mrs Palmer has been a homemaker and carer for most of their married life, the judgement should favour her."

Her face flushed over as she deliberately skirted around the fiasco of the tax credits and Dr Carrion's letter.

But Elizabeth wasn't fooled, she knew when she was being fobbed off.

"There was something else bothering Mrs Palmer, she was furious and of course speechless when I told her John had resigned. I actually felt for her. Can you understand how she must feel?"

"Yes, I know, it's not perfect timing."

Elizabeth sat bolt upright in her chair.

"Not perfect timing?" she said as she slapped the desk again, "it's positively fucking disastrous timing, fucking disastrous, the poor bitch has been well and truly shafted by both of you and it's me that will have to pick up the pieces, this firm could be ruined because of your actions, we will be a laughing stock."

Her eyes burned into Louise as she pressed on.

"I'm speaking to Gilbert this evening, I want to get to the bottom of this. Mrs Palmer insinuated that John fucked up and if he has you can tell him I'll be coming after him," she smiled, "and you too for that matter," she added with a hint of menace.

"Is that all Elizabeth? Can I go?"

Louise stood up, she'd heard enough and headed towards the door, not waiting for a response.

"You'll regret jumping ship and following John like his little bloody lap dog. When you're no use to him he'll drop you like a stone. There is only one person John looks after and that's himself."

The words faded away as Louise made her escape and walked out of the Saxtons' offices free of the files which had weighed her down for many months now. As she headed towards her car she felt the pulse of her phone as it vibrated in her pocket. Her urgency to answer outweighed her desire to get away from Elizabeth and that bloody building. She knew it was her partner in crime calling her.

"Hello."

"Have you done it?"

"Yes," she replied without hesitation

"You didn't say where we were going I hope?"

"No John, I kept quiet, although Elizabeth was livid, she's had clients onto her already including Mrs Palmer and she's not happy at all."

John ignored the comment sliding over it like a skater on ice.

"Saxtons' are behind us Louise, we are joining the biggest law firm in the north east and you and I are going to be heading up the Family Law Department. Don't get caught up in trivial matters."

"It's Mrs Palmer John, I feel sorry for her, she's-"

Bennett cut her off abruptly.

"She's a client, they come, they go, don't ever get emotionally attached."

"But John, surely we have a responsibility?"

"Yes, a responsibility to bill them for as many hours as we can, nothing more. Mrs Palmer is yesterday's news, you and I have bigger fish to fry, believe me."

Louise was stunned into silence wondering if she had just made the biggest mistake of her life.

"And one other thing," John said, "take yourself along to Carphone Warehouse on the way home and pick up a new SIM card with a new number."

"Yes John."

"The last thing we want are our old clients pestering the fucking life out of us."

I didn't linger long on the phone after Elizabeth Henshaw blurted out that John had resigned. My anger evaporated as my head went into a tailspin, what the hell did she mean he'd left? I couldn't quite register the information in my battered brain as I stood outside the courthouse, the day's events still fresh in my mind. He'd not given me one word of warning he was leaving and the cruelest blow of all, he had chosen the day of my hearing to make his announcement. How could he have left me so high and dry? He'd worked on my case for a full year and I'd paid him a king's ransom for his services then out of nowhere he gets up and leaves. Not to mention that he'd well and truly fucked up, he'd made some enormous blunders and now he expected everyone else to deal with the fallout.

There was only one other person who could help me, Louise, and yet she'd wasted no time making her getaway as soon as we'd walked out of the court, barely saying her goodbyes. Did she know he was leaving? She must have.

I returned home from the court that evening looking and feeling like a wrung out old rag. Thank God Abigail had been there waiting to drive me home. Mentally and physically I was exhausted and any energy I'd been holding in reserve all these months had well and truly expired that day. There was nothing left. As Abigail pulled her car onto the driveway I was welcomed by Victoria and Alexandra who were both perched at the front door ready to greet us. We'd had a silent journey home and I was feeling no more enthused to rake over the day's events with my other two children. I was sure the pair of them had been expecting me to be carrying home the Judge's decision clasped in hand. I saw how the disappointment had registered on both their faces when I made it clear Porter hadn't made his judgement and in fact he was going to take at least a week to do so.

I slowly made my way up the stairs to my bedroom, desperate to strip off my formal attire and change into a loose fitting tracksuit. I'd promised them I'd be back down and give them a run-down of the day's events. They waited in vain, because once I'd slung my suit back on its hanger and closed the wardrobe door, I collapsed onto the cushioned mattress of my bed, my head throbbing as the events of the day spun around my mind with such velocity I felt dizzy. Then I was out for the count, dead to the world.

For the first few days after the court hearing my body was determined to keep up its rebellion, forcing me to rest. Exhaustion had transpired into illness and the morning after the court hearing I could barely move.

I had expected to wake up refreshed after my twelve hour marathon sleep, instead my body had other plans for me. As my eyes opened the next morning, the sun seemed blinding as its uncensored rays forced their way through the bedroom window. I shut my eyes tightly yet still I could feel my head bursting with pressure, the slightest movement causing an intense sharp pain to race through my skull as if a metal skewer was being hammered into it.

I was forced to remain in bed virtually all of that day dosing myself up with painkillers in an attempt to shift the pain. Nothing worked. It didn't even make a dent in it. I was conscious of the need to speak to Louise but just couldn't lift myself from the mattress. It was only after I'd been glued to my mattress a third day did Victoria intervene, insisting I should visit the doctor.

"For God sake mother you need to get yourself sorted, how can you hope to take care of Alexandra if you don't look after yourself first?"

She was right of course and I eventually succumbed to the pressure and made my way to the doctor surgery where the no nonsense practitioner was quick to scribble off an illegible prescription for antibiotics.

"It's sinusitis," he said, "but you are also mentally and physically exhausted."

No surprise there.

It was only when the antibiotics kicked in and I was feeling their full effect did my brain fog begin to clear sufficiently for my focus to return to John, Louise and of course Gilbert and the court hearing. Thoughts of the pending judgement were never far from my mind, yet I'd been sufficiently floored that I didn't even have the energy or the desire to contact anyone at the Saxton's office. Now I was on the mend I was ready to speak to Louise as soon as I could.

I dialled her mobile number.

The number you have called has not been recognised.

Strange, I thought and just as I was about to recheck the number my own mobile rang and Saxtons name flashed across the display screen.

It was Karen, I instantly recognised her cold clinical voice.

"Hello Mrs Palmer."

My response was upbeat, disguising the panic welling up inside me, I knew there was a purpose to her call and it wasn't a social chat, Karen didn't do chat.

"Morning Karen, how can I help you?"

"I have a message from Elizabeth, she's emailed you the draft judgement, she received it this morning from the court."

For a second I was lost for words, there were so many questions I needed to ask, the first being why hadn't Louise rang me and why was I hearing this news from Karen.? Surely Louise or Elizabeth should have taken a minute out of their day to ring me and run through the judgement personally. The rage was building up inside me once more, yet as much as I wanted to voice my anger I had an even stronger desire to get off the phone and onto my emails pronto.

"Thank you Karen, can you tell Louise and Elizabeth I'll be in touch within the hour."

"But Mrs Palmer I – "

"Goodbye," I said before ending the call and raced through the house at breakneck speed to find my laptop.

I sat staring at the twenty-five page word document absolutely gob smacked. I read it word for word yet nothing sank in, I couldn't believe it, I was totally numb. My hand reached for the phone, my fingers tapping in the Saxtons' number. Without any need for prompting they ran across the keypad of their own accord .

"Hello Saxtons, can I help you?"

"Put me through to Louise," I said bluntly.

"I'll transfer you to Elizabeth, she'll have a word with you Mrs Palmer," Karen said before I had the chance to reply. Was the woman even listening to me? I wanted to speak to Louise not Elizabeth. Just as I was about to ring off and redial, Elizabeth answered.

"Hello Mrs Palmer, Karen tells me you want to speak to Louise."

"That's right, I do want to speak to her so why has she put me through to you?"

There was a brief silence before she spoke.

"I'm afraid it won't be possible to speak to Louise, she tendered her resignation on the day of the Hearing."

"They've both left?" I screamed down the phone.

"I know Mrs Palmer," she said, "I'm as upset as you are."

"Upset Elizabeth, you have no idea. They've fucked me over and left me high and dry, I just don't believe it."

"I fully understand Mrs Palmer."

"Have you read Porter's judgement?" I continued, my voice almost exploding with rage, "it's a mockery."

"I've spoken to Gilbert," she waded in, "he wants a meeting as soon as possible. I was thinking Friday morning 8.30am, can you make it?"

"Can I make it Elizabeth, this is my life we're talking about. Can I fucking make it, are you serious?"

My exasperation was all too apparent as Elizabeth continued to try and appease me.

"I will be at the meeting too, Mrs Palmer and I want to assure you there will be no charge for either mine or Mr Gilbert's time."

I couldn't help myself, all my composure had long since escaped me.

"That's big of you Elizabeth, you're all fucking heart, I've paid you nearly sixty grand for your team of so called experts and when the going got too tough for them they jumped ship."

"Please Mrs Palmer, I'm trying to help, give me a little respect and curb your language, this isn't Friday night in the Bigg Market."

And of course she was right, she clearly knew nothing about my cunning Lawyer's plans and that of his able assistant. She too had been left up shit creek without a paddle. God knows what was going through her mind. I felt the need to apologise but all I could think of was the mess I was in and how much that big motherfucker of a mess had cost me. Instead of apologising I simply lowered the handset onto the base station.

As I walked into Gilbert's office, I was no longer impressed by his palatial surroundings, my eyes were firmly fixed on the man himself who was mincing his way across the room, hand outstretched in readiness to greet us.

"Hello Mrs Palmer, hello Mrs Henshaw," his theatrics all too apparent, wasn't that the measure of the man I thought, all show and no substance.

“Please take a seat,” his hand directed us to the conference table.

I sat down in the leather-padded seat as I struggled to keep my council whilst Mr Gilbert fussed over whether we preferred milk and sugar in our coffee.

“I’ll play Mum,” he said as he poured the steaming hot coffee into small china cups. I watched his every move as he relaxed back into his chair swirling the teaspoon around in his cup as he held court.

“Well Mrs Palmer, let me just say- “

I couldn’t help myself, I cut him off mid-sentence, letting rip as the motley pair looked helplessly on.

“I think I’ll start Mr Gilbert, have you seen the judgement?” My hand was shaking with rage as I held the offending article mid-air. “I got fifty percent of the house and pensions, that’s it. He got to keep his business account, he doesn’t have to pay back any of the £55000 he emptied from the deposit account and I even have to pay him £4000 for the fucking grand piano.”

They sat in total silence, not daring to utter a word.

“And the maintenance, £1000 a month for three years, a grand fucking total of £36000 while he walks away with his fat salary that he never disclosed to the court.”

Eventually Gilbert spoke, albeit almost in a whisper.

“I think if you look at Porter’s judgement, he’s hasn’t applied the compensation principle because he’s of the opinion there is a risk Mr Palmer will not be able to work in future because of his eye condition.”

I saw red again.

“And why did that happen? The man has had it for thirty years and it hasn’t affected him yet, he plays golf off three, he runs, he cycles, he does anything he wants, it doesn’t affect him in the slightest.”

I leaned across the desk.

“Tell me why you failed to persuade the Judge that it was all a fraud, tell me why you failed to prove that his mother’s Will was a fraud? Tell me why you failed to prove his real earnings instead of the fairy stories he told the court and tell me why you couldn’t include one single fucking share holding?”

I turned to Elizabeth.

“Tell me why Bennett fucked me over by failing to disclose my tax credits.”

Elizabeth started to shake her head.

"But I – "

"You didn't know Elizabeth?" I said.

"No, I -"

I looked down at page six of the judgement.

"I'll read it for you shall I? Mrs Palmer clearly mislead the court by failing to disclose the tax credits."

"I'm sorry," she said.

"And you didn't know about the Doctor's letter, or should I say both of them that Louise sent in the court bundle by mistake. It made me look as if I had the Doctor fiddle her report so that Alexandra could stay in the house."

Elizabeth shook her head, her mouth open, trying to say something but there were no words.

"Your team screwed me over Elizabeth and then they walked away."

Eventually Gilbert found his voice.

"I still think we should appeal Mrs Palmer, I believe you have a good chance, do you not agree Mrs Henshaw?"

He had placed Elizabeth on the spot as she considered her response. I studied her carefully.

"Yes I do believe you have a strong case Mrs Palmer, you've been a housewife and carer all your married life."

She was lying, guilt and dishonesty were written right across her face.

"You really think so Elizabeth?"

"Yes."

I held the paper in front of me.

"Will this judgement win me any points in an appeal? "I lowered my head and read from the judgement again. "I accept the honest and open evidence from Angela Maddison and Tina Palmer and Mr Palmer's reasoning for lying to his children about his relationship with Angela Maddison and furthermore I'm not satisfied there was any plot or plan for Mr Palmer to inherit his mother's estate at a later date. On the other hand I find Annette Palmer's evidence less than reliable."

Elizabeth's soulless eyes stared at me as she allowed me to go on without interruption.

"Will my argument have any credit after what Porter has written in black and white? He's basically saying I've lied to the court."

My voice, which had been on the verge of cracking, regained some of its composure as the anger hardened my words.

"How does it look Mr Gilbert?" I blasted across the table. "Your cross examinations didn't get us very far did they?"

Gilbert's face flushed. I saw him for the pathetic excuse for a man he was.

"I'm sorry Mrs Palmer, so terribly sorry," he reiterated almost in a whisper.

Exhaustion and frustration overtook me as I sank back into the chair and it occurred to me there was nothing either of them could offer me other than a few apologies and some faint hope that we could appeal the judgement. My eyes fixed on Gilbert once more as I continued my onslaught.

"Mr Gilbert, I could have stood up in that courtroom myself, a person with no legal training whatsoever and I could have got the same result."

I was cutting into his pride, puncturing his ego with each word. In that moment I couldn't have cared less and to my shame I relished sticking the knife in even deeper.

"In fact, if I'm honest you couldn't have got me any less, I didn't actually get 50% if you put Stuart's savings and company account into the mix. How did you manage that or is it all in a day's work then you just move on to the next case?"

He had no argument, his podgy, round face now masked in a blush.

"I agree Mrs Palmer, I can't believe the judgement."

Elizabeth, desperate to jump to Gilbert's defence took the floor, her flame red hair mirroring the fire in her voice.

"I do not think you can rest all the blame at Mr Gilbert's door, let's not forget it was John Bennett who made the two big mistakes."

I almost broke out into laughter as she stated the obvious

"Forget Elizabeth, how could I forget? Porter has told the whole fucking world I'm a liar. It's a public document there for all to see. I will not forget that it was John Bennett, your man, who was responsible for tarnishing my reputation."

Gilbert who was obviously feeling vindicated from blame, showed renewed vigour.

"I think we should get back to the point and talk about the appeal,

I would like to put things right and draft a skeleton argument in support of your right to appeal."

Elizabeth nodded her head

"Yes I agree."

I sighed deeply.

"And how much is this all going to cost me? Have either of you got a figure to hand?" I questioned as they looked on blankly. "How much more money are you going to screw out of me?"

I reached from my bag, I'd just about heard enough. I stood up and made my way across the room to the large panelled door. I turned back to look at the pair who were clearly stunned by my outburst yet emotionally detached, it wasn't their life going down the toilet. I couldn't help thinking back to the beginning when I'd first embarked on my journey, I'd had such faith in John Bennett and the law for that matter. Wasn't it England I lived in? Didn't we have the best legal system in the world where honesty and fairness prevailed?

"I've paid you £60000 Elizabeth, care to take a guess at how much Stuart paid his team, the team that clearly won?"

Elizabeth looked puzzled as she directed her gaze towards Gilbert. She wasn't in court at the hearing so she didn't have a clue.

I took a couple of steps towards her.

"Guess Elizabeth, guess how much the winning team charged my husband?"

Elizabeth shook her head ever so slowly, Gilbert looked away, his eyes found a painting on the far wall, he knew what was coming.

"£14000 Elizabeth."

Her jaw fell open.

"I've paid you £46000 more than my ex-husband paid his team and your lot blew it."

She was stunned into silence, she had no answers.

"It will probably cost me thousands to appeal and what are my chances of success?"

Elizabeth eventually found her voice as she shrugged her shoulders.

"It's impossible to say Mrs Palmer, winning the right to appeal is very difficult, I won't lie to you."

"And my chances of winning?" I asked.

Mr Gilbert chipped in.

"As Elizabeth said, winning won't be easy."

"So you keep saying," I said as I turned back towards the door.

I couldn't listen to another word. My hand could barely grasp the large, oversized door knob. Eventually I managed to wrench the door open, ready to make my escape yet not before I left my parting shot.

"Well I know one thing, whatever the outcome, you two still get your money isn't that right?"

Gilbert looked back towards the painting on the wall as Elizabeth met my gaze but said nothing.

"Solicitors and Barristers," I said, "you lot win every fucking time."

44

In my naivety I thought that once I had received Porter's judgement my humiliation would be complete, however, there was worse to come, salt was going to be generously rubbed into my wounds as Elizabeth informed me there was to be a thirty-minute hearing in front of Porter so he could hand down his judgement. What was the point? I'd read the judgement word for word several times, as had Stuart and his team, Gilbert and Elizabeth. The point was the big, shambolic game that was British Divorce Law.

"It's merely a formality Annette," she said, "and if you can't face it I'll go alone as your representative."

I could have opted out, hidden under the coat tails of my self-elected solicitor, it would have been so easy to stay away and yet my pride wouldn't allow it. Once I'd had a few days to lick my wounds my mind was made up, I would go into that courtroom with my head held high. Porter might think I was a liar and a home wrecker, but I knew the truth as did my ex-husband and more importantly my children and that was all that mattered to me.

I'd convinced myself that confronting Stuart after his victory couldn't be any worse than having to tell Alexandra we'd have to move house. There had been the inevitable tears as the last residue of hope she'd clung on to all these months was lost. The image of her face as I broke the news cut deep, a verse from Philip Larkin resonated in my mind. 'They fuck you up your mum and dad. They may not mean to but they do.'

I'd sat helplessly cradling my daughter in my arms as she bravely tried to fight back the tears and it ripped the heart right from my chest.

As it turned out Stuart didn't show up for the hearing. A part of me would have liked to think that deep down within the recesses of his conscience there was part of him that didn't want to rub my nose in it, yet in reality I knew he probably had better things to do than to wave his victory flag in front of my face.

Bentley was there of course, sitting so close I could smell the sweet odour of his cheap cologne waft about the still air of the Judge's Chambers. I fixed my eyes on the slimy toad as he made his humble apologies for his client's absence, which Porter readily accepted without question. Then my gaze was forced to turn to Porter himself as he handed down his judgement, his voice still as weak as water yet ironically it carried the weight of lead. As he recited his well-rehearsed speech I was determined not to look away or show any emotion. I would not be defeated by any of these people. Porter hadn't noticed my defiant stance, the man didn't bat an eye lid as he delivered his finding in a uncompassionate manner.

He touched on the maintenance payments, a particularly touchy subject.

"I am satisfied that three years is a sufficient time period for Mrs Palmer to re-establish herself into the career in which she qualified and full time earnings of up to £50000 a year is not unrealistic. A £2400 monthly allowance until then will allow her to maintain her current standard of living for her family."

He explained how the maintenance payment of a £1000 would top up my other credits and he saw no reason why Stuart should pay any more. Bastard, I thought as his sermon drew to an end and Elizabeth, right on cue, got to her feet ready to deliver her piece.

We'd already discussed what she was going to say before we'd entered the chamber. Gilbert had taken the liberty to draft his skeleton argument in readiness, should I decide to go ahead with the appeal. I'd battled with that decision since walking out of his office the day we had the autopsy on the judgement. I didn't want to waste another penny of my dwindling resources on legal fees if I had no real chance of success, yet I couldn't ignore the fact that both Gilbert and Elizabeth had both been confident that I had a good case and I couldn't get away from the fact that Stuart had lied to the court. He'd hidden money and lied about his salary, the severity of his eye condition and his mother's will. It had not been a level playing field.

With only minutes to spare before we went into Porter's Chambers I'd told my team I wanted to go ahead, I was determined Stuart wasn't going to get away with it.

"Well Annette," she had said, "once Porter hands down his judgement I need to ask him for permission to appeal and he'll say no, I can guarantee it."

"What?" I questioned, my ignorance of the law all too apparent.

Elizabeth responded as if she was speaking to a child, her sharp voice slow and deliberate.

"The Judge will very rarely grant an appeal because it would suggest that there were flaws within his own judgement and he'll not admit to that."

I shook my head.

"What a farce, what's the point of even asking him then?"

"Because that's the order of the process, the law, he'll say no and then we'll need to make another application to appeal to another Judge within 21 days."

What a shambles, what a fucking mockery asking a Judge to rule against his own judgement.

As we sat in the stuffy chamber I noticed Elizabeth's approach was in sharp contrast to John's maverick tactics, he was more willing to challenge his opponent and the judge for that matter. The woman had a sharp tongue outside the Judge's Chambers yet inside, her voice had lost its cutting edge, there was no bite in her argument as she resorted to using Gilbert's grounds of appeal as the framework to plead her case to the unrelenting judge.

Porter looked on with downcast eyes, his jaw set in grit determination not to budge. As she drew to a close, he didn't give a microsecond of thought to her argument before flatly refusing her request to appeal.

I watched Bentley sit up in his chair, satisfaction spreading across his face, he knew the balance of power had swung in his direction and as he took to the floor I could see confidence oozing out of every pore.

"Can I suggest Sir, that the marital family home be put up for sale immediately."

He was barely able to hide his delight as he relished broaching the subject that caused me the greatest pain. Panic engulfed me as I was forced to entertain for the first time since the whole saga began, the idea we'd actually have to move out of the family home. It was no longer a far-fetched nightmare, it was now a reality and a situation I could no longer avoid. My heart sank for a moment before Porter offered me a small vestige of hope.

"Once the Order has been sealed, the family home can be marketed Mr Bentley, not before."

And then, as quickly as it had started it was over. As I walked out of Porter's Chambers I held an inkling of hope that maybe we could delay the house sale at least until my appeal could be heard. I voiced my views to Elizabeth as I tried to keep pace with her swift step on the way to the exit. She stopped in her tracks, her expression indicative of someone who thought they were talking to an imbecile, once again her voice was slow sharp and direct.

"Unfortunately not, nothing stops while we wait for your appeal to be heard. The order will be drafted and signed and the house will be marketed and sold if a buyer is found." She looked me straight in the eye. "The sale will go through, Porter's Judgement will be carried out to the letter."

"But that's ridiculous," I said. "It's a sham. So if several months down the line they find in my favour and the house has been sold there's nothing I can do about it?"

She shrugged her shoulders.

"Sorry Annette, I don't make the rules. Your appeal could take months and months and do you think your husband is going to be happy and sit back and wait?"

"Then what's the point of an appeal?"

"To get you a better deal."

"But all I'm interested in is keeping the house."

She shook her head.

"It isn't going to happen Annette, but let's not jump ahead, we have to get over the first hurdle which is getting permission."

As she hurried towards the exit she barked out her final warning.

"Mrs Palmer, I can't reiterate enough that the appeal will be a lengthy process and you must prepare yourself for the long-haul. Her voice trailed off into the distance as she raced down the steps.

"What's the fucking point?" I muttered under my breath.

I walked down the steps of the courthouse. I could feel a soft spray of drizzle against my skin as a light breeze lifted a dank mist from the Tyne drawing its spray up towards the building. It was a miserable day in all respects. I watched as Elizabeth's form grew smaller and smaller as she gradually disappeared from sight. Fear flagged up in my mind once more, could I really trust this woman with the next stage of my legal debacle?

After the Court Judgement Reading my day-to-day dealings with Elizabeth almost ceased. Because she had agreed not to charge until after the appeal I had been passed on to the junior members of staff whose job it now was to prepare the draft order for Porter's signature. Bentley was shrewd enough to realise he was dealing with the minions of the firm and played them like a cat would a mouse. He questioned their every move which inevitably created more paperwork as letters and emails passed between the fractured parties, all the while I was incurring even more costs, which at some point in the future I'd have to pay, regardless whether I won or lost an appeal.

Strangely enough I began to accept my situation and the reality that I wouldn't be able to stay in the house. And even then Stuart was twisting the knife when a letter arrived demanding half the furniture from the marital home. I contacted Emma, my new paralegal. (Junior.) The ball was in my court this time as I had already started showing perspective buyers around the house. I told Stuart he could have half of everything. I would take a chainsaw to every stick of furniture and a Stanley Knife to every carpet in the house if that's what he insisted on and of course I would be more than happy to continue to show the house to anyone the Estate Agent sent over. Stuart was in no doubt that I would have carried out my threat to the letter. Strangely enough he caved in and graciously allowed me to keep the furniture.

In truth I had calmed down to a smouldering rage type state. Until that is, oil was thrown onto the fire just a week after Alexandra blew the candles out on her 18th birthday cake. All hell broke loose once more and I found myself marching into the Saxtons' offices demanding to see Elizabeth. I was told to sit down and wait in the reception area. An hour had passed when I'd had enough and eventually took matters into my own hands and told Karen I was going up to Elizabeth's office whether she liked it or not. Strangely enough Karen hadn't turned a hair and instead of putting up a resistance she was unusually helpful.

"Mrs Henshaw office is up the stairs, straight along the corridor, third on the right, you can't miss it Mrs Palmer," she shouted as I stormed off.

I wrapped my knuckles on the door to Elizabeth's office, but didn't wait for a polite invite to enter. Instead I opened the door and walked in. She was on the phone, her back reclining into the chair, shoes kicked off as her feet rested on the corner of the desk. Her eyes nearly popped out of her head and within a flash she jumped up and made her excuses to the person on the other end.

"Would you mind if I call you back in a few moments, there's something I need to deal with," she said.

"Good morning Elizabeth, what a lovely day it is," I said sarcastically

She responded in a voice that did little to disguise her annoyance, she avoided the pleasantries.

"It's not appropriate to barge into my office Mrs Palmer, you don't have an appointment so unfortunately it's a case of waiting until I have time to see you."

"Well I don't have any more time to wait Elizabeth, because I've been sitting down there an hour. You clearly don't have any clients so I'm sure you will afford me the luxury of a ten minute meeting?"

She composed herself.

"I suppose so, what is it that's so important?"

I bit my tongue. I took a second or two to compose myself.

"Well Elizabeth, I've discovered another Saxtons' cock up of mammoth proportion which is going to leave me with a shortfall of £1400 a month."

"I have no idea what you're talking about Mrs Palmer, can you get to the point, I have an appointment with a client soon," she said, looking at her watch.

"Well Mrs Henshaw, my daughter turned eighteen last week and it turns out that I'm no longer entitled to Child Tax Credit, Family Allowance and not least, my ex-husbands CSA payment for her maintenance. They have all been terminated with immediate effect."

She shook her head slowly, shrugged her shoulders as if to say so what.

"Porter calculated my needs at £2400 a month, £1400 of that amount I was already receiving by way of those benefits and therefore the maintenance amount he awarded me was £1000?"

"Yes," she said, "I follow."

"It was John Bennett who told me to apply for Alexandra's maintenance via the CSA, the stupid fucker failed to say it would stop when she reached the age of eighteen, the same with the Tax Credits and Child Benefit."

She was immediately on the defensive.

"I'm at a loss how you can lay blame for that particular situation at Saxtons' door Mrs Palmer."

Her dismissive stance only served to ruffle a few more of my feathers. My fury was building as I spelt out the reality of my situation.

"Overnight my monthly income has been reduced by £1400. Porter based his judgement on a three year period, he assumed I would be receiving £2400 a month for three years."

The penny dropped, the enormity of the situation sank in and yet she was determined that her firm would not take any direct blame.

"Mrs Palmer, were you not aware these payments would stop when Alexandra finished school?"

"The Child Benefit yes, but your top lawyer told me the other payments would last until she had completed her university studies."

Her response was less than courteous, her sharp cutting tones all too evident.

"Mrs Palmer we aren't here to nurse maid you, you're a grown woman who is more than capable of finding out how and when you qualify for these benefits."

The red flag was now waving in front of my eyes and like a bull kicking its front hooves I was ready to charge.

"I didn't know Elizabeth, I'm a housewife not a solicitor, that's what I paid you for," I bellowed.

"But you should have known," she said rather half-heartedly. "You're a parent, you should have made it your job to know."

I had her. She'd stepped right into my trap.

I flopped into the seat and drew a hand across my furrowed brow. I took a breath and sighed.

"Did you know Elizabeth, did Gilbert, did Bennett? Did any of you fucking know?"

She shook her head, then nodded.

"I …yes."

"Wasn't it somebodies job to know?" I asked gently. "Wasn't it a legal responsibility to stand up at that original hearing to inform the judge that his calculations were incorrect?"

"No, I…"

"Shouldn't somebody have said in court that the payments wouldn't in fact last three years?"

She was floundering because she didn't know. Gilbert had also overlooked the fact that Alexandra was eighteen, as had the Judge and Bennett had categorically assured me that the payments would be in force right throughout her university years.

I saw it in her face, in her eyes, in her body language as she squirmed uncomfortably because she knew that not one, but all three members of the Saxtons' Family Law Team had yet again failed to raise a crucial point relating to my settlement.

I pinched hard at the bridge of my nose in an attempt to relieve the tension.

"Let me ask you just one question Elizabeth," I said.

Her mouth opened, I thought she was about to speak but she said nothing. I think I detected a very slight nod of her head.

"If Porter had been made aware at the hearing that these benefits were going to stop in a matter of weeks after his judgement, do you not agree the maintenance payment he awarded me would have been more than £1000 per month?"

"Yes, I can see where you're coming from Mrs Palmer, but-"

I held up my hand and stopped her in mid-sentence.

"Stop!"

"But-"

"That's all I wanted to hear."

I realised at that moment that my gut feelings had been right all along, I could no longer suppress my instincts, I didn't trust this woman.

"Your fired," I said calmly, "and I want my case files back."

She immediately straightened up in her chair, her defences already up as her brain deciphered the information.

"What are you talking about fired, have you lost your senses, we're waiting for the draft order to be signed by Porter, you're going to appeal, its madness to change solicitors so late in the day."

I felt a calmness sweep over me as if a weight had been lifted from my shoulders, my composure intact I remained resolute in my decision.

"I no longer trust your company or you for that matter Elizabeth.

You lot have bled me dry with your extortionate charges."

"We've worked very hard on your case Mrs Palmer and I can assure you all our time is accounted for, your fees were not excessive."

I sat up, placed my cupped fists at the bottom of my chin and smiled. I spoke in a whisper.

"Your team fucked up Elizabeth, you fucked up not once but several times and Bentley walked all over you. You were complacent and negligent. Your work was sloppy, your calculations way off and you charged me five times more than the other side for the privilege and to top it all off, your wonderful team turned their back on me and ran for the hills before the job was completed."

I knew I was getting to her, every movement she made screamed help. She wanted out of there, her embarrassment clearly evident. She tapped her pen against the desk as she struggled to suppress her anger.

"I think my next point of call is the Ombudsman," I said. "Once they see how negligent you've been they might agree that your fee's have been excessive."

Elizabeth dived across the desk and reached for the phone, punching in numbers.

"You're threatening me now, I've just about had enough."

She almost screamed into the handset.

"Freddie can you come into the office immediately."

My composure was no less evident to the outward eye although my heart began to pump rapidly, she was bringing in the husband, she meant business.

He was barely through the door when her screeching hit him head on. I sat back in my seat, not saying a word and allowed Elizabeth to fill him in on the details. When he eventually spoke to me his approach was a far cry from his wife's. He was calm and collected and fully aware of the big picture. He wanted to reason with me.

"So you are dispensing with our services and considering going to the Ombudsman?"

"I've already had tentative talks with the Ombudsman," I said, "and they have no doubt there is a case to answer."

The colour drained from Elizabeth's face as she sank back into her seat.

He hesitated for a second or two, composing his thoughts.

"That's you prerogative Mrs Palmer, but may I remind you that you still have a considerable account to settle. If you are saying you no longer wish us to act for you, it will need to be settled immediately."

Elizabeth flew into action again as she reached for the phone.

"Get me the balance on Mrs Palmers account please Karen, I want it right up to date and include the Gilbert fee and the usual charge for this meeting, bill her twice, for my time and Freddie's."

She was going to regret saying that.

I sat back in my chair as we waited in silence for the response from the other end of the line.

The phone rang about two minutes later.

"Thank you," she said as she placed the receiver down, a hint of a smile returning to her face.

"The balance on your account is currently £23542.26, you'll need to pay it in full immediately or I'll be forced to take action."

"That's not going to happen," I said. "When I initiate a grievance procedure with the Ombudsman the account is frozen until he reaches a decision," I smiled, "surely you know that Elizabeth?"

Elizabeth was practically doing a war dance around her desk as she took to her stocking feet and started to pace the floor, ranting a raving.

Her husband however, was exactly the opposite, a picture of calmness.

"Mrs Palmer, we acknowledge Mr Bennett has made some mistakes-"

"Your whole team made mistakes Mr Henshaw, including your wife," I interrupted, "your latest fuck up has cost me £1400 a month or £50000 if you calculate it over a three year period."

"Yes… but.."

I detected the first sign of discomfort in the normally cool exterior.

"We have no intention of letting the matter go. We are currently taking legal action against Mr Bennett and your case will be brought up and it will help us in our claim against him."

"I'm glad to hear it," I said, "so you admit he made mistakes?"

"Yes."

"And that he shouldn't have walked to another firm at such a crucial stage in proceedings?"

"I agree."

He gave me the smile of a man who had the knowledge of the law firmly in his corner whereas my understanding of the legal system could be safely printed on the back of a postage stamp."

And yet I had him by the balls and his smug smile never left his face. This only riled me more.

"So you admit Bennett was negligent and complacent?" I questioned and I remained calm as I sat forward in my chair so close, I picked up a faint smell of mint toothpaste lifting from his breath.

He laughed out loud.

"Hah! I can see what you're trying to do now, you want us to admit we screwed up."

"You did."

"And no doubt you'll be wanting a reduction in your bill."

I kept quiet.

He leaned over towards his wife and whispered in her ear.

"Mrs Palmer, if you can stay here for ten minutes, my wife and I are just going to take a quick coffee. Do you mind?"

"Not at all," I said, "you take as long as you like."

The Henshaws walked back into the office exactly thirteen minutes later. They sat down behind the desk.

Freddie was clearly the spokesperson.

"Mrs Palmer, we appreciate Mr Bennett has made mistakes and on that basis we would be prepared to knock £7000 off your bill on the understanding you agree to drop any further claims against our company and you agree that we can use your case files in any legal claim against Mr Bennett."

I dropped my head into my hands. After a few seconds I looked up.

"Your last fuck up cost me fifty grand and you want to pay me off with just seven, are you both idiots?"

Elizabeth was quick to chip in.

"That's our final offer, take it or leave it."

I stood and picked my handbag from the floor.

"I'll leave it thank you," I said.

I took two steps towards the door and turned around.

"Tomorrow, first thing, I'll visit my MP and make such a stink about my private records being used without my consent they'll have no other choice but to raise my concerns with the Lord Chief Justice.

By lunchtime I'll be with the local press and I'll tell them my sob story and you never know it might get picked up by one of the nationals."

My eyes fixed on Freddie's cold glare, his mouth twitching slightly as my words hit a sensitive nerve.

I continued.

"By early afternoon I will have reported you to the Solicitors Regulatory Authority for professional misconduct, negligence, complacency and irregular billing. I'll throw in the fact that your record keeping is sub-standard and on one occasion you even overlooked twelve months out of office hours costing me an additional £9000. And let's not forget the Ombudsman. I will have drafted a formal letter of complaint to him by early evening."

I reached into my handbag and threw a letter onto their desk.

"Here's my formal complaint to Saxtons. The Ombudsmen said I had to deliver that to you before he can look into my case."

The Henshaws glared at each other and as my heart pounded hard in my rib cage, I felt it was about to jump out of my chest. I walked out through the door and made my way down the stairs and out into the car park.

Freddie Henshaw caught up with me as I opened my car door. He agreed to waive the outstanding bill in its entirety on the condition that I wouldn't pursue any legal actions against his company.

"I want my files as well, every last one of them, I'll collect them tomorrow."

He nodded in agreement.

"I'll have a formal letter drawn up that your bill has been paid in full."

There were no more pleasantries, not even a hand shake and as I climbed into the car I

collapsed my head onto the steering wheel and cried tears of relief. They were gone, thank Christ for that, at last I was rid of the Saxtons.

And as I pulled out of the car park and into the heavy traffic I couldn't help thinking about my performance in that office. I was in no doubt that I handled myself well and my argument, attention to detail and recollection of the facts, not to mention persuasive powers, had been far superior to anything Bennett, Gilbert or Elizabeth Henshaw had managed during the entire duration of my case.

45

For the first time since Stuart had left me, I felt vulnerable once more and yet I also felt a strange confidence building up inside me. The Saxtons' clock was no longer ticking and it slowly sank in that I had won a huge victory against my inept solicitors. £23000 was a huge deal for me and I had to keep reminding myself that it wasn't a dream after all. The Henshaws had caved in, despite their years of legal knowledge, the organisation behind them and against all odds I had won. I let the words sink in. Several days research and the confidence to speak and take them both on had won through in the end and I was quietly satisfied with my performance.

However, it hit me hard that I was now on my own. Saxtons had sent Bentley a letter and said that all correspondence should be redirected to my home address. Effectively I was now representing myself and the gloves were off and Steedman wasted no time trying to bully me into submission. Thankfully though, the Final Order had been signed by Porter so any attempt on Steedman's part to manipulate the wording or contents of the order wouldn't wash with me, though it didn't stop him from trying. In the end he accepted it, but instead, he turned his attention to the sale of the family home. It was clear Stuart wanted it to be sold on his terms.

There had been no shortage of viewers keen to invade my space and look in every nook and cranny of my beloved home. The offers weren't slow to come in either, yet with the UK housing market at rock bottom, they all fell well below the asking price. I wanted to hold out and try and get the £650000 both parties had originally agreed to, however, after the house had been on the market little over than a month, Stuart's impatience became all too evident and he let loose his bully boy solicitor to do his dirty work. He sent me several intimidating letters insisting that I accept an offer on the property that was £70000 less than the asking price. I refused and reminded him about the figure we had both agreed on. Steedman wasted no time and sent me a letter stating that if I didn't accept the offer he would make an emergency application to the court and a Judge would force me to sell the house.

Again I stood my ground, but incredibly, just two weeks later I received a letter giving me a time and date for my appointment with the Judge.

Walking into the Judge's Chambers without a solicitor or a barrister by my side was a lonely journey and I was sure Stuart and Steedman could almost smell my fear as they cast me a pitiful sideways glance. The change in Stuart's demeanour was all too evident as he strutted into court in a relaxed mood, no longer barking orders in Steedman's direction. I remained unfazed, confident I'd done my homework and prepared for what I thought would be a persuasive argument. Again it was down to research and I came armed with details of identical properties in and around the area that had sold for amounts exceeding £700000. And to support my argument I'd had three independent estate agents submit their written valuations all of which, without exception, had valued the house in excess of £650000. And there was more, for good measure I threw in a Financial Times article that stated house prices had reached rock bottom and the only way to go was up. I read the whole article to the Judge. The Times housing expert had forecast a significant property price rise within a six month period. I pitched my case with confidence despite no legal knowledge to guide me through the protocol of the court. I was on my feet for over twenty minutes and by the time I sat down I was sure I had convinced the Judge that £580000 was way below the true worth of the house. I asked for another few months in which time I was confident that a far higher offer would be brought to the table which would be beneficial for both of us.

It was Steedman's turn and his argument was very simple. He presented the Judge with the seven offers that had been submitted to the Estate Agent, all of them considerably lower than the asking price. He was on his feet for no more than two minutes, handing the Judge the Estate Agent's letter detailing the highest offer of £580000.

As he sat back down in his seat I suppressed a smile. I certainly didn't want to appear too confident but couldn't help feeling that his argument had been lacking in substance.

The Judge studied his notes and moved a series of papers around the desk in front of him. We sat in respective silence awaiting his judgement.

He cleared his throat. There was no explanation, no reasons behind his decision.

"I'm in full agreement with Mr Steedman, I'm going to order the house be sold to Mr and Mrs Nulty for £580000." He turned to Steedman. "You can instruct the agent and the conveyancers to begin legal proceedings."

My reaction was automatic. I stood.

"You can't be serious?"

"I beg your pardon," he said. "I can assure you I am deadly serious Mrs Palmer."

"It's seventy thousand less than the valuation price," I said in desperation.

"I'm quite aware of that Mrs Palmer, but agents valuations are always on the high side anyway."

I glanced at Steedman and Stuart. They were already on their feet gathering their possessions ready to make a quick getaway. I looked back to the Judge who had also stood.

"But Sir, I-"

The Judge held up a hand stopping me dead.

"That's my decision Mrs Palmer, and that's final."

The whole sorry episode had opened my eyes as to how vulnerable I had become and I couldn't make any sense of the Judge's ruling. Had he simply ruled against me because I'd had no legal representation? Had I in some way overstepped the mark? Was he sexist? It seemed to me that Steedman hadn't made any sort of effort and yet I had spent some time preparing my argument, utilising several professional papers and opinions and I delivered them in a structured manner. I also had evidence to back everything up. It wasn't right, something told me that his decision had been made long before I'd even entered the courtroom. I tried to put it behind me but I was devastated and the more I replayed the court scene in my head, the more convinced I was that I had been stitched up.

I'd lost. There was no appeal, no questioning the Judge's decision and as he'd said, it was final.

I tried to put that terrible day behind me, because I still had to decide whether I wanted to appeal Porter's decision on the hearing. I needed advice but after the Saxtons debacle I was reluctant to engage a new solicitor and start the merry go round of fees again. I'd made some enquires, yet soon discovered legal advice was never free, a solicitor's clock was always ticking translating time into money. I visited several companies offering 'free initial consultations,' and as soon as I'd relayed the long saga of my case, they'd pitch their terms, between £2500 just to read my case files and thereafter a ridiculous hourly rate, hours that I had no control over. Once bitten twice shy was the phrase which immediately sprang to mind as I listened to their friendly pitch. I'd let them finish their spiel before making my escape on the pretense I'd get back to them, which of course I had no intention of doing. The truth was I didn't trust solicitors anymore, to my mind they were a bunch of charlatans best avoided.

Yet I knew I had to do something, my request to appeal was in limbo, lodged at the courthouse collecting dust on a shelf in the Clerk's Office. I'd let the situation ride, my mind had been preoccupied with the house sale and after the last court fiasco I knew if I had any chance of my appeal getting off the ground it needed a gigantic push from someone who could lend it some weight.

Then it suddenly came to me during one of those nights when sleep escaped me and I lay worrying until the small hours of the morning about everything and nothing. I would be a litigant in person and go directly to a barrister to seek his opinion, hadn't John and Elizabeth done much the same? As I glanced over the numerous files neatly stacked at the foot of my bed, illuminated by the scant light passing through the bedroom curtains, I knew I had all the information I needed and I certainly didn't need a middle man racking up additional costs.

Finding Simon Murdoch had been no mean feat. I trawled the website for hours looking for the right person who'd be willing to deal with a litigant in person and I was beginning to realise barristers preferred to work with solicitors and not a layperson who would need to be guided through the minefield of the British Legal System.

Murdoch on the other hand was more than happy to open up his office door to Joe Public and his pedigree on paper was second to none. My intuition had guided me to him, I'd browsed around his company's website and each time my curser moved, much like a glass around an Ouija board, it always landed back at his Chambers in Leeds and then onto his profile. I must have read his profile a dozen times before I mustered the courage to call.

Once I passed the careful vetting of Murdoch's clerk and deposited £200 in their bank account as payment for a thirty-minute telephone conversation with the man himself, I was allocated a time slot the following day. As I punched in the Leeds area code and the rest of the number I wondered if this was another waste of money.

His loud voice interrupted my negative thought pattern.

"Hello Mrs Palmer, can you hear me?"

"Yes," I said, "yes, I can hear you fine."

I quickly ran through the outline of my case, all the while conscious of the limited time we had to speak.

"Mrs Palmer can I stop you?" he said, "I can't give you any advice until I see some of your case files."

Here we go I thought, he wants more money, he's hooked me up and now he wants to reel me in. I posed the question and waited for his response.

"Absolutely nothing Mrs Palmer, I wouldn't expect any payment for that."

What the fuck?

I was lost for words, had the man just said he didn't want payment?

"Listen very carefully Mrs Palmer, can you please send me the Judgement, the signed Order and the court bundle from your final hearing? You did say you were in possession of all your files?" he added.

"Yes, yes I am, that's not a problem," enthusiasm radiating from my voice.

"Send them down express delivery tomorrow. I'm working in Newcastle next Friday, I've booked the 6.35pm train back to Leeds, it would be very helpful if you could meet me at the County Hotel opposite the station at 5.15pm. I can return the files to you then and we can talk about your appeal.

"Yes," I hesitated before adding, "and how much will this meeting cost Mr Murdoch?"

"Very expensive," he said.

That's more like it.

"If you could stretch to buying me a cup of coffee or a beer while we chat, that will be all it will cost you," he said laughing.

I almost fell back into my chair, unable to comprehend that he was a man of the law with a spark of humility and a sense of humour. I was almost in a state of shock as I said goodbye and replaced the handset.

I wasted no time packing up the paperwork into a sturdy box and called a courier from the Yellow Pages. Only then did I focus my attention onto more domestic issues. The house sale was moving fast, out of desperation I'd managed to find myself a place only a stone's throw from my beloved house, yet a million miles away by way of style and size. The house had been let out to neglectful tenants and looked a sorry sight. As I strutted around my soon to be new home I couldn't stop the feeling of melancholy sweeping over me. Maybe it was the woodchip wallpaper hanging off the walls barely disguising the patches of mold lurking in every corner or the musty smell lifting from the thread bare carpets, whatever the reason I knew the place was a far cry from the home I would be leaving behind in a matter of days. As much as I cajoled myself into thinking otherwise I couldn't stop the tears rolling down my face as I closed the door behind me, desperate to get away from the repressive hole that was soon to be called home. I cursed my ex-husband for the speed at which everything had happened. This was a stopgap I told myself, I had rented it for a six month period, surely something better would come along?

Simon Murdoch looked nothing like the picture I'd viewed on his profile shot. I'd passed him twice in the reception area of the County Hotel. He'd obviously noticed me pacing up and down the foyer confused, he jumped to his feet shouting in my direction

"Mrs Palmer."

I may not have recognised the image but the voice was unmistakable. He beckoned me over and without delay ushered me to a seat he'd found in a secluded corner set back from the general activity around us. There was a coffee pot on the table and two cups. Once he'd introduced himself and poured me a coffee there was no time wasted on pleasantries, he had a message to deliver then a train to catch. My files were spread out on a small table and I watched quietly as he flicked through the judgement.

His first question was not what I expected.

"Is your ex-husband a Freemason?" he said out of the blue.

"No, not to my knowledge," I replied.

"I ask, because it's as clear as the nose on my face the Judge has been biased in his decision, especially when he forced the house sale. Something is seriously wrong with this judgement, it's an absolute mockery from start to finish."

At last, I thought, someone who is not afraid to tell it as it is. However, any joy I felt when I heard Mr Murdoch's first few words were short lived. Almost as soon as he had delivered his strong opinion on how flawed the judgement was he went on to explain how difficult it was to be granted the right to appeal. He didn't pull any punches and told me that winning the right to appeal would be a walk in the park compared too actually winning it.

"There are so many hurdles to jump," he said.

He picked up a sheet of paper from the table.

"Division of the joint assets is clearly unfair, given your domestic circumstances."

"It was unfair," I said, "in the previous hearing the Judge was looking at a split of 65/35 in my favour."

He nodded his head.

"The Judgement does seem very unfair, however the Judge has discretion under the matrimonial clauses act and he has made a decision within those boundaries. There is no court in the land that will say he hasn't stayed within those parameters, I can guarantee that. It's a shame you don't live in the south of England, divorce is a postcode lottery, the further north you go the more inclined the judges are to award a fifty fifty split much like Scottish Law and you're practically living on the border of Scotland. Judges in the North East have a different outlook to their London counterparts."

"You're kidding me."

He shook his head.

"I'm afraid not Mrs Palmer."

He sighed, no doubt realising from the expression on my face it wasn't what I wanted to hear.

"You have to prove that the Judge was plainly wrong and in this instance it would be almost impossible.

I took a generous gulp of my coffee in an attempt to calm my nerves.

"So that's it?" I said.

He threw me a sheepish glance as if he was pondering whether to go any further.

"Well, there is an area where he was clearly wrong."

I stiffened up, he had my full attention.

"He was crystal ball gazing when he assumed you would only need three years of maintenance, at which point he is suggesting you'd be sufficiently independent and earning a salary of nearly £50000 a year," he smiled. "To be honest, if you managed to secure a salary of half that amount, you'd be doing well."

"So you think I have grounds to appeal?" I asked, my voice almost pleading for him to deliver the right answer.

He pressed his lips together as if willing himself to hold back on the words I didn't want to hear, yet he couldn't stop himself knocking down any hope I held like a breeze blowing over a house of cards.

"I didn't say that Mrs Palmer, I'm afraid it's extremely rare for anyone to be granted permission to appeal. Most appeals are unsuccessful, mainly because the courts want finality and they purposely make it very difficult to appeal a judgement."

I leaned back in my seat and let out a deep sigh.

His eyes no longer looked so bright and the lines in his face were deepening.

"You've got to have a very strong case."

"And I haven't?"

I could see empathy written all over his face which shocked me, it was the first genuine gesture of compassion I'd witnessed from anyone with any legal title stamped on their credentials. However, I could read between the lines and he was telling me that I'd be walking uphill with a ton weight on my back and I had to be ready for the fight.

He moved on.

"Mrs Palmer, I'd have to be a stupid man not to see what your husband and Tina Palmer have done, it's very clear they have committed a fraudulent act. It was a ruse to keep his mother's money out of the divorce settlement, it's as clear as day and yet you haven't a scrap of solid evidence to support your claim. I would be foolish to advise you to pursue an appeal based on nothing."

"And what about the maintenance factor?" I said, although I held no hope his answer would be positive.

He glanced at his watch, I knew time was ticking away, he had a train to catch.

He shook his head.

"Difficult."

"That bad?"

Murdoch drained the last of his coffee and placed the cup back on the table. He had painted a very clear picture, so vivid I couldn't ignore his advice although every bone in my body desperately wanted to. I wanted him to say something positive to keep my determination to fight alive. Instead he was about to throw cold water on the last spark of hope I clung to.

"Even if you appeal the maintenance decision, Mr Palmer is going to counter argue that it's too high and that he is unable to work and his earnings are decreasing. Can you be sure that the £1000 a month you've been awarded may not be revised to a lower amount if he presents a strong enough case?"

I recoiled in horror.

"That could happen?"

"Of course it could, it's unlikely but it could happen."

Of course it could happen, this was Stuart Palmer and his scheming sidekick Steedman.

"It's more than a possibility Mr Murdoch," I said, "my ex-husband has managed to fool the courts thus far. I've no doubt he can do it again."

"So it appears," he said, as he began to pack his belongings up.

We walked out of the lobby together and as we approached the glass panelled doors leading onto the street, he reached inside his jacket pocket and pulled out a business card.

"Mrs Palmer take my card, think over what I've said today and give me ring when you've reached a decision, let me know either way."

"Thanks."

"Ultimately it's your decision and not mine to make."

He said his farewells and started to walk away but then he suddenly stopped and turned.

"Some days when I see the law abused as it has been in your case, I feel ashamed to call myself a barrister. Today is such a day Mrs Palmer."

I watched him fade away as he walked across the road, his image lost as he mingled in with the busy crowds making their way into the train station. He was a decent man I thought, as I walked away with a heavy heart, barely aware of the rain bouncing like stair rods on the ground, soaking me to the skin.

The removal men had sat patiently outside my house for two hours, the furniture was packed and ready to be offloaded into the new house, the only hold up was the endless waiting for the bank to transfer the funds. I'd had a full complement of willing helpers to pack and clean and by 3pm we were finished. There was nothing else any of us could do except wait. The call came in at 3.30pm and we could finally make our way to our rented property. The removal men closed the doors on the wagon and set off to drive the short distance to the new house. I'd almost forgotten how much junk we'd accumulated despite being brutal, and what no longer had a function went directly into a skip or to the charity shop. I tried to take a positive viewpoint, we weren't able to stay in the family home yet we would have the comfort of our familiar belongings around us.

Abigail reminded me of the final task that still had to be carried out, the one I was least looking forward to.

"Do you want me to take the keys around to the estate agent Mum?"

Handing in the keys to the house I adored was always going to be tough, Abigail wasn't sure how I would react, I'd been in a tentative mood all day.

"No I'm fine, you make sure Alexandra is alright, I'll drop the keys off."

"Okay, if that's what you want Mum," she added, before heading off down the drive to her car.

I was on my own, it was time to say my goodbyes to the home that held so many memories, most of them special.

I slowly walked around the garden, my eyes picking out the various shrubs that had been there as long as I could remember. I wanted to take one last look, the autumn had put paid to the last of the summer flowers, yet still there was a sweet scent lifting from the greenery. I took a deep breath, exhaling slowly as my mind cast back in time. I could almost see the girls as little children running around the garden barefoot in their swimming costumes, trying to escape the water hose I had been commissioned to hold and douse them with at every opportunity. Their shrieks of joy and laughter rang out in my ears as I remembered how they'd run into its path and when the ice cold water hit their bare skin they'd howl even louder. How many times had we played that same game in the summer days, when they were young and life seemed almost perfect? When the memories became almost too unbearable, I made my way back into the house locking the patio door behind me for the last time. Slowly I made my way around the house briefly entering each room and lingering just long enough to relive my own special memories. I was reluctant to leave.

I became aware of a heavy knocking on the front door that forced me to snap back into reality. I walked along the hallway and opened the door.

It was Mr and Mrs Nulty, the new owners. They were early and quickly announced there was no need to go to the Estate Agent. Their solicitor had informed them less than an hour ago that all the necessary financial actions had been completed and the house was officially theirs. They barged right past me, all social graces lost, now their money had been deposited in my bank account they knew their rights and weren't slow to share them.

"Have you got the house keys Mrs Palmer?" Mr Nulty said, holding his hand out palm up waiting for me to deliver them into his greedy paws.

Reluctantly I dropped them into his outstretched hand.

"Thank you, we must get on, the removal men are on their way and we want the furniture offloaded before dark."

His face showed no sympathy, no emotion and he was oblivious to the fact my heart was slowing being yanked out of my chest.

As I walked down the path, I held the tears in as long as I could. The floodgates opened as soon as I reached the privacy of my car, the house had been the final straw, it represented all that I'd lost and more. I cried for twenty minutes and tried hard to compose myself. It was time to make the call I'd been putting off for some time. I reached into the pocket of my bag and retrieved the crumpled card as I slowly tapped the numbers in my phone, my blurred vision trying desperately to read the numbers. The phone rang for what seemed like an age. I rubbed the snot and tears from my face and tried to regain some sort composure. It wasn't the right time to call, yet I knew if I didn't do it in that instance I never would. Eventually I heard his strong voice in my ear.

"Hello can I help you?"

"It's Mrs Palmer," I said, trying desperately to hold back the tears.

"Hi Mrs Palmer, how are you?"

It wasn't the time for pleasantries.

"I've made up my mind."

"Yes."

"I'm not going to go ahead with the appeal."

46

Three Years Later

I was just about to close down my laptop for the day when the unwelcome Skype message flashed across the screen. My heart sank as I saw Gerry Holme's bubbled image appear just above a line of text.

Hi Annette have you a minute? I've booked the conference pod meet you in 5

My heart sank, Gerry Holme, my new boss. Shit! Not again.

I lifted my head from my workstation and peered over the sea of computers running in rows along the vast, characterless open plan misery of an office. I could just about see the top of Holme's fat, useless head, visible above his computer screen. I knew why he'd called a meeting. There would be some urgent work that needed to be completed for a client that evening. An extra hour or two on the working day and I would have no choice in the matter. We sat only a few feet away from one another, it would have been more than logical if he had walked the short distance to my desk to make his request, however as I'd discovered since re-entering the wonderful new world of the workplace only twelve months previously, we don't actually do much talking, communicating via Skype or email the preferred method even if we are sitting on adjacent desks.

Since the first day I'd reluctantly walked into the BGC flagship office, I was forced to acknowledge things had moved on a pace from my day, now my working environment was fluid and they'd laughed at me when I'd asked where my desk was. I'd plonk myself wherever a work station became available, set up my computer allowing me to remotely access clients' accounts and off I'd go. With no fixed abode, we minor associates were expected to move around the office like Bedouins in the desert. I was the first to admit it had been a huge learning curve returning to work and it was a trajectory I was still coming to terms with. Not least of all the additional hours I was expected to work, although there was no evidence of my effort on my monthly pay slip, my overtime was unpaid and incidentally I was earning less than a third of what Judge Porter had said I would. Before I gathered together my notepad and computer in preparation for my meeting, I reluctantly made the inevitable call home.

"Alexandra it's going to be another late one, you just have your dinner chick I'll heat mine up in the microwave when I get home."

There was no resistance only disappointment in her voice, this was our new life, a one we all had to accept and get on with.

Work wasn't the only change, since my divorce three years previously, life had not been without its trials and tribulations. After spending the first six months in the dingy rented accommodation throwing good money away on rent, we'd eventually found somewhere to live. I'd been persistent in my search for the right home and had made it my mission to cozy up with every estate agent lined up along the High Street. I was a familiar face with the girls in the front of the shops manning the sales desks and it was known that I was a cash buyer with no house to sell so they were keen to show me what they had to offer.

It was no surprise when eventually I received a call from Helen, a particularly helpful agent, who couldn't wait to tell me about a bargain house that had just come on the market.

"It's a deceased gentleman and his family are keen to get rid of it quickly. Go and view it Annette before anyone else gets wind of it. It's just within your price range," she said with more than a hint of enthusiasm in her voice knowing it was exactly what I was looking for.

On reflection I truly believe the house had been meant for us. As soon as I opened the battered old panelled front door, with the wobbly Yale lock making it difficult to turn the key, I knew I'd stepped into a home once more. Admittedly the swirly patterned carpets, stone fireplace and avocado bathroom suite were offensive to the eyes and a throwback to the seventies, yet it felt right. It was spotlessly clean although it carried the stale musty smell of a house that had been unlived in for a long period of time. I wasn't put off one bit, my intuition told me it was going to be mine and after a cheeky offer along with more than a little persistence, I secured the deal.

The house I had wanted so much came with a hefty price tag, it left me practically broke. Virtually every penny I had left from the divorce settlement had been ploughed into that cranky old house with the dodgy front door.

But it was worth it, I was grateful to have a new sense of purpose and a project to focus my mind on. With Alexandra on the mend her grip on me had slackened off over the months and I watched with pride as she began to spread her wings once more, each day branching a little further away as friends began to populate her life again and she prepared to start her studies at Newcastle University. I redirected the energy I'd spent on my daughter to creating a home which proved to be an exhausting challenge at times. Most evenings I'd fall into bed physically shattered, my joints aching after spending the day bagging rubble from an internal wall we'd knocked down or clearing the overgrown garden of its never ending weeds or painting and decorating. The list of jobs went on and with little spare cash I was the only labourer I could afford.

For a while at least, when I was preoccupied with the house, all thoughts of Stuart and his solicitor Bentley were relegated to the back of my mind. It had been no surprise to me that the insincere promises Stuart had made in court about his desire to build a relationship with his children had amounted to nothing. They'd not heard a word from him. I knew, that despite my children's bravado they were extremely hurt, it was now as clear as crystal that he had abandoned them altogether. It was brought home on one occasion where he'd passed Abigail in the street and had failed to acknowledge her presence. She told me their eyes had locked together. Abigail gave a slight smile more than ready to listen to what he had to say as she stopped walking. He looked the other way and crossed over the road in a deliberate attempt to avoid her. She told her sisters the story when she arrived home, tears welling up in her eyes. The girls needed no clearer evidence where they stood in their dad's life and eventually as the months passed any reference they might have once made to him in conversation disappeared altogether. He may well have faded away completely if it were not for the fact Judge Porter had ordered him to pay £1000 into my bank account on the 1st of every month. It was the one link that bound us together.

With no other form of income, more often than not I was short of cash and desperately waiting for the maintenance payment to be deposited into my bank account as the depleting balance crept into the red each month. I'd anxiously await its arrival yet with his demonic humour in full play he would ensure it was nigh on midnight before he'd reluctantly commit his index finger to pressing the confirm payment and send tab. It was all a game to him and even though he had clearly won in the big stakes financial court battle he still couldn't help himself and had to keep twisting the knife. Not one word had passed between us since the court hearing, yet his actions spoke volumes. The selfish twat still wanted to lord his authority over me, he wasn't quite ready to relinquish the power he'd been wielding over me for twenty-three years.

I knew the day was coming when he'd fail to make the payment altogether and it came to fruition twenty months into the thirty-six month payment schedule.

It had sent me into a panic and my pleas to Steedman had gone unheard. With no other form of income I had no choice but to take a trip to the benefit office, begging bowl in hand to wait for state charity to be doled out to me. What level would Stuart lower me to next I thought as I'd sat in front of a stern faced bitch who'd delved into my personal circumstances only relenting to give me income support when she was totally convinced I had fuck all else to live on. Her face pouted in total disgust as she stamped my docket, awarding me a measly £73.10 for the week. As I left the office I was forced to walk past the druggies and drunks sitting on the steps by the dole office. On the grand scale of low points in my life this was surely up there at the top of the list.

I sent several strongly worded letters to Steedman and he replied stating his client was no longer working and had been living on unemployment benefit. There was also an underlying threat that he was considering going back to the court to have the Maintenance Order varied to take into account his clients change in financial circumstances. At one time his tactics might have intimidated me but not on this occasion, I didn't turn a hair reading the words he'd spitefully committed to paper. I knew he'd not yet bought the four bedroomed house he'd so desperately needed so his children could stay with him and that his huge settlement from the divorce was still intact and no doubt mothballed in some bank vault gathering both dust and interest in equal measure. Unfazed by the starkness of Steedman's letter, I pursued my claim for the £3000 arrears through the Magistrates Court. Stuart turned up to the hearing dressed as the local hobo pleading poverty again. I presented my case to the panel of magistrates trying to remain calm, I didn't want to display any anger or malice because I now realised anger was a wasted energy in a court of law, the legal eyes would fall in my direction and see me as the antagonist and villain and I didn't want that. Although I kept my cool and presented Porter's signed Order which I knew no one in that particular court had the power to overturn, the magistrate still ended up showing the smirking bastard some leniency, allowing him to pay the arrears in £500 installments over a six months period. Hearing over, I watched him walk out in front of me with a spring in his step, a sense of victory evident,

After the court appearance the money was on time every month, although with each payment he attached a note

24 of 36

23 of 36

22 of 36 …….

There were no words merely figures that needed no explanation. They served as a stark reminder time was ticking against me and I had to find paid employment. It was when the note on the bank transfer read 33 of 36 that I eventually secure myself a job. I discovered after making numerous applications and then having received an equal number of rejection letters, the job market for a middle-aged woman who'd had a twenty year career gap was not a welcoming one. I would have liked to think when I eventually got the job at BGC they'd chosen me because they saw potential in me. Yet as I sat at my transient desk working like a Trojan trying to complete the task Gerry had kindly bestowed on me before disappearing home himself, I'd realised BGC hadn't spotted potential they'd spotted cheap labour at sixteen grand a year. Murdoch's voice resonated in my head once more;

The judge was crystal ball gazing when he suggested you would be earning £48000 a year.

My interest in Stuart Palmer had been resurrected since the maintenance debacle and because his contribution to my coffers was now coming to an end and his slimy solicitor had said he was unemployed curiosity pulled me like a magnet to investigate my ex-husband affairs once more. As always the easiest place to start was Google, which provided a trail to the Companies House register where it confirmed Palmer wasn't in fact unemployed, he'd landed himself the position of Company Secretary for a chemical manufacturing company based outside Durham. Having scrutinized their annual returns it was evident the company wasn't small fry either, with a sixty million turnover they must have been knocking out Paracetamol tablets at a rate of knots and as Company Secretary, Palmer would be getting a fair cut, no doubt a six figure sum.

Having stumbled upon that golden nugget of priceless information it made me realise I had nothing to lose by making an application to the court to extend the Maintenance Order.

Once my mind was made up the process gained its own momentum, after I'd notified Steedman of my decision and made a formal request to the court it seemed to take no time at all for the court letter to arrive through the door listing the schedule of events. A hearing was set to be heard in front of Judge Marshall at the end of the following month and there was a tight deadline for exchanging financial statements and lodging both completed statements and questionnaires with the court. Although I knew I was up against a solicitor who, like a ferret, could wiggle his way out of anything, the prospect was not a daunting one. The processes and procedures were all too familiar to me and I'd told myself on more than one occasion that it would cost me nothing, I wasn't going to be building up solicitors fees because I would be representing myself.

The hearing was just days away and I was reasonably happy with all of my preplanning, but something else was about to trigger two days of furious activity, something I would end up bringing to the attention of Judge Marshall at the end of the day's proceedings.

I had been driving along the A69 after visiting a friend in Carlisle when I just happened to realise I was coming up towards the piece of land that had been owned by Stuart's mother, the land she had left to Tina Palmer in her inheritance, the land where a very successful roadside cafeteria stood. I looked in my rear view mirror and slowed down as I approached it. The car park was full of cars, vans and lorries and there were a dozen questions flying around my head. I couldn't help wondering what sort of rent Tina would be receiving and more importantly where that rent was being directed. I was still in no doubt that the inheritance had all been a scam, no doubt that any income would be handed straight over to Stuart with a little backhander finding its way into Tina's pocket. It had been over three years since the Will had been executed. Was it possible that the land had been sold without my knowledge?

When I arrived home I decided to give the Land Registry office a call just to satisfy my curiosity. The softly spoken gentleman on the other end of the line had no sense of urgency in his voice as I asked him how difficult it was to get the details on a piece of land.

"Have you got the Land Registry Number?" he asked.

"No, unfortunately not, however the location is quiet distinctive."

I gave him the name of the café and the exact location on the A69.

"Let me bring up Google maps," he said, "and I'll find it for you."

The line went quiet for what seemed like an age, yet I could still hear the tapping of his computer in the background.

"Yes I think this is the one you're looking for, it's just set back from the road on the A69 would that be right?"

"Yes that's it," i said, the joy in my voice all too evident.

He reeled off the number.

"It's TZ7450249. Is that all I can help you with?"

I was dumbstruck for a second because during my divorce proceedings both Louise and John had said that they were unable to find out the number or any details relating to the land and yet a mere amateur like me had been able to secure the necessary information within two minutes. Terrified he might put the phone down on me before I'd finished, I cut in.

"Yes, I was wondering if you could tell me who owns the land."

"Wait one moment." he said once more.

"Tina Palmer," he said, his voice hesitant as if he was reading a document.

"Thank you for your help."

"Wait one moment," he said, "sorry, it used to be Tina Palmer who owned the land but I have a paper copy of a recent development. I do apologise, there's nothing on our computer records yet."

"No problem."

I recall thinking that she had obviously sold the land and her and Stuart had set up a secret trust fund to which Stuart would undoubtedly be the main beneficiary. His voice interrupted my thoughts.

"From our records the land transferred from an Olive Palmer to Tina Ann Palmer, however it's now in the name of Stuart Palmer."

"She's sold the land?" I asked.

There was another pause, the sound of papers being shuffled again and then he uttered a sentence that I couldn't quite take in.

"No, not sold, she has transferred the land to Mr Stuart Palmer for nil consideration."

"Fuck off! You're kidding me."

"I beg your pardon madam."

"Sorry, I'm so sorry, please forgive me."

My brain was doing summersaults at this point yet still I couldn't quite believe it, the cynic in me was sure there must be a catch.

"Could you repeat what you've just said?"

"Yes certainly. The land is in Stuart Palmers name," he said.

"He hasn't bought it?"

"No."

"She transferred it to him free of charge?"

"Yes. Nil consideration."

The information had sunk in. I couldn't believe they had been that stupid. Why hadn't they created a bogus sale? Surely it would have been the sensible thing to do and so simple to fiddle. Stamp Duty, that was why. The greedy bastard had wanted to avoid the stamp duty. I was thinking on my feet. His mother's house in Gosforth Park, I had the Land Registry number for that in my purse.

"Thank you," I said. "Could you help me with one more thing?"

"Certainly madam."

I located the piece of paper.

"Is it possible to tell me who is the registered owner of TY3416589?"

Once again I waited in silence as he clicked away on his computer, this time my heart galloped away as the anticipation became almost unbearable. Surely Stuart couldn't have been so irrational with this property, a house with an actual number and a street and a land

Registry number so easy to get a hold of a four year old child could look it up.

His steady voice calmed my nerves when he eventually fired back an answer.

"The property is in Mr Stuart Palmers name, it transferred directly to him from Tina Palmer, once again for nil consideration."

"Not sold?"

"No."

"Thank you."

I asked him for copies of both land registry documents and gave him my credit card details over the phone. I paid extra for next day delivery.

I sank back in my seat and took a huge deep breath. This was huge, this was the evidence of a huge fraud that my husband had committed, a fraud I had accused him of in open court and the Judge had totally ignored it. It needed handled with care. I needed advice and quickly, with the hearing days away there was no time to waste. Within minutes of ending my call with the Land Registry, the phone was in my hand once more, urgently I tapped the numbers in.

"Hello Dunstable Chambers," the efficient voice on the other end of the line said without delay.

"Hello, I need to speak to Mr Murdoch directly, can you put me through to him please?"

47

"Sorry Mrs Palmer I'm afraid Mr Murdoch isn't going to be available for the foreseeable future, he's taking some leave from work at the moment," the receptionist said in a matter of fact manner.

His voice rang in my ears and although I couldn't see his face I realised he'd already dismissed my call, he was involved in other matters. I could hear the commotion around him in the background as he tried to get me off the phone as quickly as he could.

I persisted.

"I really need to speak to him, he has given me advice in the past and I want his opinion once more."

The man's bland voice had turned a little snappy and short.

"As I've already said it's not possible to speak to Mr Murdoch at the moment."

"Is he on holiday? Have you any idea when he's returning?"

"Mr Murdoch isn't available for consultation that's all I can tell you, I'll make a note that you've called Mrs Palmer and he may contact you at a later date but that's the best I can do."

Before I could reply he ended the call.

"Good day Mrs Palmer."

It was the story of my life, so close and yet so far. What the hell was I going to do I thought to myself as I made my way to the fridge, retrieved the chilled bottle of wine from the cooler and poured myself a generous measure. I took two large gulps, the acidic taste immediately hitting the back of my throat causing me to wince before it trickled down my gullet and began to hit the intended spot. My mind was racing. I needed to think clearly. Alcohol didn't solve the problem yet it certainly slowed the pace of my thoughts. In truth the news from the Land Registry had hit me like a sledgehammer, I was almost numb and not quite able to comprehend the magnitude of my find. As I sat with my wine, its effect began to release the full extent of my imagination. I convinced myself Stuart's greed and impatience must have eventually got the better of him and sound reasoning and logic had flown out the window. Why on earth would he take the risk of transferring the property and land into his name before the maintenance payments had come to an end and all connections between him and me were totally severed? Surely it would have been wise to leave it in Tina Palmer's name until he knew for sure I wasn't coming after him for a second bite of the cherry? The truth of the matter, I'd concluded, was Stuart Palmer didn't trust anyone least of all his ex-sister in law who had been left as gatekeeper in charge of his fortune. I allowed myself a little smile as I took another mouthful of wine. The stupid, stupid bastard.

As much as I could rejoice in my find, refilling my glass with another hefty measure of wine as way of celebration, I wasn't quite sure what I could do with my explosive information. Without Murdoch to turn to there was no other legal route I could take. I had neither the cash nor the inclination to hire another solicitor. I'd been burnt already by John Bennett and Saxtons and still had the scars to prove it. I wasn't about to put my hand into the fire for a second time. My past experience had taught me that any solicitor looking at my case afresh would demand a king's ransom just to read my stockpile of case files. There was nobody I could trust and no such thing as free advice and the only legal person I'd met with one ounce of common decency was Murdoch, who to my disappointment was nowhere to be found.

I had sat on my find for days not telling a soul although I don't know how I'd managed to keep my council. Even when the Land Registry letter arrived through the front door and I held the hard copy in my hand I still kept quiet mainly because I knew it would be met with a frosty reception from the girls. I'd already made the mistake of telling the three of them I had made an application to have the maintenance payments extended. We had been sitting around the dinner table having a leisurely evening meal when I'd dropped that particular bombshell and it exploded right in my face. All hell broke loose and they weren't shy in telling me they thought I was mad dredging everything up again. It was Alexandra who kicked up the biggest fuss although she was only the mouth piece for the other two, who clearly offered her their full support as they nodded in agreement. She laid into me and there was real anger in her normally sweet gentle voice.

"For God's sake mum, can't you let it go and just get on with your life? Forget about my Dad, I'm sure he's forgotten about you."

I'd been just as passionate with my response as the cut of her sharp comment hit me hard, knocking the wind out of me and I needed no reminding that her Dad didn't give me a second thought.

"This is my life Alexandra and as much as I'd like to erase the past I can't." I shouted at her. "I'm working every hour God sends for a bloody pittance with barely enough money to see me to the end of the month. Do you honestly believe that's fair when we know your Dad's hidden so much money?"

She shrugged her shoulders, clearly taken aback at my response.

"And no doubt he's earning way in excess of anything I'd ever hope to make."

And yet my words fell on deaf ears, they didn't want to know. Alexandra had already cast aside her half eaten lunch and was hotfooting it out of the kitchen, her head shaking in disgust.

"Forget it Mum, you'll do want you want anyway. it doesn't matter what any of us think. When have you ever listened to us?"

When have you ever listened to us? It was a sharp note to end on and it had echoed in my head on more than one occasion. Guilt was never far behind the thought.

I didn't mention the maintenance hearing from that point on, I now knew exactly where the girls stood on the matter. Since the divorce hearing we'd found a happy equilibrium in our new family of four plus boyfriends of course. Abigail had even ditched her bouncer bo' and had found herself a lad with more brains than brawn. Victoria appeared to be just as happy in her relationship and was even contemplating taking the plunge and moving in with him. All three girls seemed happy, I had to question my own motives as to why was I so intent on causing more upheaval for my children when they thought it had all been put to bed long ago?

I knew the pain it could cause, yet the nagging doubts wouldn't go away and my overwhelming desire to nail the lying bastard of an ex-husband seemed to outweigh their needs and everything else for that matter.

And now I had the evidence from the Land Registry there was no turning back and my determination to forge ahead was reinforced when Steedman and I exchanged the obligatory Form E's, outlining our financial affairs ahead of the maintenance hearing.

Steedman, as usual, had prayed on my legal naivety, cunningly he'd exploited the law to his clients advantage ensuring they completed only the abbreviated version of the form which conveniently for Palmer omitted listing assets such as land and shares and properties. This was infuriating because I knew he did indeed possess land and shares and properties. Nevertheless there was still more than enough listed on the scant sheets of paper to make my blood boil as my eyes scanned the list of his declared liquid assets:

Bonds - £460000
ISA's- £31100
Premium Bonds £40000
Current Account £15320
Deposit Account £35701

My fury grew as I totted up the figures and I almost fell off my kitchen chair when I realised there was nearly £600000 in liquid cash. Six hundred fucking thousand pounds!!

I moved onto the section itemizing his monthly net income:
Net income from employment £5000
Other Monthly Income;
Interest £,800
Rent Received after tax £1926

The rent received figure immediately jumped out at me, it could only be the monies received from land rent for the café on the A69 because I knew he wasn't renting out his mother's property. I'd passed it numerous times over recent years and on every occasion the blinds had been drawn and it was apparent the property had been decommissioned.

I could hardly believe what was staring back at me on the printed page, nearly£9000 a month net income. £9000 and that didn't include the bitch's income. They'd be living it up like fucking millionaires. Eventually rage got the better of me as I mindlessly screwed the sheets up in my hand before flinging them on the kitchen floor. The papers flew in all directions and I knew I'd have to pick them up at some point but I didn't care because my mind was preoccupied with how the penny pinching bastard had treated me and the kids all these years. Not so much as a birthday card for his children and no offer of maintenance for Alexandra since the CSA had stopped in 2012 and even then he'd had the fucking audacity to ask for a £250 refund for overpayment. The man was a blatant liar and I'd witnessed first-hand Stuart's total fabrications of the truth in both the High Court and then the Magistrates Court where only months previously he'd been pleading poverty and asking for leniency with the maintenance payments because he only had £73 a week to live on. I knew without a shadow of a doubt there was no level to which the man would not stoop and I wasn't going to let him get away with it any longer. Despite all my misgivings about the girls and the trauma it would cause them, they'd have to understand, I couldn't let it go, it was like a maggot nibbling away at my very core and I wouldn't sleep until I'd nailed him to the cross and ousted him for the fraudulent prick he truly was.

From that moment on I spent my days, or the time I had available between work commitments, investigating and researching the legal process as well as dredging through both his bank and credit card statements he'd been forced to include with his Financial Statement. Once again Steedman had boxed clever and only supplied six months of statements instead of the usual twelve months. I didn't let the matter pass without a fight, I'd sent more than one written request to Steedman asking for his client to complete the detailed form E as well as asking for him to supply twelve months of bank and credit card statements. It fell on deaf ears, he ignored all my appeals, no doubt shredding each of my many letters in the recycling bin after giving them the once over. Steedman had dismissed me as some sort of joke, in his mind I posed no great threat because I wasn't legally trained and was therefore no match for him.

I got no backing from the court either. They also ignored my numerous written requests as I pleaded with them to order Stuart to complete the full version of form E. There had been no response, not even an acknowledgement of my correspondence as if the legal boys club had simply dismissed me with a wave of their hand.

It was like trying to wade through mud getting anywhere with Steedman or the court. I researched that I was entitled to compile a reasonable questionnaire that Stuart would have to give answers too. It was my legal right and I'd taken a lot of time compiling twenty-one questions asking Steedman to provide additional crucial information that I believed would help my case. I received a reply. Next to each of the twenty-one questions Steedman's response had been the same.

The Respondent has disclosed sufficient information to show that he has the necessary income to meet any such reasonable Maintenance Order the Court should determine the Applicant requires, giving due consideration to all of the circumstances.

Steedman was sending me on a wild goose chase and the courts through their total lack of action were assisting him in his quest to fob me off.

Despite everything I still remained resolute in my determination not to engage another solicitor. As I battled on, my thoughts would periodically return to Murdoch. I'd tried his office another twice and on the final occasion had pressed them for his personal number.

"I can't divulge such information Mrs Palmer," he'd said in an abrupt manner before putting the phone down on me.

I'd wracked my brains trying to remember where I'd put the crumpled old business card Murdoch had given me outside the County Hotel. I knew I wouldn't have deliberately thrown it away, my intention would have been to keep it in case I might need it at a later date yet I'd had the upheaval of two house moves since then and I wasn't the world's best at filing information and keeping it safe. I knew it would be like finding a needle in a haystack and yet I knew I would never find it unless I jumped into the haystack. And so I began my search on a wet Sunday morning and vowed that I wouldn't give up until I had exhausted all possibilities. The house was literally ransacked in the process, handbags, purses, draws and cupboards were scattered out onto tables ,beds and floors. I'd been at it for almost three hours and sat at the end of my bed feeling exhausted and considered a glass of wine. My eyes fell on the pile of legal files sat at the foot of my bed. It made sense. Could it be hidden in there?

I spent a good hour on the bedroom floor meticulously wading through each file, sheet by sheet. I'd almost given up the ghost when I came across a poly pocket full of hand written notes I'd made at one point or another. I tipped the packet onto the floor, there must have been over a hundred notes in there and I started to read a few of them. I'd turned over no more than half a dozen scraps of paper when it seemed to appear out of the blue, slipping out from a folded sheet of paper onto the floor, face up, Simon Murdoch's embossed name standing out boldly in black ink. I held it to my chest for a good minute as if it were a precious keepsake I'd recovered my heart pounding with relief. As I tapped the numbers into my phone it occurred to me that the number could have changed. It had been three years since he gave me the card.

My heart was firmly in my mouth as I waited for him to answer, I knew I was taking liberties ringing him on his private number on a Sunday and felt a little awkward although it didn't stop me from hanging onto the phone listening to the dial tone ring out which was a good sign. At the least the number was still in service. It seemed to take forever for him to pick up and I could feel my heart banging out of my chest as I waited, then relief flooded through every pore of my body as I heard his voice.

"Hello can I help you?"

An embarrassment swept over me, it was a Sunday.

'I'm sorry to disturb you Mr Murdoch, you may remember me, its Mrs Annette Palmer and you gave me advice on a potential appeal I hoped to lodge against my final divorce settlement."

He remained silent prompting me to sketch in a little more of the detail.

"If you remember, I believed my ex-husband had inherited his mother's estate and he and his sister had set up some sort of secret trust to ensure it was kept out of the divorce settlement."

Bingo the penny dropped.

"Yes Mrs Palmer, I remember your case very clearly, indeed I do."

I let out a deep sigh of relief into my cupped hand.

I picked up from the lilt in his voice that he was keen to hear what I had to say which dispelled my initial awkwardness.

"I need your help and I am more than happy to pay for your time Mr Murdoch, if you…"

He cut me off dead in my tracks.

"Mrs Palmer, you could save a little time and money by getting to the point of your call, let's not worry about any fee until we know if I can be of any help to you."

There was a softness in his voice that I could only interpret as tiredness, maybe I'd interrupted a Sunday snooze but nevertheless I continued on my mission giving him a blow by blow account of events, not least the fact I'd found evidence my ex-husband was in receipt of his mother's estate.

He listened intently as I banged on interjecting with an occasional 'yes' which assured me he was still on the line. The grand finale of my briefing being the fact I was now in possession of the Land Registry documents that proved Stuart was the owner of his Mother's land and property and that it had been transferred to him for nil consideration.

"Are you sure the evidence you have in your possession is authentic Mrs Palmer?" he questioned.

"Yes Mr Murdoch I have the documents here in front of me. They are official copies from the Land Registry."

"When is the hearing Mrs Palmer?" he said, I detected an urgency in his voice.

"Tomorrow morning 11 am," I replied, the panic rising in me as I said the words out loud.

"Oh shit," he muttered.

"Exactly," I said. "That's why I'm calling you on a Sunday, I'm so sorry."

There was a brief pause before he spoke.

"You must understand Mrs Palmer I can only offer advice on the information you've given me this evening and without having your case file or the evidence to hand it is very difficult to ensure the advice I'm offering is correct."

I picked up the cautious tone. I knew he was reluctant to commit himself without seeing the facts on paper.

"Listen to me very carefully Mrs Palmer, the way I see it is there are two elements to this case, first you want to set aside the previous order based on fraud for what appears to be a deliberate intention to mislead the court. Secondly, there is the application to extend the maintenance payments. Am I correct?"

"Yes that's right."

I felt a shift in the burden of responsibility move from my shoulders to his but the feeling wouldn't last as he brought me back to reality.

"Do you realise how difficult your task is tomorrow?" he said like a scolding teacher then before allowing me a chance to respond he went on.

"You have no solicitor to guide you and quite frankly the law relating to an appeal is complex. I must warn you Mrs Palmer it is very rare indeed for a Judge to grant you a right to appeal, very rare." he added for good measure as my heart sank to the floor.

He was painting a clear picture, the odds were not stacked in my favour.

"I understand what you're telling me Mr Murdoch," I said, "yet we both know my ex-husband lied to me and the court, I can't let it go."

The flatness in my voice was all too evident, I knew he'd heard it too. Not wanting to dampen my spirits any further he threw me a lifeline.

"We'll do the best we can Mrs Palmer. I am going to put some notes together for you and I will email them across to you in the morning at 9am. You must read everything I have written down very carefully. You have your work cut out so it is imperative you follow my instruction to the letter."

"Yes."

I was almost speechless, I'd never expected this.

"I must go now I have a family reunion tonight but remember you must read my notes, follow them to the letter and ring me after you have read them."

"Yes, thank you so much, we'll speak tomorrow." I said in a hesitant voice as the feeling of fear engulfed me once more.

"Don't thank me yet Mrs Palmer," he said, "the day ahead of you is not going to be an easy one."

"Thank you so much, I don't know how to thank you enough."

"Good Luck Mrs Palmer, you are going to need it."

48

Murdoch's email and the attachment hit my inbox in at 7.34 am the following morning. I couldn't quite believe it as I read and reread and studied the five page document full of advice, suggestions and sound reasoning. It must have taken him hours to prepare. At nine o'clock I called him and he spoke to me for well over forty minutes not once mentioning any fees or costs, but time and time again he reminded me what a daunting task I faced to get the Judge to consider suspending the original financial court order pending an appeal. I asked him several times what my chances were but he wouldn't commit himself. I took notes as I spoke to him and towards the end of the conversation I actually felt as if everything was sinking in and there was a part of me that ,although nervous, was looking forward to the fight ahead. I thanked him enormously and he asked me to call him as soon as the hearing ended.

"Be lucky," he said as the conversation came to a close.

"I don't know how to thank you," I said.

"No need for any thank you at this stage Mrs Palmer, just get in there and do your best."

Judge Rutledge had a cocky, self-assured manner about him. I'd quickly came to the conclusion the moment I'd clapped eyes on him. He casually reclined in his high back leather chair scanning my Statement of Affairs, his paws quickly flicking through its contents nonchalantly.

I took my seat and unloaded my bundle of paper on the desk in front of me. I knew the drill well enough to realise not a word would be spoken until Rutledge opened his mouth and commenced proceedings. I used the stillness of the moment to compose myself as I cast a glance at Stuart and Steedman who were merely an arms stretch across the table from me. They appeared in relaxed mode, confident, perhaps even a little arrogant. They had no idea of the time bomb I was about to unleash, a time bomb sitting just a few feet away from them.

And yet it was clearly apparent that I posed no real threat to either of them, they thought the day's events would be merely an inconvenient formality. There was no lawyer by my side, no barrister, no one fighting my corner. It was going to be all too easy for them. I must have cast a lonely, vulnerable image sitting without a legal firewall by my side to take the brunt of the heat now heading my way.

I became aware that Judge Rutledge had cleared his throat, it was time for proceedings to begin and as I looked up I could see the he was looking straight at me.

"So you want your maintenance order extended Mrs Palmer, is that right?"

"Yes it is sir, my income is very low and substantially less than Judge Porter predicted it would be three years ago."

"First things first Mrs Palmer, let's not race ahead of ourselves. Just answer the question."

He looked up and gave a little grin, I noticed Stuart smiled right on cue and even Steedman allowed himself a little laugh.

"I know you're keen to put your legal skills to the test."

He turned his attention back to me as he browsed the statement of affairs that was still clasped in his hands.

"I'll let you start Mrs Palmer, as you're the Appellant."

His tone was mocking, sexist, patronising. It was all too evident and I reluctantly acknowledged the course the proceedings were going to take. He was trying to make a show and highlight my legal inadequacies and didn't care for the idea of some layperson prancing into his court acting like a modern day Erin Brockovich thinking she could outwit the legal fraternity. The Judge was on Steedman's side, part of the old boys network and was determined to out me and knock me down to size.

No pressure I thought as all eyes were focused in my direction. I took my time to look at the bundle of papers I'd brought into court.

On top of the pile lay Murdoch's email he'd sent that morning. I focussed on the words he'd drummed into me earlier in the day.

There are two elements to the case, you want to extend the Periodic Payments Order and set aside the original financial order.

I was lost in my thoughts, my mind playing over the crucial aspects of our conversation that morning.

"Mrs Palmer sorry to interrupt you but it is only a thirty-minute hearing."

Deal with the variation of maintenance first, it's a good place to start.

"Mrs Palmer."

My mouth was so dry it caused the inside of my lips to stick to the front of my teeth preventing me from speaking. I could almost feel Murdoch's presence behind me prodding me in the back.

Get up there and do it Mrs Palmer.

I took a deep breath. I stood. I spoke.

"I would like to make an application to extend the Periodic Payments Order made in 2012."

The burden is on you to show the judge you have struggled over the last three years and you need to convince him that the new job offers no certainty or security.

I didn't hold back in telling Rutledge that although I had a job, the salary was significantly less than the amount Judge Porter had forecast I'd be earning three years after my divorce and I didn't omit to mention I was still working my probationary period, drumming in the fact my future was very uncertain. Rutledge appeared to be nodding in all the right places that propelled me to continue my onslaught as I raised the subject of my daughter and her needs.

"Alexandra is still a dependent. She's in her third year at university and since July 2012 my ex-husband has not contributed one single penny towards her upkeep."

As soon as I'd mentioned Stuart's shortcomings Steedman raised himself from his sluggish slumber and pounced.

"Mr Palmer paid CSA payments until his daughter reached the age of eighteen as was his legal requirement and I understand Alexandra inherited money from her Aunt which could be used to support her through university."

The smarmy bastard had fallen right into my trap.

I raised my eyes in the direction of my ex-husband, shaking my head in mock disbelief.

Stick to the task in hand and do not turn it into a pub brawl.

My response was measured.

"Surely my ex-husband and his lawyer are aware that his Aunt specifically stipulated in her Will that the girls weren't to receive their inheritance until they reached the age of twenty five."

"Is this right Mr Steedman?" The Judge questioned.

Steedman fumbled with his notes.

"I believe so Sir."

"And how old is Alexandra?

"Alexandra is twenty one Sir," he said, almost apologetically.

It was the turning point, a huge turning point in which the Judge realised that although not legally trained I had in fact spent a little time on my research and that Steedman and his client had perhaps approached the proceedings a little more casually than the Judge would have liked. He made a few notes as Steedman and Stuart whispered a few words to each other.

I seized the moment.

"Your Honour, I request an extension of the periodic payments to capitalize my claim under section 37 of the Matrimonial Clauses Act 1973."

It was only one sentence but the impact was extraordinary. It was as if the whole courtroom had been given a shake. Steedman sat bolt upright in his chair as Stuart lowered his eyes to the floor and began shaking his head and the Judge leaned forward as if at last he was taking me seriously.

He spoke.

"Let us move on, you want to capitalise maintenance if you are awarded an extension?"

"Yes that is correct," I responded. "Mr Palmer has failed to complete the detailed Form E and has only provided six months of bank and credit card statements."

I paused as Rutledge padded his hand around the pile of paper on his desk looking for his copy of Steedman's submission. Once he had it to hand I continued.

"I have asked my ex-husband a number of supplementary questions and he has failed to answer any of them. I would ask that Mr Palmer is ordered to complete the detailed Form E and provide twelve months bank statements and answer the questions I have asked."

My questions caused an immediate reaction from Steedman, as I knew it would. The relaxed manner was no longer evident and there was even a hint of agitation present in his response.

"As I have already stated to Mrs Palmer my client has disclosed enough information to show he has sufficient income to meet any reasonable Maintenance Order the court imposes."

Rutledge scanned the paper work, no doubt noting the healthy balance in Stuart's bank account and his monthly income.

"I believe Mr Steedman is right," he said. "If we decide to extend the maintenance period Mr Palmer has shown the court sufficient evidence that he is financially able to meet it." He lifted his glasses onto the brow of his head. "Anything else Mrs Palmer?"

Categorically state that you want to make an application to set aside the original financial order. Make sure you tell the Judge that they lied and that you believe fraud has taken place.

I reached into the poly pocket on the desk in front of me and retrieved two bundles containing the Land Registry Documents I'd photocopied that morning, the fresh smell of the ink still lingered on the paper as I lifted them out of the sleeve.

"Yes, your Honour, I would like to make an application to revoke the original financial order."

The judge leaned back in his seat and smiled as he spoke. Patronisation was back on the agenda.

"Oh would you indeed?"

"Yes Sir."

Stuart leaned over to Steedman as he whispered into his ear, a smug grin was plastered across his face.

"You believe that the honourable Judge Porter has somehow slipped up Mrs Palmer, you wish to challenge his decision despite his years of experience and legal training?"

I shook my head. I was in dangerous territory.

Don't criticise the original Judge. There was no evidence of the fraud, the Judge based his decision relating to the facts available at that time.

"I believe his decision was correct at the time Sir."

"Good, I'm glad to hear it."

The judge made an air circle with his right hand urging me to continue.

I took a deep breath yet I was now speaking with an air of confidence.

"I accused my husband of lying and I accused him of fraud. He said he did not inherit his mother's estate and that everything went to his sister in law. At the time I said it was a scam and I predicted that within a short period of time the truth would come out."

Show the Judge a copy of Porter's Draft Judgement.

I retrieved Porter's Judgement from the file and handed it across to Rutledge, all the while the words continuing to flow from my mouth.

"Mr Palmer insisted at the time he was not a beneficiary in his Mother's Will and had no interest in making a claim against her estate."

I told the Judge that his Mother's estate was valued at £1.6 million and if Stuart had inherited that amount of money it would have made a huge difference to my maintenance settlement. As the Judge studied the judgement I read him page 13, paragraph 2, Judge Porter's summary.

I focussed in on the paragraph and read it verbatim.

"I am satisfied that there is no evidence to suggest that there is any arrangement now or in the future between the husband and Tina Palmer to transfer any of the estate into his name. A mere suspicion on the part of the wife of such an arrangement is not enough to establish a case on the balance of probabilities."

I waited patiently as the Judge went through his notes. He pulled out a piece of A4 paper from the bundle in front of him.

"Yes," he said. "I have it here, specifically Mr Palmer's mothers property and a valuable piece of land in Northumberland?"

"Yes Sir."

He looked up.

"Are you telling me that Mr Palmer now owns the land and property?"

Steedman jumped up.

"Objection Sir."

"Sit down Mr Bentley," the Judge snapped.

"Yes Sir," I said.

He turned to address me again.

"And you have evidence."

"Yes Sir."

As I spoke I handed Rutledge the copies of the Land Registry documents. I also slid a copy over to Steedman. It was the moment I'd been waiting for since entering the room.

"These are the Land Registry documents for Jesmond, his Mother's home and for the land at Redburn. They clearly show that the land and the property were transferred from Tina Palmer to Mr Stuart Palmer for nil consideration."

The Judge looked up in exasperation as he raised his voice.

"Nil consideration Mr Steedman?" he questioned, "your client didn't even buy them?"

Stuart had turned a ghostly shade of white. Not so fucking smug now, I thought. I could see Stuart was beginning to fall apart as he sank lower into his seat, his face turning red with rage as he spat his dummy out of his pram, throwing the documents back in Steedman's direction and vigorously shaking his head.

I went straight for the jugular.

"Sir, I wish to apply to set aside the original Order based on the clear evidence that a fraud has taken place, a fraud that has impacted heavily on my standard of living for the last three years."

Steedman who had been struck dumb since I'd handed him the Land Registry documents eventually found his voice. I could see from the contorted expression on his face he was consumed with rage which was not the slimy little ferrets usual disposition, his composure was always intact, yet not on this particular day.

"At the time of the original hearing my client had no knowledge of the fact Tina Palmer had any intention of handing the land and property over to him."

"Did he not Mr Steedman?" I piped up, determined he was not going to make light of the situation, as was his usual ploy.

"I warned the court at the time this would happen but no one would listen to me."

I leaned across the table slightly, bringing force to my words. I was savouring every moment.

"Your client has committed fraud Mr Steedman and you had full knowledge of that fraud, there was a deliberate intention to mislead the court."

The reaction was as I had expected, my ex-husband completely lost it as he jumped to his feet and spat out his words.

"You stupid bitch, Tina Palmer has a free choice, she chose to transfer the land and property to me, there was no agreement between us."

And yet his words were false, insincere and it was clear he hadn't even convinced himself let alone the Judge. I didn't flinch, the fact was I enjoyed his reaction, I could feel his fear radiating across the table. The man was terrified. Fucking coward, how had it taken me all these years to see him for what he really was? He continued to shout at me in a fit of rage, he wanted a reaction. He got none.

Rutledge ordered him to sit down.

"Mr Palmer can you be quiet or I will have you removed from the room. That is quite disgraceful behaviour."

He looked at his watch, time was running out.

"Can I ask you to tie things up Mr Steedman, this was only supposed to last thirty minutes. Why hasn't Mr Palmer completed form E and why has he not answered Mrs Palmer's questions which appear perfectly reasonable to me?"

The tide had turned in my favour and Steedman's frustration was almost palatable as he tried to string a weak statement together with no conviction whatsoever. I had dropped a bombshell into their laps and everything else was of no significance. I knew as the hearing dragged on Stuart was gradually falling apart. I'd been married to him too many years not to spot the tell tale signs. His right eye was beginning to twitch ever so slightly and his fingernails were pressed hard against his mouth as he tried to resist the urge to bite them down to the skin. Eventually Rutledge stopped Steedman mid-sentence.

"I think I've heard enough. It is pointless at this time to proceed with the application to extend the periodic maintenance payments after what we have just heard. Mrs Palmer has requested permission to appeal the original order, that's the decision I need to focus on, nothing else."

The Judge left the room.

We sat in silence for what seemed like an eternity and I thought back to my early morning call with Murdoch and one of the final things he said.

You're unlikely to be given permission to appeal Mrs Palmer, don't build your hopes up.

And yet as I looked across the desk and analysed the body language of the two goons sitting opposite me I sensed victory, I could smell it, I could sense it. The door opened in the far corner of the room and the Judge walked in.

"Mrs Palmer, you have exactly two weeks from today to make your application for permission to appeal the original Order. If you miss that deadline then your right to make that application will be lost for ever."

He leaned forward on his desk, his slightly elevated position peering down on me, the shadow of his dark frame intimidated me.

"Let me warn you again Mrs Palmer, the likelihood of you being given that permission to appeal is remote, and even if you get over that high hurdle you are unlikely to win the appeal. I suggest you take this two week period to consider your options. You will start to incur legal costs and waste the limited resources you have at your disposal on a battle you probably won't win."

I considered his advice for all of two seconds, go and fuck yourself Rutledge, I thought as I gave a weary smile and thanked him for his time.

Stuart and Steedman bolted out of the court at break neck speed and made their way directly into one of the vacant conference rooms dotted along the corridor just outside the Judge's Chambers.

I sauntered along with no sense of urgency. I was only heading back to work and I was in no great rush to get there. For the first time in weeks my spirits had been lifted and I wanted to savour the moment for a little while longer. I stopped at the room where Stuart and Steedman had entered and took my time to peer through the glass-panelled wall. I couldn't hear a sound through the sound proof glass yet I knew from Stuart's body language he was shouting and Steedman was trying to calm him. The pair of them were totally engrossed in their heightened conversation and totally unaware of my presence and just watching their obvious discord gave me a small sense of satisfaction. I turned and walked away, there was another matter I needed to take care of. Murdoch would be waiting for my call it was spot on the time I said I would ring him.

"Mr Murdoch its Mrs Palmer, I've just come out of court and the Judge has given me two weeks to submit my request for permission to appeal the Order."

The line went silent for a second before there was an exuberant cheer from the other end of the line. It threw me for a second, it wasn't a characteristic I associated with Murdoch.

"I can't believe it Mrs Palmer, well done. I didn't think you'd get this far, it's quite unbelievable."

I gave him the condensed version of the day as he listened carefully. He told me several times that although it was a victory of sorts I still had a massive uphill struggle, first I had to win the right to appeal and if I was lucky enough to get that far he warned me winning an appeal was almost unheard of.

As the conversation drew to a conclusion he gave me one final piece of advice.

"I urge you Mrs Palmer, if your ex-husband offers to settle out of court, you snatch his hand off."

49

In truth I hadn't known where to start on my appeal. Rutledge had given me two weeks to make my application but with no real clue of what to include in the paperwork that I had to supply to the court it hadn't taken long for me to feel totally overwhelmed at the prospect.

For the first five days I did nothing but procrastinate, promising myself each evening, after I'd recovered from my days shift at work, I'd make a start. Although I had no great love for solicitors, I'd wished I had one acting for my and I could offload my mountain of files and say there you go get on with it.

Murdoch had made an offer to prepare the Grounds of Appeal that I knew were prerequisites to making my application to appeal. His offer had been tempting and I may well have taken him up on it if I hadn't been informed of his fee structure. With Christmas just around the corner and no savings to my name I couldn't justify spending such an amount on a course of action which I'd been told on more than one occasion I had no real chance of winning. Nevertheless, when I told Murdoch I was going it alone he still sent me an attachment by email on how I should draft the documents and had even taken the time to list the relevant cases he said might offer weight to my argument.

You have my phone number if you get stuck Mrs Palmer, were the closing comments on his last email. He may well regret those words I'd thought as I filed his email in the Murdoch folder for future reference. The man was a saint.

On day six, after a generous measure of gin and tonic to calm my nerves, I eventually got down to business, spreading my numerous case files across the kitchen table. My first task was to reacquaint myself with the contents of my case notes. No mean task, there was so much to bloody read and I spent most of that evening and the next looking through paper after paper. Eventually after referring to Murdoch's notes and resorting to surfing the Internet, where I found a helpful YouTube tutorial on the subject, I set about my work. The job had been an arduous one and most evenings I'd found myself burning the midnight oil, pot of coffee by my side, trying to eloquently formulate into the written word how Stuart and Tina Palmer had tried to mislead the court through their fraudulent act. I'd only fully appreciated the enormity of my chore at the eleventh hour when the deadline was merely hours away. I saved my draft word document ready to be printed off and then started to work on the Appellants Notice, a mandatory court form.

For a skilled solicitor I had no doubt it would have been a doddle to complete yet for me it proved to be a little more tricky as I tried to decipher exactly what the bullet point questions were asking of me. To top off my trauma, the court submission required three copies of everything. Looking at the growing pile of papers I began to realise there was a vast amount of photocopying to be done too. I had to resort to using my ancient old printer, which had the capacity to copy one sheet of paper at a time and my heart sank as I scanned the first page knowing there was 114 pages to follow. Surely the bloody the ink would hold out long enough to complete the task.

I'd been awake for the best part of the night, printing, checking then rechecking each bundle in preparation for submission to the court the following morning. I hadn't made it to bed at all and my head was still slumped across the kitchen table in a sound sleep when Alexandra marched down the stairs the next morning in search of some breakfast. I practically jumped out of my skin as the sound of her heavy foot padded across the kitchen floor.

"It's 9am Mum, aren't you getting ready for work?" she said in a mocking tone as she eyed me up and down with a disapproving look on her face.

I raised my aching head from the table, the last thing on my mind was work, my application had to be into the court before10am and I was still half asleep and wearing my clothes from the previous day. With Rutledge's words resonating in my head 'If you miss that deadline, then your right to make that application will be lost for good.' I hot footed it into the shower, dressed quickly and literally threw myself out of the front door.

Thankfully Alexandra had agreed to be my chauffeur which saved me time and with the morning rush hour traffic having long since subsided we were able to speed along to the Court House without delay. I abandoned Alexandra as we pulled up to a stop at a set of red traffic lights directly opposite the entrance.

"Bye chic, love ya," I said before sprinting across the main road and up the steep steps into the Court. To my amazement I'd managed to make it as I noticed the clock on the wall read 9.57. I walked up to the desk and handed over the three hefty bundles to the court clerk. Once the Appeal bundles were in his hands and I held the receipt of their time of delivery in mine, I gave a heavy sigh of relief.

"Have a good weekend," he said cheerfully.

Miraculously I had made it and now I was at the mercy of the court but for the first time in a long while I breathed a deep sigh of relief and allowed myself to relax.

The feeling of peace and calm lasted most of that day or at least until I was sitting in front of the telly that every evening, cup of coffee in hand, watching the six o'clock news. It was Fiona Bruce, the BBC anchor newsreader who caught my attention as she recited directly from autocue the day's headlines. The newsreaders sharp crystal voice reverberated in my ear as I tried to listen to her over Alexandra's attempts to tell me about the events of her day.

"Mum are you listening to me, I got sixty five percent for my last essay."

I tried to listen, this was important.

"Shush for a second Alexandra," I snapped as I nudged her out of the way.

My ears had already filtered out the sound of her voice in an effort to listen to the news report which had attracted my attention as I began to realise it bore an uncanny similarity to my own circumstances. Fiona Bruce stood directly outside the London Law Courts. It was clearly a huge news item when the leading anchor was transmitting in real time on location. She braced herself against the cold autumnal weather her words echoed out as I sat captivated by what she was saying.

'In a landmark judgement the Supreme Court has unanimously

granted two women, Alison Sharland and Varsha Gohil the right to appeal their financial settlement in their divorce due to their husbands not providing full disclosure at the time of their original financial settlement.'

Grabbing the remote control I turned up the volume just in time to see events from earlier in the day being replayed. The camera panned to two ladies as they left the court building, their faces beaming. Mrs Sharland stepped forward to a swarm of awaiting journalists. The cameras were clicking, reporters jostling for position as she made a statement.

'I'm relieved and delighted that the Supreme Court Judges have ruled in our favour. I hope that their decision sends out a message to everyone going through a divorce that they cannot lie in the family courts and get away with it. My legal battle has never been about the money, it has always been about the principle.'

Her statement went on yet already her words were blurring away as my thoughts began to compare their circumstances to my own situation. Would it make a difference to my case I thought, as my eyes remained glued to the screen. The coverage had switched back to real time, now a leading Divorce Lawyer was giving his view on the days ruling, I turned the volume up even louder.

'This ruling will open the floodgates for other women whose husbands have tried to mislead the court and hide their assets. It is sending out a clear message, dishonesty in any legal proceedings should not be tolerated. The Supreme Court has confirmed that the Family Court is not an exception to the general rule and that it is no more acceptable to lie there than it is in any other court.

"Too fucking right," I muttered under my breath.

It seemed so surreal that on the day I'd submitted my application to appeal there had been this landmark ruling. As I powered up my computer and searched around I eventually hit upon both judgements that must have been released almost simultaneously to the ruling being handed down. I practically fell off my chair as I read the detail of both cases, in particular Mrs Sharland's situation, which had all the hallmarks of my own. A lengthy marriage, three children, one of which had special needs, the couple separated and soon after she discovered fraudulent none disclosure by the husband. As I read on I became even more convinced these two cases must surely add some bearing on my application. I knew at that precise moment I needed to make the Judge, who would be dealing with my case, aware of the outcome of the Supreme Court Judgements. He would likely know anyway but I couldn't take that chance. It was national news, rocking the world of every family law solicitor up and down the country. Steedman would be notified and he was well aware of his client's attempts to defraud the court. I would submit copies of the judgements, pointing out their relevance to my case. But it was Friday evening and I could do nothing. The deadline had passed. Would they even except any additional information? I printed out three copies of the Sharland and Gohil judgements, preparing a covering letter requesting the documents be added to my Appeal application and reached for the wine bottle.

When Monday morning arrived, instead of heading to work I made a detour to the Law Courts on the quayside. I came face to face with a grumpy slip of a girl who clearly had the Monday morning blues. I knew I had to tread carefully, I needed her to add the additional notes to my application and because it was past the deadline date I wasn't sure the clerks would be prepared to do that for me. I'd decided to play it dumb, capitalizing on the fact I was a litigant in person who had no legal knowledge of the system. Judging from the girl's hostile expression it was going to be a challenge to convince her. As she spoke her rough, unrelenting voice confirmed my suspicions.

"Sorry, you can't add any additional information if you've already submitted your application,"

As she turned to a colleague for help I noticed her name tag. Jade, I'm here to help you.

"Julie, this lady's made an application to Appeal an Order, the deadline was Friday, it's too late to add additional notes innit?"

"She's too late darling," Julie called back in agreement

I wasn't going to take no for an answer.

"I would be extremely grateful if you could add these judgements, it would really help my case." I pleaded

"It's not the normal protocol," she snapped back.

"I'm so sorry to ask, I'm a litigant in person so I wasn't aware I couldn't add anything after the deadline date."

Jade threw an unsympathetic look as she shrugged her shoulders.

"Doesn't matter if you are a lawyer or a barrister or even the Pope, rules are rules and we can't accept anything after the deadline.

There's nothing you can say or do that will change my decision."

I looked into Jade's eyes. I read pain and more. There was bitterness, hostility, they were devoid of hope and she was here to do her job, nothing more. I guessed she had a family in the rougher suburbs of Newcastle, a single parent for sure. It was time to change tact.

I let out a sigh, leaned forward and spoke in a barely audible whisper.

"Look Jade love, if I can add these papers to my appeal I might just be able to extend my maintenance payments from the bastard who has ruined my life."

Jade looked up.

"He walked away with the younger model, cast me and his girls to one side and left me without a fucking pot to piss in."

Did I detect a slight shake of her head, sympathy, a crack in her hard exterior?

"How long were you married?" she asked.

"Twenty three years."

"The cunt," she said.

"Quite," I replied, taken aback.

"They are all a bunch of cunts," she said. "Give it here, I'll add it to the bundle."

I was speechless as Jade reached across the desk and took the paperwork.

She rubbed the back of my hand.

"I hope it helps pet, I really do."

I watched as Jade stood and walked away with my papers in her hand. She stopped at Julie's desk and whispered a few words and then walked away out of sight through a door on the far side of the office.

There was a God after all, I thought to myself.

As I made my way out of the courthouse, my hands free from the copies of the Supreme Court Judgements I'd carried into the building minutes earlier, it suddenly dawned on me that for the second time in a matter of days I was walking out of that court house feeling I had achieved the impossible.

I expected it to take weeks to hear back from the court because my past experience had taught me it was usually the way of things within the Family Law Courts. So as I picked up the letter from the hall table as I stepped through the front door after another long day at my corporate sweatshop I casually opened the envelope. The heading suddenly leapt from the page. In the Family Court at Newcastle Upon Tyne.

I'd only submitted my application 10 days previously, surely not?

I must have read that one page document at least a half dozen times.

IT IS ORDERED THAT

1. The application for permission to appeal out of time and the application for variation of maintenance are listed before The Honourable Mr Justice Poulton for directions.
2. The parties shall submit a bundle (including the required case management documentation) in advance of the hearing in accordance with PD27A
3. The substantive hearing is likely to be listed before a High Court Judge within the next 90 days, dates to be confirmed.

As I sat at the kitchen table gulping my coffee, the letter fixed flat on the table in front of me. I read and reread the words. It appeared to be good news. I came to the conclusion they were telling me in long winded legal jargon that a Judge named Poulton was ultimately going to say whether I could or could not appeal my case. Even though it was in black and white I still didn't quite trust my own opinion so I messaged Murdoch. My message was short and to the point.

Can you clarify the meaning of the attached letter I received from the court today?

Annette

Within five minutes I heard the ping of my phone informing me there was a new message in my inbox. Impatiently I opened the envelope icon, it was Murdoch blunt and to the point.

Annette

It's great news, you have been listed before the Resident High Court Judge to plead your case for appeal. This is VERY unusual, but daily costs are now being incurred – YOU SHOULD TRY AND SETTLE THIS WITH THE OTHER SIDE - If you lose you will have to pay the costs of the other side which will be at least £10000. Please contact Steedman and tell him you are willing to settle. You have won the first battle but don't try and go it alone and win the war. I urge you.

I read Murdoch's words of caution more than once. I had respect for the man there was no doubt, yet my determination was resolute.

Fuck Steedman and fuck Stuart, fuck the lot of them.

Hell would freeze over before I'd pick up the phone to Steedman and tell him that I was prepared to settle.

50

I arrived at the courthouse at 1.15pm and it occurred to me as I climbed the steep steps to the building lugging a heavy load of files in my wake that it had been the first time in my entire life I'd managed to be early for anything. As I entered the building somewhat nervously I noticed the barristers and solicitors mingling in the corridors with their clients and my anxiety notched up a little. I questioned what the hell I was doing there. It sank in. I was alone with not a soul in the world to fight my cause. I bit my lip, closed my eyes and took a deep breath as a feeling of overwhelming fear washed over me. I walked over to the reception area and as I signed in my hands were visibly shaking, almost uncontrollably as I dropped the pen twice in quick succession. I had to give myself a firm talking to as I made my way up the stairs to the Family Court, the same mantra playing over in over in my head like a broken record, your decision, fucking get on with it.

Murdoch had hinted that an out of court settlement may result prior to the hearing but since we'd received notification of the date of the application to appeal, both Stuart and his seedy solicitor had been conspicuous by their silence. There had been only one enquiry on their part, Steedman had been keen to know if I intended having legal representation before the Honourable Justice Poulton while at the same time notifying me that they were wheeling in the big boys, a barrister called Mr Quinn of Garden Chambers, London. I didn't reply and left the bastard guessing, playing him at his own game but the realisation that it was three against one really hit me. I didn't want or need the challenge of having to compete against a skilled barrister, it was bad enough dealing with Steedman.

I dropped a quick message to Murdoch, it would do no harm asking if he had any knowledge of the man. Murdoch wasted no time replying. His words had made my blood run cold.

Your ex-husband is a VERY crafty man, his barrister works from the same chambers as His Honourable Justice Poulton. Barrister and Judge know each other very well and he is one of the best Family Law specialists in the UK. He is expensive, I suspect your husband will be paying a premium for his services, circa 20K. I urge you to make contact with Steedman and settle out of court ASAP.

And as I walked into court I couldn't help thinking how happy team Stuart would be in just a few minutes time when the reality that I was completely on my own sank in.

As I took my seat in the formal court room I so wished I could have turned back the clock, swallowed my pride and contacted Steedman to discuss an out of court settlement. But no, I had said fuck them all.

As I laid my court bundle out in front of me, fuck them all didn't seem such a good strategy after all.

What chance did I realistically have pitted against an experienced solicitor and a barrister who was evidently in cahoots with the Judge? I was a middle-aged housewife with no legal experience in opposition against a QC and a solicitor with over fifty years legal years between them. It was David and Goliath, Custer's last stand, the siege of the Alamo, who the fuck had I been kidding?

Desperate to see the opposition, my eyes instinctively wandered across to Quinn who was sitting on the bench parallel to my own. Steedman and Stuart sat directly behind him. I could see my ex-husband tongue lashing Steedman as usual but there was something erroneous about his whole demeanour. I stared for a few seconds and then suddenly it struck me. Stuart was terrified, he was fucking petrified and it was written all over him from top to toe. His once glowing complexion looked almost sallow as if he was going to throw up and I could almost smell his fear as it seeped across the room and it lifted my spirits for a moment. That was until my gaze finally rested upon the sharp cut Quinn, with the Saville Row pin stripe suit and tortoise framed spectacles sitting on the bridge of his nose looking every inch the legal guru. I couldn't stop my eyes rolling to the ceiling in despair as my thoughts inevitably moved onto the girls.

How the hell would they react if I lost my case and had to find close to £20000 to cover their Fathers legal fees? I didn't have to ponder long. I only had to recall the conversation we'd had a few days previously. I could vividly recall three sets of bewildered eyes staring at me in disbelief when I told them I was definitely going ahead. I remember not giving a damn about their opinions or feelings, my motherly compassion lost as my determination to see my day in court was resolute and apparent in every word I uttered.

"The court is taking my case very seriously," I argued in my defence, "and my application to appeal is being heard in front of Justice Poulton. If he gives me permission to appeal I am going to fight on," I said as I continued to prepare the evening meal trying to make light of the situation.

It was Alexandra who was the first to throw her hat into the ring.

"And how much is this all going to cost Mum? We've got no money left, can you not get it in to your head the only thing we own is the house?"

Her index and middle finger pointed to her head like a loaded revolver, her actions as expressive as her spoken word.

I tried to fob her off, reluctant to shade in the details and tell her the brutal facts that if I lost the case I'd have to fork out thousands of pounds that I didn't have. As it happened no words were needed, her razor sharp mind had figured out my little omission straightaway. No doubt past experiences had taught her there was always financial consequences when solicitors were involved.

She wasted no time telling me what she thought.

"Mum, if we have to sell this house to pay your debts I will never forgive you," she looked towards her sisters for support and they nodded in agreement, "in fact I'll bloody well hate you."

She stood as she slammed her empty coffee cup onto the table. Her mute sisters stood in a show of unity and all three took off out of the kitchen together, the front door slamming in their wake. I knew her words had been slightly over dramatic, she'd probably hate me for a fortnight and no doubt forgiveness would eventually follow yet the sentiment was heart felt, they wanted to draw a line under the whole thing and move on and I knew that going back to court wasn't going to allow that to happen.

I was snapped back to the present as the court usher raised his voice.

"Court rise," the court usher barked as Justice Poulton walked into the court room, caped and gowned as if he was going to pass the death sentence. I was taken aback slightly as I had only been used to seeing the Judges suited and booted, never in full court regalia, his crimson gown a stark contrast to the normal bland, grey surroundings.

We stood to attention as Poulton took his seat and nodded for us to take ours. Once the formalities were over and the caps had been doffed, proceedings began in earnest. All eyes were on me at this point.

Poulton was well aware of my legal naivety and was quick to offer guidance and with no edge to his manner.

In a firm but gentle voice he was the first to speak.

"Mrs Palmer you are up first, take as much time as you need to present your argument."

His eyes turned to Mr Quinn who sat at ease in his chair looking every inch like a man who wasn't the least bit threatened by his opposition.

"Mr Quinn, as Mrs Palmer is a litigant in person we need to help her as much as possible, she must be allowed to present her argument without interruption."

Both men gave each other a knowing glance before Quinn nodded in agreement.

The exchange unnerved me slightly. Was Quinn in the habit of shooting the opposition down in flames I thought as I raised myself gingerly from the seat. I held my nerve as I took to the stage, grit and determination set in and as my words began to flow all the inhibitions I'd had when I had entered the court melted away.

Apart from a faint buzzing sound, which I assumed to be the air conditioning, the only other sound heard above the stifling silences of the courtroom was my voice. My audience was still and captive as I relayed the chronology of our marriage and events leading to the appeal. When eventually I broached the subject of Olive Palmer's death and the implications on my divorce settlement, Quinn stirred in his seat. I could just about see him from the corner of my eye, rifling through his papers. I tried to stay focussed, I had practiced this speech a hundred times in front of the bedroom mirror and I had to get it out. I carried on as I raised my voice slightly in an attempt to drown out the rustle of the paper that appeared amplified in the stillness of the room.

"At the final hearing we were led to believe my husband had been disinherited by his mother, her estate in its entirety left to her daughter in law, Tina Palmer. My legal team and I warned the Court that his mother would never do this to her only surviving son."

I took another much needed breath.

"I told the court that my ex-husband would someday receive the lion's share of his mother's estate and this is now the case."

I paused for a fraction of a second to reclaim my breath. Poulton spoke, filling the void.

"Are you suggesting that Mr Palmer now owns his late mother's estate?"

Finding my voice I was eager to relay my version of events.

"He does your Honour and furthermore he has benefited from that estate as a result of fraud."

Quinn jumped to his feet.

"Objection."

The Judge looked at Quinn and signalled to him to sit down.

"Overruled Mr Quinn, let us hear what Mrs Palmer has to say."

Before he allowed me to continue he warned me not to point any fingers of accusation. He said it was an open court and I should be careful not to slander the character of my ex-husband with false and malicious statements.

"I am well aware of the law relating to slander Sir," I said.

"Very good," he replied, "then carry on."

"I believed at the time that there had been an agreement reached between my husband and Tina Palmer to ring fence Mrs Palmer's estate and keep it separate from the matrimonial finances."

Stuart let out a long exaggerated sigh in an attempt to put me off. It didn't.

"Mrs Palmer's estate was valued in excess of £1.6 million and he was well aware that if that kind of money had been taken into account at the final hearing it would have significantly altered the financial outcome."

Quinn was on his feet again like a terrier sniffing out a rat.

"Objection your honour, Mrs Palmer is not a mind reader and therefore cannot surmise what Judge Porter's decision would have been. There is no evidence of an arrangement between Tina Palmer and Mr Palmer, neither is there evidence of any deception being practiced," he gave a sarcastic smile, "Mrs Palmer has created this fanciful idea to meet her own ends."

He laughed dramatically at the end of his statement, causing Steedman to break out into a broad smile in an attempt to show his camaraderie to Quinn, who was now in full flow and still going.

"In order to demonstrate a misdemeanour the wife must have cogent evidence and there is none."

"Mr Quinn, I have the evidence in front of me as do you," I said.

My hand glided through the court bundle I'd painstakingly put together only nights before the hearing. Each page in the pack was committed to memory and it took little effort on my part to find the Land Registry documents which I held up in the air.

Quinn tried to gloss over them.

"Your Honour, they are Land Registry documents which show a simple transfer. It's hardly evidence of fraud."

I wanted to jump in but my attention was drawn to Judge Poulton who seemed more than interested in what I had provided him with. He read for a full minute before looking up over the top of his glasses.

"Transferred for nil consideration?" he questioned as he shook his head.

Quinn was caught flat-footed and started to confer with Steedman. I sat back patiently enjoying every second. Quinn could have the floor, Quinn could have as many minutes and as many words as he wanted but when it was my turn I was determined to make an impact.

He was backtracking making no attempt to hide the fact that the estate was in Stuart's name.

"It is irrelevant your honour, the law on inherited money is clear and not subject to equitable distribution. I fail to see the point of Mrs Palmer's claims."

His words were empty, almost meaningless as he quoted some Judge called Mostyn and his ruling on inherited assets. The Barrister from London was rambling, I knew it, the Judge knew it and team Steedman knew it too. I couldn't compete with his legal wrangling but he had fallen so easily into my net assuming that I was looking for a slice of Olive Palmer's estate.

I knew I had to hit the Judge with cold hard facts. I jumped in and reclaimed the stage much to Quinn's annoyance and surprise.

"I never wanted to make any claim against the capital your Honour. I'm simply stating that an inheritance of that size would have produced a substantial income at the time of my original settlement. That income would have impacted heavily on the maintenance payments for my family."

"So you keep saying," Quinn mumbled.

I kept quiet. The Judge had picked up a pen and I noticed that he was pushing a few buttons on a calculator. I half expected Quinn to jump in again but he remained seated.

I picked up the sheet of paper from my file.

"Sir," I said.

"Yes Mrs Palmer."

"I have an estimate of the income my husband could have received at the time of my settlement if he hadn't conned the court."

Quinn jumped up.

"Objection."

"Sit down Mr Quinn."

I held up the paper and read from it but in reality the figures were etched into my brain.

The Judge nodded in my direction. I kept it brief.

"Sir, I estimate that my husband's monthly net income would have be in the region of £17000 a month."

Steedman, Stuart and the bigwig barrister collapsed into collective fits of laughter, the ridiculous scene looked as if it had been almost choreographed. Even Judge Poulton couldn't suppress a smile.

He was the first to speak.

"Mrs Palmer, I do appreciate that you are a layperson when it comes to court proceedings but we must try to keep ourselves in the real world."

I walked over to where he sat and handed him a copy of the calculation.

His eyes settled on the figures as I spoke.

"My husband was a Company Accountant and his take home pay at the time was just short of £5000 per month, despite the two year old tax return he fobbed the court off with originally. I have evidence that he was cohabiting with Ms Maddison who at the time earned only slightly less than him. I'm reliably informed she took home £4000 a month."

"Objection your honour, pure hearsay."

"Sustained," he said, "cohabitation is very hard to prove Mrs Palmer."

"Agreed," I said, "but he walked out on his family to be with Ms Maddison, believe me they were living under the same roof."

The Judge nodded his head slightly and waived his hand in a gesture for me to continue.

I raised my voice slightly.

"He's a compulsive liar your Honour, he lied about his income, lied about his mother's estate, lied about his domestic arrangement and even lied about his eye condition. He lied from start to finish to stop his family receiving a reasonable amount of money to live on."

"Objection."

"He's a liar," I said, "a liar and a fraudster."

"Objection."

"It's all there in black and white your Honour, the man is a perjurer."

"Objection."

The Judge took control of the courtroom as he lowered his voice and gave me a stern lecture on courtroom etiquette. His words went in one ear and out of the other. I had made my voice heard and that was what mattered. He made a few scribbles on his notepad and asked me where the other £8000 a month income came from.

"That's easy Sir," I said, "a 6% income would produce £96000 a year from £1.6 million, or £8000 a month. I was told by a financial adviser to base my calculation on that conservative figure. He assured me a 6% return is very realistic."

I glanced at my paper, time to conclude I thought.

"He was living with her Sir," I emphasised, "that's nine thousand net income from salary and eight from investments. £17000 is a decent monthly income in anyone's language while Judge Porter felt sure that an award of a £1000 a month for me and three girls was more than enough."

"Objection, my client's income is not the issue here."

At this point in proceedings a strange thing happened. Judge Poulton eased back in his seat and said nothing. Either something was sinking in or he was enjoying the brawl, two boxers, an amateur and a pro and for once the amateur was holding their own.

The scrap was on and we were in the final round, nothing between us on the Judge's cards.

"His income is irrelevant," Quinn repeated.

"On the contrary," I said, "if he had inherited the estate at the time that would have been his income. The fact of the matter is Mr Palmer and Tina Palmer committed a fraud to con the Judge."

Quinn threw his hands up in the air in frustration.

"You have no proof."

"Tina Palmer was merely the caretaker of Mrs Palmer's money until Mr Palmer thought it a safe time to transfer everything into his name." I turned to Stuart, whose face had turned a deathly shade of grey. "You committed fraud Mr Palmer, you knew exactly what you were doing. You lied in court as did Tina Palmer, in my book that is fraud and when I leave here today and explain the details to Northumbria Police I'm sure they will agree with me."

The Barrister lost it. His eyes had been fixed firmly on me but he now directed his attention to Poulton, who at this stage sat in complete silence.

He almost shouted at the Judge.

"The fact that Tina Palmer made a decision to transfer land and property to Mr Palmer does not suggest fraud has been committed."

Quinn was rambling again, debating the finer points of English law. It was his last throw of the dice yet he chose to ignore the income aspect completely. He had changed the subject completely.

"Your Honour, in circumstances where an application is made out of time, the court should only grant permission to appeal where there is a real prospect of success. I quote Judge Mostyn again who described a real prospect of success as one that has a better than 50:50 chance of success?"

His eyes met Poulton's who at this juncture was sitting perfectly still, his body language giving no indication of his opinion either way and yet I couldn't help thinking that these two men were from the same chambers. Was this all a farce, part of the big legal game?

Quinn waffled on, he was beginning to monopolise the court with his strong voice and legal superiority, I knew the longer he stood making himself heard the more likely the judge would listen, I had to stop him in his tracks.

I interrupted him mid-sentence.

"Your Honour, given the circumstances surrounding my case I believe that I have a reasonable prospect of success."

Poulton raised his eyebrows.

Reading from my carefully prepared script I drilled home my point.

"My husband was presented to the court as a disinherited son receiving nothing at all and with an eye condition that prevented him from working. There can be no other logical explanation for this metaphorical rags to riches scenario, other than it was agreed prior to the death of his Mother that Tina Palmer would hold the estate in safe keeping until it was deemed an appropriate time to transfer it to Mr Palmer and that is exactly what has happened."

"Objection."

I continued. My speech was lengthy and I knew Quinn was waiting in the wings desperate to take the stage and make his closing pleas. My parting shot needed to be strong. Like a Shakespearean actor I delivered lines from a case Murdoch had brought to my attention. I could almost hear his voice projecting through my mouth, the words weren't my own they were so alien to anything I would have ever said naturally.

"Both my ex-husband and Tina Palmer committed a fraud and lied under oath to the court. No court in this land will allow a person to keep an advantage which they have obtained by fraud, no judgment of a court, no order of a Minister can be allowed to stand if it has been obtained by fraud. Fraud unravels everything and that's why the original ruling has to go to appeal."

Eventually I finished and I sank back down into my seat.

"Thank you Mrs Palmer," Poulton said in smooth voice before asking Quinn for his closing statement.

There was nothing in there that I hadn't heard already and it bordered on boring.

The Judge announced there would be a ten minute recess after which he would deliver his judgement. Immediately panic set in. Ten minutes! What can he do in ten minutes? I concluded he'd prepared his speech and therefore his decision before he'd even entered the courtroom. I thought the worst and the blood pumped around my veins and for the first time since I'd started my crusade I fully considered the impact of losing my right to appeal and the effect it would have on the girls. It would crush them if I went home empty handed with a huge debt hanging over me because if I lost I would need to cover his legal fees too.

It all seemed so very civilised as Poulton began to pass his judgement, there was no noise from the other side. Stuart sat still, his head lowered in his hands looking at the floor while his two comrades scribbled notes, as was the way of all legal men. I made a half-hearted attempt to take notes, yet I struggled to keep pace. As his speech went on and on I sensed he was reading from a carefully prepared script, his words washed over me. Poulton rambled through the legal jargon and with each turn of each word he seemed to sway from favouring Quinn's argument then my own. He gave nothing away.

I gazed at my watch. Poulton had been talking for twenty-three minutes and I questioned how a ten minute recess could produce a twenty-three minute speech. It was rigged. It was the final nail in the coffin of the Mr and Mrs Palmer divorce game and I was about to be shafted yet again.

"And therefore I have reached my decision based on what I have heard today."

I sat bolt upright and a strange sensation washed over me.

"I am going to grant Mrs Palmer the right to Appeal."

"Court rise," the usher announced as team Stuart and I stood slowly.

Had he just said that? I thought to myself. Did he just grant me the right to appeal?

Stuart collapsed dramatically into his seat as the Judge walked from the room and Steedman wasted no time fussing over him. Quinn busied himself collecting a few papers together and as my eyes penetrated into the top of his head I prayed that he would look up and face his nemesis.

Eventually there was nowhere else to look and our eyes met.

There was a moment of awkwardness but he found his tongue.

"Don't get overconfident Mrs Palmer," he said, "you haven't got a cat in hell's chance of winning this."

I reached for my handbag.

"Sorry Mr Quinn I haven't got time for small talk, I have an important meeting with Northumbria Police about a fraud case I happen to have stumbled upon."

By now the three of them were all sitting in a neat, little line.

"Let's not do anything too hasty Mrs Palmer."

"I'll bid you all good day gentlemen," I said, "fuck you Steedman and fuck you too Mr Quinn and last but not least fuck you too Mr Palmer."

I slung my handbag over my shoulder and left the courtroom with a smile on my face bigger than the mouth of the River Tyne.

51

I walked calmly down the corridor heading towards the main waiting area even though I wanted to pump my fists in the air and shout to the world that I had won. It was as if I was walking on air. I wanted to pinch myself to be sure I wasn't dreaming, me, Annette Palmer, downtrodden housewife and single parent who'd never won a thing in her entire life had achieved the impossible. For once in this whole sorry fiasco I'd come up trumps although I was wise enough to realise one fine day didn't make a summer. I'd escaped paying Stuart's legal feels on the day, yet his costs would be accruing against the next hearing and as Murdoch had taken great pains to point out to me, if it got to a final hearing and I lost I would be responsible for all of my ex-husbands legal fees which could be in the region of £50000.

It was a sobering thought as I heard the heavy steps of the opposition coming up behind me. The muffled sounds of their voices caught my attention, Quinn's Public School drawl stood out above the other two, his voice amplified by the fact the corridors and waiting areas were almost deserted. I checked my phone, it was almost 4pm, we'd been thrashing it out in the courtroom for the best part of two hours. As I made my way to the main stairwell, I quickened my pace slightly hoping to increase the gap between us. The last thing I wanted was any hassle from Stuart and his crew, I'd had my fill of the lot of them for one day.

I made my way down the staircase, my gaze was drawn to the twinkling lights reflecting through the glass panelled windows. It was dusk outside, the winter light had almost faded and the banks of the

Tyne were lit up with a myriad of colours, the reflections dancing off the choppy current of the river. An inner peace washed over me for a few seconds until I heard Quinn's voice echoing down the staircase.

"Mrs Palmer can we have a word please?"

I glanced up, his head leaned over the stair railings and our eyes locked together. His face was expressionless as he reiterated his request.

"Could we have a word?"

Part of me wanted to ignore him, desperate to get out of the building and back to my family who I knew would be anxiously waiting for me to get home. There could only be one reason why they wanted to speak, they wanted to settle out of court, the last thing they wanted was to go to appeal.

Murdoch said that if I won the right to appeal they'd want to settle and he urged me to do just that. Going through with the appeal was a huge risk and yet part of me wanted my day in court with them. I was also scared of the odds stacked against me. Three against one, fifty years of legal experience compared to just a couple of months playing at the game. I pictured the scene, how could I possibly sit down with them and negotiate a fair settlement?

I looked back up the staircase.

"I have to be going Mr Quinn, I want to get back to my family."

"Please Mrs Palmer, just hear me out, just give me ten minutes of your time."

There was desperation in his voice and I sensed it immediately. Suddenly the thought of sitting down around a table with team Palmer didn't seem so daunting. What harm could it do to listen?

Quinn led me, without another word, to one of the many client conference rooms where Stuart and Steedman were already sitting in silence. My eyes glanced from one to the other but they both avoided eye contact. They looked like a pair of naughty schoolboys who'd been hauled up in front of the headmaster. As I took my seat directly opposite the three men I somehow sensed I held a few aces in my hand. As much as I feared the duo of skilled negotiators I guessed that Quinn must have told the pair something they hadn't wanted to hear.

As I placed my handbag and files onto the floor I opened up the dialogue with a big broad smile.

"So what can I do for you gentlemen?"

Quinn looked at Steedman who gave a slight nod and then he responded.

"We would like to discuss a capitalised maintenance settlement."

I turned to Stuart.

"Is that right Mr Palmer, you want to settle?"

He lowered his eyes.

"After three long years you've decided to do the honourable thing and look after your family?"

He shook his head as he buried his face into his hands. I was enjoying every second.

Steedman broke the silence.

"The Judge made it perfectly clear he would like both parties to attempt an out of court settlement. Mr Palmer is happy to do that."

My ex-husband still kept his head down, his chin cupped in one hand. I couldn't take my eyes off him.

"You have no realistic chance of winning Mrs Palmer," Quinn said, "the evidence you have is at best flimsy. Could you sustain the costs if you were to lose the Appeal?"

His voice appeared to soften as if he had a genuine concern for my predicament. It was false, I could see right through them.

"Mrs Palmer, we would like to reach an amicable agreement because you are fighting a battle you cannot possibly hope to win. If we can put it to bed this evening you and Mr Palmer can get on with your lives."

I leaned back in my chair.

"I'm happy to take my chances in court. Why waste your time trying to talk me out of making my Appeal if you're so convinced I can't win? If that's your attempt at mediation Mr Quinn I think it's quite pathetic."

I stood up from the table and reached for my handbag.

"Hold on Mrs Palmer," Steedman growled, "my client would like to make you an offer."

Now he had my attention.

I sat back down.

"Go on then make your offer. I'm all ears," I said.

Before Steedman had the opportunity to say another word, Quinn bounced in.

"Mr Palmer is willing to offer you £30000 as a one off payment."

As he said the words with complete conviction I nearly fell off my chair with shock. This time there was no acting, I was absolutely stunned as the three men looked at me blankly. When I'd composed myself sufficiently I gave him my answer.

"Are you three monkey's fucking serious?"

My head was shaking in disbelief. I bent forward across the table and I was almost in touching distance of Stuart, I could smell his musky cologne, his favourite.

"You call me in here to talk about an offer like that, it's a fucking insult."

Steedman was first to respond as he told me it was more than fair. For the first time since I'd walked into the room Stuart looked in my direction. I could see the hate in his eyes, he had nothing but contempt for me. Once it would have cut like a knife, now it bounced of me. His opinion of me no longer mattered.

We may well have been locked in a deadly stare indefinitely if it weren't for Quinn interrupting the deadlock.

"Can you give us a moment Mrs Palmer," he said as he gestured to Steedman and Stuart beckoning for them to follow as he stood up and walked out of the room. I sat in quiet isolation as the three of them made their way into the corridor.

I took a deep breath and was in two minds to stand and walk away. But I composed myself hanging on Murdoch's words to settle. I tried to steady my nerve knowing I had them on the run, yet how far were they prepared to go. Steedman had come in with a ridiculous offer but common sense told me if he was starting at £30000 they were prepared to go far higher. Nevertheless I felt it was evident that their final figure was going to fall way short of my expectations. What would Murdoch say, what would his advice be I wondered? I lifted my bag from the floor and quickly rummaged through to find my phone. There were two missed calls and three text messages, all from the girls wondering what had happened in court. I quickly text them back.

Still at court will be home soon.

I text Murdoch.

Won the right to appeal, they want to settle, can you advise what sort of offer I should be looking to accept?

I had just sent my message when the door opened and the three men marched back into the room. Stuart slumped in his chair, his agitation growing by the second. He was about to pop at any moment I thought as I laid my phone on the table and crossed my hands in front of me. Quinn broke the silence.

"Mr Palmer wishes to increase his offer to £50000, it's his final offer, take it or leave it."

Just then my phone pinged. It was a reply from Murdoch. I took my time, ignored Team Palmer and opened the message.

Brilliant news! I would suggest anything the region of £50000 is a day well spent in court but follow your own intuition as it is only your tenacity which has got you this far.

I looked up and smiled. I had it, I had been offered the amount that Murdoch suggested we settle on. He was right of course, no costs or fees and fifty thousand in the bank. I pictured the scene at home later that evening. I'd walk in with a ridiculously expensive bottle of champagne and announce to the girls that although I had lost numerous battles along the way at least I had won the war.

I studied Steedman, he was clearly confidant it was an offer I couldn't refuse.

I sat back in my chair and took a deep breath before speaking. I looked directly at Stuart.

"Unlike you Stuart, I'm not a greedy person. All I ever wanted was enough money to care for our daughters, to live the same lifestyle we were used to. I never wanted all of your wealth or your Mother's estate. This should have been sorted out three years ago."

Steedman nodded in agreement, he sensed a settlement was near.

"I wanted £2400 a month, that was all. That was what Judge Porter said was a fair income."

Steedman had picked a pen up and began to scribble on his legal pad. He couldn't hold back as he started to patronise me.

"I think that's a reasonable figure Mrs Palmer, I think we could work something out on those calculations."

It was Quinn's turn to speak.

"We'll give you £2400 a month for a two year period, a payment just short of £60000 Mrs Palmer. We are happy to round it up to sixty thousand."

I nodded my head slightly.

Stuart's reaction was priceless as he turned towards Quinn in shock. The high flying, brother in arms Barrister to the Judge had just given away another precious ten grand as easily as that. It was a legal poker game and Quinn had just shown his hand.

Steedman picked up where Quinn had left off.

"Sixty thousand pounds Mrs Palmer, on the proviso you make no other claim for capital or maintenance."

It was my turn to scribble a few figures. I wrote £2400 on a notepad and turned it around so they could read it.

"That figure is more than acceptable," I said.

"Good," Quinn said, "we can get the documentation drawn up immediately."

I held up my hand.

"I'm not finished."

I turned to Stuart.

"My dear ex-husband, you lied and you cheated and you took your daughters to hell and back. How dare you think that two years maintenance payments will buy me off."

Stuart immediately jumped from his chair.

"You mad deranged bitch. I told you she's a greedy cow," he shouted, "she'll be sticking another two years on just for the hell of it."

His menacing presence was not new to me. I'd witnessed it many times yet this was the first time I wasn't intimidated by him. I didn't flinch. I remained calm.

"I'm prepared to settle out of court for the three years payment shit you've put me through."

Steedman had worked it out on his calculator.

"That's £86000 Mrs Palmer, that's simply unacceptable."

Stuart was on his feet.

"What the hell makes you think you deserve eighty six grand?"

His attack on me was so venomous I could feel droplets of his airborne spit touch my cheek. I reached into my bag for a handkerchief and wiped off the traces of his saliva. Quinn was clearly agitated that the meeting he was chairing had gone awry and he tried to regain control.

"Sit down Mr Palmer please."

Stuart pulled his chair away from the table like a scolded schoolboy and placed it at a right angle towards Steedman. I couldn't have cared less, I could be talking to the back of his head but he was going to listen to me. I was determined to make my point.

"You robbed me of twenty three years Stuart, the chance to spend time with someone who genuinely loved me."

Steedman and Quinn were looking in all directions, the conversation stepping into a territory way out of their comfort zone. Stuart didn't engage either, his eyes fixed to the floor once more.

I turned towards Quinn.

"I've wasted my life on this fucking lying twat of a man who subjected me to years of mental abuse and torture and he is going to pay for it with the precious cash he's been trying to hide ever since he walked out on me."

Quinn didn't entertain my argument.

"Unfortunately for you Mrs Palmer the law doesn't work that way, it is only interested in the financial investment, there is no concern for the emotional investment," he said as he gathered his papers together. "This meeting isn't going anywhere, you clearly do not want to accept Mr Palmers offer of £60000 and I see no point in continuing."

Quinn stood and Steedman was quick to follow suit. They stood but they made no attempt to walk. It was at that exact moment I knew I had them exactly where I wanted them.

"Sit down gentlemen," I said softly, "you've no intention of walking away and you know it. If we don't settle this tonight I will take my husband down. Mr Quinn, Mr Steedman, your client has committed fraud and he lied to the court under oath."

Stuart's head collapsed onto the table, the theatrics of his gesture was almost comical. Quinn was desperate not to inflame the situation any further.

"Stop being ridiculous Mrs Palmer."

"Ridiculous?" I questioned. "I think not, your client could face up to seven years in prison if he is found guilty."

I could see Stuart's face turning red, I needed to turn the vice as tight as I could get it.

"When you eventually get out of prison you'll never find employment again Stuart, a convicted criminal working as an accountant. I don't think so. You'll lose your practicing certificate for sure." I said calmly.

"You've got no evidence against me, a fucking Land Registry document is that it?" he challenged.

I sat back and smiled.

"Oh I have a lot more than that Mr Palmer. I have an open fucking book to hit you with."

I turned to Quinn.

"Did your client tell you he was executor of his Aunts Will of which my children were the beneficiaries?"

Quinn shrugged his shoulders.

"Your client and his mother skimmed off the Aunt's money for themselves," I said, "he was supposed to be paying a £1000 a month to his Aunt to rent her flat."

"And I did pay it," Stuart shouted

"No you didn't, the money never hit your Aunts account." I fired back, "you wouldn't pass the executors accounts on to the girls because you knew the figures didn't add up. She was banged up in a home with dementia and you and your Mother used her money as your own."

"Bollocks," he screamed again.

Quinn was shaking his head as I continued.

"As you know embezzlement can carry up to ten years in prison gentlemen. And by the way as well as the police I'll also be informing HMRC that Mr Palmer has lied about his income."

Stuart was unable to hold his tongue.

"What the fuck are you talking about now?" he shouted, his voice so loud the sound reverberated around the room.

"Your tax returns fall way short of showing what you were actually earning at the time and I would suggest that as well as trying to hide your forty seven share holdings from me you also hid the dividends from the tax man."

Quinn looked on bemused unlike Steedman who twisted in his chair, he knew more than he was letting on.

"Fraud, perjury, embezzlement and tax evasion," I said, "you take your pick."

Stuart's arms were flaying in all directions. I was hitting a nerve all right, his eye began to twitch and I noticed as we locked horns across the table that he had begun to perspire.

"I've got nothing to hide," he shouted running his hand through his hair, another sign the stress levels were rising

"Good, then you've nothing to worry about," I replied in a matter of fact manner.

Steedman was unable to hold his tongue, he waded in.

"If you believed Mr Palmer lied on his tax return why didn't you report it sooner."

I looked at the man in total disbelief.

"I didn't think you were that stupid Mr Steedman. Why would I report him when I was getting maintenance payments from him? He's an accountant and if he had been robbing the taxman he'd lose his practicing certificate and his income. Do you really need me to join up all the dots for you?"

"See what a mad fucking cow she is?" he said, looking from Steedman to Quinn and back to Steedman for support.

Both men sat in silence.

Quinn was the first to speak.

"Tell me want you want Mrs Palmer."

It was the moment I'd been waiting for. I picked up my pen and next to the £2400 on the notepad I wrote the figure 13.

"I don't understand," Steedman said.

"It's simple enough," I said, "I want three years maintenance back payments and another ten years on top for good measure."

Quinn's jaw almost hit the table.

"You want thirteen years maintenance payments?"

"Yes."

"You have to be kidding?" Steedman said.

"£374000," I said.

Quinn was about to open his mouth when Steedman shouted over him.

"That is not going to happen, even if you won your appeal you wouldn't get a settlement anywhere near that."

"Perhaps not," I said, "but what price can Mr Palmer put on his liberty and his reputation?"

Steedman was furious. He was on his feet and holding onto Stuart's shoulder in attempt to keep his client from launching across the table at me.

"Mrs Palmer, please let's be realistic." Quinn interjected, "I'm sure my client can stretch to three years payments."

"Thirteen," I said.

Steedman launched his own attack calling me deluded, a black mailer, saying he would be more than happy to go to appeal with his client.

It was time to get personal.

"I'll take my chance at appeal Steedman, it will give me a chance to show the court the Ombudsman's report exonerating me from any wrongdoing."

Steedman was lost for words, he had no idea that I had been to the Ombudsman.

"And I also intend to report you to the Solicitors Regulatory Authority."

"On what grounds," he said, a look of shock and indignation on his face.

"On the grounds you've taken advantage of the fact I am a litigant in person, your bullying tactics, your misleading and deceitful behaviour, deliberately withholding critical information. I've got all the emails you sent me. You need to look at the Law Society's recommendations on dealing with litigants in person, you've breached every one of them," I said, "so when I'm finished with the Police and the Inland Revenue I'm moving in on you. I'll also be informing the DVLA there's a fucking idiot, who swore under oath he was practically blind, still driving a car."

I turned the notepad back around towards me. In big letters I jotted down,

'POLICE FRAUD SQUAD - EMBEZZLEMENT TEAM - INLAND REVENUE - SOLICITORS REGULATORY AUTHORITY

"I hope you don't mind," I said, "I need to make a note or two just in case I forget."

Quinn stood again.

"Gentlemen can I have a word in private please."

The deflated pair followed him like lap dogs out of the room and I breathed a huge sigh of relief because I had done something of which I was proud. I hadn't caved in, I hadn't given up the fight and if push came to shove I was ready to take them on in the courts once again.

My thoughts were interrupted once more as the three men walked back into the room. I could feel my heartbeat increasing and there was a subdued silence as they took their seats, but their somber faces gave nothing away.

It was Quinn who did the talking, his voice slow and deliberate.

"Our client will agree to give you £250000."

I shook my head and sat in compete silence.

They threw four more figures at me edging ever closer to the magical figure equating to thirteen years maintenance.

Stuart screamed and cursed at me and Quinn tried to calm him down.

I remained silent.

With a deep sigh Quinn eventually caved in.

"Our client will pay you the £374000. You make no other claim for capital or maintenance and you will drop all malicious and slanderous threats about his character. You will not contact the Police, HMRC or the DVLA nor will you lodge any paperwork with the Solicitors Regulatory Authority."

I could hardly believe what I was hearing but I held my composure and my dignity. Steedman and Stuart couldn't look at me, as they remained silent. What a coward Stuart was, terrified of his own shadow. I'd put the fear of God into him and he'd crumbled like a pack of cards.

I said nothing at first, I wanted to savour the moment, but as the seconds stretched out to the point of becoming excruciatingly long I was forced to break the silence.

"I want the draft order drawn up and signed this evening."

Stuart looked at me angrily and then to Steedman as he nodded in agreement.

"Yes we agree," Quinn said. "We'll draw it up now if you're prepared to wait."

"Yes I'm happy to wait, I've got all the time in the world Mr Quinn," I said calmly. "Add a clause that if the money does not hit my account in three working days the deal is off."

I looked at my husband who was on his feet and ranting again.

"Impossible, how the fuck am I going to find that sort of money in three days?"

I reached into my file and pulled out a sheet of paper that I passed across the desk. "Have you forgotten Stuart? You have nearly £600000 in liquid assets."

I stood and gathered up my things.

"I'm going to wait in the foyer, bring me the draft order when its ready to sign."

Steedman had already opened up his laptop and started to type. I left the room and sent a text to Murdoch. It read,

I managed to squeeze them for £374000. Did I do well?

He simply sent a photograph of 'The scream,' by Edvard Munch.

Thirty-seven minutes later they called me back into the room and

I read over the two-page document before I signed it. They took a copy and I kept one for myself.

There were no pleasantries, my husband was not magnanimous in defeat as he scowled and grumbled and cursed his way through the final proceedings.

At last it was all over and he stood. He couldn't wait to get out of there.

"Not so fast, where do you think you're going?" I said bluntly.

He didn't say a word he just stopped in his tracks like a frightened dog waiting for his master's next command.

"Home," he whimpered.

"I think you've forgotten something Stuart."

He cocked his head to one side not quiet understanding what I meant. I obliged him one last time.

"We've agreed my settlement but we haven't talked about what you're going to give to the girls. I think you better take a seat again, we're not done yet."

Epilogue

Dear Stuart,

Do you ever wonder about your old life or is it just a distant memory banished to the recesses of your brain? For me it seems like a lifetime ago since I walked out of that courthouse for the very last time. Do you remember how you stood at the top of the court steps watching as I climbed into my taxi? I recall I glanced up and there you were hands firmly planted in the pockets of your overcoat as the cold breeze whipped up from the Tyne, a deflated expression planted across your face. I'd never seen you in such a state, every time we went into court you'd always been brimming with an arrogant confidence, sincerely believing that the cards were stacked in your favour. Strangely enough, I recall feeling a sense of sadness and even pity as I stared back at you from the rear view window. I've no idea why you'd aroused such feelings in me and in truth it was fleeting and it was quickly replaced with a feeling of euphoria, the only thing on my mind was getting home to tell the girls it was over once and for all.

You should have seen them Stuart, all three were huddled together around the kitchen table holding hands like they were about to hold a séance, a look of dread on each of their faces. I instantly knew what they'd been thinking, how much money has she wasted on legal fees now? I didn't prolong their misery, I couldn't keep the smile from my face a moment longer.

"It's all over," I squealed with delight, "we've settled out of court and your Dad has just handed me nearly £400000."

After the initial tears of relief when we'd kissed and hugged, there was this buzz of excitement and I can assure you the champagne corks popped that evening. It was Bollinger if my memory serves me correctly.

The celebrations didn't stop there either. We carried on in party spirit up to and throughout the Christmas season. I don't have to remind you how the girls and I love Christmas. That year was even better and I'd gone one step further surprising them with a spur of the moment trip to New York for New Year's Eve, courtesy of the money you'd grudgingly deposited in my bank account. Can you imagine, there we were standing in Time Square surrounded by thousands of people cheering and hugging as the clock struck midnight, ticker tape falling from the sky onto our heads as the sound of Auld Lang Syne blasted out above the ruckus of the crowd.

The smiles on your daughter's faces were priceless Stuart. I took hundreds of photographs, but some things just can't be caught on camera. I remember as we walked back to our hotel bursting with laughter and the joys of life, I had felt the same tinge of sadness as I had outside the courthouse and again your defeated image jumped into my head. I wondered why, then it suddenly dawned on me, I was sad you'd missed a truly magical moment with your girls.

It led me to ponder, do you ever wonder what's going on in your children's lives Stuart? Don't you long to hear them say Dad again? Dad can you do this? Dad can we have this? Dad can you give us a lift?

When the girl were young you'd walk in through the front door and the three of them would pelt along the hallway, screaming your name, Daddy, Daddy, as they competed for your attention. I'm sad to have to tell you that you've lost your title now. They don't have a Dad anymore, your just Stuart, plain old Stuart.

It gives me a warm feeling knowing I still count in their lives, I matter to all our three children.

Now I have been given the honour of being both Mum and Dad to our girls and I must say I've adjusted to my new role. When Abigail walked down the aisle it was me she chose to be by her side, to walk the steps you should have walked as her Dad. The day was magical and I was bursting with pride yet once again thoughts of you came to my head for a nanosecond, then it struck me. You will never experience a sense of pride a parent has for a child who is doing spectacular things with their life. The pride I felt when against all odds, Alexandra graduated with first class honours. I was there, as she stood capped and gowned, posing for the photographs, grinning from ear to ear. It was the same pride I'd felt when Victoria announced she was packing in her job to go travelling around the world. And as I waved her off at the airport, yes I was worried to death, yet still so immensely proud that my headstrong and independent girl was setting off on the adventure of a lifetime.

I can say without reservation our children have given me so much pleasure, they are gifts that keep on giving Stuart. If I'm honest I only fully appreciated this fact after Abigail placed our baby grandson into my arms. Can you imagine my sheer joy being able to hold this beautiful child, the spitting image of his mother, knowing he was my grandchild. I'd not experienced such joy since our three little bundles arrived into the world?

I often wonder what you would have made of our grandson George, I know you were so desperate for us to have a boy. You can't deny it, it hadn't gone unnoticed, the disappointment was etched on your face each time the midwife said "It's a girl Mr Palmer."

There are so many things I could tell you about our Gorgeous George as I keep insisting on calling him, although now he tells me, "I nearly four Nana I'm a big boy, babies are gorgeous not big boys."

I smile every time he says those cute little words. He melts my heart if I'm honest and he can wrap me around his little finger. He's such a clever boy we often sit for hours reading storybooks or playing outside on the grass. I'm convinced he's going to be a sportsman. Maybe he's inherited some of his sporting enthusiasm from you although I never say the words out loud. I'm forbidden to mention your name when George is around, Abigail has such strong opinions on the matter and she hasn't held back sharing her thoughts

"I'd never allow Stuart to hurt my child the same way he hurt me and my sisters," she's said on more than one occasion.

She has a point Stuart, all three girls carry the scars from your rejection. They hide them well beneath the layers of happy memories they make each day, yet if we delve deep enough, their emotions are still very raw.

I often wonder do you ever get the slightest pang of guilt when you think about how you've let your children down so very badly? Shouldn't a Dad worth his salt always be there for his children come hell or high water. Not you it would seem.

I've wondered for years if you have any regrets and now I know with certainty you do have some regrets. I saw it in your face that day in the park. It was the first day I'd clapped eyes on you since the court hearing. Wasn't it a special day Stuart, one you'll never forget, the first time you met your grandson. Who'd have thought our worlds would collide and you'd be walking around Exhibition Park on the same afternoon as me, Abigail and George. Of course we were happily oblivious to your presence as Abigail and I took it in turns to push George on the swings. He's a bundle of energy that boy, I thought we'd never get a chance to take the weight off our feet and sit on the park bench for a while and watch George play. Eventually he did run out of steam and started playing in the sandpit with his new found friend, Verity. I'm convinced you must have been watching from a distance, we could have only taken our eyes off him for less than a moment then the next time we looked he was right over the other side of the park. Did you call him over I wonder? In shock we both jumped up from our seats, calling his name, the panic in our voices was obvious to all around as parents and children turned their heads to stare in our direction. It was Abigail who saw him first standing next to a strange man, she ran over and I was quick on her heel. George's red anorak stood out like a beacon, yet you were just a dark silhouette. It was only when we were both feet away your image came into sharp focus and it dawned on us, it was you, Stuart Palmer. Abigail stopped dead in her tracks as she looked from her child to you then me. I didn't say a word this was Abigail's call, a fork in the road so to speak and it was only she who could decide which path to take. I smiled at our daughter. It was my way of giving her permission to do what she thought was right in that awkward moment. As I stared at you I couldn't stop myself from thinking, this is how it should have been if our lives had turned out to be the fairy tale I imagined it was going to be when I was young and naive. You certainly looked very much the Grandpa crouched down meeting George on his level.

"What's your name son?" I heard you say in a gentle voice but George just stood looking at you like you were some sort of alien and of course you were alien to him. I recall you glanced up at Abigail with sheepish eyes, were you looking for a way back into her life?

We will ever know the answer because Abigail had clearly made her mind up as she raced towards her son and lifted him clear away from you into her arms.

"I've told you before about speaking to strangers George."

By fuck I bet that hurt Stuart!

What a legacy to leave to your grandchildren, nothing, absolutely fuck all. How does it feel knowing you will never leave a mark on their lives?

I so wanted to post this letter off to you Stuart, twist the knife a little further. Yet even I can't be so ruthless to you and believe me where your concerned I can be merciless. As my final act of charity to you I've decided this letter will never reach the post box. I'm going to spare you from knowing the extent of the contempt and hatred, yes hatred, that your daughters have for you because you tore their perfect little world to shreds.

I hope she was worth it Stuart.

Have the life you deserve my darling.

Annette

Printed in Great Britain
by Amazon